McGhee in the Gloaming

McGhee in the Gloaming

Bob Hazy

ANOMIE HOLLOW

P R E S S

2640 Tam O'Shanter Dr.
El Dorado Hills, CA 95762

Copyright © 2016 Bob Hazy

ISBN: 0997541504
ISBN 13: 9780997541502
Library of Congress Control Number: 2016910478
Anomie Hollow Press
Cover Painting: Yukon Raft near Ruby, AK, by Bob Hazy

Dedication

For my Father and Mother who blazed the trail...
For my brothers Jim and Tom, the two best brothers a guy could have...
For my son Nathan, who has yet to find his way: adventure awaits you....

Contents

Preface   ix
Prologue   xi

On the Margin   1
Never Far Enough   37
Most of the Way   63
One Certain Sunset   95
Old Men   107
Kite   131
Stones   145
The Cherry Man   165
Confessions in the Gloaming   185
Losing Les   209
The Calendar Lagniappe   265
Drift   303
Remember the Sea   339
Holy Orders of the Olives   363
Fully Meets   389
The Boney Pile   405

Soldier's Wounds   433
McGhee's Road   465
The Math Idiot   487
A Dublin Homily   503
The Baptism of Frosty McGhee   537
Kite Weather   559
Signal and Noise   575
The Dust Magi   621

Epilogue   641
Chapter Illustrations   657
Acknowledgements   667
Author Biography   669

Preface

There always seems to be one last thing to write, as if it would ever, or could ever, be sufficient. And so it is as I hurry to complete this task before it is too late. I'd rather not leave this thing unsaid after spending so many words to say what feels like everything else. How many times have I done that – neglect the title, forget to format, omit the cover – after spending so much time meticulously tending to the content. To wit, if you get one thing from this preface, let it be this most important message: persevere.

I almost didn't persevere myself, very nearly abandoning the enterprise at the outset. But to no one's greater surprise than myself, I sit here nearly finished, relieved. So, like the salmon, I can flop onto the river's bank and die knowing I've fulfilled the only imperative that I've ever actually known. So be it. The deed is done, and I can rest my head in peace, finally free of it.

It may help to know this story consists of twenty-four chapters, one per each hour of the day, though these stories can cover days or months or even years. Together these hours from across my life form a quilt that is my best day, the most significant hours of a lifetime, stitched together. It is something like what Joyce did for Leopold Bloom, only my day covers my lifetime. That seems more telling, doesn't it, than just one day at twenty-five or fifty-five or seventy? That said, the stories are not in order, though in this telling you'll soon acquire the perspective I did not have in the living of it. I hope this will be useful as you accumulate the wisdom of my later experiences so that you can see them as I see them now that my candle has grown short. That is my hope, anyway, such as it is, knowing that words can never capture this elusive thing called living.

Fran McGhee

Fran McGhee
May 1991

Prologue

An Atheist's Prayer (of Sorts)

There have been countless 3:00 a.m.'s in which I did nothing. I switched off the light, went to bed, and tried to forget this beast inside, strapped it down for another night. Please let this not be one of those defeats.

There is so much to confess, so much to reveal, so much ground to cover and so little time, I don't know where to start. There's my heap of regret – which at times seems so tall I can't see past it. There are my loves to recall and the adventures, the people who made it matter, and those who didn't. There's the vast wasteland of time in between the greatest of moments. There's the fear I've had inside. There's the shame of barnacle laziness that anchors my feet to the ground and my ass to the chair. There's all that unrealized potential, rotting like so much wasted fruit. There's so much to do as the barman says *it's time* that I feel my heart implode, almost too small to beat any longer.

And yet . . . it's one of those rare nights when the wind is just right, car noises wafting in, with restless dogs barking from distant neighborhoods bothered by the stillness. And then there's that other dog, with long plaintive wailing, full-throated and sad, like a whale searching for its mate that's been hauled on deck and lies bleeding from deep punctures. That howl calls to me, turns my head, and says there is an antidote to this fucking sickness welling up inside that this is all there is.

These things are converging to squeeze my head in a vice of imperative, to whip the dancing procrastinator with one last warning: there are no further chances, and this is the last possible moment.

So it ends now. In spite of all the sensible reasons to abandon this pursuit, and the senseless reasons, too; in spite of how easy it would be to sleep and lose myself in dreams, despite the sun of the morning that nearly wipes away this sorrow, and in the name of the gloaming before then, I will commit this tale to paper. This will be my story, so help me god.

Francis McGhee
Sewickley, PA

On the Margin

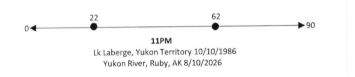

11PM
Lk Laberge, Yukon Territory 10/10/1986
Yukon River, Ruby, AK 8/10/2026

It was the end, and McGhee knew it: snow was flying in squalls, ice was flowing on the Yukon, and soon the land would be cold and dead. It was time to depart, and further delay might result in being stuck in Alaska for the season, unprepared for it. The mud ruts of the road were starting to freeze with crusty puddles in the wells. The channels were jerking the wheel back and forth in his friend Matt's hands as he struggled to control the truck, McGhee banging his head on the window more than once. They were driving in Matt's pickup as they made their way down the hill into the Ruby valley, then back up toward the flat hilltop just at the back side of the village. Both men were silent but preoccupied: Matt with his preparations for the upcoming dark days of winter, McGhee with his lack of a plan beyond that moment.

McGhee absently broke the silence as he stared out the window. "I had an odd dream last night."

Matt looked over, hands lightly on the wheel, careful to keep his fingers out of the middle where they could get trapped in the supports. "Lots of guys break thumbs this time of year. Ya gotta drive like this, really careful," he said. Then, realizing he'd missed what McGhee had said, added, "What?"

McGhee looked over, but the caution didn't register. He was already on the way out. "You wanna hear about my dream or not?"

Matt laughed. "Sounds like you wanna tell it, so don't let me stop ya."

McGhee grunted, smiling himself. "Well . . . it was short. Only went on about five seconds."

"So this won't be a long story then . . . ," Matt said pulling the truck into the long graveled meadow that was the airstrip. A small plane was still taxiing in from the far end.

"It was mostly just a string of words. No moving images, but maybe just an old black and white still of an old guy with a beard. I'm not sure." McGhee stopped talking, watching the plane roll in, the propeller stuttering to a stop.

"Well?" Matt said.

"Well what?" McGhee said, looking over at him. "Oh . . . I think it was a man's voice, like one of those scratchy recordings of Robert Frost or something. The voice just said, *The blood takes the handle.*"

"*The blood takes the handle?* That's it?" Matt said, cracking the door to get out but remaining seated.

"Yeah. Not a question, like you said it, but yeah."

"*The blood takes the handle.* Like that?" he said.

"Close . . . ," McGhee said, "but more like in the middle of a stanza. Only I woke up."

Matt tilted his head, scratching at it. "What's it mean, you figure?"

"I don't know . . . ," McGhee said, shrugging, "but it felt significant."

"You think it's a reference to something?" Matt said, laying his arm across the wheel.

"I don't know. I don't think so," McGhee said shrugging again.

Matt stepped out, leaning against the door to look back over Ruby and the Yukon flowing behind it. Ice floes were visible in the current, growing thick. It wouldn't be long until they met and the whole thing froze solid. Leaning back in, he looked at McGhee. "Well, I like it anyway. Start your novel with that . . . ," he said, slamming the door shut before McGhee could respond.

"What novel?" McGhee called after him, but he was already striding around to the bed where McGhee's duffle bag lay. McGhee hopped out, leaning against the bed as Matt hauled out the bag. "What novel?" he repeated.

Matt stopped, looking at McGhee. "We both know you're gonna write a novel. You need to write it. It's obvious. Or maybe *you* haven't figured that out yet." Matt hauled the bag onto his shoulder, patting McGhee on the back as he walked by.

At the airstrip, visibility was a quarter mile or less. McGhee was cold, but Matt didn't even have a coat, though he did hunch his shoulders a bit and had one hand jammed into his jeans pocket. He wore a slightly nervous look, smiling, which said they might never see each other again. The stakes with the deteriorating weather were about to get a lot more serious, and this would be the last opportunity to escape before regular flights to Fairbanks stopped.

They both knew it was important for him to go, but McGhee was reluctant to move.

"You know . . . I don't really need to go . . . ," McGhee protested.

"Yes, you *really* need to go . . . ," Matt said laughing. "You have *no* idea."

"I could stick it out . . . ," McGhee objected. "How bad could winter be?"

Matt laughed again. "You'd die," he said. It was clear he meant it, though it was more a matter of fact than personal indictment. Winters in central Alaska were brutal and long, claiming many lives from those who underestimated its severity. McGhee understood it was true, but felt obliged to push back: he knew Matt was sad to see him go. As it turned out, they hadn't spent much time together the whole of his six weeks out there. Matt had taken a barge job shortly after he got there, but he understood: Matt pretty much had to take the gig because regular paying jobs rarely existed in the bush, except fleetingly, and the extra cash would fund months if not a whole year of his life out there. That barge job had lasted more than a month, so he didn't get back until the week before McGhee was to depart.

"I don't think I'd die . . . ," McGhee objected, enjoying the banter, though it wasn't the proper time for it. The bush pilot was already tossing the pack of the other traveler into the back of the Piper Cherokee, hustling to head out before it got any worse. He wanted to get into Fairbanks before the storm descended upon their destination, making any thought of air travel, primitive as it seemed to McGhee, impossible.

"Not right away. You'd break something most likely. An ankle. Worse, a thigh. Then you'd sit against a tree and freeze to death. *Then* you'd be dead," Matt said, gesturing with his hands to indicate an ankle problem, then the more devastating femur break.

"And where would you be?" McGhee said.

"Inside, *stupid*," Matt said, laughing again.

"Well, I'm coming back . . . ," McGhee protested, conceding defeat.

"I know you will . . . ," Matt said, though it wasn't clear either of them believed it. McGhee was saying it to convince himself, and Matt was saying it to get him on the plane.

"I mean it . . . ," McGhee said, sticking out his hand.

"I know you mean it . . . ," Matt said, taking it for a firm shake. "I'm glad you came out. I doubt I'll ever see another Yalie in these parts . . . ," he said, releasing his hand. "Now you have some idea of what I was talking about back in New Haven. With that short story of mine about talking to Ford and Hope over the phone, and the pines pouring in, and the cold."

McGhee smiled. "Yeah, I guess I do . . . ," he said, nodding his head.

It was time to get into the plane – the other traveler was in – and the pilot was completing his pre-flight check of flaps for ice. McGhee saw Matt as he hadn't quite seen him before: a man of this place, and not a man of the east where he had first known him, in the middle of a poor city in college. That reality – the reality of youthful and academic experience – had been fully abstract and illusory, an insubstantial and safe existence devoid of actual bodily risk. Matt had wisdom where McGhee did not, had faced adversity and had tested his mettle. He'd come in as an older transfer student and McGhee liked him immediately because he was different. And as they'd gotten to know one another, Matt had invited him up to see the land for himself.

"Thanks, Matt," McGhee said.

"You're welcome, man . . . ," Matt said, smiling broadly, but he didn't laugh this time. Shaking his head and rubbing his neck, he looked at McGhee. "The blood takes the handle – it'll take a while to unpack that," he said, holding the door open as McGhee climbed in and buckled the restraint.

Matt tapped twice on the door after securing it shut to signal the pilot he was good to go.

Once the door was ready, the pilot throttled the engine to spin the plane and start down the strip immediately. As the Cherokee winged around to the west and swung back over the airfield, McGhee could see Matt already in his truck, driving back down the hill into Ruby.

When the wheels of the 737 touched the tarmac in Fairbanks, McGhee realized two things at the same time: he had kept his promise to return, and it had taken him almost forty years to do it – in just a few months it'd be forty exactly, which in part explained why he booked the flight when he did: any later in the year (past August) and he wouldn't have enough light during the day, and if it wasn't then, it might be another ten years, and who knew what would happen by then. He was pretty sure Matt was still there, though they hadn't talked all that time. Somewhere back in the late nineties they had exchanged email, but that was about it. So perhaps it was less *sure* than *strongly suspected*, but at this stage of his life, that was enough. Besides, he liked the absurdity of it and had rehearsed the phone call in his head many times over the years:

"Matt?"

"Uh, yeah?"

"It's McGhee."

"Ok."

They'd both enjoy pretending it was absolutely ordinary to pick up a conversation after forty years without giving the gap its due. So he imagined it'd be like that, but before he'd get to it, he had something to do first.

At the car rental counter, the attendant looked to be about nineteen, with red hair and acne where the apples of his cheeks should be. The young man started talking as soon as McGhee veered toward the counter from the concourse. "Mr. McGhee?" he asked, but continued, "We have a midsize for you today if that will be okay. A white Chevy . . . ."

His front teeth were large and locked into a perpetual smile, which, when combined with his large brown eyes and scruff on his chin, gave him the distinct aspect of a beaver. It also didn't help he was chewing a Ticonderoga pencil, quite effectively, nor the large fur hat on his head apparently fashioned of short brown spiky fur. McGhee stopped five feet from the workstation to accentuate his question. "How did you know my name was McGhee?" he asked, tilting his roller bag again to resume his approach.

As McGhee reached the counter, the young man stopped chewing and started talking, staring at him while he did so, unblinking. McGhee watched to see when he might close his eyes, but it was a full thirty seconds before the attendant did so, his eyes closing at slightly different times.

"We only got one reservation this afternoon . . . ," the kid said, starting to spin his monitor around, only it wouldn't turn any further, and he resorted to pointing at it. "See?" he said, though McGhee made no effort to check for himself.

"Got it . . . ," McGhee said.

Looking between McGhee and the monitor and McGhee again, he realized he wasn't going to look, so he shrugged. "Suit yourself . . . ," he said, smiling again, his large teeth happily capping his lower lip as he started typing. He wasn't even looking at the keyboard, but his hands were jumping all over as he glanced at the screen once or twice to make sure he was in the right field, cringing once when he apparently mistyped, with three exaggerated strikes on the backspace before he resumed the onslaught of data entry, smiling again.

"Ok . . . ," the kid said, stopping the typing, though his fingers remained in the standard typing position, "you're *NOT* taking this car into the Arctic Circle, are you?" His smile broadened and he winked at McGhee, resuming his typing. "Didn't *think* so . . . ," he said, still looking at McGhee. McGhee remained fascinated that the young man didn't blink except once a minute or so, and only marginally followed the constant monologue the kid continued to spit out.

"*But if you did* . . . ," the young man said, "if you did go up the Dalton Highway, and drove about forty, maybe fifty miles an hour, it wouldn't be too bad. I mean, you'd make it, coz there's gas right there at the Yukon River Camp, which you should definitely get coz there's nothing 'til Coldfoot, and you should take some water and get a knife and maybe a bag to sleep in just in case, and a fishing rod wouldn't hurt, if you was going up into the Circle, but like you said, you ain't, so it doesn't matter." The entire time the young man didn't blink and didn't stop typing, though once his speech was done, he did both, simultaneously.

Out in the lot McGhee sat in the car with the engine idling. It'd be the longest stretch he'd driven in a while, maybe since CA 395 in California, and the thought of it brought a smile to his face.

The Cherokee bounced twice on the runway at Fairbanks before sticking, but it was the sight of buildings and civilization that held McGhee's attention. It had not been that long since he was in a town, a city, but the scale and the pace and the feel of it was jarring, short as his tenure was in the wild. And by regular city standards, it wasn't very busy at all, but there were cars and planes and people moving about, and the sheer bustle of it surprised him. Such was his re-entry into to the commerce of domesticated men.

Only when he was transiting the airplane gate, which was little more than a small corrugated metal building adjacent to the fueling station where the planes rolled in, and had passed through the cyclone fence, did his next steps even occur to him. His thoughts turned back to his car, which he had parked (and basically abandoned as far as he knew, since his return was unclear) back in August. It vaguely occurred to him that he had done nothing to prepare the car to sit, or for the weather, or anything else. Other than making sure the windows were rolled up, he had done nothing, and the thought that he should probably have done more suddenly dawned on him.

The driver side door creaked open and he plopped into the seat before realizing he hadn't seen the key for the last six weeks. Luckily, it was slightly heavier than the rest of his possessions, or denser at least, and had slipped to the very bottom of his military duffle that his cousin David had given him before leaving. So after some fishing, his arm stuck in up to the pit, and his hand swinging around through the bits that had strained there, he found the key, attached to nothing else, and pulled his arm back out, victorious.

The celebration was short-lived, however, as the car wouldn't so much as *click* when he turned the key in the ignition. "Shit," he said. "Shit, shit, shit . . . ," he said again after a few more tries, and he sat back into the bucket, the Naugahyde cracking worse than ever, the cold making it still more brittle than its age demanded. Staring at the dashboard, McGhee grabbed the steering wheel to thunk his head against it. The motion reminded him of the trip he and Matt had taken the fall of their senior year, only twelve months before, up to Maine where Matt had been born.

They were in the same Datsun, the one McGhee had inherited from his brother who had moved on to something better (a Camaro), driving into the darkness, when they remembered they had a case of beer chilling on ice in the back. Matt reached back to get a couple bottles, but realized they hadn't remembered to bring an opener. Helpfully, McGhee pulled the key from the ignition to use for the job, the ignition being loose from its one hundred thousand tough miles. He'd always found it amusing he could do so while driving and that the car would continue running. It had been a novelty, and this time allowed them to continue hurtling 70 mph into the darkness. Matt merrily set to work to open the bottles, when there was a sudden *clink* upon the second one, and he held up two pieces to show him.

"That wasn't your only ignition key, was it?" he had said.

For a while outside Fairbanks the Dalton was paved, but that didn't last too long: inside the city limits and ten miles out it wasn't bad, but after that the locals left the pavement to fend for itself, at the mercy of the merciless frost, making what had been a smooth driving asset into a washboard designed to shake screws loose, bust axles, and otherwise convince drivers they'd made a mistake. Seeing the transition to packed mud and gravel McGhee's heart sank, though he continued on, but after five minutes on the new surface, he was glad for it. For although it would seem less amenable to modern vehicles, the opposite proved to be true. Where asphalt resisted the incessant heaving of the cold, the packed rock and mud flowed with it, allowing it to resist the cracking power which rendered more solid surfaces a wreck. Upon realizing this, McGhee smiled to himself, remembering other such realizations from long ago, where his city-based wisdom was supplanted by bush knowledge to the contrary. Relaxing, he found a good speed just below fifty where his rental wouldn't skate on the loose gravel, but he could make decent progress.

It wasn't long before off to his right, he could see a structure running parallel to the road, which moved closer to the road as he went, and he realized he was seeing the pipeline to the North Slope. The larger trees near town had given way to the scrubby, thin pines of the taiga and tundra, permitting increasing vistas to the north. Cresting a small rise, he suddenly could see off to the horizon and the endless straight road, or nearly so, with its steel companion running alongside, like a faithful dog, cresting the far-off hill just as the road did. He remembered his concept of the pipeline through the years — abstract and symbolic of man's need to siphon riches from the earth — and how different it was to see it. In his aloneness, he was glad for a symbol of man, such as it was, to remind him there were at least vestiges of others, even if they were absent.

There were no other cars, either behind or in front, or coming in the opposite direction, and he found himself utterly alone. Allowing the car to drift to a stop, pulled slightly into the margin, he shut off the engine to listen. Stepping out, he walked in front of the car for a look at the landscape, realizing he had to urinate. For a few moments, there was no sound but that of his piddling in the thawed dust until that subsided, and he heard far off the light sound of a bird screeching, then the heavy caw of a raven, the two suddenly bursting from the trees, the small bird in chase as the heavier black bird retreated. A breeze emerged, too, whistling lightly in those pines, reaching his ears in little bursts, cool like the thawing Pennsylvania winds of March, even though it was August. It had in it the briefness of the season, the apex of warmth which wasn't so warm, bespeaking a soon turn to the colder. And though the sky was a brilliant blue, with tiny clouds dotted out toward the horizon, he knew he was a stranger there and needed to continue because such luxuries and ruminations bespoke a tourist. Though he had no aspirations to be a genuine bush man, he recalled the necessity to observe the local sensibilities to avoid trouble.

A few hours later, McGhee crested a small hill, navigating a couple curves before it straightened again, lining up the road with a bridge as the view opened more broadly, exposing the Yukon, stretching each direction, wide and brown, running slowly to the west and the Bering Sea. There was no traffic on the bridge either, so he slowed as he crossed, looking downstream toward Ruby, about two hundred miles west as the water flowed. He could see just off to the side of the bridge on the northern bank a crude ramp was built of earth ending in the water. A barge was moored there, offloading 55-gallon drums, some lumber and other supplies. On the hull *Ruby Marine* was painted in neat white letters.

McGhee looked at Matt, then back to the road, accepting one of the bottles, taking a large swig, followed by a burp. They'd been driving in darkness for hours and it was late, moving toward midnight. No car shops would be open, even if they could find one out there in the thinning wilderness of Maine.

"Yeah, that was the only key," McGhee said. Matt laughed, shaking his head.

"So *why* did you hand me your only ignition key?" Matt asked, smiling broadly, showing his white teeth below his ruddy and bushy mustache, pushing up his horn-rim glasses for emphasis. "*That* was pretty dumb."

"Yeah," McGhee agreed, nodding, having another swig from the bottle. "I'm guessing we're pretty fucked then."

Matt held both sides of the broken key in his hands, pushing them together over and over again, holding them up for McGhee to ponder. "You see this?" he said, showing them again. "This is what we in the bush call a setback . . . ."

"Maybe we'll find a shop up ahead?" McGhee asked, hopefully, but Matt laughed again.

"Sure. A midnight Datsun shop in rural Maine. There's gotta be lots of those . . . ," Matt laughed again. He seemed to be enjoying the dilemma as he looked at his friend, which wasn't lost on McGhee.

"What?" he said, looking from Matt to the road and back again.

"You have no idea how *screwed* you could be, right?" Matt said. McGhee could feel a lesson coming on, but he knew he deserved it.

"You do that out in the bush and you die. Pure and simple. They might not even find your body."

"What would happen to my body?" McGhee asked, following the wrong thread as he seemed prone to do at times.

"Not that that's the point, but you could be *way* out in the middle of nowhere on a Snow-Go, where no one goes. Even then, lots of things would enjoy eating you. Bears, lynx, wolves. And wolverines. Eagles. Even ravens . . . ," Matt continued, scratching the five day's growth on his chin. "Pretty much everything," he concluded with a shrug. "They might find your shoes, so you should write your name in them. Just to close the loop."

"Thanks for the advice," McGhee said, looking back to the road. "But what do we do now?"

Matt tossed the keys on the floor. "I know what *I'm* gonna do . . . ," Matt said, reaching into the back seat for a pink bakery box on the floor. "*I'm* gonna have some pie."

Back in New Hampshire they'd pulled off in a small town for dinner, and on the way out some Girl Scouts were having a bake sale. They had the usual boxed cookies, which McGhee was eyeing, but Matt called him off to the side. "Ever see a pie like that?" he said, motioning to the table. Among the custom baked goods sat a pie with an enormous puffed top. The lady chaperoning the kids leaned over. "We don't slice the top, so it gets big with steam," she said, smiling at them. She crossed her large arms in front of her, her forearms drooping with her own pie encounters.

"Looks like a Jiffy-Pop popcorn . . . ," McGhee said, looking to Matt.

"What kind?" Matt said, turning back to the woman.

"Cinnamon apple . . . ," she said proudly. "Picked 'em myself . . . ," she continued, tilting her head.

"We'll take it . . . ," Matt said, "if you can give us a couple forks to go with it. We're on the road."

Lifting up her large handbag, she plopped it on the card table, which wiggled slightly under its weight. Fishing around inside, she stuck out her tongue as she felt around. "Just because you look like nice guys . . . ," she said, pulling out two plastic forks.

"You carry forks in your purse?" McGhee said, then noticing Matt's look, added, "Thanks ma'am."

Opening the box in his lap Matt wiped his fork on his pants, then went through the gaping hole in the pastry canopy like a careful surgeon, extracting an apple slice, some crust, and sugary filling in a heaping load.

"So you're gonna eat pie while we're in crisis?" McGhee said, reaching over to tap the box.

"Uh-huh . . . ," Matt said, stuffing the pie in his mouth. "Helps me think," he said, chewing and smiling.

McGhee looked out into the road ahead. It was dark – they'd gotten deep into the state already – beyond any street lights or signs of civilization, except the road itself. The road was lined with pines, and the sky was clear but dim. The only light they saw was from the headlamps peering down road, and the bugs that flashed as they flew before them, like hovering snow.

"You got any other keys?" Matt said suddenly, his attention focused back in the box, fishing for more dessert.

"Maybe, yeah . . . you mean like car keys, right?" McGhee said. Matt laughed.

"Yeah, like car keys," he said shaking his head, jamming another forkful in his mouth.

Reaching in his pocket, McGhee pulled out another set. "For my brother's Camaro. Why?" He handed them over to Matt, who held them up, straining to see them in the darkness.

Reaching up, Matt switched on the dome light. "That's better . . . ," he said, inspecting them. "They might work," he said, then went back to eating his pie.

"What?" McGhee said, looking from the road back to him, but he was hunched over the box. "How does that work?"

"It's a primitive ignition in these cars. Simple key. GM cars, too, like the Camaro. So the key might work. These keys are both smaller than the Datsun's, so one will probably fit in so we can twist the ignition and fire the starter. We can try it when we're ready to stop. Worst case, I'll just hotwire it . . . ."

McGhee remembered that was the first time he saw Matt differently – that he was used to adversity and obstacles, and was used to solving them – though he wasn't fully convinced until they stopped later and tried it. Matt just smiled when it worked and the engine turned over. That was McGhee's first glimpse of him as an Alaskan, used to making due, though it was deep in Maine, and all because of the lack of a simple thing like a bottle opener.

At the end of the bridge the road resumed its trek north, but widened off to the left where a hand-painted sign for the Yukon River Camp shone in crude white letters on plywood. It was the stop that the rental-counter kid had reminded him was the only stop for gas along the Dalton, but he was going to pull in anyway. The view of the landing from the bridge had assured that. But rather than head for gas directly, he kept his eyes open for another turn down to the earthen ramp he had seen from above, which emerged as he expected, as an ad hoc cut into the brush on the left. A D9 Cat responsible for it still sat on the side where it had pushed its last pile of soil and trees and rocks out of the way to recondition the ramp for the season. Heading down, he pulled over to the left on the edge so there'd be room for others to pass. A pickup was backed down to the water where the barge was nearly done offloading, and someone was on the bed of the truck wrangling a drum.

The walking along the edge was difficult due to the clods of earth pressed to the side, but the rest of the road, such as it was, was like the Dalton, consisting of pressed mud and gravel. It only took a minute or two to reach the barge and the water's edge, so McGhee stood stretching and admiring the river from that angle. There was some commotion in the mouth of the barge, with some banging and swearing where men unseen were struggling with something heavy and metallic. Suddenly the top of a head with just the eyes showing appeared over the barge edge, looking at him.

"You wanna give us a hand with this?" the man asked.

It took a few seconds for McGhee to realize the man was talking to him, but he waved, making his way around the front.

Another man in full length shop-overalls was bent over the front of a machine that looked to be a generator, and though the generator had wheels, it was anchored with straps to a pallet, and their efforts to slide it had resulted in a fitting falling off with a clang, but little progress otherwise. When the man stood, he leaned backward, pushing his fist into the small of his back and let out a moan. It was all familiar to McGhee and suddenly cast him back in recollection.

"Karl?" McGhee said, approaching.

"Yeah?" the man said, swinging around, wiping his brow with a dirty red cloth. When his eyes met McGhee's, he didn't recognize him at once, but after a moment, his eyes broke into a smile, his lips curling at the edge.

"Jesus . . . risen from the dead," he said, stepping over to McGhee, stretching out his hand. Turning his head, he called over his shoulder: "Matt, you better get over here . . . ," not letting familiarity enter his voice to give it away.

From around the corner, another man ran in, worried. "You all right?" he asked concerned, but stopped in his tracks.

"Jesus . . . ," he said. "You're late . . . ," he continued, stepping over and pushed between Karl and McGhee to grab him in a hug. He, too, wore the full length green coveralls, emblazoned with *Ruby Marine* on the left, and his red and white name tag on the right, smudged and scuffed, with a little seam blowout at the shoulder.

McGhee looked at both of them, speechless, shaking his head.

"Enough small talk . . . you gonna help with this or what?" Matt said, stepping back to grab a corner of the generator. Karl laughed, walking over to grab another corner. Matt pointed to a third corner, then waved McGhee in. "It's heavy. Take it easy. You've come a long way to get crushed now . . . ," he said, laughing.

The three, with the truck owner, too, were able to jostle the wheels free and roll the unit off the gate of the barge and up to the truck. The gate of the truck was a power lift and was lowered into position already, so they tipped the unit back against the bed, and with some delicate balancing and muscle and mechanical assistance, were able to get the generator loaded and secured with straps.

Once the truck started up the ramp with its load, Matt started the trudge up behind it. "Let's get some grub before heading back to Ruby," he said, talking over his shoulder. Then after a moment, he turned again to clarify: "By the way, you're coming with us."

Stepping out of his car again, McGhee looked at the Datsun. *What would Matt do?* he thought to himself, and just as quickly, it came to him. Luckily, no one was parked in front of his spot, and it was angled down a slight incline. It had become a habit of his to park that way, as the battery had died more than once already, and he'd mastered the skill of the push-start. Reaching in, he straightened the wheel, wiggled the stick to make sure it was in neutral, and made sure the key was in the ON position. Leaning in to the door joint, he pushed with his chest, his feet planted behind him at a heavy angle, his right hand on the wheel.

The tires had frozen slightly to the pavement, but after a little rocking, it wasn't too hard to break it out and get it rolling.

Matt had taught him that, too, only with a dog sled. Ten seconds later he was jogging beside it as it got up to speed, and he jumped into the bucket, pushed in the clutch, and shifted into first before instantly popping the clutch again to engage the engine. The old car wheezed under the stress, but complied, grumbling, as it tossed out some black exhaust before settling into its reliable hum. Depressing the clutch, he came to a stop and swung the door shut, engine idling. It was indeed time to go, and he knew he should take advantage of the weather window to get on the road. Every mile further south he got increased his chances of making it the whole way home without getting stuck, which, as he had learned in the bush, was the way to manage risk, and which for them, was synonymous with survival. It wasn't yet noon, so he'd be able to get down the road and make good progress before he pulled over and slept for the night, or at least caught a few hours before the cold forced him awake again.

He'd lost the cover to the atlas sometime back in the summer in Anchorage, or perhaps it was Seattle before that – he couldn't remember. Still, it came in handy, for he needed a refresher on the cleanest path south. Pulling over just outside the airport, he spread the Alaska pages open on his lap, creasing the book horizontally slightly to keep it open. He'd need to head down Alaska Route 2 south east past Tok Junction, where in June he had turned south and west to Anchorage on the way in.

Merging back into traffic, he pointed his hatchback east a few miles until signs for his highway appeared, and he began his turn, out and away from the apogee of his travels back toward the ALCAN highway, which he knew would take him homeward.

<hr />

Out on the river, Matt piloted the barge into the main channel near the bend, heading her west toward Ruby. McGhee found a place near the bow where the gate of the barge plowed through the water so he could lean against it and look out, feeling the cool air and spray on his face. Though it had been forty years, it reminded him of the trip he'd done with Karl and Julie, though the barge didn't yield to the swells the way the skiff had. It was warmer, too, somewhat, being August rather than September for his last visit, though the warmth in the air had a thinness to it to remind him it would be receding soon. The darkness of the stunted trees on shore reminded him of that journey, too, and as they got just a mile down river from the camp where they'd eaten, all vestiges of civilization fell away, and it was just them in the barge, and the great gray river, and the stillness peculiar to the north. The sky was brilliant blue, with a few light clouds, the sun warm on his cheeks, and he smiled into it.

Though standing in his lean against the gate, McGhee was nearly napping as the gentle bobbing of the craft lulled him asleep. A light pat on his shoulder let him know Karl had joined him there, his shoulders hunched up as he dangled his forearms over the gate to look out down river, his chin resting on the metal.

"Sorry about the Kaskae thing . . . ," Karl said, tilting his head to look over at McGhee, one eye squinting due to the sun. He was smiling as he said it, though, so it was more of a reminder than an apology, and after looking at McGhee a few seconds he just looked back over the swells breaking on the flat hull.

It had been the last time he'd seen Karl before he headed up river to trap, and the day before McGhee flew out. Karl and Julie were loading the skiff with gear and his sled dogs for the trip. The sky had been clear and bright then, too, but cold. It had snowed two feet the night before, so it was difficult treading along the ramp. Most of the dogs were loaded, but Karl had asked him to get the last one – Kaskae – his lead dog at the far end of the run where the dogs had been staged to await transport. He wasn't the familiar picture of a husky at all, but some kind of mutt, short and stocky, powerful shoulders, odd patches all over him, some smooth, some rough, some black, some brown, some gray, with one brown eye, one blue. When their eyes met, Kaskae's tongue dangling, it felt more like he was looking at a peer than a beast of burden, there was that attitude to him. Karl had told McGhee to grab him by the collar before unclipping him, and just as he did, Karl whistled for him to rally over. Dutifully, Kaskae had taken off, strong and confident and unwavering, yanking McGhee off his feet to tow him through the snow, plowing as he went, as fast as he could run, with no problem at all. Twenty yards later, McGhee came to a stop near Karl's feet, his jacket packed with snow, as was his face and beard and shirt and pants. The recollection made McGhee laugh and he looked at Karl.

"So how is that dog?" McGhee said, regretting it as soon as he said it, but it was too late and Karl just shook his head.

"You think I have a forty-five-year-old dog, McGhee?" he said, smiling broadly, but it faded slightly as he remembered him. "Best lead I ever had, and I had a lot of 'em . . . . A lot of heart in that dog."

McGhee nodded, looking out again. Some birds were flying low out over the water, their wingtips nearly touching the surface but they didn't, from off their starboard the whole way to port where they disappeared in the glare of the sun on the water. Other than the lapping of the water on the bow, and the low hum of the screws in the water behind, it was soundless, and it was good.

"So how's Julie, then?" McGhee asked, more cautious, but by Karl's look, he could see it didn't matter.

"Lost her, too . . . ," he said, his voice catching slightly, which he diverted into clearing his throat. "Almost ten years now. Fought it hard, but the cancer eventually got her . . . ."

A small loud speaker crackled to life behind them, tucked beneath the cab.

"Karl, you wanna steer a while?" Matt called out.

Looking back over his shoulder, Karl nodded with exaggeration so Matt could see him, then leaned back to standing, patting McGhee on the shoulder.

"Forty years is a long time. We're old men now . . . ," Karl said smiling and rubbing his beard. What had once been solid dark had grown longer and frosted. Only vestiges of the young beard remained, but the smile was the same.

⸙

Alaska Route 2 wound out of Fairbanks, falling south and east along the Tanana most of the two hundred miles to Tok. It was endless conifers and birch and tundra, set against snowy mountains, mile after mile, occasional breaks opening to show the river it was tracing, wide and brooding, like the Yukon, carving into a landscape that seemed to give it reluctant portage where they were locked in perpetual struggle but mutual benefit. McGhee had new respect for rivers and what they meant, well beyond the scenic blue map lines he'd seen them as before or admired from bridges, to something more meaningful and useful and menacing.

And so it was that McGhee found himself leaving Alaska, winding back the miles he had unwound on his outbound journey. Since sometime back in December or January it had been his plan – the full extent of it – to flee the east coast after getting out of school and drive to the north. Matt had casually invited him to come up and see for himself what it was like, and the moment he said it, it had become McGhee's plan, and the more he thought of it, the more sense it made. While most of his friends were heading off to grad school to become lawyers or doctors, or to jump into industry to find their way, McGhee wanted nothing of that. He wasn't sure what he wanted – in fact had little idea for a direction – but one thing he knew was what he didn't want: to put his neck into the yoke of conventional employment. He'd had a taste of that the summer before as an intern at xCopy Inc., and though he could see doing it and had even enjoyed some of it, he didn't think it was for him. Though it was only three months, the sense of it unfurled for him as he looked into the future of it and it didn't feel like the right path. Worse still, he had met a few other interns for whom it was exactly what they wanted and they excelled and thrived while all he could focus upon was his wanting. He knew there was an open door for him there if it came to that – those were their literal parting words to him, for they liked the potential he had shown – but if he could help it, if he could find another path that proved viable, he'd prefer to make a go of that, whatever it was. So his flight to the north was more away from things he didn't like than toward something specific, but now that was done, too. As he drove he sensed the closing arms of his future nudging him toward decisions usually prefaced with notions of responsibility, and it settled on him as would a pall.

Out at the bow of the barge, McGhee got another slap on the back, harder than Karl's. Matt stood staring at him, smiling. There was some gray in the temples, which translated into his mustache, still lining his mouth in a vague seventies-style cut he recognized and was glad to see.

"So you were heading up to the Circle you said?" Matt said, leaning against the gate, one toe of his rubber boot kicked over and stood on end. "There's nothing up there, you know. Not a line. Nothing. I think they got a sign there now . . . ."

"Yeah, I figured . . . ," McGhee said, smiling back. "It was just something I wanted to do."

"Well, you're heading back to Ruby, now. We'll be back at Yukon River Camp in a couple days . . . I guess you can go then."

"Thanks . . . I was hoping to see Ruby somehow anyway, but hadn't planned that yet. Was hoping to run into you, too."

Matt laughed. "Come on and help me set up. We're gonna have a fire . . . ," he said, walking back over the deck toward the side of the barge. McGhee scanned the deck, noticing the wood planking across it, wondering how that would work. Tucked along the edge where Matt was undoing some bungee cords, a piece of sheet metal five feet on a side leaned out as it was freed. Each grabbing a side, Matt led them back toward the bow, and they set the sheet in front of it on top of the deck. Walking further back toward the captain's bridge of the barge there were some tarps in the corner, bungeed and holding something bulky in place. Tossing them aside, McGhee saw there was a 55-gallon drum there with a gap cut in the front, exposing almost half of it. Two metal guides had been welded along the top and bottom where the removed piece could be slipped in and slid across like a door. In that there were torched slots to let air in. A five-inch hole in the top had a foot of metal pipe sticking up for exhaust.

"Our stove . . . ," Matt said, laughing. "Let's move it over . . . ," he said, grabbing one side of it.

They placed it on the steel sheet and Matt jiggled it until it was stable in place against the bow and on the sheet. Grabbing a couple bungees, he hooked into some hooks welded to the back, then secured it to the bow, looping through bars there to hold it in place. "There . . . ," he said when he finally stood up. "We can't have this thing tipping if it gets rough later."

The afternoon waned into evening, and the evening gave way to dusk. Matt disappeared into the bridge again to spell Karl and guide the barge into a corner of the river where they could anchor for the night. As Karl carried an armload of split wood out to the stove he explained to McGhee they didn't run the river at night since the draw of the barge was deeper and demanded more attention than their skiff and raft had in the old days, and it wouldn't be safe to run at night. They'd leave at first light and be back in town by dinner, assuming they didn't have any trouble. McGhee followed Karl back and forth as he continued preparations, carrying wood when he did, then camp chairs for them to sit, then food to cook on top of the stove, then sleeping bags they'd stowed. When the weather was nice and not so cold, they'd sleep out on the deck by the stove. It was something they enjoyed doing when they could, when the weather permitted, and the air was warm enough to allow it.

When the anchor was set and the running lights lit, in case someone else was running at night and might run into them otherwise, all three set to lighting the fire and preparing the food. They had some moose in foil packets already and some foiled potatoes and carrots (which they dropped into the front of the stove where they could retrieve them), and a coffee urn. Night had fallen, though it was slow and incomplete, never reaching full darkness as it was still mid-August. It was nine before they ate and almost ten before they settled into their chairs to poke at the fire and digest.

The drum had worked well as a stove, and now with its door slid full open, it cast a warm glow onto the deck and the three men camped in front of it. The air began to have a slight chill in it, and as Matt noticed McGhee sliding his chair in closer to the fire, he put a hand on his knee to stop him. Running back into the darkness he disappeared a moment, but McGhee could hear him rummaging in the wood pile, deep thunks indicating he was tossing wood aside, until he heard several other thunks of a higher timbre. Returning, Matt had several sticks of birch in his arms, four inches round, cut to length but not split. Handing one to McGhee, he motioned for him to throw it in.

The bark ignited almost instantly, throwing off a blast of heat that pushed McGhee back. "I forgot about that . . . ," he said, looking over to Matt and Karl. They were both watching him and seemed to be enjoying the spectacle of it and the company of their friend.

Settling back into his chair, McGhee was warmer and stared into the fire. It reminded him of being a younger man and of his adventures on the river long ago. The same seemed to occur to Karl, for he spoke of them.

"Ever hear back from your bottle?" he asked, though he continued staring into the fire. "The one you tossed in back then, with the note inside. That was one hell of a letter, man . . . ," he said, his mouth curling up at the corner at the thought of it.

"Hold a sec . . . ," McGhee said, climbing out of his chair to disappear back along the deck toward where he had stowed his gear. Returning a moment later, he tossed a frosted green bottle into Karl's lap.

"This time it's full . . . ," he said, patting Karl on the shoulder.

"*Oh, man* . . . ," Karl said, cradling it in his hands, trying to read the label in the firelight. "Same stuff then?"

Matt leaned over to have a look. "Sounds like I missed a party . . . ," Matt said, leaning back in his chair.

Karl twisted open the cork with a merry *thwig* sound and took a sniff. "May I?" he said, holding it up to McGhee.

McGhee nodded, smiling. "Only forty years late . . . ," McGhee said. Karl tipped the bottle back and took a long pull on it before tipping it right again, and smacked his lips before handing the bottle to Matt. "Cap?" he said. Matt accepted the bottle, but took a more judicious sip.

"We were out on the river . . . ," Karl said, taking the bottle back from Matt before handing it to McGhee. "It was the wood run. Wind had come up in the day and wrecked the raft, so we were drifting at night. A drizzle came in and it was cool. We had the potbelly in the skiff and McGhee and I stood by the pipe all night holding on with our wet gloves. McGhee had a bottle then, but only a couple sips left. When it was done, he put in a real nice letter thanking his brother for it. And something about the journey not taken . . . ."

"So how are your brothers?" Matt asked, looking to McGhee.

McGhee held the bottle in his lap, thinking, then took a swig from it, wiping his lips on his sleeve before answering. "Don't talk to them much . . . ," he said. "I had a bit of a falling out with Les. Talked to Wil about six months ago."

"Which brother was that letter to, again? The one in the bottle?" Karl asked, reaching over for another drink.

"That was Les . . . ," McGhee said, handing the Courvoisier over.

"Seemed like you were pretty fond of him them . . . ," he said, pulling out the cork, but letting the bottle rest on his stomach. "What happened?"

McGhee shrugged. "Family shit . . . ," he said, staring into the fire. "Actually haven't talked to him in ten years."

"Money?" Matt asked, grabbing the bottle away from Karl before he'd had a chance to drink, but he didn't protest.

"Something like that . . . ," McGhee said. "Estate stuff. Really, it was kinda stupid. At the time it really pissed me off, though . . . ."

"So why doncha call 'em?" Karl said, looking over. "I lost my brother a couple years back. Kind of a douchebag, but I still miss 'em."

"Habit, I guess . . . ," McGhee said, motioning to get the bottle back.

Matt took another small sip, letting out a satisfied groan as he handed it over. "Pretty smooth . . . ," he said.

"Gets harder the longer I don't talk to him. Of course, he hasn't called me either. Got a Christmas card, though, about five years back. From his wife. It had his name on it, but it was her handwriting . . . I think."

"Well, that's *something* . . . ," Karl said.

"Yeah, that's something . . . ," McGhee said, taking another swig. The cognac was sweet on the tongue but warm in the throat and the belly. "Funny how time gets away from ya. One minute you're twenty-two, then next you're sixty . . . ."

"Sixty-two as I recall . . . ," Matt said.

"Thanks . . . ," McGhee said, raising the bottle in toast and taking another swig before handing it over to Matt.

"Hey . . . it was my turn . . . ," Karl objected as the bottle passed in front of him, but he made no move to intercept it.

McGhee shuffled his chair in another inch closer to the fire and sighed. "I just woulda thought I'd have gotten more done . . . ," he said, staring into the flames. "You sure that thing's safe?" he said to no one in particular, but they ignored him. The edges of the can seemed to be glowing, but McGhee thought that might have been the cognac hitting his system instead. "There always seemed to be so much time. Maybe too much."

"I think it's just about right . . . ," Karl said, reaching for the bottle. "I'm not sure how much more I can take, but it's been a good ride . . . ," he said, then added, "pretty good anyway."

"I used to look at old men, think about how much they had done. Listen to their stories. It made sense to me they'd done a lot, since they were old. But it doesn't have to work out that way. It's easy to waste time," McGhee said, tapping the burn barrel with his toe.

Karl looked at Matt, then at McGhee. "Not out here, it isn't," he said.

"Damn straight," Matt said, nodding. "So, you out here looking for your youth?" he added, laughing. "That's way up river, but you can't get there from here . . . ."

"Guess I felt like I had some loose ends here . . . ," McGhee said. Karl handed him the bottle, but McGhee let it rest on his knee.

"Like the Arctic Circle?" Matt said.

"Yeah, and other things . . . ," McGhee said, looking over. "Just wanted to see how things turned out for you. And you, too, Karl."

"Well, you're lookin' at it . . . ," Matt said, waving his arm around. "Some of it anyway. Got a wife – Amy – couple-a kids, too."

"Hey, wasn't that the name of that new teacher we saw that day in Ruby?" McGhee said.

"You *saw* her?" Matt said, surprised, shaking his head. "Yeah, that's my Amy."

"Hell yeah, I remember. You told me to stay away from her, that I had a whole world of women to go after, but that one was yours."

"Really? I said that?" Matt said, reaching over for the bottle. "I don't remember that at all."

"That's coz you're old . . . ,"Karl said.

"I got two years on you Karl. I can still take you . . . ,"Matt said, tipping the bottle back for another little swig.

"If I'm dead drunk, maybe. And ya got some help . . . ," Karl said, grabbing the bottle back again.

Standing up, Matt stretched and yawned, twisting at the waist right, then left to stretch. "We'd better call it," he said, yawning again. We got an early day tomorrow." Stepping over to McGhee, he stretched out his hand, then pulled him out of the chair, standing, but didn't let his hand go.

"You let me know when you sort things out. I'm still waiting on that book'a yours . . . ," he said smiling, then released his hand to grab a bag and unfurl it. "Spent forty years thinkin' of that line-a yours and still haven't figured it out."

It didn't take long for the light snores of Karl and Matt to let McGhee know they'd drifted off already. As for him, he lay awake, looking for the darkest section of sky to see the aurora, but it wouldn't come, as it wasn't the season for it.

The best part of the driving for the young McGhee was that it gave him miles and miles to think, and he believed that after all that driving – perhaps hoped is more accurate – that the solution would occur to him to avoid the fate of soul-crushing boredom a while longer. At least he'd gotten past September which had always spelled school for as long as he could remember, and he wasn't in it. That was a good deal of his flight, too: the previous four years had been hard on him and wasn't what he had expected. For as long as he could remember, college had been his destination and he hadn't needed to think any further. For most of his life, the train tracks led to that destination, and it was far enough out to be his plan. And he had expected something to blossom during his time there – in the cloistered and fecund environment that was Yale – such that his plan would become evident. But it was harder than he expected. The academics were intense and oppressive and he instantly had found he was behind, far behind, when, from his experience he had always been far ahead. That was hard to accept, but over time he found his stumbling way, though he felt he had lost a lot of blood in the process. His love for the sciences had been damaged, or perhaps it was just his ego. There were dark days when his grip upon physics loosened until he lost it all together, fleeing to math, only to discover it wasn't to be his home either. Science had been his identity for as long as he could remember, though in retrospect, it was more the trappings of it, the fun, the facts, than the performance of it. He saw its cold execution in lonely labs, the processing of data, the thin victories of percentages versus the sweeping glory of his youthful fantasies. It, too, became work, its joy drained until it was another lifeless pursuit, more drudgery and mind-numbing analysis than euphoric epiphany. Truth remained elusive while details filled in the cracks and solidified into a road of toil. So where he expected to learn the grand truths of the universe, he instead learned a more troubling and personal truth about himself: that he didn't have the will to do it, and that he could succumb to laziness just as he had criticized in his high school colleagues a few short years before. But as was his way – the way of the dilettante – he sought solace in other areas where he dabbled.

There, too, he had found frustration. When confronted by superiority in the past, though that didn't happen often, he'd point to his other talents, thinking, "But can you . . . ," as he flexed his skills in varied pursuits that never found their match. That is, not until that same challenging environment, where there were others similarly renaissance in their perspective. Only they were better there, too. His drawings weren't the best, though they showed potential, but he wasn't willing to expend the effort to truly master it, shunning instruction, afraid. Worse still, his poems and writing seemed juvenile in comparison to his colleagues, some of whom were published already, but most of whom seemed to have a better mastery of the medium, of words. It had been a sad awakening, when, as a freshman, he learned everything he had been taught about exposition was wrong. That his strict structure wasn't the picture of discipline, but was a noose about the neck of his ideas. That his prose was rife with colloquial usage, that his perspective was parochial, that even his insights fell short of the real questions that his peers raced ahead to grasp, consider, and expose in nuanced arguments. In short, it was perhaps there even more than in the sciences that he learned his limits, and that they were significant. These affronts had collected en masse for him, so that by the end of school he was done with it, content to move in a different direction, which seemed more defined and bounded and shaped by dislikes and fear and defeat rather than passion for anything specific, forcing him to wonder if Alaska had been an adventure at all, or merely a retreat.

Such were McGhee's ruminations along that part of Alaska 2 until he noticed his perseveration and shook his head, then shook it again to dispel that avenue of recollections. Those thoughts belonged in the short mountains of the east where he'd arrive eventually, but for the time being, he needed to process *this* summer, for he suspected there was truth to mine there yet, and the exposure he'd had might lead somewhere, if only he could think of it.

As he finally drove north to the Circle, he thought of Ruby and how little it had changed. There were fewer white men than there used to be, the cold pressing them out to leave the hardier Athabaskans behind. Otherwise, it had looked about the same: the houses and shacks a bit more dilapidated, the main street just as rough and shorter than he remembered, either end having shriveled or been abandoned. The only new thing he could see was Matt's cabin up on the shoulder of the hill, but even that was largely abandoned, only used for spare nights he had to spend in town when travelling the river. But it was good to see it and to see his memory was intact, even if the real version had aged in his absence.

They'd made it to the Yukon River Camp mid-morning, and Matt held McGhee's hand in both of his. "You can always come back . . . ," he had said, but this time they both knew he probably wouldn't.

The air was clear but cooler than it had been when he started driving the previous week. Still, the weather was fine, and landscape remained green with fresh shoots, though clusters of fireweed bloomed magenta in the margins signifying fall was near. So when he saw the sign for the Circle and the pullout filled with RVs and temporary travelers, he wished it had been further and continued past, looking in but not stopping, lest some eager tourist wanted to engage and pull him from his reveries.

About fifty miles into the Circle, maybe ten miles south of Coldfoot, McGhee pulled his car into a wide spot on the side of the road, and shut it down. Reaching into his pack, he removed a red-kerchief-wrapped object and stepped out of the car.

By the edge there were mosses and lichens growing around some rocks, thriving in the short summer. It was easy to lift them, exposing the earth, and easier than he imagined to excavate a small cavity. Standing, he pulled the packet from his pocket and unwrapped it in his palm, exposing what was in there: his dad's old wristwatch, leather straps stiff from lack of use, the watch stopped at eleven.

One night he had been sitting with him at the VA hospital just before he died. Mr. McGhee was in a sweat, which wasn't unusual for him those days, but there wasn't much the nurses or McGhee could do, other than keep a cool washcloth on his forehead. McGhee kept vigil into the late evening. His father wasn't delirious, but he was close to it, or perhaps he was seeing past the edge already. He had said it reminded him of his bouts with malaria, back at the end of the war. He and the guys in the ward used to joke – during the sweats – that they wished they could be in Alaska all of a sudden. It made him laugh to think of it, and he regretted never having seen it. It was the last he ever laughed as far as McGhee knew.

Wrapping it again, he stooped to slide it in the small hole, then pushed some dirt back over it before replacing the lichen and moss, tamping it into place. No one would know what was there, but he would, and he sighed, less satisfied at having done it, than sad his father had never seen it for himself.

McGhee's Datsun was getting close to Whitehorse, Yukon Territory, late, and he planned to stop there, but didn't make it. A sign eight miles west of town pointed left and north toward a lake he didn't know was there, and he found himself on the road to it before he even knew he had turned.

The road was dark and lonely, but he knew he had to take it, winding back into the hills, away from town and the bustle of humanity. And as a view of the lake opened before him over a gentle rise, just there before him, he was close to the headwaters of the Yukon. It was near where the mighty river came from, and where that Robert Service poem from his youth was set, the words flooding back to him suddenly:

> *The Northern Lights have seen queer sights,*
> *But the queerest they ever did see*
> *Was that night on the marge of Lake Lebarge*
> *I cremated Sam McGee . . . .*

Pulling into the widening of the road that became the lake's edge, McGhee turned off the lights and engine to listen. Stepping in front of his Datsun, he leaned on the hood to absorb the moment, and it was good.

All was quiet and still. It took a few minutes for his eyes to adjust to the darkness, but it gradually revealed its detail, its dark beauty, subtle beneath a starry sky, black trees silhouetted against it, the gentle lapping of the water on its hidden shore. Up above, the aurora blazed in green curtains, fringed in pink and yellow, waving madly, then peacefully, but always silent. In the distance a loon called out for him to hear, him alone, for there was no one else to hear it, and the message of the summer suddenly settled upon him, light as the cool air on his cheek: that, though he'd go home, he'd likely never truly get there, for no matter what he did or where he went, whomever he loved or lost, he might forever find himself on the margin.

Never Far Enough

3PM
Butler, PA 11/11/1971

McGhee's mother had grown up in Pittsburgh, so it was natural for her to want to go there. That said, she didn't want to go too often. It seemed she had run just far enough to be out of its clutches, but remained close enough when she needed go back, one day at a time. In retrospect, perhaps she might have been a bit afraid of her sisters and that they might pull her back into that life, into their lives, that she'd consciously left behind. As an older man, McGhee got that, though he couldn't imagine returning himself. But once he'd lost his personal tie to the area, he felt a bit like a kite with a cut string: free to go where he wanted, but without the tension in his chest to define himself against. This in turn reminded him that his brothers used to have kite fights out in the yard, a large skewer sharpened on one end of the box, or the diamond, depending on the kite. When he was a kid, he couldn't understand how

37

they got them to swoop at each other, or the point of it at all – to tear the other to shreds – and now with the intervening years, he couldn't remember who won, either. He just remembered the kites pulling at their strings like captives wound too tight around his brothers' purple fingers as they pulled and pulled. Somehow it meant something, but he wasn't sure what, neither then, nor in recollection. Sometimes, though, he felt like the kite in shreds, even as a boy. Looking back, many of his earliest recollections had that flavor.

On one such occasion, it was about three in the afternoon on a Saturday when it happened, up by the crest of Duncan Avenue, on the way back from what McGhee thought was birthday shopping, but was really more of an excuse for his parents to get out, have a talk, and go to the city. He was oblivious to most things like that, being seven – going on eight the next day – and it was natural to have that thought in his head, because at that age the world is barely larger than one's head, and its mission little more than keeping one fed and perhaps entertained. Such is the scope of a boy that age. That said, even then he wasn't oblivious to everything.

It was getting toward mid-November, so the trees were bare but for the final few dead leaves that hung on. They'd usually be on the Chestnuts at the back of the yard – not the apple trees: those gave up their leaves quickly, like at the first sign of cold the trees said they were done with it and were going to sleep. The yard had been something of an apple orchard once upon a time, but not like the precision operations one sees these days, with trees in lines and optimized for height and picking. No, these were all sorts of apple trees – Jonathans and Baldwins and others that weren't good for making pies, no matter how much sugar his mother used, and she certainly tried. But up toward the end of the yard, where it met the field where the cows came down to the edge, those trees were different still: Choke Cherry, Maple, Sassafras, Chestnut. They were the line of defense, a wall to keep things in and keep things out, which separated fields in the old days, keeping cows and apples apart. Those trees held out longer like holding their leaves was a point of honor. McGhee watched them from the rear picture window, and they were signaling the swift change of seasons, and because of that, his birthday.

By then, birthdays had already become something of a disappointment. It was his own fault and he knew it, which had already become a source of some personal guilt. That was probably the first time he had any involvement in the gift selection; until then his mom seemed to know what to get, or at least, what she got was exactly the right thing, or close enough. Was it four when he got Laddy – the big stuffed German Shepherd? He was in a pose lying on his stomach, tongue out, and rear legs swept around to hold him upright, with a nice long tail. He was a good dog – quiet – but provided most of the friendship he needed. McGhee supplied the dialog, but he knew Laddy generally supported his positions: wonder at the digging in the field beyond the Choke Cherry, annoyance with the boots and snow suit he had to wear to go out and play, fear of the plastic yellow placemat that hurt his mother's eye. Laddy didn't say it, but McGhee knew he must agree, and he knew enough not to tell his brothers, either, because they were old and said he was a baby and only played with him when there wasn't anything good on TV, and even then, played with him more like he was a toy than a brother. So Laddy was that indispensable friend, even better than Bill Kennedy was, his imaginary friend who really wasn't substantial at all and, frankly, just came into being because he heard somehow that kids his age sometimes have imaginary friends. Laddy was much better than that, and that was age four, so birthdays were still good then. But five was different.

He desperately wanted to want something in particular, but lacking much exposure to anything, even via the TV, he had no ideas whatsoever. This, of course, perplexed his mother who just wanted to get him something nice — something nice for a five-year-old that is — and be done with it. This emerged as a minor issue sometime around Halloween that year, but escalated in vast importance (at least in McGhee's head) until the day before his birthday. And after three circuits through Bill's Bargain, where his toys mostly came from when his mom had other shopping to do, she eventually stopped and looked down at him and said: "Just pick something, Franny!"

They were in front of a display for something new — at least new to McGhee — so he chose that: a Nerf basketball and hoop. It was perfect. It was a set. A big box. It required some assembly. It was a big-kid game. His mom scooped it up and tossed it into the cart, next to Borax and Clorox and steel wool and dishwashing detergent. The open-faced box rode on the top, lighter than the rest of the cart contents, and he watched it through more shopping, through the line to buy it, through the door and into the car. Even there he was able to keep an eye on it in the way-back of the station wagon where it floated to the top, again. Then he watched her take it inside, put it on the table, then into the closet in the hall where the coats hung, because it wasn't his birthday yet.

What hadn't occurred to either of them, least of all his mother, was that this time he knew what he was getting, and further, knew where it was. In short, these facts haunted him. He managed to forget about it one hour when he watched Mr. Rogers, but as soon as that was done, it floated up from the depths of his otherwise vacant head, floated up to sit at the very forefront of his thoughts, just like it had done in the cart. It was only four thirty, too, and it wasn't even dark yet, so he'd have to wait almost an entire day before he could take it out.

That evening, he took to asking his mother about it every few minutes: Was it safe in the closet? Was it even still in there? Was she going to wrap it? When might he expect to get it? – until, finally, the look of exasperation on his mother's face became noticeable to his father, who uttered just one word – "Franny . . . !" – in that tone that meant he'd better give it a rest.

Somehow he managed to hold his tongue the rest of the evening, even though it was on his mind. His mother helped him get to sleep eventually, though it was fitful and full of Nerf fantasies. In his dreams he'd hang it on his door, low at first until he became good, then they'd put it higher for him. He'd spin in the air. He'd dunk it. He'd toss it from impossibly far away and it would swish through the stiff nylon net. Somewhere about four in the morning, these dreams pushed him awake, his eyes snapping open. It would be a long time yet, but he couldn't stand it. He lay there trying to sleep, but there was no sleep left in him. After such an eternity he convinced himself he must have waited long enough – it couldn't be too long until they were getting up anyway – and surely it would be OK to ask his mother for just an idea when he might be allowed to have it.

Sneaking into his parents' bedroom, he marched up to his mother's side of the bed. He thought his noise would surely wake her – his footsteps on the wood, the creaking, the scuffing of his feet (which he added at the end, because it wasn't so far to walk anyway) – but she remained motionless. He watched her sleeping form for a solid minute before resolving to reach out and poke her on the shoulder. A moment later a sleepy, "Hmmm?" emerged from the dark still lump that was his mother.

"So when can I have it?" he asked.

"Hmm? What? Why aren't you in bed? What time is it?" she asked, her voice increasing in annoyance the more awake she became, the last coming as she rolled over to grab the little boxy clock to stare bleary-eyed into its face. The light orange glow said five to five. "Are you kidding me?" she said sitting up. Her movement in the bed woke the bear next to her.

"What's going on?" he heard his dad say. "What? — is something wrong?" he said, struggling to the surface from a deep sleep. McGhee was realizing it may not have been a good idea, but still, they were awake now, so he pushed ahead.

"I was just wondering if I could have . . . ," he said, his voice shrinking the further he went.

"What?" his mom said.

"Huh?" his dad said.

"You know . . . ," McGhee said. "The thing. The birthday thing. The Nerf . . . ." There was a thirty- second pause which he suspected she was using to see if he went away, but he didn't. He shifted slightly on his feet, causing a small squeak from the floor boards.

"Fine . . . ," his mother said, tossing the covers open to put her feet down. Stuffing her toes into her slippers, she began scuffing over the wood. "You know, I haven't even wrapped it, but if you just *can't wait any longer*, then . . . ." Grabbing her robe, she brushed past McGhee on her way out. He followed close behind her, running into her at the closet where she stopped to open the door. She grabbed the box, swung the door closed and moved to the kitchen and switched on the light.

"Here . . . ," she said plopping it on the kitchen table. "I hope you're happy. I'm going to bed." The box had barely come to rest before she was padding back to bed down the hall in her slippers.

McGhee climbed up on the chair to give it a look: one open-faced box, containing one large sponge ball, one plastic hoop, and an attached fish-line net. McGhee put his arms around the box, staring into it. It wasn't much, not nearly as good as he imagined, even though he had seen it, and worse, it was all there was. This was his birthday, it was done already at five in the morning, and the realization he'd just blown it flooded over him suddenly. Before he could control it, the tears started, and more than that, sniffs which mounted and mounted until, finally, he erupted in uncontrollable sobbing. He didn't even need to take it out of the package. It was there, plain and dull, and his fifth birthday was a complete disaster. He was inconsolable — not even Laddy could help him as he watched from his perch in the dining room. From behind him, he heard the door to his parents' room open, and he heard the padding of his mother's slippers returning, but it didn't matter. It wouldn't matter what she said. She said nothing and just put her hand on top of his head and pulled him to her. And then, in his father's voice, he heard him say, "Oh Franny . . . it'll be OK."

The age five debacle seemed like ancient history, but birthdays already filled McGhee with an odd sensation of apprehension, a lumpy mix of anticipation and dread. He knew birthdays didn't have to go well, and this time for his eighth, he'd do his best to make it at least decent. No, this time, they weren't going to Bill's Bargain, either: they would go most of the way to Pittsburgh so it would have to be different. There were *real* toy stores there, so surely he'd find something worthy. Still, he was a bit worried — he'd already been all over the other small toy-store in town, and there wasn't a thing there that caught his interest, which had almost never happened before.

When they didn't go to Bill's Bargain, and they were waiting for his dad to come out of the store where he worked, sometimes they'd wander a few doors up the street to Aland's. It looked a bit like one of those old west stores from *Gunsmoke* – he didn't have the words to describe such things – crammed between two other nameless stores, a single wood step leading up and into the heart of it. The two front windows on either side of the entrance were stacked with good things: scooters and sling shots, lawn games and trains. Inside, it only got better. The wooden floors were ancient and dusty and creaking, soft to the step, even for a boy, with cracks between the boards leading to the dark underneath, and dim above from the toys blocking light. It was stacked floor to ceiling with stuff, things hanging off shelves up to the top, and the ceiling had stuff dangling, too, the whole way across. There were sombreros, hats with feathers, bows and arrows, wagons and peddle cars, pup-tents, parachutes and piñatas, balsa-wood glid-ers, and runner sleds. The further back into the store, the more stuff there was to see, until, finally, in the deepest recesses, one reached the rubber masks and kites and BB guns and magnifying glasses, the aisle narrowing the whole way until further passage was impossible. He usually found something there, but not this time. Even at the register, where he used to get the bag of peas and the thick straw peashooters, there wasn't anything. Even the Pez dispensers left him cold, and they used to always work. No, he'd have to go further, out of town, and when he looked up at his mom, she read it in his face. "We'll go this Saturday . . . ," she said, and smiled at the old man behind the counter. "Sorry Mr. Aland . . . ," she said, corralling McGhee to leave. "Nothing today."

Before heading back home his mother made a detour by the church: she slowed down near the parking lot by the bank. People were streaming in and out, carrying baskets and baked goods and candles and programs. McGhee's mother had both hands on the wheel as she looked on, watching a few minutes, until McGhee started to fidget in his seat. As they drove away, he noticed that expression he saw on her face sometimes, the one she'd get when her sister Stell called to tell her of her troubles.

Once out of town, her mood improved the closer to home they got. She was reassuring and said she was sure they'd find the perfect thing, so he thought so, too. He liked when she said things like that, so sometimes he'd pretend he didn't hear it, just to have her repeat it, which she did, dutifully.

Because he was so much younger than his brothers, he spent a lot of time with her. Especially when he was little. He'd help her with the laundry Mondays, and watch her sing to the washing machine. When he got a little older, he still liked to play around her feet, though he became a little self-conscious of it: he'd taken recently to asking her if he was a *mama's boy* which he'd heard about at school, and she'd laugh and assure him he was not, even if he asked several times an hour. So he had no reason to doubt her, even if she seemed a little distracted. She'd been so busy lately working at the sewing machine, and he watched her through her sewing hour as he played on the painted cement floor: he'd set his armies to conflict around the cabinet of her machine, narrating the harrowing feats of daring his men were performing, though they remained stoic with their plastic green expressions. She was working on that quilt, and it seemed to go on forever.

Somewhere back in the spring she got the idea for it, or rather, circumstances led her to think of it. She'd never done a quilt before, though she had done plenty of sewing: clothes, fixes, hems, the occasional pillow. And she'd made plenty of pant suits which she wore, out of the house even, in public. They were on the boxy side, but she said they were *comfortable*, which actually seemed to mean that they were easier to sew, and a little too big.

All of this was lost on McGhee – he was just happy when she set to working at her machine. When she was really into it, she'd hum or even break into a verse of an old song. McGhee liked that, even though he feigned embarrassment when she did so. But this latest project – the quilt – was much more ambitious than anything she had done before and required more materials than she had ever used. There were the various fabrics. There was the design, which she said she was only using as a guideline, only it ended up looking mostly just like it. There was the batting. And there were the drawings – she made several, many even – trying to get one particular part right.

Tuesdays she still worked at the rectory for a couple hours. McGhee would land at the Sanderson's because Mary was always home and happy to help out, and McGhee could play with David, his first-ever friend. He was a year ahead of McGhee, so he seemed significantly older. They'd play in the basement with his collection of peddle cars, though David always got the fire engine, and he had the stupid sedan, which was apparently a Desoto, even though he didn't know what that really was. They'd race in tighter and tighter circles until they couldn't turn any tighter, then in one instant, crash the cars together in a cataclysmic collision that often as not sent them sprawling onto the cement floor, and one or both in need of multiple Band-Aids. One time McGhee flew out but somehow landed on his feet, mostly, though he was propelled headlong into the tall rack of canned tomatoes. When Mary raced down the wood stairs she discovered the rack toppled and weeks of boiled Ball jars broken on the floor, the rack resting over his body showing only his wriggling legs. The tomatoes made it look bad, so when he emerged unscathed, she was more relieved than anything – he heard her praying as she dug through the wreckage to pull him out. Such were his Tuesday adventures.

For her part, his mom was glad to get out of the house. She'd been a secretary before she was married, living in Pittsburgh and working down town with the other professionals. Moving to the small town had been hard for her. She said it was always what she wanted, but once she had it, she always wondered a little bit whether it had actually been the right thing. When the rectory job emerged right after getting married, she jumped at it. The pay wasn't much but it helped – more than that, though, it was just a little like the life she remembered. It was lucky she could type and take steno, so she became the administrative assistant to the Monsignor himself. She'd take his calls, take dictation, then write up her correspondence – all with her flawless skills honed in the big city to the south. Once the kids came along, she had to scale back her duties there. By the time McGhee was school age, she was down to one day a week, but she was reluctant to let it go. It wasn't really enough to meet the needs of the Monsignor, but he seemed to sense she needed it even more than he did, so he made due. Sometimes she'd even take a few pieces home and tap them out on her typewriter. She said he always thanked her for it, too, though there wasn't overtime.

It was in this capacity that she learned of the Harvest Festival and the declining finances of the church. The Monsignor even confided in her, while he was dictating a letter to the bishop in the Pittsburgh diocese, that this year they were expected to make up some of the difference through sales at the festival. Though they had had festivals every year, this year it seemed the stakes were higher. Her position might even be on the line, as there might not be funding for any staff at all. The Monsignor even shuddered as he admitted he didn't know the first thing about using a typewriter, and he feared the impression it would make if he couldn't have his correspondence rendered in crisp, clear triplicate.

So the idea emerged to solicit goods to sell for the festival, anything from baking to home-canned goods, to other crafts. It probably wouldn't generate more than a hundred dollars he said, but every bit would help, and further, it would show "the powers that be" that St. Paul parish was deserving of whatever extra help they could spare. Such were the realities of the political environment of the diocese, and such became the inspiration for the quilt. And once she suggested it to the Monsignor, he heartily endorsed the idea of a "custom quilt" and said that might even get them more than he imagined.

That night, she set to thinking about the project, talking to McGhee's father about the time it would take, and the materials. This latter part would be an unexpected expense, but she argued she could get most of what she needed from the remnants bin, and that she had some fabric left over from a couple of her projects, so really, the biggest expense would be for the batting, and that wouldn't be much. She even offered to stop buying tomato soup – which was her favorite, and which she considered something of an indulgence – to fund it. "No need for that, honey. Go ahead," he had said, and she kissed him, right in front of McGhee, which made him a little squeamish, like her singing did.

That was April, or was it May – McGhee had the impression it had gone on forever, though upon reflection he realized he wasn't in school much after she started, so maybe it was even June. She had set out the tables in the back of the basement, beyond the finished part where the washing machine and dryer and sewing machine lived. Clearly it would be something of a production: she unfolded the tissue-paper pattern on the table she had purchased at the Kmart, carefully unfolding and unfolding and unfolding until it hung over the edges of both tables. Then she took out a pen and started marking up two or three areas where she thought it should be different, looking at her little note-card drawings while she did it, until after a few days of fretting and thinking and reviewing, she looked at McGhee and said, "OK."

She had a set of big shears she used to cut the fabric — not the regular scissors she used for ordinary things and paper. These she kept in a drawer of the baby dresser in the corner where she stowed her sewing supplies, wrapped in a lightly oiled rag. One time McGhee reached to touch them (he liked to touch everything), and she yelled, "No!" He pulled back his hand and looked at her — she didn't yell very often. "These . . . ," she said, lifting the shears, "are *very* sharp, and special. I don't want you to hurt yourself, or them, either." Her look was earnest and serious. She didn't usually look so determined on her normal projects. Still, he didn't really like scissors anyway as they never quite worked the way he planned, so he was content to nod and watch her. At least he was content to watch her the first fifteen minutes. She was very deliberate and careful as she cut, and the cuts were slow and precise. After several minutes, she carefully laid the shears back down and lifted the piece in her hand, each end of the arcing piece draped over the edges of her palm. "One down and a hundred to go," she said happily. That was enough for McGhee who sucked in his lips in a smile and ran off to find something more amusing.

McGhee would circle back now and then to check progress, and after a few hours was disappointed to find there was merely a very short pile of cut pieces and nothing resembling the blanket he expected. On her end, his mom was happy with the progress — more than twenty pieces cut — though the disappointment registering in McGhee's eyes was enough for her to push it aside and head to the kitchen to start dinner. And that's how it was for days and days until the actual sewing began, and even then the progress was slow. It would eventually be a queen-sized quilt, but the more she sewed, the bigger that seemed to be. When she'd finally done the edge around a corner, successfully gathering and then sandwiching the batting between the four pieces it required, she held it up. McGhee was there to see it, but his shrug was enough to have her push it aside for yet another day.

It was a hot summer, which made the work in the basement that much more tolerable: the expanse of cement floors, tile, and cinder block walls made for something of a natural refrigerator, albeit not a very cold one. Still, it was preferable to the upstairs which could be sweltering, despite the fans constantly agitating the air. Her allergies and headaches seemed to be worse in the summer, or perhaps these were other ills and aches that came with her time of life. The basement, though, remained a refuge for her, and for McGhee, and while she worked in the back on the quilt, pulling more and more pieces through the machine, she'd have *The Guiding Light* on TV, or *The Secret Storm*, her "stories," which made the whole thing something better than merely tolerable, and as even McGhee could perceive, she actually enjoyed it. She had a look that he liked to see, though he could never have described it, for, again, he didn't have the words just yet. It just seemed she was more herself in those moments when she was lost at the machine, and would emerge from those prolonged sessions smiling.

Just after Labor Day he had to go back to school, which he hated, but he'd run downstairs each day when he got home to see the progress. By mid-September it was taking shape: the full field was completed, or at least filled in, and the end seemed within view. Time was drawing close as the festival was less than a month away, so she re-doubled her efforts and worked longer into the evening, sometimes even after dinner. She had begun working on the theme of the quilt and set to cutting more panels for that purpose.

She drew several designs, then set to cutting out the silhouettes of several women in hats which she then applied onto the surface, overlapping so they looked like a crowd. Some were white, some brown, and some shades in between. Finally, at the front she crafted a face from many pieces of a woman looking straight on, peering out from the quilt. McGhee was surprised it looked so good, because he had never known his mother to draw a face like that. His father drew now and then, and he assumed he'd gotten his interest in drawing from him, but with that face crafted from fabric, he wasn't so sure. When he asked her who she was, his mother smiled at him. "It's a secret," she said. Then the next day she sewed 1-9-2-0 on it, and a word he didn't know, then it went into a big box that she put in the trunk of the car. It was six days to the festival, so she had just made it.

She was all smiles that Tuesday, the one before Saturday's Harvest Festival, when she dropped McGhee at the Sanderson's. So he was surprised he was only there an hour before she returned — his visits usually ran all afternoon. Her eyes were red and puffy, and Mary hugged her in the driveway by the car.

McGhee wasn't sure why they didn't go into the festival and had only driven by, but he was glad since he didn't want to go anyway. The church smelled weird and was dark, even in the basement where they had those fluorescent lights. He was far more concerned with his birthday, which was just a week away, wondering how to avoid repeating the disaster of his fifth. Even though Aland's had been a bust, he was pretty sure he'd be able to avoid it, though, since they were going most of the way to Pittsburgh, and his mom had promised they'd find something anyway.

So that Saturday they got up a little early – it was about the last Saturday his dad would have before the Christmas rush when he worked all the time – and they piled into the car. The older boys stayed home to do "homework," or so they said, so it was just an outing for the three of them. McGhee liked it that way sometimes since he had their full attention. His mother was quiet, though, staring through the windshield in thought. Eventually his dad switched on the radio and tuned in a Pens game on KDKA. His mother looked sideways at her husband a few times until he noticed her, but she didn't say anything. For his part, McGhee was occupied with deliberations and looking out the window.

McGhee didn't notice when his mom lowered the hockey game to talk to his dad, and he didn't notice the look on her face either. She'd worked at the rectory a long time. Mr. McGhee sighed and was silent for a minute. Eventually he said it wasn't unexpected, so she shouldn't feel bad. She looked half better, but Mr. McGhee didn't seem to notice, turning up the game again. Myron Cope was explaining some subtlety of goal tending, to which Mr. McGhee said he was "such a twit."

It wasn't a very nice day: the sky was low and gray and gloomy and cold, but McGhee was in a good mood. He was hopeful, sitting in the back and looking out the window as they zoomed down Route 8 toward the city. He was watching for snow flurries which he always liked, especially on school days when they might portend a disruption to his regular schedule. There was nothing better than to wake up to a fresh snow and listen to the radio to hear his school was cancelled. It was early yet for snow days, but it wouldn't be long. His birthday signaled the start of that season, and his thoughts revolved merrily about the prospect of missing school. The bare trees whizzed by the window, half-heartedly flanked by sparse yellow grass. The leaves scuttled across the road ahead of them in the crosswind like skittish people in the moments before a rainstorm.

They made it most of the way to Pittsburgh but stopped on the outskirts of the city where a Toys-R-Us occupied a full city block. McKnight road had become one of those suburban shopping meccas for the city. The Pittsburgh skyline was visible on the horizon and McGhee pointed, but his mother didn't take notice, instead closing the car door and lightly pushing him on the back to get moving.

Inside, it was already winding up for Christmas. An elf on a ladder was stowing tinsel around a bell near the top of a pole close to the ceiling. He wondered briefly how that might work, with Santa and so few elves, though he already suspected he wasn't privy to the full story. He knew enough to leave it alone, though, so he walked by the elf onward toward the games. Sometime during the week he had an idea he might like a game, so he was single-minded in his intent to look into that first. His parents were just thankful he had something of a plan and followed in his wake. They hung back to talk as he went off, though they kept him in sight.

By the time they caught up to him he was staring like a pointer-dog at one game in particular: *Battling Tops*. Never mind it would require someone to play with, and his brothers, being teenagers, were as likely to request extra lima beans as sit to play a game with him, but he imagined it would be fun anyway. His mother nodded, and he slid it off the shelf. It was a pleasantly large and heavy box — he liked the heft of it and how substantial it was. The kids on the cover seemed to having a blast playing it, too, so after momentary hesitation he looked up at her and nodded. On the way to the register, she picked a few small things for him, asking if he might like those, too. It was buzzing in his ears, to which he'd learned to say, yes, which he dutifully did with a smile on his face – he didn't want to do anything to jeopardize the main prize he held. Once through check out, a tremendous weight lifted from his shoulders: he had found something good and would not be repeating his dismal fifth, and the relief registered in broad smiles and over-response to everything his parents said to him. For her part, a slight smile made it through her expression, which, if McGhee had come to regard it, looked as gray as the weather. On the way out, an elf offered McGhee a complimentary bag of popcorn, and it was enough to complete his ecstasy. His dad stopped him, smiling himself, putting a hand on his shoulder: "Just don't wipe your hands on your pants, OK?" McGhee nodded his assent, like it was the most important directive he had ever received.

The bag barely fit over the box, punching its corners out in all directions of the plastic. With his mom's permission, he jiggled it out of the bag in the back seat as they left the lot. He balanced the box on his knees, delighted that they found the heft significant, too. "It looks really good, huh Mom?" he asked over the bench seat.

Leaning back over the seat, she looked at him. "I bet it'll be real fun, Franny . . . ," she said. He saw that as a good sign.

Now they had completed their mission, everything seemed a bit easier: his mom and dad were talking a bit in the front. After a silence, his eyes raised to look at them when he heard his mom say, "Sorry . . . ," to his dad.

His father looked over, but didn't say anything immediately, returning his gaze to the road. After a few moments, he relented. "It wasn't much money, but we're gonna miss it . . . ," he said finally.

She looked at him, her eyes watering slightly. She put her hand on his shoulder to rub it. She still had her leather gloves on, so they made a little squeaky noise. "So, what did he say?" his father said.

She pulled her hand back, lowering her head, but didn't say anything. Mr. McGhee looked over at her a few seconds, then looked back at the road. "Was he mad?" he continued.

Raising her head, she looked over at him. "He said it didn't have anything to do with the quilt, but . . . ," her voice trailed off. He waited for her to continue, but she did not. They drove on in silence a few minutes. They communicated that way sometimes — in little bursts — then they'd sit and process until the next question came.

"We can always use it at home . . . ," he said. "So what was it, anyway? I never even got to see it before you took it in," he said. "Was it that bad?"

McGhee had become aware of the conversation, and still swelling with well-being, wanted to help. "It wasn't bad at all!" he blurted out. "It had a really cool woman on it . . . ."

Mr. McGhee looked at his wife. "Clothed?" he asked her, a smirk curving into his voice.

She smacked him on the shoulder. "Yes, clothed . . . ," she said. She couldn't contain a momentary smile, though she suppressed it again. She kept looking at him, but didn't say anything.

"And?" he said. Eventually he looked at her.

"It was Susan Anthony . . . ," she said.

"Who?" he said.

"Susan Anthony. Susan *B.* Anthony . . . ," she said, her voice hanging on the *B.* Mr. McGhee still had a blank stare.

"You don't know who Susan B. Anthony is?" she asked him, allowing some incredulity to creep into her voice.

He just shook his head. "Nope."

"Women's *suffrage?*" she said, her voice leading him.

Suddenly McGhee put it together. "Oh, that was the 'S' word on the quilt, Mom, right?" he said.

"You're kidding, right?" Mr. McGhee said. "You made a suffrage quilt for the Monsignor's bake sale?" he said. He kept looking from the road, to his wife, and back to the road again. She didn't say anything, but he kept after her. "You had to know he'd *hate* that . . . ," he said. His tone was somewhere between disbelief and consternation. "He's a friggin' *Monsignor* for Crissake . . . ."

Her head was bowed and her voice was low. "He did say he thought I meant the Virgin Mary when I had said there'd be a woman on it . . . ," she said, "and that I'd gone a little too far . . . ."

"What were you thinking?" he went on, though he didn't look at her when he said it. McGhee's mother didn't look at her husband, either, her head still lowered and her hands in her lap. "Sorry . . . ," she said again, her voice low and small.

McGhee felt bad for her, though he didn't exactly understand what was going on. She'd been working at the rectory as long as he could remember, and she was proud of that. He could tell she was, every time Tuesday rolled around and it was time to go to David's house. Mrs. Sanderson was proud of her, too; she'd never gone to any business school, nor learned to type or take dictation, at least not officially. Sometimes Tuesday afternoons, before she'd come back for him, Mrs. Sanderson would give him some fresh hot buns to eat — a tiny bit of butter melting inside already — and sit with him to tell him about his mother. How she came from the city. How she'd worked for *Herbick & Held*. How she'd supported her mom, toward the end when she couldn't work anymore herself. It was a big change for her to leave the city, to start a new life in a new place. She was "courageous," she had said, and when McGhee looked up at her, she was nodding to him. "Courageous," she said again, pointing at him. "Because in those days it was *hard* for girls like her, making their way in the city, then going off to start a new life like she did. And look what she did . . . a beautiful home, a good husband – your dad – and three lovely boys." She pulled the tissue from her sleeve where she always kept it and wiped her nose. "You boys should be *very* proud."

The road was a little curvy there, spilling McGhee's popcorn on the floor. His father saw it out of the corner of his eye. "Franny, you pick that up. I don't want it getting under the seat here." McGhee got down behind the bench and started grabbing after the kernels. His dad didn't seem mad exactly, but with the tone of the discussion, he didn't want to be a source of further frustration.

It was about three in the afternoon, and Duncan Avenue had a nasty turn over the crest of the next hill. McGhee rolled gently against the seat as the brakes applied. He heard his dad say, "Dammit," a moment before the sound of crunching, screeching metal, the squeal of tires sent sideways on the cold asphalt, and the finale of glass bits rolling on the pavement. The car came to a sudden stop, askew in the lanes of traffic.

McGhee wasn't sure what had happened and looked over the seat. Both of his dad's hands were clenched on the wheel. His mother had both hands clutched to the sides of her head. Steam was coming up over the hood which was crinkled in a couple feet, accordion style. A rapping on the driver side window brought them out of stasis. It was a young man in an army jacket. The name patch on his breast said *Danko.*

"You guys alright?" he yelled in through the inch gap in the window. "You alright?" he repeated.

Mr. McGhee turned to his son: "You OK, Franny?" he asked. "Honey?" he said, pivoting to his wife. Both nodded, but no words came out.

"Hold on a sec . . . ," Danko said, leaning back from the car. "I saw the whole thing. Lemme see if I can get a plate." Before Mr. McGhee could say anything, the young man was dashing off down the street behind their car. McGhee turned to watch him, and his bobbing head kept going until it disappeared completely over the hill.

The rest of it was something of a blur: the police materialized within a few minutes. Once the immediate shock wore off, Mr. and Mrs. McGhee were recounting the story over and over to each other, and asking Franny if he had seen anything, and noting how lucky it was that he had spilled the popcorn at the exact moment he did, sending him to the floor after it, and considering how it could have been, if he hadn't. They "shuddered to think of it."

They stayed in the car until the police asked them to step out, then poured out to have a look: the front driver side was caved in most of the way back to the mirror — Mr. McGhee tried to get out his side but couldn't, so he had to slide across the bench to get out behind his wife. McGhee's mom opened the door for him on her side to avoid the traffic. Meanwhile, the cars streamed by slowly as drivers and passengers and kids in the back seats craned their necks and pushed noses against windows for a good look. One of the cops stood in the middle of traffic, directing it around the wreck, waving with impatience as the cars inevitably slowed to see the carnage. The three McGhees gathered in front, staring at their car: the bent-in wheel sat at an odd angle like a broken leg. Fluid was bleeding onto the street, creating steam on the engine as it flowed out forming a green tongue licking its way slowly along the pavement. The left headlamp looked out sideways like a large glass eye, dead and staring skyward. McGhee crinkled his nose and covered it with a glove. His mom smiled and leaned down to acknowledge his face: "Poosey dinkies," she said, which she always said when something smelled bad.

His dad was talking to the cop when McGhee noticed Danko jogging back up over the hill toward them. His army jacket was flapping in the wind which was chilly — sometime in the last bit the drizzle had converted over to flurries, only they weren't so merry as he watched them. By the time Danko made it back to the car, he leaned against it, head down and out of breath, which was coming out as steam in the cold air. McGhee's father had forgotten about him until that moment, then put his hand on the cop's shoulder to interject: "This guy said he saw the whole thing . . . ," he said.

The cop nodded and stepped over toward the young man. "Is that right?" he asked, his voice somewhat forceful. It was clear he didn't want to dilly dally. Danko, looked up from his bent pose, and seeing it was a cop, stood at attention. "You in the army, son?" the cop asked. His tone softened a bit.

The young man nodded. "Yes sir," he said. "On leave though . . . ," he continued. "For the holidays."

"Glad to hear it," the cop continued. "So what's the story?"

"This guy . . . ," he said, pointing down the road over the hill, "this priest crossed over the line and smacked into these here people. I mean, their car. Just right over the line and *boom*. Saw the whole thing . . . ."

The cop looked at Mr. McGhee then back to the kid. "Priest?" the cop asked. Mr. McGhee looked at his wife and a shadow passed over her brow.

Danko was recovering from his jog and shifted his stance before answering. "Yeah. *Priest*," he said, leaning in. "So, once I checked on these people," he said motioning to the McGhees, "I hoofed it over the hill to see if I could get a plate. He skidded off the road down there . . . ," he said, motioning again over the hill. I ran up to his window and rapped on it — he was hunched over the wheel a bit, but rolled it down — the window I mean. That's when I saw his collar . . . ," he said, pausing a moment. "And smelled it." He finished talking, his expression curled into a wry half-smile and he shook his head.

"Smelled it?" the cop asked, his pen stopping on his pad. He looked at the young man and his eyebrows went from frowning to knowing. "Oh . . . ," he said. "Beer then?" he asked, his expression matching the young man.

"More like bourbon I'd guess . . . ," the young man said. "But I don't know. It was *something* though . . . ." The cop set to writing it down, then clicked off his pen. "He still down there . . . Danko?" he said, looking at the name patch on his jacket.

"Hell no . . . ," Danko said. Looking over at the McGhees he looked sheepish. "Sorry, ma'am," he said. "No sir," he said, returning his glance to the cop. "Once he saw me, he peeled out down Duncan. Almost ran over my foot, too."

"Great . . . ," the cop said, looking back at Mr. McGhee, then back at Danko. "I don't suppose . . . ," he continued, but Danko cut him off.

"Why yes I did!" he said, and held up his left hand. Scrawled across his palm in blue ballpoint was the priest's plate number. He wiggled a Bic pen in his right hand, smiling.

Mr. McGhee stepped over to Danko and stuck out his hand. "Thank you very much young man . . . ," he said. Danko wiped his hand on his pants before accepting the handshake and smiled at him. "Happy to do it, man . . . ," he said.

Just before the tow-truck pulled away with the car, McGhee reached into the back seat for his game, clutching it to his chest. His mother pulled him close, and his father pulled them both against his shoulder.

McGhee overheard the hushed discussion of his mother and father in the kitchen sometime after that: it turned out it was scotch,

and pills, too. Apparently the priest's church was anxious for the
McGhees to forget. For his part, McGhee couldn't understand how
his mom lost the job at the rectory, or why the quilt was bad even
though it wasn't, why the Monsignor wouldn't let her work there
anymore, and why another priest would go out and drink scotch in
the middle of the afternoon and wreck into people. It was all very
confusing, but it seemed like it made some sense, only not in a way
McGhee could figure out.

The check from the church let them install air conditioning the
next spring, so they didn't have to hide in the basement anymore
to escape the heat. Still, there was more damage to repair than the
check could cover.

One afternoon that November, McGhee saw his mom hand his
father a screwdriver. He couldn't hear what she said, but she nodded sadly. His dad said he didn't have to, but she insisted, wrapping
his fingers closed around the driver. He walked down the stairs
and into the back of the basement, followed by his wife. Kneeling,
he unscrewed the sewing machine from its cabinet. It was a 1952
Singer – she'd been using it ever since they were married – but she
didn't want to touch it anymore, or even see it, at least not for a
while. Mr. McGhee put it into a box just large enough to hold it,
folding the four flaps of the box closed. His mom took it from him,
and stood there looking at him. It was heavy in the middle, and she
cradled it to keep it safe, just before she slid it onto the shelf by the
washing machine.

Most of the Way

21

0 ◄——————●—————————————————————► 90

7AM
New Haven, CT to
Pittsburgh, PA 12/23/1984

As usual, finals were a blood bath, and McGhee stared into his response to the last question wondering how it had happened again. But unlike the past, McGhee just closed the bluebook, tossed it onto the proctor's desk and ran for the door. It was the end of yet another round of finals and it was disappointing – not what he had been used to in high school – but the sound of the exit closing behind him offered some relief. It was that time of year when his thoughts would turn to the holidays, which for him, really meant he might actually get some sleep. It seemed like it had been weeks since his last decent rest, and between the coffee and those little yellow helpers from his roommate, he'd gone longer without sleep than he ever had before. Or maybe that was really last year – he couldn't remember – but that was the other thing: this year it didn't matter as much and wasn't as surprising. He was beaten and was learning to be on autopilot and merely hoped to make it through. What had before been cause for soul searching and self-doubt had settled in to mere confirmation of under-achievement. It had become a marathon now, and he simply had to keep going.

One thing was becoming a constant: he hadn't packed in the spring, either. Freshman year he used to plan his return more carefully – actually anticipate the journey and sweat the details – but he was past that now. The commute through New York City still stressed him, even though he wouldn't admit it: half his class was from the city, so that would have been too damaging to reveal, but that wasn't the worst part. The worst part was discovering *he* was the country bumpkin this time: the averted eyes when he used the wrong word, the stifled smiles when his Appalachian accent crept out late in the evening, his pedestrian and thin opinions. So it seemed those revelations found their way into the simplest moments to remind him he was alien and behind. And even though the city wasn't any less daunting than it used to be, he now looked at it as a Darwinian test: if he didn't make it home due to misfortune on those streets, he simply wasn't meant to make it. Such was his mental process when exhaustion and amphetamines replaced sounder thought.

Stuffing what seemed ten days-worth of underwear and shirts into his duffle he headed out; with some luck, most of it would be clean. He had to run half-way to the train station, and the chain smoking wasn't helping, either. Hands on knees he coughed and coughed near the Knights of Columbus building. When he stood again he saw stars but had to run right through them to make his train. The conductor was stepping in the door when he hit the platform and waved him over to hurry, barely making it on. His hands were on his knees again – this time he thought his spleen hurt, or something like it because he didn't know what a spleen actually was – when the conductor asked for his ticket. He fished it out and handed it up without looking. With a quick punch the conductor jammed it back in his hand. "Merry Christmas," he said.

McGhee tilted his head to look up at him and scanned his name tag. He wasn't exactly smiling, but he wasn't scowling either. Standing up, McGhee looked at him. "Conductor Sharon – that's kinda funny," McGhee said, but the conductor stared back blankly.

"There'r some seats up there," he said, motioning further into the car.

The train was old and made of screeching pale metal, cold linoleum floors, glass and chrome with a crappy fluorescent light one ballast shy of fully operational. The seats were cold hard green Naugahyde, that much harder for the coldness of the car. Still, it felt good to collapse into the seat, jammed into the corner like a sack of coffee. Outside New Haven began to slide by, first slowly, then with increasing pace. At first he kept his eye on a building as it went by, but he got tired of moving his head until it all started to blur. Zipping by, the poor city dissolved into structures and weeds and artifacts of decay. Drooping lines looped down then swept up, drooped down and swung up as poles interjected to lift them. There were clothes lines between some of the buildings – something red, dangling, zipped by, just before a sheet of rain splashed his window. He'd been lucky to miss that – New Haven had a way of sensing when you could least handle further adversity before unleashing torrents of cold rain upon you. It wasn't a rational thing, but he knew the rain was meant for him, only he had missed it this time. The thought nearly curved the corner of his lips into a smile.

As he sank further into the corner, the exhaustion finally caught up to him in a wave, forcing him to nod off, sending him adrift into uneasy dreams. His mind tumbled into the dark, recollecting another trip on that same train last year. It was another journey home, in the spring he thought, because it seemed so nice, upon which he'd met Sonja. He knew she was the editor of that campus magazine he hated — a monthly dedicated, in his estimation, to pretentious poetry and tedious stories. Each issue, the aspiring writers and poets submitted their works for admiration, the more oblique and obtuse the better. McGhee had looked forward to reading it when he first heard of it, but upon inspection found each work more impenetrable than the last. So when he stumbled upon a month's-worth of submissions one very late evening in his residential college library, he acted on impulse to take the lot of it and relieve the world of at least one load of dreck, or so he saw it. Within a week his conscience got the better of him and he put it back, but the damage was done and the issue was delayed. He was not proud he had done it — on the contrary, it was yet another demonstration of his misplacement there, and the thought of it burned as a bright reminder of it. But though he hated the magazine, he had admired Sonja from afar.

Sonja was clever and pretty and was actually *doing* something productive, and the thought of that bothered him deeply, not because she was doing it, but because he was not. He was barely surviving while she was actually thriving. Still, he was drawn to her and when he found her receptive to conversation, his heart leapt, for it had been so long since he had engaged a woman in dialog. And it was good conversation, ranging across many things, each smiling at recollections, chiming in with details to supplement the other, and her smile was carefree. It was another school break, so they were both in good spirits, creating a window of connection opportunity. So it had seemed like such a natural thing to casually disclose what he had done — he was sure she'd understand, only she didn't. She couldn't understand such an act, and in that moment, he knew he was the source of disappointment to her, and worse, that his recollection of those events was accurate in its bleak assessment of his character.

McGhee jolted awake as the car skipped in its track. Rain was still streaming over the windows, backlit by the cold thin gray ceiling of clouds. Sometimes it'd go for days like that, as if that was as good as it'd get, varying from dark gray to light, but no better. Only in the spring, when classes ended would the clouds part to reveal blue – just in time to go home. But that would be some months: he'd be back and go through another cycle before then, and it was just too far away to even think of yet.

Adjusting the foam headset pads from his Walkman he settled back into the corner to nap. He was playing a tape with nothing but Neil Young's *Expecting to Fly* recorded on it, over and over. There must have been ten copies there, and he'd probably listened to it a couple thousand times. Somehow when he closed his eyes and listened to it, the clouds parted for him and he'd see a warm sky from his youth in the summer, far away from his current confusion, long before even his fall was foretold, in which it seemed easier. It was a comforting illusion and he crawled into that restful cocoon, such as he could while stranded on a train headed into darkness.

McGhee's neck was stiff when he started awake again. They were in the tunnel already, moving into Grand Central, shuffling along slowly, the car clicking and clacking through the dark-timbered underworld. The imagery wasn't lost on him, but he didn't want to surrender to it: instead, he wanted to turn his gaze forward, to three weeks devoid of study and doubt to be filled with banquets of turkey, dopey movies, and late-night cruising with the boys through the VA grounds. And by some miracle, he could feel the pall lifting and with it, the first glimmers of holiday relief.

The rest of the car was waking and the passengers were beginning to stir. The lady across from McGhee was gathering her shopping bags together which crinkled with every movement and tightening of her grip. Up ahead, the conductor was talking to a kid, smiling. He couldn't make out the words, but they seemed to be having a good chat they both enjoyed. The young man was smiling – his white teeth flashing against his dark skin. The conductor had his arms crossed and was balanced, leaning against a pole, his feet crossed with one foot resting on a toe. His smile was broad and easy, looking like he might be Irish, with red in his cheeks and puffs of silver hair jutting from beneath his cap. In keeping with McGhee's thoughts which were turning toward home again, he was heartened to see it: his hometown didn't have much of that, being entirely Caucasian with only a few exceptions. So it was cheering to witness a tiny bit of harmony, such as it was. He'd wished he'd done more to engage the conductor getting on, and planned to say good-bye to him on the way out. Just then the car slowed more still and the conductor shook the kid's hand, walking toward the front of the car, then out through the door. There was a louder clack-clacking as he opened it and stepped through, until it shut behind him and he was gone.

Grand Central was a cacophony of people and noise. Clasping his backpack tight and his gym bag with the clothes, he tucked his head down and made for the door. Blasts of colder air announced he was getting closer to the outside world. Turning back a second, he gazed over the vast space of the central station: the vault was mostly lit from the high windows, and though the sky seemed white with overcast, it threw enough light to illuminate the floor, showing dust motes in the air. The cavernous room was nearly uniform gray and cold in its granite block construction, except in the waiting area where a few wooden pews spread across a section of the floor and around the edge. Stranded travelers reclined there, or sat, mixed in with the homeless. It was at times hard to tell them apart, except the homeless seemed more stationary, and there were their gazes which bespoke nowhere to go. The travelers always looked a little more harried, even though they were stuck alongside them. Then there were the shopping carts heaped with stuff – clothing and other bits of urban flotsam – he was wondering why the cops had let them in or how they'd even made it through the narrow doors. It must have created a huge blockage, like a thrombosis, as people collected behind them and built up pressure until they were pushed through. The image weighed on the buoyancy he was trying to muster when he found himself confronting the sadness again, only more directly.

Realizing he was creating a minor blockage of his own, he turned to leave, but found his path blocked by a homeless man before him. Their eyes met: he was weathered and wrinkled, dark-skinned with darker freckles, yellowing eyes, sparse teeth and a sparser frosty beard, his look blank. They stared at one another a moment, neither speaking immediately.

"Repent," he said eventually, his eyes having sudden focus and purpose. McGhee looked at him a moment remembering his dream from the train, and his ad hoc confession.

"I did," McGhee said finally. "And I'm sorry to say it didn't go well . . . ."

The man's eyes searched McGhee's, and he smiled. He was surprised to get a response, and if nothing else, it seemed to tell him he was there and not the forgotten invisible after all. "OK," he said, and stepped aside. McGhee fished out a crumpled dollar from his pocket and handed it to him, then pushed by with the rest of the human current.

In the cab to the Port Authority, he tried to ignore its smell but wasn't successful: it was a choking mix of something bad – he couldn't tell what – and women's perfume. He wasn't sure which part was worse, either, but the combination achieved an unholy synergy that was definitely worse still. He wondered if the woman, confronted by the same aroma had taken measures to improve the situation with a spritz of her scent. Or maybe she just wore such vast amounts it infused the space on its own, evaporating from her skin. He reached for the window switch to lower it, but it was broken. It made him wish he could have afforded to fly home from New Haven, but he pushed it from his mind as soon as it presented: there was no way they could afford that.

The Port Authority had the expected charm of a gigantic bus station, though not quite in the same scale as Grand Central Terminal. His ticket in hand, McGhee plopped into one of plastic cup seats to wait. It was instantly uncomfortable, as if he'd been sitting for hours already even though it was just seconds. It was slippery (no doubt for cleaning purposes), and regardless of his attempts he slid into a slouch. Across from him a man with two kids watched McGhee. They both leaned against him from either side, asleep. The man didn't look that much older than McGhee, probably late twenties, but he looked tired. His cap was slightly ajar, but it seemed he might wear it that way by intention: his dark hair was indented with its shape, like perhaps the cap might move a bit but generally sat within the depression it had made there. He had a couple day's growth on his chin and cheeks, a dark stubble the same color as his eyes. Dark circles under them completed the image of a man in transit. His lips were moving slightly and inaudibly, though his eyes were on McGhee.

Standing suddenly the man leaned forward toward him. The kids collapsed together into his vacant seat, miraculously holding each other up while they remained asleep. "You have a little something . . . ," he said reaching toward McGhee's cheek.

Leaning back, McGhee raised his hand. "That's OK," he said in protest, but the man gently persisted.

"That's OK, I'll . . . get it . . . ," he said, reaching in to brush the sandy crystal away lightly. He spoke with an accent, haltingly. He was European, though McGhee couldn't place it. Once done, the man settled back in between his kids, nestling in with a slight wiggle. He didn't look back at them but raised his arms around them, pulling them closer, all the time watching McGhee.

Leaning forward again, the kids collapsed together just as before. Stretching out his hand, his lips curled into a smile. "Excuse me . . . ," he said by way of apology, "I am Sergey . . . from Ukraine." McGhee took his hand and shook it. It was warm and moist — it wasn't the hand of a laborer — but the shake was firm. He immediately launched into an explanation: McGhee looked like an intelligent American, which he found interesting. Then he apologized again when he noticed the wry smile flicker on McGhee's lips and realized he had again tripped over — in his words — *the invisible culture that is America*. He explained his English training did not include things like social conventions. He was constantly getting himself into trouble — the last time a woman had brought in a policeman.

"It's not our custom to touch the face of strangers . . . ," McGhee explained, shaking his head, "nor to make such personal observations . . . but I appreciate the compliment," he said, smiling.

When it came time to board the bus, McGhee helped him with two suitcases. They reminded him of the valises his parents had from back in the fifties which they still used, leather bands around the edges and simulated fabric grain over cardboard. McGhee was glad for the diversion, and Sergey had his arms full with two sleeping children and bags draped over his shoulders. He was aware that everything Sergey had in the world was in those cases and bags. Sergey explained his wife had died last year of the flu, and that she was his last connection to his homeland. He went on to ask McGhee for an explanation of New Jersey, but McGhee was at a loss.

"It's just a state," he said, realizing it wasn't very satisfactory. It occurred to him, though he didn't know much about the Soviet Union, that regional identity meant something there it didn't mean in the U.S. Still, some part of him envied Sergey for the adventure he was having, involuntary as it was, as he was starting a new life while McGhee still had school indenturement in his foreseeable future, and it wasn't turning out to be what he expected. "What part?" McGhee asked, hoping to provide a better answer.

"Prince Town," Sergey said. "No, Prince-ton. Princeton."

McGhee nodded. "Right. Princeton. It's a nice place – very pretty and out in the country. Good school, too."

"Yes!" Sergey said, getting excited. "I'll be teaching there. Associate Professor – though I was already tenured in Kiev."

"Wow . . . ," McGhee said. "What subject?"

"Electrical engineering – processing of signals is my area."

McGhee smiled, though it had as much sadness as amusement. "I used to *love* physics . . . and math," he said, his voice trailing off. "Until partial differential equations . . . ," McGhee said. "They *killed* my love for it."

Sergey threw his head back, sighing loudly, causing his kids to stir, but he curled his hands onto each of their foreheads, stroking them back to sleep, before leaning forward again. "I *hate* them . . . differential equations," he said, whispering as if in confidence. "I should not admit that," he said, lowering his head. It sounded like he was chastising himself, and he looked to McGhee. "You should not feel bad about that. They are the *ugly children* of mathematics," he said, scrunching up his face. "Useful, yes, but better for someone else to do," he said smiling. "Unfortunately, I *am* that someone else . . . but I curse them." Sergey pursed his lips as if to spit, then realizing he was in America, inside a building, swallowed his saliva uncomfortably. "I forget I can't spit in America. This is difficult for me . . . ," he said, smiling sheepishly.

McGhee barely had time to scribble his number on a shred of paper and thrust it into Sergey's hand when he realized how late he was as the bus pulled into his stop. The bus dropped McGhee at Newark Airport only thirty-five minutes before his flight – the last of the night – so he had to run for his gate. He was supposed to have more than an hour, but the bus ran late, which put him into a traffic jam. As he ran down the stairs of the bus, he glanced back – Sergey had his hand up, waving with a smile.

McGhee was flying PeopleExpress – possibly the cheapest airline on earth – and had no ticket. He'd have to get one at the gate, but that had always worked. Security was light, but there were families clogging both of the lines feeding through. Further complicating the flow, they were rookie flyers taking their time with boxes and bags and conducting arguments with ill-behaved children while everyone watched. By the time he made it through he had a little over ten minutes to get to the gate before takeoff – it was ten gates down, but he'd make it. The thought actually occurred to him that he was early and he let his pace slow. By the time he made it, the attendants at the counter were doing final checks. There was one guy ahead of him, but it wasn't clear if he was waiting or not. He didn't have the typical vigilance of one waiting to catch the eye of an attendant. McGhee tapped him on the shoulder to ask, but got an immediate question instead.

"You got a ticket, man?" he asked hopefully. By the sound of it, McGhee suspected trouble. "Uh . . . no," he answered reluctantly.

"Then you're screwed like me . . . ," he said turning back to watch the women behind the counter. Grabbing up his bag, the young man pushed the rest of his stuff to the side – sliding a duffle on the floor with his foot collecting a few cigarette butts in the process. Zipping up his Notre Dame letter jacket, he looked frustrated. One of the attendants moved back to the desk, so McGhee rushed the counter.

"I need a seat . . . ," he blurted out. "Is it really sold out?" he asked. His tone was plaintive and pathetic. He hoped it would make a difference, but it didn't.

"I'm sorry, hun," she said sympathetically, looking up from her list. "We're completely oversold . . . ," she finished, tilting her head to the side. It was that little head tilt that got him. There was no coming back from that, but it didn't stop McGhee from trying.

"I don't suppose I could wait list . . .?" he asked hopefully.

She smiled sadly, her head still tilted. "Cleared that ten minutes ago . . . ," she said. He waited for her to offer a suggestion, but she just stared at him.

Two people had lined up behind him and were stirring impatiently. One last look at the attendant revealed she still had that sad look on her face – she was just waiting for him to move aside – so after some final fidgeting, he did.

It had never happened to him before: he'd done this commute five or six times already. Though it was usually close, he'd always made it on a flight – admittedly, the last one several times. And then, too, there were usually later flights, but not this time. He wouldn't get on this flight or a later one. He wouldn't get to watch while they pushed that weird little cash register cart down the aisle. He wouldn't pay his nineteen dollars for the flight to Pittsburgh. He was stuck.

There wasn't anything else to do, so he watched the final prep. The review of the list. The hushed discussion over the mic with the attendants on the plane. The flip-up of the doorstop. The final clank of the gate door slamming shut with him on the wrong side of it.

Just as he was coming out of his haze of disbelief he realized he wasn't alone. There was a crowd of guys and one young woman clustered around having the identical experience. Two of the guys – the older ones behind him in line – were in something of a panic. They were talking to each other, alternating whispers and something louder, then separated, somehow inviting the others around into their circle. The guy who was in front of McGhee perked up as one of the older guys spoke to him. "You have to get to Pittsburgh tonight?" he asked.

It was a stupid question. They all had to get to Pittsburgh, but it served its rhetorical purpose. Zipping his college letter jacket again, the young man jammed his hands into his pockets in disgust, nodding silently. Those standing around started to magically converge on this discussion: there was the guy around forty travelling with the young woman – McGhee figured it was his daughter until he pulled her close and kissed her on the lips while he put his arm around her shoulder; there were the two guys driving the discussion, both dressed as wise-guys in their late fifties with slacks, shiny shoes, leather jackets, slick hair, shirts open down the chest to show chains and little gold crosses; a gray rabbi; and McGhee. The shorter of the wise-guys pointed to each of them in turn with his pinky, like he was counting a hundred people. "Six," he finally said.

The taller wise-guy stepped into the circle, hunched over a bit, his hand on his chin. He was apparently thinking, though no words were coming out. The man with the young woman started to say something he found amusing – he was laughing as he started – but the wise guy held up his hand to stop him, which then became a single pointer finger. It wasn't menacing – he just apparently needed silence to think. Finally, he raised his head and uttered one word: "Car."

The short wise-guy stepped in beside him. "You think, Jonnie?" he said.

"Why not . . . ?" Jonnie said. It was like they were practiced in saying the fewest words possible to communicate. Jonnie nodded. "Car," he said again, swinging his head around to look at the group, convinced he was right.

The short guy commenced counting again, stopping half way to start again. "But six?" he said finally. "Maybe a van or something . . . ?"

"Frankie, you're a genius," he said, snapping his fingers, leaving his fingers out to point around the group. "Anybody got plastic?" he asked. McGhee shook his head and shrugged. The rabbi didn't seem to follow. The man and the girl looked on blankly.

Finally, as Jonnie reached the letter-jacket, the young man asked, "Why?"

"And you are?" Jonnie asked. It was studied and ingratiating, manipulative and transparent.

"Pat," the young man answered, wary. His hands were still in his pockets and he appeared uneasy.

Jonnie looked at him intently. "If you'll use the plastic to get us a van . . . ," he said pausing. He looked around the group, eyebrows raised. It was some kind of question to the group. McGhee shrugged and that was enough. "If you use the plastic . . . ," he repeated, "Frankie and I will cover it when we get to Pittsburgh."

Pat looked skeptical. "Why don't you use *your* card?" he asked. Jonnie was dumfounded, his palms up. "What – you don't want a free ride to Pittsburgh . . . ?" he asked rhetorically, looking around at his audience. "Sounds like a good deal to me . . . ," he said, frowning. "Maybe that's just me?" he asked, turning to the others. "We'd just . . . prefer . . . ," he said, haltingly, "to not leave so much of a trail. We're good for it . . . but if you don't want . . . ," he said, his voice drifting off, his head tilted to the side, eyebrows high, frowning even more.

Pat was on the spot and he wasn't comfortable. Four pairs of eyes were on him – the Rabbi was oblivious to the process, though he tried to look engaged. Eventually, he looked at Pat, too.

"Fine," Pat said shrugging, caving to the pressure. "I'll do it . . . ."

"Good!" Jonnie said, immediately launching into a walk before he wheeled back to the counter. The attendants were talking and he held up his hand. Stopping, they looked at him. "The rental cars would be . . . ?" he asked. It was the same tone he used with Pat initially: ingratiating yet insistent. The attendants stared at him until one had the presence of mind to point back down the hall.

"Thanks hun . . . ," he said, wheeling on his heel and walking through the group. Apparently Jonnie was in charge, and the group followed him down the corridor.

McGhee found himself walking beside the man and woman. His hair was straggly and dirty blond, like he was using it to cover more of his head than it naturally would cover on its own. He wore an old army jacket and jeans over Converse shoes, untied. He noticed McGhee looking at him, removed his arm from around the girl and extended his hand. As their hands clasped, he pulled him closer. "What's up with those guys?" he asked, smiling. It was instantly conspiratorial and McGhee liked it. "Oh, and I'm Buzzy," the guy said. "And this here is Bunny." The girl peered around Buzzy to smile at McGhee. She was nubile and thin, somewhere shy of maturity. Her white tank-top draped open as she reached

over to shake his hand, her breasts free of confinement. He shook
her hand and smiled, averting his eyes, but she caught him.

"Nice to meet ya . . . ," she said smiling coyly. She held his
hand momentarily longer than he held hers, forcing their eyes to
meet again. For McGhee, her glance was just short of flirtatious
but was clearly conspiratorial, too.

"So . . . like, how old are you anyway?" McGhee asked Bunny.
He was rather surprised it slipped out, but it was on his mind.

"Sixteen," she said. If she'd had gum, he knew she would have
snapped it.

"Isn't she great?" Buzzy said, accelerating his step to catch the
bunch ahead.

It was late by the time they made it to the rental counter, and
it was dead. Commotion ensued as Frankie and Jonnie became
excited and started talking in whispers again, Jonnie pushing his
jacket back at the hip to think. Pat was there, too, as the plastic
guy, but the others hovered around. At the far end of the counter
sat an old red phone. McGhee moved over to it for a look: it had a
dial, but it was glued in position, the cord was ancient and simple
with a cloth covering fraying near the receiver end. He picked
it up and instantly got a voice. "Hertz . . . ," the voice said, and
nothing else.

"Uh, yeah, we're at the counter . . . ?" McGhee said, his voice
trailing up.

"Yeah?" the voice responded. It wasn't enough apparently.

"Yeah. And there's . . . no . . . one . . . here," McGhee went on.

"It *is* eleven-thirty . . . . Hold a sec . . . ," the voice said, then
music came on instantly. It was a Muzak version of a Beatles song.
McGhee smirked, looking up at the others. They had stopped debat-
ing and were watching him. Jonnie shrugged, palms out. McGhee
shrugged back. "Hold music . . . ," he said. "Muzak *Helter Skelter* . . . ."

Hearing that, Buzzy flew into a tizzy, running his hands over his forehead and pushing his fuzzy hair back. "It should be *illegal* . . . ," he said. Bunny wrapped her hands around his waist and pushed her head into his chest. "It's OK, hun . . . ," she said. "They don't know any better . . . ."

The music cut off and the voice said someone would be out in a second. From the office they could hear some rustling. A woman emerged, packed into a brown polyester suit. Her blouse billowed out around her vest, and she had a colorful scarf around her neck at an angle that looked like she had just pulled it on over her head. Her hair wasn't going anywhere though – it looked to be held in place with a few extra layers of hairspray, a curl permanently laminated in place on her forehead. Her hands came to rest on the keyboard where she paused a second. With a sigh, she looked up at them, scanning the assembly with some amusement.

"I don't suppose you have a reservation?" she said. Despite her entrance she seemed friendly, if guarded. Pat stepped up to talk to her, but Jonnie leaned in. "We all . . . ," he began, swirling his hand in the air, "just got bumped from a flight. So we're looking for a van." It wasn't entirely accurate and McGhee considered objecting, but it didn't matter. The woman shook her head, smiling, and began tapping keys.

"So where ya going, anyway . . . ," she said absently.

Pat leaned in. "Pittsburgh . . . ," he said.

"Pittsburgh?" she said, laughing lightly.

"Yeah, Pittsburgh . . . ," Pat said defensively, but Jonnie stepped in.

"Honey, sooner or later we all go to Pittsburgh . . . ," he said, with a shrug for emphasis. She stopped typing a moment to look at him, then resumed her search.

There was a burst of typing, then silence, she shook her head again, then another burst. She leaned into the monitor, raised her hand and began tracing the screen with a very long fingernail. She shook her head again, then set to the keyboard with another flurry of taps. She did this three times before she stopped, leaned in, then smiled at Jonnie, then Pat, then Jonnie again. "We got . . . *one*," she said.

Jonnie instantly pounded on the counter: "All right!" It startled the attendant and she looked at him, her hands still on the keyboard.

Frankie leaned in. "He does that. *Sorry*," he said. Jonnie and Frankie retreated from the counter as Pat leaned in with his card. The attendant took it from him, but kept her eye on Jonnie. Looking over to Pat she smiled again, tapping at the keys.

"That is gonna be one *looong* ride," she said to him, her eyes darting to meet his, her lips curling at the edge.

Out in the lot the troop moved along the line of cars. The clouds that had been hanging low had begun to drop something of a drizzle, or perhaps worse. McGhee saw some of the spots on his coat were water while others were more solid. Through the pink glow of the lot's lamps, wet lines came down, some clumpy, some not, though on the ground it was only water. Stepping off the curb, McGhee discovered the half-inch puddle he expected was deeper, his canvas tennis shoes instantly sopping up the cold water.

Releasing Bunny momentarily, Buzzy put his arm around his shoulder. "*Man* . . . ," he said, shaking his head. That was it. McGhee looked up from his shoe to see him smiling at him.

Releasing him, Buzzy clapped, then grabbed Bunny's hand to jog after the others.

It was a long white van, the kind churches use, with a bench in the middle and a bench in the back. Pat took the first leg driving with Jonnie next to him riding shotgun. Frankie sat behind Jonnie and Bunny was squished in the middle – luckily there was no hump on the floor – with Buzzy against the window. That left the back bench for McGhee and the Rabbi, which was fine with McGhee. He had visions of napping, which would be easier out of sight in the way back. That was his thought anyway.

McGhee was glad not to be driving – leaving Newark airport always got him turned around on those few occasions he did it. It was like the roads weren't thought out at all, or perhaps they paved over cart paths, but whatever sensibility got them that way, it wasn't a sensibility he had any interest in understanding.

It was a tough night for driving: the precipitation went from drizzle to steady light rain, the traffic was bad as it always was in Jersey, and there was construction. There was always construction, though it never seemed anything ever got constructed. It took most of an hour to get out of the cars and up to a decent speed. They finally got past the last of the urban areas sometime after one, but Pat kept driving. Just after the tollbooth into Pennsylvania, he pulled over into a wide spot by the road, spent. Jonnie jumped into the driver's seat and Frankie took shotgun. Pat didn't seem sure it was a good thing to switch, but he was done. The van was on his card, but by then he was too tired to protest. They were off again in a minute without a break, and Pat slumped against the van door, almost instantly asleep.

Bunny was napping against Buzzy's shoulder, but he leaned around to look at Pat. Looking back he caught McGhee's eye.

Jonnie and Frankie were having some discussion up front. Frankie was incessantly tuning the radio to pull in songs, or perhaps he was creating cover for their chat, which was barely an audible murmur over the car noise. Buzzy motioned for McGhee to lean in.

"You figure they're *connected* . . . ," he whispered, motioning his head and eyes toward the front. McGhee had been wondering the same thing. He'd seen such characters in the movies, but that was all remote from his experience. He'd grown up in a small steel and corn town north of Pittsburgh and those things never happened there, at least not on his side of town. Still, he had to keep reminding himself he wasn't in the backwater anymore. It seemed he had that realization a couple times a day now to explain his new reality, but he never got used to it. There was always that little fact remaining to disturb his peace of mind, and he wondered if he'd ever reclaim it again. The thought filled him with a shadow of sadness, but he was content for the moment to be going home and let his head cool down from the onslaught which was school. Leaning back, McGhee smiled and shrugged in response. He didn't want to disturb the balance, even if Buzzy was oblivious to it.

Beside McGhee, the Rabbi was quiet, looking straight ahead. He hadn't said a word. From his position leaning back into his corner, McGhee could look at him undetected. He must have been in his late sixties by the look of him. He had sparse beard on his cheeks, frosted somewhat, that culminated in a larger goatee on his chin. Occasionally he'd stroke it, pulled down slowly until he reached the point of whiskers several inches below, his lips invisible beneath his mustache. None of it was trimmed, and years of apparent uneven growth had given it a natural, wild appearance. The others in the van had made themselves more comfortable, opening jackets and relaxing for the long ride, but not him. His black wool coat remained buttoned and belted. He even continued to wear his black Borsalino hat which went the whole way to the ceiling of the van. It had a flat, satin lined lip around a broad brim with a satin hatband around the crown. As his eyes adjusted to the darkness, McGhee could see faint scuffs around the brim and even some threadbare satin where he no doubt grabbed it. The same was true of the coat, now that he had time to review it at leisure. It was neat and tidy but showed similar signs of wear. McGhee closed his eyes and began to drift. The steady beat of rain on the windshield and the hum of the tires lulled him into a semi-sleep — as good as it gets when one travels and sleeps in a tilted-vertical position.

His thoughts tumbled through darkness and exhaustion, turning to something floating in the back of his head, not even a thought, so unformed it was. He couldn't get his arms around it, which seemed to be its most defining feature. It had no name, and as such, had no convenient handle by which to grab it for examination. He knew it had to do with himself, with home, with leaving it, and the untethered feeling he now had almost all the time as a feeling of helplessness. What he thought he knew slipped from his grasp, evaporating. It seemed to be the only thing he did know — that he didn't know anything and that he was powerless in the face of it — but that certainty wasn't comforting. Yet, he knew within that thought it had a name, and perhaps that bothered him most — that he couldn't get at it, even though it sat unexamined, inexorable and waiting for him. It didn't have the allure of a present, or any of that anticipation. Instead, he felt something of dread, unknown as it was, as if it would speak a truth he wasn't prepared to hear.

Within another instant and just as he stopped pondering it, the thought took shape and had become a box, sitting on his mother's kitchen table. It was always her table, even though his dad sat there for dinner. The kitchen was her domain, with the spritely brightness she gave it, singing to the radio when the right song came on.

But that box sat there, old and dilapidated, like something sad from the basement hauled out from time to time as a reminder. It had old paper tape on it, the kind with strings in it – why would anyone put strings in tape he remembered wondering every time he saw it, the tape frayed but the stringy bones intact (perhaps that was their purpose after all) – the box collapsing on the top, the flaps forgetting their stiffness as the corrugation fell in upon itself, imploding. He'd seen her put it there, cradling the bottom for the central heaviness of the content, with that sad face she had – he didn't like that face – so he knew he shouldn't like the box either, that it contained some terrible sadness that his mother had become steward of. It never remained on the table when his dad came home from work, only remaining out during the day, sometimes for a few hours. And when the box did come out, he knew to turn away and flee, which he did, running in little bare feet up to the sweaty sash of the window which he used to pull up and look outside ten seconds at a time, just above his tippy toes.

Rain streaked down the window, but he could see his dad out there working in the yard, pushing load after load in the wheelbarrow, making the new yard of the house into an older yard, then an old one, one dirt load at a time, improving what had been a flat lot with modest variation. It must be Wednesday he thought – that's when Dad came home early for lunch and stayed, so it must be Wednesday, or maybe it was Saturday, even though it didn't feel like Saturday because he didn't sense the looming church mass they went to in the evening, even though he didn't have to go, yet. He recalled the box on the table, wondering why it was out, a welling slight panic, until he forgot it again.

A merry little gusher of water emerged near the street where the downspout water came out in the ditch, and he knew it must be raining hard, though his father only looked wet from the sweat and he wondered why the rain wasn't touching him if it rained hard enough for the gusher to gush. Though it seemed it must be April, the rain outside suddenly made him cold and he retreated, running the vast distance from the window to the couch where he threw himself into the gap underneath, and where the vent let out the warm air when the furnace clicked on. The warm air enveloped him, but he felt cold. He felt cold.

Starting awake, McGhee realized the van had come to a stop. "Piss break . . . ," he heard Jonnie call out. The side door of the van gaped open already, the cold damp air pouring in, and the others had climbed out and were stretching. The Rabbi sat looking at him, expectantly, his elbow on the bench ahead, ready to launch out as soon as McGhee cleared the way.

The Hardees sign at the Pennsylvania I-80 rest stop glowed orange through the sleet which was doing its best to collect in the looping cups of the illuminated letters. Even their tops were capped in slushy precipitation, though half-hearted and threatening to slide off at any moment. The troop was already starting to trudge up the hill, though Pat remained behind to lock the van. The Rabbi went on ahead clearly motivated but cautious in his sliding steps. McGhee stretched by the van as Pat turned the key in the lock. He pulled on the handle twice to make sure it was locked, then turned away before returning to try the passenger door to make sure it was locked, too. It reminded McGhee of the risk he took, on his behalf, too, and he stuck out his hand.

"McGhee," he said. Pat stopped to look at him, then took his hand.

"McGregor," he said in response. "You seem like the only normal guy in the crew," Pat said. "You figure those guys are connected?" he asked, his lips curling into a smile.

"That's *exactly* what Buzzy said . . . ," McGhee mumbled.

"No shit, Sherlock," Pat said, laughing. "Everyone heard that . . . ," he continued, anticipating McGhee's question. "Even Frankie and Jonnie . . . . They were snickering over it like a coupla twelve-year olds."

"How did I miss *that?*" McGhee asked, scratching his head as the two started up the little hill toward the others.

"You kidding me? You were sawing logs, man . . . ," Pat said.

McGhee stopped momentarily. "I was snoring then?"

"Uh, *yeah* you were snorin'," Pat said. "No sweat, man. It was better-n the chantin'." He continued up the hill, the sleet starting to collect on his letter jacket.

"Chanting? What chanting?" McGhee said hurrying after him. Pat turned to look back at him but kept walking.

"The Rabbi, man," Pat said. "He had a little thing in his hand – a little book or somethin' – and started rockin' back and forth. Sounded like a prayer or somethin'. Started just whisperin' it, kinda, then it was more like singin'. You seriously didn't hear anya that?"

Inside, the rest-stop was dead. The metal security curtain was mostly drawn around the *Rest Shoppe* where the travel knick-knacks resided: snow globes, ancient CDs of Lawrence Welk and polka hits, bumper stickers stating "*I* ♥ *Intercourse, PA,*" cashew nougat logs and thimbles. An old black man had a rolling-bucket in the corner, sloshing gray water onto the ancient aggregate floor. His mop was the same color, but he stopped moving to lean on it and watch the parade. Jonnie was already striding from the restroom over toward the food area. Another illuminated Hardees sign sat along the edge of the ceiling where it dropped down a couple feet for the seating area; the two "EEs" were dark, prompting some comment from Frankie who was trailing after him. Jonnie sneered over his shoulder but kept moving. Buzzy and Bunny emerged in synchrony from their respective restrooms, falling in line behind Frankie with the Rabbi close behind them. McGhee and Pat did the same.

At the counter behind the aluminum rail, the group bunched in a log jam. There was a waitress at the counter perking up for the sudden flood of customers. Her badge said *Margaret Elizabeth*, but she insisted they all call her Madge. She was spilling out of a mustard-color uniform with white piping and white lapels, her cap matching and held in place by ten bobby-pins atop a pile of hair styled in the fifties. She looked to be pushing sixty, which put her in Jonnie's sweet spot. He instantly took to calling her *Madge Doll*, or just *Doll*, explaining the situation, their travels across the state, and could she please feed them before they all "expired." After his speech there was a pause while she looked at him, feigning displeasure. Putting her hand on her hip, she waved across the bar of fried foods and vats of soup, "It's all yours, hun," she said with a husky voice. The ensuing flirts flew in both directions, each reveling in the opportunity to talk as much as possible.

Jonnie was at the front of the line, leading the procession while everyone behind loaded their trays. There was a prevailing assumption he'd pick up the tab, so there were extra apples, fries and cellophaned pieces of pie that had been fresh the day before. Stopping by a huge black plastic kettle, Jonnie pointed.

"Chowder," Madge said.

Jonnie was beside himself. Tossing open the lid, he grabbed a large Styrofoam drinking cup and dipped the whole thing into the kettle. Pulling it out, he let the drips settle back into the pot over his fingers, then chugged it. Frankie followed suit, getting nudged back out when Jonnie went for seconds, chugging that one, too. He set the empty cup on his tray, chowder still streaming down the sides. Pulling out twenty napkins from a dispenser, he mopped his fingers. Sliding his empty tray up to the register, he looked back over the line, wiping his lips with the soiled napkins and using one of his clean fingers to make a circle in the air. Madge began ringing up the line. Jonnie motioned with his chin to Frankie who pulled a roll of bills out of his pocket and peeled off a fifty. Madge started making change, but Jonnie put his hand on hers. "No, doll. The rest's for you . . . ," he said magnanimously. Frankie closed his wallet, nodding his assent.

Jonnie and Frankie chose the closest table to the register, Jonnie continuing his courtship of Madge. Buzzy and Bunny chose the next table as there wasn't enough room to fit them all at any of the small tables. The Rabbi joined them, clutching a single apple. McGhee settled there, too, with a tubular sandwich in foil marked "Cheesesteak" and some fries. He'd wanted some of the chowder, but the antics had changed his mind. Pat, bringing up the rear, headed to their table which was already crowded, but Jonnie called him over. "Got one for you here . . . ," he called, sliding out a chair noisily on the floor. There was no avoiding the invitation, so he wheeled on his heel and pretended he hadn't seen them there.

Bunny was messing with Buzzy's hair. "Don't you love his fro?" she said, turning to McGhee.

Buzzy laughed. "He doesn't give a *shit* about my hair, hun. Guys don't do that." She smiled, wrapping her hand behind his neck for a quick rub. "So what's your story, kid?" Buzzy asked McGhee. He set to unwrapping the sandwich he got, too, but he kept looking up at McGhee.

McGhee wasn't sure what to share – he never was. Buzzy seemed friendly enough, or at least not hostile, so he relaxed a bit. "Heading home from school," he offered, starting to unwrap his cheesesteak. It had been steaming in the foil under the fry lamp for quite a while; half of the bun was mushy with condensation. "Shit," he said. "I hate that," he continued, staring down at it.

Buzzy pushed back his chair and went to the condiment station, returning with a fork. "Here," he said, handing it to McGhee. "I'd say that happens about seventy percent of the time for me," he said. "I get that a lot, being on the road." McGhee knew a leading comment when he heard it and prodded for more.

"Well . . . ," Buzzy began.

Bunny pushed his shoulder. "On come on, hun, don't be bashful." She looked at McGhee, chewing on a French fry. "He's so humble. That's what I *love* about him," she said, bending in to stop chewing and kiss him on the lips. "He's *really good* at playing the drums, aren't ya hun," she said, encouraging him to continue. Leaning over toward McGhee she whispered: "He's *famous* . . . ."

"Yeah . . . yeah," Buzzy continued. "I've been playing a *long* time. Back in the day I played with CrazyHorse for a while . . . ," he said, nodding. He took a huge bite of his sandwich. It was so large he couldn't talk, but perhaps that was by design. Bunny pushed her hand through his hair again and kissed him on the ear.

Just then the Rabbi started choking on his apple. It was faint at first but became more pronounced as the bite slid the wrong direction. He reached out for something to drink, but there wasn't anything to give him. Bunny ran over to the fountain and returned with a plastic cup of water. He grasped it in both hands taking a sip, but it didn't seem to help. Suddenly a big thump landed on his back, dislodging the piece into his cup of water. Jonnie stood over him, proud of himself. "Ain't no fuckin' Rabbi dying on my watch . . . ," he said. "Am I right?"

The Rabbi was startled, but thankful. He extended his hand to Jonnie. He waited a moment, then took it. "You're alright . . . ," he said to the Rabbi. It seemed to go beyond the momentary crisis, but there were no further words to explain it. The Rabbi bowed his head and mumbled something, but it wasn't English.

Buzzy laughed. "I wonder what the hell he makes of this whole thing?" he said, looking at McGhee. "The poor bastard doesn't speak a lick of English, and we didn't know this whole time."

The Rabbi objected: "A little . . . ," he said, holding up two fingers an inch apart. He smiled faintly, and the table erupted in laughter. Fishing out the apple bit from his water, he wrapped it tidily in a napkin then drank the cup in one gulp.

Back at the van Buzzy offered to drive. Jonnie seemed tired of it already and Frankie was nursing a sour stomach, so Jonnie tossed him the keys. Pat shared the first bench with the guys, and McGhee loaded in behind with the Rabbi. What had been a slushy mix had drifted back into pure rain for the moment, only twice as hard as before. Buzzy had to turn the wipers to the high setting, so they set to slapping the rain from the windshield as fast as they could. It was raining so hard they couldn't even crack the windows – otherwise those on the front bench would be drenched.

Somehow that seemed the perfect time for Buzzy to light up. Unrolling the sleeve of his jacket he took a little hand-rolled smoke from his cuff and handed it to Bunny. She laughed liked he'd said the funniest thing in the world and said, "Amazing . . . ." Their eyes locked momentarily in gooey love while she ignited the jay.

In the way back McGhee was calculating the odds of his survival if the van flipped over. It didn't take long for the sweet and illicit smell of reefer to wend its way back through the cabin. When the beams of oncoming traffic illuminated the air, the blue smoke lit up like a local rain cloud. Frankie couldn't take it, so he tapped Bunny on the shoulder to roll down the window a bit. "But it's raining?" she objected, but based on the slight scowl on his face, she complied.

Sensing a party, Jonnie wasn't going to be left out. "Hey, give us a hit of that . . . ," he said, reaching up between them.

Buzzy turned to look at Jonnie, smoke escaping from his tight lips, then began laughing so his whole head disappeared in a cloud of smoke. *"All right, man!"* he said, handing over the stub to Jonnie.

He deftly pinched the roach between his fingers, sucking in the smoke for nearly thirty seconds. Holding it in, he handed the butt to Bunny. After a couple grunts and squeaks he finally let it out. "That *there* is some *good . . . shit . . .* ," he said, patting Buzzy on the shoulder.

The breeze from the cracked window had pushed the cloud firmly to the back of the van. The side windows in the back could tilt out a bit with a lever. McGhee and the Rabbi seemed to discover this simultaneously, both popping their windows like corks, draining the bulk of it. It wasn't that McGhee objected to it — he didn't really care — except that it had become a bit difficult to breathe. He stuck his nose into the crack of his window and the cool air felt good and fresh. He'd had a few minutes of breaths when he realized he was hearing something behind him.

Across the bench the Rabbi had unrolled something in his lap. He was gently rocking back and forth, his lips moving slightly. The whispering and hissing of his guttural words achieved ignition as his voice transitioned into a light chant. His curls were bouncing slightly as he rocked, keeping time with his verses.

From then on the rain subsided to a mild drizzle. The sky went from black to blue and then to a leaden gray as they drove into morning. Somehow the Rabbi communicated where his place was, just east of the airport in Shadyside, which was on the way. He was the first out and shook everyone's hand and bowed to the van as it pulled away. He remained in the street until the van turned the corner and he disappeared from view.

McGhee could see in Pat's face what he was thinking: he hoped Jonnie and Frankie would make good on their promise once they got to the airport. McGhee planned such things, budgeted very carefully as he didn't have much cash to spend even in the best of times. If they welched on their promise, it'd be a lean Christmas, and he didn't want to ask his parents for more money, either. College was hard enough on them. By the looks of Pat, he was in the same situation only the whole thing was on his card, so it was worse for him.

At the airport, Jonnie and Frankie had the van divert to long-term parking. Frankie was leaning up between Buzzy and Bunny, directing them left, and right and straight and right again. Finally he said, "Here . . . ," and the van came to a quick little stop by the curb. Jonnie popped the door, then turned over his shoulder to Pat. "Don't worry . . . wait a second," he said. Helping Frankie out, they both stretched like old men, hands on hips, twisting like a black and white calisthenics movie from health class. McGhee expected them to start marching down the row, but they stopped at the very first car in the nearest possible slot: a red Ferrari. It wasn't the newest model year, but was new enough, in fine shape and even clean but for some rain and a small patch of slush on the roof.

Frankie climbed in, signaling back with a queen's wave. Jonnie reached in from the driver side, fished around a console then returned with another billfold. Looking in at Pat, he smiled. "So what's the damage?" he said, fingers poised inside along a stack of bills.

Everyone in the van looked at each other. "Holy shit . . . ," Buzzy said under his breath, but the rest heard him and laughed. Pat pulled out a folded and wrinkled pink slip from his pocket then ran his finger down to the bottom line. "One-oh-six-sixty-nine . . . ," he said finally.

With a satisfied frown, Jonnie pulled out a wad of bills. "Not so bad . . . ," he said. "Not nineteen bucks, but we made it back didn't we?" He held out a hundred, a five, and a one. "You guys can cover the sixty-nine cents I imagine?" he said, smirking. Pat took the bills, nodding. They were all nodding.

"Well fellas, it's been real . . . ," Jonnie said, adjusting his pants with a snort before turning on his heel to go. They watched from the van as the Ferrari started with a low rumble, but pulled away before Jonnie had a chance to gun the engine.

It was 7:00 a.m., puddles marking the lot in gray coldness when McGhee stepped out of the van. Pat gave him a salute and wry smile. "Stay cool, man," he said. Buzzy stuck out his hand for a shake, and Bunny leaned out to kiss him on the cheek. Buzzy even honked twice as he pulled away. It had been a long time since he'd heard such a thing, and he was surprised to find such welcome in the company of strangers. It was looking like it'd be a good day after all.

McGhee was sure his dad was waiting for him already near arrivals since he had called ahead from Dubois. It made him smile to think of his dad sitting in the Volaré, waiting for him, though each time he returned he felt a little further away. Maybe this time he'd make it the whole way home.

One Certain Sunset

7PM
Tucson, AZ 6/18/1998

There really wasn't much to do on his project on the last afternoon – a couple deliveries and one pick-up his boss had asked him to do – so McGhee had been thinking it might be nice to get out of town a couple hours. He wasn't home, but for being away, this wasn't his idea of a good time, either. He loved the locale, Tucson, but work was work, and he seldom got to enjoy it unless he made the effort to carve out a little time for himself. When he'd go on the road, he figured he ought to get a little something out of it, whether that was a decent local meal or a nice view of new scenery or some strolling through an interesting market. That was what he called the *old-school* mode of business travel, even though he wasn't so old himself. It went with his self-perception that he was rather beyond his years in sensibility, and more tired of the

routine than he had a right to be. Still, it was his natural disposition, and he'd indulge it especially when no one was around to see
it. He sensed he was on the cusp of transition from that era of employment and travel, and something newer which hollowed out and
eliminated the good parts for the traveler leaving only the business
tailings behind. It wasn't like his days at *xCopy Inc.* – the behemoth
corporation – a few years before when cost and time weren't such
pressing considerations. The prospect annoyed him, even though
he wasn't much of a business traveler to begin with – his travels had
been pretty tactical of late – but that was beside the point. *What's
in it for a guy on the road if not a little entertainment in the margin?* he
thought. He wasn't talking about anything lavish of any kind, just
a few minutes to himself and a chance to clear his head. *That* was
his plan anyway.

Luckily Nick hadn't called yet, and seven was getting close,
which they had agreed was day's-end, so he figured he was in the
clear. Still, McGhee had the nagging suspicion Nick would do
something to screw that up – he did have a habit of calling just after
those deadlines, or sometimes a minute or two before, with some
extra piece of work. McGhee usually saw it as a way to yank his
chain, even if it was legitimate. Just a way to milk a little more value from him on his own time. His work was, in fact, that dull these
days, and even the lack of genuine basis for affront galled him. So
this time, as he saw the deadline looming, he turned off his phone
at 6:57. *Screw him* he said to himself, pressing the power key with
extra pressure just to make sure it really turned off. Then, unsure
it was off, he pressed it again, just to make certain, but managed
to turn it on again – he never was sure it worked – so, fumbling
with it he took the battery out entirely. "*Fuck 'em,*" he said out loud
this time, smiling to himself, the unwitnessed mutiny buoying his
spirits. Unwitnessed, that is, except for the lady next to him in the

grocery where he was standing, who frowned at him, motioning with her head toward her son in the cart.

Wheeling his wobbly head around and over backwards toward McGhee, he screamed, "Fagaa!" merrily.

"Thanks . . . ," she said, but McGhee was already two steps down the aisle.

Outside, the air was perfect and the sun was low enough in the sky to be a little less relentless than it was the rest of the day. It wasn't so hot, which is saying something for Tucson in mid-June, when it's just as likely to be one hundred degrees as anything, but it wasn't so bad, and rolling down the window presented a warm but tolerable breeze. Ninety-something most likely, though it wasn't a Houston ninety, or even New Orleans. The dryness of the air always made it hard for him to guess accurately. The stickiness he was used to in his youth in Pennsylvania to gauge how uncomfortable he was, and hence the temperature, didn't work at all in such climes. By the time he felt the temperature in the West, it was usually quite hot, and he wasn't feeling it at all, so it was good. Such was the utter lack of distraction he had at the moment, and quickly forgetting about Nick and his imagined affronts, he reached for the radio knob of the rental car.

The first acoustic notes of Van Morrison's *Into the Mystic* came out of the speakers, and it was another good sign. Usually he'd land in the middle of some crap song, but not this time – this time he smiled, twisted the volume knob up, pleased. It was as loud as it would go, and for once, the speakers of the car he had rented didn't sound awful. Leaning back, he let the melody flow over him, like it had the first time he'd heard it back in Jersey.

He'd been cruising down the Garden State Parkway, far enough south to be out of the industrial wasteland that was Newark, that land where the lovely smell of baking bread wasn't the smell of baking bread at all, but instead was the yellow smoke belching out of towering smokestacks, no doubt some industrial process for creating pesticide or petroleum distillates. No, that time was good, too, beyond all that filth, and he was driving through Cheesequake State Park, looking over the marshes filled with cattails and tall grasses swaying in the breeze near the coast, and the sky was filled with fluffy clouds scudding east on the wind, only mostly blocking the sun. He was heading to some meeting in South Jersey and was glad to be out of his cubicle when the same song came on. Though he knew it was seventies vintage, he also knew he hadn't heard it before. It had a nice baseline, simple lyrics he could understand, light strumming, and swelling horns that sung of escape. In short, it was the combination of discovery and a melody worthy of it, the happy collision of a moment and the perfect song. That might have been a perfect moment had it not been bound and contained within the confines of New Jersey, which, try as he might, never felt like where he was supposed to be.

As a kid living north of Pittsburgh, McGhee would listen to the trucks out on PA 422 at night during the summer. The windows were open, and the breeze would carry those sounds to his room, lilting in and out like a soft voice calling to him. He liked it when the trucks heading down the hill used their Jake brakes to decelerate – they sounded like exhausted animals, tired from an endless trek in the West. And he liked the down shift of those other trucks, heading the other way, west, straining to take the hill. In every one of those moments he imagined they were off to Arizona – somewhere different than Pennsylvania, somewhere hot and dry and wild. So when he had a chance to visit Arizona, he'd remember those times, though not so much when he was in Phoenix, which had much of the sprawling charm of Newark, only with better food. And on those occasions when he could head north to the Mogollon Rim or the Canyon, or south into the more primitive-feeling Tucson, he felt he was in the real Arizona. It was to those places his mind had wandered on those sleepless nights, and he sought on every such occasion – when he found himself in those environs – to take advantage of it.

So it seemed things might be lining up for him, at least for the moment – his work was done, the prospect of an interruption was limited, the weather was fine and temperate, and he was in a landscape he'd always felt drawn to. He was glad to leave I-10, too, for smaller, less-travelled roads. Turning west on Speedway, he headed out of town. He'd heard there was a half-decent spot to watch a sunset and figured he'd check it out. He'd be heading back east in the morning, so this was a last chance, at least for this visit, at doing something better than sleep in his cheap motel room. It was good to have something else to do, and he adjusted in his seat. His arm was draped over the wheel, and the cars stayed ahead and behind, perfectly balanced, as he held his own in a small gap in traffic. He noticed on his wristwatch it was the eighteenth of June – his brother Les's birthday – and the thought occurred to him to call him, but a glance at his disemboweled phone was enough to discourage it. There'd be time enough for that later. He was enjoying the change in scenery: it had slid into the residential side of town, stucco houses with Mesquite and Palo Verde in the yards, prickly pear by the end of the drive.

McGhee liked the sensation of tracing a small town's evolution, from its urban trappings by the highway – strip malls, restaurants, hotels, heavy traffic and light industry – out toward the edges when the land still had the upper hand on humanity. Something about that transition suggested to him that the process might be reversible, that men were only tenants on the land, at its discretion. He knew it was illusion, but he liked it anyway, delighting as the scars of civilization peeled away, as homes spread further apart, as their styles became more varied, as the poor became apparent on the fringe where watering stopped and desert began, and where the rocks hadn't moved except for erosion in a hundred thousand years. These observations helped quiet his head, and he welcomed the quiet.

As he drove, the street eventually narrowed to a road, becoming more twisty, with fewer and fewer traffic lights, then fewer street lights, then on into stop signs. Before long they diminished, too, and the edges of the road changed from nicely paved bike lanes, to thin-lined edges, to crumbling pavement margins marked with orange BUMP signs festooned with sprays of scrub grass and short blades of prickly pear. What had been a wide valley sprawling to the south was narrowing as he made his way into the hills along the right, where Speedway became West Gates Pass Road. A ridge line began tracing his path, injecting bends into the road as it intruded, until finally the road dove into the hills themselves.

The further out he went, and the more the rest of his mental ripples settled, the more the last bits of distraction surfaced. Welling up, like the slightest pressure on a saturated sponge, recollections of a woman came to him. It had been a year since Kate, and with the thought of her his grip on the wheel tightened momentarily. But that theme seemed content for once to sit at the margin of his mind for the moment, just out of the light's edge. It wasn't that he had come to terms with it – he doubted he ever would – but he was simply weary, and somehow the less he fought them back, the more they were content to sit just beyond his focus. Thoughts of her would still come to him on occasion, causing him to wonder after her and how her life went on without him, even though he didn't feel his had, not really. Still, there was a calmness to his thoughts that felt new, perhaps a resignation, so that the thoughts seemed less commanding and he could turn away from them, when he was ready if he wanted to, though he didn't think that moment had come just yet. They remained like an echo, and he listened to them fading like one calling into the vastness with no expectation of an answer. Such were his ruminations as the road wound into the hills.

Around such a bend arose *Tucson Mountain Park* more quickly than he expected, and he veered into the lot a few seconds before he realized he had even done it. It was his destination, but he wasn't aware of it so much as his driving mind was. It wasn't a large lot, but was empty except for two other cars. Shutting off the engine, he rolled down the window to listen. Somewhere unseen a couple cicadas were vibrating their abdomens in summer noise, then relaxed to let their buzzing subside. Otherwise, it was silent.

The lot was at the foot of a large hill, or small mountain, topped with a tiny butte. Off to the north a mile, a distant ridge comprised of more righteous mountains moved past his spot toward the west. Two paths left the lot from a common origin – one went toward the higher ridge line, up through scree until it disappeared among boulders in a gulch. It must have been a mile at least. The other headed straight ahead from McGhee, switching back and forth up the hill in front of him, and seemed the better choice.

He was mildly put out by the cars there and the people they implied – he wanted to be alone – until he saw two small groups trailing up the path toward the taller ridge of mountain. *Like I'd climb that* . . . he thought to himself, getting out of the car to take a look. Something distasteful seemed to pervade that observation, unpleasant and judgmental, so he pushed it out of his head. *Good for them*, he thought, *but that's not my path*. Once the sentiment was recast, like most such things, he chose to ignore judgment altogether, and the lack of thought remaining pleased him.

It was quiet, and it was good.

The air was stirring just slightly, not enough to shake the spare weeds in between the scrub and cactus, but just enough to register on his cheek. Now and then the slight clicks of scree on the path behind the hikers would reach him, but no human sounds: the hikers apparently had sense enough not to ruin the silence with their voices.

The path ahead hooked left, then went nearly straight up the side of the hill until becoming switchbacks half way. It must have been several hundred feet vertical, but seemed about the right scale of challenge McGhee was prepared to endure. He wasn't even sure he knew how he knew of this place – it wasn't like he knew anyone in Tucson – and he wasn't the type to strike up a conversation with those he met. His interactions lately were mostly with waitresses, counter people in stores, check-out clerks and gas station attendants. His expression didn't invite conversation; his interactions were transactional and brief, seldom more than a handful of change and a brief grunt when obligatory greetings came his way. So that probably wasn't it. He kept his head down on his project, too, so it wasn't that, either.

Trudging up the hill, he thought he could have heard of the park at Denny's the day before. Though he rarely talked, he sometimes would sit near others and would listen to their conversations. The violation this represented didn't concern him – he wasn't going to tell anyone, and he certainly didn't care about the details – but at some level he needed occasional *social adjacency*. That was his term for it. It was a means to satisfy what he considered a vestigial need for contact without actually engaging in talk. So this seemed the most likely means he had heard it. He'd hear snippets of sentiments, like *Fred's got cancer*, or *Syed is coming soon*, or *Hammond is such an asshole* – that sort of thing – but rarely enough to assemble a story. But now and then there'd be more interesting disclosures. Truckers talked of roads and stops and construction and weather and food. They were passing through like he was, so their conversations were useful to him more often. Still, that might not be right either, for how would they know of a local park? Or now and then, when he was in the mood, he'd sit at the counter and have some pie and coffee, and risk actual conversation, though he certainly discouraged it. That seemed more likely for park information in this case, though he couldn't recall something like that, either. Or maybe it was just at a coffee shop, but why would those people mention a place like this? The rumination was working though – he was halfway up before he had to stop, so he turned to look back.

Down below he saw his rental car. He had overshot his space and was over the line on the left. *How hard could it be to park in an empty lot* he thought to himself, but he stopped the thought, closing his eyes to let it go, and turned back to the hill. He was trying to be in the moment and such thoughts were unproductive. Leaning into the path, he pushed on his knee with his hand to get moving again. Up wasn't so far anymore. He was surprised to find he was enjoying the physical exertion, though he didn't let the thought take shape lest he destroy it with further observation. But once his mind cleared, he suddenly remembered where he had heard of the park: Nells.

The tail end the day before, Nick had called him late to drop into a real estate office. Of course, it was on the north end of town, when he was already on the south side, so he had to take I-10 to get there, and relatively speaking, the cars were thick. By the time he got there, Nells was by the door, coat over his arm, a loaded ring of keys hanging from the door kept open with his foot, office dark. Despite his apparent hurry, he was nice enough, and couldn't avoid his realtor urges to feel-out McGhee about the area, whether he might be looking for something. That turned into five minutes of discussion about a nice three-bed two-bath owner-financed ranch west of town, and the nice park down the street. "Great views of the valley, and sunset . . . ahhh . . . ," Nells said, putting his hand to his chest. "Whatever you do, check out Tucson Mountain Park for a sunset before you go," he said, putting a hand on McGhee's sleeve. Then he handed McGhee three thick manila envelopes with closing papers for something, twisted the key in the lock, and waved bye over his head as he swept around the corner of a Mercedes.

So the park mystery was solved, and McGhee shook his head, glad to be rid of the question. He didn't like the idea of holes in his recollection – signs of a failing brain – which seemed to be happening more than they used to, so the resolution was welcome. Again, his head cleared, and he resumed his summiting, limited as it was.

The path was dusty and dry through several more switchbacks and around boulders until it leveled near the top. There were no others there as the path finished in a curl around a large flat stone at the summit, save another jutting rock beside it to lean against. McGhee did just that, tipping against the warm stone slightly and facing to the west with a full view across the valley.

The sun glowed orange low on the horizon. Just to the north, the other ridge jutted out into the valley, too, though it was far enough away not to block the vista. Saguaro dotted the walls of the canyon as it opened to the west, up to the very crest where they stood in silhouette against the sky. It was a light blue, almost white, set against the dull taupe of the terrain, gaining in whiteness as it spilled over the ridge and into the valley, spreading out to the distant edge where the land met the sky. It had been a hotter day earlier, and the land relaxed in the dissipating heat. Gentle small hills rolled into the distance, where another small range jutted up from the landscape to broker that sky's edge. A small foot sign said

Old Tucson lay out there somewhere, but after tracing a few dusty roads to what might, or might not, be an intersection in the distance, he gave up looking, realizing he didn't care to see it anyway.

McGhee stared into the expanse without a thought in his head. There was no regret or worry, nothing pending, nothing open. No conversations dangling, no real woman troubles to bother him, though memories of Kate still lingered. No children either for that matter, either of his own to remember, or others nearby to bother him. He closed his eyes and there was simply nothing to occupy his attention other than the moment. He caught his mind pondering even this and let it dribble in small then smaller beats to complete stillness. His heart, pounding from the climb, gradually subsided into its normal beat. What had been a mounting bead of sweat on his brow disappeared in the dry air and the sensation of the slight breeze returned. There was nothing but the moment, and to his recollection, this had not happened more than once or twice before, and it was good.

Looking over his shoulder, he could see the shadow of his hill casting far back toward the city. Sunlight glinted on a few windows there, orange, wavering slightly with the distance. Putting his hands behind his head, he leaned back fully against the stone, resting his hands on the warm rock. Words were forming lightly in his head like the beginning lines of something and he enjoyed the sensation. There was no pressure from them, only the tickling sensation of a poem about to emerge, and he realized it had been a long time since he'd been relaxed enough for that to occur.

He could look directly into the sun without discomfort. The dust in the air made it a warm orange. Where it was setting, the sky was grayer, with a diffuse smoke or something, permitting full view of the disk. He had imagined sights like this as a kid, back when he thought of Arizona, but had never seen it, not this way, though he had been in the area several times. It was better in the moment than he could have envisioned, and he knew it was because he was there. Not only was he there in person, but his mind wasn't anywhere else. And he knew he couldn't take it with him, but could only have the recollection. Adjusting his hips, his back loosened still further, and out there he finally saw what he had travelled for, and knew it would always remain where it was, on the horizon, in that one certain sunset.

Old Men

23
0 ———————————————————————————— 90
8PM
Deadwood, SD 5/20/1987

He heard the truck long before he saw it, struggling to make the hill but hidden from view around the bend, down below where he was dropped an hour before. He thought it might be easier to get a lift higher on the hill – one of those hitchhiking notions which are an equal mixture of reason, hope and superstition – so he'd trudged up a couple hundred yards, and if nothing else, the exertion gave him the illusion of progress. Still, the lateness was worrying him as the sun was already behind the mountain where he perched deep in the Black Hills, and he worried he might not get to see the men, and further, that he had no idea how he'd spend the night. But that was hours down the road – distant future. For the moment, the urgency was to get to the right mountain.

Throughout his trudge up the hill he'd dutifully held out his thumb, but nothing. One car pulled over ahead of him, but tore out sending gravel back once the driver's cigarette was lit. Someone else shouted something inaudible – it wasn't nasty – some sort of joke – as if he could hear any of it as they whipped by at fifty miles an hour. They waved, though, so it was something. But it was getting late, and once he reached his perch, he thought he needed something – a sign – to get more attention. Grabbing a notebook from his pack, he fished for a marker, his arm in up to the pit in his full-length army duffle (his companion since at least Alaska), which had been a present from his cousin. Thin, dense stuff always filtered to the bottom, but he found it without too much problem. Jamming his hand in his pocket, he pulled out some change, picking out a nickel, a penny and a quarter. It wasn't too hard to get Washington's profile – the design of the quarter helped there. So did the penny. Jefferson was a total toss-up – but he figured he'd get the point across. He was just finishing the fill of Washington's dark profile when the truck came into view.

It was an old red Ford pickup, originally assembled some time back in the fifties, now held together by something other than bolts, its fenders wiggling with the effort against the hill. The small chrome hubcap domes were dented, then dented some more, like calypso drums, turning slowly as the wheels chewed into the incline. It almost seemed a shame when he rolled to a stop, right in front of McGhee – the thought occurred to him it might not get moving again, but he was willing to give it a shot as the hour was late and he'd take any ride he could get. The driver was an old man and motioned with his hand. "Hop in . . . and throw your pack in the back, there's not much room up here . . . ," he said. McGhee looked at the seat with misgiving: the Naugahyde of the bench had seen better days – the stitching had finally completed its perforation along the quilted surface, and the foam underneath was protruding the full width of the seat, along multiple seams. On top, there was a clear layer of dirt, lots of papers and pieces of mail, and an empty sack from a drive-thru. Swiping it all on the floor, the driver repeated, "Get in . . . we don't have all day," and even before McGhee was seated and his door fully latched, the driver manhandled the shift into gear with considerable grinding and the truck lurched slowly forward, seemingly reluctant to begin the climb again. They were moving, only slightly faster than walking speed at first, but it picked up until finally they merged into traffic, other cars whizzing by, sweeping into the other lane to give them room.

For McGhee's part, it was nice to be moving again. He had just resigned himself to missing Rushmore, but it seemed he might make it now after all. The road was a nice three-lane, freshly paved, curling up and around the mountain, two lanes up, one down. It seemed they were probably within ten miles, so barring further problems, it should still be light. It was mid-May, so it'd stay light fairly late and the air was warm with only the slightest late spring chill remaining in it. The driver looked to be pretty old to McGhee – probably in his seventies – and he'd spent a lot of that time in the sun. His hands were enormous and calloused, wrapped around the thin steering wheel. He wore a green John Deere cap, mesh, so the air would flow through, and had thick, meaty ears. His face was weathered, and he wore old glasses, horn-rimmed on the top, wire underneath, of the style his dad used to wear he remembered from when he was still a kid. And though the man didn't have a beard, he had a few day's-growth on his chin, with a bushy silver mustache on his upper lip. When he'd run his hard hand on his hard chin, it sounded like wood on sandpaper, only he didn't know which might be which. For his part, the driver was sizing him up, too.

"So how long ya standing there?" the man said, looking from the road to McGhee and back again.

"An hour, maybe . . . ," McGhee said, resting his elbow on the frame of the window. "Thanks for the lift – I was starting to think I'd miss it."

"Yeah, well, we ain't there yet," he said, shaking his head. "I think this damned thing might explode before then," he said, taking his hand off the wheel to smack the dash. Looking over at McGhee, he extended his hand. "The name's Bud. Bud Taylor . . . ."

McGhee shook his hand. "I go by McGhee," he responded.

Bud shook his head. "Fair enough," he said, looking back to the road. "I musta passed a hundred o' you guys out there on the road," he continued, looking out through the windshield like the road might change any minute. "Know why I picked ya up?" he asked, turning to look at McGhee.

"My sign?" McGhee guessed.

"You're *damn right*, your sign," he said, nodding again. "Only one with enough goddamned sense to be creative," he said, looking back at McGhee, smiling, his lips curling in, his cheeks accentuating his smile with folds on ridges on wrinkles. McGhee rather suspected there might be missing teeth, but there weren't – they were old but complete and straight, shining and just visible under his mustache. The net impression was hard and weathered, like the wind and sun and earth had swirled into his makeup from years of exposure.

"So, three . . . ," Bud said, looking at McGhee. "Why only three?" Bud motioned to the notebook in McGhee's lap, still folded open to his sign.

Looking down, McGhee saw the sign and put it together. "Oh, well . . . ," he started, somewhat embarrassed. "I couldn't remember the fourth guy."

"*Jesus!*" Bud said slamming his hand on the wheel. "I think he's the whole reason for the thing . . . ," Bud said. "Roosevelt. Theodore Roosevelt?" He kept looking back and forth from the road to McGhee, incredulous he could forget the fourth president.

McGhee shrugged. "I wouldn't have had a coin, anyway," he said, showing Bud the penny, nickel and quarter still sitting in his palm.

"Damn," Bud said, slamming the wheel again. "Now that's creative. And those likenesses aren't bad either," he said, motioning to the sign again.

Settling in, they both fell silent, looking through the windshield. Tall, dark pines lined the road as they climbed the hill. The sky was blue and falling into late evening, half full of clouds, or perhaps half empty – McGhee wasn't sure which position to take – scudding slowly eastward, smashed out and gray in the middle, but with bright silver and white edges with growing hints of orange. McGhee motioned up toward the sky, and Bud leaned into the windshield.

"I love it when they do that . . . ," McGhee said. "The clouds. I love that." Bud turned to him and smiled.

"Farmer's friend . . . ," he said, nodding. "Spent the better part of sixty years praying for those."

McGhee scanned him again, noticing coverall jeans over a thin checked long sleeve shirt and white t-shirt underneath. Suddenly it made sense to him. "Farmer?"

Bud looked at him. "Yeah. Taters. Got a spread up near Pocatello." Both his hands were on the wheel, and they seemed to involuntarily knead it lightly, almost like a reflex. "Been a couple weeks since I was there and was gettin' kinda antsy to get back . . . was down in Santa Fe. Got a daughter down there. Nice kid but bad luck. Husband died. Got two kids, so I figured

I'd help her out a couple weeks. Workin' on a nursing certificate. Almost got it, too. Wouldn't-a helped Billy none, though. Poor kid was changing a tire on his truck and got clipped by somebody. Never even stopped."

His grip tightened on the wheel as he thought of it, but gradually loosened, his brows relaxing, and his easy smile returning, though with some sadness in it.

"Water under the bridge, now . . . ," he said, tilting his head. "Funny how life works. And here I am, a couple heart attacks already, but I just don't seem to stay dead. Doesn't seem right somehow."

McGhee was content to listen, and Bud seemed content to talk. They were getting close to the monument, but had a couple miles to go yet.

"Got to Cheyenne and just couldn't keep going home. Found myself taking the road here instead. Seeing the presidents makes me feel better, somehow . . . ." He shook his head slowly, his smile broadening at the thought of it. "Ever see 'em before?" Bud asked, turning to McGhee.

"First time," McGhee said. "Was in the area and thought I'd take a look."

"So, I take it you're not from around here, then?"

"Pennsylvania . . . ," McGhee answered. "Near Pittsburgh. A small steel and corn town."

Bud shook his head again. "So how does that work, you being in the area?" he asked.

"Long story," McGhee said.

Bud shrugged. "I got time . . . ," he said. "Lots of it."

McGhee scratched his head, thinking. "Well, I was helping a roommate deliver some furniture down to Albuquerque. Been hitching since Durango. Stopped in Boulder."

"That's your version of a long story?" Bud said, laughing. "I fart longer'n that," he said.

Up ahead a sign directed them into a lot and they parked close to where the path fed up into the trees. There was a handful of other cars, but it was mostly empty. Bud didn't bother to lock the truck as they walked away, and he read McGhee's mind. "Who would steal that thing?" he said, putting his arm around McGhee's shoulder for a reassuring pat. "Now you're gonna like this . . . ," he said as they started up the path.

The sun was set, but the sky remained bright and the air still decently warm. The smell of pines enveloped them as they moved deeper into the woods. Bud walked with a lumbering gate, as if he were more used to being stooped over than walking fully upright, like each step was a step toward leaning over again. It was quiet, though a slight breeze through the pines made a light, breathy noise. It wasn't far before the pines parted and they had their first glimpse of the hill and saw Washington's gaze peering off to the south. McGhee's impulse was to run toward it, but he held back. Somehow the slow and steady walk felt right to him, and especially with the company, he was content to take it slow. It was only another few yards anyway before the trees opened fully and they walked onto the viewing platform, behind the building, the wall of granite before them in the distance, nearly in silhouette against the evening sky.

"My god . . . ," McGhee said, his mouth remaining open. Bud laughed quietly and patted him on the shoulder again. "Better than you thought, right?" he said.

McGhee was speechless, staring up at them. The magnitude of the task was astounding: granite rubble lay at the foot of the mountain beneath each of the stone faces. Light wisps of orange cloud hung above them still illuminated by the sun. Low rays of sunlight made the faces glow, as if living men had been captured in the majesty of sunset, frozen in the enormity of their stature, and by their humanity. It wasn't at all what McGhee expected, and only when Bud handed him his embroidered hanky did he realize his eyes were wet.

"It's OK," Bud said. "I cried the first time I saw it, too."

Standing there they looked in silence, and it was good.

On the patio, the scene was repeated, families marching to the edge, leaning on the wall to stare up the monument. McGhee alternated from looking at the stone faces to those around him — their experiences seemed universal. Some cried, the more stoic held it in, but all were affected. Behind them near the café there was some bustle, but it all subsided when they looked up at the mountain. When McGhee looked back at Bud, he was still staring up at the faces, smiling, then realizing McGhee was watching him, he looked over.

"It's never disappointing," he said, shaking his head. "Gets me every time. Wish everything was that reliable." Looking back to the hill, McGhee leaned into the wall again.

"I love stuff like this," McGhee began, "so it's always been on my list. I knew I wanted to see it. I didn't expect the emotion, though." He paused, still looking up, propping up his head in the crook of his elbow. "The funny thing is, it's not really the patriotic part that gets me. Don't get me wrong . . . ," he said, tilting his head to look at Bud. He didn't want to offend him with his youthful sentiments, even though he wasn't sure what they were, either.

Bud nodded, putting his fist on his hip. "Me, neither," he said. "But what is it, exactly?"

Looking back up, McGhee focused on Washington. His gaze toward the horizon filled him with emotion again, so he dabbed at his eyes before answering. "I guess . . . when you read the history books it's easy to forget they were real men. Only . . . they risked their lives and made a difference, for something they believed in, when they couldn't really know how it would turn out. And they look so wise – makes me wish I could have known them." He fell silent a moment, staring up at the old men. "I wish I had some of that."

Bud moved closer to him, put his arm around his shoulder again. "How do you know you don't?" Bud said. McGhee looked up at him, and he had a kind, knowing smile.

As long as he could remember, he'd always liked older people – the older the better – much more so than his peers. He'd had friends, of course, but when it came to really connecting, it was always the older men who seemed to understand him. Mr. McCandless, his neighbor – he was a farmer, too – he was like that. They never actually discussed much of significance. More often than not it was the weather, everyday life, stripped of the abstract. From his experience, they were old enough to see past the senselessness, past the distraction, past the competition, past the fear, to the essential, and they always had that slight smile. They wouldn't have said it themselves; in fact, they'd disdain such labels, but they seemed to see the essence of it, and in their presence, their calm warmed him.

Bud still stared at him, studying his face. The thoughts played there like clouds, alternating between sun and shade.

"I feel like I'm always afraid," McGhee said.

Bud patted his shoulder and grabbed the hanky from McGhee, blowing his nose into it before stuffing it into his pocket. He laughed and shook his head. "You're a funny kid, McGhee," he said, smiling more broadly. "You're hitching across the country, alone, out in the middle of nowhere, and *that* doesn't scare you." Lifting his hand he gently thunked McGhee on the forehead with his palm. "It's easy, kid," he said. "Just stop thinking so much."

With a couple last looks, Bud and McGhee moved away from the veranda, back toward the truck. Looking down at McGhee, Bud seemed to anticipate his thoughts. "I'm not ready to let you go yet, young man. How about dinner in Deadwood?" It was just dawning on McGhee he didn't have a plan after Rushmore, so he smiled gratefully.

In the cab, Bud paused, key in the ignition. "I always wonder if ol' Betsy'll start," he said, leaning in for a careful turn. Grrr . . . Grrr, Grrr. Bud looked at McGhee. "She usually does that." He turned the key again and it started, reluctantly at first, then finding her rhythm, she settled into a low hum.

It still wasn't dark, but the trees hung over the road with their thick needles, mostly hiding the last light of the sky. Winding down the hills, the view opened a bit as the road spread before them. Bud suddenly turned to McGhee, a serious look on his face. "I never been east of the Mississippi," he said. McGhee wasn't sure if that was a confession or not: his tone had more defiance in it than repentance.

McGhee shrugged. "I've been to forty-nine states so far. Haven't hit Hawaii yet."

Delighted, Bud slammed on the wheel again with his hand. "All right then. Now you gotta tell me _why_ I should go east . . . ."

It seemed like an easy question to McGhee, until he tried to answer it. "Well . . . ," he began, but nothing came out immediately. Bud kept switching his gaze from the road to McGhee and back again, but he remained silent.

"Oh, come on, you can do better'n that . . . ," Bud said finally.

"Yeah, yeah, I know. OK . . . well there's New York." Bud immediately shook his head.

"Hate cities," he said. "Next."

Mentally, McGhee was crossing Boston and Atlanta and Washington and every other eastern city from his list. "Beaches . . . all of Florida," McGhee said, brightening with the thought.

"Seen beaches, all up and down the west coast. Can't be better'n that . . . ," he said.

"The water's warmer though . . . ," McGhee objected.

"Don't swim. Next," Bud retorted, shaking his head again, but McGhee was ready.

"Smoky Mountain National Park," he said, raising a finger for emphasis.

Bud shook his head. "You call those mountains?" he said.

"Acadia National Park in Maine. Beautiful, first place in continental US to see the sunrise?" McGhee said.

Bud had to think about that, tilting his head. "That's an awful long way to go to see a sunrise . . . ," he said eventually. "But maybe."

They were getting into the outskirts of Deadwood, but McGhee was running low on ideas. "What do you *like*, anyway?" McGhee asked. The frustration in his voice was feigned, and Bud enjoyed the back and forth, smiling at McGhee in response.

"Trains," he said.

"Trains . . . ," McGhee repeated. "Did you see that one back in Keystone?" Bud shook his head. "Rode it. Back in '63. But that doesn't count, that's out *here*."

"I know, I know . . . ," McGhee said, sensing his time was running out, then it occurred to him. "OK, I got it," he said, smiling, waiting for Bud to ask.

"So what you want ta eat anyway?" Bud said, changing the subject.

"No, no, no," McGhee said, wagging his finger at him. "The Smithsonian . . . ," he said, crossing his arms in triumph. "You *gotta* see that."

"They got trains?" Bud asked, turning into the drive of a diner. It wasn't quite on the main drag of town, but looked to be a local spot, marginally less touristy than most of the other stuff. "I like going to these towns," Bud said, "until I realize everyone else does, too. I hate people," he said, shaking his head, then smiling. "Most of the time. Herds of 'em. Give me cows any day."

"I thought you grew potatoes?" McGhee said, stepping out of the truck.

"Don't mean I can't prefer cows," Bud retorted, slamming his door shut. "Prefer potatoes, too, but that didn't seem like a fair comparison."

"Present company excepted?" McGhee said, coyly pointing at his own chest.

"Depends . . . ," Bud said, stopping to look at him. "What kinda potatoes?"

The front door creaked when it opened, with a little bell near the top tinkling. At the counter, three old men turned their heads to look at them, then went back to staring at their coffees. It had four, maybe five tables, but most were empty. The proprietor behind the counter was drying cups with a white rag, and he whipped it over his shoulder, grabbing a couple menus. "Anywhere you want, gentlemen . . . ," he said, swinging around the register and motioning to the tables.

Bud picked the furthest back, then hurried his step to get the furthest seat facing the door. "Can't be too careful in Deadwood," he said, slowly lowering himself into the seat. It creaked with his weight, but held steady like it had been doing for thirty years. Bud looked around approvingly, leaning over to McGhee. "I like when the kitschy old stuff is really just stuff that's been there since it was actually new," he said.

McGhee scanned the place, but wasn't sure. "How can you tell?" he asked, leaning in with him.

" 'Cause I *remember* it, that's how," he said, banging his fingers against the edge of the table. Picking up the menu, he took to studying his options. McGhee did, too, though he usually just ordered a burger or something cheap.

"You got any money for this?" Bud asked, still looking into his menu.

McGhee glanced at him, but copied Bud's focus on the menu. "Some . . . ," he said, somewhat warily.

Bud let out a garumpf, took off his hat to wipe his forehead, then put it back, smiling at McGhee. "Which means you're broke," he said, smiling again and shaking his head, resuming his read of the menu. "Don't matter anyhow. This one's on me." Taking off his glasses, he folded them and stuffed them in his pocket.

The proprietor came over, pad folded back and took their orders, collecting their menus under his arm. The order went up on a metal wheel in the cook's window that he spun, wobbling several times before it came to a rest. That squeaked, too.

"So where ya headed tonight, anyway?" Bud asked, folding his fingers in front of himself on the table.

McGhee was drinking his water, which he gulped until it was gone. "You gotta take it where you can get it . . . ," he said, wiggling the cup, then after wiping the water from his thin beard and mustache, added, "Minneapolis."

"*Jesus* . . . ," Bud said, rubbing his neck with one of his thick hands. "Well, you ain't gettin' there tonight." McGhee shrugged, picking up his glass again, but realizing it was empty, put it down. Bud slid his water glass over to McGhee. "That's gotta be five hundred miles, anyway . . . ."

"More like six hundred . . . ," McGhee said, lifting the glass in toast to Bud, then downed that one, too.

"You gonna stay somewhere?" Bud said, sounding concerned, "or push through?" McGhee shrugged.

"Just gonna keep going. It'll be all right . . . ," he said, smiling weakly. They both knew Bud would offer to put him up in some flop if he wanted, but somehow that violated the unstated rules of hitchhiking.

Bud matched his smile and shrugged also. "I'll get you out to I-90 then, after supper. I can take that the whole way back to Pocatello," he said, throwing a thumb over his shoulder.

A low voice from the counter rumbled: "Free Taters for Outta Staters . . . ." It was an old man in jeans and flannel, a faded red Vets cap on his head. A spray of white hair shot out from his shirt, and from around the edges of his hat. He was twisted on his stool, looking over at them.

Bud twisted in his chair to look over, then turned back to McGhee, before shouting over his shoulder with alarming volume, "Harry *fuckin'* Garber."

The restaurant went silent. Bud sat there, shaking his head. After a few seconds, he laughed loudly, slapped the table with both hands and pushed his chair back with his thighs striding over to the counter. The man on the counter stool stood, too. Bud put his hands on his shoulders, and the man tried to do the same to Bud, only a beat late, opting instead to wrap his arms around Bud and pull him in for a hug. Putting an arm over the man's shoulder, Bud turned back. "McGhee, get over here. I guess you oughta meet this old fool, too . . . ."

The food was arriving, so McGhee stole a bite before wiping his hands on his jeans and stepping over.

"This here is Harry Garber," Bud said. "We come up together, 'til he skinned out anyway. Navy?" he said, turning to the old man again.

"Marines," Harry said with a grunt. He knew Bud knew, and it made him laugh to think of it. Pulling a red kerchief from his pocket he mopped around his lips, laughing and coughing with phlegmatic intensity, before stuffing the kerchief in his pocket again.

McGhee shook the old man's hand. "Yeah, I think everybody knows your name now . . . ," he said, snickering. The few remaining patrons went back to their dinners content to ignore the spectacle.

"Taylor always was a blowhard . . . ," Harry said, slapping him on the arm. Looking over his shoulder, he motioned with his chin to his mates at the bar. "This here is my posse . . . ," he said. "Jerry . . . ," he said, the bearded man tipping his cap, "and Beef." The other, larger old man on the stool just looked at them blinking. He had something of the aspect of a bulldog, jowls hanging, a saggy neck underneath, his mouth drooping open at the corners.

"So what are we eatin'?" Harry asked, dropping his arm from Bud's shoulder to step around to their table. "Bud's buying . . . . Boys?" As if on command, Jerry and Beef shuffled over to the table, Beef grabbing an extra chair from the next table over. "Mike – can you bring us some menus?"

"You know the whole goddamned thing already . . . ," Mike said, not budging.

"Humor me . . . ," Harry said. Sighing, Mike grabbed two menus and handed them to Jerry and Beef, but Harry ignored the affront. "I'll take the Au Jus thing," he said. "How about you guys?"

Beef looked at him, incredulous. "Can I have, like, a second here?" Jerry nodded, too.

"Fine . . . ," Harry said, turning to look back at Bud. "So who's the kid?"

Bud was about to take a bite of the sandwich he'd ordered, but rested his arms again.

"Like I said, this here is McGhee . . . ," he mumbled through his food, his tone somewhere between annoyance and amusement. He raised the sandwich to his lips, but Harry intervened with a hand on his arm, lowering it again.

"We've established that," Harry said.

"Can I eat here?" Bud asked, shrugging off Harry's hand. He moved the sandwich quickly to his mouth, taking a large bite. Looking over from Bud, Harry stared at McGhee.

"You're not his, are ya?" he said, then, saying *McGhee* to himself, he held up his hand. "Na, that wouldn't work."

McGhee wiped his mouth with his napkin. "No relation," he said. "We were both heading to Rushmore and Bud here gave me a lift."

"So you're from Pocatello, too?" Harry asked, his faced screwed up in confusion.

"No, we just met on the road."

"So you're, like, hitchhiking?" Harry said.

McGhee nodded. "Yep."

Harry shook his head, violently. "What a damn-fool thing . . . ."

"That's what I said . . . ," Bud said, his mouth still full of chewing.

"No you didn't . . . ," McGhee objected.

"Well . . . ," Bud said, shaking his head at an angle. "I was *thinking* it."

"I hitched the whole way, once . . . ," Harry said, motioning from one side of the diner to the other.

"Oh, and that was a good idea?" McGhee retorted, smiling.

"Fine . . . ," Harry said, beaten, then smiled. He liked that McGhee pushed back and reached across to smack him lightly in the shoulder with his fist. Jerry tapped the table in front of Beef who gave a slight nod, then waved at Mike to call him over. "Barkeep, fill 'er up," Harry said, holding up his coffee cup to intercept him, before Jerry could get his order in. Beef took the opportunity to hold up his menu and point, Mike nodding as he scribbled.

Bud was looking back and forth between them, smiling as he chewed. "The three stooges . . . ," he said, leaning toward McGhee but motioning toward the others with his chin, a trickle of dressing escaping the corner of his mouth.

"Curly," Harry said.

"Larry," Jerry said.

Beef sighed. "Shit," he said.

Once they started chuckling, they couldn't stop, all five of them, nearly falling silent until one would chuckle, setting the whole group in motion again. Only when their food arrived did the men get past it and set to the serious task of eating. Bud and McGhee finished before the others, so continued their conversation.

"So . . . the Smithsonian . . . ," Bud said. "Forgot about that. Pretty good, huh?"

McGhee nodded. "Yeah, it really is. It's actually a whole slew of museums. My favorite is the Air & Space, but there are lots, including one with trains and steam engines – can't remember which one."

Jerry looked up from his plate, talking through a mouth full of food. "Beef used ta fly." Beef nodded. Harry elbowed Bud and leaned over.

"I'd like to see that plane . . . ," he said, and they all laughed again. Beef chuckled, too, but craned his neck, cracking it in the process.

"I hate when you do that . . . ," Jerry said, "especially when we're eating here . . . ." He motioned to his plate. Beef reached over and grabbed the last wing from his plate and laid it atop his salad.

"Problem solved," Beef said, smiling broadly.

Jerry pushed his plate away, rubbing his stomach. "I was sick of 'em anyway."

"What kind of planes?" McGhee asked, then, calling over their heads, "Can I get a Coke?" to Mike, who was monitoring their progress from the counter.

Beef was in the process of removing every morsel of chicken from the bones of the wing. "Corsairs, from a carrier in the Pacific. Jets later. Did a stint at Edwards flying test."

Jerry leaned toward Harry and whispered, "More like crashing 'em."

"Wow . . . ," McGhee said. "Ever meet Yeager?" Beef nodded, moving on to the skin and sinew of the wing.

"Yeah, I knew Chuck. And Neil. All those guys. Peckers every one of 'em . . . ," he said, licking his fingers.

"Really?" McGhee asked, grabbing the Coke from Mike as he dropped it off.

"No, not really," Beef said, "just makes a better story. They were good guys . . . ," he said, casually dropping the bones on a little plate and settling back into his salad. "Just yankin' yer chain, kid . . . ."

"How about you, Bud?" Harry asked, turning back to his old chum. Bud shrugged.

"Not much to tell, really. Just been growing taters forever. Dad passed about twenty years back." A cloud moved over Harry's face.

"Sorry to hear that. He was a good sort. Shouldn't be surprising though – we're old now. Just about everyone's dead." Looking to his right, Harry noticed Jerry nodding off. "Even Jerry here, though nobody's told 'em yet . . . ," he said, giving him a poke with his elbow, startling him awake.

"Always loved that sign on your farm by I-90," Harry said, looking back to Bud, then to McGhee. "Free Taters for Out-of-Staters," he said. "Giant frickin' thing. Pure genius, that was. Even set up a potato stand at the rest stop. Only in Pocatello . . . ," he said, smiling again. "Haven't been there in a *looong* time." Pulling out his red kerchief, he hacked a bit, quickly wiping his lips, then replacing it again. "Hey, remember that piece of shit truck you used ta drive?" he said, brightening again.

"Still do . . . ," Bud said. "She's out in the lot now, just waitin' for me to get in her again."

"You always did have an unnatural relationship with that thing," Harry said, shaking his head, thinking. "Bunny, or something, wasn't it?" Harry said, scratching his head.

"Betsy, and don't ya go makin' fun of her, now . . . ," Bud said, throwing his own elbow at Harry. "She got McGhee, here, and me to the presidents." Harry looked over to McGhee, his face screwed up in a wrinkly smile.

"First time?" he asked and McGhee nodded. "Cry?" he asked, McGhee shrugging, then nodding.

"Still gets me . . . ," Harry said. "So, what's your plan, kid?" he asked suddenly. McGhee leaned back in his chair.

"Well, I just got out of school last year. Spent some time up north, but haven't figured it out yet," he said, shrugging again.

"You sure shrug a lot," Jerry said, leaning in. Beef nodded, and shrugged himself, and nodded again.

McGhee stopped himself from shrugging, self-conscious. "Well, you guys ask a lot of shrug questions . . . ," he said in his defense. He looked at Bud for support, but he shrugged. "They got a point," he said.

"You just shrugged, though," McGhee said, pointing at him and looking to the others for back up, but didn't get it.

"He does it right," Harry said.   On cue, Beef and Jerry shrugged. "Yeah, he does."

"So, what's the difference?" McGhee said, leaning onto the table, still avoiding the urge.

"When Bud does it," Beef said, pointing at him with his fork, "it's in *addition* to his answer."

"And when you do it," Jerry said, "it *is* your answer."

"'Cause you don't got nothin' else . . . ," Beef said. He waited a second, and shrugged.

"It's like saying uh, uh, uh all the time," Harry said.

"Only quieter," Beef said.

"Still means your tank is empty," Bud said, tilting his head to look at McGhee. There was a kindly smile there – the others had it, too. Only, McGhee didn't know what the joke was, if it was one.

Harry looked at him again. "So . . . what's your *plan*, kid?" he asked again, more slowly. McGhee leaned back in his chair, quiet. Harry leaned back, too, his chair creaking with his weight, and he rubbed the arms with his hands. They were worn and old, but comfortable.

"I have no idea . . . ," he said finally. The others looked at each other, then McGhee.

"You can shrug now," Jerry said, smiling.

"Our friend here . . . ," Bud began, "has a bit of a problem. He thinks too much."

A chorus of "Ahhhhh . . . ," arose from the other three men.

"We never had time for that . . . ," Harry said. "Too busy finding stuff to eat, workin' . . . ," he said.

"You got yourself a girl yet?" Jerry asked, leaning in.

"Not really, no . . . ," McGhee said, shrugging again.

"Good shrug . . . ," Beef said, under his breath.

"Well, get yerself a girl – that'll solve that right quick . . . ," Harry said.

Bud leaned over to him, snickering. "You got that right."

"So, whatcha thinkin' about?" Jerry asked. McGhee looked back at him, his interest seemed earnest.

"Stuff . . . ," McGhee said.

"You can't shrug on that one . . . ," Beef said. "That doesn't count."

"Enough with the shrugging . . . ," Jerry said, turning to Beef, his hand up to stop the rolling review. "What kinda stuff?" he asked, turning back to McGhee.

McGhee leaned back in his chair, tipping up on two legs slightly and put his hands behind his head to think. Reflexively, the other men leaned back in their chairs, too, each creaking under their own loads. "Jesus . . . ," Bud said, "sounds like the chairs are in pain."

"Sometimes it just feels like I'm running . . . ," McGhee said, finally. "Feels like I gotta go, because the place where I am isn't right, only anywhere I go isn't right, either."

"Symptom," Harry pronounced.

Jerry nodded. "Yeah, that's not it," Beef agreed.

"You know what they're talking about?" Bud asked, leaning into the table again.

McGhee looked a bit confused, or worse, resigned. "Not exactly, no . . . ," he admitted.

"No matter where you go, there you are . . . ," Jerry said, nodding.

"Who said that again?" Harry asked, wrinkling his face.

"Yogi Berra," Beef said.

Jerry smacked him on the back of the head. "Confucius, you idiot . . . ," he said.

Beef resorted to mumbling. "Yogi said it, too."

"Don't look so glum, kid," Harry said, reaching over to tap his arm. "It just means you take your problems with you, that's all. Once you figure that out, you're half way to fixing 'em."

Sitting up, McGhee shook his head. "No offense, guys, but that's pretty obvious . . . ."

"Fair enough," Bud said, rubbing his neck again, nodding. "Then what is it?"

McGhee grabbed his drink, but only held it, looking at the plastic tumbler. "I guess I'm afraid of failing . . . ," he said, looking up at them. "And even trying. If I don't try, I won't fail, right? Only, it makes me miserable."

Bud reached over and patted him on the shoulder. "Don't be so hard on yourself, McGhee," he said. "You got a whole life ahead."

"Look at Beef, there," Jerry said, smiling. "He crashed two planes into carriers before he was done."

"Three," Beef clarified.

"I thought it was four . . . ," Harry said, turning to him.

"It was three, countin' that trainer," Beef said, "only I don't usually count it. Rudder stuck."

Bud leaned in. "See, he was just too stupid to quit. That's your problem right there." Spinning around, Bud waved Mike over. "We need an ice cream rescue over here . . . ."

It wasn't what McGhee expected of an evening in the Black Hills – he had no expectations – but that's what he'd come to love about it, about roaming. Right there in that moment, he found he enjoyed the company of old men, to be one of them in communion, if briefly, and forget the life that bothered him in favor of living it, if only he could remember to do so. And as they settled into their cups, each man had his thoughts and pondered them in silence. Entire lives, and hardships, and loves and disappointments and even fulfilment, carved in their faces, in the corners of their eyes, time recorded there, for all to see.

So it was easy for McGhee to smile as he saw it emerge, all on its own, in the natural order of things he was learning to observe: Bud staring off over McGhee's shoulder, Harry looking straight out, Beef sandwiched in between, pushing his wire-rims up, and Jerry looking out past Bud stroking his beard. He'd only seen it an hour before, and here he had his own personal Rushmore, each of their weathered faces lost in thought, pondering their mortality and the folly of youth over dessert, revealing their humanity one spoonful at a time.

Kite

12 Noon
San Francisco, CA 10/31/1988

She was writing a poem on the back of a customer check still attached to her pad, the old receipts pushed back as far as they'd go and the carbon yanked out to give her room. The shop buzzed around her, but she heard none of it, hand on her hip with a cheap pen jammed in her fingers, her knuckles white with the pressure when she pushed into the pad. Her hair was up, mostly in a bun, but it was less stylish than convenient, meant to keep it out of the way, casually swept into a ball, except a few strands that had escaped and hung loose about her neck, free. It was light brown, or perhaps dark blonde – a color not easily described – which made it all the more attractive to McGhee. And the dark green apron, looped over her head and tied smartly about her waist showed just enough of her figure and lines, that once noticed, became unforgettable to him. That pose – by the wait station, one tennis shoe twisted atop the other, hip out, hand there as fist and penned, eyes in her pad, oblivious to everything else – was the pose he'd remember forever.

He was working at xCopy Inc. down the street, so it wasn't hard to get coffee on the way in, and on the way out, too, once he had noticed her. Then he started with a break in the morning, and one in the afternoon until he was stopping four or five times a day at the shop and was making something of a spectacle of himself. The other baristas noticed his presence long before Kate did and started teasing her when he came in – McGhee trying to appear casual but invariably looking anxious – nudging each other with knowing glances and even occasionally snapping their small white dishtowels toward Kate to alert her to the presence of her suitor. He had a preferred table near the door where he'd sit, too, watching her conspicuously, but utterly unaware how obvious he was on his perch, staring. So eventually, in part to stop the incessant teasing, but also, once she became aware of it to stop the staring, she walked up to McGhee just as he entered the shop, planted herself in front of him, and said, "What?"

He had imagined such a moment many times – in fact every time he had come in over the last few weeks – but found himself without words only able to squeeze out a weak, "Uhh . . . ," as he looked into her eyes. From the distance, he hadn't been able to see their color exactly, though he suspected they might be blue. In fact, they were not, but were a nice gray with tinges of green, or perhaps hazel, around the edges. Her lashes were long but natural, her face thin, taut even, with youth just pushing into womanhood. Her lips were neither full nor thin, but had lovely edges creating a ridge around them, where they collected under her nose, which he noted was a tad on the pointy side, though attractive. He found himself cataloging these things, then realized he'd been staring another ten seconds, his eyes scanning her face. "Uhh . . . what do you mean, *What?*" he clarified.

Kate stared back at him, her eyes switching focus from one of his eyes to the other, scanning him back. Shifting her weight to her other foot, her brows crinkled slightly. Pointing to his customary seat next to them, she commanded, "Sit," then spun on her heel to head toward the end of the bar where the baristas were clustered, watching. "What?" she barked at them, scattering them like rats under a flashlight, except one: a tall, tousled young man with long red hair and a puffy red beard remained staring at her, his mouth open. Stopping in front of him, she looked up at him. "Alright, Randall. Make his usual . . . ."

For his part McGhee was paralyzed in the spotlight of recognition, glued at the table until further orders. Eventually, Randall started out to deliver a cappuccino, cup rattling in the saucer, until Kate intercepted him half way, sweeping it out of his hand in a smooth motion toward him. Her expression was stern, except her lips just barely formed a smile in one corner. Setting it down in front of McGhee, she dragged out the opposite wood chair noisily on the floor, plopped into it, put both elbows on the table and propped her chin on her palms, silent.

A part of McGhee's brain was running away with him, exploring scenarios, pondering meaning, wondering if it was too late to escape. The other part began speaking, even to his surprise, because he had no idea what to say.

"Is this what dating you would be like?" he said.

So that's how it started. Though McGhee had known women before, and had even had a few minor relationships, this was entirely different. Where before there were dates, increasing closeness and a build to moderate warmth, this was nothing like those times.

This was immediate, strong, all-encompassing and easy. From that first day, which turned into a first evening together walking Market and the streets of Union Square, their conversations skipped past the normal first pleasantries. Though they were the same age – twenty-five – Kate was still a junior at SF State. She'd taken a year abroad in France, which turned into eighteen months to her parents' dismay (a man was involved), changed her major three times, but was pretty sure she liked studying film, which McGhee helpfully pointed out trained her perfectly to be a barista. One might think she would have been offended, but she loved it, in turn jabbing McGhee at his weak points, and in this way they knitted together strong bonds in days that others might take years to develop. For purely practical reasons, or so they told each other, six weeks later they decided to become roommates and share expenses. They both knew there was far more to it than that, but were both wise enough, or at least knew themselves enough, not to label it further.

They'd found a nice bright apartment near Broadway and Sansome, top floor and high enough to capture morning sunlight and the wafting fumes of Chinese from Henry's Hunan at noon. And though it was up four flights of stairs, the walk up was certainly worth it. Out the corner window they could just glimpse a sliver of the bay between a couple buildings. Some evenings, McGhee would lean there watching the boats pass through the little gap where he could see them, whether they be sailboats or container ships making for port in Oakland. In a rare fit of handiness, McGhee even built a makeshift window seat as the window went nearly to the floor, with only a narrow column in the corner before it continued onto other windows facing opposite them. They could just see over the edge of the next building where there was a small roof garden tended by a small Asian man who always seemed to be working there with a small hand-hoe and a bucket and a hose.

Kate was partial to watching the garden when she sat across from McGhee, a collection of poems in her lap she'd tilt to review, then reorder. Sometimes she'd write them, too, staring out the window between lines to watch the man tend his tiny crops. In the finer weather, usually the fall, she could raise the sash on that window (the others only tilted out for some reason) and get a clearer view and a bit of the breeze. Invariably, the Asian man would hear the creak and slap of the sash as it went up and banged, and once he noticed Kate sitting there, he'd take off his work glove and wave over at her, bowing his head repeatedly and smiling. Eventually, Kate ran into him in the street and introduced herself while he bowed deeply. From then on when he waved, he'd yell her name, which sounded more like *Kite* than Kate, and she'd yell back, "Good afternoon Mr. Chung," and smile as widely as possible, like she was on stage, so he could see it from that distance. She'd look back over at McGhee who always watched the exchange with intent, mostly because it gave her such pleasure, and she glowed after each such interaction, limited as they were. If it was early enough, a little direct sunlight would light her up, warming her, and the transformation transfixed McGhee. Though she always glowed from the inside out, when combined with the sunlight, she became luminous, and though they were the same age, McGhee was struck by her youth and health and happiness, and it warmed him. And in those moments, sometimes she'd lean over to kiss him and he'd slide his hand behind her head to pull her a little closer to catch her lips, warm from the sun, which always probed his just enough to be playful.

For his part, McGhee was happy. The internship consumed his days, and he rather liked playing at being a young manager in a large corporation in a good city with a steady, though modest, income. At first the days were long, and the prospect of staying in his cubicle, extracting reports from endless data sources was difficult, but he grew to tolerate it. He'd find ways to amuse himself, playing with formats, looking for patterns, deriving (what he considered) marginally more interesting inferences from the numbers than were asked for, and other extraneous activities. He made some friends – others likewise caught in the web of corporate America who were hungry for distraction. They discussed movies, places to see in the city, planned getting beers at new bars. These things made his days tolerable and built into weeks, then months, and eventually years. Throughout this, though, he always had an unshakeable suspicion he was an imposter in this world, and sometimes at night this thought would haunt him.

Meanwhile, Kate buckled down, and with some help from McGhee pushed through the last few semesters of her program. Though he'd been an unremarkable student himself, he did find the lessons he'd learned in writing particularly helpful, and though late, these lessons blossomed in his head and he found writing papers with Kate to be enjoyable and that he had some skill with it. For her part, Kate was perpetually incapable of getting her thoughts out in anything other than poetry, so the exposition help was a relief. In the course of these collaborations they became even closer, completing each other's thoughts to create essays on all manner of literature and films, delighting in the destruction of literary and film criticism in favor of pragmatic interpretation. By the time of her graduation, Kate was ready to get out, and McGhee was glad for the partnership they had forged. It was something he never expected, had not even conceived, yet finding it was a delightful and surprising and satisfying discovery.

For her part, Kate took a job at a local photographic studio in the Castro which, though not film related exactly, allowed her to feel she wasn't entirely moving in the wrong direction.

She'd taken to carrying a Leica around with her in the city, snapping mostly dark black and white photos of bicycles, children and dogs stuffing their snouts into unsuspecting stranger's crotches. McGhee delighted in their subversion, and they'd frequently lie awake late looking at the pictures, snickering with a flashlight under the covers at the surprised expressions of those violated by the dogs. Kate would sometimes share her poems, too, and she began pairing them with some of the photos, then began writing for them directly. She'd get in the heads of those in her pictures, even the dogs, and the results were amusing and good. Before long, she was combining them onto large prints — one of the benefits of her job at the studio — and had the better ones plastered on the walls of their apartment. Still, it wasn't quite perfect for McGhee, though it was close.

What had begun as faint misgivings in McGhee regarding his job, grew in his mind. Sometimes at night he'd wake up and stare at the ceiling, rising from a dream in which someone was chastising him for something. The words weren't clear, but he internalized the criticism, and over time the tone of the words seemed like they must be coming from his brother Les. He couldn't see the person: it was like they were sitting somewhere at sunset, beside one another but looking out, and they might have been having iced tea — he wasn't sure why that mattered, but it did. The ease of the setting — he couldn't really see it either — seemed like it was his parents' place, back when their yard still had trees, the large apples of the orchard where they built with the GI Bill. There was a stillness to it, when the summer heat abated and the humidity fell, that he'd never found again. It had that feel to it, and though he couldn't see it, it bothered him and soothed him at the same time. He was sitting with someone telling him he needed to do more, and though the words didn't include disappointment exactly, they conveyed that exact sentiment: the notion of wasted potential. And given the facts, his facts and recollections, McGhee concluded it had to be Les uttering them.

He'd watch the ceiling fan turning slowly above him, and it seemed like another clock, ticking his life away with each slow rotation. Eventually, he'd turn his head to look at Kate, and his thoughts would move to her. She'd sleep on her side most nights, usually facing him, her head atop her folded hands on the pillow. Even in the dark he could sense her features, and he'd listen to her slow and constant breathing. She'd sleep in a white tank-top, covers usually ajar, and he could just make out the curves of her breasts, heaving slowly. Even when she was asleep her beauty moved him and he was glad to have her. He was glad, too, she seemed to be finding her way, one little bit at a time, and he envied the light in her eyes when she was hard at work assembling her pictures, laying them out on her drafting table, making edits to the poetry, drawing crops on the photos to tune them just right. So in those moments, he'd fall asleep thinking of her, and it brought something like peace to him, at least until the morning.

It didn't take much longer – a year perhaps – for McGhee to realize that despite his moderate success at work that it wasn't the work he wanted to be doing. He could imagine promotions, some of which happened, but no path along that course ended in a place he wanted to be. Worse, he wasn't sure where he wanted to be instead or what he might be doing. He took to doing some writing in the evenings, and in his free days, some painting, which he hadn't done since college. Both were helpful to him and he realized his day job didn't have to fulfill everything for him. This trick worked for a while, too – perhaps a couple years – but began to wear thin over time. The time he spent in the evenings grew longer, his weekends were consumed, until he looked with resentment upon the nine hours each day locked away from these pursuits, or something else entirely, and the peace of mind he lost on either end anticipating them, or replaying affronts perceived and real afterwards.

Sometime during that period Kate had her first show – a little gallery down by the wharf catering to tourists with too much money and a burning desire to spend it. She'd only placed five pieces there – it wasn't just her show – and they all sold in a day or two. It wasn't much money, but it fed something in her, and if anything, she was more luminous still. The next show she had fifteen pieces, and they sold, too, prompting the gallery to suggest they have a regular arrangement with her. Her photo studio was supportive of her efforts and never suggested she pay for the mounting expenses of her budding career, but she felt bad about it. Before long she had an arrangement there, too, paying for supplies as the gallery suggested she create series of her prints – why do one-offs when a series would yield more profit was their reasoning – so she went into productions of them. She had to reduce her hours doing the studio's work, but the money was a bit better, and the studio was making something, too, so everyone was happy. With the extra money, Kate and McGhee went shopping and bought their first new couch – they'd been living on consignment pieces forever – and Kate proudly sat on the new set, rubbing the suede in her fingers with satisfaction. McGhee marveled at her and hugged her and kissed her, though something inside him felt a little broken.

Throughout this time, McGhee had been rather productive, too, alternating between painting and writing, depending on which muse moved him. It was clear to him his work life was necessary but wasn't going to ever be enough for him. He was

resigned to this, though it left him wanting something else for satisfaction.   He'd taken to hanging some of his paintings on the walls,
which to his eye were decent but not great, but he liked to see his
handiwork on display.   Kate, too, had her work on the walls, only
her work was exploding and there was much more of it to choose
from.   Only her favorites went up, but even these were mounting, and they were professional due to her attention to detail and
the benefits of working in a professional studio.   Once the shows
started, her output increased, too, and before long McGhee saw
her deliberating over which to have on their walls at any moment
because they were out of room.   She would never have suggested
taking McGhee's work down because she loved him, and further,
she argued, his work was better than hers, though neither of them
believed her when she said it.   It was clear to McGhee he'd have to
be the one to take action, so he did, removing his largest work – a
landscape of the bay – to make room for two of Kate's.   He argued
it made sense, and after some spirited but slightly hollow protests
to the contrary, she acquiesced.   This worked, until the next time,
and the time after that, until he only had one left in the hall by the
door, where his favorite remained.   It wasn't even a painting at all,
but just a charcoal he'd done of a roommate in college.   The slide
stopped there, and there were no further removals of his work,
though McGhee thought he saw on a few occasions a fleeting but
mild look of disapproval on her brow when Kate brushed past his
sketch.

They had their combined thirtieth birthday party one Sunday
on the roof – they had only been born ten days apart as it turned
out – looking out over the bay to the east, and Mr. Chung's garden on the roof jutting into their view to the south. They lived
on the top floor anyway, so it wasn't so far above the garden that
he couldn't see them.   He waved to them and bowed while Kate

cupped her hands around her mouth to call her greeting to him. He called back that he had seen her pictures in that Sunday's paper and that he liked them, which was news to her. After dinner, they went and bought ten copies after tearing through one to find a review of her show with several photos of her work. After that, their phone started ringing as other galleries were looking for shows or to resell her prints. McGhee had to take those calls when she was at the studio, trying to keep up with demand, and by the time she'd come home he'd have three or four such requests to hand her. One such call was an agent who wanted to represent her, and after some deliberation, she agreed it might be a good idea to off-load some of the logistics. Those were heady days, and McGhee enjoyed Kate's success almost as much as she did.

Whatever hesitation there might have been in Kate when she started out, tentatively feeling for an entry position, then growing into it, was gone. McGhee marveled at the ease with which she adapted to the changing situation, building out the things that needed building to meet the new demands. She eventually hired a young woman to help, "Just an intern," she told McGhee, shrugging with a smile, like it was just as unbelievable to her as anybody else, and it was. When she was working and McGhee would approach her with a cup of tea and touch her bare shoulder, she'd always break from her work to turn to him with a smile and, "Thank you." She'd even clasp his hand over her shoulder and hold onto his fingers an extra beat before she let them go and grabbed her markup pen again. It was like she was rising up before him, buoyed by the wind and climbing effortlessly. It was magical and he loved her, but began to wonder if he was enough for her.

He began to notice in bed, too, her confidence welling. She'd always been a willing and generous partner, as anxious to please

as be pleased – but something was different. As time went by
she felt freer to take the initiative, even be a little inventive as
their sessions included something of a pursuit, in which he was
both the pursuer and the pursued. Where she had followed his
lead before, he found her sometimes leading but always smiling
and tender as she did so. It engendered a fresh excitement into
their healthy physical lives and also a bit of the unknown. For
McGhee, it was a novel experience, but he liked it. Most of him
liked it, that is, because some of him felt slightly threatened by it
as he felt his leadership becoming full partnership, and perhaps
trending further.

To her credit, Kate was sensitive to the change, and once
she'd seen a few fleeting moments of doubt cross McGhee's
dark eyebrows, she knew enough to pull back gently and smile
at him, allowing him to resume pursuit. Once they were done
and she cuddled in the crook of his arm, she looked up at him, a
bit of sadness in her eyes, though her lips still smiled. She told
him it was OK and that he could tell her anything, so he did
and they talked deep into the night. By the end of it, McGhee
was more convinced than ever that he was deeply in love with
her but feared perhaps her love wasn't as deep as his own. He
knew he needed her, but he wasn't sure the opposite was true.
He also knew that he was too young to know what should come
next, or how to fix it, and the thoughts filled him with empty
dread.

On towards morning while she slept, he awoke from a dream
and lay looking at the fan, slowly turning. This time it had been
Mr. Chung's voice calling, "Kite, Kite . . . ," and she was rising up
on a string into the breeze, held firmly in place by a string wrapped
tight in McGhee's fingers. Her arms were out and she was smiling,
sailing into the sun and looking away out toward some horizon he

could not see. Looking over at Kate he saw her sleepy eyes looking at him. "I love you . . . ," he whispered, his face on his arm. Smiling, she closed her eyes, but he was pretty sure she was already gone.

Stones

47

0 ←——————————————————————————————→ 90

1AM

St. Francis Memorial, San Francisco, CA

The waiting room was a clean, well-lighted place, but gave McGhee no solace as he had waited too long – as usual – to make the drive in. He'd been turning in his sheets since 10:00 p.m. or so, first from the vague backache, which he only slowly came to recognize, then pinpoint, then diagnose. Then, as usual, he tried to convince himself it was his imagination, or perhaps something else, adding up the probabilities for those things to just above fifty percent, which, for the purposes of tricking himself was enough to justify another hour of position shifting, pillow flipping, trips to the sink and sighs. Only when there was a sudden jab, slightly more insistent and focused, accompanied by a quick impulse to throw up, did he resolve to go in, but by that time it was, of course, too late.

The whole thing was a monumental inconvenience. He'd have to lie and tell them someone was coming in for him – otherwise they'd never give him morphine. And then, he might actually break down and try to find a friend to give him a lift after all, but he knew that was unlikely as he didn't quite know anyone well enough to do that, or whom he'd feel comfortable enough imposing upon, especially at that hour. Brushing his teeth, he thought about the options – Andy might not mind. And it'd probably be at least three or four hours at the ER before he was ready to go, so it wouldn't be *that* early. Pulling on his pants, each gyration of which bothered his lower back made him think it might just be tweaked after all, leading to another thirty minutes of sitting, deliberating, until the full wave of nausea hit, and he knew what it was for sure, or mostly. OK, so it'd be 5:30 a.m. before he got out, almost blue in the east, which made that dreaded call that much easier to make if he had to, and he was pretty sure he would.

Luckily it wasn't that far, and the length of the trip might just fit between the waves of increasing discomfort and sickness rolling in. He waited in the car for the current wave to subside, adjusting in his seat to find the elusive angle of comfort, switching on the ignition, so he'd be ready to go. Once it was gone, or almost gone, or at least tolerable, he shifted into reverse and got out and moving. He also knew that the waves wouldn't go on indefinitely, that they would soon merge into a growing tide with no trough to help him, swelling into a tsunami of discomfort, and that this wave might actually be the last before that happened, making such unaided transit impossible. Taking some back streets he avoided several lights, and even ran one, making a left after looking, because the prospect of waiting through ninety seconds of witless redness at an empty intersection seemed like an absurd existential challenge to his sensibilities. It was only after making the turn that he saw the cop car parked along the side, the cop watching him execute his premeditated disregard for law and order. He flipped on his lights – had McGhee for certain – but turned them off again. Still, he swung out from the curb, doing a U-ey to follow McGhee right into the parking lot of St. Francis Memorial. He even raced ahead to open the door for him as he made his way in, pausing to throw up behind a juniper just outside, patting him on the shoulder and helping him to the In-Take desk.

Looking up from her phone, the attendant glanced back and forth between them. "He in your custody, officer?" she asked, putting her hand on the receiver of her phone, ready.

"Uhh, no . . . ," he said. "Just saw him comin' in . . . ."

McGhee was pale, one hand pushing hard into his lower right side, but he managed a smile. The pain was subsiding slightly, mostly due to the shifted internals from being sick behind the bush. "The officer was kind enough to give me an escort after blowing through a light at Broadway," he explained.

Taking his name and insurance info, she generated a band and had it on his wrist moments later. "We'll have you back in a jiffy. Take a seat . . . ," she said, motioning to the waiting area.

Moving over, McGhee sat in one of the extra wide seats they'd placed to anticipate larger clientele, shifting in his seat again. In the background, he could hear the cop talking to the attendant in a low voice, but couldn't make it out. Under better circumstances he might have been able to hear, but his attention was focused on his pain which, mounting again, proved unignorable.

A few moments later the seat next to him groaned with the weight of the officer. The walkie-talkie at his shoulder was squawking with chatter, so he turned down the gain to make it less annoying. He was looking at McGhee, a half smile on his face. He was a rather stalky black man, and the vest made him look even bulkier and uncomfortable, though his aspect tended toward kindly.

"Stones?" the officer asked. From his tone he seemed familiar with it, the sympathy including a knowing sense to it. Shifting his belt, the gear there seemed to dig into him less, and he looked more comfortable. McGhee wished he could do the same, but comfort was not possible. Noticing his name plate, McGhee smiled, though the pain contorted it.

"I used to have an imaginary friend named Kennedy," he said weakly, sticking out his hand. "When I was five or so . . . ."

Taking it, the cop said, "It wasn't Bill Kennedy, was it?" shaking it warmly.

His hand was soft but strong, and McGhee wondered at that combination, the strength and softness, then the name. "Yeah, it was," he said, looking the officer over. "Funny that he grew up to be a cop," he said.

"And black, I bet . . . ," Officer Kennedy said, laughing softly.

"Thanks for the escort . . . ," McGhee said. "I don't think I could have handled a ticket just then . . . ."

Kennedy shook his head, taking off his hat and placing it on the seat next to him. "Yeah, I kinda figured that," he said. His head was wrinkled, with barely any hair, crenulations in his scalp a phrenologist would have loved, ending in slight rolls at his neck where his tight collar gathered them in a tight package of deep blue. "I was gonna pull you over, 'til I saw your expression. Figured I'd see if you were on your way in . . . ."

McGhee winced, another wave mounting, but managed another smile through it.

"Had a stone myself a couple years back," the officer said, shaking his head again. "Man, they suck . . . ."

McGhee nodded, shifting again, scanning the walls for the restroom.

"It's over there . . . ," Officer Kennedy said, motioning around the corner. "In case you need to make a run for it . . . ."

Without acknowledging, McGhee launched out of his chair, the attendant looking around her desk partition in alarm. The officer raised his hand to calm her. "Been there . . . ," he called out to her, smiling. "Better get him back to put him outta his misery." Moments later a nurse emerged from the door, looking to the officer for guidance. Motioning toward the restroom, she nodded, pulling out a wheelchair behind her to collect him.

In the back, they parked McGhee in one of the triage areas, each separated by a curtain that could be drawn for privacy, but left his open to keep an eye on him. They had him change into a loose gown and crawl onto an examination bed to wait. He wasn't there long before a radiology tech showed up at the nurse station to whisk him off for an image of his gut. The young man was all business, scurrying around the dim room, moving the table into position, lowering the boom and pushing the button that made it all buzz for a second just after he said, "Hold still . . . ." Stepping out, he swung the boom back and had his arm under McGhee's legs, getting him transport-ready again. End to end it was five minutes, which made McGhee hopeful the whole enterprise might go quickly this time, but by the time he was waiting another forty-five minutes back on the triage bed, those hopes faded to zero. During that time his pain had mounted several times, and despite calling for the nurse and her coming to have a look before disappearing again, his entreaties didn't have the desired effect. He was ready to pounce the next time she came and began speaking as soon as she appeared, but a young Resident popped out from behind her, and behind him, a barely older Attending Physician. Fanning out, they stood around the foot of his bed.

The Attending grabbed McGhee's chart and had a look, flipping back a few pages before handing it to the Resident. "Go for it . . . ," he said casually, leaning against the wall to watch.

Looking at the Attending, McGhee let out a low groan. "I hate you already . . . ," he said, to which the Attending just smiled.

"Hurts, huh?" he said loudly to McGhee, like he was used to talking to geriatrics, then realizing he was stepping on the Resident's moment, put up both hands, saying, "Go ahead," before folding his arms again.

McGhee looked at the Resident who was ponderously studying his chart in silence. After a full minute of this, the Attending cleared his throat to move the process along; the Resident was apparently tuned into this cue and looked up at McGhee. To his eye, the short, skinny young man was probably twenty-five or twenty-six and looked like he was stamped out of some newbie doctor machine in the sky: meticulously groomed, short hair, trimmed side burns, manicure. His wire-rimmed spectacles were round, as were his eyes, with serious correction in the lenses making them appear microscopic. His white lab coat was perfect with his name stitched in pristine red letters on his left breast: *Dr. Trepanier*, and he stood with the stiffness of a young man discovering his occupation actually involved dealing with human beings.

The Resident cleared his throat and looked at the Attending, who nodded empathetically, before he returned his gaze to McGhee. "You have a stone," the Resident said.

"OK, nice job Zeke," the Attending said, standing from his leaning perch against the wall. Whipping his stethoscope from around his neck, the rubber of the tips made a wriggling noise as he separated them to jam them in his ears. Pushing the bell against McGhee's chest, he kept talking. "You smoke?" he asked, listening to McGhee's lungs.

"Now and then . . . ," McGhee answered.

"Shush . . . ," the Attending said, listening to his heart a moment, then moving the bell, listening again. Yanking the ends from his ears, he looked at McGhee. "Stop doing that," he said. He'd apparently had some gum trapped in the edge of his mouth, which he freed, chewing it with some determination. "So like Zeke said . . . ," and pausing, lowered his head a moment before raising it again, "so like *Dr. Trepanker* said," he corrected himself, "you have a kidney stone. Just a couple millimeters. Shouldn't be too bad. Ever had one before?" Leaning back, he looked into McGhee's eyes, then focused on the right, then the left, then both again. "You takin' anything for the pain?"

"Yeah. A couple years back. And some ibuprofen . . . ," McGhee offered, wincing again.

The Attending was looking through the chart again, but shook his head. "Right. So I'm guessing you'd describe your current condition as . . . *uncomfortable?*" he said, smiling back at McGhee. He didn't wait for a response, but stepped over to McGhee, patting him lightly on the knee. "You're gonna feel a whole lot better in ten minutes," he said, then turned to the nurse. "Let's get him ten milligram IM morphine right now, and I'll write a scrip for hydrocodone . . . remind me to do that. I gotta get back to the kid with the eye issue . . . ," he said, handing the chart to the Resident, but still talking to the nurse. He disappeared around the corner, but reappeared immediately: "And let Dr. Trepanker admin the shot . . . ," he said, tapping the door frame before disappearing again.

The nurse looked at the Resident and shrugged. "Tre-pan-ier," he said, scanning between the nurse and McGhee. Raising her eyebrows, she said nothing, ducking behind the curtain. The Resident clasped McGhee's chart to his chest with both arms, silent.

The latest wave of pain was subsiding, slightly, so McGhee scanned the young doctor. He was remarkably motionless, a little robotic, standing at attention. "So how long you been on this rotation?" McGhee asked eventually.

Dr. Trepanier looked at his watch. "Twenty-three minutes," he answered, but didn't elaborate immediately. After a minute of silence, he added, "Psych was my last posting. I think I liked that one better."

McGhee laughed, but the compression in his gut from it set him squirming in pain. The nurse returned with a stainless kidney tray with a prepped shot inside rolling around, hard plastic rattling in the metal tray. "All right . . . ," she said to McGhee, smiling slightly. "Show us some cheek, please . . . Dr.?"

It was like she pushed his switch. Reaching in his pocket, he donned some blue rubber gloves with a snap and grabbed the alcohol pad from the tray in his left hand, the syringe in his right. Feeling with two fingers of his right hand, he found a target area on McGhee's gluteus and swabbed it six or seven times, then looked at him. "Don't tense up," he said, then swinging his arm a foot he casually jammed the needle into his butt. Once it was set he slowly started to depress the plunger. Leaving it there, the Resident looked away to yawn a moment, the nurse's eyes bugging out. He remained clueless, however, maintaining his glacial pace, slowly pulling the needle out at the end, plopping it into the tray and snapping off his gloves.

"Yeah, stick with Psych, doc . . . ," McGhee said, leaning back on the bed, but the Resident was gone already.

The nurse stepped to his bedside, pulling the sheet up over him. "You'll start to feel better almost immediately," she said smiling sympathetically. "Take a nap — we don't need the bed right away. Slow night," she said, patting him on the shoulder.

Closing his eyes, he heard the rings of his curtain slide shut to give him some privacy. It didn't even take a minute for him to feel the edge leaving, and within a few more, the pain was sliding warmly into the periphery. That warm relief, the absolute reprieve from discomfort, almost made it worth the pain to get that feeling, which went well beyond physical ministration into other realms of relaxation normally not within his reach, and it was good. It was somewhere past three in the morning, and in the absence of pain he noticed his exhaustion welling, and he thankfully gave himself over to it, slipping quickly toward dreams.

He reveled in the moment, the descent into an infinitely soft blanket, wrapping him in fuzzy comfort, and he sought to hold onto consciousness a moment longer and trace his route from clarity to oblivion. He was in a hospital bed, somewhat stiff and angled, but it seemed to be softening beneath him, melting like butter. The air on his face was slightly cool, but even that seemed to lift off his skin, buoyed by the glow from within. Then he smelled daisies and knew he'd crossed the boundary, drifting into a delicious twilight, floating just above sleep, suspended in perfection.

Somehow it was December, too, though it wasn't, and the snow outside looked so inviting through the window. Les and Wil were out there, sledding down the hill. He could see the first part of it until they disappeared around the bushes near the crest, but he could hear their voices, thrilled and high pitched with exhilaration. There were other voices, too, like theirs, and he wanted to be out there with them, but he was too little, and he wondered what it would be like when he, too, was one of the older boys, wondering what they'd talk about as they pulled the ropes on their sleds back up the hill, the metal runners on the snow, the wood creaking with every pull, he being one of them, one of the older boys himself.

Then he was older still, but his brothers were gone or mostly gone anyway, and he was with the neighbor kids, running and chasing, and there was a girl there named Ann, and he liked her yellow hair, how light it was with the sunshine in it, and how later that day he'd hide on the hill near her house and call out, "I love you Ann! I love you Ann!" and how she never heard him, and how he knew she never would, and how he knew he was too young for that anyway, but had wanted to try.

So when he met Janine, he knew that was different, and he was smitten for what seemed forever, throughout elementary, and past it really, reading each day as omen of closer or further from her, until she was gone entirely, or what he had of her, which was nothing but his young longing, though he didn't know what that meant, not really. And so on, and so on, getting closer to that elusive love he yearned for. Each time he approached what he wanted, but couldn't quite get it, until one moment he found himself across from just the right one, Kate, and he knew the moment had finally arrived.

It was raining, or maybe it wasn't – it was both somehow. His face was hot, but that was his hand there perhaps: the rest of the coffee shop was disappearing, blacking out, leaving her face in front of him, floating on her hands, and she looked at him like she knew what he was thinking, because it seemed maybe she'd had that same experience, too – those approaches on approaches without getting there until that exact moment, when they arrived there in synchrony. And he recalled that feeling in his heart – a welling, like it would come out of him and did – and that she met it, perfectly coming to rest, next to him, where she belonged.

When she held him that first time, it was the first time he wasn't scared. She was completely his, her warmth against him, looking into his eyes with the same gaze he knew he was giving her, and for the first time he lost himself in another, in warm oblivion, at peace with himself and with her, entirely. Her lips took his softly and he caressed them, he holding her against him as they slipped away, between moments where nothing could follow. He'd never known love until that moment, and he lay there, spent and relieved that he'd finally, finally, found it.

McGhee recalled those moments of lassitude, but it was an old memory, and the more he thought of it, the further it seemed to recede, as if the mere recollection were enough to make it more remote, as if his fingertips reaching for it kept bumping it further back on the shelf, until finally, he nearly couldn't reach it at all. So his mind let it go, softly, content to hunt for others nearly as good, which he found nearby, and though it wasn't the first time, it was early with her, and very nearly just as sweet. And so it was he continued perusing recollections until he noticed they didn't have quite the same flavor, that perhaps he had strayed from the simpler category of closeness to one just next door, on matters of happiness in general. There, too, it started sweet, but grew more nuanced over time. There were so many parts to it – to his side of it in particular – that made it harder to keep happiness in focus, so many spinning plates on sticks to manage that their sheer number made him weary, and even when they didn't need tending, their incessant wobbles bothered him, even when he was otherwise content. And for a while this bothering was a private matter, unknown to Kate or unacknowledged, until that, too, fell aside, and he saw it in her eyes, and it went well beyond acknowledgement toward something else, like resignation, which he couldn't bear to see. He knew he wholly owned that, that he had manufactured it out of his own insecurity and that he had no one to blame but himself, at least until it gave her license to move on, which she did nearly imperceptibly, until she was gone. He just wished she had been patient enough to wait it out, or better, to have called it out for what it was, and loved him despite his best efforts to screw it up. If she'd loved him better, she'd have seen that and done that. Then again, she was as young as he was, so how could he expect that? He couldn't, though he could wish she were that much better, just a little bit better.

McGhee felt himself hovering over those recollections, able to look right and left and just see at the far edges of his sight the full collection, from start to finish, and realized that from them arose an essence, not quite a full and warm aroma, but a more subtle redolence of general sweetness with only the faintest tinge of regret. And with that, he grabbed the very last card in the card-catalog and read it, and though it wasn't the last time they had talked, wasn't even close to the end, really, of their cohabitation and relationship, it was the moment when vague feelings made the transcendent transition into actual words, and she uttered them, out loud, for them both to hear and ponder: "I'm not sure we're going to make it."

Both her elbows were on the table, splayed out. He remembered her white skin, or nearly so, on the dark, rough wood of the table in that dark Thai restaurant down the street from their place where they used to go to do their planning, their conspiring, only this time it was the opposite of that, an unwinding of sorts, and she started it with those words, tentative sounding but with many thoughts behind them, far more than she let on, but with the certainty of her tone, there must have been, or so it seemed to McGhee. He couldn't know for sure, in part because he was never sure of anything, but also because he had just started to notice a film in her words, between what she said and what she meant, or more precisely, between what she said and what they ultimately implied, and he realized she had learned to manage him, and that, worse, it was necessary to do so. It was a terrible revelation, and he lowered his head. Kate noticed and lifted his chin gently with her hand. "What?" she had said, more kindly than the first time she'd said it, and that only made it worse, because he had already decided to be sad, and at that age, his moods were sticky traps, and she'd learned it was best to just leave him be, which might have been the worst part of all.

Once he found himself in that mood, he'd sometimes permit himself to wallow in analysis, which, for purposes of their relationship, and when focused upon, was never a good thing. It took another six months to wind down, but it was all there in that moment, except for the meticulous unpacking. She'd be travelling a bit — more than a bit — down to LA where there were some shows, and up in Santa Barbara, and in Laguna, too, and in Huntington. She made it seem like the logistics were heavy on her, and to be fair, they were, but underneath it all, she loved it, loved what it meant, and it made her glow with pride, and that, *that* was something she had that he did not, and he wanted it. It had seemed this thing of hers had happened without her really thinking about it, as if she'd planned to think about doing something eventually, and in the meantime, it just happened for her and blossomed and was the perfect thing for her without even trying. And though she had just said they might not make it, talk had turned to the details of her life, each logistical piece yet another indication of her success and his lack of it. He knew it wasn't right for him to feel that – he reproached himself almost constantly for it – but she should see that, shouldn't she? Shouldn't she know him well enough by then? Shouldn't that be as important, or almost? But then again, what could she do? What should she do? Repress it, deny the details, minimize them to avoid the issue? Or did she see it and not care? More likely she saw it, and didn't know what to do, either, and in the absence of a solution, eventually, she just had to march on with those details because they demanded it, and like she said, she'd think about it later, but in the meantime her life was happening, and what was wrong with that anyway? He then realized she had actually said those words: *What was wrong with that anyway?*– he hadn't imagined them – so another unutterable had become real, right over that dark wood, where they used to plan together, but seemed to be planning separately all of a sudden.

That's where her studio in Laguna came from, from that dis-cussion, and though it started as an actual studio, morphed into a studio apartment – just for a while – that just made "sense." That was her word for it, and he pondered it. It was something he might have said himself, only he didn't, so it hung in the air, or at least in his ears, like a new way to consider their love, and its apparent impediment to her progress.

The memory became too painful to continue, so McGhee let it go. No matter how many times he revisited that card, it never became clear enough for him – how much it was him, or how much Kate. She'd urged him to go with her the first few times, then they became simple invitations, but he couldn't go, or wouldn't – he didn't really have the days to do it, and further, didn't want to spend his precious vacation trailing after her from gallery to gallery, hearing how well it was all going, watching her from the back, managing her growing life without him as she receded into her success. And when he took that trip with Paul to Turkey, it seemed to signal something for Kate, or gave her permission to move on with more confidence, or at least more focus, though she did promise they'd sort it out at some point, which he knew even then would never happen. So when he overheard her on the phone one day say the hushed words, "grown apart", and another time her whispers admitting to some friend, "Not really . . . ," regarding their love life, these sentiments became a little annealed stone of imperfection that he swallowed, rough and irritating, that stuck just below his sternum, lodged like the nidus of a pearl in his gut to ponder and coat until he could bear it, only that never quite happened. Even in the arms of others later, even in the tender care he found in Dublin, the pain in his gut remained.

It was in this way McGhee found himself pondering the stone in his gut without surprise and with no small measure of regret and culpability. He could see it there, lodged and inflamed, his body incapable of accepting it to make it something better than it was. It was an ugly thing, rough and ragged, and upon inspection, more complex than he had imagined. Lifting it out, small as it was, he held it in his hand and he realized the other dark marks and pieces came from elsewhere, and recognized them with some sadness, and even rancor, causing him to mumble in his dreams and for the nurse to approach and ask him, "Who's Les, hun?" but he remained lost to dreaming.

It wasn't so long ago his mother had passed, which was the end of a long, slow spiral of decline. She'd been reluctant to leave the house once his father had died, and only after collapsing in the bathroom, undiscovered for seven hours as she slumped, wedged between the wall and the toilet, would she entertain doing so. It was really the broken hip that did it – with the surgery and physical therapy – that got her to move, provisionally, into assisted living.

That was a trial in its own right, with Wil three hundred miles east, Les in Wyoming, and himself in California – logistically, it was a challenge for all of them, especially Wil, who bore the heaviest burden being closest. So when it came to light Les had wanted her to sell shortly after that so he could cash out, it made a difficult situation that much worse, especially for McGhee, and hurtful.

For his part, McGhee couldn't see the hurry. And as the youngest, his ties to the property probably remained the strongest of the three of them. Add to this that he was easily the most sentimental of the three – he knew it, too, though he hated it mentioned out loud – he found the thought nearly as impossible as losing his mother herself, which happened shortly thereafter anyway, rendering the whole debate a matter of *when* and not *if*. But perhaps it was more the *how* of it than anything because it all started so civilly.

They'd had a call on the phone, generally catching up, discussing all matters related to their mother's care and otherwise, and it only seemed an afterthought near the end when Les brought it up. Wil was willing to entertain it, though his reaction leaned more toward waiting, in part, because, as they all knew, she was against it. It was only in the next call that Les mentioned he had spoken to her about it, and that she thought it might be time to move ahead, which was most certainly news to Wil and McGhee, and more than a little surprising given her steadfast opposition in every such conversation in the past. Still, it was progress toward what they all knew was inevitable, and despite the surprise of it, was welcome news. For McGhee, it meant they'd need to start thinking of it, which in turn implied it would be some time *out there* in the future, perhaps not far, but long enough to ignore for the moment. So it was surprising to Wil, and astonishing to McGhee, that on the next call they learned Les had identified an agent in the area to handle the matter. It was entirely unlike Les to dabble in such things – he was notoriously reluctant to manage any such affairs, including his own – something which McGhee felt he shared with Les. Wil was the dutiful son when it came to those things, but for his part he was glad to have one less thing to manage and worry about.

It was about that time McGhee made his way back to see her, which he couldn't do very often, but which seemed to be necessary to say his good-bye. Wil had communicated and Les had substantiated the urgency of the matter, because what had been a long, slow decline had, of late, become more precipitous. So his head was full of these thoughts when he saw her, slumped in her wingback chair, crossword puzzle book in her lap, listless. She looked sad to him, and he did his best to raise her spirits, making tea without even being asked to, doling cookies out on the plate. Only what he thought was troubling her, her decline, was in fact, not the thing on her mind at all, but the impending loss of the house – her home for almost sixty years – just to make a loan to her oldest son.

McGhee didn't understand at all, and in fact, chalked it up to her diminished faculties. After cleaning the teapot and stowing the cups and replacing the unfinished cookies in the cupboard, and reinstalling her in the wingback chair, he placed *that* call to Wil, who likewise had no idea what it might be about, and suggested adding in Les to clear it up. So it was then, while McGhee paced the hall outside his mother's apartment, that they learned more of Les's recent discussions with their mother, and that he had indeed suggested selling the house, and, by the way, would she mind loaning him some funds against those proceeds. Oh, he made it sound like *she* had suggested it, almost anyway, and it was only after more discussion that he had agreed to accept it. Of course, this was all Les's recollection, and Wil and McGhee would have come to the same conclusion, he told them.

Both McGhee and Wil were silent a few moments, though Wil did proceed to ask Les more questions, but McGhee wasn't hearing most of that. He'd stuck his head back into the apartment to look in on her, and seeing his mother slumped there, glum, staring toward the window with whatever spark she had had remaining, extinguished, and he lowered the phone, putting it back in his pocket to head inside. He didn't hear their protests, either, though he imagined them, especially Les's.

That night, she complained of something in her gut, retching a few times before they hauled her off to the ER as a precaution, and the next morning she was gone, McGhee staring at her, letting her go and watching the imperceptible transition of her from his mother, and all that meant, to nothingness, and he felt his ribcage collapse a little with the absolute knowledge it was over.

With that, the dreaming McGhee found himself staring once again at the stone in his hand. Misshapen as it was, he began to think it had a name, and that name was McGhee. It was a strange revelation, and he hovered there wondering at it, that it was his identity, that he took these things that shaped him and wrapped them in this place to bother him. McGhee. McGhee. "Mr. McGhee . . . ?"

When he opened his eyes, the nurse was looking down at him, her hand lightly on his shoulder. She was looking at him, kindly, but slightly worried. "How was your nap?" she asked, stepping on the floor pedal to raise the top of the bed. Groggy, he rubbed his eyes, gradually realizing where he was, reaching for his side where the pain had been, but it was gone.

"How long was I out?" he asked looking at her, but the Attending answered from the other side of the bed.

"An hour . . . ," he said, leaning in with his stethoscope, "though it didn't seem so restful. You were thrashing a good deal of the time. Never saw that before on morphine," he said, moving the cup around on McGhee's chest, then wrapping it around his neck. "Unfortunately, we need the bed. Car wreck . . . ," he said, then turning to the nurse, "Make sure he gets the filters and the scrip," he said, holding up a page from his pad before slipping it under the clip on McGhee's chart.

It felt good to be in his clothes again, but as they wheeled toward the exit, he realized he probably shouldn't drive, wondering how to finesse it with them. Reaching around to hit the door opener, the nurse seemed to read his thoughts.

"Your friend is here to take you home," she said sweetly, and he couldn't imagine who it could be.

Officer Kennedy was waiting by the door and smiled at him as he emerged. "Figured you could use a lift," he said, putting his hand on his belt, and it suddenly made sense to McGhee, his head still swirling with his dreams, that the only one who would ever be there for him, really there for him, would be imaginary.

The Cherry Man

0 ◄————————●————————————► 90
       30
      6AM
Istanbul, Turkey 9/21/1994

He couldn't sleep, even with the twenty-hour plane ride and cab and walk through the dark city; his mind was lost in some time zone over the Atlantic, leaving him restless on a hard bed meant for smaller Europeans or Turks, but he was OK with it. They'd let the window open as it was still mid-September and the air was warm, gently mounting as slight breeze just barely enough to stir the plain white sheers there along the edges. Based on the movement in the sheets on the next bed over, he knew Paul was awake, too, only he wasn't sure it was a good idea to speak yet. He must have had some sleep as they'd collapsed at ten or so and it was much later, but it was all a blur, and he was content to stare at the ceiling, watching the fan slowly cycle. He did notice his state was good for one thing, though – his thoughts of home, Kate and work – those things couldn't grip his mind and he was free to bathe in the lassitude of exhaustion, thoughtless.

McGhee did notice, once he thought to look, that the sky was no longer black, but had slipped into deep blue and even further, throwing the faintest light into the room. It was spare and simple. White walls and ceiling, tile floor, pedestal basin, one glass. The foreignness was reassuring – he most certainly was not home – and the difference reminded him he was on the road, only this time, beyond the edge of what he knew. Putting his arms behind his head, he rolled to look out, the light just barely revealing a minaret, dark against the lightening sky. It was only moments later that the tones started, and even his ears knew he was truly away.

It began low at first, sounding like static, so he couldn't be sure he heard anything at all, but built moments later, a solitary man's voice wailing a call to prayer. The initial bars were low and sonorous, but quickly built into higher tones, escalating in volume and urgency.

"You hearing that?" Paul asked from dead silence, his voice clear indicating he'd been awake for a while. McGhee cleared his throat quietly to acknowledge before speaking.

"Everyone is hearing that . . . ," McGhee said, getting up on one elbow to look over. "I think that's the point." There was just enough light in the room to see his friend. Paul's arms were behind his head, but he was looking over, too.

"We're not in Kansas anymore," Paul said, then laughed with his typical guttural tone, "You ready to head out yet?"

McGhee felt around on the little table, grabbing his watch, then pressing buttons until it lit up. "It's only five thirty . . . ," he objected, though it didn't sound confident, and he knew it. Throwing his legs over the edge, he stretched and made his way to the basin. "Feels like I've been awake for a while, though . . . ," he said, looking at the faucet handles. In the low light, they looked to be the same, so he turned the left, but only cold water came out. Resolving to get warm, he turned the other, too, but after a minute, the stream remained cold.

"Well . . . you stopped snoring an hour ago . . . ," Paul said, pulling himself up but content to lean against the wall and watch. He was shirtless, his knees pulled to his chest, his arms behind his head again.

McGhee looked over his shoulder, cold water dripping from his nose. Paul had that gotcha look on his face he was fond of making, and McGhee turned back to the basin. The water remained cold, but he forged ahead. It felt good anyway, washing away the hours of travel and restless sleep. As retribution, he quickly flicked the light switch on, then looking over his shoulder, smiled. "Turning up the lights . . . ," he said while Paul covered his eyes.

"Thanks . . . ," Paul said, finally putting his feet on the floor. "Let's get out and see what this city's about . . . ."

There was an urn of coffee in the lobby which was small and spartan, like the room. Beside it, small cups and saucers lay, both of them opting for cups only. It was a thick Turkish brew of some kind with a foamy dark head which they downed quickly. McGhee decided it was good after all that the cups were small, because it was high octane and any more might toss his balance over the edge.

Outside, Paul started his march and McGhee pulled up next to him. "I just wanna walk . . . ," Paul said, looking over at McGhee, who nodded.

"Sounds good to me," he said. Walking down the alley, the street broadened into a square. Off to the left, the minaret he had seen in the distance was now clearer in the light, surrounded by many others circling a large domed building off to the north.

Paul was looking into a map, then noticing McGhee's glance skyward, traced with his finger over the map. "Looks like the Blue Mosque," he said, looking up himself. The wailing was continuing, echoing through the streets. Though the hour was early, there were some people stirring in the square, preparing for another day. The air was clear and perfect and just warm enough to keep a chill from them.

The buildings behind them spread out, a mishmash of Byzantine and European architecture dating back hundreds of years at least, but mostly further still. It was the old section of the city, the Fatih District of Istanbul, some form of which had been there a couple thousand years. In front of them, an obelisk stood, rising up seventy-five feet into the sky. Walking over to it, Paul put his hand on the railing of the fence around it, tracing the markings with his outstretched hand. The symbols on it were alien and strange, and he turned to McGhee and smiled. "Cool, huh?"

McGhee was studying a plaque in front of it. "Holy shit . . . ," he said, but continued reading to himself. "Made around 1425 BC in Egypt," he continued, "but was moved here 390 AD." They both craned their necks looking up the side, then circled it, stumbling over the cobbles of the square as they moved. Looking at each other, they welled with something like glee, though suppressed the urge to show it.

An inviting avenue led off to the southeast, so they moved on. The sun hadn't quite risen yet, but the streets were becoming more active. Most of those moving seemed to be shop owners getting their places ready for the morning. Men were using long metal poles to twist awnings out from the shadows, or hoses to wash down the sidewalk in front of their places, or washing the steps of whatever dust the night had left. Once off the square, the flavor changed to more residential, though the buildings remained varied and formal. Some of the buildings had a distinct European flavor, wrought iron railings and fences on small front yards, alternating between French and Spanish and Italian. Others looked more Eastern, displaying marble columns. Others still were somewhere in between, combining Greek elements into the mix. Many had tiny yards in front, hemmed in by more wrought iron fences which supported vining plants. Morning glories – blue, and purple and white – bloomed there and were beginning to open for the day, too, like the rest of the city.

Some blocks down, beyond the low grade, they began to smell bread or something baking, and they found themselves following their noses to its source. The door was open and the owner, seeing the first customers of the day, pushed his brush broom into the corner and shooed them into his shop. There were countless baked goods there already, radiating their warmth, only Paul and McGhee didn't recognize anything but a few baguettes. The owner shook his head, though, instead directing them to another bin, empty. Holding up his hand, he disappeared into the back, behind a curtain, emerging a few moments later with a flat metal implement on a large pole, two flatbreads steaming on it, fresh from the oven. Tipping them into the bin, he then bowed and tipped his hand toward the basket in offering. They were too hot to hold more than a few seconds in their grasp. Both McGhee and Paul juggled theirs, hand to hand, ripping them into steamy shreds and stuffing them into their mouths. The shop owner was delighted, smiling and laughing in his language, utterly indecipherable, trying to push them out without paying, but McGhee managed to slip him fifty kurus in coins he'd collected at the airport the night before. The little man was thankful, wrapping his thin weathered fingers over the coins, sliding them noisily back and forth in his grasp, bowing repeatedly.

On their way out, a wave of little girls pushed their way into the shop, one after the other. They were all dressed identically in navy blue uniforms and white shirts, immaculate and starched, a small red patch on their left breast with a gold cross in the middle. McGhee and Paul dodged as they flooded around them. Those toward the back took notice of the tall strangers, waving and squeaking to them in their language, as inscrutable as the shop owner's, merry and animated. Some girls blushed, turning their cute brown faces to each other shyly, looking back a moment with dark eyes, before turning away again, laughing. Looking down the avenue, they followed the trail of them to where they emanated from another vaguely European building, larger than the houses around, gray granite bricks brooding in a large artifice, pushed nearly to the edge of the street. Above the door read an old sign they could just half make out: *Armenian Catolik Rahibe Okul, Istanbul*. Just below it, a nun standing on the threshold monitored the students, her hands hidden in the opposite sleeves of her habit. Smiling at them, she bowed slightly, keeping a watchful eye while the girls still parted around her, spilling onto the steps like puppies.

The sun was just edging to the horizon, catching only the tips of the minarets in the distance, like they were dipped in gold and stabbing into the clear blue cloudless sky. The street they were on began tipping more steeply downhill, though still gently, and curved off to the left as it did so. Following it they emerged onto a frontage road running along the water close by. "The Bosporus . . . ," Paul said smiling at it, then back to McGhee, and back again to savor it. For his part, McGhee was largely ignorant of Turkish history, but Paul wasn't. He proceeded to begin rattling off various bits and pieces of stories that happened there, transition of power, the time of Constantinople. McGhee only half-listened though, content to let it wash over him, and with it clean him of his ruminations, bad and good, from back home. He didn't want those thoughts to intrude on the moment, and in that moment, it was good.

On their left, they slowly traced along a wall capped with ivy. They were strolling more slowly now, warming in the sun now risen over the water, some food in their bellies, content. Eventually the wall opened into a small arch and steps, but the gap was closed with another iron gate. Looking in, they saw the courtyard of another school, a madrasa perhaps, as the students looked more Eastern and staid. At the far end of the courtyard, the building towered over them with a small dome in the middle, old stone supports holding it up and forming the edge of the open space. No one spied them looking in and they watched the activity a while before moving on, down the wall to the end of the block. Crossing the street, they walked along the water's edge, busy with enterprising men bringing in the early catch from their small boats, tugging nets over the gunwales with strong hands, smiling at each other, cigarettes tucked in every smile's corner, puffing smoke like they ran on steam. Eventually, the edge broadened into a half-round space jutting out into the water where tilted wooden cases sat for display of their fish, striped mackerel arranged in neat rows and columns, gleaming in the morning light, their last gasps only minutes before.

Pulling up to a large flat boulder, McGhee sat, leaning against another stone. "Let's break here a minute . . . ," he said, looking out over the wide, watery passage. He tugged his cap lower on his forehead to stare toward the sun, over the water, under the bridge which officially connected the west and the east. "Seems like a good place to watch a while." Paul didn't answer, but stopped beside him, pulling out the map again. Tracing his finger along it, he looked up, first over the water, then further along the dock, which curled back around the city, disappearing behind more buildings and another mosque.

"I'm glad we came . . . ," McGhee said, mostly to himself. Finally sitting, Paul took out a bandana and wrapped it around his head. He was tall and muscular, his head similarly angular with barely a shadow of hair. It was early yet, but the sun was growing stronger by the moment, and he disdained other headwear for some reason McGhee never thought to ask about.

"Yeah . . . ," Paul said. "It's good to get out – really out, I mean." Paul had his eyes closed, listening. "It even sounds different," he said.

McGhee looked at him and understood. It wasn't at all like California, and it was impossible to imagine it was, as it did indeed sound different: the constant Turkish yammering, the sound of men working at a pace their own, gathering nets and fish, the puttering diesel cars and trucks zipping past, tiny horns bleating, those girls skipping with their alien cadence, singing songs in that foreign tongue, the wailing which they could hear again in the distance. His life was receding and he was glad to let it go. He closed his eyes, absorbing the sounds, then the smells, too, slipping away in the enjoyment of it.

Somewhere near them there was grilling with the smell of wood-smoke commingling with the aroma of roasting fish and chicken and kabobs of mutton. As the trucks passed, a light wave of diesel displaced the food smells, then waves of smoke from the fisherman, and the smell of the sea itself, riding low in the nose as the salt and standing fish wafted in. Even a blind man would know he was far away from home, he thought, and he reveled in his immersion, nearly napping as he soaked it in with the strong sunshine, the light breezes, and the feeling of true escape. It was always elusive for him, but he had found relief, for the moment.

Wending their way up the street, they curved back into the city, up a deep, narrow alley between buildings leaning against each other for support where they each seemed to hold up the other. Eventually, the sky above disappeared as canvas tarps covered the walk, then it became a solid roof, the street itself disappearing as they moved into the Grand Bazaar. Salesmen and women hovered by their stalls, looking at them languidly, sizing them up for sales, but generally deciding they weren't worth the effort to even stand from their stools. Some of the women smiled at them meekly, but averted their eyes, even as a few muttered something in Turkish and waved their hand over their wares. There were silver bangles, baked baubles, silk scarves, brass bins and skeins of yarn, brass swords, baskets of beans and peppers and yams and tomatoes, small buckets of olives, brown and black and green, blackish-brown, deep brown, reddish-brown, and nearly yellow, but not quite. One table held a huge, orange mountain of fresh saffron blossoms, dried and delicate, lightly floral and inviting. Tables held immense piles of spice, redolent and deep-colored, red and green and yellow and brown. Next door a vendor had several vertical rotisseries of mutton Doner Kabob meat roasting, the fumes rising to collect under the ancient roof overhead, fanning out beneath the blue-tiled arches to contribute to the overall aroma of the market, the man there merrily carving out thin wafers of the meat with a long machete as it cooked to wrap in warm pitas they'd use to catch the meat directly from the fire. And on and on, past thick carpets and thin kilims, hand painted images of heroes and illicit artifacts for sale, until finally emerging on the far side, they found themselves on a regular city street, more Western than anything they had seen, but still foreign, in need of lunch.

The presence of several old Turks, sockless in hard shoes, in front of a small restaurant beckoned to them, and looking at each other they resolved to eat there without speaking a word, taking a table next to them. Both Paul and McGhee disdained ever looking like a tourist, though that section of the city had many of them, so they tried their best to fit in, but that was of course hopeless. Still, they tried for the dignified reserve the old men had, the slowness and measured emotion, and in that, at least, they matched the customers around them. A waiter showed up quickly with a tight cotton apron tied around his waist, two menus slung under his arm and two strange cups, which he placed in front of them quickly, the liquid nearly jostling out of the central glass fixture, but not quite, three cubes of sugar and small spoon on each of the saucers. "Apple tea . . . ," he said in clear but accented English, anticipating their question like he answered it a hundred times a day. Snapping the menus from under his arm, his efficient routine was a blur to them: he had them in their hands with alarming speed and was off before they had any opportunity to ask questions, but it didn't matter because they had none, and besides, they were busy studying the slow movements of the old men.

Their tea cups were interesting, though: four feet crafted from swooshes of some cheap base metal, sweeping up in a tight basin squeezing hold, by friction apparently, a tall narrow glass in the middle, filled with light brown fluid, steaming. It had the vague odor and flavor of apples but was bitter to McGhee's taste, so he swished a cube of sugar in before sipping again, then another, then the third, deciding they had served three for some reason after all. Paul drank his straight in small sips, watching McGhee's process with some disapproval, but said nothing. Once fully sugared, McGhee found it tolerable and enjoyed it, if only for the strangeness and presentation. As for food, luckily the menu had English subtitles, and they both opted for the fresh fish which they soon discovered was, of course, mackerel. Other than the fish, which was scorched on the edges but otherwise intact, the plates were spare, only consisting of a Mediterranean relish of some kind comprised of diced tomatoes and cucumber in a very light vinaigrette. In short, it proved to be a good meal for them as their digestion was still variable from the long flight, lack of sleep, and long walk they'd had that morning.

Somehow it had gotten well past noon, and the shadows of the buildings mostly filled the street, though there were occasional sunbeams cutting through, splashing the cobbled street in warmth. The men at the next table remained, talking among themselves, smoking and drinking tea. As for McGhee and Paul, once finished with the food, they pushed their plates back to relax and have more tea, for neither was inclined to move any further for the moment.

Like McGhee, Paul could be a man of few words, except when the occasion moved him. Motioning slightly with his hand, to keep it discreet, he looked toward the old men.

"I love watching that . . . ," Paul said, McGhee turning his glance slightly to refresh his view of them. "I learn a lot watching the old men of a culture – they set the tone . . . ," he continued, then almost as an afterthought, "and the old women, too, of course."

Shifting his chair slightly, McGhee could watch them more closely without turning his head, but did so just enough to remain inconspicuous. He nodded, looking at Paul. "There's some truth to that, I think . . . ," he said. His travels had been more limited than Paul's, mostly domestic, so he was careful not to overstep. Paul was also the older by seven or eight years, so he usually fell into a deferential role, not quite like with his older brothers, but somewhere in between. Paul was well-traveled, and in fact, this was some of the attraction for McGhee in their friendship and as explorers. And McGhee enjoyed it when Paul slipped into his more pedantic gear, pointing out the obvious and subtle alike with the same enthusiasm. Mostly, McGhee liked Paul because he wasn't ordinary, or at least strived to be less so, with gusto.

"I wonder if they're retired . . . ," McGhee said, leaning in, aware the concept was probably ridiculous.

Paul took the bait, rolling his eyes, before taking it seriously. "Who knows if that even applies here. At least they're outside . . . doing *something*." In his fashion, he'd taken the idea and done something with it. "In the US, they'd probably be in a home by now . . . ," Paul continued, leaning back in his seat. "Just shoot me if it comes to that . . . ," he said, laughing. Reaching into his pack, he pulled out a cigar. "We're staying a while, no?" he said, holding it up to show McGhee. For his part, McGhee pulled out one of the last of his cigarettes and lit it. Paul's cigar created a cloud of smoke, obscuring him, but realizing it was creating too much at the table, took to blowing it up and away into the air beyond the patio. "I hate that about the US – the old don't have the place they used to. We park them in places to forget them. Used to be they'd be part of the family to the end. I bet that's how it works here. That's how it is in Asia . . . ," Paul continued, then paused to refresh the end of his cigar. "That's one of the best things about travel," he said. "It restores my faith in *humanity* . . . at least a little."

"Don't you ever get sick of it – the travel?" McGhee asked, leaning back himself. "You're on the road a lot. I'd think that'd get tiring after a while."

"Not really, no . . . ," Paul said, shaking his head, then stopped to stare at McGhee. He'd strike a philosophical pose now and then, which McGhee found amusing. "What?" Paul asked, maintaining his pose.

"Nothing . . . ," McGhee said, but he couldn't suppress his smile.

"You smiled . . . just then. What was it?" Paul objected. McGhee considered answering, but thought better of it, diverting slightly.

"I haven't traveled as much as you. I find it rewarding. I just don't think I could sustain it. Living out of a suitcase, I mean."

Paul continued staring at him, waiting for him to continue. "Go on . . . ," he said, content to listen.

McGhee tapped the ash from his cigarette, taking a long draw. He'd taken to blowing the smoke up, too, though he aimed to make it less conspicuous than Paul. He was enjoying the moment, and most especially, the opportunity to get at an itch for him that was difficult to scratch. For all their differences, McGhee felt a closer kinship to Paul than he did to most other people, a general alignment about one key thing: living with intent.

"I guess . . . I've felt of late that I've become too much of a . . . consumer," McGhee said, struggling to get at it. "I need more than that. I need to contribute . . . ."

"And this has *what* to do with traveling, *exactly?*" Paul said, tilting his head. It was another pose he liked to take, and McGhee recognized it. When he was skeptical, he'd assume that look, prepared to strike, though it was less about killing his opponent in debate than pushing the conversation in a clearer direction.

Just then the waiter showed up with two more cups of tea, removing the empties, no intervention required. McGhee took to swishing the sugar into solution to Paul's consternation.

"Got enough sugar there?" he asked sarcastically, then laughed, throwing his head back before looking at McGhee with a broad smile on his face.

"Smart ass . . . ," McGhee said, stealing an extra cube from Paul's saucer. "So it's like this," he continued. "For me, the travel is good, but that's the consumer part. It doesn't become useful to me unless I process it somehow and produce something. That makes it mine . . . ."

"So, like writing or something?" Paul said, reaching into his backpack. Pulling out a leather-covered notebook, curved from constant packing, he plopped it onto the table and flattened it out a few times before leaning back, though the cover resumed its curl anyway. "That's why I journal everything," he continued, leaning it to grab up the notebook again and leaf through it. "I got it all in here. All of my trips . . . there are other books, too. This is just the latest. Got 'em all at home, stacked up, waiting."

"Waiting for what?" McGhee asked. Most of the sugar had dissolved, but he was impatient and sipping at it already. The light apple flavor was growing on him.

"Ahhh . . . ," Paul said, taking a draw on his cigar. "My novel."

McGhee nodded. "Yeah, that's what I'm talking about. Or maybe poetry, even though I can't stand reading it . . . ," he added, snickering. Smoke protruded then retreated rapidly with each such noise, finally escaping in a long exhale.

"Nothing wrong with poetry . . . ," Paul confirmed, nodding. "I write a little, but it sucks. But that's not the point, is it? It's that you *do* it at *all*, right?"

"Yeah," McGhee agreed, though he tipped his head and rubbed his neck. "Though it's better if it's decent . . . ."

Paul pointed at McGhee, then his finger turned into a slight wag. "That's stronger in you than in me, my young friend. I can see that," he said, nodding confidently.

"Now it's your turn to *go on*," McGhee said, amused to turn the tables on Paul.

Tapping his cigar on the ash tray, he nodded. "Fair enough . . . ." Paul took a long drag on his cigar, puffing, allowing the smoke to escape around the end, then another, and another. "I don't have the same illusions you do . . . ," he said. "Of greatness." Paul's eyes narrowed, his lips forming into a smile, since he knew he'd hit on something.

"Delusions, maybe . . . ," McGhee acquiesced.

"See, right *there!*" Paul said, pointing at him with the cigar. "Right *there* . . . ." He took another puff. "Right there. It was all in there."

McGhee was on to Paul's occasional buffoonery, but this wasn't it, and he knew it. "Go on . . . ," he said, warily.

"Well . . . you're a complicated young man, McGhee," he said, leaning back to savor the thrust that was coming.

"You're not so much older, Paul," McGhee interjected, pre-empting the strike.

"Granted," Paul said, "but in some ways you are a *lot* younger than I." McGhee thought he understood, but wanted to hear it in words. He knew enough to shut up when the moment demanded it. Leaning forward, Paul pulled his chair in, leaning on the table to point with his cigar again. "So it's like this: you need fame more than I do, or something like it. You need an audience, and you're young enough to still believe it might happen. And you're good enough that you might just be right. Only you're afraid to want it, to take it, to make it happen."

McGhee stubbed out his cigarette but immediately lit another, taking a long draw, but saying nothing. He sighed, smoke coming out his nose in two jets, resigned to the truth of it.

"And *that*, my friend . . . ," Paul continued, but paused. Uncertainty appeared on his face as he was suddenly reluctant to continue."

"What?" McGhee asked, impatience seeping into his voice. Paul remained silent, grabbing his tea finally to have a sip. McGhee likewise pulled into the table, splaying out his elbows on it. "What?" he repeated, this time with some entreaty.

"You know I'm just a blowhard half the time . . . ," Paul said, avoiding the subject.

"Only half?" McGhee said, smiling halfway himself, then laughing lightly. Paul laughed, too. "Well played, my friend," he said.

"What?" McGhee repeated again, more softly still. "I'm not letting you off with a comment like that . . . ."

"All right . . . ," Paul said, resolving to go on. "*That* is your problem with Kate."

McGhee was surprised at the direction their conversation had taken, sitting back again. "Uh oh . . . ," he said, watching Paul, "Here it comes." All affectation was gone from his friend, and he wanted to hear it, what he himself had thought, but had never spoken out loud.

Paul shrugged, carving the ash on his cigar in the tray, but leaving it there to smoke on its own. Looking over at McGhee, he leaned back again, letting his arms trace the arms of his metal bistro chair, relaxed. "You know I don't know shit about women, right?" Paul conceded.

"You don't . . . ," McGhee agreed. "And you do – like any man I guess, only more so, I'd say."

Paul threw his head back, laughing. "Exactly," he agreed, happy they'd landed in the same place.

"OK, that understood," he continued, his posture seeping back into his delivery, "the way I see it, you can't stand that about Kate, that's all."

McGhee shook his head, confused. "What *that*, exactly?" he asked, though careful to temper his tone to be even, neither defensive nor hostile.

"That. *That!*" Paul said, leaning in again, "That she's doing it *at all*. That she's going for it, when you can't . . . or won't." Grabbing his cigar again, he took to stoking his furnace, smoky puffs emanating from his mouth as he spoke. "Well . . . ," he said, laughing slightly, but shaking his head, "you can't stand it that she's got her *art thing* going," he said, throwing air quotes with his fingers, "that she's making a go of it and it's working."

"What's with the air quotes?" McGhee said, making them himself, realizing he knew already.

Paul tilted his head, looking at him with his best penetrating gaze. "Oh, come on . . . ," he said, laughing more insistently. "The worst part is that *shit* she produces that passes for art . . . ," Paul said, taking a puff on his cigar. "You *know* that, and it kills you."

McGhee shook his head. "It sells . . . ," he objected, though his heart wasn't in it.

Paul pounced, leaning in. "*There!*" he said, smiling with satisfaction. "And it *galls* you, doesn't it?"

McGhee was silent, splayed out, like a bug pinned to cardboard, wriggling but defenseless. He wouldn't go there, though. "I feel like I'm losing her . . . ," he admitted, sighing again. "Losing her to *it* . . . ."

Paul shook his head. "No . . . it's worse than that," he said. "You feel like she's *choosing* her shitty art *over* you – that's what gets under your skin. And other things . . . ." Putting his arms behind his head, he took another puff on his cigar.

"Such as?" McGhee asked, shifting in his chair.

Paul shrugged, sighing. "That shit job of yours, for one thing . . . ," he said. McGhee just looked at him, silent. "It's fuckin' killing you, can't you see that?"

Picking up his cigarette, McGhee took a long drag, then shrugged himself. "Yeah."

"So quit already," Paul said. Leaning back, he threw one elbow over the corner of the chair back.

"It's not that easy . . . ," McGhee objected, weakly.

"Yeah, it is . . . ," Paul responded, staring at him. "Only you're too scared to do it . . . ."

"Yeah, I guess I am, 'cause I don't know what *else* to do instead . . . ," McGhee countered.

Paul shook his head. "No, you *do* know, only you don't want to *do* it."

McGhee thought for a second, then leaned in. "What – you mean *write?*"

Paul shrugged, puffing on his cigar.

"I gotta pay rent," McGhee countered, disgusted he found himself making that argument.

"That's why it's a game for the young man, my friend. It's easier before you own things. Have obligations. But other guys our age do it," Paul responded.

"I don't see you doing it . . . ," McGhee said, his frustration mounting.

Paul shrugged again. "I'm not as miserable as you."

"Nice . . . ," McGhee answered, staring at Paul, then laughed.

Paul laughed, too. "Between Kate and that job, you're getting crushed . . . ."

"Jesus, Paul . . . ," McGhee said, returning his gaze. "Some things are best left unsaid . . . ."

Paul looked at him, motionless. "Leaving them formless, without words, doesn't make them less real," Paul retorted, though his tone was sympathetic.

"That's my entire coping strategy, buddy," McGhee admitted, shaking his head.

"And that's why you're miserable . . . ," Paul said, smiling slightly at first, then laughing. "Me, too, as it turns out," he said. Raising his glass he leaned over until McGhee did the same, clinking its metal frame lightly against his friend's. "To delicious misery, and the bitch of a muse she is . . . ," Paul said in toast, his glass aloft. Their eyes met, and despite where his thoughts had run, McGhee was glad for his company. For better or worse, there wasn't anyone else who would tell him these things, and he needed to hear it. Raising his glass, too, they both drained their tea like it was something much stronger.

The shadows had grown long but the air was warm and just barely moist. Kids were getting out of school, racing up the sidewalk against the flow of older men streaming down. Hawkers were calling them in to view carpets, and the call to prayer was ringing again in their ears. Men were roasting mutton on spits, while others walked the streets with round pretzels stacked on skewers selling two for a dollar. They had strayed into the tar pit of commerce without even knowing it, but it was OK as the onslaught of noise and distraction was welcome, abrading McGhee's gloom until nothing but a light glow remained. He'd escaped again, if only for a little while.

Weaving through at a pace his own which was slower, another man about their age was trudging up the hill, hunched over with both hands over his shoulder to hold his load. On his back he carried a large ornate silver jug nearly as long as he was, feeding a bassoon tube over his shoulder, which he pinched between his fingers while grasping the strap, shouting, though not loudly, "Shiraz, Shiraz, soguk shiraz." He came to a rest before them, slinging his jug onto the sidewalk with a sandy clunk, standing more erect, but they could see he was feeling it in his back. He smiled at them, tired, half his teeth missing. "Cold cherry juice . . . ," he said, breathless but in surprisingly clear English, holding out a plastic cup to them.

Paul held up his hands, then looked at McGhee. "I wouldn't," he said.

McGhee looked at Paul, then the man. His clothes were rags, up through the cloth wrapped around his head. His eyes were dark and tired, but there was warmness in them. McGhee smiled at Paul, shifting his weight to his other foot.

"With any luck, it'll kill me then," he said and gave a quick nod to the man. Tipping the tall jug slightly, he filled the plastic cup with the juice from the tube and handed it to McGhee. Holding it up to view the liquid, it was a deep red against the long rays of the evening sun. Then, toasting Paul, he tossed it back, cold and sweet, the best thing he'd tasted in a very long time.

Confessions in the Gloaming

5AM
McKees Rocks, PA 12/18/2023

McGhee sat on the cement step, shivering, pulling up the lapels of his jacket, but it wasn't enough. The sky was just turning blue from black, the deep blue indicating night was giving way to morning, but wasn't through with its bleak treatment of McKees Rocks, PA. A flank of clouds covered part of the sky coming in from the west and was throwing snow flurries, though it seemed to portend worse. He'd sat that step many mornings, waiting. Ray wouldn't be in for another hour, but it wasn't worth going home to sleep, which had become a euphemism for his restless nights in the sheets. With some luck, there might be something for him to do there, that is, if Ray was caught up after the parade of losers working their way through Rudy's bar last night. McGhee didn't recall how they'd met, but knew he liked him and how he tended to those coming in for the *sacraments*, as he called them, nightly. He'd been working on some writing himself, so for once he wasn't one of them. He might be tonight, though, if the words wouldn't come.

A light scuffing of soles caught his attention too late; in the distance a man in a long dark coat and black hat had already altered his course – the scuffing was his turn no doubt – and was heading straight for McGhee. *Jesus Christ* he muttered, adjusting his collar and trying to push his head even further into his wool cap, but there was no escape. It wasn't the first time a man of the cloth would try to save him, and he readied himself for an assault. Two polished shoes came to rest just under the view of his bill. Looking up, he was surprised and a bit amused, though more relieved than any-thing. "Mark . . . ," he said, but the man remained silent a moment.

Two eyes peered down at him, just visible under the fur ruff on the front of his cap pulled low on his forehead. Two ear flaps were folded down, too, though their ends weren't tied under his chin, the white patch of his collar bracketed by darkness. The lapels of his black wool long-coat were up, too, to cover the gap, but they weren't quite enough to do it on their own, so his left hand clasped them closed with a leather glove. He, too, was shaking a bit, but had some red in his cheeks and beads of moisture on his forehead. *How can he be sweating in this cold,* McGhee thought, but said nothing. Pulling out a waxed bag from his coat, the priest thrust it toward McGhee.

"Doughnut, Franny?" he asked. McGhee thought about it a second, gears grinding. Was it worth losing a little heat to grab the bag? – Maybe. He grabbed the bag without saying anything. Inside there were plain doughnuts. *What is it with priests and plain doughnuts,* he mumbled to himself. "Would it be a fuckin' sin to get some iced ones?" he said, stuffing his hand in. They were still warm and it felt good on his fingers. He regretted his words instantly but said nothing, pulling out two. Rolling up the bag tightly he handed it back to the priest. The first bite was warm and sweet. Despite the lack of frosting, it tasted good and was just what he needed. The priest was right, and he almost hated him for it, but couldn't bring himself to.

For his part, Fr. Chepelsky seemed unfazed by this treatment, but it didn't matter — he'd grown used to it with much of his flock. Scrunching up his nose, he wiped it on his shoulder, looking down Island Avenue toward where it dumped into Chartiers. It was a tough street that had seen better days: fifty years back it was bustling and fit, but the cold and cracking frost had taken its toll, as had chronic neglect. Now, it was in the same slow decline as the rest of western Pennsylvania, slipping into decay one flake of cement at a time. A street cleaner sat at the corner, humming with its tubercular vacuum sucking at a drain. A city worker in an orange vest was kneeling beside the truck poking underneath with the handle of a shop broom trying to free something from the whirling brushes. Suddenly it grabbed the stick with a *wham* and simultaneous *snap*, throwing out the fragments a moment later.

"*Motherfuck!*" the worker screamed, jumping back and shaking his hand, looking at the back of it, then shaking it some more. The sudden strike on his cold knuckles had thrown his hand into the frozen asphalt for a double hit. Looking around, his shoulders went slack when he saw the priest. After hesitating a moment, he called out, "Sorry Father . . . ," waving weakly.

Fr. Chepelsky waved back quickly before stuffing his free hand back into his coat. He looked over at McGhee, shrugging. "Sometimes I feel like a cop."

"Should have been Irish then," McGhee said, finishing off the first donut. "Coulda swung both ways, then."

McGhee's wry smile reminded Fr. Chepelsky of a kid he once knew. Staring down at him, he said nothing. He wasn't sure what to make of McGhee exactly. His words had always seemed to wriggle between meanings, even way back in high school, and the fresh reminder took him back. McGhee had always been hard to pin down: even when he was friendly, he was complicated. Looking back, he usually never knew, but he also knew this time wasn't any more serious than it ever had been. Sometimes days later, he'd recall yet another layer of pun, and he'd wonder. Still, despite the repartee, it seemed founded on an odd respect, or perhaps the remnant of some vestigial childhood expectation. It was better than nothing. For him, his ministry was like farming on rocks, where he'd take any hint of green as a positive sign, even if it were a weed. He felt something like a sermon coming on, and the faintest smile curled at the corner of his lips. That was, of course, a mistake.

"What?" McGhee said, taking notice, but looking away. He took any such gap as an opportunity, and delighted in them. "Looks like the Holy Ghost is tickling your ass with a feather . . . . You're getting that *homily* look. Better save it for Sunday."

"You gonna miss, Franny?" he asked. He seemed to know the substance of the answer, but enjoyed asking anyway.

"Miss what? You mean *mass*?" McGhee asked, looking up. Fr. Chepelsky's eyes were still kind, and a little mischievous, like they'd always been.

Back at St. Michaels, the day they'd met, more than fifty years before, Chepelsky was out of breath, having just beat Adams, who was fast, too, but not as fast as he was. He was pushing his fist into his side to dull the pain, his shirt-tail untucked and his face sweaty. Even then he had the habit of holding his face down and looking out the top of his eyes, just under his brows, which was odd for a kid to do. First grade, or maybe second – even that was growing foggy for McGhee — they used to race down that hill: hard shoes slapping into the pavement, running flat out down the steep grade to the speed bump, where they'd have to pull up quick or risk skidding on the gravel. A crash had only happened once, but was enough: that was the last race for any of them. O'Connor, who wasn't so fast or coordinated as it turned out, hit that gravel, and that was it. Headlong into the curb just beyond, teeth everywhere. The fact he was a redhead didn't help either: the blood on his skin looked especially bright, Sister Teresa there holding the handkerchief up to his mouth with the blood flowing through, freely, deep red, his wiry hair starting back and forth as he choked back sobs and spit out gobs of god knows what, waiting for the ambulance. That's what he thought of when he looked at Chepelsky. His eyes were still that color of hazel-brown, though rather than see them then, he recalled that moment, and though they now had wrinkles at the edges and his frame had grown stalky, he saw the lanky seven-year-old version anyway.

"Whatcha thinking, Francis?" the Father said, adjusting his feet.

"Remember when O'Connor smacked the curb?" he said, finally shifting his gaze to meet the priest's.

Fr. Chepelsky winced reflexively. "Jesus, McGhee, what made you think of *that?*"

McGhee smiled. He liked that he could get his friend to relax and slip back into his old posture, if only for a second. "Dunno . . . ," McGhee said, shrugging. "Was just thinking of the day we met. Can't believe you became a priest . . . ."

"Happens to the best of us . . . ," Fr. Chepelsky said, shrugging himself. The pun was so slight, it evaded McGhee's notice, or he chose to ignore it.

"They did a nice job with his teeth . . . ," McGhee said.

Fr. Chepelsky shifted again. "Move over . . . ," he said, sliding onto the step next to McGhee. There wasn't much to protect from the wind, which wasn't so strong but was enough to push the cold air in with more immediacy. The two men sat next to each other, McGhee lost in thought.

"Whatcha doing out here, Franny?" Fr. Chepelsky said, his tone friendly, but probing.

McGhee threw a thumb over his shoulder. "Waiting for Ray to open up . . . ," he said by way of explanation, but it wasn't satisfactory.

"No . . . ," Fr. Chepelsky said, "I mean out *here*," he said, whipping his glove finger around before stuffing it into his pit again. "Was surprised to hear you were back. Weren't you out in the Bay Area a long time?"

McGhee nodded, but said nothing immediately, eventually relenting. "It's colder than I remember."

Fr. Chepelsky slapped him lightly on the back of the head. "Doesn't help sitting out like this, numb-nuts."

McGhee smiled at the familiarity, and the insubordination. "I'll head back . . . eventually."

Fr. Chepelsky snickered. "Smart, coming out for the winter . . . ."

"Bastard . . . ," McGhee said, swinging his head around, but smiling more broadly.

"Jesus, McGhee . . . ," Fr. Chepelsky said, shaking his head.

"You said it, not me," McGhee followed.

"OK, truce . . . ," the priest said, holding up his hands.

"Looks more like surrender, boyo . . . ," McGhee continued.

Folding his hands in his lap, Fr. Chepelsky looked at him intently. "You should try it, sometime, Franny . . . ," he said, smiling softly. The conversation was teetering on the edge of seriousness, but McGhee chose to divert instead.

Standing up, McGhee turned to look down at him. "So . . . we gonna eat or what?"

"Whatcha thinkin'?" the Father said, looking up at him, McGhee shrugging. "Mary Anne's doesn't open 'til six-thirty . . . ," he continued, scrunching up his face and rubbing his nose on his shoulder again.

"Eat'n Park then . . . ," McGhee said, shuffling off a step, then turning. "You coming?" Reaching out an arm, McGhee pulled him standing.

"Whatcha call those doughnuts, then?" Fr. Chepelsky said, jogging to catch up.

"Appetizers . . . ," McGhee said, hunching up his shoulders, starting the march to Chartiers.

It wasn't a long walk, but it was cold, and as the street opened by the light at the intersection, the wind whipped down from the west, blasting them hard with something between flurries and sleet. It was an old street, too, and every time McGhee saw it, he knew exactly where he was: clapboard houses hung above the street, their stoops spilling right down to the sidewalk, cement calving off in flat pieces where the ice had thrown them. Mixed in were businesses, run up to the street's margin, teetering, a narrow sidewalk away, their yellow bricks edged with soot, mortar dark, too, from the smoke of industry long gone. Signs hung there with unreadable paint, but everyone knew what they said anyway. The sidewalk slabs tilted unevenly, right then left, then right again, like sheets of broken ice on an urban river of asphalt, nipped at the edges by cracking frost, too, seams exposing dormant weeds flash-frozen by the winter but ready for a cruel April to pull them back again from the dead. All along the way, Father Chepelsky kept his head down to avoid the wind, though it was at their backs after the turn east, but McGhee didn't. He wanted to see it all, let it wash over him, cold and dirty and hard, and what might have been dispiriting to others, if they saw it at all, filled him with something like satisfaction.

In a lot that had the air of being something else, where something else must have stood but was long gone, cleared out to the edges where the buildings resumed as if nothing had happened, the new Eat'n Park stood, unnaturally fresh like a green shoot after a fire. McGhee didn't like it for that reason, through no fault of its own, but the options were limited, especially at that hour. Fr. Chepelsky shrugged and looked up the street. The steam of his breath shone against the growing blueness of the sky. It was quiet enough to hear the tiny click of the street light change half a block down, winking orange, then weakly gray, meaning the cold must have gotten to it, or perhaps it was realizing the night was close to over.

"Supposed to snow more later . . . ," McGhee said, seeming to read his mind, one hand on the handle.

The priest looked over at McGhee and found him staring back. "You ever gonna open that door, Francis?"

Inside, a busboy was running a floor cleaner, letting it slide back and forth fluidly over the fake small terracotta tiles lined with Cartesian precision, oblivious to their entrance, headphones over his head, his back to the door, a long white wipe-cloth dangling from his rear pocket nearly to the floor. Spying them from afar, the hostess marched the length of the restaurant to reach them, hitching up her step in the middle to expedite her arrival. Walking past the busboy, she punched him in the shoulder, but otherwise didn't acknowledge him. "What did I do?" he whined, allowing the handle to rest on his pelvis as he removed his earphones, then spying the customers, said, "Oh . . . ."

The hostess was short and bright and cute with a long blond ponytail and a badge that said *Britney.* Escorting them back to a booth, she kept talking over her shoulder to them with instructions: "The salad bar isn't up yet, but you probably don't want that anyway."

Fr. Chepelsky nodded, smirking.

Looking ahead a few steps, she started in again: "Your server will be Gina. She'll be right with you. We are running a special on waffles and eggs. You can ask her about it." Spinning on the ball of her foot, she fanned out the menus to herd them into a booth in the corner, windowless.

Looking around, McGhee noticed the rest of the place was empty, except for one guy who appeared on the edge of homelessness with three shopping bags crushed into his side of the booth, nursing a cup of coffee and some toast. On second thought, perhaps he had crossed that line after all, McGhee concluded.

"Can we sit over there?" McGhee said, motioning toward the middle of the outer edge by the windows. Momentary disappointment flickered over Britney's brow, but she recovered with a bright, "Sure!"

Fr. Chepelsky had already sat but stood up, leaning over to McGhee. "Good call. I always forget you can do that."

Marching to the new spot, Britney repeated her maneuver, like a gymnast's dismount, but she'd gone one booth too far for McGhee's taste.

"This one OK?" he asked, stopping short.

Again, her brows flickered, then relaxed. "Sure!" she said, stepping up, though her dismount didn't quite work from that angle without the pirouette, and the menus struck the partition when she fanned them, knocking them on the floor.

Fr. Chepelsky stooped to gather them as Britney threw her hands to her cheeks, flustered. "I'm . . . so . . . sorry . . . ," she said, shaking her head.

"You're doing fine, Britney," McGhee said, smiling at her.

"I second that," Fr. Chepelsky said, handing McGhee one of the menus before tilting his jacket off his shoulder and tossing it into the booth. Both seemed to empathize with her situation, trying to match her gravity.

"It's my first day . . . ," Britney said. "I was practicing at home."

"It shows . . . ," McGhee said, nodding.

"I was in Cheer at Sto-Rox, so I thought this would be easy, but it isn't . . . ," she said, confiding in them.

"You'll get it . . . ," Fr. Chepelsky said, then realizing she might take that badly, added, "You're doing well already."

Shifting on her feet she smiled, touching his sleeve. "Ahhh. That's sweet . . . ," she said, her bubbly-self returning immediately.

As she left, McGhee discretely watched her exit but said nothing, taking a sip from his ice water, but it wasn't quite discrete enough.

"I saw that . . . ," Fr. Chepelsky said, leaning in.

"I don't know how you do it . . . ," McGhee said, shaking his head, the intention clear to the priest.

"Lots of meditation," Fr. Chepelsky said, raising his glass to McGhee.

"So that's what you call it?" McGhee said, snickering.

"That'll be three full Rosaries, Franny . . . ," Fr. Chepelsky said, taking a sip from his glass.

"What . . . ? Penance? For what?" McGhee complained, though enjoying the exchange.

Fr. Chepelsky leaned back, twisting his water glass in slow rotation, looking at his old friend. The years hadn't been unkind to

McGhee, though he looked older. There wasn't as much hair, of course, and what was left was mostly gray with some of the dirty blond still showing through. He was heavier, too, but wore it well, and he still moved without difficulty, though his gait remained unusual. It had been many years since they'd had a meal together, so it was a welcome surprise to find him like that, even in the dark cold of the morning in a jacket better suited to more temperate climates. Still, the serendipity of their meeting made him smile, though he'd learned over the years to trust in its provenance, or perhaps providence.

"So you're traveling alone, I take it?" Fr. Chepelsky asked. It had been so long since they talked that he realized he didn't know the first thing about his old friend.

McGhee nodded, then downed some of his water.

"Kinda surprised you never married . . . ," he said, watching McGhee, "but maybe not so surprised."

McGhee watched him back, considering. "Who said I didn't?" he said.

Just then Gina showed up to take their orders, and she was all business. She knew the menu by heart, the options, the combinations, the shortcuts to the best deals, combining their orders and recombining them, yielding a cheaper price and hash browns on top of it, but Fr. Chepelsky never took his eyes off McGhee. Once she had moved on, he cleared his throat. "You were saying . . . ?" he said, unwilling to let the thread drop.

"So I'm heading back in April, I think . . . ," McGhee said coyly, but the priest shook his head.

"Nuh-uh," he said. Leaning in, he whispered: "You were *married*?"

McGhee shrugged. "Yep," he said. Gina returned with two coffee cups and a carafe and set to pouring, disappearing again in a flash. McGhee emptied a couple creamers in his, stirring slowly, but Fr. Chepelsky just watched.

"How long?" he asked, once McGhee was through with his distractions.

"Couple years," McGhee said, matter of factly. "Her name was Tess."

Fr. Chepelsky leaned back, but then leaned in again. "What happened?"

"Didn't work out . . . ," McGhee said, shrugging again. "She wasn't the one."

"You sure shrug a lot . . . ," Fr. Chepelsky said.

"I've heard that," McGhee responded, his face screwed up into something like a smile, though it looked more like resignation or regret, or at least recognition of the absurdity of it.

"So, when was this, anyway?" Fr. Chepelsky said, still struggling with the news.

"Almost twenty years ago, now . . . ," McGhee answered. He raised the cup to his lips, carefully sipping at the coffee. It was hot – steam rose from it profusely, though it wasn't cold in the restaurant – his lips tentatively drawing it in, first a bit, then more aggressively once he'd established it wasn't so hot after all.

Fr. Chepelsky had his finger threaded through the cup handle, but it remained in the saucer. "How's it possible I didn't know that?"

McGhee shrugged again, then noticing it, laughed. "I guess I do shrug a lot," he said. Suddenly, he felt the years between them, the distance, and he regretted it. "When I left home, I never looked back. Lost track of everybody, and hoped they lost track of me . . . ."

Leaning back again, the Father finally drank his coffee, but looked puzzled. "But why?" he said. "It wasn't that bad, was it?"

McGhee smiled, sighing as he did. He took to twisting his cup in the saucer. "No, not really. It wasn't like that, though I never thought I'd stay. I just had to go, and wanted to disappear."

Shaking his head, Fr. Chepelsky objected. "I still don't get it. A lot of people looked up to you back then."

"I seriously doubt that . . . ," McGhee countered.

"Remember that soccer game when you told Hector you had a Yale meeting in Pittsburgh, then you showed up at game time and ran down the hill dressed as a chicken? We won that game because of that. We totally sucked, but that nearly killed Hector, and they fell apart."

McGhee laughed. "Nearly forgot that."

"And then you disappeared," Fr. Chepelsky said, shaking his head. "So what happened?"

McGhee picked up a sugar packet and began playing with it in his fingers, folding it then straightening again. "I . . . ," he started, pausing a long while. "I was beaten."

"How?" Fr. Chepelsky asked, leaning in. Looking up, McGhee met his eyes again, and remembered how kind they had always been, even back then when they were both just kids.

"I let fear in," McGhee said, folding his lips over. "And it fucked me up."

Leaning back, Fr. Chepelsky pushed with both hands on the edge of the table, shaking his head. "Jesus, Franny . . . ," he said. "You were in the *big* leagues. What'd you expect?"

Tilting his head, McGhee smiled coyly. "Taking the Lord's name in vain – I think that'll be three full Rosaries, Chepelsky."

"No . . . ," Fr. Chepelsky said, leaning back in, holding up a finger. "There's more to it than that . . . ."

"Oh, so now you're a therapist, too?" McGhee said, playfully.

"Yeah, well, more than you know . . . ," Fr. Chepelsky said, shaking his head. "You can't stop there, or it'll drive you crazy. Seems like you lost your faith in yourself or something . . . ."

McGhee shrugged again, laughing, low at first, then out loud. "You think?" he managed to get out, then kept laughing. "Sorry . . . but another guy in your line of work already told me that."

Even the busboy, who was wrapping the electric cord up in lassos on the hook of the floor cleaner, looked over until Britney got him to stop staring by punching him again. Seeing McGhee had noticed, she wrapped her fingers into a small megaphone around her lips. "This idiot's my boyfriend . . . ," she called over, then waved.

Fr. Chepelsky sat back looking at him, smiling slightly on the edges, but in the middle his eyes were sad, and McGhee saw it, dampening his laughter. "So you keep company with wise men, then . . . ," the Father said, coyly sipping his coffee.

Gina delivered their breakfasts, efficiently plopping their plates and plates and plates, and hot sauce, and ketchup, before topping off their cups. Looking between their faces, she knew not to ask, and retreated. They set to eating, each lost in his own thoughts until their plates were empty and they pushed them back.

Wiping his mouth, the priest took a few pulls on his coffee, letting it settle noisily back in the saucer. "So . . . Tess wasn't the one, then?" he said. Full bellies had let the gloom dissipate somewhat, but he wasn't about to let it go.

McGhee shook his head, tilting it slightly. "Indeed, she was not." Lifting his cup halfway, he continued: "Seemed like a good idea. Only, my heart wasn't in it. I know who is, though . . . ," he said, leading, but Fr. Chepelsky missed it.

"Almost got married myself . . . ," the priest said suddenly, shaking his head. "Just before I decided on seminary."

"So what happened?" McGhee said, leaning in. It was a time of revelations, and he enjoyed being on the other side of the interrogator's lamp.

"Didn't work out . . . ," Fr. Chepelsky said, smiling.

"Not the right one?" McGhee continued, draining his cup. Pouring from the carafe, only a trickle came out, and he held it up with a jiggle for Gina to see, but she was already in route with a replacement.

"No, she was the right one . . . ," he said, staring into his cup. "I wasn't."

"She turn you down, then?" McGhee said, refilling his cup, then topping off his friend's.

Fr. Chepelsky shook his head. "No, wasn't like that. Got right up to Valentines. Had the ring and everything, only I couldn't do it."

"Oh man . . . . How did *that* play out?" McGhee asked, pressing, but not too hard.

Fr. Chepelsky was quiet, twisting his cup, watching the steam. "Got to the night before. I was pretty excited actually. Got a call from my dad. He said he thought he was supposed to call me – he was like that – you remember how he was?"

McGhee laughed. "When the plant closed, that seemed to kill him a little bit. I remember him sitting with the garage door open in that lawn chair, looking out, like he'd been gut-punched."

The priest nodded. "Exactly. And he got real religious after that. Used to go to church every morning. The 5:30 at St. Paul's . . . ."

"Didn't know that part . . . ," McGhee said, wagging his head a bit.

"So Dad calls me and says he was *told* to call me, only he won't say by whom, only I knew. So I told him my plans, and he was real quiet."

"Had he met the girl? What was her name?"

Fr. Chepelsky leaned back, looking at McGhee. "Hell yeah, he met her. It was Sandy."

McGhee let out a laugh. Looking over, Britney waved again.

"Your neighbor – literally, the girl next door," McGhee whispered, leaning in. "You were gonna marry *that Sandy*?"

"What's wrong with Sandy?" Fr. Chepelsky said defensively. "She was nice. Better than nice."

"No, no – nothing is wrong with Sandy. I just had no idea it ever got that serious," McGhee said, smiling.

"You were gone, remember?" Fr. Chepelsky said, more serious than he had been.

McGhee retreated, reaching for the water. "No, it's just so . . . ," McGhee said, his voice trailing off.

"Cliché?" Fr. Chepelsky said. "Yeah, that bothered me a bit, too. Not enough, though. I really loved her . . . ."

McGhee nodded in acknowledgement. "So what did your dad say?" McGhee said, sipping at his water.

Fr. Chepelsky stared into his cup, recalling the conversation. To McGhee, it seemed like he was actually hearing it, for his aspect darkened, but he didn't speak right away.

"Mostly . . . he just listened," Fr. Chepelsky said eventually. "I was really into it. Laying out the plan – getting a job, where we might live, helping her finish school – all that." He fell silent again, then looked at McGhee. "I wish we could smoke in here . . . ," he said looking around.

McGhee grabbed the check. "Let's ride, then . . . ," he said looking at his friend, then slid out of the booth. "Only, I need a pit-stop first after these eighteen cups of coffee . . . ."

"Me first," Fr. Chepelsky said, grabbing his coat and striding toward the restroom. Lucky for them, the restroom had two urinals, so there was no waiting.

McGhee noted his friend's brow remained serious, and he thought to remedy that. "That water sure is cold . . . ," McGhee said, staring straight ahead. He'd broken the men's code of silence, but for good reason. He could sense Fr. Chepelsky turned his head slightly, then straightened out again.

Uttering in a low, husky voice, "and *deep,* too," Fr. Chepelsky completed the juvenile joke from their youth.

Both men began to chuckle, then commenced laughing, their voices filling the small space. The door cracked open and the busboy stuck his head in, headphones around his neck. "Britney wanted me to check on you guys . . . ," he said weakly.

Outside, the air was brisk and their breath showed with the heat of much coffee in their guts. The wind fought their trudge up Chartiers, but they were fortified against it, though in no hurry. Fr. Chepelsky fished out a pack of Salem menthols, squishing one out toward McGhee. He hadn't smoked cigarettes in years, but he took one anyway, tapping it on his watch to pack the tobacco.

"Old habits die hard," Fr. Chepelsky said, his cigarette wiggling as he spoke, then ignited it with a cigar lighter, the noisy jet instantly creating a cloud of smoke. Tossing it to McGhee, he followed suit, handing it back to the priest.

"So, you were laying it out for your dad . . . ," McGhee said, exhaling half from his mouth, the rest from his nose.

Fr. Chepelsky nodded. "Right. So I get to the end of it, and he's really quiet. He was always like that when he had something to say — you had to pull it out of him," he said, using both hands to show it. "So . . . I just come right out and ask him what he thinks. And he's quiet. And I say, 'Dad, what do you think?' again, and he just says, 'No.'"

"Just '*No*'?" McGhee said, looking over.

"Just 'No'," Fr. Chepelsky said, shaking his head, taking a long drag on the cigarette.

The two walked along in silence a few strides. "So then what?" McGhee asked finally.

"So . . . I asked him, '*Why not?*'"

"Were you, like, *mad* at that point?" McGhee asked. He couldn't imagine an exchange like that with his father, but he had been a different sort of man. He wouldn't have intruded — in fact, he hadn't intruded when he'd had that conversation with him.

"Not mad . . . No, not mad. More like crestfallen," Fr. Chepelsky said, looking over at McGhee.

"I haven't ever heard that word actually *spoken* . . . ," McGhee said. "Congratulations."

"Whatever . . . So I ask him, 'Why not?' and after a bit he tells me he had just had a dream. Clear as day. I was a priest, and he was so happy and proud, and he was dialing the phone to tell me that before he was even fully awake."

McGhee stopped walking. "Wait," he said. "You became a priest because your dad had a *dream?*"

Fr. Chepelsky shrugged, stopping, too. "Not *exactly* . . . but *kinda*," he said.

"No way . . . ," McGhee said, shaking his head.

"He said he thought it was the Holy Spirit . . . ," Fr. Chepelsky said. "There was some fire in the dream."

"Jesus . . . ," McGhee said, shaking his head, laughing lightly, but more from disbelief.

"No . . . the *Holy Spirit*," Fr. Chepelsky corrected him, leaning in with a sly smile. "And he figured he was the messenger . . . ."

"God . . . ," McGhee said, shaking his head. "That's just too much."

"No . . . the *Holy Spirit*," Fr. Chepelsky said again, though more seriously.

"All right, enough with the Trinity already," McGhee said. "That always gave me nightmares . . . ," he said, trailing off.

They resumed walking again. The sun still wasn't up, but it was a lot lighter, and there were a few people about dusting the light snow from windshields with their sweepers, or shoveling their steps, billows of steam from their mouths, even though it wasn't so heavy this time.

"Come to think of it . . . ," Fr. Chepelsky began, turning his body toward McGhee to speak the words, "I bet you wish you had an intervention like that . . . With Tess, I mean . . . ."

McGhee glanced at him, but continued walking. "Nope," he said.

Fr. Chepelsky laughed merrily, subsiding into a smile. "Could have saved you a lot of trouble," he said, looking over again.

McGhee shook his head. "No, thanks," he said. "I'll take the trouble."

Fr. Chepelsky laughed again. "What sense does that make?"

McGhee swung his head around, looking at his friend. "You really wanna debate *sense* with me?" McGhee said, jovial but firm.

Fr. Chepelsky shrugged. "Sure . . . ," he said. Though his lips looked like a frown, they were more of a smile. McGhee loved the whole picture of him, and it made him smile: his hair stuck out at all angles from under the hat, which rode high on his head, like a ship in the mop he still had, with the unsecured earflaps flapping as he walked like an exuberant puppy.

"OK, so suppose I took that deal . . . ," McGhee began.

"The Tess intervention?"

"Yeah, the Tess intervention. Maybe that's a good thing. Maybe it's not."

"I can't see how it's not, but OK, you've taken the deal," Fr. Chepelsky said, nodding.

McGhee nodded, too. "Now, look what I have to trade to get it . . . ," he continued.

Fr. Chepelsky thought a second, then looked over at him. "Loneliness, doubt and years of strife?" he asked, straight-faced, though his lips curled into another smile.

McGhee let out a laugh, taking another drag on his smoke. "OK, perhaps a bit, but it's all imaginary, isn't it?"

Fr. Chepelsky frowned again, only it wasn't sadness. "Maybe . . . ," he said. "But that's where faith comes in . . . ."

McGhee put his hand on his friend's shoulder to stop him. "See, my life doesn't require that."

"I feel sorry for you, then . . . ," Fr. Chepelsky said, his frown looking more genuine.

McGhee shook his head. "If I were to ever say that to a *religious*, I'd be crucified."

Fr. Chepelsky smiled. "Nice word choice," he acknowledged. "And you do have a point. Tolerance isn't so common, is it? I apologize . . . ."

"So, going back to that deal, I can trade some short-term solace in exchange for admitting a huge logical gap in my world view. That's how I see *that* deal . . . ."

Fr. Chepelsky nodded his head, or perhaps it was shaking – the motion was unclear – but McGhee knew better than to expect surrender. "So . . . you know everything, then?"

"I never said that . . . ," McGhee said, shaking his head. "I don't know anything, not really, but that doesn't mean I'll willingly accept something that doesn't make sense when there's a more likely explanation."

"Occam's Razor isn't a law, you know . . . ," Fr. Chepelsky said, holding up a finger. "Just being *likely* doesn't make it *true* . . . ."

"True . . . ," McGhee admitted, tilting his head. "But it's a pretty good rule of thumb. And I don't abandon it without a good reason."

"So, you're saying I don't have a good reason, then?" Fr. Chepelsky said, looking at McGhee, waiting until their eyes met.

McGhee shrugged. "Yeah, I guess I'm saying that. Sorry."

Fr. Chepelsky shook his head, laughing. "I think feeling like I'm part of something bigger is worth it. Not to mention the shield against doubt and loneliness – that's pretty nice . . . ."

Turning the corner, they faced back up Island Avenue toward Rudy's, finally out of the wind. Ray was outside in the distance, pouring a basin of water into the margin by the road's edge but was too far away yet for him to notice them.

"So, you're saying . . . ," McGhee said, continuing the debate, "just because it feels good is the reason to do it?" He enjoyed the irony of it, though he contained the full gravity of his rejoinder, out of deference. He'd been hit with that argument before, and it felt good to turn it around for once.

"No . . . ," Fr. Chepelsky said, stopping and holding up a hand. "Because it feels *right*."

"But what does your head tell you about it?" McGhee said, crossing his arms.

"It's not really a head thing," Fr. Chepelsky said, putting his hand on McGhee's shoulder. "It's more of a *soul* thing."

McGhee rolled his eyes, but Fr. Chepelsky kept on.

"You telling me you don't feel like there's a soul in you?" he said, looking into his friend's eyes.

"Sure I do," McGhee admitted. "Just like I really wanna believe in Santa Claus. Only, it's not real."

"How do you know that?" Fr. Chepelsky objected.

"You mean about Santa Claus?" McGhee asked, deadpan.

"No I don't *fuckin'* mean *Santa Claus*," Fr. Chepelsky said, annoyed. Raising his eyes, he crossed himself.

McGhee shrugged again. "Well, you can't prove a negative. But the burden of proof is on you, then, isn't it?"

"There is no burden of proof," Fr. Chepelsky objected. "And from where I sit, that's a pretty strong denial: you feel the presence of your soul, but you deny it . . . ."

"I need more than a feeling, Mark. In the end, all I got is my brain, and it tells me there's nothing else."

"Isn't that a little self-serving for your brain to tell you that? Isn't that a little *hubris*? Isn't there some *delusion* to that?"

McGhee smiled. "Nice try . . . ," he said, shaking his head, "but that's not a real tautology. You're using your brain, too, so you can't discount it like that . . . ."

"I'm not *just* using my brain, though. I'm using my heart, too . . . ," Fr. Chepelsky said.

McGhee tilted his head. "Really, Mark?"

"You know what I mean," Fr. Chepelsky said. Dropping the butt on the sidewalk, he crushed it under his sole. "It's not just about evidence."

McGhee turned to him stopping again. "Yeah, but why *wouldn't* a benevolent god provide some evidence, then?"

"Who says he didn't?" he said, exhaling the last of his smoke. "Besides, it's more about faith, now isn't it?"

"So, you mean Jesus and the Bible and all that?" McGhee said. "As evidence, I mean."

"Forget the Bible," he said. "But yeah, Jesus."

McGhee laughed. "Can I quote you on that?"

Fr. Chepelsky cocked his head: "*But yeah, Jesus* — sounds like a bumper sticker."

McGhee shook his head. "Nice — no, the other part."

"I know better than to debate the Bible . . . ," Fr. Chepelsky said. "It's not literal anyway."

"So, faith, then . . . ," McGhee said. "It boils down to having faith because you want to, then?"

"Yeah, that, and other things . . . ," Fr. Chepelsky said. "I see it all over . . . ."

"You mean *intelligent design*, then?" McGhee asked, winding up, but Fr. Chepelsky wouldn't take the bait.

"Not really, no. Just how things play out. I've seen too much to think I can understand everything."

"So you have to take that leap, though?" McGhee asked. "You know, you have to check your reason at the door."

"Naa. Not really . . . ," Fr. Chepelsky said. "Besides, there are worse things."

"Such as?" McGhee asked.

"The loneliness, for one thing. I'm not strong enough to bear it," Fr. Chepelsky said. "It's just too sad to consider. That when it's over, it's just . . . over."

"Who's showing hubris now?" McGhee said, smiling.

"That's not hubris, Franny. That's more like . . . ," he said, but his voice trailed off.

"Desperation?" McGhee offered helpfully.

Fr. Chepelsky laughed. "I was thinking it's more like *hope*."

They'd finally made it to the stoop at Rudy's, which wasn't much more than a crumbling edge where they'd sat earlier. Still, it wasn't quite so grim as it had appeared in the cold darkness, the light improving its aspect markedly.

Ray was standing there looking at McGhee, wiping his dirty hands on a dirtier rag. "You ready?"

"What are you doing here, anyway Franny?" Fr. Chepelsky said, but McGhee was quiet, looking sheepish.

"Oh *fuck all*, I don't care if he knows . . . ," Ray said to McGhee, then lowered his head. "Sorry Father."

"No worries, Ray . . . ," Fr. Chepelsky said, lowering his head, too.

Looking up, McGhee glanced back and forth between them. Shrugging again, he patted Fr. Chepelsky on the shoulder. "We're working on our reading skills," he said. "Ray might even get his GED one of these days, right Ray?"

Ray nodded. "Seems like maybe you're not the only do-gooder roaming these godforsaken streets, Father . . . ."

Fr. Chepelsky smiled. "Perhaps not so godforsaken, Ray," he said, looking from Ray back to McGhee.

McGhee shook his head, sighing. With that, he opened the door and stepped into the darkness, alone.

Losing Les

```
              65
0 ◄─────────────────────────●────────► 90
            10AM
      Rawlins, WY 11/15/2028
```

Somewhere around hour ten of the drive McGhee began to hallucinate, convincing himself he could drive the whole way from San Francisco to Rawlins, Wyoming in one sitting, and even more absurdly, on one tank of gas. There was no way that was ever going to happen but perhaps was understandable because his brother was dead, and he wasn't in his right mind at all. As evidence, his bag only had a toothbrush and a jacket in it, which was the stranger because he chose the larger bag since he knew he'd be gone for a while and wasn't even sure how long. That's why he elected to drive in the first place. So when he heaved the large bag into the car, he even remarked to himself it was lighter than usual, and the sound of a singular toothbrush rolling around within it did nothing to break him out of his stupor. In short, it was very clear to him this was not supposed to happen — he fully expected to die first and even preferred that might be the case (assuming it was painless and quick) just so he could avoid the hassle and discomfort of dealing with in-laws he only marginally knew and tolerated in the first place (this was the true dividend of dying early, or at least before his brothers) – so, the unexpected happening simply threw his mind into some indeterminate state, like a transmission stuck between gears, and his ability to operate was thus impaired. That said, he found this state to feel like something of a buzz, which he found oddly pleasant, so he made no effort to break the spell.

It should be no surprise, then, that he ran out of gas along I-80 somewhere in the western half of Nevada. Lucky for him his brother had died in November, just after his own birthday, so it wasn't so hot, because if he had died in July and he had tried that stunt, he could very well have died himself out there walking along the highway in that heat. It had been a few hours since his phone had drained, and he certainly didn't have an auto club membership, so he would have been walking regardless. He definitely would not have thought of, nor cared to, flag down a motorist to use their phone. In fact, while he walked along the road, he didn't even have his thumb out, and was content to walk the whole way to Winnemucca, even though it was a good twenty miles there yet. This partially explains why the old red pickup pulling over just ahead of him caused him to stop in his march momentarily as he actually considered walking past it. It was only his recollection of another such pickup truck, many years before that got him to relent and grab the handle at all.

He was glad the driver looked to be Mexican. Maybe he didn't even speak English, or so McGhee hoped – he didn't think he was in the mood for conversation. For McGhee, this was just about as good as he could hope for, so he slid onto the bench, clicked the door shut, smiled weakly at the driver, who returned the exact same expression. He shifted into gear as he checked the big mirror on his side before getting back on the road. It was practically a formality that he checked the mirror at all – there hadn't been a car along that stretch for several minutes – but it did seem to follow the general flow of the driver's disposition, coasting slowly toward the end of a work day. Despite the lateness of the season, he was sweaty and rather grimy. He had little flecks of bark and grass along his arms in patches and a half-moon of perspiration under his arm, which he had draped over the wheel. His shirt had been red once upon a time but had bleached into something like an earthy pink. His work pants had been dark green, or perhaps olive, but with the incessant sprays of water and pesticide, manure and animal urine they had attained a special color of their own. His right pants pocket was ripped an extra inch at the edge where he had a pair of shears jammed in and sprung off catch, something he apparently needed at his reach every single moment. The pants ended jammed into tall rubber boots with the excess fabric gathering around his shins and calves. The boots had a half-dried slurry of mud on them, or as McGhee suspected, based on the slight odor, shit.

He might not even have been aware of it, but McGhee was secretly glad he had run out of gas. First, he was in no hurry to make it to Rawlins, which in his estimation was little more than a wide spot with a gas station and a bait shop. Why Les had chosen to live there he didn't know, either, except he did know – it was because of Clara Ann – but he remained in denial, even though Les had been there at least thirty years, or so the math seemed to indicate. Second, he was rather tired of driving, which he hadn't even realized. He'd always driven a lot, sometimes for pleasure and sometimes when on projects, and enjoyed it. He'd never driven a truck, though, because as much as he liked it, that seemed a little extreme, even for him. That said, he still enjoyed it – he enjoyed the pace of it, the slowness of progress, and the simultaneous surprise of arriving long before he ever expected to. He never tired of that sensation. But in this case, he'd been driving five or six hours straight and he was just physically tired, even though that thought never fully formed in his head, even when the engine started stuttering and he drifted to a stop in the gravel margin twenty miles west of Winnemucca. And he secretly liked having a bit of company, too, language-locked as it was behind a stoic companion. The solitariness of his journey and its purpose would at times come at him, bubbling up through the rocks and bricks that were his foundation and nearly send him reeling. Family mortality might generally follow birth order, but not in his case from his perspective, and though he had no reasonable explanation to support this supposition, this assumption regarding his mortality had somehow baked into a solid and foundational mud brick in his head, and the disintegration of it was at once surprising and baffling.

It was in this state of flux and exhaustion that McGhee began mumbling to himself, and due to his general solitary existence, was utterly unaware he was doing so. After a few minutes of these private exchanges, which were mildly animated, the driver could take it no longer.

"Don't make me sorry I picked you up, *pendejo* . . . ," he said, looking over at McGhee. His glance was serious, but melted as he chuckled to himself. "I just picked you up coz that seat has a friggin' stupid spring in it that starts squeaking when I get over sixty-five and it reminds me of that old lady getting banged by that a-hole across the street. So far's I'm concerned, you're just some ugly ballast, vato . . . ."

He looked over at McGhee, both hands on the wheel, jerking it back and forth to keep it steady. McGhee looked back at him, but said nothing. As far as McGhee was concerned, the interruption was a sudden curiosity, and he was content to follow the flow.

"So what the fug you doin' out on this road anyway, walkin'?" the man asked. His tone didn't have its original bite, so McGhee adjusted, too, to match it. It was the hitchhiker penalty: you always have to engage the driver to keep the ball rolling – those are the rules, and that's the trade: conversation for transport.

"Ran out of gas . . . ," he said, shifting his gaze to look out the windshield. The wiper was broken on his side, leaving vast swaths of mud and bugs smooshed in arcs across his view.

"No shit . . . ," the man said. "And you got no can, right?" he laughed to himself. "Now that's some good planning. You sure you're not a Mexican?" he asked. His tone had softened considerably, and he seemed to be in something approximating a good mood.

"Definitely not a Mexican," McGhee said.

"Something wrong with being a Mexican?" the man asked.

McGhee looked at him again. He was smiling more broadly now, and the gold of a couple teeth flanking his incisors flashed in the evening sunshine from the mirror. McGhee didn't say anything, his smile wry and curved into his cheek, not sure what to make of him.

"Hey, you're the a-hole that started talking," the man said, looking back at the road. "Me, I'm just makin' conversation," he said. He looked back at McGhee, lifting his ancient John Deere ball cap off his messy black hair to wipe his forehead against his shoulder. The whole motion seemed automatic, like he did it a hundred times a day, and the hat settled back into position as his head moved under the hat versus the other way around.

The driver saw McGhee wasn't sure where he was going with the conversation, so he rubbed his hand across his shirt then stuck it out. "Jaime," he said. McGhee took it.

"McGhee. And thanks for the lift . . . ," he said. "You work around here?"

"Yep. Augustana Farms. Just back there," he said motioning over his shoulder. "You actually ran out of gas on it," he continued. "Your car oughta be alright for a while . . . unless my guys find it. They'll strip that fugger bare."

McGhee looked at him. He had a funny delivery and he enjoyed it. "Didn't look like a farm . . . ," he said, throwing his elbow out the window and putting a foot on the dash.

"You don't know dick about farms, then. Comfy?" he said, tossing his chin toward McGhee's foot.

"Gettin' there . . . ," McGhee said, stretching a bit. Jaime reached across, knocking his foot off the dash to open the glove box.

"Have a snort of that then . . . ," he said, waving toward the box. A thin silver flask shone in the light. Behind it sat an old .38 long which gave McGhee pause. He looked at Jaime, who was noticing the gun, too.

"Coyotes," he said. "We're lousy with 'em out here. They love chicken more than I do . . . ."

McGhee grabbed out the flask, closed the box and put his foot back up. He took a long pull on the flask, and shook his head with a shudder. "What the hell is *that*?" he said when he found his voice again.

Jaime snorted out loud – his voice had a sing-song tone to it when he laughed, merry and guttural. "*That* is San Marcos . . . ," he said. It didn't appear to register with McGhee, so he continued. "Mexican Brandy . . . ?" he said, his voice rolling up to a question at the end. McGhee took another swig, wincing as he pushed it down. "Smooth . . . ," he said, offering the flask to Jaime.

He looked in both mirrors, then smiled at McGhee. "Can never be too careful, right?" he said, grabbing it. "Take it a sec . . . ," he said, letting go of the wheel to tilt his head way back to take several gulps. McGhee steered while Jaime lowered his head for a pause, then shook with another bout of laughter. Up ahead a service station appeared on the right — dilapidated like something out of the fifties, odd wings flung up on the corners of the roof above the cashier and station store. McGhee thought they'd be turning in, but Jaime gave it more gas. McGhee had to veer back onto the road. He looked at Jaime, who was looking back at him. He hadn't been in a hurry to take the wheel back, but he casually grabbed it again.

"You, my friend, need more than gas . . . ," he said. He paused a moment to let that sink in. "You don't appear to be in much of a hurry, am I right?" He took another swig and handed the flask back to McGhee. McGhee took it, but didn't drink right away. He wasn't sure where this was going, so he just looked at Jaime.

Jaime broke out in laughter again. "No, my friend, you are *not* my type," he said. "Now, my *wife*, she's my type. And I think what you really need is some professional grade Mexican food. She's making Pozole tonight and that's what you *really* need."

McGhee considered protesting, but when he thought of getting back on the road to Rawlins, he sighed. "That actually sounds about right," he said, and took another long pull on the flask, laughing right along with Jaime the rest of the way.

Winnemucca was low and sprawling in the sun in the distance, but they turned off the road before getting there, veering right at the airport exit and curving around the edge of the tarmac toward what appeared to be an abandoned man camp, or mostly abandoned. The entrance said *Hycroft*, but the placard had slipped all but one of its bolts and rotated until one corner rested on scrubby soil. A prickly pear nestled in its spare shade, nearly obscuring the sign's tagline: *A Champion Community*. The units near the front were wholly abandoned, some doors swinging open, others missing doors entirely. Since the drilling dried up, so did the men who occupied those units, seeking their fortunes elsewhere. As is the way of things, others had followed behind them to reclaim those resources, either squatting or something like it, and it seemed there wasn't money in putting out the new occupants, so signs of life emerged the further they went into the camp. Near the back end, most of the units were full, with kids spilling into the street playing whiffle ball and soccer, sometimes at the same time. One kid wearing an enormous and battered lacrosse helmet, hearing the car, lifted his goalie stick and waved the others from the street to let them pass. Jaime stopped at the goalie and rolled down his window.

"Go tell Mom we have company . . . ," he said, rolling up the window to the ensuing protests that involved, "middle of the game," and "so not fair." Looking in the mirror as they drove off, McGhee saw the kid take off the helmet, drop it in the weeds and kick it in disgust. A chorus of, "Leave the stick, leave the stick," rose from the other players, but he didn't, trotting after the car and jeering at them as he did.

Looking at McGhee, Jaime shook his head. "Luis can be a little shit, but his heart is good," he said by way of explanation. "You got kids?" McGhee shook his head. "Really?" Jaime said, swerving at the last second to avoid a tricycle in the street. "I got three," he said. "Want one?" he asked, serious momentarily until he couldn't contain another laugh. "Seriously, don't tell my wife I said that . . . ," he said, looking skyward and crossing himself.

After a couple quick turns, they pulled up to a unit on the edge of the camp, facing a hundred yards of desert before it dissolved into the end of a runway for the airport. It was a small prefab, made for two men, at one time tidy and solid, but those days had passed. The siding facing south and west had been beaten by the sun into a peeling mess, though the other sides looked marginally better. It was tan, like every other unit in the camp, with a black asphalt roof. The gutter on one edge tipped down with its downspout hanging a foot out into the air with nothing to drink. Still, some smoke rose from its tin chimney, and kids were slamming the metal screen door as they went in and out incessantly. A little girl sat on the corner of the stoop, playing with a doll. Upon inspection, McGhee noticed it was missing an arm, but it didn't seem to bother her as she was having an animated dialog with her about the absolute necessity of getting busy to make dinner because they had company coming. At that moment, Luis came busting out of the door and nearly ran into Jaime. "Mom says fine," he said, attempting to dart around his father to launch into the yard and away.

"Whoa, bub," Jaime said, catching a corner of his shirt as he tried to squeeze past. Luis's shoulders went slack with resignation.

"Now what?" he said with all the attitude an eleven-year-old boy could muster.

"You watch it, mister," Jaime said, moving into a boxing pose. "I can take you out and make another any time I want . . . ," he said, shadow boxing the boy. Luis instantly joined the match, reaching in to jab Jaime in the gut, just as Jaime put his hand on top of his head to hold him back. Luis kept throwing punches, but started laughing as he did. Jaime looked at McGhee. "See what you're missing?" he said. Turning back to Luis, he grabbed both sides of his head. "Grills. Go . . . ."

"Ahhh . . . ," Luis said, wriggling free, but jumping off the porch toward the three Webers arranged in a little U in the yard near the door. "It's Manny's turn. I did it last time . . . ," he continued, slamming open the lid of the first one, then hoisting a bag of charcoal on his knee before spilling the dark briquettes inside. "How many this time?" he asked, jiggling a few more chunks onto the pile.

"Just two. Do the black one, too . . . ," Jaime said, waving at the far grill. Looking back to McGhee, he motioned to the girl on the stoop. "That's my little Chispita . . . ," he said. "Have a seat. Want a cold one?" Jaime opened the door and went inside before waiting for an answer. The girl was wearing a neat cornflower blue dress and white socks with little flats, though the latter had scuffed toes, and only one of the straps remained attached. McGhee sat beside her, but she didn't seem to take notice, continuing her conversation with the doll.

"We have to be good coz papa's bringing home another stray and mama sez . . . ." She stopped suddenly, and held out her doll to McGhee without actually looking at him. "You wanna play with her? Mama sez I should share, so here . . . ."

McGhee looked at the doll. Aside from missing an arm, half of its hair was pulled out, it was grimy with smudges and scuffs, and one eye remained closed, suggesting she'd endured some violence. "What's her name?" he said, grabbing the doll by a foot before cradling it in his palm.

The little girl looked up at him. "Barbie. Duh," she said. "All dolls are called Barbie. I thought 'dults know that already," she said. She smiled, one of her front teeth missing, but with a stub coming in. McGhee snickered at her attitude, turning the doll over in his hand.

"So what happened to her arm?" he asked.

"Luis pulled it out. Papa called him culito, too, and Mama yelled at him. He tried to put it back, but it wouldn't stay in. They never do, though. See?" She reached beside her leg and pulled out another doll, a man, this one missing both arms and both legs. "He's s'posed to be called Joe, but Papa calls him Matt." McGhee laughed. "That's an old joke . . . ," he said, handing the doll back to her.

"I don't gitit," she said, stroking the hair remaining on the doll. McGhee wondered how to explain it, but the door opened, Jaime calling back to someone in Spanish. His hand on the door had two longnecks jammed between his fingers. A faint response came from inside, to which he laughed, letting the door slam shut. The remains of a doorbell hung by the door and Jaime stuck each bottle inside the gaping box in turn, popping off the lids before handing one to McGhee. It was a *Tecate*, though half of the label had sweated off or dissolved in some ice bath. Jogging down the stairs, Jaime motioned for him to follow.

McGhee turned to the girl: "Bye Chispita . . . ," he said, patting her on the head.

"I'm Cece. Just Papa calls me that," she said. McGhee looked at Jaime.

"Means *little spark*," Jaime said, walking backward a step before resuming his march.

McGhee followed Jaime around the house. In the back, facing the airfield, sat two aluminum lawn chairs. The yard was strewn with toys – a *Big Wheel* locked in place by some tall scrub grass, a backstop like the one he'd seen in the street, only the netting had seen better days, three soccer balls (deflated), a batting tee bent over to a forty-five-degree angle, and a hammock. Jaime noticed McGhee looking at the balls.

"Tell me, how does a kid *break* a soccer ball?" he asked McGhee. He held up his beer and McGhee clinked his bottle against it. "Cheers," Jaime said. Both fell silent, looking out from the yard and down the runway.

"Very noisy?" McGhee asked eventually.

Jaime looked at McGhee, then the runway, then back at McGhee. "You mean the planes? – Naaa. Not really. Small planes mostly, you know, Comanche, Beechcraft and such. Now and then one of those Lears. They're kinda loud, but not so many. I just like to look at the runways. Reminds me of travel . . . ."

McGhee looked at him. He must have been about forty, maybe forty-five, though working outside was hard on his skin. He had a little gray in the temples, but looked pretty fit, not counting a small belly. His work shirt said *Augustana Farms* on one side, and *Jaime* on the other in a white oval, but was now unbuttoned down to his navel, revealing a white t-shirt.

"So where you from?" McGhee asked him, still looking at the runway.

"Right there . . . ," Jaime said, pointing over his shoulder with the bottle. McGhee looked at him, but didn't say anything. "Oh . . . You mean in Mexico?" Jaime continued, helpfully.

McGhee nodded, taking another swig.

"San Antonio," Jaime said, taking a drink himself.

"There's a San Antonio in Mexico?" McGhee asked, finally looking at him. Jaime was smiling again.

"How the hell should I know? I'm from Texas," he said, laughing again, then coughing, then laughing some more. "You gringos always fall for that . . . ," he said.

Just then a little window on the backside of the house slapped open and a stream of Spanish spilled out in a woman's voice. Jaime leaned forward in his chair, yelling over his shoulder, "Si, Si . . . ."

Standing, he stretched, pushing in the small of his back. "Time to get the meat on . . . ," he said. McGhee started to get up, but Jaime urged him to stay put, which he was glad to do.

It was a fine evening – the sun just below the mountains fifty miles to the west. Though November, it was unseasonably warm – almost seventy degrees. The sky was white near the horizon, continuing through a light blue, then darker hues the whole way to the east where it was already past dusk. McGhee was glad for the diversion, but his thoughts turned back to his journey, his car by the highway, and Les waiting for him in Rawlins, laying in a box. He thought of Clara Ann bustling in that kitchen of theirs, probably making casseroles, and receiving tureens from sad neighbors. Everyone seemed to like Les. He was pretty affable – even McGhee had to admit that, though he was reluctant to do so. He wondered about that, then remembered some of the reasons. It was the accumulation of bits of conversation, looks of disapproval – the house. Mostly little things that summed in McGhee's head to a vague discomfort at the thought of Les. But despite those things, he knew the real reason for his ambivalence: Les had known him when he was a young man, and that reminded him of all he hadn't done, the writing he'd started and abandoned, unfinished, the roaming. Things were different with his brother Wil.

The thought of his brother was beginning to cloud his otherwise pleasant evening, so McGhee pushed those thoughts out, draining the rest of his beer in several long gulps. Either the brandy or the beer, or more likely both, were starting to have the desired effect. The slight buzz started to raise his mood: he noticed a thin sliver of moon in the sky to the west, just above the glow where the sun had set. He could see the rest of the disk, just barely visible as a slightly darker shade of blue than the surrounding sky. His reverie was broken by an emerging racket over his shoulder.

Luis and another boy were dragging a folding table around the house and yelling at each other, Luis in English, the other in Spanish. They stopped momentarily when they saw McGhee, then resumed their back and forth.

"Stop banging it, Manny," Luis said over his shoulder, who was leading the parade.

"Yo no soy," the other said. Luis came to a full stop and turned around to look at him.

"And stop picking your nose, *pendejo*," he said before resuming the task.

"Yo no soy," the boy said sniffling. He reached for his nose, but used his wrist to wipe it, as if that made a difference.

"And speak English . . . We've got company," Luis said, banging the table on the ground. The two set to extending the legs, but the smaller boy had difficulty with the first one.

Seeing his trouble, McGhee stood to help, but sat down again, his head spinning slowly. "Uh oh . . . ," he said.

The young boy, noticing McGhee's collapse, whispered to Luis: "El gringo se borracho."

Luis, glancing over at McGhee looked back at his brother. "Ninguna mierda, Sherlock."

Jaime wheeled around the corner, a glass of tea in one hand and a beer in his other. He handed the tea to McGhee before going over to the boys. With a flurry of Spanish, he helped extend the stuck leg and got the table upright. Luis ran back around the house, Manny trailing after him. A minute later, each boy emerged with two folding chairs, Manny dragging them as they were slightly too long for him to carry outright.

Watching the production made McGhee dizzy, so he turned back to watch the runway. In the distance, a small plane was taxiing to the far end of the tarmac, turning to face him. He could just barely hear it, a low hum wafting in and out on the breeze. He took a sip of the tea – just right, no sugar – and it seemed to immediately cool his brain. The tannins of the tea were strong, but not too strong, its light, clean earthiness a welcome counter to the hops of the Tecate. He took another drink, allowing it to wash his palate clear. In the distance he could hear the whine of the plane increase in pitch; it was still too far to see much of it, but it was coming directly at him. Moments later it was lifting from the tarmac, a duster heading to the fields. The wings were broad and light, dispensing tubes and spray nozzles visible as it flew directly over, banking west in a graceful arc. It didn't go very high before it dipped again, swooping low over another field just beyond a hedgerow and disappeared. He kept watching, rewarded in a few seconds as it swung up and out from the field, banking hard right to line up for another pass.

"I love that . . . ," Jaime said over his shoulder. "I thought living by the airport would suck, but I gotta say, I still love that . . . ." McGhee looked up at him. Jaime was staring after the plane, holding his hand over his eyes like a bill to get a slightly better view. "Ready to eat?" he asked McGhee.

"You just put the meat on . . . ," McGhee said.

"That was almost an hour ago, amigo . . . ," Jaime replied, snickering. The boys came in and said you were a little . . . you know, so I brought you the tea. Man . . . that brandy musta hit you hard."

Standing, McGhee found the spinning had gone. Looking at Jaime, he smiled sheepishly. "Sorry," he said, holding up the tea with a slight jiggle. "This is good."

Jaime walked over to him and slapped him on the back. "That's good, coz I got some killer tequila for later . . . ," he said, gently pushing him over toward the table. The kids were already seated, legs dangling for Manny and Cece, though Manny could touch his toes if he tried. Cece still had the doll and was talking to it. Jaime led him to the far end of the table where his wife was placing an armload of serving dishes. Looking up, she smiled and bowed her head slightly. He reached out to receive a bowl with each hand and placed them further along the table, before turning back to her.

"I'm McGhee . . . ," he said, extending his hand now that hers were free.

She looked at him, her smile warm but shy. "Ximena . . . ," she said, taking his hand softly. She held onto it a moment, flipping it over to look into his palm before slapping it and laughing. "That's it? McGhee?" she said, turning to head back into the kitchen. When he didn't follow immediately, she stopped and turned, placing her hand on her hip. "Well, come on, make yourself useful . . . ," she said. He looked at Jaime who shrugged.

"You heard the woman . . . ," he said. "I only work here."

Inside, it was a single room, like a studio apartment. Though it was small and five people lived there, it was tidy. Along the right side was a bunk bed, with a third level close to the ceiling, and the bottom level just above the floor. A boxed *Candyland* game sat on the lowest level with Matt the poor boy-doll on top. A ladder ran up the corner made of angle-iron with wood rungs. Luis's lacrosse helmet hung from the top bunk where the corner pole jutted up a few inches. Along the back wall was a double bed, neatly made with the corners tucked in navy-style. The Berber on the floor ended at the foot of the bed where linoleum began for the kitchen area. Ximena was at the cooktop, flipping tortillas in a skillet, one after the other, then loading them into a terracotta warmer. Dropping the lid over it with a rattle, she swept it off the counter and handed it to McGhee. "Here," she said. He grabbed it underneath, but quickly moved his hands to the flanges along the edge.

"It's hot," she said, looking at him and smiling, as if he were a stupid man. She stepped back to the stove, shaking her head. "Where did he find you, anyway?" she said, moving in to the sink to wash her hands, looking over her shoulder at him.

"Along 80," McGhee said. She kept looking at him but didn't say anything. "I ran out of gas," he continued, feeling further explanation was necessary. She still didn't say anything, but switched off the water and rubbed her hands on a small towel at her waist. Walking up to him, she stopped, looking up at him.

"He gave you some of that brandy, didn't he?" she said. She didn't need to hear an answer – she could read it in his face.

"It's OK," she said, walking back to the sink. "He's like that. Always picking up strays. Where ya from?" she said, opening the fridge for a plate of radishes and another covered with cucumbers and jicama. "I like 'em cold," she continued, not waiting for an answer. "Makes 'em crisper." In the corner by the refrigerator a half-table was jammed against the wall, and on it a large serving bowl, steaming. Suspending the plates above the bowl with two fingers, she picked up the bowl with the rest. "Let's go . . . ," she said. "I sure hope you like Pozole, coz that's what we're having. And cabrito. He always has to have some grilled meat. You see all those grills?" Breezing past him, Ximena nudged the door open with her elbow, waiting for McGhee to catch up. Just as he did, she let the door go with a bang against the warmer in his hand. "You gotta be faster, vato . . . ," she said, smiling over her shoulder.

Out at the table, Jaime was dismantling a rack of cabrito ribs onto a plate. Luis was picking at them, so Jaime alternated cutting at the ribs and swatting his son's hand away. It seemed like a familiar game: Luis timed his intrusions in the gaps between the swats, to Jaime's consternation, though it looked more like resignation with a touch of amusement. Manny was reading a book, his finger tracing out the words, and Cece was flying Barbie over her plate like a little kite. Once Ximena appeared, Luis yanked back his hand, Manny hid the book, and Barbie landed beside the little girl's leg on her seat. She was sitting on her knees so she could reach the table as she seemed to be making sure she was at least as high as Manny.

Once Ximena and McGhee had placed their loads on the table and taken seats, by some unseen command the whole crew lowered their heads, including McGhee, once he realized he was the only one not doing so. Jaime, without looking at him, said, "Luis, you wanna say grace?"

Luis instantly said, "Grace," and the crew awoke from their poses, grabbing spoons and plates and bowls and scooping the contents of each dish before passing them along, whether the next in line was ready or not. Jaime looked at McGhee: "Botanas?" Then, looking to Cece, he asked her to hand the cool plates to McGhee. "They go first," Jaime said by way of explanation, "though, as you can see, first doesn't matter much." Luis was pulling a third rib from the cabrito plate until he noticed his mother's cold stare and put it back. The table became quiet while Cece leaned up on the table, and carefully, with both hands, handed the plate of cucumbers and jicama to McGhee. He wasn't going to reach for it, but once he held it, he could smell the faint scent of lime rising from the pieces and they suddenly seemed more attractive to him. Taking two of each, he set to eating them – cool, and fresh and clean with a light lime flavor and salt, crunchy and satisfying, with a burst of light flavors.

"Wow . . . ," he said, surprising even himself, to which Ximena laughed. She handed him a bowl of Pozole. Fidgeting off his chair, Manny grabbed a couple corn tortillas and walked around his sister to McGhee.

"You gotta eat these with it, otherwise it's just soup . . . ," Manny said, holding them up, folded like a couple pieces of paper. Ximena smiled at him, then at McGhee, blushing.

"He's the good one . . . ," Jaime called from the other end of the table. Luis punched him on the shoulder while Ximena glared in his direction. Raising his palms in explanation, he resumed his eating, heads down, on his own bowl. Meanwhile, each time a dish reached Cece, she placed some on McGhee's plate before loading her own. She'd already placed two ribs there and some more tortillas.

McGhee thanked her but realized two eyes were on him, waiting. Manny wanted to see what he thought of the soup, though to McGhee's eye, with its thickness, it looked more like stew. Ripping his tortilla, he scooped up a cube of pork, some chilies and several kernels of hominy. The red broth dripped over the edge and, despite his best efforts, trickled down his chin as he jammed the loose mixture into his mouth. At once he had an explosion of flavor, savory and warm and chewy and hot.

"Wow . . . ," he said again, looking at Ximena, then at Manny: "You're right – I can't imagine it without the tortilla."

Gratified, Manny shook his head and set to eating his own bowl. "El gringo tiene sentido," Manny said, slurping his spoon. The table erupted in laughter, laughing even harder when Luis cuffed him on the back of the head, saying, "English, butthead . . . ."

Gnawing on the last of his ribs, McGhee thought to compliment Jaime on his skills. "This is the best barbecue I've ever had . . . ," he said, motioning with his chin toward Jaime. Jaime kept chewing, looking at McGhee.

"So you like goat then?" he asked casually, pausing to lick some sauce from his fingers.

McGhee's chewing came to a sudden stop, the table watching him. Tilting his head to the side, he began nodding slowing. "I guess I actually do . . . ," he said, resuming his chewing.

Jaime immediately collapsed into his chair, beside himself laughing. Luis held up a rib and went "Naa-aa," like a goat toward McGhee, further sending the rest into rounds of laughter.

It was dark by the time they finished, cleared the dishes, and stowed the table and chairs. McGhee was thinking it was about time to get back on the road, staring up at the sky. Orion already showed clearly, a smudge just visible below the belt. Jaime appeared beside him with a different idea, however, holding up a bottle of tequila in one hand, and two tall shot glasses in the other. McGhee protested, but Jaime insisted. "Just one . . . ," he said.

Jaime motioned over to the lawn chairs where they had sat earlier, plopping into one of them with a satisfied sigh. McGhee followed, strolling hands in pockets but didn't sit immediately, looking over the airport. Dark had settled, deep blue almost down to the hills where the faintest remnant of a light sky remained. He felt a tap at the hip and turned to see Jaime leaning out with his arm extended, a shot of tequila for him in his hand. Taking it, he saluted Jaime. "Thanks for an excellent meal . . . ," he said, tossing it back in one swing. It was smooth, growing in warmth as it slid down. Jaime raised his glass to him then followed suit.

Jaime let out a sigh, then motioned to the chair. "Take a load off, man . . . ," he said.

McGhee settled into the lawn chair with a squeak. Off to the east a few miles, the lights of Winnemucca twinkled pink and blue and white in the desert air. Despite the lateness of the season, the air remained tolerably warm, or perhaps the tequila was doing its job. He felt a sense of ease settle over himself, relaxing his shoulders; he was content to stare into the distance. Jaime offered him some more, but he shook his head. "I'm good," he said, tipping the glass again to drink the last drop, then dropped it carefully into the scrubby grass by his seat. Jaime put the bottle down and his glass, too, looking east as well.

"You looked like you could really use a ride . . . ," Jaime said, still looking east. "Sometimes, you just sense that about a guy. Like you'd worn your horse down and were gonna walk your way out of the desert."

McGhee looked at him. Jaime had a knowing look on his face, each arm on his chair, his hands dangling down. McGhee looked east again.

"My brother died yesterday . . . ," McGhee began. There was a long silence, but Jaime didn't break it. "I'm not sure how I feel about that. He wasn't supposed to die yet, but he did. We weren't on the best terms. He lived in Rawlins, so it was easy to grow apart, too . . . ."

"Rawlins . . . ?"

"Wyoming," McGhee said. Jaime shook his head and hunched up in his chair, elbows on his knees.

"How long since ya'd seen him?" he asked.

"Ten years," McGhee said, then reconsidered: "Twelve actually." He shuffled his feet on the ground. It was dusty where the aluminum of the chair had worn the thin grass away. His shoe slid through the dust, small pebbles underneath rolling with a small thunder beneath his sole.

"That's a long time," Jaime said finally. "Were ya mad at 'im?"

McGhee could tell the prospect of that bothered him, almost hurt him, and could see the slight anguish in his face, in the crow's feet by his eyes. "Sorta . . . ," McGhee said. "But not mad enough not to talk for twelve years, though. It just sort of happened."

Jaime leaned back again. "Yeah . . . I got a brother, too. Francisco. Cisco. We don't talk neither."

"He back in San Antonio?"

"Dunno," Jaime responded, shrugging. "Maybe, I guess. He was a guest of the state a while . . . up at CA Holliday. Always thought that name was . . . *ironic* . . . ."

McGhee looked at him. Jaime looked uncomfortable with the recollection, so he let it alone.

McGhee reached down for his shot glass, lightly tapping it on the aluminum arm of his chair. Jaime looked over, his eyes just red enough to see in the darkness. "I don't think one is gonna do it . . . ," he said, forcing Jaime to smile. He reached down to grab the bottle and his glass. Filling them both, Jaime kept the bottle in his lap. This time they sipped them.

"It's funny . . . ," McGhee said, sipping again. "When I was young, I wondered what it would be like to get old. I sure didn't think it'd be like this. I woulda thought I'd have figured it out by now . . . ."

Jaime smiled, raising his glass. "You got that right," Jaime said. He looked at McGhee, taking stock of him. Of the two, McGhee was the senior by perhaps twenty years, maybe twenty-five. His hair was more salt than pepper, but still some of the darker color remained, particularly along the edges of his short beard. His face showed the passage of time, but more in the expression of it than in tangible aging. His eyes had a weariness to them suggesting hardship or perhaps it was chronic sadness which had left something like a light frown imposed over a barely perceptible smile. It wasn't a smile of happiness either, but more a smile born of wisdom, or at least experience, a kind of acknowledgement of prevailing irony and his inescapable place in it.

In the distance, an eighteen-wheeler moved along I-80, the sound of its Jake brake reaching them on the lightly wafting breeze. They could see the running lights on it, though more wasn't visible from that distance.

"I always think of the road when I hear that . . . ," Jaime said. "Always have. Sometimes I think about getting on 80 and just heading east." He shrugged, taking another sip from his glass.

McGhee looked at him, then back toward the receding lights. "I was like that," he said. "Then I spent about thirty years doing it. Roaming. Now it's just a road, and I'm just a guy stuck on it. It's only romantic when you're looking out your window from home. Doesn't look the same through a windshield." McGhee leaned back in his chair, his tall glass between his hands, rolling slowly, warming from the heat of his palms. Looking skyward, he motioned toward it with his chin. "You see Orion there?" he asked. Jaime looked up and nodded. "And see that smudge below the belt?"

Jaime strained to see it, then looked to McGhee. "Sort of . . . ."

"Exactly," McGhee said, nodding. "Now try looking just to the right of the smudge. See it now?"

Jaime tried it, then smiled. "Better . . . I can see it better, anyway, not great though."

McGhee looked up again. "That's the Great Nebula of Orion. It's light years across and right in front of you, and you can hardly see it, until you're looking a little bit in the wrong direction. Life is like that . . . ," McGhee said, falling silent. He took another sip, but kept looking up. "At least for me it is."

Jaime looked down from the sky to look at McGhee. "Sounds pretty lonely . . . ," he said.

McGhee shrugged, looking back toward the airport and city lights in the distance. "Yeah," he said finally. "I've just never been comfortable wherever I am. Never. Always looked better over there . . . ," he said, motioning out into the dark.

"The airport?" Jaime said. McGhee looked at him and laughed. Jaime was glad for it and laughed himself.

"Yeah, the airport . . . ," McGhee said, holding out his glass for a refill. Jaime obliged, stuffing the cork back in the bottle afterward with a pleasing plug sound.

"My brother Les was never like that . . . ." McGhee continued. "Once he got out to Wyoming, he put down roots and never left. Never understood *how* he could do that. Had a wife, a kid, a spread – the whole nine yards."

"So you were jealous then?" Jaime asked.

McGhee looked over at him, then back out. "Naaa. Not really. It just seemed he didn't go far enough. Do enough. But maybe that's just me – just how I see things. Seemed to work for him." Headlights in the distance swept across their spot as a car turned into the airport, then continued a U-turn and became taillights heading back down the frontage road. "So maybe I was mad about that. Or maybe I was just annoyed that he mighta been right."

"Everybody's got their own road, man . . . ," Jaime said.

McGhee sighed. "Maybe. But seems I missed mine a while ago . . . ," he said. "Seems like every time I tried to get it going, I lost my way – too lazy to follow through, or maybe just too afraid of what I'd find if I did."

Ximena appeared by Jaime's shoulder, holding a sleeping bag. She kissed him on top of the head. "For your friend . . . ," she said, holding up the bag. Jaime looked over at McGhee.

"Hope you don't mind the hammock. Usually too cold this time of year, but tonight's s'posed to be pretty warm. I sleep there in the summertime most nights. I love the stars . . . ."

"Thank you, Ximena . . . ," McGhee said, raising his glass. "I wasn't looking forward to crashing in the car . . . ." She looked at Jaime, perplexed. He said something in Spanish and she smiled back at McGhee.

"Her English is good, but not quite that good . . . ," he said. Standing, Jaime stretched again. "I guess it's that time. I get going about six. I hope that's not too early for ya. We can get fuel at the *Gas-n-Go* before we head back to your car. I got a gas can . . . ."

McGhee rolled out the bag into the hammock, then checked Jaime's house window before slipping off his jeans and sliding into the bedroll. As he drifted off, he almost saw Orion's nebula straight on, but not quite.

∽∽∽

It was cool in the morning when he said good-bye to Jaime, next to his car. The sun wasn't up yet — the sky was just switching from black to the deepest blue. Steam rose from his coffee, and from Jaime's giant rubber-clad chrome travel mug. McGhee started his car, then stepped out, extending his hand. "I think you were right . . . ," he said to Jaime.

"'Bout what?" he said.

"I needed something other than gas. Thanks."

Jaime held onto his hand, covering it with his other. "There are a lot of good roads, McGhee. Don't worry so much about the one you're on. Now get out of here already . . . ."

Some miles down the road, when the sun had risen, he found himself thinking of the night before and the solace he'd found again in the company of strangers, and how they saved him. Opening the glove box, he pulled out a couple pages he found there and pen and tossed it onto the seat beside him; there was a stirring he might capture later if the mood was right.

Somewhere just west of Salt Lake the gas light came on, and this time, McGhee was sensible enough to obey it. Taking an exit for Tooele, he found gas at the end of the ramp at a Flying J. Stepping out he discovered he was stiff, either from the sitting or from the hammock, though he suspected the sitting because he had slept better in the hammock than he had in recent memory, and that, he suspected, may have involved the brandy or the beer or the Pozole or the tequila. Whatever the explanation, the evening brought a slight smile to his face, even if his back was complaining, and the smile, slight as it was, wasn't a familiar sensation. Across the lot, a family was pouring out of a place called *Earl's* which looked a lot like a *Denny's*, and it occurred to him, as if a revelation were required, that he was hungry.

From inside he could look down the highway he was about to drive, and he didn't look forward to it. Though he usually liked getting on the road and getting out, this was different. Usually others supplied the destination – projects or whatever – but this time the destination was his and he didn't like it. He didn't look forward to pulling into Rawlins, and he wasn't sure what kind of face to show to Clara Ann. He knew it wasn't nice, but he would have liked it better if she were the one in the box rather than his brother – she had a way of getting under his skin, without even trying. She seemed to know everyone in Rawlins and their secrets, and she told them like it was her duty to do so. It didn't matter if the listener were from out of town. And there was Les lying in that box, probably smiling because he'd finally get some rest from the incessant whispering. The thought almost brought another smile to McGhee's face, but he suppressed it. He let his dread of Rawlins subside as the miles of driving he'd already done came back into his head.

The drive reminded him of a McPhee book he'd read, almost back in his college days, about the geology of the road he was on – Interstate 80 – the whole way across the United States. He'd driven it many times now, but usually his destinations were demanding his attention, or something else was. This time was different. He was seeing the scrub grass and tumble weeds of the basins, he was feeling the climbs of the ranges, over and over, in a slow cycle from basin to range, basin to range, like slow waves of America washing over him. And he realized each of those exits along the road was home to people who had settled in their riffles like so much gold dust. He felt like the tailings that never settled, though, moving through the machine to spill on the pile of rocks at the end. Still, it felt better to see it than not see it at all, and it offered some comfort to have a mental model for it.

The waitress slipped a cup of coffee under his chin which had slumped onto his palms, which in turn had pushed his tired elbows apart on the table. He looked up at her for explanation.

"Looked like ya could use it, hun . . . ," she said, pulling a pencil from behind her ear and folding back pages on her pad. "You need to look at the menu?"

He looked up at her, leaning back into the bench of the booth. "I don't know if I should have breakfast or lunch," he said.

She shifted her weight to the other foot and chewed her gum a few times. "It's *Denny's*, hun. It doesn't matter."

McGhee swung his head to look out the window, then back at her. "I thought it was *Earl's?*" McGhee said.

Her head was tilted and she was looking back down on him. "Used ta be a *Denny's*," she said, chewing her gum for emphasis.

A short, dumpy man in a short-sleeved white shirt and carrying a pad came up behind her and gently put his hand on her shoulder. "I'll take it, Deb . . . ," he said. Shrugging, she pushed off before McGhee could say anything.

"Mind if I join you?" the man said, sliding into the booth across from McGhee without waiting for a response. McGhee looked at him, then grabbed the metal creamer and spilled some into his coffee.

"I must look awful," McGhee said. "This happened to me yesterday, too . . . ."

"Earl Hobbs . . . ," the man said laughing, extending his hand across the table. "I'm the manager."

"Uh oh . . . ," McGhee said, shaking his hand. "Am I in trouble?"

Earl shook his head. "No, no, no – not at all. Maybe you just have one of those faces. I saw you come in and thought I'd sit with you. I like to sit with a customer now and then. Long as they don't mind . . . ?" His voice went up with the question, and he held his palms out. McGhee motioned it was fine, so Earl settled onto his elbows.

"You come in from 80 I bet . . . ," Earl said. "Oh, wait . . . ," he interrupted himself, motioning for Deb to return. "Have Armando make him one of his special scrambles. You know, the steak one . . . ."

Scribbling on the pad, she clicked off her pen. "Sure thing, boss . . . ," she said, retreating to the wait station to key in the order.

"It's kinda like breakfast and lunch mixed together . . . ," he said to McGhee. He fidgeted with a sugar packet. He didn't have much hair left on his head, and what was there was white. He had a friendly face with wrinkles upon wrinkles and loose skin, collecting as jowls, then flowing under his chin like a rabbit's dewlap. His ears were big and meaty, matching his nose, which had continued to grow long after the rest of him tapped out. "So you heading far?" he asked.

"Rawlins . . . ," McGhee answered as he was moving his cup to his lips. It was very hot, so after a careful sip, he added, "Wyoming." By way of recognition, Earl nodded his head and frowned.

"I been there . . . ," he said, his nod converting to something of a shake. "Long time ago, though. Speckt it's changed since then. Musta been about '79 or so – hard to believe that's fifty years. Not much goin' there as I recall. No offense . . . ."

McGhee smirked, blowing on his coffee. "None taken. My brother lives there . . . ," he said, then after a few seconds, corrected himself. "He lived there. He died Wednesday," he volunteered, a bit surprised he had done so. He had taken a vow of silence on the subject about a hundred miles back on the road in his inner dialog, but it didn't last long. Earl became a little more stoic, still slowly bending the packet in his hands.

"That's tough. You guys close?" he asked.

McGhee twisted his cup in his saucer, then twisted it again. "Not really," he said, looking up at Earl. Earl was nodding and shaking again.

"My brothers are all dead," he said. Looking up for Deb, he motioned to McGhee's cup and held up two fingers and pointed at himself. "I'm the last one left," he said. "Got a sister, though," he continued. "If there's one thing we LDS do well is procreate." He pointed at the black name badge on his shirt. It said *Elder Hobbs* on it, and he was half smiling. "One of the kids made it up for me. Kinda a joke. I always stuck with the white shirts. I was Elder Hobbs about the same time I hit Rawlins."

McGhee didn't seem to be following, so Earl continued. "I did my mission out there. Was kinda hoping for Paris."

Recognition appeared on McGhee's brow and he smiled. "Oh . . . ," he said, taking another sip of his coffee. Something in his tone got Earl to lean in.

"Don't worry," he said, "I won't baptize you with that coffee or anything . . . ," he said, smiling broadly. "The older I get, the more I leave people alone . . . ," he said. McGhee looked at him, a smile curved up on one side. "Mostly," Earl said.

Deb arrived with the scramble for McGhee, and a cup for Earl. She poured from an orange-covered carafe up to the top of the cup. "Thanks, Deb . . . ," he said, looking up at her and moving the cup in front of him. McGhee set to shoveling the egg, steak and potato mixture, leaning it to improve the yield with his fork. Earl started dumping sugar in his cup like he wouldn't stop, halted when he noticed McGhee's gaze, then poured a little more before putting it back.

Earl sat looking out the window while McGhee ate, watching the cars zoom along 80 in the distance. "Nice day for driving . . . ," he said, turning back to McGhee.

McGhee looked out the window, too. "I guess . . . ," he said, then relented seeing Earl's interest. "Better than the last time I drove this stretch anyway," he said, loading another forkful in his mouth. "It was snowing like mad then . . . . Got stuck in Salt Lake."

Earl nodded. "Better there than up in the mountains." Earl stopped talking, but seemed to have something on his mind. He took to fidgeting with another sugar packet.

"What?" McGhee asked through a mouthful of scramble. Earl fidgeted in his seat.

"Well . . . ," Earl began. "So . . . you ever write a eulogy?" he asked, looking McGhee in the eye suddenly.

McGhee pushed the bolus of food down his throat and set his fork on his plate. "Why?" he asked, some wariness entering his voice.

"Well . . . ," Earl began, messing with the packet again. "I gotta write a eulogy for a close friend . . . . Since you mentioned your brother . . . ," Earl explained, trailing off to silence. McGhee picked up his napkin, cleaned the corners of his mouth and shifted in his seat, looking at Earl. McGhee put both of hands on the edge of the table.

"Look, Earl . . . ," he began, but the words escaped him. Earl's bushy white eyebrows were furrowed, and he looked rather uncomfortable. McGhee's shoulders went slack and he looked back to his plate, lifting the fork again. "Don't you have someone else who could help? You don't even know me – hell, I don't even know the guy . . . ."

McGhee was talking himself out of the job, but Earl kept up his gaze. Something about its sadness caught McGhee's attention – the look of sudden mortality and the reality that went with it – and he instantly understood there was no friend after all. When the truth of the matter dawned on McGhee, he dropped his fork on his plate. In the next booth over, a trucker turned his head slightly at the noise, but knew enough to mind his own business.

McGhee leaned in, staring back into Earl's gaze. "You've *got* to be kidding . . . . Don't ya have some family?" Earl shook his head, continuing his stare. "Some friends?" Earl shrugged, shaking his head some more. "Church?"

Earl finally lowered his gaze, resuming his slow tumble of the sugar packet. "I don't want that . . . ," he said, his voice low and quiet.

McGhee leaned back in his seat, placing his hands behind his head, then folded his elbows beside his temples, closing his eyes.

"So what is it?" he said from between his arms, low, like Earl's voice was.

"I got the cancer . . . ," he said, not looking up. "Pancreas." McGhee opened his eyes and lowered his arms. Earl was still staring at the packet. "I don't want to write my own, and I don't want some random church fool writing it neither . . . . They don't know me from Aaron."

McGhee couldn't help being incredulous. "But I'm a total *stranger* . . . ," he said, leaning in again.

Earl looked up, finally, smiling weakly. "I kinda like the sound of that. I've spent most of the last fifty years in the company of strangers . . . right here," he said, motioning around the restaurant. McGhee looked over toward the counter where seat after seat was occupied by loners who wandered in from the road. "Strangers *are* my people . . . ," Earl said. "Started as a dish-worsher," he said, his accent coming out. "Got to manager five years after that. Bought the damn place ten years back. They were gonna close it down, so I just bought it. Most of these folks don't have any place else to go. Leaving the whole damn thing to a trust so it'll just go on when I'm gone. Like a train on a big round track." Earl brightened, nodding to McGhee's plate. "'Sides, I'll throw in lunch . . . ," he said, laughing quietly.

"All right, all right . . . ," McGhee said finally, raising his palms in surrender.

Earl smiled, lifting the pad from the bench next to him. Taking a pen from his pocket, he clicked the end before dropping it onto the paper. Sliding the pad across, Earl smiled at McGhee. "OK, it should go something like this . . . ."

The big highway sign west of Rawlins said, "Caution: Windy Conditions," but McGhee didn't need a sign to tell him that; though he had a midsize Subaru, he was getting blown all over the road, and he was just glad he wasn't in something bigger. The trucks were circling the wagons, riding in convoys of six or eight, and actually driving under the speed limit and staying out of the fast lane. For his part, it made the driving a bit more challenging, and hence interesting, and further, less sleep-inducing than the relentless sun he had had overhead since well before Salt Lake. He did miss the more temperate air there, however, since it dropped from sixty at noon, to only thirty-four as he was pulling in.

He had forgotten what the approach to Rawlins was like, and as he cut through the small hills just west of town, he was hoping for something of a reveal but was disappointed. More high-plains scrub grass, a few signs, and a steel pre-fab building in the distance. It reminded him of his first impression years before, a prevailing question of *why here?* Still, he was trying to suppress his impulse to form negative sentiments and relax. Then again, any place that has a prison as a historical site isn't exactly putting its best foot forward. Relaxing wasn't his usual MO, but he figured the next twenty-four hours would be stressful enough. He had planned to get to town yesterday, but was glad for the diversions and rather relished arriving late. Les would be in the ground in the morning, and he'd be seeing all the scenery in reverse soon thereafter.

There was, of course, a standing invitation for McGhee to stay at his brother's house, but he'd no sooner do that than sing in public. No, the *Sunset Motel* on West Pine was more to his liking. Quiet, industrial, and with not the remotest possibility of running into a relative or teary grieving friend. He pulled into the lot, signed in at the office and went to his room before any thought of going to the house. In one motion he stripped the spread off the bed, spun it like cotton candy into a ball around his arms and tossed it into the corner: the stories of bedspread filth had taught him that lesson long ago. And like a tree, he collapsed corner to corner across the mattress nearly instantly asleep, even though it was only four o'clock in the afternoon.

McGhee wasn't asleep long – perhaps an hour – before something forced him awake, sweating. He was having one of his usual dreams in which he was late for class or something important, and once again he was about to screw it up. The sensation of impending shame propelled him toward consciousness, though he remained disoriented. The room was dark, and when looked out the window, the sky wasn't much lighter. Momentarily he wasn't sure where he was – the denatured white walls and generic furniture could have placed him anywhere in his travels – leaving him adrift in years of roaming, but like a light mist, recollection fell upon him, and with it a vague sadness.

Glancing at his wrist, he saw it was only five thirty, so it wasn't such a disaster after all. He couldn't avoid the inevitable any longer, so after brushing his teeth (he had no paste) and splashing his face, he grabbed the jacket out of his bag, the only other thing he had remembered to bring. A disturbing wrinkle ran down the right front, through the lapel and down to the pocket, like a fault line through otherwise decent wool. Moistening his hand in the hot water, he tried pressing out the wrinkle with his palms running up and down the line, one inside, one out. After a few passes, the spasm of the wrinkle seemed to be easing and he judged it good enough.

It had been a long time since he had been in Rawlins, but he still knew the way. McGhee was sure to stay on the opposite side of town, small at it was. Still, he was able to find his way to the end of

Darnley Road, then down the dirt road without a name for another mile to where his brother had his spread. He had fifteen acres of prime scrub all his own, with a little ranch-style house on the corner and a little barn near it for the stuff he needed to run the operation. McGhee smiled to himself as the word "operation" occurred to him – that was Les's word for it. Really, he had a couple horses and chickens, and otherwise the place was a wasteland. Behind the barn sat three cars, the entirety of Les's automotive history, and one school bus with weeds growing through the block that he'd gotten from god-knows-where for god-knows-what reason, only it seemed to fit with the godforsaken landscape. Such was McGhee's recollection, but he couldn't see most of that when his headlights swept into the yard. He stopped at the end of the drive for a moment, the dust cloud following his car catching him ten seconds later, obscuring the little he could see in the dark. The porch light was on, and there was an old late nineties Ford pickup poking half way out of the garage, but otherwise, no activity. Pulling in behind the pickup, he shut off the engine.

The metal storm door on the front squeaked open momentarily, then shut again. He could hear a young man's voice say, "Mom, he's here." McGhee waited a moment, wondering if Clara Ann would stick her head out, too, but she didn't.

Even though there was a doorbell by the door, he wrapped his knuckles on the metal, which set the thing buzzing when the aluminum filigree inset began to vibrate. A tall, thin young man came from the recesses of the house and popped the door open. He looked sad, but his gaze brightened. "Uncle Fran!" he said, stepping out, and wrapping his arms around his shoulders.

"Mikey?" McGhee said, unsure of himself, because he didn't quite recognize the young man hugging him, though he looked familiar, as if from distant memory.

"Mike," he said, "I'm Mike now, but yeah . . . ." He leaned back to look at McGhee. To McGhee's eyes, however, he was Les at twenty, and despite his attempts to anticipate what this moment might be like and steel himself against it, he was speechless. Mike read his gaze and smirked. "Yeah, everyone says I look like Dad."

"Yeah . . . ," McGhee managed to get out, but he was stuck looking at him. In the background he heard Clara Ann approaching, something he never thought he'd appreciate until that very moment, for staring at the young Les was unnerving to McGhee. He didn't even realize he was shaking his hand, and had continued to hold onto it. Clara Ann patted her son on the shoulder, then hip checked him out of the way.

"All right, Fran, my turn . . . ," she said, putting her arms around him and hugging him close, and patting him on the back lightly. She put her head against his chest, the top of her hair coming up to his chin. She looked up at him and they gazed at one another in silence.

Her hair was different than he remembered, straight, light brown or maybe a little dirty blond. She was older, and the skin of her face was weathered, though she still had a patch of freckles across her nose and cheeks. He was struck, however, by the look in her eyes, which like her hair were hard to describe: somewhere between blue and green and hazel, though the net effect was pleasing. But it wasn't the color that struck him, but the look of them in the corners. Where he had known (or thought he knew) an insipid woman, wisdom had collected adding a touch of humor and sadness. She smiled.

"You look tired . . . ," she said, patting him on the chest. "Come on in and I'll fix you a plate."

Clara Ann disappeared around a corner into the kitchen; Mike motioned to a spot on an ancient leather couch by the wall next to a little corner table with a Craftsman style lamp, a warm tortoise shade glowing above a wood base. The table itself was mission style. Elsewhere there was dark wood paneling, owing to the vintage of the house, but across from the couch a river-rock hearth surrounded a broad fireplace. He remembered when Les put it in twenty years back, and the struggle he had removing the seventies-style façade that had been there. It had become an old fireplace in the interim, seeing many fires, including the one glowing mostly in embers at that moment. Those stylistic touches reminded McGhee of his brother, and as he plopped into the seat with a satisfying poof, the net sensation of being in his brother's place brought a lump to his throat.

In the distance he heard a door slam and the beeps of a microwave moments before its hum. Above the mantle on the wall was a painting of a lake in a dark frame. It seemed to fit the décor, and he continued scanning, until he remembered the picture. Looking back to it, he suddenly recalled painting it, though he had no idea where it had gone after he did so, or that Les had kept it. It was an odd sensation to him – seeing the painting, forming an opinion of it, then realizing it was actually his. His impulse, upon realizing it was his, was to discount it, but given this sequence of events, he was forced to acknowledge it was probably better than that. He was also surprised Les would hang it, let alone in his living room. From his recollection, Les never seemed to get that part of him, or at least McGhee didn't think so.

Mike was watching his uncle assimilate the room, sitting in a leather cigar chair off to the side. Once McGhee sensed his gaze, he looked at his nephew.

"You still paint, Uncle Fran?" he asked. McGhee looked at him, still struck by the resemblance to his brother. He was a little lanky, but substantial. Dark hair swept across his forehead, and he had handsome, angular features. He had the Adam's apple of a young man, and a thin beard across his chin and early mustache. His red and white flannel shirt was unbuttoned down to his waist, a navy T-shirt underneath, jeans below with hems worn ragged by his heels where they must have dragged.

"Naaa . . . ," McGhee said finally, scrunching up his lips. "Not in a long time."

Mike kept watching him, his arms stretched out along the arms of the chair, hands dangling. "So, how does that happen?" Mike said.

McGhee leaned back in the couch, the leather adjusting with a soft squeal. "What do you mean?" he asked, stalling for time. He was wondering how one explains aging to a kid, only nothing was forming in his head.

"I mean . . . ," Mike began, "one day you're painting, and the next you're not. It's the last one. Did you know it was the last one? Did you *decide* to stop?" His earnestness was disarming and warm at the same time. Lucky for McGhee Clara Ann came in with a plate in one hand, utensils wrapped in a napkin in the other.

"Mike, clear a space for your uncle on the coffee table so he can eat. And quit with the questions already – he just drove like a million miles to get here . . . ."

Mike obliged, sliding the material on the table into a pile: *Scientific American*, an Ansel Adams issue of *Photography*, an exploded copy of the Sunday *NY Times*, sections strewn about with the book review folded back to an article. "There ya go, Unc," he said, plopping back into his chair, the cushions huffing with his weight, slight as it was. Clara set the plate in front of him, then pulled up an oak rocker from in front of the fire.

McGhee looked at the plate, and it appeared safe enough: a couple slices of prime rib with a dab of horseradish on the side, a pile of mashed potatoes with gravy, and some kind of slaw of cabbage, carrots and cranberries, not too moist with dressing. He had to admit it looked good, and the knot in his stomach was responding to the stimulus whether he wanted it to or not. Leaning in, he unfurled the napkin and silverware, breathing in the aroma from the plate. He smiled slightly, to which Clara Ann clapped her hands lightly.

"High praise from Fran," she said, looking over at her son, then back to McGhee. She watched him as he started chewing on a piece of the beef. His enjoyment was clear, and her pleasure at it was obvious.

"I was a little surprised you didn't fly . . . ," she said. "That's a hell of a drive. Kinda pretty, though, if you like desert and geology. Les always liked that . . . ," she said, bringing the conversation back to her dead husband. Mike sniffled a little bit at mention of his dad. McGhee noticed the rims of his eyes were a bit red, though the sniffle was the only other outward sign of grieving from his nephew.

McGhee looked at his sister in-law sitting in the chair. It had been Les's. He knew that to be the case because he had given it to him fifteen years before. He'd been passing through – probably the last time he did – and they went to some sort of rummage sale. Les was looking for tools, and McGhee came upon the rocker, tucked back in the corner and stacked with a couple boxes of glassware: Ball jars, pickle jars, ash trays and the like. It didn't even have a label on it, but he got the owner down to a decent price anyway. It turned out it was some sort of estate sale. The owner's kids were running it as the old man had just moved into assisted living on the far side of town. At the time the irony of the sale couldn't be apparent to McGhee, but in this moment, it was. It reminded him of the rift he had with his brother, and his ensuing ambivalence.

Clara Ann saw his brow darken and seemed to know his thoughts. Looking over at Mike, she struck her parental pose. "What?" he asked automatically.

"Can you get that VSOP of your dad's and a couple glasses?" Mike disappeared around the corner, toward the other end of the house where Les's den was.

"You mean the Courvoisier?" he called out from the distance.

Craning her neck, she paused a moment, listening until the remote rustling stopped. "Yeah – the green bottle. It's about half full I think . . . ."

She looked back at McGhee, already half way through his plate. "I figured you could use a drink . . . ," she said. "And far be it from me not to join you." Her smile was weak but genuine. For his part, he couldn't help but being surprised by her, and it made him wonder if it was just another case where he had written off someone without sufficient consideration, or just by mistake. The older he got, the more often he realized his snap judgments might be in error, or just the notion of judging at all, wrongheaded.

Mike winged around the corner, a green bottle in one hand, three whiskey glasses trapped between in his fingers in the other. When he saw his mother's gaze, he was ready. "What?" he said, though it was clearly less of a question than a statement of moral authority. He set the glasses down and uncorked the bottle with a thwig, pouring a finger's worth into each.

"You see what I have to deal with?" Clara Ann said, looking at McGhee. Her displeasure was feigned, and it made McGhee smile. Clara Ann smiled, too. "Now that's what I like to see, Fran . . . ," she said, leaning back for a couple rocks in her chair.

McGhee pushed his plate aside, grabbing two of the glasses. He handed one to Clara Ann, and to Mike's delight, the other to him. He raised it to his mother in mock toast.

"Already colluding . . . ," she said, laughing.

"I think I should get to have *one* drink with my nephew, Clara Ann . . . ," McGhee said, toasting both of them. "How old are you now, anyway?" he asked Mike.

"Twenty next week . . . ," he answered, his nose in the glass, sniffing the cognac.

"Close enough . . . ," McGhee said, officially raising his glass. "To Les . . . ."

Clara Ann and Mike each obliged with their glasses, then took sips. McGhee tipped his glass the whole way back, holding it in his mouth a moment to feel the warmth build before sending it down. It reminded him of a similar drink out in the dark of the Yukon years before, but he kept the recollection to himself.

"All right, *Unc!*" his nephew said, smiling over at his mom.

"Michael . . . ," Clara Ann said, tilting her head in disapproval. His enthusiasm drained immediately, but he maintained a surreptitious smirk. The entire interaction amused McGhee and he leaned back into the leather.

"I once read a letter . . . ," Clara Ann said, taking another sip of her glass, "sent from a young man in Alaska. Something about *the love of one brother for another.* Very touching, that letter . . . ."

McGhee was looking at her, the glow of the VSOP building slowly in his stomach like a little campfire. "He kept that?" he said, pushing his empty glass back toward Mike. Unplugging the bottle again, he refilled his uncle's glass dutifully. Then he poured another dash into his own glass before replacing the cork.

"Michael . . . ," his mother said again. "I taught you better than that," she said, pausing a moment, before extending her glass in his direction. "Don't forget your mamma . . . ." Mike unplugged the bottle again, delighted to indulge her. Looking back at McGhee, she smiled again. Reaching into the gaping pocket of her sweater, she pulled out a couple notebook pages, folding into a neat quarter square. "Yeah, he kept it . . . ," she said. Leaning forward, she held it by a corner, extending it as far as she could to McGhee.

Accepting the pages, McGhee inspected it. Slight coffee stains adorned the back, and the thin red margin line was disrupted where some water had smudged it. Despite the age of it, it still didn't lie quite flat, the fold defiantly springing the corners apart an inch. The paper had yellowed and aged, but otherwise had remained intact. He unfolded it and began to look at the words he had penned more than forty years before.

"He kept that in his vest pocket . . . ," Clara Ann said proudly. "One time or another he showed most people who flowed through *The Pie Tin*."

McGhee looked up. "The *Pie Tin?*"

"Our coffee shop," Mike volunteered.

"Got it about a dozen years back . . . ," Clara Ann said. "Spent most of his time down there, during the days anyway . . . ."

"Other side of town . . . ," Mike said. "Across from the *No-Tell Motel*." His mother looked at him again, though his smirk remained.

"I never figured Les for that line of work . . . ," McGhee said, looking between them.

"Oh *yeah* . . . ," Clara Ann said, her brows accentuating her words. "He *loved* it. Ever since Lulu threw him and he hurt his back, he had to find something less physical to do . . . ."

"That horse was such an a-hole . . . ," Michael said.

"*Michael* . . . ," Clara Ann said, rolling her eyes at him.

McGhee was quiet a moment, processing. He had another sip, then set the glass down. "I guess I missed a lot."

Clara Ann nodded sympathetically. "Yeah," she said. She pulled her legs under her on the chair, and wrapped her sweater closer. "You know . . . ," she continued, "that's what he did with the money . . . ."

McGhee picked up his glass again, leaning back into the couch. As he sipped, he stretched his arm along the back of the cushion and crossed his legs. "I always wondered what he did with it. Wondered *why* we had to sell . . . ." He took a long slow swig from his glass holding onto it in his mouth before swallowing. "I was pretty mad at him for that. Wil didn't want to sell either."

Clara Ann nodded. "Yeah, I know. Les did, too."

"Sell what?" Mike said. He leaned forward to drag his chair closer into the circle. He didn't want to miss anything, and as they were discussing ancient family history, he wanted to hear all of it. Once he settled in again, he looked between them, back and forth. "Sell what?" he asked again.

Clara Ann raised her glass at McGhee. "It was your house," she said. "You tell it."

McGhee looked at Mike, struck again by the look of him. "You're a dead ringer for your dad," he said.

"Yeah, I know," he said. "Sell what?" His mother frowned at him, tilting her head.

Resigned, McGhee shrugged. "Our mom's house," he said finally. "She'd moved into assisted living. It was the house I grew up in – we all did. We didn't *need* to sell it yet. She had enough money from Dad . . . ," he said, then clarified: "Your granddad – to live there at Winter Haven a couple years yet."

"But then she died . . . ," Clara Ann interjected. At once she realized she shouldn't interrupt, holding up her hands and mouthing *sorry*.

"That's right . . . ," McGhee acknowledged, shrugging again. "She died. So I guess it didn't really matter, did it?" McGhee's eyes met Clara Ann's, and she tilted her head. Her eyes appeared watery and she nodded, but said nothing. "Somehow it mattered to me, though . . . ," McGhee said, finishing his glass. He slid it slowly toward the bottle. Mike quietly refilled it, then offered more to his mother.

She shook her head. "You guys drink faster than me."

McGhee pulled his glass close but didn't drink it. "I don't know why it mattered to me so much. It wasn't like I was gonna move back there and live. Wil neither, though I think he was mostly going along with me because I wanted it so bad. He was always supportive of my sentimentality. Where is he, anyway?" McGhee said, turning back to Clara Ann.

"Left about an hour ago. Had a 6:00 a.m. from back east, so he was pretty whipped. He'll be back in the morning."

"How'd he look?" McGhee said, turning to Mike.

"Old," Mike said immediately.

Clara Ann picked up a pillow lying next to her rocker and threw it at him, hitting him square on the head. "Michael!" she said.

"No, wait . . . ," Mike said, leaning forward. His hands were fully extended, fingers apart, like he was trying to grasp a ball that wouldn't come into focus. McGhee saw the youth of his fingers, of the gesture, of the grappling instinct. Looking over at Clara Ann, she smiled at him. She saw the same things when she looked at Mike, though she kept it to herself.

"So you and dad didn't speak all those years because of *that?*"

McGhee nodded his head. "Yeah, that, and other things I suppose. You might have wondered how he would have gotten the money out. Turns out he talked Grandma into giving him his share . . . ."

Clara Ann cocked her head. "Well . . . ," she began, "it wasn't *exactly* like that," she objected. "He was telling her about his plans, when he got the money to do it, and she offered."

McGhee shifted his pose, pulling his arms in, elbows on knees. "She was out of her mind," he pushed back. Clara Ann shrugged, cradling her glass in her hands. "I told Les to wait," she said. "I just want to give him a fair shake."

McGhee looked at her. She seemed so much more reasonable than he remembered, and he liked the new version of her. Looking around the room, McGhee saw Les everywhere. The dark hardwood floors were his — broad boards, a little old fashioned. Sconces on the walls with little Western sculptures: a cowboy roping a calf, a chuck wagon, a calf sheltering under a heifer. A narrow wall near the kitchen had a long, thin Navajo weave in taupe, brown, burnt orange, and oxblood red. In between the decorations, the walls were an off-white, setting off the dark wood trim which he put in himself. McGhee never had the talent for that kind of work, and he wondered where his brother had picked it up. Everything in the room tied together with nice touches, comfortable. As he drank it in, his shoulders relaxed. There was no point in re-litigating those events, and further, his certainty had waned over the years. He was experiencing an unexpected communion with his brother, perhaps facilitated by the brandy, or Mike, or Clara Ann, or all of it.

Looking at his watch, he saw it was getting late. "We have a big day tomorrow . . . ," he said, rising to go. As soon as he was up, though, his head was swimming and he sat down again, steadying himself against the arm of the couch.

"Mike, why don't you get that fuzzy blanket from the hall . . . ," Clara Ann said, grabbing another throw pillow and leaning over toward McGhee. She tucked it into the opposite corner from where he sat and patted him on the shoulder. "You've had a long day . . . ."

He nodded, tipping over toward the pillow and pulling his feet nearly onto the sofa. He wasn't sure if it was lack of energy, or awareness he still had his loafers on, but his feet remained dangling over the edge. Clara Ann caught his legs under one arm while she slipped off his shoes with her free hand, spilling his legs onto the leather. He shifted his position on the cushions, and they adjusted with him, huffing out their air to accommodate his body. His eyes were closed as he nestled his head into the pillow. The yarn of it was a little rough, but he liked the feel of it, a sigh escaping him as he settled in.

Mike returned with the blanket, spreading it over him. It was alpaca, with a South American design, instantly warm and cozy.

"Good night, Uncle Fran," Mike said, snapping off the light. As he retreated, he wasn't sure, but he thought he thought he heard his uncle whisper, "Goodnight, Les."

Around eight the next morning the house started buzzing with activity, making further sleep impossible. Sitting up suddenly, it took a moment for McGhee to get his bearings. On the coffee table was a large glass of water – a thoughtful anticipation of his state – and he grabbed it thankfully, downing it in straight gulps. He was still getting his head straight when he realized someone was sitting in the chair where Mike had sat the night before. The man leaned out of the shadow, the scant light from the kitchen illuminating half his face. "Francis . . . ," he said.

McGhee didn't need the light to know it was Wil. Even before he leaned forward, or spoke his name, he suspected it was him. Ever since he was little he knew when Wil was in the room, even when he was quiet. Though Wil was eight years older, he seemed to look younger to McGhee. He had the gray in the temples, and a few lines in the corners of his eyes. His body was noticeably older, too, not having the buoyant suspension of a younger man any longer, but still something in his aspect lent him youth, at least relatively. He certainly looked younger than McGhee felt at that moment.

"I woulda stayed later if I knew you were coming in . . . ," Wil said, a slight hint of reproach hiding in his sentiment. It brought back the recollection of previous conversations – he had always been like that. His words always seemed to be slipping between two meanings, or have a hidden footing. It happened too often to be coincidence, but he'd learned to expect it, accept it, and some-times, even enjoy the ambiguity of it.

"I wasn't sure myself," McGhee parried, standing slowly, then walking over to his brother. He extended his hand and it was met warmly as he stood to hug him. "How did ya hear?" Wil asked him.

"Clara Ann called me. Day before yesterday. Seems like a long time ago already . . . ," McGhee said, settling back into the couch.

Wil lifted a cup and saucer from the floor next to the chair – its table remained near the fireplace from where Mike had dragged it. "She still makes good coffee . . . ," Wil said, having a sip. On cue, Clara Ann wheeled into the room with another cup.

"There ya go . . . ," she said, landing it with a rattle in front of McGhee. "Still just cream, right?" she said, but didn't wait for an answer. She knew the McGhee boys, and there was no need for such updates once a person knew them. She was gone before he even thought to thank her.

Once she was out of earshot, McGhee motioned toward her wake. "She like you remember?" he asked, taking a sip. It was scalding hot, but good, so he had another.

"Substantially . . . ," Wil said, smiling. "A little calmer maybe." He had a sip from his cup, replacing it in his saucer to avoid any rattle. He'd always been like that — careful to avoid extraneous noise — and it was something McGhee appreciated, largely doing the same. His brothers were older enough that it was almost like having extra parents around when he was a kid, so much of his sensibility came from them.

"So he was at the shop, I guess . . . ," Wil said, setting the saucer in his lap. He had his legs crossed, so he had to adjust the saucer to lay flat.

"Yeah, I never got the story actually. Forgot to ask Clara Ann when she called. Just jumped in the car and started driving . . . ."

"And you don't have your phone, apparently . . . ," Wil said, slipping his from the pocket of his jacket and wiggling it between his thumb and forefinger. "I called you, like, ten times . . . ."

There it was again — that tone — but it was more familiar than annoying to McGhee. It made him smile to think of it, goading Wil to continue.

"What?" Wil said, smiling himself. "You're more aloof than ever . . . ." Watching McGhee, he paused to lift his cup, but didn't drink. He seemed to expect some comeback, but lacking that, he finally raised the cup to his lips.

"Dead . . . ," McGhee said, slapping his phone onto the table with a little too much force. Alarmed, Clara Ann looked around the corner. "You guys fighting in here?" she asked. Her tone was just right — a mix of amusement and cynicism — something they both sensed was more an imprint of Les upon her than her natural tendency.

"Naaaa . . . ," Wil said. "Fran was just demonstrating why his phone doesn't work — it tends to land hard," he said, smiling into his coffee cup.

"Actually . . . ," McGhee said, by way of defense, "I left the charger at home. Died before I got out of California and didn't get around to getting one on the way." Looking over at Wil, he shrugged. "Sorry. I should have called you." Wil was satisfied, this time slurping his coffee as he sipped it.

"No worries . . . ," he said. "I'm guessing you just wanted to be alone. Wendy gave me a wide berth, too. You were the only one I reached out to, though . . . ," he said. There was a loneliness in his voice, prevailing over the reproach. Clara Ann disappeared again around the corner, and the brothers stared at one another. Leaning forward, Wil put the cup on the ground again, leaning with his elbows on his knees.

"So he was at the coffee shop, pretty early I guess. Busboy came in around seven and found him slumped over the register holding a roll of quarters. Musta been pretty quick. His nitro was still in his pocket."

McGhee lowered his head. "Something else I didn't know . . . ," he said.

From around the corner, McGhee heard Clara Ann's voice call to him: "Maybe you should freshen up, Fran. We gotta get going in about twenty . . . ."

In front of the basin, McGhee let the water run until it was hot, then splashed it into his face, then did it again, and again. Looking at himself, he saw the water dripping from his eyebrows, the edges of his gray hair, and the ends of his thin, mixed beard. It was less a beard than a lack of shaving, but it had always been that way. His eyes were red around the edges, and he looked tired. He wondered how many times his brother had done the same thing, and what he was thinking Wednesday, the morning he died. The stubble was working its way down his neck, getting scratchy, so he opened the cabinet behind the mirror in search of a razor. There were a couple plastic razors there, and one he recognized: an old-school brass-handled, double-edged razor, versus the more modern disposables beside it. He knew that was Les's because he knew it was his dad's before him. Way back when they were cleaning out his dad's stuff after he died, he had seen it in their old cabinet. He'd left it, but apparently Les had not. The blade looked tolerable, and his dad's old brass-handled brush was there, too. Grabbing it, he closed the mirror. Staring back at him was some mix of his dad and mom and even his brothers. Using the bar soap, he lathered in his hand then swept the thin mixture on his neck. He liked the heft of the brass handle, but the blade wasn't so sharp anymore, scraping across his neck with difficulty. This was what he wanted, however, and the shave satisfied a need for connection he didn't even know he had. Once done, he looked tolerably good, awake even, and was ready.

There was a viewing at the parlor for family and close friends. He expected the room to be sparse, but it was packed up to the far end where the box was, containing his brother. McGhee wasn't anxious to have a look, in fact resolved not to look, but some inexorable force mixed the room and McGhee with it, sweeping him slowly toward the casket. En route, several visitors told him they saw Les every day at the shop, and told him of his kindness. He smiled politely, but secretly thought it was ironic they all knew his brother better than he did. While he was in one such chat with an old woman who was crying about *The Pie Tin*, and how it wouldn't be the same without Les, he was interrupted at his elbow.

An old man in an ancient army jacket that said *NAM* on the back with a peace symbol under it had grabbed McGhee by the arm. His pull was insistent, including some weight; otherwise, he was standing with a metal crutch that ran up his forearm with a support. "You his brother?" he asked.

Turning toward the tug and the question, he looked over the man's head, then realized that, by virtue of the bend in the man's back, the man's eyes were much lower. Looking into them, he saw they were watery blue. On either side of his head two large hearing aids projected from his ears, surrounded by tufts of white hair. A white beard and mustache entirely obscured his mouth, making it still harder to understand him. McGhee had to lean in to hear the man, even though he was raising his voice.

"Yes, I am . . . ," he answered, "Fran McGhee." He freed the man's hand from his sleeve to shake it, even though it was his left. His second crutch dangled from his forearm as the man shook his hand, but he didn't let go, instead holding onto McGhee's fingers. His eyes were blinking slowly, and his lips seemed to be moving, but nothing audible was emerging.

Leaning in closer, McGhee was suddenly hit with a blast of words from the deaf man: "Your brother saved me . . . ," he said, bowing his head slightly. Pulling McGhee by the hand, he tugged him toward the casket. Walking slowly the remaining few feet, he continued talking. "I used to sit outside that shop-a his," the old man said. "Even when it got cold. Once your brother bought the place, he brought me in to sit at the counter. I sat there the better part of the last ten years."

They both looked into the box together. Les looked old to McGhee, but the expression on his face looked, if not happy, content. His silver hair was neatly groomed, his nose hair clipped, his mustache trimmed, and his chin remained clean. Something in the lines of his nose and cheeks reminded him of his father in the same pose thirty years back. Even his eyebrows had the lines of his father. As the oldest of the McGhee boys, he always seemed to be in the lead, so maybe he took that from their father. Below, he wore a white snap cowboy shirt with brown stitching, and a vest, a watch chain visible from his pocket. On his midsection sat a white cowboy hat — one he had clearly worn to being comfortable on his head — below that, jeans and boots. He'd always said he wouldn't be caught dead in a suit, which brought a slight smile to McGhee's face.

The old man squeezed his hand to get McGhee's attention, tugging to have him lean over. "He was very kind to me . . . even gave me jobs to do sometimes. Hard to find something for an old cripple like me to do, but he did. Let me wrap his change now and then. Pennies mostly. Quarters sometimes."

"I didn't even know he had a coffee shop 'til last night . . . ," McGhee said, but the old man didn't seem to hear.

"He'd talk about you . . . ," the old man said, "and Wil, but mostly you." The old man paused to look up at him, his eyes moister than before, welling in the corners. "Said he was sorry," the old man said. He nodded his head, finally releasing McGhee's hand. "Just wanted to pass that along. I'll let you say good-bye to your brother . . . ." With that, the old man reset the crutch on his arm and slowly moved aside.

From behind, the funeral director was shooing the non-family from the room for the final family good-byes. Appearing beside McGhee, Clara Ann put her hand on his shoulder, rubbing his back a little bit. Her eyes were moist, but she was strong. Behind her, Mike put his arms around her waist, resting his head on top of his mother's. On his right, Wil leaned in.

"You and Les always used to have kite fights. Remember that?" McGhee said. He couldn't take his eyes off Les, lying so still.

"He always won . . . ," Wil said, his voice catching at the end. McGhee turned to look at Wil, then back to Les.

Clara Ann leaned in and kissed Les lightly on the forehead. "Bye, hun . . . ," she said, turning around to cry into Mike's chest. McGhee wasn't sure how he did it, but Mike remained stoic – sad, but dry in the eyes. Wil leaned over to McGhee to whisper: "That's *exactly* what Les would have done."

The procession to St. Joseph's cemetery was slow, but it didn't take long. The cars stopped near the northeast corner by a rock outcropping and a copse of cottonwoods. It was late in the year, but some of the cotton still clung to the edges of the grass, and some of the leaves, brown and dry, scuttled noisily across the pavement in the breeze. Other leaves, still holding on, whipped furiously in the slight gusts, but otherwise quivered, through alternating glints of sunshine, throwing shadow dapples on the grass beneath. Fresh earth lay on a matt near an open grave, and the funeral men carefully extracted the coffin from the hearse, sliding it onto a rolling cart, then solemnly rolling it toward the opening.

A Catholic priest in black came over to the limo where the family sat while one of the funeral-men opened the door for them. Clara Ann stepped out first, and seeing the priest, walked to him. "Thanks for coming, Father." He shook his head knowingly.

"I know Les wasn't a religious man," he said to her, "but I thought I'd look on anyway. He was a good man."

By the time they made it to the grave, Les's casket was suspended over the hole on the supports, waiting to be lowered. A small collection of friends had assembled there already, and the family moved to join them. McGhee mixed among them, coming to rest beside the old man he'd met at the funeral home. He looked up at McGhee, smiling sadly at him, but said nothing. Everyone stared at the box, lost in their own thoughts. Though the priest assumed a position at the head-end of the grave, he, too, remained silent, his head lowered, eyes closed. After a minute of silence, it became clear no one was officiating, but the head undertaker was prepared. Scanning the small crowd he spoke to the assembled:

"Before we commend our friend and brother and father and husband, Les, to the earth, would anyone like to speak?"

Clara Ann gave a quick shake of her head, raising a handkerchief to her nose, a red one, like the one peering out of Les's pocket most days. Mike had assumed the same position he had at the
home, hugging his mother from behind. He cleared his throat,
twice, before managing, "Bye, Dad . . . ," before the tears obliter-
ated any chance he had to speak further. Wil clutched his hands in
front of himself, a frown cemented in place to prevent the same.
The undertaker began to fidget, raising his arm to signal the other
men to commence lowering, but McGhee intervened, raising his
hand. The undertaker saw the signal, staying the actions of the
others with a slight gesture of his hand.

McGhee stepped forward, looking across the faces. Reaching
into the chest pocket of his jacket, he pulled out a couple pages, folded in quarters. Unfolding the newer one, he held it in his right hand,
reaching out with his left to touch the casket. The metal of it was
cold in the November breeze, even though the morning was brilliant.
He cleared his throat to speak, unsure what would come out.

"I wrote this a couple days ago, but it seems appropriate . . . ,"
he said, clearing his throat again:

> Here lies a man who spent his days
> in the company of strangers,
> caring for them when they were alone,
> feeding them when they could not pay,
> listening to them when there was no one to listen,
> wishing for nothing in return
> except friendship.
> Remember his kindness.

There were a few whimpers from the audience, but the silence
continued. Unfolding the second, older sheet, he paused to look

at the casket, then the crowd. Both Mike and Wil were looking at him. Clara Ann cried quietly into Les's hanky, searching for his scent.

The paper was old and faded, but he could only make it through the first couple lines:

> Les:
> I thought you should know about the note I stuck in the bottle you gave me for graduation:
> *To the finder of this bottle:*
> *This letter speaks of the love of one brother for another, of adventures taken and missed, and lives well-lived.*

Folding the sheets, McGhee lowered his head, and with that, the undertaker nodded to his men to proceed.

At the house, McGhee extended his hand to Wil, but Wil hugged him anyway. Mike shook his hand and gave him a small paper lunch bag, folded neatly over. "From Dad . . . ," he said. Clara Ann waved, pulling her shawl closer over her shoulders.

Back at his motel, where he collected his things, McGhee saw *The Pie Tin* was across the street. A small wooden panel dangled below the sign, ragged edges and rustic with wood-burned letters: *Proprietor: Les McGhee.* The wind made it creak as it swung, but it held, constant. Through the window, he could see the goings-on, which continued in Les's absence. Above the register, on a wall sconce sat an antique Singer sewing machine. Above it, along a shelf floating just below the ceiling, sat an old runner sled, tilted for better viewing, *Flexible Flyer* still faintly visible in red paint. He stopped at the door, however, smiling to himself again. *This was Les's place . . . best leave it be*, he thought, and didn't go in, stepping away as he convinced himself it was time to go.

Half way out of town, McGhee opened the paper bag Mike had given him, spilling the contents into his hand. He pulled over to inspect the thing in his palm, skidding into the gravel. It all came back: it was a little plastic orange top from the game he got for his birthday almost sixty years before, still emblazoned with its name, *Hurricane Hank*. Les had said he'd never give it back, but it seemed to be a time for relenting. The sky was brilliant and the clouds raced east on the wind, but he didn't see any of it as he sat by the road for most of the next hour and cried.

The Calendar Lagniappe

1PM
New Orleans, LA 6/15/1979
Nashville, TN 12/24/1983

McGhee bugged out of New Orleans early – it was done for him – and he wanted to get home by Christmas. After seven straight hours of driving Wil's red '82 Camaro, the passing stripes had merged to form a connect-the-dots from the Big Easy to Nashville. Les was going to let him crash there, and with some luck, might go back with him to western Pennsylvania and the rest of the family, but it wasn't likely, or so Les had told him already. For McGhee, it was only his second winter break from college, so he wasn't about to miss Christmas at home, which somehow still remained unthinkable. He'd flown into the city the afternoon before to retrieve Wil's car and had been listening to *Every Breath You Take* most of the way, reinforcing himself in an odd frame of mind. By the time he'd gotten to the Nashville outskirts, it had drummed into the lower portions of his brain, right next to the hum of tires and an engine red-lining most of the way. That very hum lulled him into frequent recollections of a warm city which had gone cold for him and just wasn't the same anymore. And he was pretty sure it never could be.

—————◦◦◦—————

Back when he was fifteen, he'd had his first trip to the city, and it was different for him then. He was different then, too, unsullied, though it was lost on him at the time.

It was dark and hot, the sheets reflecting his body heat, the stifling air carrying the smell of brackish water, even inside with his eyes closed, with shallow breaths. Still, he liked it and what it portended. The ceiling fan wasn't offering any relief either, broken in the darkness, barely visible against the high ceiling when he thought to look again, hanging on a long pole, but still ten feet above, lifeless. McGhee lay still, hoping that would help, but it didn't: he could feel the beading sweat on his neck collecting in the little well below his Adam's apple, one ticklish drop at a time, but it was something to divert his mind. That is, it was a diversion until he felt a new sensation all of a sudden, just barely, which he thought to be perhaps a mosquito, lightly landed. When he finally resolved to sweep it away, he felt more resistance than a dust-like insect would offer, much more substance. It was like a chip of wood, though moving, and when he thought to smell his fingers, because he was smelling something bad, they registered a disgusting and indescribable odor of putrefaction. Clicking on his light, he discovered he was sharing his pillow with a two-inch cockroach, twitching its feelers, disturbed by his swat from drinking at the small hollow of his throat. So that was it for sleep on that bed, his first night in town.

The common room was spare with the decorations of a mid-twenties male: a scratchy old couch, a coffee table (to hold random items), and a small TV on a stand with rabbit ears at skew angles to collect the local stations. The floors were wood with a Mexican carpet under the table, fringe mangled and caught with detritus on the floor. It was a little easier to sleep out there with the windows open, and he knew Wil would be out early to work long before he'd rise. Somewhere around 4:00 a.m. he thought the heat might subside enough to sleep, and he resigned himself to languishing in the swelter until exhaustion took him. At least he didn't think the roaches would find him there, or he held out hope for it. In the darkness he tipped his head to look out the window – outside, the Quarter still hummed in the distance, though he felt it more than heard it out toward the pink clouds illuminated by what he assumed or imagined to be sin, over the tired roofs between him and there.

Moving to the window, McGhee looked out. It must have been after two or so in the morning, but a couple old black men were converged at the corner. One leaned against a wood phone pole, another had pulled out a lawn chair and was sitting beside it, wiping his head. Their shadows cast in the tired street light at their feet, looking as miserable in the heat as they were. Miserable, that is, until their voices rose and sounded otherwise, deep but merry guttural laughs at unheard jokes. With that, he went back to the couch and eventually slipped into uneasy sleep.

One moment he was hearing the laughs outside and the next those sounds had become the dull roar of the jet engine humming just outside the hull, his eyes closed as he tried to sleep on the flight in. Though his eyes were shut, his thoughts turned to the young woman sitting next to him, though she seemed mature to McGhee – already in her life, in her twenties, mostly an adult. Still, her limbs were young, peach fuzz on her arms, raising in goose flesh as the AC was cold in the plane. She seemed to be in a slow writhe in her seat, which brought to mind her breasts heaving with her slow breaths beneath her shirt – if only she'd take his hand he'd hold it, touching her palm lightly, and when she put her head on his shoulder, he'd feel her warm breath there on his ear and catch her whispering something, though he couldn't quite make it out, with her little whimpering laugh after it in some conspiracy only they knew.

But he'd have to pull back from it – there was time enough for that later – for he was on his first adventure, out and away from his home, off somewhere – he had momentary panic when he couldn't remember where – though that dissipated, too, even though he never quite recalled where he was going. He resolved it didn't really matter, and that what did, was that he had finally gotten out, gotten started on his way, even if he didn't know where that way might be. There was relief to that, a sigh, and once that sigh had settled in, a sense of excitement, for the day had finally come he was old enough to go. So as he slipped into that sleep within his sleep, content to drift and let the current take him where it would, it seemed the sun had come in under the shade and was heating him to a slow bake, draining the momentary relief he had finally begun to enjoy.

It was somewhere around 11:00 a.m. the light from the window hit him on the couch and the warmth had built again to the point where further sleep was impossible. Resigned to this fact, he threw his feet onto the floor, groggy. Though the sleep wasn't good, he was excited to get out and explore the city as he'd only gotten in late the night before. He wasn't sure a shower would help either, but he opted for it anyway only to discover once the warmish water was done and he'd toweled off, sweat instantly replaced it. The humidity of the bathroom was barely more than that of the ambient air, so he leaned on the sink, swiped the moisture from the mirror and considered shaving, though it wasn't really necessary: his chin barely had fuzz on it, and his lip only had the lightest shadow of early growth, thin and mostly bleached from the sun. Toweling off his hair, long and curly, he realized it'd likely stay wet regardless of his attempts to dry it, and that he didn't really care anyway.

He had packed like a rookie from Pennsylvania with no knowledge of June in Louisiana – mostly long shirts and long pants – so it would be a moist day unless he managed to find air conditioning, which wasn't his objective, but might become necessary the way it seemed to be going. So once he had his long sleeved snap shirt and long cords on, he made his way down the steps to where Wil had said the bike was stowed and pulled it out. Other than some rust on the rims and dust on the seat, it looked OK – a cheap ten-speed – and he was ready for the road.

From what Wil had told him, he could follow Rampart the whole way into the Quarter, and though he'd have to watch for cars going the other way, it wouldn't be too far. It was a narrow residential street, though not like any he'd seen before: dilapidated houses and cars and corner grocers spilled sweaty people into the street, or so they appeared to McGhee. Sleeveless ribbed white undershirts seemed to be the standard for the young men, with huge crescent wet marks under the arms; many of the older men wore the same, only the incessant wetness over years of wear had formed yellow stains instead. The young men were thin, but the old men had broken their bodies, and had exploded in their clothes, oozing out of them in sweaty rolls. Still, some wore nice hats, maroon and red and deep blue, with black satin bands and an occasional feather; they smiled and waved at him as he rolled by. The houses – even the poor ones – still showed a pride of style even as they collapsed in decay, while the nice ones displayed the same esthetic, though with fresh paint and repaired siding. Thick clapboard was the standard for all in that street, whether they were small, thin houses, trailing back from the sidewalk, each end an entrance to a duplex, or spread out double-wide, stacked in stories, as nicer homes. The doors had wide trim around them, festooned at the top with crowns of flashing wood, other crowns reaching up in the corners to meet the roofs, fanning out in fancy filigree, vaguely evoking the French history there. Even the older and poorer houses had it, though the moulding looked the worse for wear, and the paint was fresh forty years earlier. And whether they were old or new, the colors spanned the rainbow in blues and greens and yellows and reds, the older betraying their ages with paint flakes leaning off in bendy arches, aching for some kid to peel.

Once McGhee crossed Esplanade, everything changed. He'd come to a stop after crossing it, looking down the street and from there he could see the Quarter opening before him. Rampart seemed the other edge of the frame, so he headed down Esplanade, past Burgundy and Dauphine, chancing upon Bourbon, which he'd heard of, so he headed in that way. Though it still appeared residential, the buildings went to mostly two stories and looked more interesting still – the upper floors mostly had balconies of elaborate wrought iron with roofs hanging over, corners filled with baskets of flowers – impatiens like the ones his dad had in the back yard – gushing out in colors, swinging around the poles holding up the soffits, dancing their way down several feet. Along the street, most of the doors looked like tall shutters, old paint in bright colors peeling but looking significant to his eye, like official history rather than abject decay. Pressing on, the buildings continued to improve, until in the heart of it, they were brick, their shutters newly painted, their flowers choreographed on each corner, gas flames sputtering in lamps, even in the day time. The corners all had nice signs, seraph white on black fields, painted with names he'd heard of somewhere: Orleans, Royal, Toulouse. Though most of the streets had cars on them, there were people, too, milling about, absorbing the atmosphere, cameras hanging from every neck, children holding mothers' hands, and mothers covering eyes where saucy signs or painted women sprung from doorways (he assumed they must be women) and walked the streets, spilling out of their bustiers like mini Mardi Gras floats personified.

After riding a while, he came to a stop at St. Ann and Decatur on the corner of Jackson Square, putting his foot down to rest a while. Artists had set up the whole way around the edge, drawing patrons for ten dollars, or showing their wares under umbrellas to ward off the heat, even though everyone knew the heat was in the moisture anyway, and umbrellas couldn't do anything about that.

Directly across Decatur, the *Café Du Monde* sat, huge open terrace and ceiling fans whirling feverishly, black men in white service hats and aprons dashing about with trays of chicory coffee and plates containing mountains of powdered sugar. Wil had thought to suggest he try it, so leaning his bike against a post, he moved over and took a seat at a table. Most of the attendants were young men in their twenties, running back and forth with a skip to their step, but an old black man made his way to his table, leaning with both hands on the edge, looking at him. He must have been seventy, his face hanging and tired, but he smiled anyway, rubbing a moist cloth on his neck, shaking his head.

"Mind if I sit a minute, son . . . ?" he asked, but didn't wait for an answer. Dragging out a chair with scrape and squeal on the floor, he carefully lined up before he landed with a slow speed plop on it and a long sigh to go with it. "That sure is better," he said. His cap was at an angle but seemed clamped to his head, or perhaps it was his head gripping it instead. His bags pulled his eyes open a little extra, red along the edges where they met the yellow where the whites should be, and his irises ringed with milky age. "Been standin' all day an' I'm a bit tired."

McGhee stuck out his hand, surprising the old man who looked at him. "Fran McGhee," he said.

The old man blinked, breaking into a wide smile. "Willy Robinson," he said, extending his meaty hand and clasping McGhee's, tightly. After the shake, Willy nodded approvingly. "You got a strong shake, son. That's real good."

"You do, too . . . ," McGhee responded. Willy laughed, low and slow, rolling like a little bit of thunder, deep from his chest.

Willy pulled the cloth from his neck, still smiling, rubbing his hands on it. "So what kin I getcha?"

McGhee shrugged. "Not sure what you got . . . ."

"Really?" Willy said, delighted. "That's so cute."

McGhee looked dismayed. "Cute?"

Willy's eyes got big. "No, man . . . I just get snotty tourists here all the time, readin' their travel books and whatnot. It's nice to hear somethin' different . . . ."

"Oh . . . ," McGhee said, brightening. "So what ya got?"

"Beignets," Willy said, "and Café au Lait, and Chic'ry . . . ." Rubbing his neck, he looked at McGhee. "Only I don't s'pose you want none-a that."

"Those beignets – donuts or something?" McGhee asked.

"Yeah . . . ," he said, then raised his hand. "Oh, we got chocolate milk, too."

"All right then," McGhee said. "Bring me some of that."

Willy prepared to stand, putting his hands on the table, but didn't get up. "That was a little too quick," he said, laughing again.

McGhee folded his hands, looking at Willy. "No hurry, man. So . . . what should I do here?"

Willy's face went slack. "You mean in No-Luns?"

"Yeah, in No-Luns . . . ," McGhee said, matching his pronunciation, straight faced.

Willy busted out in his low laugh again, shaking his head. "That's so cute . . . ," he said, then holding up his hand, "Sorry . . . you know what I mean." Leaning back in his chair he threw one arm over the peg on one corner. "Well . . . you're too young to drink, I'd guess . . . ," he said, smiling, the corner of his mouth pulled back, just a bit wry, but friendly.

"Yeah . . . ," McGhee said, sitting up a little straighter. "I'm fifteen, so I guess not."

Willy shook his head again, then had a thought. "You like music?" Willy asked. "Coz I know just what you should do then . . . ." A young waiter was zipping by, and Willy caught his sleeve. "Hey Stevie, could you bring my friend here an order and some milk?"

"Chocolate?" he asked, looking between Willy and McGhee.

Willy nodded, letting go of his sleeve. "Extra sugar, too . . . ," he said, turning his head to call *thanks* after the receding waiter.

Leaning back on the table, Willy looked serious. "OK now, you know where Royal is yet and St. Peter?" Willy waved his hand past Jackson square. "Oh, you'll find it . . . ," he said, wiping his forehead with the cloth. "All right. Now you go down there, next to *Pat O'Brien's*," he said, holding up his hands to make a circle. "Big round sign. Green I think. It's all pink outside – easier to find that . . . ," he said. He was visualizing it and McGhee watched him, like he was having a vision. Opening up his hands, he leaned in, like it was a confidence. "Right next to it – don't look like nothin' – there's a place called *The Preservation Hall*. Crappy old windows – all yellow and stained, shutters fallin' off practic'ly, ain't been painted in forever, little doorway. Got a trombone case up there says *Preservation* on it. Ever hear of it?" McGhee nodded, but wasn't sure. Willy laughed again. "Man, you're killin' me . . . ," he said smiling. "OK, so go in there. Usually a line, but it's worth it. Couple bucks is all. Just don't gawk in the window, or you'll be sorry . . . ," he said, all serious. McGhee nodded solemnly, which made Willy laugh again.

Just then Stevie showed up with a plate mounded in powdered sugar, just a hint of an edge peeking out in one spot, like a sudden tiny blizzard had snowed-in a mini ski lodge.

"Go right ahead an' dig in. I better get back to it," Willy said, but waited, hands posed to hoist him again.

McGhee tugged at a corner, freeing one, but had to drop it immediately, the oil still hot on the surface. Willy shook his head. "Gotta eat it hot," he said. "That's the best way anyhow . . . ."

McGhee grabbed at another edge of the dough pillow covered in sugar, easier on the fingers and stuffed it into his mouth. It was warm and sweet and crunchy, and after one bite, he kept crunching, stuffing the remainder in his mouth, his fingers instantly hunting in the snow for the next one to devour, the powdered sugar already lining his lips and cheek. Willy watched the transformation on his face, satisfied.

"Good, huh?" he said, shaking his head and smiling. "I love that part – watching the first bite. Never get tired of that." Pushing himself up, Willy looked at McGhee. "You enjoy that now, and come back after you been to the Hall and tell me *alllll* about it . . . ."

Fortified with sugar and fat, and more sugar, McGhee made his way to his bike and curved around Jackson Square, dodging pedestrians messing with cameras seeming more intent on capturing the memories rather than having them, the artists patiently fielding questions, but hoping they'd sit for a fee. At the far end, the streets opened again and he made his way down St. Peter. It wasn't more than a couple blocks before *O'Brien's* opened up on the left, and just beyond, he found his objective. A small line of people waited outside under the trombone case, but he was thankful for the guidance because he would have missed it otherwise. Stowing his bike by a pole, he joined them next to the windows.

In front of him, a family waited to go in; the woman squinted into her AAA tour book while the man loaded film in his old camera, feeding the film in where the edge would catch on the winder. Down below, a three or four-year-old was bouncing, tugging at the edge of his mother's skirt. He smiled up at McGhee and waved, hiding behind her knees before peeking out again. Once she was done reading, she looked in the window, but it was dim and stained, both inside and out. Leaning in, she formed her hands around her eyes to keep out the light. "Hun . . . ," she said, keeping her focus inward. "You gotta see this." She motioned with her hand for him to join her, so he leaned in, too.

"Gees . . . . They're right there!" he said, one hand on his camera still, the other shielding his eyes. Just then a snare rim-shot from inside made it outside and the crowd inside laughed, clapping. From down below, the little boy laughed, too, looking at McGhee, then looking at his parents, then at him again. Rubbing his eyes, he grabbed his mom's skirt again.

It wasn't much later the attendant came out and led them into the hall, collecting their fees. McGhee stood in the back, which was a little cheaper still, but it wasn't so large inside, and leaning against a pole, he took a casual pose, hoping at some level to look marginally less like a tourist, if that was even possible. Somehow it was already important to him to avoid that, and more importantly, not to be that — the greedy consumer of cultures like a meal to be gobbled down — and to blend in, if he could, and immerse himself in its atmosphere instead. By contrast, the family from the line had rushed to the very front bench to get the best seat possible, right in front of the little platform where the band was set up.

The walls were covered with posters and pictures and memorabilia, coated in the same dust and yellow nicotine exhalations which had coated the windows themselves, lending an unhealthy but authentic patina to everything. The wood was weathered and worn, edges sanded smooth and shiny on the benches, black marks on the square posts holding up the roof and rafters where countless others had leaned since it had opened. From those rafters hung dusty threads, swung slowly through the air by the low-speed circulating ceiling fans. To the side, a little plaque hung on two hooks, indicating the players would be *Sweet Emma's Band*, the sign crudely painted in red on a small fragment of a slat of some kind — perhaps even a siding clapboard like he'd seen on the way into town.

When Sweet Emma came in, frail and ancient, one of the younger members of the band helped her onto the platform at her elbow, and she made her way to the upright piano against the wall, where she could play and sing and look out. The others made their way to the drums, the clarinet on the stand, the banjo, the trombone balanced on the bell, the trumpet and the huge wood base balanced in the other corner, though in all it wasn't more than ten feet across for all of them.

Almost as soon as they had alighted at their stations, they began to play a slow blues melody of some kind, the band spokesman shuffling to the front. "Welcome to No-Luns," the man said, "from Sweet Emma's Preservation Hall Jazz Band . . . ." Pointing at each one of members, he introduced them, their instrument coming to the fore of the melody as they bowed their heads, until he finally got to Sweet Emma herself, and she twisted on the bench and spoke:

"We hope you like our music . . . ," she said, her voice cracking and weak, but everyone clapped, or mostly, for McGhee wasn't sure that was the right thing to do, so he waited. Twisting back, she tapped on the keys lightly, but it was perfect, fitting in like a kid snuggling between his parents Sunday morning. After a few notes, she turned the other way to the band, saying, "A Good Man . . . ," and they instantly transitioned into a new song, running several bars until they'd all gotten in sync. Sweet Emma hit the keys a little harder, and they reduced their volume as she prepared to sing:

> *A good man is hard to find,*
> *You always get the other kind . . . .*

Her voice was light and thin, but the band helped her, their tones muted but woven into a blanket of warm melody. At the end of her verse, everyone stood, clapping, and for his part, McGhee had to clap, too.

From there, the band cycled through several more tunes, each instrument taking its turn in the playing cycle, as it appeared was their standard method of playing. Near the end, the spokesman shuffled forward again, the roar of the music dimming so he could speak.

"We want to thank you ladies and gentlemen for coming to see us . . . ." The band instantly became louder again for a few bars, before dimming again.

"Now, when you go out, be sure to tell those folks not to look in the window . . . ," he said, turning slightly with his arm out toward it. "We don't want 'em lookin' foolish now . . . ." Just then, on cue, spectators were looking in, hands cradling their eyes to peer through the glass, and the man on drums hit a rim-shot with his snare. Everyone laughed, even the family on the front bench, though they exchanged sheepish glances as the music wound down.

⚬⚬⚬

McGhee had never been to Nashville but had a decent map and rudimentary directions from Les; he was a firm believer that the struggle would make McGhee stronger so left the directions high level. He always seemed to fall into that role with his little brother – instructor – so McGhee was used to it. He'd adapted to it long ago, developing countermeasures to defeat these instructional impulses: pulling into a *7-Eleven* just inside the city limits, he got directions from the attendant there. Even without ever having been there, he was conflicted about the city anyway: his family didn't abide country music, as it seemed to them to be the taste of others drawn to the melodramatic themes of strife and alcoholic misery. No – without saying it out loud, for they wouldn't do that – the McGhees silently disdained country music, its stars, its sacred ground, and its stations of the cross, where Elvis did this, or Dolly said that. *The Grand Ol' Opry* was just a large building he'd never go to, so Nashville had remained a dark and blank patch on his aspirational map, and he was fine with that. So the detour to it, far from a welcome adventure, was more of a mild endurance test. Such were his thoughts on Nashville, and while he was at it, Tennessee in general. Other than seeing Les, there wasn't much else for him.

Winding through streets and turns, left and right and left again, he eventually pulled into a lot protected from the street by a short L-shaped building which, judging by the number on it, was where his brother lived with two roommates. The others were residents at Vanderbilt, and according to Les, there was rarely more than one of them there at a time as they progressed peristaltically through the bowels of their rotations. And as for Les, this was just the latest of his roamings, so he wasn't sure what he'd get when he rapped his knuckles on the hollow wood door, and in fact got nothing at all, until the second round of knocking. He was persistent with his tapping, and eventually heard the deadbolt turn, revealing a sleepy brother: he looked like a hedgehog, rather ruffled and groggy, though it was two in the afternoon. He wore his hair long then, an attempt to make up with length what he lacked in coverage, and the sleep had rendered it shrub-like in its bramble appearance, asymmetric with mounting mounds on one side, some thin spots on the other. He yawned while waving in McGhee, turning to walk toward the sink, then thought better of it, remembering to turn and hug his little brother first before resuming his quest for a splash of water. At the sink, the water was cold and he didn't have the patience to wait for the hot, and shuddered as he splashed it repeatedly into his eyes. Water dripped from his nose and all parts of his face out to the very edges of his frizzy hair. It was teased thin, wisps burnt from endless blow drying and all manner of product meant to preserve it. Finally looking back at McGhee, he smiled at him.

"What time ya leave New Orleans?" he asked. Moving over to the fridge, he opened it up for a look. Reaching in, he pulled out a long neck, then held it out to McGhee. "You want?" he asked. McGhee shook his head, so he closed the icebox and knocked off the lid on the edge of the counter. Tipping it up, he took a few long pulls before continuing. "So when'd ya leave again?"

McGhee moved over to a sofa, pushing aside several newspapers and magazines to clear a landing place before plopping down.

"Dunno. Seven maybe . . . ," he said, throwing his arm up along the back edge along the pillows.

Les leaned against the counter, looking at McGhee, his aspect darkening with recollection. "So . . . how'd it go?" he asked tentatively. Putting down the bottle, he took to running his fingers through his long hair, carefully teasing out the tangles, then pushing the hair back into shape, adjusting the general distribution to even things out.

"OK, I guess . . . considering," McGhee said. Their eyes met, both reluctant to discuss the recent events in New Orleans. Moving over, Les plopped into a recliner across from McGhee.

"Well, it sure was nice for you do to that for Wil – I know he wasn't up to do it himself. It's good to see you nonetheless . . . ," he said, smiling at his brother. "How's school?"

McGhee lowered his head, then looked away. Realizing that was telling, he looked back at his brother. "OK, I guess . . . ," he said, smiling.

"Pretty tough, huh?" Les asked, taking another swig from his bottle.

"You could say that . . . ," McGhee said, nodding.

Looking around, McGhee surveyed the place as his eyes adjusted to the darkness. It was dim and messy – the small north-facing windows lining the top edge of the wall were covered by grim, cheap brown curtains that didn't admit much light, seemingly by design, and where the light made it through, dust motes floated in the air, making him consider the air he was breathing. The floor had dark brown shag, visible in patches under the sprinkled newspapers strewn like a slow-speed paper explosion had occurred, a side-effect of the marginal hoarding dysfunction apparent. The walls had dark paneling, too, completing the general image of a mid-seventies depressive décor in zero danger of a *Better Homes* photo exposé. That said, Les seemed oblivious to the effect, and he sat watching his younger brother, still smiling at him.

Once McGhee looked at him again, he pointed his bottle at him, pushing down the last swig in his mouth. "You hungry?" he asked, standing, scanning for his pants which were stuck running up a broom and step stool in the corner, hastily thrown, one leg inside out, the other dangling. Jingling the belt free and thrusting an arm in, he pulled them right side out and stepped into them, grabbing his wallet and keys from the counter. "Ready?"

Outside, McGhee walked toward the only other car in the lot, but Les turned the other way, spinning to signal his brother. "There's a diner down the street. I figured we could walk . . . ."

The area was semi-residential with squat businesses intermixed with small houses and little strips of two and three shops for nails and haircuts and beauty supplies and music stores advertising two-for-one guitar strings and lessons. The sky wasn't helping much with a low, cold ceiling that wasn't precipitating, but seemed bent on it if it could find the moisture to cry. Still, it was better than the apartment, and the fresh air felt good to McGhee. It was better, too, than the oppressive moisture of the New Orleans air, which for McGhee had turned a corner from welcome warmth to something darker and strangling.

"You talk to Mom and Dad yet?" Les asked as they walked down the block.

"Not since yesterday," McGhee said. "Told 'em I'd be heading out today, wasn't sure if you'd be coming back with me or not."

Les shook his head slowly. "Don't think I'll make it this year," he said, frowning slightly. McGhee wasn't sure if he was seeing regret or grim satisfaction at the fact, Les's face hard to read. Sometimes he seemed to enjoy deprivation, like such penance had a peculiar resignation to it, and he recognized that impulse, feeling those notions himself, though he'd just as soon not have those feelings visit him, especially at the moment. The prospect of getting home and forgetting his mission, and most important-ly, the cause of it, was welcome, as deluded and impossible as he knew it would be.

Embedded in another small strip of shops, they made it to *The Old Kaw-Liga*, a diner marked with a wooden Indian at the door jammed in between other shops, all showing window paint, each yammering for attention with garish swaths of color advertising specials. The diner had eggs and corned-beef hash and grits and cornmeal mush for sale, and thirty-cent bottomless coffee. The door creaked as Les opened it, getting stuck halfway open as it hit some rough spot in its rotation with an extra groan before releasing entirely, like an extra test to assess the resolve of those endeavor-ing to enter. "I love this place . . . ," Les said, his smile as broad as it ever was.

As they slid into a booth, a waitress dropped two mugs in front of them, brown and heavy with a clunk on the Formica, not even waiting for acknowledgment before sloshing them full with a hasty pour from the glass carafe – caffeine with no options – sugar and cream on a little saucer spinning to a rattling stop dead center be-tween them. "You guys need a minute?" she asked, dealing out menus as she said it, detecting hesitation in the same instant; spin-ning on her toe she looked back at the counter and the cook's shelf and stepped away before there was any chance for equivocation.

Looking over the menu, McGhee asked his brother for guid-ance. "What's good here?" he asked, opening it, tri-folds expand-ing to reveal endless breakfast options and marginal lunch fare.

"Honestly . . . ," Les said, shrugging, "nothing." He laughed a bit as he said it. He seemed to enjoy the irony of loving a diner with mediocre food. Just then, the waitress was back, ballpoint on her pad, ready. Les looked up at her: "Dry whole wheat toast, two eggs worth of egg beaters, OJ," he rattled off. Looking over at McGhee, she signaled it was his chance. Folding the menu, he looked up at her, too. She looked tired, mid-forties, dishwater hair escaping from behind her ear, dangling, her expression permanently underwhelmed.

"OK, uhh. Corned beef hash, two regular eggs over hard, grits," he said. She chewed her gum twice before stowing it again in her cheek.

"Number seven, then. Minus the browns," she said, then realizing he had no idea, she shook her head, scribbling. "Forty cents cheaper that way," she said, catching a wisp of hair to jam it back behind her ear as she stowed the pen there.

"You talk to Wil?" Les asked McGhee, averting his eyes to look into his coffee.

McGhee was sipping his cup but paused for an, "Mmm-hmm," before taking another drink. "I called him in Jersey yesterday. He's driving to Butler tomorrow," he said.

Les nodded. "That's good. It'll be a tough holiday for him." McGhee nodded but didn't respond, but Les pushed on.

"How you handling it?" he asked. He wasn't usually much for uncomfortable talk but seemed compelled by something, perhaps his sense of elder-brother duty. His smile was pressed closer to a frown, so McGhee obliged him to just get past it.

"OK, I guess . . . ," McGhee said, matching Les's frown. "I just think of Wil, and it makes it easier."

Les nodded. "Yeah, I get that. That was a hell of a call for Wil to get on Thanksgiving," he said, his voice trailing off.

"You ever meet Honey, then? — I don't remember . . . ," McGhee said, spinning his cup in his saucer. Les shrugged, shaking his head.

Just then, McGhee noticed a light, lilting tune playing in the background. It was a few bars into a new song when he noticed he was hearing *Knights in White Satin;* the melody seemed to complete the mood. Les noticed as well, cocking his head to listen, just before his eyes locked onto McGhee.

"You hearing that?" he asked. McGhee nodded but said nothing. "I love when that happens," Les said, grabbing his cup, blowing the steam away. "Suddenly it's like you're in a movie. The music is swelling and the camera pans back."

McGhee nodded. "I know what you mean." Emotion was welling in his throat, but he swallowed hard to suppress it.

Les nodded, too. "I always heard music in my head when reading Dostoevsky," he said. "Huge, swelling melodies . . . ."

"Really?" McGhee said, stirring his coffee. "That's funny. Like Tchaikovsky?"

"More like Mussorgsky — those dark passages. Visceral. Dostoevsky had those moments over and over again, pulling out human nature. Like grabbing a blanket from a trunk that's been in storage a long time, but you forgot all about it, only it has that familiarity. It has that smell you'd forgotten, the one that takes you back to those times you encountered it before but never thought to speak of it. It's that immediate. And you don't think of the words. You just get it in your gut, like a little punch, only he's smiling when he does it. He loves man and hates him in the same instant — it's kinda delicious, isn't it?"

McGhee nodded. "Thanks for telling me to read *The Brothers.* Made me wish I could write like that . . . ."

"Those are some big shoes, amigo . . . ," Les said, shaking his head, his smile returning. "You doing any writing up there in New Haven?

McGhee shook his head. "Just papers for class, which suck . . . ," he said. "And I get blasted on them. Feel like I'm in eighth grade with Mrs. Tomosavic, only worse if that's possible."

"Gees . . . ," Les said. "I remember that. She was *tough*. Good though . . . ," he said. "How about physics, then? How's that?"

McGhee darkened, thinking. "Dropped thermo . . . ," he said, pouring more cream in his coffee, watching it swirl, reluctant to disturb the beauty of it.

"What?" Les said, leaning in. "What happened?"

McGhee shrugged. "It beat me," he said, looking up to meet Les's eyes. They were sympathetic, but surprised.

"Jesus . . . ," Les said, shaking his head. "Was it the math?"

McGhee tilted his head, nodding slightly. "It just drained my confidence. I was feeling crushed by it. Seemed like it would be it or me, and it wasn't gonna be me."

"That whole winnowing thing they do sucks . . . ," Les said, frowning and smoldering. "It's not meant to knock out guys like you . . . ."

McGhee smiled weakly. "Thanks bro . . . ," he said. "I didn't think so either. Feels weird to be on the outside now. Never expected that."

Just then the waitress returned with their food, plates stacked along her arm like a circus juggler. McGhee and Les began eating, silent. The hash was satisfying and salty and oozing grease, as was the rest of it. "You had it about right," McGhee said, smiling while he chewed. "But I love it, too."

Les nodded, smiling. "Somehow it works, in spite of itself," he said, speaking through a mouthful of toast. "Sometimes when things suck, I just like to wallow in this place," he said. "It's good to have a place like that. A place to go. Not so clean though."

The fluorescent light above flickered dim, then popped back on, as if on cue. "Right," McGhee said, grinning. "Not so well lighted, neither . . . ."

Rolling out of the *Preservation Hall* onto St. Peter, McGhee squinted in the sunlight, stepping back under the balcony for some relief. The music had been good – better than that really – and finally got his mood aligned with the city. He'd sort of felt like he was still searching, even after the *Café du Monde*, but now he was pretty sure he'd found it, even if it was in the company of other tourists. At least he hadn't been one of the gawkers at the window, so he was a little proud of that – mostly because he'd learned that from a local and had had the sense to follow the advice.

He was leaning against the wall just down from the entrance from the Hall, watching the current of people flow by, when he realized he himself was being watched. To his right, there was a young man leaning just like he was next to the door at *Pat O'Brien's*, looking at him, arms crossed, looking more local than everyone else; he wore a purple hat, ringed in pink satin, and red garter gathers on his sleeves by his elbows. McGhee didn't have anything to do, and once he saw him, he thought to investigate, as everyone else seemed to be moving except the two of them. Walking over, he leaned against the wall next to him.

The young man seemed to be a few years older than McGhee was, but not that much. His skin was light brown – in between black and white – and his hair was short in tight curls, light brown, or dark blond. He had a gold stud in his ear and wore an easy smile. "You from around here?" McGhee asked him, and he shook his head with a definitive single shake.

"Sure am," he said, extending his hand. "Freddy . . . ." McGhee shook it, introducing himself.

"You like that show?" Freddy asked smiling, and McGhee nodded.

"Even better than I expected."

Freddy cocked his head proudly. "An institution, that . . . ," he said, smiling up and out, then looking at McGhee. "What brings you in?"

"Visiting my brother . . . ," he said. "Flew in from Pennsylvania yesterday." He liked the sound of his voice saying that — *flew in* — like he did that a lot. No one had to know it was his first time on a plane going somewhere, and he expected — definitely hoped — he'd be doing more of that. The pride must have shown on his face because Freddy smiled, too.

"Wish I could do that sometime," he said, shaking his head, looking down to his feet, before looking back at McGhee. "Seems like a long way away, though . . . ," he said, smiling a little sadly and hopefully at the same time.

"So whatcha doing out here?" McGhee asked, swishing his finger around in a circle in the air.

"Me?" Freddy asked, pointing to himself. "I'm tappin'." McGhee looked lost, shrugging.

Breaking into a smile, Freddy leaned over. "Watch then . . . ," he said, then standing from his spot he looked down to his right foot which clicked once, rapidly, then stopped. He looked as confused as McGhee, looking back at him, then looked back at his foot. This time it clicked twice. Clamping both hands just above his right knee he looked back to McGhee smiling, but his left foot clicked three times and he looked dismayed again. Switching his hands to his left leg, he clamped down hard on it, shaking his head, looking back at McGhee.

Others on the sidewalk took notice of the racket, stopping to see what the matter was. Freddy held his pose again, smiling with some relief, but his right foot started tapping rapidly on the sidewalk, clicks emerging like a little machine gun rattling on the cracked cement there. It was so fast McGhee couldn't even see his foot move. Freddy watched his leg with the same disbelief as the others gathering around the commotion, gradually releasing his hold on his left leg. It remained still a moment, then began its own tap, countering the taps of the right, in between the impossibly short intervals, until they became so rapid it seemed he could almost hover on the tapping and he slid out over the curb and began sliding in a circle on his feet, moving imperceptibly, until finally he broke into a light tap dance outright, smiling at the circle of people growing around him. Turning around, he kept tapping, facing the curb, using it against his toe for alternate taps, then began running up and down the curb, faster and faster.

A man from within *Pat O'Brien's* brought out three wooden steps, all stuck together and slid it over to him, where he stopped it just above the curb with a single tap and a gap, clapping in the same syncopation suddenly, and he began tapping with his left toe on the street, then the curb, then the first step. "Thank you, Mr. Bojangles . . . ," he said, flashing his smile, resuming the tap, moving into a full step dance right there, the wooden step stool resonating with his taps, his claps augmenting them in an impossibly fast and complex rhythm, some claps on his thighs and backside, to the delight of the crowd. His head was gyrating, and he began spinning, his arms twirling, his feet keeping time through it all like a perfect metronome. Running up and down the steps, he tapped and tapped, and finally, just when it couldn't get better, he went to the top of the steps and did a full back flip onto the street, landing mid-tap on the cobbles, showing surprise like the rest of the crowd that it worked.

The crowd broke out into wild applause, and just then Freddy took a knee, knocking his hat so it'd roll down his arm into his hand. Parents handed change to children who walked it over, dropping it in before sheepishly retreating back to them again. A tall German traveler walked over and dropped in a five-dollar bill, Freddy acknowledging it with a wide smile. Once the last of them had contributed or drifted away, Freddy made his way back to McGhee, falling into his original pose against the wall, his chest heaving, out of breath still, looking at him.

"I feel a little stupid," McGhee said, smiling weakly. "I fell right into that . . . ," he said, shaking his head and wiping his forehead.

"No, man, don't . . . ," Freddy said. "You were just a part of the show, man. Like we all are . . . ."

Despite the protest, McGhee looked a little glum, but Freddy wouldn't have it.

"You're eighteen, right, more or less?"

"Uh . . . ," McGhee said, unsure how to respond.

"More or *less* . . . ," Freddy repeated, tipping his head in, smiling.

"More or *less* . . . ," McGhee said, acquiescing, his smile returning because there was no alternative but to go with the flow of it.

"And let me guess . . . you ain't never had no *Hurricane*, have ya?" Freddy continued. McGhee looked confused again.

"I don't really have much . . . ," McGhee said, patting his pockets, but Freddy wouldn't have any of that either.

"First one's free. Least when I ask they is . . . ," he said, pulling McGhee away from the wall and pushing him into the darkness of *Pat O'Brien's*. He had to let his eyes adjust from the blinding sunshine, but he could hear standard New Orleans jazz in the background. Freddy was pulling him by the sleeve anyway, and cut good naturedly between a couple patrons, signaling the bartender.

"Set one up for McGhee here, on me . . . ," he said. The bartender eyed McGhee warily, drying a glass, but then shrugged. Grabbing a pitcher, he poured a tall shapely glass full of pink liquid clinking with small ice cubes the height of it, stuffing in a thin straw before sliding it out to him.

Once he began sipping, he didn't stop. Freddy patted him on the back and had to get back out on the street but warmly shook his hand before departing. It had been so hot, and so bright, and the air so moist McGhee thought he might wring out drops of moisture from it if he turned too fast. And this drink was so sweet — didn't taste anything at all hardly but punch and juices and just a little something else under the explosion of flavors, and he hadn't had anything to eat either other than the beignets, but that wasn't much, and the punch cut right through all of it, quenching something deep inside, immediately and completely. When there was just the faintest pink remaining, trapped between the cubes of ice, he shook it to make it fall and be suckable through the straw, the rasping indicating that, too, was exhausted — much as he was becoming.

It couldn't have been more than twenty minutes before he was done, and he thought to head for the door. It was only when he was hit by the heat outside, full force and moist and relentless, that he realized the drink was probably stronger than he thought, but by then it was, of course, too late. He made it to his bike, even got it unlocked, and began riding, but the extra degrees of freedom did not improve his situation. He was feeling his head wobble already but had the unsettled feeling he was still very far from the end of it. It wasn't but a couple blocks before he had to come to a stop with some urgency, the percolation of the bumpy streets raising the unwelcome prospect of sickness. He leaned off the bike, clasping onto the bare trunk of a crepe myrtle there, his eyes rolling back, his gut taking over with an involuntary and violent retching. He managed to aim with some success toward the roots of the tree in its skirt of suckers growing from the base there. He was clasping the tree, on his knees for some minutes when he realized there was a hand placed on his shoulder. He wiped his mouth before looking up to see her, a youngish woman leaning in, smiling sadly, but rubbing his arm lightly.

"Why don't you come in a minute . . . ," she said kindly. "Don't worry about your bike. I got that . . . ," she said, leaning it against the tree, looping the lock around the trunk. "I live right here . . . ," she said motioning to the steps a few feet away.

McGhee was powerless to object, but didn't want to refuse anyway, nodding thankfully. "I don't know what happened," he said, shaking his head slowly, raising his hand to his creased forehead.

"I know . . . ," she said, guiding him up the steps and after some key fumbling, into the first floor flat there right inside the entrance.

It was all a blur to McGhee, happy to be out of the sun, collapsing into a wood-frame chair with square lime pillows. He closed his eyes, leaning his head back, but the tumbling started in his head, and he pulled it erect again, opening his eyes, struggling to push through the spin and right the ship, his gaze finally fixing on the mantle where a collection of small figurines stood, arranged in small groups or families, then by couples, and some singular pieces, usually men. They seemed crude upholsteries of burlap, clothed in jackets and hats and pants, all eyes Xs, noseless and mouthless, dumb and odd. Just then the woman came back to him with a tumbler full of water and helped him drink it, almost forced it, tipping it faster than he could swallow, but he couldn't object lest it pour across his chest. Once finished, she thunked it on the table next to him by a tall lamp whose pole disappeared below, ending up above in a lacy, yellowed shade. Sitting herself, slowly, she came to rest across from him, looking into his eyes.

Despite the water, his head was swimming, and the alcohol was still making matters worse, though he'd thrown up the bulk of it. Just before he lost consciousness, he felt her put her head under his armpit and help him stand, then walk, around the kitchen area, back where it got darker in the apartment, and she allowed him to roll off her shoulder and onto a bed, where everything slipped away, absolutely gone.

Out on the street, Les and McGhee began the stroll back to Les's apartment. The air in the diner had been warm, but outside it was close to brisk, though the geography of Nashville wouldn't let it get very cold, at least at that time of day. Tired from the drive, McGhee was glad for it, inhaling deeply to let the cold invade his lungs and give him a jolt of sobriety from his road weariness. The coffee was helping, too, so the combined effect approximated something like a second wind, and he was feeling a little rejuvenated.

Les seemed lost in thought, however, his hands in his pockets, eyes on the sidewalk. After half a block, McGhee took notice of his brother's silence and thought to ask.

"Something wrong?" McGhee said, taking a moment to enjoy the steam his breath was making in the air.

Les looked over, then resumed his stare at the slabs of the sidewalk. It appeared he was getting into one of his pensive moods.

"You worried about Wil?" McGhee asked, looking over sideways at him. "Because I think he's doing pretty good, considering . . . ."

Les shook his head. "Naa . . . ," walking a few more steps before continuing. "More worried about you, actually." He looked over at McGhee, his eyes a little sad.

"Me?" McGhee said, laughing, though the end of his laugh had a nervous twinge to it.

Les nodded. "Yeah, you," he said. "I remember those days – sophomore year – when you're past the freshman excitement, deep in the depths of it. Too far from the end to see the light at the end of the tunnel, too immersed to see the shape of it. Seems like everything you thought you knew is up for grabs. Sense seems optional. And there you got that load of work – so hard – can drive a guy to break if he can't see past it."

Les didn't provide direct guidance often, or talk of his own experience, even though McGhee knew it was always in there, informing his thoughts. Les wasn't exactly stoic, but was certainly reticent; his experience appeared to cause him some discomfort. Perhaps it was shell-shock, an injury from growing up too fast, or an enduring sense of loss. He'd seen the edges of it before in his brother, only this time it was like McGhee was seeing it fresh for the first time and in a new way: he'd never fully understood his brother's demeanor, not really, but this time he was *recognizing* it from the inside, and the revelation surprised him that he, too, was becoming affected the same way.

The thought gave McGhee pause, and he fell into reflection, joining Les in his silence. It wasn't like it was back in high school, when the future simply looked bright, devoid of detail, but unlimited. Somehow, those gates of limitation had started gathering in the margins, snapping in by degrees, fencing off options, even ones he had no intention of considering. He didn't like the feeling of limitation at all, especially when that limitation was found to originate within himself. He had once thought of himself doing anything, and perhaps everything, and that now looked more like a dim and remote possibility than something likely. And it wasn't just the withdrawal from physics, either – it was broader and deeper than that – which meant he was fully-bounded in his potential, and he could feel the realization dimming his internal light as a result. He'd always prided himself in being a Renaissance man, good in many things, yet uncommitted to any one of them. It even seemed he might be good enough to avoid the moniker of dilettante, which to his young mind seemed the only legitimate refutation of remaining uncommitted to any single passion. But now the fences were gathering out there in the mist, just beyond his view – he could feel them – and he was coming to the realization there was something far worse than being a dilettante after all, and that was being deluded.

McGhee smiled at Les, but it was empty. "I think I finally know what you mean," he said, nodding grimly.

McGhee's recognition seemed heartening to Les, and his face brightened. "Well, that's good. That's the critical part – recognition. Once you start to see the shape of it, you get your main weapon back . . . ," Les said.

"Which is?" McGhee asked, looking straight ahead.

"Perspective," Les said, then more emphatically, "*Perspective*." After a few more steps, Les continued. "I hate to tell you, but you're about to lose everything, if you haven't already." Leaning in, Les peered into McGhee's eyes, first one, then the other, then both. "Yeah, you know what I mean. That confidence you had as a kid that everything makes sense starts to fall apart, and once you feel it, it's too late to hold onto any of it, even if you wanted to. It's like you had a nice building with just a few cracks, and you start looking at it, and the more you do, it starts to crumble and it gets smashed into bricks, not even two of them stuck together. I was about your age when I told Mom and Dad I didn't believe in God anymore – that's when that was happening for me."

"I remember that," McGhee said, smiling, his lips curved in the corner.

"You know, Mom and Dad asked me to talk to you last year about the church thing . . . ," Les continued, his eyes wide. "They wanted me to tell you to go, but I wouldn't do it. They were mad . . . . I'm pretty sure they blame me for all of that."

McGhee nodded his head. "Yeah, they probably do. But I wanted to thank you for that. For breaking the trail. It must have been hard. Especially at Notre Dame . . . ."

Les laughed. "Not really . . . everybody was falling apart . . . ," he said. "Anyway, I heard what the priest did for you. That was pretty cool . . . ."

McGhee looked at him. "Yeah, no kidding. It was pretty dicey there a while. Mom especially was pretty rabid. They said they wouldn't send me back to Yale if I didn't go to church."

"Yeah . . . . I know . . . ," Les said, frowning again. "What made you think of talking to the priest?"

"Desperation, I guess . . . ," McGhee said, pushing his hair back from his forehead. "I had no idea what else to do."

"So how did that play out, then?" Les said. Sheepishly, he took a pack of Carltons out of his pocket and shook one loose. When McGhee noticed, he shook his head. "Fell off the wagon again . . . ," Les said, pausing to strike a match and fire it up. Exhaling strongly, he looked up, pushing out the last of the smoke. "That's better," he said, then looking at McGhee, paused again. "I still blame myself for getting you started."

"It was more Wil than you . . . ," McGhee said, matching his smile, which was a bit ironic-looking. "But I take responsibility for it."

Les nodded. "Thanks for that, then," he said.

"So the priest was very reasonable," McGhee said, taking up the thread again. "He listened to what I had to say. Went into his own philosophy, which wasn't so far from mine, really, and he seemed to understand. Mostly, he saw the futility of making me attend, and how that was likely to do more damage than good. Most of it was him talking to himself about it, then offering to intervene with Mom and Dad."

"Mom," Les clarified.

"Yeah, Mom . . . ," McGhee agreed. "So about a week later they called and said they'd had a long conversation with the pastor and they were reconsidering."

"Jesus . . . ," Les said, taking another drag from his cigarette.

"No kidding," McGhee said. "Very cool for him to do that. And you know what – I think I'll remember what he did for me for a very long time. That was one hell of an act of kindness, and I bet that'll be the high water mark for me and religion."

Les nodded as they turned into the back lot where his apartment sat. "I bet that was a huge load off your mind . . . ," he said, shaking his head in thought. "Now you just have to handle the rest of it." Les reached over and punched McGhee lightly in the shoulder. "I know you can do it, even if you don't . . . ."

When he opened his eyes, the ceiling fan above him was slowly circulating, the ancient motor humming slightly, white sheers by the window stirring, spread around the face of a window AC unit which was doing its best to dry and cool the air. He hadn't been so comfortable in a couple days, since getting to the city in fact, and he was thankful for it. Add to that the feel of clean sheets against his skin, which was odd, because he couldn't recall getting undressed – the fog in his head was still dissipating, but was much improved from earlier. Odder, still, was the sensation of an arm draped over him, bent at the elbow, with a hand resting lightly on his shoulder. Then there was the feeling, under the sheets and out of view, of her naked thigh on his, her whole body heaving slightly with her light breathing as she slept next to him.

He only vaguely recalled her rescue of him at the curb in his dire state and the glass of water, but everything after that was a very dim blur and nearly non-existent. Still, he wasn't alarmed, which surprised him because he'd never been in this position before, and since it was so large a part of his adolescent psyche, he found some relief believing something had happened, largely due to his mental absence. Adjusting his position slightly, he could look at her, and her sleeping face looked peaceful.

He'd have to guess she was in her late twenties or maybe early thirties, with chocolate skin and fine features, the remains of plum lipstick along the edges of her mouth, the edges of which were clear and sensual, neither too large nor too small. Her brows were fine, too, lending a friendly look to her face, or better yet, kindly. In that moment as he looked at her, her eyes slowly opened, and rather than register any alarm, she smiled sweetly at him.

She cleared her throat, looking from one eye to the other. "Feeling better, I hope?" she said.

"Much . . . ," McGhee said, returning her smile, though it registered his confusion.

"You were a total gentleman . . . ," she said, moving her hand to rest on his chest, stroking it slightly. McGhee sighed, some combination of relief and disappointment flitting across his brow as he looked at her. With that, her aspect changed, registering a mischievous smile. "But I wasn't . . . ," she said, keeping her eyes on his, then laughing lightly. Lifting her hand from his chest, she held it out for a shake. "Molly . . . ," she said, like a serious introduction.

Her hand was soft in his, but he shook it as she offered it. "McGhee . . . ," he said, then reconsidering, added, "Fran McGhee."

"Well, Fran McGhee, how about something to drink . . . ," she said, tossing the sheet back, rolling off the bed to stretch. She was tall and thin, small-breasted but shapely, like a dancer, entirely naked, on her toes like on pointe, arms above, curling in, spinning slightly. Her silhouette showed against the white sheers, perfect and lovely.

"Uhh . . . ," he said, holding up a palm. "Not sure about the drink . . . ," he continued, raising himself on an elbow.

Grabbing a large men's button down shirt from the dresser, Molly hunched it over her shoulders, threading two buttons on the front. Shaking her head to look at him, she stopped. "Really?" she laughed, putting a hand on her hip. "Just juice for you, hun . . . ." Smiling she strode past and he watched her disappear around the door jamb, swinging around it on one hand as she went by.

Taking the sheet off himself, McGhee confirmed he was also totally naked, which he suspected already. His clothes were strewn on the floor and he set to collecting them and dressing himself as quickly as possible. In the other room, Molly switched on music, and he recognized the notes of the *Tin Roof Blues*, as he'd just heard it at the Hall earlier, before he had fallen apart. He spied himself in the large oval standing mirror in the corner, his hair tamped down on one side, where he'd slept, and hamster-like on the other, disheveled. He straightened it a bit with his fingers on both sides, evening it out, decent, then tucked the tails of his shirt in. He looked different to himself in the mirror, though he couldn't put a finger on it.

In the outer room, McGhee saw the lime chair where he originally landed but chose to remain standing, instead walking over to the mantle where the dolls were clumped. Picking one up, he looked into the face of it – blank – and called to Molly. "What's up with these things?" he said, holding it up with a jiggle.

Sticking her head around the edge of the kitchen area, her eyes got big. "Better put Jake down . . . He wouldn't like that," she said, disappearing again.

Looking back at the burlap figure, he noticed the X eyes were stitches of crude brown thread, but more distressing, he discovered that tacked to the side of the head was lock of real hair. "Shit . . . ," he said, hastily replacing the doll on the mantle.

Coming around the corner with two glasses of orange juice, she handed one to McGhee, sipping the other, before toasting the mantle. "Oh, don't worry . . . ," she said. "It mostly doesn't even work . . . ."

It wasn't quite comforting to McGhee, but the orange juice was good and he gulped it down, feeling like his body was drawing it in directly, even before it reached his stomach. Molly smiled sweetly, watching him. Her eyes were brown and soft, and despite the circumstances, he was glad it had been her.

"I put your bike by the tree . . . ," she said, reading his face.

By the door she paused looking up at him, grabbing two handfuls of his shirt to pull him close, then pressed herself against him. Her breasts were warm against his chest under the shirt, and she lay her head on his chest a moment, listening.

"You have a strong heart, Fran McGhee," she said, and kissed him slowly before she pushed him gently out and closed the door.

McGhee paused at the bottom of the steps to his brother's walkup duplex, not sure what he'd find up there, but resolved to go in. The tenants from the other side were making their way down – Ben and Jen as he learned – who said he looked like Wil a bit, and they were sorry and everything, and did he want them to let him in and even go in with him. He said it was fine, and he could feel their eyes on his back as he climbed the wooden stairs, squeaking with each step.

The door cracked open when he turned the key – the seal around the edge hadn't been broken in a month, and it sprung open a little with a sudden pop, like the door had swollen a bit. Wil would be coming through to do a cleanup later, that is, if he couldn't get the property management company to do it. In the meantime, he'd sent McGhee down to get the car, which he'd left for Honey to drive. Wil had said he didn't have to go in if he didn't want to, but he said he would, which at that moment he regretted a bit, but which he knew he wanted to do anyway.

Inside it was hot and close and dark, and he dragged a few of the dim curtains open to let light it. The air still had the stale smell of the swamp which he remembered, but it didn't carry the exotic feeling for him anymore, and just stunk. Dust swirled in the air where the sun cut in, shining on the old kitchen table – red Formica with chrome around the edges – it had a newspaper on it, a milk glass, dried milk clinging to the lower edges, a bowl and spoon, cereal dried and stuck to the sides. Out in the common room, it looked like he remembered: the scratchy couch remained, itself strewn with papers, the table covered, too, in various articles of life, as if the whole thing were flash-frozen in an instant where no further movement would be possible.

Just beyond, the master bedroom yawned open and dark. On the one hand, he was glad there was no tape over it to bar his entrance, but on the other, that might have been sufficient to stop him if it was there. He knew he had to look, though, and moved slowly through the living room where he had slept four years before, when he was so excited to be there.

Stopping at the doorway, he leaned against the jamb, looking inside, staring at the bed. The sheets were still twisted from someone who had slept there, but there was no more evidence. There was no pill jar on the nightstand, though an empty water glass remained, lipstick on the edge. Walking over, McGhee stood by the foot of the bed in silence. He'd never known death before, not like that. And he'd known Honey – at least a little – he knew her well enough to know what her absence would mean to Wil. He imagined her voice, low until it wasn't, racing up the register when she laughed with that wild creole cadence, like some wild creature escaping. He smiled to remember it, though he noticed, too, his cheeks were wet, and he rubbed his eyes at the folly of it, at the sadness, and perhaps, even the inevitability.

As he turned to go, he glanced at the wall next to the bed, and found it there, Honey's calendar pinned up, not quite straight. It was that little extra bit of darkness he had hoped would not be there, and somewhere in his head he heard Sweet Emma's band playing *A Closer Walk with Thee*.

McGhee couldn't convince Les to return with him – he had some work shift or other, though McGhee suspected he didn't want to go this time anyway, not really – so he decided he'd just push on and try to get home before the weather turned for the worse.

Les grabbed him by the shoulders, looked into his eyes, then pulled him in for a hug. "It'll get better, kid . . . ," he said. McGhee hugged him, too, patting his back a couple times before releasing.

Out on I-65, McGhee got the car up to eighty just past the edge of Nashville, heading into late afternoon. He wasn't sure he'd make it by midnight, but it was worth a try. The nose of the tape was peering out of the deck in the dash, and he tried not to push it in, but had to. Wil had said Honey used to say it was their song, only when she said it, something would catch in her voice, or so he said. *Every Breath You Take* oozed out of the speakers again, and he settled in for a long drive, not looking into the empty bucket next to him but once or twice. There sat the calendar folded back to November, red Xs crossing out every day except for those from the twenty-fourth onward, which were empty, and always would be.

Drift

3AM
Yukon River, Ruby, AK 9/26/1986

About one that afternoon the river took a turn for the worse. The sun was brilliant but cold, doing little to warm the landscape which was already tilting toward winter with an inexorable slant. The banks of stunted and dark pines slipped away silently as the boat and raft drifted without power. What had been flat water began to knap from a wind blowing straight at them up the river, raising choppy waves of two and three feet.

The day before Karl packed supplies into the twenty-foot skiff, checking and rechecking to make sure he hadn't missed anything. He tucked a thirty-ought-six under the gunwale after wrapping it in a sheet of Visqueen. He noticed McGhee watching him, then turned back to it. "Bears . . . ," he said by way of explanation, standing erect again, then pushing in the small of his back. By the look of him he was somewhere in his mid-thirties, but a thick beard made him look older. Julie was checking the foodstuffs in the pack. It'd be a short trip, but they wanted to make sure to anticipate delay. Things always went wrong in the bush, and the Yukon would take you if you let it, or something else would. Such was the guidance from Karl. Julie looked up long enough to nod and shrug, then went back to her inventory. McGhee helped Karl manhandle two 55-gallon drums of fuel into the bow and stern of the boat respectively – balance was key. Rubberized straps helped secure things in place, though the drums would move where they wanted if the river didn't cooperate. Karl tossed his chainsaw on top of a loose tarp near the bow to hold it down. Surveying the skiff he stood in silence a moment, eventually looking over at Julie and motioning for McGhee to get in. It was time to go.

The mission was to restock Karl's winter cabin some sixty miles upriver, then collect driftwood to bring back down river to stock the house in town. He'd be trapping his line for a good two months once the snow flew, and it was getting late. The river would freeze within weeks, and the opportunity to get large loads of supplies upriver would be gone for the season. He could tow a small sled behind his snow machine when he went up later on the river ice once the river was solid, but that wouldn't work for the fuel load or the lumber either. Then there was the dog food to haul; most of his work on the line would be by dog sled, and he had to haul a couple hundred pounds of air-dried salmon to feed them. They'd eat a hot gruel of fish soup most of the winter, but not if he didn't get it up there in the first place. Overall the load was just shy of a ton, and there wasn't much room left for the crew. Karl and Julie sat near the engine and McGhee plopped into the tarp next to the saw. "Better stow that blade . . . ," Karl said, motioning to the exposed chain by McGhee's thigh. "It'll cut ya just falling into it," he said. Leaning back against a cold wood stove in the middle of the skiff, McGhee looked into the wind that was mounting as they got up to speed.

The land was desolate and devoid of human touch. A sullen sky lay low over the river portending weather, though nothing fell for the moment. Around the bend, the river had cut into the bank, creating a bluff of thirty feet. From the stern behind him he heard Karl say, "The Boneyard". Looking over his shoulder he saw him motion to the bank he had been observing. That was where Ford had said he found that tusk, though McGhee was sworn to secrecy. There were tough rules and penalties for collecting ivory from the boneyard, and he didn't want any trouble. He had the tusk laying out in the tall grass behind his house. A good seven-footer he said, that'd collect a real premium once he got it to market. It struck McGhee as odd that he didn't seem to care it came from an extinct animal – a Wooly Mammoth – dead for ten thousand years. To Ford it was just another piece of income. As he was coming to understand, subsistence was very real in the bush, and the land didn't give up much without a fight. What in the abstract seemed questionable and conflicting, in practice was totally understand-able. More than that, it was imperative. The imposition of rules from distant authorities seemed absurd when faced with survival. To the young McGhee, this was a useful realization. It wasn't what he learned in school, but it was just as valuable. Perhaps more so.

The air was a brisk twenty-eight degrees and with the wind, colder still. Along the edges there wasn't much bank visible in most places. In some areas, where the land jutted into the water the river pushed back, eroding the trees from the edge. They'd tilt from their perches along the bluffs until they finally succumbed to the water's abrasion. Occasional surges on the river would end the job, pulling entire trees into the current. As they proceeded, they'd see trunks lined along the edge, or sometimes, afloat in the river coming the opposite way. Karl kept his eye out, steering wide of them, driving the skiff upriver against the current. The water was gray against the sky, broad as it was, melting away against the clouds in a mist, or fog, or just indiscernible horizon. It wasn't clear to McGhee what was ahead, but the water seemed to be open for the moment. It was nearly a mile across at many points, so there was room to maneuver if necessary. The drone of the engine helped lull McGhee into something of a doze, though his eyes remained partly open. Dark trees melted past, endless trees, stunted and thin, doing their best to push up into the gray, and down into the still-frozen earth. Endless trees and trees and trees, and no sign at all of human perversion. Miles of endless, untouched wilderness.

The tenor of the engine dropped slightly, then more quickly as the skiff nosed into the north shore of the river. Just off the river's edge, a barely discernible path emerged from the otherwise pristine shore. A small beach – no more than seven or eight feet wide, but wider than any area up or down the nearby edge – presented itself for the skiff to edge up onto the shore with a gravelly grind. Karl had been intending to catch McGhee napping, but he was already stirring and wasn't alarmed. Karl grunted that he'd been robbed of his fun, but Julie didn't notice: she was pulling the pack from under another tarp at the back of the boat and was already plunged into it, searching. Her hand emerged with an apple. Handing up a slice to him, McGhee was thankful for it. He was trying to be a good guest and not bother them with his lower-48 sensibilities, but his stomach was grumbling a bit. They'd been on the river a couple hours and that loading effort was draining. He knew, too, that he'd be expected to haul, among other things, those drums out of the skiff and up the shore to the cabin, which would be harder still. The apple was hard and crisp and sweet, and his gut rendered it with immediacy. This wasn't lost on Julie who watched him while Karl worked the ropes, so she handed him another piece.

"Thanks," McGhee said, but she was already back to helping Karl. It was an unspoken understanding that McGhee wasn't used to the lifestyle, but they were too courteous to speak of it openly.

The cabin wasn't too far in from the edge of the river, perhaps twenty-five yards, so it could have been worse. That said, the bank did have a two-foot lip to navigate where higher waters had carved their will. For most of the provisions heading to the cabin it wasn't a problem, but the drums were another story. Both Karl and McGhee working hard managed to tip the drum up onto the ledge of shore. Tipping it again on edge they got it upright, then went back for the second to perform the same operation. Once both were up on the edge, Karl moved to the first one, tipped it slightly and began rolling it carefully on its edge along the path toward the cabin. McGhee did his best to copy the maneuver but struggled, either tipping too much or too little as he rolled. Finishing quickly, Karl ran back to give McGhee a hand.

Coming up from behind, Julie patted him on the shoulder. "Usually I have to do that," she said.

Smiling, McGhee looked at her. "No problem," he said, relieved someone seemed to think he was useful.

The cabin was rough but solid. Karl had to remove some bear-proofing before they could enter: a spiked threshold mat consisting of a board with seven-inch spikes pounded through sat by the doorway. Karl smiled wryly as he called it his *welcome mat*. Boards nailed over the door held it secure. There was evidence of many nail holes around the boards indicating this had been the trusted security method for years. Inside, the cabin was low and dark, not much more than standing height in the middle. Toward the back sat a kettle stove on the floor which led to a pipe poking up through the roof. Two rough tables lined the front and left sides, and something of a cot lined the right. Traps hung in the corner in front of the only window, a small one-foot square pane still dark from the bear-cover on the outside. Just below the window sat a square of insulation that seemed to fit the window's size and McGhee assumed it was used to stop heat loss when there wasn't enough light to see anyway. According to Karl it could get to sixty below out there, so it was necessary to trap in the heat however one could.

Julie lit a kerosene lamp and the rest of the cabin came into view, such as it was. Rafters above formed a rudimentary roof structure. More traps hung there, as well as other tools, such as skinning knives, a pick, another chain saw and various bits for field repair. Behind the stove was another small table, and above it was a crate tacked to the wall for an ad hoc cabinet. It contained two coffee cups, two plates, two table knives, two forks, two spoons and a bowl. The small table had a red and white checked towel draped over both ends. It was the sole splash of color in the cabin, but had lost most of it to many seasons of washing and wringing and scrubbing. Still, it was neat in its own way, lending a touch of comfort to an otherwise spare existence. It was not a picture of luxury, but was comfortable enough, which seemed to be the standard in these parts.

McGhee noticed he was the only one left in the cabin, so stepped out to help. He didn't want the perception to build he was a slacker and wanted to pull his weight. Karl had gone back to the boat and Julie was already stacking some planks. Trailing back to the river he found Karl gathering up items in his arms, struggling to carry as much as he could in his next load. McGhee reached out to accept it from him, and Karl eased his pace to look at him. "You're doing fine...," he said handing his load over and turning back to grab more stuff. He was apparently tuned-in to the young man's anxiety.

McGhee wasn't sure where to put the stuff, so he stood on the threshold with his arms full, waiting. Julie was back inside, bustling behind the stove.

From behind him he heard, "No, no, no . . . ," as Karl caught up with his own armload. "This stuff doesn't go in the cabin," he said motioning with his chin toward McGhee. "It goes in the cache."

"But it's food . . . and . . . ," McGhee objected, but his voice trailed off as he noticed Karl's expression. It was set to patient, or something like it. He was waiting for McGhee to talk himself out, which McGhee realized he had just done.

"That's the surest way to get a bear in your cabin," Karl said by way of explanation. Waving him over with his head, he led the way to the cache. Twenty yards or so away, to the west, he noticed clumping in the trees as they walked up to them. Four trees each less than six inches in diameter sat growing roughly at the corners of a square. A makeshift ladder of old lumber and some split rails led up into the nest about fifteen feet off the ground. It looked like a tree house, only there were no windows. Pulling a hammer from his belt, Karl climbed the ladder and pried the bear protection from the top: a sheet of plywood with rows of spikes pounded through facing out and down the ladder for the last four steps. A board over the small door provided another layer of security. He opened it carefully but stood back clear of the opening while wrapping an arm around one side of the ladder. "You never know what might have gotten in there . . . ," he said cautiously. Karl motioned toward the top of the cache, then waved the hammer in a circle. "It isn't exactly Fort Knox." He didn't want to surprise anything that might be hunkering inside, and he didn't want to fall off the ladder either. It was obvious by his movements that he did these things automatically, that they resided in his muscle memory as much as in his consciousness. "Falling out in the bush is a major reason guys don't come home . . . ," Karl said absently, moving closer to peer into the dark opening. He pulled out a small flashlight he had tucked away somewhere and snapped it on. "Not because the fall kills you either – that'd be too easy. Usually a guy breaks his leg, or maybe blows out a knee." Turning to look over his shoulder down the ladder, his lips curved into a slight smile. "You didn't see any hospitals on the way out here, didja?" he asked.

"Ahh . . . no . . . ," McGhee said, shrugging.

"Well, there's not one in Ruby either," he said, turning back to the cache. Climbing up, half his body disappeared into the hole. He could barely fit through the gap and had to maneuver diagonally to get his shoulders in. After some rustling and gyration, he pulled back out of the gap with some effort. He could see the puzzled look on McGhee's face and continued his instruction.

"You make the door little so bears can't get in, either. That won't stop them from ripping it apart if they're motivated, though." Motioning to the heap of stores on the ground, McGhee began handing up the dried salmon for the dogs and other foodstuffs for the camp. Stuffing the materials through the hole, Karl kept up the monologue. "Bears are bad," he said, "but for my money, wolverines are worse. They're just fuckin' ornery bastards and . . . ," he said pushing a large package through the opening with successive thrusts and grunts: "tricky . . . little . . . sonsabitches." After inspecting his work, he looked down at McGhee. "Their claws will open you up real quick," he said, panting a bit from the effort, "and they're smart and fast as hell. No way they'll miss if you're in striking distance and they get it in their head they can beat you. And they always, *always* have that in their head. Best give 'em a wide berth and carry your gun." His hand moved down to his belt. McGhee hadn't noticed before, but a woven Gore-Tex holster in camouflage jutted down his side. "Forty-five works best," he said. "They have thick skulls. So do bears. I've seen a round glance off more than once. Thank god it's usually enough to discourage 'em, though."

Once the stores were stowed, Karl replaced the door, then the cache's *welcome mat*. Julie was in the door of the cabin. She appeared to be done with her chores and watched the two coming back. No review was required – they didn't need to discuss what was needed or done on either end. Karl simply swung the door shut and grabbed up the bar to replace it with long spikes. A *welcome mat* went in place there, too. Standing back, Karl stared at the cabin for a moment in silence. It was becoming a familiar pose, McGhee thought. Something of a conscious habit, born of necessity and the inherent difficulty of bush life. There was no coming back, not without considerable risk and inconvenience, so trips were planned and minimized. If he'd forgotten something, he'd likely be without it for months, alone. Looking up from his thoughts he glanced from McGhee to Julie and back again. "Time for the real work . . . ," he said, stepping off the porch onto the path toward the river.

"Real work?" McGhee asked, chasing after him.

The plan wasn't clear to McGhee, but he was getting used to that. It involved collecting wood and heading back, but beyond that, he had no detail. He was glad for the momentary respite, however, and settled back into his place in the bow atop the crumpled tarp. Heading back down river, the breeze wasn't as strong in his face, and he was glad of it. The wind was following the current down river and it made the journey slightly warmer than the trip up had been.

Twenty miles or so downriver, the skiff's motor changed tempo and McGhee could feel the boat turning into shore. It was a slight bend in the river where the current had left a shoal of gravel which in turn left a wide band of coarse sand, or small gravel, or both. It was a natural place for things to fall out of the current or get snagged in the confused currents of water and wash ashore. This flotsam had included various things that had become unmoored higher up the river – several floats from small boats or barges, half a port-o-john which came from god-knows-where, a few bottles, and various other indicators of humanity. McGhee found it odd to see as there was so little evidence of humanity otherwise. He then realized he was seeing the distillation of a thousand miles of river and concluded it wasn't so much after all.

Other than the refuse, the beach was populated with much wood: endless stumps had washed ashore, complete with large root-balls stripped of soil. Many had burned edges and tips, and most showed what at one time had been a clean cut by a chainsaw – further evidence of human presence. Endless soaking and floating and collisions had left them broken and battered and black. The good news was there were whole trees there, too, conveniently stripped of most branches, except nubs which remained where some river violence had relieved the trees of their members. Karl had selected this place for good reason: the trees there would be enough for his plans and supply-wood for the winter. Surveying the wood available he looked pleased. "Saw this on the way up . . . ," he said, stepping over some logs that lay close to the water. Somehow it became clear to McGhee as he started to get into the local mind-set that the convenience of the limbless trees close by water wasn't a total coincidence. It was Karl's target all along, and he knew to look for it. The lack of limbs meant less work to clean them, and the proximity to the edge meant less effort to get them afloat again.

Without words, the plan suddenly became manifest: they'd construct a raft of these trees and float them back downriver to Ruby.

As Karl scoped out the wood situation, Julie dragged the tent pack up the beach to slightly higher ground. It was roughly cylindrical, a foot in diameter, five feet long, and heavy enough to carve a slight path in the sandy gravel along the way. Tugging the tent from the canvas bag, she began to spread it out, tossing the larger rocks from the area to make for more comfort later, and to avoid damage to the under-mat of the structure. Unfolding the tent revealed a surprisingly large footprint. McGhee went around best he could flattening out the lay of the flaccid structure toward each of the corners. The plop of a small bag near his boot revealed his next task – staking the corners in place. Just as it occurred to him he'd need to pound them in, a hammer landed next to the small bag. Looking up at Julie he saw her waving her hand to get going. The stakes were long and flanged at the end to catch the tent loop, but the driving in of them wasn't hard as the sandy gravel yielded with modest blows from the hammer. By the time he was done with them – there were six – Julie was assembling the aluminum poles and jamming them through the support sleeves to erect the tent. It wasn't ten minutes but Julie had the tent up and was working on guide-lines to further secure the structure. "You don't know how bad camping can suck until you've been blown around in a loose tent . . . ," she said over her shoulder to McGhee.

"Great," McGhee said smiling, but she was too busy to notice.

Down by the water, Karl was priming the saw to get to work. It made a few asthmatic, guttural sounds but wouldn't catch. Grabbing the blade, he carefully dragged the chain around a quarter of the length, then checked the spark plug. Blowing into the cap he smacked the cable end on the housing to dislodge what might be there, or might not. Putting a little spit on his pinky, he jammed it into the cap and twisted back and forth. Satisfied, he snapped it back into place and grabbed the cord. First try it wheezed to life, tentatively, then roaring as he exercised the saw. It had been some time since he used it, so he sent the chain rolling several times to get it oiled, warm and ready. Moments later the first spray of saw dust flew up over him in a huge fan tail, the engine straining with the thickness of the wood it chewed. It was a large tree, perhaps fifteen inches at the base, which given the size of many of the stunted trees, was substantial. After another twenty seconds of sustained cutting, the root ball fell free and the trunk, relieved of its load, shifted up with a groan. Though the tree didn't have many of its limbs left, only nubs, Karl moved along the length to trim the longer ones flush with the trunk. By the far end, he knocked off the tip of the tree where it had shrunk to six inches in diameter. Overall, it was at least a phone pole in length of perhaps forty feet. Allowing the saw to stop, he stood erect, pushing in the small of his back with some satisfaction. "One down, thirty to go" he said, scanning for his next victim.

After another hour of cutting, the beach had a cluster of ten or twelve prepped trunks for the raft. Julie had built a small fire in front of the tent, downwind slightly to avoid smoke, or worse, fire in the tent itself. Fire placement was something of an art, but by this time an automatic skill she exercised without thought. She built a slight windscreen on the upriver side from rounded cobbles on the beach to protect it. Getting a good set of embers would come in handy later when it came time to cook potatoes and the rest of the camp meal.

McGhee helped Karl wrestle the logs into rough alignment as close to the water as possible. They made a width of ten feet or so, but needed some rotation to minimize the gaps along the length.

Using two pike poles with hinged hooks near the end to grab the logs with some leverage, the two adjusted their attitude to Karl's satisfaction. Karl made it clear it needed to be constructed half in the water to avoid problems later, most notably, not being able to get it the rest of the way in. He'd use the boat engine to pull it in the rest of the way while Julie and McGhee pushed from shore when it was ready. Once the logs were wrangled in place, parallel to make a platform, he went back to several of the decapitated tree tops to rip them flat lengthwise to create cross-spars. Laying them across the logs he spaced the four spars across at intervals to give the raft strength. Seeing the state of progress, Julie brought the hand drill over from the skiff for the next phase of the process. It was an old steel auger, four feet long, with a foot of bit, three feet of shaft and a wooden T handle on top for twisting. It would be necessary to auger three or four holes per each end spar, down through the raft logs beneath to hold them in place. Taking turns it would take a few hours to complete.

Karl took the first shift and drilled an entire hole by himself, through fifteen inches of spar and log. Seeing the process, McGhee went next at the other end of the spar, but wasn't able to complete the hole himself. After several stops, with decreasing runs between the breaks, Julie spelled him while he collapsed on a nearby root ball stump still fresh from the cutting. Karl went among the branch stubs looking for suitably straight limbs to make into six-foot pegs, returning with an armload of candidates. McGhee, wanting to keep up, retrieved some others in case that would not be enough. Karl shaped their ends with a little chainsaw work before pounding them into the holes with a sledge. After another two hours of boring, each of the end spars had holes and were pegged into place. According to Karl, the pegs served two purposes: to hold the spars and logs together, and to provide vertical guides at the corners and middle for the stacked wood. The two central spars were easier as Karl pounded in several seven-inch spikes for those. By late afternoon, the raft was nearly done. McGhee wasn't totally clear why so many pegs were necessary, but it seemed better to remain silent on the subject. One thing was clear throughout the process: Karl was in control and didn't appear interested in questions or debate.

Walking out to the water-ward end of the raft, Karl started the saw. He looked right and left along the end surveying the irregular ends to devise an approach. After a few moments he set to cutting a notch into the end of the logs about five feet wide which roughly matched the contour of the front of the skiff. This would be for the boat to attach to the raft, nose in, as they drifted down river. When they were ready, he'd attach the skiff with ropes and rubber bungee straps for the drift back home. Once the notch was finished, he looked over his work. Glancing over at McGhee he saw he was whipped, slouching on the root-ball, watching him. "Now we're done," he said. Shifting his look to Julie, he smiled. "How about some dinner?"

Though he wouldn't admit it, McGhee liked the sound of that as his stomach had been growling most of the afternoon. It wasn't clear to him how they operated on such little fuel, but he was also sure he was used to ready-food in a way that was impossible in the bush. He'd simply have to get used to this as he had no intention of becoming anything like an annoyance.

Up by the tent there were two camp chairs by the fire, and he immediately collapsed into one of them. After a moment, he realized he'd taken one of their chairs and just as quickly launched out it, trying to look casual in the process, even though he had nothing to occupy himself. Pushing him on the shoulder, Karl told him to relax. "You're not used to this . . . ," he said, moving on and disappearing into the tent. From out of view, Karl kept talking. "I hope you like bear. We're having the last of the bear stew tonight . . . ."

By the fire, Julie leaned over and confided: "Thank God for that – we've been eating this fucking bear for months . . . ."

Nestled in the coals were foil packets containing the rest of the meal: three tight foil balls containing potatoes and a looser packet containing some wild carrots and onion. Karl emerged with a tin pot, black on the bottom with licks of black up the sides. In his other hand he had a small metal rack. Using a stick, he flattened out an area near the edge of the fire pit and tossed the rack into place. After some tapping and prodding, the rack was stable enough to hold the pot, which he immediately plopped onto the rack before pulling his hand quickly away. The lid jostled as it came to rest, revealing a light aluminum sound – steal was too heavy to lug in a pack. As McGhee was learning, everything in the bush required consideration, weight being a significant one. Karl remained on his haunches, prodding the fire with a stick. Without looking at McGhee, he went into a monologue of instruction and observation:

"You did good work today – you're hardier than you look. I'm sure you're not used to it, but you'll get there. Everything is hard out here, and there's risk everywhere. Oh . . . there's bear-sign all over around here. Probably a fishing spot. There's tracks over there," he said, motioning with his chin, just to the left of the tent, "and some scat just down the beach there. You better be careful if you step out of the tent at night to piss. Keep your eyes and ears open. If you hear grunting or huffing, it's probably a bear. Just don't run. They like to charge, and if you run, you're dead. You can't out-run a bear anyway. They go thirty-five or so." After a few moments of silence, he continued.

"Tomorrow we'll load the raft. I'll cut lengths and you can collect them. Julie'll stack. We'll be up around sunrise and should be on the river by mid-morning. With some luck we'll be back in Ruby by nightfall."

After a few moments of silence, McGhee offered to help cut the wood, too.

"You know how to run a saw?" Karl asked hopefully, finally looking at him.

"No, not really . . . ," McGhee admitted, "but I could give it a shot."

Karl laughed and shook his head. "*Hell no . . .* ," he said. "The last thing we need is to be collecting your toes and running back to Ruby. I'm pretty sure Joey couldn't get 'em back on neither . . . ."

"Joey Koyukon is sort of the town doctor . . . ," Julie said, filling in the blanks. "He's pretty good, but not that good . . . . He was a medic or something in the Army."

"So, *NO*, you can't use the saw," Karl said, resuming his speech. McGhee was secretly relieved – he could imagine toes all over the place. Karl and Julie both laughed: the scenario was playing over the young man's face. McGhee was still lost in thought when Julie pulled the pot out of the fire. Steam was escaping into the cool air from around the edge of the lid, and with it came the aroma of stew.

"Thanks . . . ," McGhee said, accepting a plate and lifting it for a sniff. "Smells good."

Julie smiled, adjusting the foiled potatoes in the fire, tossing one to McGhee. "Everything smells good when you're hungry."

McGhee didn't think twice about laying into the formless slurry on his plate, though he was marginally aware it was a new animal he was tasting. It looked like any other stew and tasted about the same. Where the normal beef taste would be, he focused his attention but didn't find much difference. It wasn't fat. It wasn't gamey. It definitely didn't taste of regular pork or chicken. It was pretty much just like beef, though a bit different, perhaps slightly porky after all, though in a way he couldn't quantify, but it didn't bother him. In fact, it was so un-disturbing he hurried through it hoping for another spoonful, but it wasn't to be had — it was indeed the last little bit they had shared. He was a little sad he hadn't stretched it out to enjoy longer. Squishing out his foil potato, he used it to gather the last few trails of stew remaining on the plate until nothing more remained but his memory of its savory taste and the brief satisfaction it afforded.

"That was pretty good . . . ," McGhee said, sitting his plate on the sand by his feet. "I thought I was gonna faint from hunger."

Julie smiled again. "Matt told us to take care of you," she said.

"I feel like a baby out here . . . . I don't think I'd survive a day on my own," McGhee said, staring into the fire.

"Oh . . . you'd make it . . . ," Karl said, his lips curling into a smile. "At least forty-eight hours anyway . . . ."

"So you went to school with Matt back east?" Julie asked, finally sitting back with her own plate.

McGhee nodded, but his expression dimmed. "Yeah . . . ," he said, but didn't go on.

Julie looked at Karl, then back to McGhee. "Well, you're not gonna get any lectures 'round here," she said, smiling slyly, "except from Karl. He's full of 'em."

Rolling up his foil into a ball, Karl tossed it at Julie. "We don't want him to get eaten now, do we?" he said, standing to brush the crumbs from his lap into the fire.

The sun was gone from the sky though some light remained. The trees appeared even darker in the gathering evening. Twenty feet away the river rolled by heading west toward Ruby and onward toward Nome. There were no sounds other than the slight crackle of the fire: no birds made noise, the river was silent, and the local human bustle was quiet. Evening was laying upon them quickly and the slight breeze crept across a threshold from welcome to chilling almost imperceptibly. It would be in the thirties before long, so it was time to button up camp and get to sleep. The rinsed pot and utensils were stowed some distance from the tent to avoid problems from wildlife, and the fire was allowed to burn low.

※

It seemed McGhee had just closed his eyes when he was shaken awake by Karl—the tent door was open and the patch of sky already shown pale blue, though it was before dawn. Julie was at the fire, stoking the coals and adding a few sticks to get more flame. There was an old blue white-speckled country coffee pot on a flat rock next to the fire, waiting. It must have been ten hours he'd slept, but it seemed only moments. The aches in his joints reminded him of the previous day's boring. Getting up on one elbow, he nodded to Karl. It was time to get moving.

It was probably seven or so, not that it mattered much; they'd work until the work was done, drift the river, then work some more. Still, McGhee was used to knowing what time it was, so he asked. "Morning," was the answer from both Karl and Julie at the same time. Julie found it amusing, but Karl was on task.

"OK, so here's how it's gonna work . . . ," he said, mostly to McGhee, since Julie knew the routine. "I'm gonna strip some more trees, then cut four-foot lengths. Your job is to get them back to the raft. Julie will stack. But first we got to float the raft, and before that we got to hook the skiff to the raft. Got it?"

McGhee nodded. "That's what the notch in the raft is for, right?" McGhee asked.

Karl nodded. "Right . . . ," he said. By his look the answer was obvious, so McGhee resumed his studious silence.

Julie handed McGhee a cup of black coffee – he wanted to ask for milk or something to cut it, but that didn't feel even remotely possible or actually necessary. Karl was chugging his cup in huge gulps, even though it was scalding hot. It didn't feel like it would be a leisurely breakfast, so much as a pit stop in a race. After a few sips, McGhee was growing to like it – it went with the surroundings: simple, relentless, unforgiving.

As he was getting toward the bottom of the cup, Julie handed him some jerky. "Salmon," she said.

Karl was already gnawing on a chunk. "It has loads of fat and energy. You're gonna need it . . . ," he said smiling. He didn't smile often – he always seemed to be worried about this risk or that task – but when he did it was genuine and warm. It was the kind of look guys in trenches give one another when shells are falling all around, or so McGhee thought. He hadn't been in the military, but he'd seen his share of war movies. As for the salmon jerky, it wasn't McGhee's idea of a breakfast, but the infusion of energy was indeed welcome.

Karl went on ahead to fix the skiff to the raft. It fit neatly into the notch he had cut and he set to strapping it in. Pulling onto the cords, he adjusted them until he couldn't budge them, satisfying himself it would hold for the journey. Stepping to the stern he started the engine. Julie and McGhee went down to wait for the sign, and when he gave it they both levered with the pike poles on the beached end of the raft. The water was running a bit higher than the night before, so with their heaving, the higher water and the tug of the engine, they were able to push the raft free. Using the engine Karl was able to bring it parallel to shore. Julie grabbed a couple spare lines Karl had set, which were attached to the pegs to pull it in the last foot or so, and tied it off to a root ball close to the water's edge. McGhee handled the other end, though made a hash of the knot he tied to another piece of drift nearby. As he walked over to where Karl had moved, Julie retied the knot to make sure it didn't come free but took care McGhee wouldn't see her redoing his work.

Out on the beach Karl's Stihl whined to life and he set to dismembering trees with alarming speed. Once a tree was de-limbed, the blade set to work on the trunk and the tone low-ered as the wood fought back against the assault. Rooster-tail plumes of dust shot up and over Karl but he paid no attention — goggles provided enough protection that he could keep his head down and focused. Before long, he waved McGhee over and the hauling began. Hauling the first log on his shoulder he wondered how he'd do this all morning. It must have weighed a hundred pounds or so he thought, and his frame compressed under the load. Back at the raft he tipped it down where the end landed with a thud. Julie grabbed the upper end and hauled it out on the raft where the first cord would lay. The raft appeared sound and solid, not straining under her weight, or the log's, which seemed about equivalent. He marveled that for a small woman she was very strong.

Once back at Karl's cutting location, there were two more seg-ments for him to carry. He realized he'd have to pick up the pace to keep up and rolled the next chunk onto his shoulder.

"Lift with your legs or your back will be a mess later . . . ," Karl shouted over the sawing, though he didn't appear to slow his cutting. It was a good reminder because McGhee already felt the strain, and the thought was just then forming how to combat it. Back at the raft when he handed off the chunk he asked how much wood they'd be gathering.

"Three or four cords I think," Julie said, handling the log next to the other already in place. "Don't worry though," she continued, seeing McGhee's dismay. "Karl and I will help. There's no way to keep up with his cutting. I'm just glad you're here to get a head start."

And so it continued through the morning, past sunrise until the sun was far up in the sky. Each time McGhee got to where Karl was cutting there were more and more chunks to lug, and the chunks got further and further away from the raft as Karl found new trees to render. Though the initial chunks seemed unbearably heavy, McGhee found something of a rhythm. He learned not to hurry, but to plod along at a constant pace. The course of logs on the raft built through the length of it, out to the last spar, then began a second course, and third. McGhee was unloading yet another log when he heard the saw go silent. Karl rose from his position, pressing into the small of his back. It had been several hours of good work and the remains of almost another twenty trees lay strewn in irregular lines across the beach. McGhee had lost pace long before, though he had kept at the work steadily. All three took a break to drink some water, have some more jerky, and survey the work before them.

The raft already held more than a cord of wood. When McGhee looked over his shoulder at it he was a bit surprised they'd made so much progress. Still, he could feel each one of the logs on his shoulder as if each had left its own peculiar dent there. Tugging off his leather gloves, McGhee looked at his hands. They were red and hot, but it seemed he had avoided blisters, which was his concern even before he started the hauling. Rubbing them together he could feel them crackle as he relieved their stress and the massage felt good. And though his shoulder was a bit sore, he smiled a little to himself that he'd been able to do it. Karl would cut a few more trees, he said, as they might just have enough soon, and then he'd help carry.

After another hour Karl was done cutting and had converted to moving the pieces. He moved with such a quick pace McGhee couldn't keep up with him. For every two McGhee carried, Karl had three and was heading back for another. The courses were well-formed enough for Karl and McGhee to place the new pieces, so Julie moved up to camp to prepare lunch and start to strike the tent. They'd need to be on the river by eleven or so to make the drift to Ruby by nightfall, so there wasn't much time to waste. Lunch consisted of a few strips of moose in the pot, mixed with some scrambled eggs and some dried onion flakes. This time the meat was more surprising than the bear had been: it was more like venison than beef, but sweeter. It wasn't exactly gamey, but was distinct from anything he'd had before. After a few bites he was clear he liked it and continued shoveling. McGhee took care not to eat so fast this time, but was delighted to learn there was another small scoop of the hash. Julie automatically dumped it over his fork when it came to rest and he looked up at her. She smiled then moved over to dump the rest on Karl's plate. "Thanks, hun . . . ," he grunted, giving her a quick smile, too. He wasn't a man for many words, but they mattered. She smacked him on the shoulder, flashing a quick smile back at him.

Karl and McGhee finished the stacking, adjusting the wood to ensure, best they could, it'd stay in place for the journey. Karl was a bit concerned they'd stacked too high and it might become unstable on the river, so they adjusted the load to lower the center of gravity. Still, the raft was sitting low in the water, which created another concern. Jumping onto the shore, Karl pushed on the raft with his foot. It didn't budge. Pressing harder, it still wouldn't move. "Shit . . . ," he said, standing back to look at the situation. The load on the raft had pressed at least one of the spar pegs into the sand, anchoring it place.

Karl went back up the beach in search of one of the pike poles. Further up the strand, the tent was collapsing as Julie struck camp. She'd already stowed the pot and other supplies in the skiff, so this was the last step. Back at the raft, Karl began fishing under the edge with the pike to find the peg wedged in the sand. At the lower end of them, the pegs weren't very thick. After a few attempts he was able to catch it with the hook on the pole. After two or three hard yanks there was a muffled snap under the water and six inches of peg floated to the surface. Karl smiled briefly and pushed on the raft, but it still didn't budge. "Shit . . . ," he said again, moving to the next spar peg. After three such operations, his push on the corner yielded movement and the raft was free. Julie arrived momentarily with the tent stowed in the bag and wrestled it over the gunwale of the skiff with a plop.

Karl didn't take more than a few seconds breath before he was in the skiff, adjusting the contents for the journey. He dragged the potbelly stove into the center of the boat and inserted a stove pipe into the top of it, rising some five feet or so to keep any smoke out of the skiff. They wouldn't be needing it during the day, but if the drift went long, they'd want to have it. Toward the back of the skiff he pulled out a pike pole and wedged it just below the engine where the aluminum frame made a gap over the corrugated hull of the craft. At the front end of the pole, he made a V with the other pike pole and another straight limb he'd stowed earlier for the purpose. Using a bungee he bundled the three together, forming something of a teepee structure. Just as the sticks constelled for McGhee and the purpose dawned on him, Karl threw a blue tarp over the long pike down the center to form a lean-to shelter. That'd be a convenient place for them to get out of the wind and sun as it was going to be a long afternoon. With that, Julie jumped in the boat, Karl fired up the engine, and within a minute they were already pulled out from shore and heading for the channel of the river. McGhee settled into his spot near the bow, nestling into the tarp for a bit of rest and to watch the river. Once the skiff and raft made it into the channel, Karl shut off the engine to conserve gas and let the current do the work. It was quiet but for the lapping of the water on the gunwales and the occasional call of ravens on the near shore scrumming over bits of found treasure.

The sun was high in the sky, but wasn't imparting much warmth. Between the latitude, time of year and the wind of the river, the sun barely warmed the air beyond its natural chill. Still, it was a fine afternoon, and with the constant muscle work of the morning, each of them were glad for the break. Karl sat in the back by the tiller, ready to fire the engine but clearly nodding off. Julie had climbed into the lean-to almost as soon as they were on the river and was napping. McGhee was leaning back against the stove, eyes closed, but apparently looking skyward in his dreams. The view had changed since the trip upriver. Now, instead of an unimpeded view across the bow of the water, the raft provided a new foreground. It also changed the nature of the ride; where there had been some buoyancy and bouncing as the water dictated with the skiff alone, with the raft, there was less of that, and it was different. It was more of a slight rolling. If anything it made napping an inexorable imperative as the movement lulled even the most vigilant to sleep.

Eventually Karl gave in to the inevitable and crawled into the lean-to. A slightly mussed Julie soon emerged from the shelter to take his watch. Ostensibly, McGhee was on watch, too, but they each knew (though it was unspoken) that he wouldn't be able to handle a crisis anyway. Julie had had an hour of sleep, so she was mostly ready for her watch, though yawning frequently as she peered over the water. McGhee was roused from his nap and stood, watching the water, too. Patches of shade swept across the river as the sun hid behind light clouds, then emerged again. The weather seemed fine.

Given the conditions, it was surprising when the wind picked up soon thereafter in the early afternoon. The knap of the river changed, going from smooth to ruffled, and from ruffled to capping within a minute. What had been a very light chop became two and three foot swells and these took turns washing over the edges of the raft. McGhee saw it as more of a curiosity than anything – the peril was lost on him. Julie called to Karl in the shelter to come out and check the wind. Between the wind catching the higher profile of the raft like a sail, and the current swirling under the wind's influence, the skiff and connected raft began to rotate. Karl emerged to see the combined craft drifting sideways down river, with increasing waves crashing broadside into the stacked wood. The raft itself began bouncing, digging deeper into oncoming swells and troughs as it found a natural bobbing rhythm with the water. This accentuated the effect of the waves.

Karl was instantly alarmed. "Fuck, fuck, fuck . . . . We're gonna lose it!" he shouted, hustling sideways up the skiff to the raft and calling back to Julie. "Use the tiller to bring us straight if you can . . . ."

Julie nodded and slammed the tiller handle to port to steer into the skid, but without power (the engine remained off), the passive effect of the tiller wasn't enough to counter the active effects of the wind and water. Karl clambered over the nose of the skiff and onto the raft, but the disintegration had already begun. It wasn't clear he could have done anything to stop it anyway, other than, perhaps, throw his body on top of the logs and will the wood back into place. The shaking and wobbling and bobbing and dashing, though not wild, were easily sufficient to undermine the friction of log on log. The water, too, aided the process by lubricating them and jostling them by degrees out of alignment. The piles were four and five feet tall in most places, and with the gyrations of the raft and the waves achieving synchrony, the logs were dislodged, and the stacks began melting away. First the top few logs, then entire courses spilled into the water. Moments later and only a few log segments remained on the raft while the rest slid into the drink.

The wind continued to blow, now less up river and more toward the southern shore. Julie and McGhee weren't sure what to do – Karl stood on the raft watching his hard work head down river. He watched several minutes in silence, until Julie pulled him out of it: "What should we do, Karl?"

After another few seconds of watching, he turned to them. "Looks like the wind that's pushing us ashore is pushing the logs, too. I think we can get 'em back maybe. Let's head to shore and see . . . ."

With that he stepped back into the skiff and made his way to the engine. Crackling to life, it allowed him to regain control of the craft and bring it in parallel with the shore. Once it was just a few feet out, Julie jumped off with a guide-line and secured it to a tree limb jutting out of the gravel. They were lucky to have come ashore along a long low sloping beach. It was about fifty feet up to the turf and tree line from the water – a lot more than most of the shoreline. Karl was already off the raft and running down the beach. The first of the logs were coming ashore and he was dragging them out of the water where further wave action couldn't get at them. McGhee trailed after him and they'd skip past each other moving down the beach to grab the next fugitive log, and the next, and the next. The chunks came ashore slowly at first, then in waves of five and seven and ten. Soon it seemed almost all of the logs had been pressed off the water by the same wind that threw them in. Gathering those clumps of logs, Karl and McGhee started forming piles up and down the beach. These ran the full length of the strand – perhaps more than a mile – when they looked over the work ahead of them.

Walking back the length of it they found Julie on the beach setting rocks in a circle for a fire. "Good idea . . . ," Karl said. He put his fist on his hip and looked directly at her, wordless.

"So what do ya think?" she said finally.

"I think we got most of it back . . . ," he said. "Only now it's waterlogged, so it's gonna be a lot heavier . . . A *lot*!"

They stood in silence again, looking at each other. "I should have started the engine sooner . . . ," he said, dejected. "I musta still been asleep. So, maybe you can make camp up here, while McGhee and I get the wood back on the raft . . . ."

Julie nodded and went to grab the large camp bag. "Come on . . . ," Karl said to McGhee, trudging past him back toward the piles of wood. The true meaning of Karl's words only sunk in when he tilted the first log segment upright and onto his shoulder. What had seemed heavy before now was crushing. Not only that, the wet wood seemed to swell with the water and regain some hardness, making its press into his shoulder that much more painful. After just carrying the first log back to the raft he felt done, but that clearly wasn't going to be the case. Karl landed just after him, plopped his log down next to McGhee's, and patted him on the shoulder before passing him to slowly walk back down the beach.

It was a painful four hours, especially the last portion with the longest walks to the furthest piles, then back up the beach. Once it was all stacked it was clear they had indeed lost some wood, though perhaps only ten or fifteen percent of the total. It was a hard-earned recovery from total disaster, but they had paid, both Karl and McGhee, at the edge of exhaustion. Julie, too, had worked hard. After setting camp and the tent and the fire, she worked to stack the wood. This time there was more care to interleave some of the logs to make what happened less likely when they got back on the river. Sliding the rounds back and forth and adjusting the piles she had repeatedly caught her fingers between hardened logs finding their position as they shifted into place. By the time the last log was stacked, they were spent.

Climbing into the tent, all three fell onto their sleeping bags and were instantly asleep. It was nearly dark when they stirred at all, and it was fully dark when they had enough energy to eat.

They were quiet around the fire, each emerging from a tunnel of exhaustion. Eventually, Julie broke the silence. "So, I guess we're doing a night drift then...," she said, looking up from the fire at Karl.

He was poking the embers with a stick, gradually waking up and eating some of the provisions they had for quick energy. He shrugged and looked at her. "Guess so . . . We kinda have to," he said. "It won't be bad – we have the stove . . . ," he continued, trying to sound hopeful. What wasn't clear was whether that was genuine, or if he was saying it to get himself prepared for the drift. After some more snacking and warming by the fire, Karl got to his feet, stiff. "OK," he said. Julie looked up at him and offered her hand so he could pull her up. McGhee did, too, and Karl laughed. Julie pulled him upright. Once up, the three set to striking camp so they could get back on the river. Within the half-hour the engine was pushing them back out into the current, where Karl turned it off and it went silent.

Though they saw stars for a while, it was short lived. By nine or so clouds made their way in from the southwest, blotting out any hint of clear sky. They made the sky a little lighter and warmer than it had been, but that was short lived, too. Before long it seemed like the clouds were as tired as the crew and began to fall out of the sky, precipitating on them as a fine drizzle. The temperature was dropping, too, as any vestige of afternoon warmth leaked from the air. Karl left the tiller to Julie's care and stepped to the middle of the boat. Checking the stovepipe, he made sure it was secure. "We'd better get this thing fired up . . . ," he said, looking up at McGhee. He tossed a few sticks he'd split into the stove, then a few larger split pieces, and finally a few solid three or four inch rounds of a foot in length or so. He grabbed an oily white container with red lettering on it and a long thin nose, squirting ten seconds worth of recycled motor oil all over the wood. "It can't help but burn with that shit on it...," he said. Tossing in a match, the wood caught quickly and he closed the little metal hatch with a squeak and a clang, latching it in place.

The skiff and raft were in the center of the channel and the river was pretty wide, more than half a mile, and perhaps wider still. Luckily the wind wasn't blowing hard, but it was cold enough. The air must have been about thirty-five degrees because they could see their breath easily, but the moisture in the air remained fluid, at least for the moment, so it wasn't quite freezing. That said, the precipitation fell more steadily, though it never quite rose to the level of a rain. After standing in it for most of an hour, their rain ponchos were mostly soaked, though the moisture couldn't reach their skin. Still, it was enough to wick most of the remaining heat from them. Now and then Karl would open the hatch on the stove to stoke the fire or adjust the amount of air getting in to increase the output. With both Karl and McGhee on watch, Julie took the opportunity to get out of the elements and crawled into the lean-to to rest.

At times the drizzle would relent and they'd be left to watch the river as it carried them. Now and then objects would appear in the drift, logs mostly, or pieces of trees, keeping pace with them as they moved in the same current. It turned out both Karl and McGhee had developed the same game, imagining a race between the raft and the newfound drifters. They'd both watch until it became apparent there was a winner, at which time they'd toss their heads back in triumph or defeat. Karl noticed McGhee crushed by one such race and asked if that was what he was doing. They then compared notes, asking if either had seen this or that piece, and how it seemed the raft would win until the root went wide and found a slightly faster channel and took the lead. This was a good discussion, but didn't end up passing much time before they fell into silence. Almost imperceptibly the sky began to gather again and fall upon them with a slight, then increasing drizzle.

It seemed this batch of mist was more persistent and thicker, for they were dripping much quicker this time. They had both taken to holding their hands close to the stove pipe to gather its warmth, but with the driving moisture, it wasn't enough to fight off the cold. Karl was the first one to reach for his leather gloves. Pushing his hands into them, he exercised his fingers to get them in the last bit to the tips. They were old gloves creased and split and abraded by years of hard labor, both soft with crenulations and hard in between where the leather had ossified with sweat and dirt. Running his hands along the arms of his poncho, first right hand sliding over left arm, then left hand down right, he collected the water that had beaded on the surface. McGhee watched the process with some interest, for it seemed counterproductive to make the gloves wet. Still, he took out his own gloves because any barrier against the cold moisture had to be better than nothing. Meanwhile, Karl got closer to the stove and stovepipe. Looking McGhee in the eye, he wrapped his fingers dangerously close to the stovepipe, but not touching. He could see McGhee's eyes bug-out as they both knew the pipe was nearly red-hot. They'd been hovering over the pipe an hour already, so were both well aware of the threshold where the warmth went from welcome to scorching. Karl was well within that threshold now. Continuing to look at McGhee he smiled slightly and fully grabbed onto the stove pipe. The moisture in the leather instantly began to sizzle, then steam. After thirty seconds or so he let go of the pipe, holding up his hands. They were steaming furiously in the cold air and incessant drizzle. This became the new game for them as each took turns holding onto the pipe. McGhee initially tried it without wetting the gloves which worked momentarily, but quickly grew too hot. Withdrawing his hands after five seconds, he had to shake them to ward off the excess heat. Karl shook his head, a wry smile on his lips. With an exaggerated motion he again wiped his hands down alternate arms to gather moisture into the gloves. McGhee shrugged, wiping his hands down his front and arms in different fashion to minimize the lesson he was taking from Karl.

Once his gloves were wet enough, McGhee set back to the stovepipe. Ringing his fingers around the pipe, he drew them closer together until he was handling the pipe in his gloves. He could feel the warmth through the leather, but it was tolerable. The moisture in the gloves went from cold to neutral, from neutral to warm, then warm to hot. The progression seemed manageable and not so fast, so the cycle was tolerable and mildly amusing. Both Karl and McGhee took to holding the pipe in this fashion, and despite the incessant and relentless drizzle, they found a diversion to ignore it. Waking some time later, Julie emerged from the lean-to to see them gripping the pipe.

"Isn't that hot?" she asked them rooting around for a thin thermos they had packed.

"Yes," they both said in synchrony, laughing low in a guttural moment of bonding.

Around one in the morning the drizzle subsided and most of the clouds receded. A small residue of haze remained to the southwest but did not grow more than a few degrees above the horizon. Otherwise, the sky was clear. Without the clouds it was darker on the water, but their eyes were well adjusted. The dark trees formed an immutable silhouette against a slightly lighter sky, a contrast of black on dark blue with stars. The Milky Way cut a band across the sky, providing a bit more ambient light for their dilated eyes. Watching the river a thought dawned on McGhee: he had a bottle of something jammed deep in his pack. It'd sure be nice to have a swig of that. He mentioned having a bit of VSOP to Karl who greeted the news with enthusiasm.

"Well break it out then . . . ," he said, grabbing McGhee's pack for him.

McGhee dove in up to his arm pit to find the bottle, but it took three tries before he came up with it. His face showed some disappointment, however, as he remembered how little remained. He thought it might be barely more than a swig or so.

"There's not much left, I'm afraid . . . ," McGhee said, explaining it had been a gift from his brother and that he'd had a small drink each night through the summer. Handing the bottle over, he motioned for Karl to have a drink.

The disappointment registered on Karl's face. The prospect of an infusion of sweet, warm alcohol was very attractive to him given the cold air, the moisture and the inactivity of waiting hours through the drift. Still, when he heard the light swish in the bottle (in fact, he shook it, too, to get measure of the remains), it was clear little more than a couple swigs were left. Taking a small snort his cheeks bulged as he stuffed the cork back in and handed the bottle back to McGhee.

Julie had retired to the lean-to again, so it was clear for McGhee to drink the remainder. Removing the cork with a pleasing thwig sound McGhee could smell the sweet cognac inside. Finally swallowing his mouthful, Karl shook his head. "Wish you had some more . . . ," he said. McGhee smiled and faced slightly away into the darkness of the river. He wanted to be alone with it just as he had been all summer. McGhee paused momentarily to think about the last drink before taking it.

His brother Les had meant to see Alaska after college, but life had gotten in the way. The night before he was to leave for the north, Les received word a job was waiting for him, so he'd have to put that trip on hold for another time. He'd given this bottle to McGhee knowing full well he'd be taking it up there, almost doing it for him. McGhee recalled this, holding onto the green glass bottle. The thought made the last swig that much harder to swallow.

"What are ya waitin' for?" Karl asked, throwing his chin toward the bottle.

"I dunno . . . ," McGhee said. "Thinkin' about my brother Les . . . and it seems like my summer is over . . . ."

Raising the jug, he poured it down his throat, holding the last of it in his mouth to savor. The cognac burned his tongue as he held it, so he let it go, down to his stomach. The warmth trailed down inside him, disappearing in his depths. Staring at the bottle, McGhee suddenly had an idea. Setting it aside, he dove into his pack again, rifling around in search of something. A minute later he emerged with an envelope and a pen.

Karl watched from down the skiff and nodded his head. "Good idea," he said.

Folding the envelope over on his knees to make it stiffer, he sat a moment with the pen hovering just over the paper. Then it came:

> "To the Finder of this Bottle:
> This letter speaks of the love of one brother for another, of adventures taken and missed, and lives well lived . . . ."

Adding his name and address he rolled the envelope into a tight tube then tucked it into the mouth of the bottle. Using his pinky he pushed it the rest of the way in – the coil of paper unfurled with the release of pressure from the bottle neck. Stuffing in the cork he twisted it into place with a quarter turn. Holding it in his hand he suddenly became sentimental, realizing he'd never hold it again. He contemplated throwing it far out into the river, beyond where he could see. Then he thought better of it. He tossed it lightly over the side, then watched the current carry it along right beside him. Karl watched it, too. It was like the game earlier, only this time they knew the thing adrift in the current. For at least twenty minutes they could see it, though the dark green glass was hard to discern once the bottle was more than a few feet from the edge of the boat. There wasn't any moon to help them either, so the tiny glints from the glass soon became indiscernible from the tiny glints of the waves all around it. At one point, McGhee was sure he could see it. Then suddenly he wasn't sure he was seeing it after all: though the glint he was tracking was the same, the confidence with which he watched it was not. There was momentary despair over the loss, then a bit of self-reproach over so silly a concern: the bottle was lost as soon as he threw it in, and it wasn't lost at all as much as freely given to the river to find its own way. These were McGhee's ruminations as the bottle finally left his view, and no glint beyond that moment ever became, even for an instant, the bottle he'd protected all summer.

Karl saw McGhee's reverie and tapped him on the knee with his boot, motioning with his jaw toward the north side of the river. It was only half a head turn, but there it was: high in the sky silent green curtains shimmered. Along their edges were highlights of magenta and sometimes yellow. They waved slowly but were always silent. McGhee had seen the aurora before, but he wasn't entirely sure he'd really *seen* it until that moment, wrapping in a loose circle high above and centered on magnetic north.

"I love those . . . ," McGhee heard Karl say. "Never get tired of them . . . ."

"Particles from the sun make the upper atmosphere glow like that . . . ," McGhee said, but Karl just laughed and lowered his head.

"You think too much, McGhee," he said, smiling at the young man. "Sometimes you just have to go with the flow."

It was about that time the howling started. First it sounded like one dog, very far away. It was a plaintive sound. McGhee thought it might be a wolf, but he wasn't sure. It wasn't quite as inconsolable as the howls he was told were from wolves. Those were forever lonely, even when they occurred in pairs and threes and fours. This howl wasn't quite so soulful, though it did come from a neighboring place. Then as McGhee listened to it, it was joined by another. The second voice was tentative at first, then grew in strength. A third and fourth added in quick succession, then perhaps four more. Karl was watching McGhee as usual, enjoying the confusion playing over his face.

"That's Ruby . . . ," Karl said, motioning in the direction of the howls. "We're probably three miles out yet, but the dogs can smell us now. We're almost home . . . ."

The chorus mounted as they continued their drift in the darkness of the river. Before long the voices of two hundred sled dogs rang to announce their presence to Ruby. The 3:00 a.m. darkness was marked with their guttural voices, some afraid and some defiant, with nips and yips and barks and growls and howls and snapping chains. The dogs knew they were there in the dark water, but not what they might portend, and not whether they be friend or foe.

Remember the Sea

40

0 ◄———————————●———————————► 90

11AM

Bordeaux, FR 5/20/2004

He lay in bed in foreign sheets, not his, reluctant to rise, not because of what he might face, but because he felt so perfect in his sleep. He was actually resting (rather than pretending), lightly floating, and thus reluctant to give it up because anything to follow was likely to be a disappointment. His eyelids were closed, but pink from the sun coming in, not so bright as to heat or disturb – on the contrary, the rays were perfectly filtered through a light sheer. He could hear it now and then flapping, tapping the dark wood framing the window he had seen the night before, just as he had caved into the sheets, exhausted. The thought of it lightly fluttering came at his mind from the side, playful and unexpected, where he wasn't accustomed to looking, not for some time, and it tickled his heart which he knew was in desperate need of it.

So it was with some reluctance he gave up his pillow when he could sleep no longer and dressed, making his way down the stairs in the back, across the small courtyard and into the main part of the house where the kitchen was, hoping for a sip of coffee. The kitchen was empty, but there were pans atop small flames on the stove, lightly bubbling, and he could hear bustling elsewhere in the flat. Pausing a moment, he decided to take one of the chairs at the small table, out of the way, to wait. He'd driven through Bordeaux some years before – ironically, on his honeymoon – and hadn't had much time to form an opinion of the city, except it seemed authentic to him: less about visitors consuming it, and more about being its own place where people lived. The inhabitants seemed content to live and die without external intervention, and he liked this sense of it. He remembered the dark church spires and narrow streets and not much else, so he was a little surprised to find himself there again, and this time by specific intention, if mostly driven by serendipity and a little desperation.

It had been a bad autumn involving the dissolution of his marriage, which he seemed to know from nearly the beginning had been a mistake but was content to make the best of it, that is, until he could not do it any longer. When Tess finally suggested they give it up, he was secretly relieved, though he shed some tears in the process. If he were honest, they were mostly compulsory tears, because just below that, he felt his heart skip a little with the prospect of escape, and despite the long route to safety which was sure to be painful and ruinous, he knew that way was his path and was glad for it. So through that fall they had hammered out the details in painful sessions, lawyers mediating, and through the winter, too, until finally when spring came back and the weather cleared, his prospects began to brighten, too, and he allowed himself to move on, at the least first few steps of it.

So when it happened he read of a program to take an apartment in a foreign city, embedded with a family, he jumped at it, resolving on Bordeaux merely by scanning a column of names and picking one he thought might suit him for a while: not so flashy, out of the way, devoid of English (the prospect of further conversation tired him), where he might just let his brain cool and his perspective settle back to normal. He'd made the arrangements that afternoon in early April and nearly forgot about it until his departure mid-May when he threw things in one suitcase, slipped a laptop in his backpack, and shuttled to the airport. Sitting there in that kitchen, he was a little surprised he had done it, but judging by the slight smile he could feel in the corner of his lips, he was already glad he did.

The kitchen was tight and packed, a smallish stove working on four burners, each busy heating, additional iron skillets hanging on pegs, cheese on the cutting board next to a small pile of diced tomatoes and fresh basil; a loaf of warm bread on the table, half sliced, knife stuck mid saw; jams and jellies and fresh butter spread; cut flowers in a thin vase, pushed back, leaning out in objection to the wall there – tulips and irises and a spray of lavender – and opposite him, a little plate with a half sausage, and an egg bleeding its yolk reaching for the toast, blocked by a fork from reaching it.

Just then a young woman walked in, apron around her neck, but undone at her waist, smiling at McGhee momentarily before a quick curtsey and turn to the stove to adjust the pans there. She called in French over her shoulder, a merry sing-song tone, causing a little man to come out of the bedroom, smiling at the guest. Sliding into the seat by his plate, he spoke in French to McGhee, but upon seeing he couldn't quite follow his quick words, he held up both hands, clapping them lightly, tilting his head.

"*Pardon moi . . .* ," he said, then cocking his head, found his English.

"Mr. McGhee . . . ," he said, "it will take me a moment to find my words for you. I speak four or five tongues, but alas, can't keep them straight always." Sticking out his hand, he introduced himself. "I am Yannick," he said, smiling.

"We met last night," McGhee said, taking his hand for a shake.

"Ahh . . . ," Yannick said, "but that was not a proper introduction. You were tired, and so were we," he said spinning in his chair to look at the young woman, throwing some words to her in French.

She spun and smiled again, looking at McGhee. "Bonjour . . . ," she said, her voice bright.

Looking back to McGhee, Yannick smiled again. "That's my beautiful wife, Lucie," he said, his pride evident.

McGhee called out a stilted, "Bon Jooor," to her back, which she acknowledged with a quick turn, before engaging the skillets again.

"How about some breakfast?" Yannick asked good-naturedly. He was reaching for a jar of preserves, but McGhee shook his head lightly.

"Coffee would be great . . . ," McGhee said, looking back.

Yannick's mouth fell open in faux horror. "Nooo!" he said. "It can't be. You're in France now, and Lucie is a wonderful cook . . . and she *loooves* it!"

Yannick spun in his chair to look at her, then back to McGhee, then to her again, excited, then back to McGhee. "Sausage . . . Ahhh, we have these wonderful little sausages from the market . . . ," he said, tossing his head back in ecstasy, then smiling at McGhee. "And if you're going to have sausages . . . ," he said, spinning to throw directions to Lucie, which she acknowledged, each one, with a nod, "you must have eggs, too," he said, turning to McGhee momentarily, then back to Lucie, with more instructions.

"Over hard then," McGhee said, capitulating, but Yannick stopped in mock horror again.

"Not so hard, no . . . ," he said, serious, looking into McGhee's eyes. "They're from a nice little chicken down the street. We know her . . . Miss . . . ahhh," he said, thinking, "*Quack*, in English, because she sounds like a geese," he said, turning to Lucie to fill her in.

She frowned, too, shaking her head *No*, then cracked two eggs into a freshly vacant skillet, sliding in a pallet of butter, sizzling beside it, then somehow under it, and a dash of wine, her thumb over the neck, admitting a splash, then another, and a third, just in case.

"And toast, too . . . ," Yannick said, almost in a panic he had forgotten, cutting two thick slices from the loaf on the table before leaning back on the chair to throw them into another pan, putting his hand on Lucie's waist to warn her and gently get around her. Then, noticing the coffee press on the stove, he half stood to retrieve it, and a mug from a little tree there, pouring it for McGhee, before sliding it across to him, careful not to spill it, with both hands. Thunking his head with his palm, he smiled again, reaching over by the flowers for a tiny pitcher of cream to hand it to McGhee.

"You know the cow, too?" McGhee asked, smirking a bit, but good-natured.

"Oui," Yannick said, serious. "She's very fat."

Spinning from the stove, Lucie spilled two perfect eggs onto a plate, grabbing off the toast gingerly, crispy and hot on the edges, light smudges of breakfasts-past on its surface, steaming. From another skillet, she poured two sausages on, petite but bursting with hot juices, sizzling, then slid the loaded plate before McGhee, smiling herself. She put a hand on Yannick's shoulder, and he looked up at her, then back at McGhee, his eyebrows wide. "Eat," he said, expectantly.

The sausage burst lightly when McGhee cut into it, flowing, and the image made Yannick laugh lightly – he put his hands together, like it was some prayer or a godsend, and skewering a wiggly piece of egg, McGhee had a bite: the flavors enveloped his tongue, savory and gooey, buttery and light with a touch of wine playing along the edges, like a clarinet in a song, merrily augmenting the taste, complex and simple, like life itself lay open in a single bite in all its glorious subtlety.

As the pleasure registered on McGhee's face, Yannick clapped with delight and Lucie smiled, too. Surveying the pans and provisions, McGhee kept eating, each bite as good as the last. "So, how many are staying with you?" he asked, scooping some egg onto a corner of the toast point. He could never recall enjoying an egg so much, runny as it was, yet it was just right, and he marveled at their wisdom and what they knew to be right about him and what he needed, without even knowing him.

Yannick, shrugged. "Just you, my friend . . . ," he said, looking over to Lucie, then back. She shrugged, too.

"This is all for *me*?" McGhee asked, surprised by it, but Yannick smiled, putting his hand on McGhee's sleeve.

"And me, too . . . ," he said, turning to smile at Lucie again, then laughed, throwing his head to the side, then realizing yet another omission thunked his head, and reached for a jar of preserves to twist it open, inhaling its aroma deeply before looking back at him.

"Do you know Mirabelles?" he asked, serious, holding the jar close to his heart.

McGhee shook his head, still chewing. "Should I?"

Tilting his head, Yannick looked sadly at McGhee. "From now on, there will be *before* Mirabelles, and everything after . . . ," he said solemnly. Extending his hand, he slid the jar toward McGhee.

Accepting the jar, McGhee looked at the label. "I'm not really a jelly guy . . . ," he said, looking at Yannick.

Yannick snatched the jar from him, cradling it again.

"Jelly! Noooo . . . ," he said, shaking his head in horror. "Jelly is for heathens . . . Philistines."

Grabbing the bottle back, McGhee looked at it again. Yannick smiled, glad he took it, though feigning loss. "What are Mirabelles anyway . . . ?" he asked, scanning the label, which was entirely French. He'd had a couple years in high school many years before but little remained. He'd hoped to work on it during his stay, but those aspirations wouldn't help him at the moment.

"They are . . . little yellow . . . ," Yannick said, searching for the word, looking to Lucie, but she shrugged. McGhee was learning the English dialogue was as lost to her as the French was to him, so when she shrugged, he shrugged, too – at least they had that.

"I can see that they're yellow . . . *jaune*," he said, pulling one French word from the mist of his memory.

"Ahh, you speak French?" Yannick said, brightening. McGhee smiled. "Un petite peu . . . ," he said, then to accentuate it, said, "Literally, *un petite peu* – a little bit."

Yannick went back to thinking of the word, then in a happy explosion, he shouted, "Plum!" loudly, then, seeing it startled them, said, "Little yellow plums," more softly.

McGhee had one wedge left of the thick toast and grabbed it, ready.

"A little butter first," Yannick said, sliding the saucer over, the creamy pile showing no signs of ever being a cold hard rectangle.

Dutifully, McGhee took the little knife there and spread a thin layer across the toast to Yannick's approval. Then, grabbing a small spoon on the table, he took a quarter's worth and spread it on the toast, looking at Yannick.

Yannick sputtered with his lips, "Pt-pt-pt . . . ," taking the spoon from him, dipping it deep into the preserves, glopping a large dollop on to the toast, lovingly spreading a thick layer across the surface with the back of the spoon with the skill of a master plasterer finishing drywall. With a shrug, he dropped the spoon on the plate by the butter. "Now . . . ," he said, gesturing with his hand before folding his arms in front of himself, his head at an angle, watching with merry disapproval.

McGhee bit in with a crunch, a full bite, for he knew anything less wouldn't do, and Yannick smiled. The bread was still warm and crusty, and the butter hit his tongue first. It wasn't like American butter, its tepid counterpart, but was warm and creamy, salty and sweet, nuanced and lovely, escorting the jam to his taste buds with a quiet fanfare, until the Mirabelles finally met them, too, sweeping past the high notes with a sweetness he'd never encountered before – not the insipid sweet he expected, but a complex melody of flavor, with tones of apricot without the bitterness, hints of its darker plum brethren, but not the sourness, unfolding almost shyly he thought, by degrees, light and airy, like the sunshine itself had been captured and rendered as food for far more than his stomach to enjoy.

"Now you understand, *mon ami* . . . ," Yannick said, smiling with approval, his laugh returning. Lucie smiled, too, turning back to the stove to tend her pans, and McGhee knew, this time, he would see France differently.

McGhee sat out on the steps in front of the house, cradling a bound drawing book in his lap with a set of watercolor pencils, a bottle of water at his side for drinking, and when he thought to do it, light smudging of the image. It wasn't a large street with houses crowding down to it, cars lining each side with barely enough room for a single car to pass down the middle. The sun was high and the sky clear with puffy clouds, shadows of the building edges carving down the middle of the street. Above him, large shutters were thrown open beside the windows which were open to the sun and breeze, their light curtains lapping out, like they wanted to play. Drawing, he became lost in thought, allowing the sun and stirring air to draw the venom of those dark days from him by degrees, like a special salve designed to heal him, and he reveled in it.

After some time, the door behind opened and Yannick stepped out, stretching in the sunshine hands on hips, looking down on him. McGhee was finishing his first picture, a quick sketch of the buildings down the street, nestled in their shadows. It wasn't great in his estimation but was a decent start, and he was satisfied it wasn't worse, but more, was glad to have done it at all, and finally feel he was moving beyond his doldrums. Sitting next to him, Yannick looked over at it, happy at what he saw.

"I like how you see my street," he said, pointing into the book with his pinky, tracing the purple shadow along the foot of the building. "I never saw it like that before – thank you."

The mists of the creative process lifting, McGhee looked over at him, finally thinking to smile.

"Thanks – the next one will be better," he promised, dismissing it.

"Then may I have that one?" Yannick said. "It sounds like you may not keep it, and it'd be a shame to lose it. "

McGhee moved to rip it from his book, but Yannick stayed his hand. "No, no, no – you can't just tear it," he said, reaching into his pocket, opening a small bone-handled pocket knife. "The tip is very sharp – you push lightly and it will come right out," he said, handing it to McGhee.

Following the instruction, McGhee pressed near the bend where the paper disappeared into the binding, and sure enough it left a thin line, cutting through cleanly but leaving the paper beneath with only the slightest crease. Folding the knife, he handed it back to Yannick, then the small page, cupping it from the corner to make it stiff to hand over. "It's still a little wet," he said, placing it on Yannick's outstretched palms.

He looked delighted to receive it, staring into it a moment. He moved his hand over it, tracing the lines again, careful not to touch it.

"Ahh . . . , Mr. McGhee, it is lovely. I shall frame it and put it in the hall."

"Fran, please . . . ," he said, extending his hand to him, and Yannick took it in both of his, shaking it warmly.

"Lucie has put out some tea and wine and cheese for us on the patio – will you come in?"

McGhee nodded, the one drawing being enough for the present. He had been starting to wonder what to do next anyway, considering a walk through the city, but didn't have quite the motivation to do so, making such an invitation perfect, if only for its timing. Yannick raced ahead with the picture to show it to Lucie, stopping long enough by the door to the kitchen to shoo McGhee on by and out to the courtyard through the hall.

Outside, there was a small table set beneath a peach tree, though the peaches it had were still small balls of fuzz, barely past the work of the bees as the tree still held some blossoms, it being

May yet. A small bird was hidden in the tree, chirping, out of view but familiar from his youth, though he couldn't name it. On the table sat a saucer of soft cheese and some crackers, a small tea pot, steaming, and a label-less bottle of red wine, half gone, cork stuffed in half way for safe keeping.

The bricks below were a bit uneven with grass growing in between, nudging them at slight angles that might have been annoying under foot, or under chair legs elsewhere but not there. It was warm, the shade of the tree pleasant, and McGhee found sitting there as good as it had been for him anywhere. There were three small wine glasses on the table, and he took the liberty of pouring some out in each of them before trying it, a cabernet, which he found to be nice and smooth.

Yannick wandered out with Lucie trailing, but though he sat around the corner on the table from McGhee, Lucie remained standing, her hand on Yannick's shoulder. She smiled at McGhee, then spoke French to Yannick, and he nodded, turning back to his guest.

"Lucie wants to give us time to talk, like men," he said laughing lightly. Leaning in, he explained her English wasn't very good anyway, and she didn't expect them to speak French, and certainly not Russian, which he further explained, was her native tongue in the Ukraine.

McGhee smiled up at her, managing the remainder of his French with a *merci beaucoup*, and a slight bow. Smiling, she curtsied and disappeared again.

Yannick spread his elbows out on the table, then reached for the little knife in the cheese, spreading brie on a cracker before stuffing it into his mouth with a little flourish and a laugh, but fell quiet, looking at McGhee.

"You look sad, my friend . . . ," Yannick said. "Like you've been hurt deeply."

McGhee looked at him, but said nothing. Yannick's face was kind – soft features, showing his smile had etched lines there over time, the way frowns do the other work on sad men's faces. They seemed to be about the same age, within a few years, and perhaps because of that and the empathy in his voice, McGhee trusted him. It wasn't something he felt often, but it put him at ease. Nodding, McGhee finished his wine, and Yannick reached for the bottle, filling it again.

"I think I explained my circumstances in my mail . . . ," he said to Yannick, leaning back in his chair.

Yannick shrugged, leaning back, too, but smiling as he did. "You seem like a decent man. It's a shame these things happen to us. I was married once before, too . . . ," he said, shaking his head, his visage darkening. "It was so wrong, I had to escape. It was crushing the life from me, the joy. I was like this . . . ," he said, holding up his thumb and index finger pinched tightly together. "Flat. Flat. Flat." Sighing deeply, he let his lips flap making a funny noise, and he laughed again. "Even in such pain we can find humor, if only in the sigh it brings," he said.

"It was like a long dream . . . ," McGhee said, reaching for a cracker. The cheese was very soft as it had sat in the sun warming while it waited and was easy to spread.

"Not a nightmare, I hope?" Yannick said, swinging his arm lightly around the peg on the corner of his chair. Though McGhee hadn't spoken of it before to anyone, he found it easy to share with his new companion.

"Not really . . . ," he said, rather sadly. "But it was like I was waking up the whole time, every day – toward the end anyway – wondering why I had decided to get married at all. To her, anyway. We weren't very well suited. I'm not even sure I was in love.

Sometimes I look at the way I was yesterday and think *I was totally insane then . . . thank goodness I'm better today*."

Yannick laughed, nodding. "But today is *tomorrow's* yesterday," he said, smiling to think of it. "I wonder if you'll think this is a dream, too, and insane."

"This insanity I don't mind so much . . . ," McGhee said, toasting Yannick with his glass.

"Ahh . . . you say that now . . . ," Yannick continued, letting his voice trail off.

McGhee shook his head lightly, lost in thought. He couldn't remember the last time he'd had a conversation like this, and he missed it. Somehow, most of the people he'd known over the years had fallen away, not that there had been a falling out. To the contrary, there had been a few friends he always enjoyed talking to – especially a few guys from his college days. They used to joke they had survived a plane crash together, so they had no choice but to be friends after that. It might have been his friend Matt who said it first, or perhaps Chris, or Ben, or Rob, or Dave – the more he thought of it, the more he recalled people he had lost touch with, and the thought bothered him.

Yannick saw the cloud darken McGhee's brow.

"Tell me my friend what you are thinking right now . . . ," Yannick said, tipping his head back slightly, but watching him as if it improved his observational skill to do so. Perhaps it was his bifocals that required it, but the pose seemed to go with the rest of Yannick's affectations.

Pulling out of his funk, McGhee looked at him. "Why? – just curious why you chose to ask that? Just now, I mean . . . ."

Yannick tipped his head back down to look at him over his glasses. "Mon ami . . . your face tells a story, every time you think of something. I just wish I had the words to go with it . . . ."

McGhee nodded slightly. "I've heard that before. I've heard that I look like I have a cloud over my head . . . ."

"A dark cloud?" Yannick asked, smiling and chuckling. McGhee nodded again, shrugging.

"You don't have a cloud, my friend. You have a whole weather system . . . ," he said, swinging his hands over his head. "You're a fascinating man to watch . . . ."

"Is it really that obvious?" McGhee asked, shifting uncomfortably in his chair.

Yannick laughed, throwing his head back, then looking at McGhee, did it again. "Oui . . . ," he said. "But I like it . . . ," he continued, tilting his head. "You're not skilled at hiding your feelings . . . ," he said, then leaned in for a confidence: "I am the same way!" Slapping the table, he folded his arms.

"I hate being transparent," McGhee said, looking into his wine glass. A small black fly had found its doom there, riding the swells of wine. Using his pinky, he reached in to fish it out.

"But no . . . ," Yannick said, leaning over again, patting McGhee on the hand. "I know where I stand with you, and I can almost see your thoughts. We share some of the same pains, I think, and it gives me comfort to see . . . ."

"OK . . . ," McGhee said, leaning back in his chair, this time throwing his elbow over the corner peg of his. "So . . . read me then . . . ."

Yannick put his elbows on his knees, leaning in for a look, first one eye then the other, then scanning him up and down. Leaning back he folded his arms again.

"You, my friend, are a *beautiful sufferer* . . . ," Yannick said, nodding once.

"Go on . . . ," McGhee said, holding his pose. He was trying not to give up any more clues, to thwart the reading, but had the uneasy feeling that was pointless, so he relaxed, sighing.

"See? I was right!" Yannick said, laughing merrily. McGhee had to smile, though it was against his will, and Yannick delighted in seeing the struggle. Holding up his hand, Yannick searched for the words, mumbling to himself in French, then giving up, looked at McGhee. "Have you read Gide? – he's one of our best."

McGhee nodded. "Some," he said. "*Lafcadio's Adventures* I think was his . . . ."

Yannick nodded. "And Sartre and Camus?" Yannick continued. Again McGhee nodded, then shrugged. "Bon, bon . . . ," he said, grabbing his chin a moment. "So . . . you are a character directly *ripped* from their pages," he said. "Merely existing makes you uncomfortable."

McGhee shrugged again. "Isn't everyone?"

Yannick laughed, tilting his head. His fondness was clear, and his delight in the examination showed in his features – in his cheeks and thick lips, which were still smiling.

"Mais non!" Yannick said, a little too loud, and he covered his mouth, laughing again. Lucie stuck her head out with a concerned look, then she waved and disappeared again. "It never occurs to most people . . . ," Yannick continued. "They skate and skate on the ice, and never think to ask how thin it is . . . ."

"Nice image . . . ," McGhee acknowledged, taking another sip of wine.

"Only you – you can't get your mind off it. You think of nothing else."

"I think that's an exaggeration," McGhee said, smiling wryly.

"Perhaps . . . just barely," Yannick said, shrugging himself. "But that is when you are most *you*. When you are *pondering*. And I bet your friends don't get that about you – if you have friends."

"I have friends . . . ," McGhee objected, though the moment he said it, he knew he was lying.

"Sure . . . sure – we all have *friends* . . . ," Yannick said. "But you secretly feel alone."

"Maybe not so secretly . . . ," McGhee said, looking at Yannick.

"Well, now you have one, at least . . . ," Yannick said, raising his glass for a little toast, then having a drink. "And I think you thought getting married might solve that for you . . . only it didn't."

"Where are you getting this?" McGhee said, sitting up straighter in his chair.

"Am I wrong, then?" Yannick asked, his eyebrows spread with the question.

"It's more complicated than that . . . ," McGhee said, crossing his arms. Twisting, he stretched a bit in the chair, and it felt good in his back where it cracked in a little muffled snap.

"Yes, yes – of course it is . . . you never really expected to find someone who really understood you. But you were hopeful. To have someone against the loneliness. But then she hurt you . . . ."

"You can see that?" McGhee asked, incredulous but open to it at the same time.

Smiling again, Yannick tilted his head. "Women always hurt us," he said, his smile less merry but more genuine in sympathy. "We are men, and that is our lot. Only there are some things we can forgive, and some . . . we cannot. For me, it's ingratitude. I can forgive *anything*, but not that."

McGhee grabbed the wine cork from the table, squishing it in his fingers, then smelling it. It had an earthy aroma and remained moist from where it had done its duty.

"Me, too. Is it wrong to want a little recognition? Even to expect it?" McGhee asked.

"Yes . . . ," Yannick countered, "it is wrong, but we are men, and we need that. It is a little bit selfish, I know, but it is who we are. But women know this about us. And when they withhold it, it is out of *spite*."

McGhee laughed, shaking his head. "Some women . . . ," he said, his brow clouding again. "There are exceptions . . . sometimes we just make it too hard."

Yannick leaned back, laughing, tilting his head, merry again. "Indeed we do . . . ," he said, "but that's when the test comes, isn't it? It's easy to love in fine weather, but harder in the storm."

"You sure love your weather metaphors . . . ," McGhee said.

"Life *is* weather," Yannick said, "of one sort or another. The good woman can see that because they know *we own the storm* and the duty to shelter them from it."

"That's a bit patronizing . . . ," McGhee said, "though there's some truth to it. But what if the storm is in here?" McGhee said, pointing to his head, "or here?" he said, pointing to his heart.

"Ahhh . . . ," Yannick said, nodding. "That's the thing, isn't it? If the storms come from inside *you*." Leaning over, Yannick tapped him on the chest. "And that's what I see in you, my friend."

McGhee sighed.

"You are an existential hero, my friend. And I *love* that about you. What you need is a woman who can love that about you, too."

"Yeah, well that wasn't Tess . . . ," McGhee said, rubbing his neck.

"Of course she wasn't . . . ," Yannick said, "because you *hid* it from her." McGhee stared at him blankly. "Because you thought you could ignore it, ignore your nature . . . . But that is folly, my friend."

"So it was my fault?" McGhee said, but Yannick immediately shook his head, making the dismissive sound with his lips again.

"No, my friend . . . . We just spend the first half of our lives, men like you and me, running from who we are, and the last half running back to it. The sacrifices you made she could not see, or understand, so they were invisible to her, and you could not expose them because their truth would have killed her."

"That's a pretty good guess . . . ," McGhee said, shaking his head, "but how do you know that?"

Yannick shrugged. "How could anyone – a normal person, that is – deal with the fact you were . . . *ambivalent* . . . about the sacrifice you made to be with her."

"The sacrifice being?" McGhee said, his lips curling into a slight smile.

"To be . . . *ordinary*," Yannick said, shrugging again. "That thought kills you, *strangles* you, a little bit every day. It was only a matter of time," he said, wringing his hands around his throat. Leaning in, elbows on knees, he whispered: "I'm better at *hiding* it than you. After all, I am an Algerian hiding in France."

Leaning back suddenly, Yannick threw his hands behind his head. "So I know *just* what you need . . . ," he said, smiling.

Yannick was careful the next morning backing the Citroen out of his little garage down the street. Even though it was a small, ancient car, it barely fit into its space, like a caterpillar in a little cocoon. Swinging the doors of the garage shut, McGhee jumped into the passenger seat. Yannick wouldn't tell him where they were going, but he was happy at the prospect of an outing. Lucie had packed a basket for them, and a thermos of wine. "It isn't that far," Yannick said, feigning disinterest to look through the windshield before tossing a smile over at McGhee.

Clouds had gathered to form a light ceiling, but it did nothing to dim McGhee's outlook, which was much improved in Yannick's company and which seemed therapeutic, even though the clouds released a light sprinkle. It was a warm rain which made all the difference, and was just enough of a spritzing to maintain the flowers and blossoms and shrubberies at vital freshness. Winding through streets and rounding roundabouts, they found their way west of the city, the buildings growing farther apart, and more modern than those in the old section where Yannick lived, to look somewhat like American stores and businesses but always with some European flair to remind him he wasn't at home. Finally, even those gave way to pine-barrens, stretching around them in all directions, endless. It was a pleasure to be in a foreign place in the company of a local – he had no concern for navigation whatsoever and such absolute confidence in their progress that he could ignore it entirely. In short, he was content in a manner which was uncommon for him, and he enjoyed it.

"I was thinking of making a trek to Barcelona while I'm here . . . ," he said, looking over at Yannick. "Would that be hard?"

Yannick wrung his hands on the steering wheel then clapped before grabbing the wheel again. "That would be excellent," he said. "You should do it. Take the train – it would be such fun."

Satisfied, McGhee nodded. "I feel a compulsion to roam Spain at some point . . . this would be a start of that."

"You were made to have Spanish adventures . . . ," Yannick said, looking over at him. "Only you need a companion – that's how knights errant always did it . . . ."

"You think I'm Don Quixote, then?" McGhee said, absently rolling down the window so he could put his elbow out. The rain had stopped, and the air was warm and moist already, though it was still early.

"No, mon ami. You do!" Yannick said, laughing. "And I'd have to agree – you seem to make windmills of everything."

"Here we go again . . . ," McGhee said, good-naturedly. He had to admit he was enjoying the running psychoanalysis, if only because he never permitted much attention to be directed at himself. It was his habit to remain as invisible as possible, to be an observer, an eyeball, floating. But recent events – the dissolution – had eroded more of himself and his well-being than he wanted to admit. The attention he was receiving felt like something of a balm to him, or perhaps a poultice, neither of which he would have sought, but the comfort was welcome.

"Care to be my *Pancho*, then?" McGhee asked, looking over.

Yannick, glanced over, then back to the road, and at him again, his face serious. "I'd be *honored*, monsieur."

"So let us consider this our first venture into the countryside, then. Only I must know our destination . . . ," McGhee pronounced, nodding.

Veering suddenly, Yannick pulled into a parking lot among the trees, slowly rolling to the far end where some small buildings rested – a creperie or little bistro (he couldn't tell), built rustic to suit the surroundings, and a park house to manage the environs. Drifting into the lot, sand spilled onto the pavement, unwilling to remain where it seemed to originate in the trees.

"Where are we?" McGhee said, stepping out for a stretch.

"Dune du Pilat . . . ," Yannick said, smiling broadly.

"Dune? Where?" McGhee said, spinning to look around, but seeing nothing but the trees. If it wasn't for the sand at the edges, he would be sure it couldn't be the case.

Grabbing the basket and a small thin blanket, Yannick swung around the car. "Monsieur . . . ?" he said, sweeping his arm out in a low bow toward the path leading between the buildings and into the forest.

The walk through the trees wasn't far before the path opened before them, spreading wide on both sides, and facing them sat an immense mountain of sand, stretching both directions as far as he could see until disappearing in a light distant bend into the trees. The dune itself must have been three hundred feet tall, or perhaps higher, but oddly – for McGhee had never seen such a thing – it had a wooden staircase built into the side of it to ease the climb, though it remained a challenge if only for the length of it.

By fifty steps in, Yannick was pressing on his knee to aid the climb, and began insisting they stop at each landing to take in the view, but it was really the extra breaths he was after. That was OK with McGhee, too, for as they ascended, he got a view of forest progressively higher as they went, hunkered in the shadow of the dune. By the time they made it to the top, they were both thoroughly winded, Yannick setting the basket aside to rest on both knees a moment before standing to take an exaggerated breath of the sea, fully inflating himself with it and smiling into the air, his arms up and out.

For his part, McGhee looked back toward the forest first, finally seeing it from up high, reaching out to the east for miles like a puffy dark green quilt. As he spun to Yannick to comment on it, his breath came short as he saw the view westward, for it was magnificent: stretching before him a thousand feet or more, the dune gently descended down to the sea in mild undulations of light, fine sand. Children played along the flanks of the dune from top to bottom, coating themselves in it like sugar, before racing to the surf to wash it away, dashing into waves and out again, tiny squeals of delight reaching the men where they stood, watching.

Just under the crest, far enough from where the people still entered the dune and off to the side, Yannick opened the blanket

sideways to allow the sea breeze to inflate it – red and black check-
ers floating on the wind – until he brought the corners down, laying out a nice square for them to sit and have their picnic. Opening
the basket, Yannick pulled out a wedge of cheese, an apple, a ba-
guette, some hard salami and some olives and pickles in a small
container, and the thermos of wine. Opening his small knife,
Yannick carved the apple and some cheese slices, some salami and
chunks of bread (pulled not cut), handing over pieces to McGhee,
and they sat munching looking toward the waves.

"So this is what I needed?" McGhee said, shielding his eyes
from the sun while looking toward the horizon before looking over
at Yannick, but he said nothing and just smiled.

"This is what we all need . . . ," he said eventually. "When
we're filled with unbearable sadness, we need some unbearable
beauty to smite it . . . . And we feel our hearts lift with a *pop,* like
a cork in the water," he said, motioning with his thumb upwards,
wiggling.

"And what if we carry our sadness with us, always?" McGhee
said.

"Then remember the sea, always . . . , or something beautiful,"
he said.

Just then, they noticed a couple hundred yards to their left,
when the winds shifted and they heard the noise of it, a small
group – two helpers, a woman and a dog, setting up in the sand.
The woman was directing the others while holding the leash of the
dog – a golden retriever – having them set a beach chair and small
table atop a blanket, which wasn't cooperating in the wind, and
a tripod behind it all, angled, to catch the view down the beach.
Pointing with her leash hand to direct them, she lost it, which the
dog sensed was his chance, and he took off running, the woman in
pursuit, first in circles across the set, knocking over the table, then

the chair, then the tripod, before the dog got up to full speed and began to gallop away directly toward the men, the woman trailing further and further behind until she fell into a walk.

"I think it smelled the salami," Yannick said, merrily turning to McGhee, laughing, then turning back to the chase, the dog just arriving.

Yannick cut a small slice and gave it to the dog, panting, not so winded as to reject the offering, but it continued its run past Yannick, stopping by McGhee to sit near him. Petting it, he looked into her eyes, wide set and sad, but smiling, too, like she bore some secret, hidden behind her inscrutable tongue. Reaching under her chin, McGhee pulled out the tab on her collar, and laughed.

"Dulcinea," he said, looking over at Yannick.

"No!" Yannick said, leaning back to look at the dog's tag.

The woman who had been striding toward them, her arms flung out with each step, got closer. She walked with the gate of a mature woman, but healthy, her heels twisting slightly in the sand with each step to show her energy. Her white oxford fluttered in the breeze, a collar blown against her chin, light brown hair blown, too, though she didn't seem to mind it. She had been walking fast, but slowed her pace as she approached, stopping ten feet away looking at them, stunned, her mouth open, then curving into a smile.

Petting the dog, McGhee didn't notice until Yannick tapped his arm, shaking his head back over his shoulder toward the woman. It almost couldn't be, yet it was.

"Kate . . . ," he said, rising to meet her.

Holy Orders of the Olives

0 ←————————————————— 74 ————→ 90

6PM
Tipaza, Coastal Algeria 7/15/2038

The place they'd taken for the summer – perhaps longer – wasn't large but suited them, especially McGhee. Once they'd finally gotten there, after a full day of travel and a plane change in Charles de Gaulle, and a taxi from the Algiers airport to near Tipaza, he walked directly through the house to the back: he'd been assured there was a nice (if distant) view of the sea, and was relieved to find just that. This had been weeks before, already, and he had spent nearly all of his waking time out there, staring into the distance. The water wasn't so far as he had feared, and in fact couldn't have been a mile, and the terrain between tumbled away in front of the property, so his view remained unimpeded. And to his delight, the wind usually came in from that direction, lightly carrying sounds of the surf with it, which were soothing to him. In short, to his relief and surprise, it was perfect.

It never would have happened at all if it weren't for his friend, Yannick, who had insisted upon it, describing it as *possibly the best place on the dear earth*, and if it hadn't been that familiar tone of hyperbolic ecstasy in his friend's voice, he might have found a reason to decline, but he could not. They had not, in fact, communicated in some time, which remained a source of guilt for McGhee, like the other relationships he had let fall into default, and he was just about to send an email to him when one popped into his inbox just under his finger posed to hit *compose*. It was sounding some vague alarm as he had not heard from McGhee, and sensed an immediate need to "intrude" once again – Yannick's word – and *pull him back into the world*. Such was his style, even in email.

So rather than write back, which was his first impulse, he dialed Yannick who immediately went into a well-reasoned and impassioned argument why they must summer in Algeria with him, or near him, as the adjacent property was available and cheap and lovely – he knew it just was what McGhee needed at that exact moment. It was practically decided – all he needed was McGhee's assent – and as he pondered the offer, Kate came in, and as was her way, looked over his shoulder to read the email and squeezed his shoulder before rubbing it, and he knew there was nothing else to do but acquiesce, the truth being they each knew, all three, that McGhee needed to be convinced to do those things he wanted and needed to do anyway.

The house itself was small and whitewashed, crafted many years before, surviving no doubt because the elements never rose above a mild rain and tepid wind, and the air remained in a narrow, temperate range most of the year. The floor was stone, polished by feet – not by intention but by years of traffic – and consisted mostly of two rooms: one for sleeping with a modest queen bed, or something about that size, for actual sizes came later than it did, and a common room with modest wood seating, with pads, and a cooking area off to the side suited to modest cooking duties. In fact, as he scanned the house, *modesty* – the word – kept coming to him at every turn from the rough-hewn trim, to the roughly flat floors, to the curtainless windows facing north to the sea, and this premise of simplicity was indeed what he needed. That said, the inside of the house was more Kate's domain than his, as she took to reading in the afternoons, and evenings, too. It was his stated mission – as his compromise to do it stipulated – that he was there to finally finish his current piece of writing, which bothered him, and he'd be sitting in the garden to do it and wished minimal interruption. Kate smiled to hear his argument, and grabbed his shoulder when she heard it, tilting her head. "Of course, Franny," she said, every time he repeated it, which seemed often.

So it was he banished himself to the garden, though he had hardly been the first to do so: rough furniture there indicated otherwise. Both sides of the yard ended in rocks rising up to conveniently conceal neighbors. In the middle a relatively flat area remained, though it was still rather rocky, gently sloping toward a bluff which dropped off before the beach appeared below and in the distance. The yard itself had been something of an olive orchard, though it seemed its productive days had largely passed and was not large enough for anything but the barest subsistence. Just off the back of the house, where the stone terrace disintegrated into the yard, organically, a wooden table sat, broad and old, polished by hands into a pleasing patina which made splinters inconceivable. The color of the wood – gray and light yellow, veined in light brown – suggested it might be olive wood, which made sense, given the propensity of the earth there to field it. The surface was silky, almost as if it still retained its olive oil past, or so he imagined, and it made sitting there a pleasure. Other than the occasional precipitation of black olives landing with a splashy plunk now and then, it was ideal, and even then, he enjoyed the reminder of orchard, though forgetting it would have been impossible even if he was blind. When he closed his eyes, the smell of olives was always present, wafting in and out, like a hovering cloud of earthy incense.

The table was nestled in a gap between trees, which had seemed to learn, or suffer through pruning, and had grown around it to accommodate occupants there, the leafy greens forming a canopy over it, though not entirely thick enough to provide shade, but admit slight and thin sunlight dapples as it shook when breeze demanded it do so. Behind it on each side sat a bench, though it had a full length back support suspended above it on rough timber at one-third intervals such that it became a tolerable place to sit for extended periods, which was exactly what he had in mind. And from that location, out through the canopy between the twisted old trunks, he could see the water, bright and blue and moving eternally. It was exactly what he had in mind for writing, though if asked, he would have been incapable of describing it. Unfolding his thin computing device the first time there on the table, he worried somehow it would not work for him, that it might wobble, or worse, sit solid but crooked. Or that it might lean at some thwarting angle to anger his old fingers or wrists which were a little tight in the mornings. The technology was already annoying enough to him that he didn't need anything else to complicate his already delicate process. If he were honest, he'd admit he'd stopped trying to truly understand his computer years before, allowing it to become a simple tool, but also relegating himself to utter helplessness in the face of its challenges. His life now had that element to it, or elements – things he knew would exceed his capacity for patience or understanding, things that seemed designed to remind him he was an old man, and at any moment a turn in the technology would leave him absolutely helpless. This offended him, for it seemed as unnecessary as it was inevitable, but he didn't hold on to such frustration, for he'd also learned such pointless rancor did him no good. Learning to let go of things was perhaps the hardest skill he had ever managed, and he secretly knew he never really let go anyway but simply allowed his discontent to spiral into a little point almost immediately, and then would agree with himself to ignore it. He was, in fact, proud of the efficient absurdity of it, and that it allowed him to move on to other things.

So that first day he opened his computer, which was the evening of his first day there, he tilted the screen to the right angle and positioned his hands upon it, gazing over the top edge to see the water in the distance under the bowing arms of olive. It worked and he was satisfied. At least in theory he could write, if the words would come. He had also realized with the passage of time that they would indeed come eventually, if he didn't think too hard or worry too much, and that, at least in his estimation, they would be good, or good enough.

And as it would turn out, during such ruminations he'd usually find he had been writing much of that time already. Those musings on aging and conflict with obsolescence had found their way onto his page, and to his mild surprise, they were tolerable in their exposition though absolutely irrelevant to what he had set out to write in the first place. This had become a common thing, especially at the beginning of a session when he wasn't quite sure where his mind was, his mental finger tracing the varied texts in his head. Only through a few paragraphs would he learn which of the many themes that visited him had burped up onto the edge of his fingers at the moment. He largely felt like a passenger a good deal of the time, along for the ride, learning the story himself just after his fingers had typed it. It was this exact sensation that kept him doing it more than anything else – the thrill of discovery, like he was a big ball of wool, and some impulse within him allowed a strand to emerge, fingered into a thread and woven into a fabric of sorts. It was this that kept him at it and gave him faith the enterprise was indeed worth it, for if the truth were spoken, it would admit he had never received that external approval he'd hoped for, and he'd learned that he must just satisfy himself because it seemed he'd never have the opportunity to satisfy anyone else.

It was in this context that he filed these ruminations away where he usually did and got back to the story he'd been writing about his mother and Les. He wasn't too far into it, and it wasn't flowing as best it could when Kate wandered out to him and sat next to him on the bench, sliding over a glass of iced tea, sipping one of her own. She'd found some mint in the yard and had thought to throw a sprig in to spruce it up. Looking at her, he lightly removed it from his glass, but leaned over and kissed her on the forehead.

"You know I hate mint . . . ," he said, smiling down at her. She'd drifted over in a lean against his shoulder, looking up at him, affection in the corners of her eyes where wrinkles had finally started to appear.

"I know . . . ," she said, smiling mischievously. "But we're here now, and it looked better with a sprig in it, and all the travel journals mentioned Moroccan Mint Tea, so it seemed right."

"Fa . . . ," he said, mildly exasperated, but it was weak in its virulence, and they both knew it. Judging by the smile on her face, all he couldn't figure out was whether it was the mint or the idea of travel journals which bugged him more, or that she knew him well enough to spin a small riddle to addle his already bothered mind.

"Do you like your spot?" she asked, looking up at him again.

"It'll do . . . ," he said, reluctant to give up his posturing, though he was melting.

"I'm glad . . . ," she said, nestling her face into his arm further, then pulling back, a fold of it pinched in her fingers. "When's the last time you washed this shirt?" she said, wrinkling her nose.

"Washed?" he asked, trailing off and looking down at her. After holding his frown a moment, he broke into a mild smile, laughing slightly, slow.

"You packed dirty clothes, didn't you? It smells old . . . ," she said, releasing it with a little pat.

"I'm old," he said, lifting his arm to wrap it around her and pull her closer, looking out.

"What's that make me then?" she said, peering up at him.

"Oh . . . you're young yet."

"How's that work?" she asked, pushing back to look at him.

"You suck the youth right out of *me* . . . ," he said, looking down at her again. Putting her head on his chest, she looked out under the trees.

"I'm glad we came . . . ," she said.

"Me, too . . . ," he said. After a few moments, he sighed, contented. "You hear that noise?" he asked.

"Yeah . . . ," Kate said, "it's lovely. The breeze in the olives. A little raspy . . . and breathy . . . . It's nice."

"I can imagine listening to that sound for the rest of my life . . . ," he said. "It soothes me, and it sounds ancient. I can imagine someone sitting here a hundred years ago – it wouldn't have been much different."

"No computer though," Kate said, looking up at him, and he nodded. "How's the writing coming?"

"Just getting started," he said, rubbing her arm lightly, distracted by the thought of it. "But it feels right . . . ."

"I was thinking of taking a walk down to the beach, take some pictures. Wanna come?" she asked.

"Raincheck . . . ," he said, pulling a few strands of hair away from her forehead to get a better look at her. "I'd like to make a little more progress. Besides . . . you'll have more fun with your camera without me."

Their eyes met, McGhee looking deeply into Kate's, and she into his. They each had a vague recollection of their younger selves and the other, and the ambivalence they felt and the confusion, but it was mostly a memory now, and it seemed little of that remained. Kate's brow remained relaxed, her focus in the moment, with McGhee, and he felt it, too, unmarred by doubt, though some of his restlessness remained. For her part, her gaze into his eyes apparently reminded her why she loved him, and she smiled.

After several weeks, McGhee had fallen into a pattern, writing in the garden in the morning, then a few hours in the afternoon. Most evenings, Yannick would intrude with suggestions for dinner, and they'd take turns hosting or visiting the other. It was only a short walk around the boulders near the edge of the house, up and around the shoulder, then down again into the drive next door where Yannick was staying with Lucie. Their house was slightly larger and better for entertaining, with their terrace outfitted with a nice round teak table and a clearer view of the water. Despite the McGhees' attempts at cooking, Lucie remained the superior chef, so the better meals were there, and they'd frequently only begin eating at eight and not get home until midnight, or even later after dessert and wine and much laughing and confidences.

One afternoon, near the end of his writing when the words were slowing, Kate brought Yannick through the house with a guest: McGhee could hear his voice filling the small space, already booming with laughter in the few moments he was there, and the voice of another – deeper and less merry, though good-spirited – prodding him to finish his last thought before turning to greet them.

"Ahh . . . Fran, I have a treat for you . . . ," Yannick said, turning to put his arm around the shoulder of the man. "My friend the physicist, the great Bijan Ganoush . . . ."

Stepping forward he extended his hand. "You might as well call me Baba – everyone else does . . . ," he said, forcing a slight smile, though it seemed genuine, if pained.

His hand was large in McGhee's, firm but soft, a combination of control and restraint, like that of a fisherman used to hauling nets and finessing his catch. He was a short man and stalky, a spray of silver chest hair emerging from his sleeveless T-shirt, a thin gold chain riding the waves of curls, an open muslin shirt rolled up at the sleeves, shorts ending at his knobby knees. He looked older than they were, though healthy and solid, the years of jostling and wear resulting in a compact, dense frame.

"Not a lot of physics to do in these parts, I imagine . . . ," McGhee said, smiling at him.

"Not if I can help it . . . ," Baba said, laughing lightly. "I prefer to let my brain languish these days . . . hence my friendship with Yannick," he said, throwing a sly smile at him.

"What? Have I been insulted again?" Yannick said, feigning surprise, then laughing. He posed to hold up a finger: "I'm insulted, therefore, I am."

"I'll bring out some mint tea, fellas . . . ," Kate said from the threshold, "except for *you* . . . ," she added, throwing a kiss to McGhee.

Once she disappeared, Baba turned to McGhee. "Don't let her go . . . ," he said, clapping him on the arm.

"I've learned my lesson . . . ," McGhee said, motioning them to the table.

Crowding in, Yannick seemed anxious to speak, starting, then adjusting, then starting again, skipping over the central back spar, then pulling his trousers out of his crack, his face screwed into a look of determined effort as he did so.

"He's endlessly amusing . . . ," Baba said, looking at McGhee. "He's worth it for the entertainment value alone." McGhee laughed, but Yannick wouldn't be silenced, sticking his arm in between them to interrupt.

"Baba . . . ," he said, leaning between them to look into Baba's face until he was pushed away, "has a little boat."

Baba shrugged. "Just an old wood twenty-foot cabin traditional. For fishing...," he said.

"And he's suggested we do an evening voyage," Yannick injected, impatient.

"It was Yannick's idea . . . ," Baba said, mildly exasperated. "I go where he tells me . . . ."

"To fish?" McGhee said, his lips curling into a distasteful grin.

"No, to sleep . . . . Of course to fish!" Yannick said, showing his palms to them both.

"I don't really *fish* . . . ," McGhee said, leaning back to cross his arms.

"It's not about fishing . . . ," Baba said, shaking his head. "Well, it is, and it isn't."

"Yes," Yannick added, nodding. "It's not."

"A fishing trip not to fish, then . . . ," McGhee clarified. "Sounds positively *existential*."

"More like *absurd* . . . ," Baba said, wagging a finger between them.

"I like this guy . . . ," McGhee said, pointing his thumb toward Baba. "So . . . . When?"

"Now . . . ," Yannick said, standing, but Baba pushed him back down.

"In a bit . . . ," Baba said.

"Lucie already packed us a basket . . . ," Yannick added.

"What about Kate?" McGhee said, looking over his shoulder for her, but she was still hidden inside.

"Lucie is coming over with another basket . . . ," Yannick added, tilting his head, all ends covered.

"But I'm still working . . . ," McGhee said, motioning to his computer.

Yannick shook his head. "No, you're done . . . ," he said, spinning the unit around for a look, then turning it to Baba. "See?"

Baba glanced at it, but didn't intrude, leaving the charade to Yannick.

Coming out, Kate approached with a serving tray and four large iced-teas, three with sprigs of mint and some raw sugar mounded in a little dish. Hip-checking McGhee, she slid into the bench next to him, sending him up and over the middle spar bump, and nearly into the branches. "Sorry hun . . . ," she said, smiling at him, and the others.

"I *like* her . . . ," Baba said, smiling at Kate.

Righting himself and brushing his shirt, McGhee looked at her. "She may be available . . . ," he said, smiling at her coyly, then added, "The boys want me to go fishing."

"Good," she said, nodding. "The sooner the better."

"And Lucie is coming over with a basket for you and her," he continued, looking at her.

"Excellent. So I won't have to torture food tonight then? — that's a win . . . ."

Looking back at Yannick and Baba, McGhee shrugged. "It looks like I'm yours...."

"Oh hun . . . ," Kate said, leaning into McGhee's lap to get at her back pocket. "Looks like your mail finally made its way here. I left the junk mail inside . . . ," she said, handing over a thin white envelope.

Unfolding some reading glasses with one hand, McGhee put them on, then tilted his head up to read the address through them, then took them off again. "Hmmf . . . ," he said, slipping it, un-opened, under his iced-tea glass.

"You're not going to open it?" Kate said, reaching to pull it back out, but he slid his hand over hers, patting it gently.

"No . . . ," he said.

Yannick looked confused. "What is it?" he asked, looking from McGhee to Kate.

"Correspondence from *The New Yorker* . . . ," Kate answered. "On the last submission I think . . . ," she said, looking at McGhee, though he wouldn't return the glance.

"I have a whole box of them already . . . ," he said, twisting his glass upon the envelope, the ring of wetness growing wider. "I figured I'd make use of this one for something," he said.

"At least they wrote back . . . ," Baba said, frowning slightly, though it seemed supportive.

"Oh, they're very polite with their rejections," McGhee said, raising his glass to toast Baba. "One feels like a veritable king while being shown the door."

"What was it about?" Yannick asked. Grabbing his iced tea, he began scooping spoon after spoon of sugar into it which fell like sand to the bottom, thick granules stacking up like small boulders.

"It was about meeting a young woman in a San Francisco coffee shop . . . ," McGhee said, shoveling sugar into his own glass, only he took to swirling the sugar with the long handle spoon in a tiny brown maelstrom. Despite the attempt, they fell out of suspension as soon as his motion stopped.

"Non-fiction then?" Baba asked, stretching his arm, bent behind his head, pulling with the other. A tuft of silver pit hair bulged out where the shirt lifted, but seeing the eyes of McGhee go there, Yannick moved Baba's shirt to cover it.

"You are with human beings today . . . ," Yannick said, leaning in.

"I forget . . . ," Baba said, but didn't lower his arm. "That's the beauty of getting old – I don't have to care anymore."

"We won't remember tomorrow anyway . . . ," Kate added, smiling at Baba.

Baba smiled back at her, raising his glass. "I like her . . . ," he said, turning to McGhee. "So it's fiction then?"

"Yeah . . . I guess. Both . . . at the same time. I never thought about it. What's the difference, right?" McGhee said.

"How's that even possible?" Kate said, leaning around to look at him. "I mean . . . you never tell me anything."

"Oh sure . . . *now* you want to know . . . ," he said, smiling, wrapping his arm around her.

"He's very mysterious . . . ," Kate said to Baba and Yannick, rubbing McGhee's chest.

Baba suddenly pulled his arm down to check the large silver watch on his wrist. "We ought to get going, to beat the tide . . . ," he said, raising his glass for a few more gulps. Taking the sprig of mint out, he chewed it lightly before dropping it back into the glass.

At the dock, McGhee didn't know anything about prepping the boat for launch, and didn't pretend to, content to watch. Near the end of it, Baba asked him if he'd tend the lines, and he was happy to; at least Yannick had Lucie's basket to manage, which he did repeatedly, moving it onboard, then off again, then back on, Baba working around them as if they were troublesome pylons. According to Yannick, Baba had come from a long line of fishermen and had worked the boats himself when young, until it was time for university. He'd had four brothers who had been fishermen, which made it easier for him to leave, as he was the only one with a head for school, but they were all dead now, and the boat traditions fell to him to continue. He bore the irony of that rather lightly, however, that he, the non-fisherman was the only fisherman left, and he performed his preparations with the deftness of an old hand, operating largely from muscle memory.

The boat itself was white with teal trim, all of the paint peeling or flaking, right down to the waterline where it had gone entirely, the name – *Pilar Pequod* – barely visible in red paint that had disintegrated in its own peculiar and particulate manner. The cabin of the boat took up half of it or more, open on the back, ending in an overhang toward the rear to offer shade. Apparently it had been in the family as long as Baba could remember – this according to Yannick – and though it wasn't their primary fishing craft, they used it frequently, especially when fishing was to be done as something other than a profession. It struck McGhee as odd any fisherman would fish in his off time to relax, but then again, he realized he'd never understood the sea as anything other than an abstract paradigm of beauty, and certainly not as an occupation or avenue for recreation.

Once they set off, the engine took over, anemically pushing them out into the harbor like its heart wasn't in it, sputtering now and then as if something in its ticker were about to expire for good. Baba didn't pay much attention to it except when it would hitch three times running (or stopped altogether), and he'd open a panel and jam his heel in to kick it, which was funny to see in sandals, especially when he lost his, caught on the battery cable and nearly fell back onto the deck, except Yannick caught him. He seemed to take its flaky performance personally, as if it were being rude in front of his company, comprising some affront to his manhood and competence as a boatman. Still, after the exasperation left his brow, which it quickly did, he'd smile and wipe his forehead with his shoulder.

After forty minutes they rounded the spit at the end of the bay and made their way out into the open water, further and further from land until they could barely see it, but came to a slight disturbance in the water where it had improbably become shallow again. Cutting the engine, Baba looked at them both. "We are here . . . ," he said, then throwing a small net over the side with tiny buoys along one edge, stood to look out, hands on hips, silent.

Leaning over, Yannick whispered to McGhee, "He's looking for *the* fish."

"*The* fish?" McGhee asked, too loud, for it attracted Baba's attention, who turned to look at them.

"Yes. *The* fish . . . ," he said, turning back to look at the water. "It lives here, by this ridge."

"His whole family has tried to catch it for many years . . . ," Yannick added, leaning over to whisper.

"I can hear you, Yannick," Baba said, still looking at the water. Yannick elbowed McGhee lightly, snickering and covering his mouth.

Turning again, Baba looked at them. "Well, let's get our lines in then . . . ," he said, stepping to the other side. Tucked under the gunwale were several rods fitted with tackle ready to fish, Baba handing one to each of them. "We all fish on that side . . . ," he said, motioning to the tip of rock just under the surface.

"He doesn't move around?" McGhee asked, accepting the rod. It had a large reel and thick line with a nasty hook caught on the hook-keeper below the lowest line-guide, holding the tip slightly bowed, the line taut.

"Of course he moves around," Baba said, sliding out a bucket of chum from the back over to where they would be stationed. "But he won't strike unless we attack his home."

"They have a relationship . . . an *adversarial* relationship," Yannick said, leaning in again.

"Are you going to do that all night?" Baba said, stirring the bucket, looking for a good piece.

"What?" Yannick said, shrugging, his palms out. "I'm filling my friend in . . . he has missed a *lot* of the story."

"Get the chairs, then . . . ," Baba said, swinging his head back under the canopy. Yannick moved further in, finding folding chairs stashed along the wall stowed behind an elastic strap. McGhee followed to help him, carrying two. Unfolding them, McGhee marveled at their ingenuity, half again as clever as a regular folding chair, unpacking twice from their compact state, remaining small when opened but substantial enough to offer comfort. Baba, seeing his admiration, stood, wincing a bit as he pushed at his back.

"I designed those," he said, some pride in his voice. "They get their strength from the weight of the person . . . simple physics, really."

"Not so simple," McGhee corrected. "Elegant . . . I love that."

Baba smiled, his first full smile since their meeting. Grabbing out a piece of coarse fish from the bucket, he grabbed McGhee's line, feeding the hook through it a few times before letting it swing. "Yannick tells me you did physics yourself, once upon a time"

McGhee laughed. "Briefly, in college. I wanted to be a physicist, but it was too brutal . . . ."

Baba smiled, grabbing out another piece of chum for Yannick, but handed it to him. "Here . . . ," he said, to Yannick's disappointment.

"But you did his . . . ," Yannick objected, looking toward McGhee, but Baba waved him off. "He's a new friend . . . ," Baba said, grabbing out a piece of his own.

"So that's how it is . . . ," Yannick said sadly, but his posturing went unnoticed.

"Yeah . . . I was too dumb to quit the science, painful as it was," Baba said, loading his hook. Once he was done, he swung it lightly over the side, releasing the baited hook to sink by the rock twenty feet or so before locking it. At the top of the gunwale there was a holster contraption to hold the base of the rod, and he slipped it in securing a catch behind the reel to stop it from loss due to a sudden jolt. McGhee and Yannick did the same with theirs, though it took them longer to get it right, and by the time they did, Baba had gone to and returned from the cabin, dragging a small cooler with a sandy grind across the deck.

Settling into the chairs, the three fell silent, looking out over the water. The boat heaved lightly on the swells which were gentle but noticeable. The canopy of the cabin extended out and over them, mostly shielding them from the sun, except that it had progressed lower in the sky to come at them from the southwest. Still, the strength of it was gone, tempered by the hour, allowing it to add warmth without baking them. The sky was a baby blue, streaked with diaphanous fans of cloud, thin to nothing, with mounting stacks of cumulus on the far eastern horizon. The air felt to be in the low eighties – warm and slightly moist, but pleasant – and the net effect was pleasing to them.

For McGhee's part, he was not accustomed to spending time this way – in the company of others in such a passive occupation, waiting – but he was finding, as predicted, the fishing was more a pretense for protracted relaxation and conversation than an object in itself. Still, the pretense of an epic family struggle against a particular fish amused him, and he found himself pondering it.

"So . . . tell me about this struggle we're in . . . ," McGhee said. "How long has it been?"

"Forty-five years . . . ," Baba said, reaching out to twang the string, then leaning back. "It started with my grandfather, toward the end of him, then my father, then my brothers . . . ."

"And you think it's the *same* fish?" McGhee said, tilting his head. Baba looked at him, smiling, then looked back to the water.

"Of course it's not the same fish . . . at least, I don't think so . . . ." Moving his hand to his chin, he stroked the stubble there with an audible rubbing.

"Then it's the son of the fish?" McGhee continued. Baba looked at him to assess the nature of the question, if there was sarcasm there, but there wasn't.

"I imagine so . . . ," Baba said eventually. "Our family against theirs . . . over generations."

"And what if you catch it?" McGhee said.

Yannick let out a *Pfft* . . . but didn't go further, for he knew the answer.

"Oh, we have . . . many times."

"And you throw it back in?"

"We throw it back it in . . . ," he said, looking over to McGhee. "You don't get that, do you?" he asked.

"So, what if I catch it then?" McGhee asked.

Baba laughed, low and slow. "Then you'll decide for yourself . . . ," he said.

It wasn't long before their struggle began, as if each one were to be tested in turn.

Yannick's line moved first with a quick pop, jostling his rod in the holster. Grabbing it out and putting it in his lap, he pulled quickly, even before Baba could advise otherwise. Yannick began reeling in, pulling back, but Baba shook his head. "He doesn't hit that way. He's just holding the bait to play with you . . . ," he said, crossing his arms to watch. Sure enough, ten seconds later, the taut line went slack, the hook leaping to the surface, empty.

Yannick looked sheepishly at Baba, reeling it up to the first guide, then dropping his pole back into the holster, disgusted. "*Merde* . . . ," he said under his breath, crossing his arms, but his mood only lasted a moment. Seconds later, his hands were behind his head and he was tilting back in the chair, his feet on the metal rail along the gunwale's lower edge. Baba continued looking at him. "You were too eager, and he knew it . . . ," he said. Yannick made a *Pfft* sound with his lips, smiling over at McGhee.

It wasn't five minutes before Baba's pole tweaked, then tweaked again. Yannick leaned over to point at it, but Baba was cool, holding up his hand. "Patient . . . ," he said. "He's kissing me to see if I'm easy . . . ," Baba said quietly. Reaching out, he removed his pole from its holster, careful not to jostle the line, but somehow the fish seemed to know. Suddenly the pole bent and the reel whizzed with line flying out fast, but still he did nothing. Twenty seconds the reel sung, then went silent, though the line remained taut. A faint release and tug tweaked the end of the pole, and Baba smiled: "He's eaten it now . . . ," he said, pulling back on the line hard to set the hook, but by the look on his face, he didn't appear satisfied. Reeling in, the line remained taut, but there was no fight in it, no struggle. After three minutes of winding, they could see over the edge of the gunwale, glimmers just below the surface, when he showed his white stomach, swimming back and forth until Baba almost had him out, and that crafty fish let the hook go, sending it with its undue tension, flying from the water straight at Baba and across his cheek, leaving a neat red line in its path before continuing on past him to land behind the men, baitless.

"That fish is evil . . . ," Yannick said, hands on the gunwale, looking into the water, then back at Baba.

The salt in his wound stung, but he said nothing, pulling out a rag from his pocket to wipe the blood away. "No . . . ," he said. "He is a worthy adversary."

Neither Baba nor Yannick re-baited their hooks, content to let McGhee have a try. Noticing this, McGhee looked at them. "I guess it falls to me, then . . . ," he said, and almost immediately, the tip of his rod dipped twice, taut then slack, taut then slack, as if the fish were taunting him, but he waited. Reaching into the ice chest, he fished around for something to drink, electing for a bottled lemonade, though there was beer and other similar drinks. Again, the rod tweaked, then again, this time the line running fast, only he left the rod holstered.

"I see you learned from us . . . ," Baba said, Yannick tipping his bottle toward McGhee.

"He fishes like a chess master . . . ," Yannick said.

McGhee smiled at the image, as did Baba, but he still didn't move to lift the rod. Over the next several minutes, the reel spun fast again and again, falling slack in between, McGhee content to sip his lemonade. After another ten minutes, the rod quiet, the reel stationary, McGhee looked at Baba.

"You have a net?" he asked, finishing his drink, letting the long neck slide through his fingers until the bottom reached the deck, rattling to a settle.

Baba looked circumspect, one eyebrow up, but stood, moving into the cabin to retrieve it. Moments later he emerged with a long pole with a looped net at the end and handed it to McGhee.

Moving to the side, McGhee looked into the sea, but there was nothing. Tipping the pole over the edge, he lowered the loop into the water, slowly, no splash evident to betray its presence, pushing it beneath the surface until he couldn't see the end, rotating it to open its face to him, though it wasn't visible.

Baba and Yannick flanked him, the men leaning with both hands on the side to watch. Neither spoke, for they knew crafty fish might hear the words of men. McGhee still did not touch the rod, but kept the pole along his arm and under his pit, the boat slowly bobbing in the swell of the slight waves.

It wasn't another two minutes before they saw it – the glimmers of his stomach – flashing deep below, coursing back and forth in front of them, then in and out, and back and forth again, first one side, then the other, like a bull fighter exposing his side to his opponent to egg him on to his doom, only the pole and line remained inert, passive in the grip of the tricky fish. These undulations continued, the glimmers growing stronger as he moved closer to the light to glimpse this new opponent who confused him, who didn't respect him enough to fight, or forgot his line entirely, or had fallen asleep in his chair, like so many fishermen had before when he'd come up to look. Unmoving, the men stalked their quarry in silence, waiting, patient, while the fish grew bolder to get a better look, his wide eye watching, dead and cold, dispassionate at what looked like statues by the white wall with green trim. Just then its nether eye caught its own glimmer, surprised at it, to be swimming near it when it hadn't appeared before at all, *what fish is this* it seemed to think, but too late, as McGhee eased the pole back, rising to attack from underneath, until the fish's last panicked attempt at escape threw it entirely into his net, caught.

"My god . . . ," Yannick said, looking at McGhee. "*That* was *magnificent!*"

Baba clapped him lightly on the back, allowing his arm to rest around his shoulder, the three men looking at the large fish wriggling in slow motion in the net, dripping, its gills sucking at the thin air for oxygen they couldn't extract, the eye looking at McGhee as much as any of them.

"You think like a fish . . . ," Yannick said, staring at McGhee, dumfounded.

Leaning over, Baba whispered in McGhee's ear: "*Now* you have that decision to make . . . ."

It was nearly eleven the next morning when McGhee awoke, still groggy from the late night. Kate had long since risen — he could hear her bustling in the other room — but it was so pleasant, he lay there thinking. The thin muslin curtain hung stiffly, goaded by a breeze into a slight swing, but wouldn't give it much flexibility, that being their dynamic. The course weave of it threw a diffuse pattern at the foot of the bed, riding the crenulations playfully reminding him of the adventure the day before. He smelled cooking, but guessed he had missed anything like breakfast, especially since the aroma reaching him was more savory and pungent than the typical Mediterranean morning fare. Drawing it in, he realized it must be fish and time for lunch, so he reluctantly put his feet down, found his slippers, and scudded out to find what was to be had.

Kate was checking a skillet, lightly sizzling with butter, crisping the under-skin on the fillets. She remained the superior cook of the two of them, not that this was any great accomplishment, but McGhee never complained. He'd learned his lesson long ago, though his recollection of this lesson was becoming foggy. Beside the skillet, a French press on the stove was steaming, the grounds still swirling in the brew. Squishing the plunger, he poured himself a mug, then spying the cream, reached for it, but stayed his hand. This was a black coffee morning, and grabbing his mug, he reached around Kate, still sliding the fillets like thin pucks in the pan, looking to foil the defense. He kissed her on the temple, causing her to smile.

"It's not ready yet . . . ," she said. "Why don't you sit in the garden and I'll call you."

At the door, he stopped, turning to ask, but Kate was more awake and well ahead of him. "Lucie brought it over this morning. Some nice Bonita filets. Yannick got them from the dock first thing . . . ."

Outside, McGhee slipped into his spot at the table, realizing as he sat that he hadn't brought the computer, mildly irked at himself, but resigned to just enjoy the coffee instead. It was still hot, doing its best to throw wisps of steam into the dry air that was too warm to accept them. It had a light brown foam around the rim – he liked that part of foreign coffee, the strength and thicker viscosity – and sipped it carefully, the rich flavor infusing him with more wakefulness suddenly. He liked that part, too – the kick to his head – and set it down, glad for it. The older he got, the more sensitive he was to caffeine, and the more he needed the intervention.

It was another perfect day, light clouds spread on light blue, peaking in beneath the olive branches which were barely stirring. Out against the blue in the distance, he could see a few white specks of boats, plowing across the bay. The beach was empty, devoid of people, and the only noise that reached him was the wispy olive breath and occasional waves breaking on the rocks, incessantly eroding.

The table was empty except for his mug, a wilted sprig of mint, and the remainder of his tea from the day before, still pinning the envelope to the wood, soaked. Grabbing the mint, he crushed it in his palms, rolling it several times before pulling his folded hands to his nose to inhale the aroma. As much as he didn't like the flavor, he enjoyed the redolence, though he'd never confessed that to Kate. It wasn't a secret, but more a private pleasure he took now and then, especially since it grew wild in the yard. Closing his eyes, he remembered the hillsides in Pennsylvania when he played there in the woods, fitting great adventures into less than a mile of rough path and creek. He had brought fresh mint to his mother, and she had run her hands through his hair, smiling.

A sudden breeze made him open his eyes, it causing a raspy sound as the envelope under the glass caught it, drawing his attention to it. Raising the glass, which had sweated through it nearly, he pulled the sopping envelope out. *The New Yorker . . .* , he thought, reading the address with a sigh, but noticed the window was vacant. A neat cut along the top revealed it had been opened leaving only the shell behind. He might have been annoyed in an earlier time, but he knew Kate well enough to know she couldn't suffer an unopened envelope, even if it was sure to contain disappointment. The thought of her cutting it open to see made him smile; whatever there had been between them – the competition, the immaturity, the confusion, the ambition – had long since dissipated, though the barest vestiges remained. Now it only served to remind him that he loved her, and why.

Trudging back in, he stopped in the doorway to look at her. She was wearing one of his white shirts, two sizes too big for her, collars opened and unbuttoned half way to her navel, the hint of her breast showing in shadow. She was scooping the fillets out of the skillet onto plates and looked over at him.

"Good timing . . . ," she said, spinning to tend the plates on the table behind her.

Holding up the envelope, he flicked it with his finger a few times to make it rattle, catching her attention. She didn't need to look at him, though she raised her head to answer. "Check the line . . . ," she said, lowering her head to tend to the plates.

She'd taken to walking the beach most mornings with her camera and had printed some pictures. Though there was no need for it, she hung them on an improvised clothes line she had strung across ten feet of the corner, looping lightly between the nails holding either end. Five pictures hung there, and two white pieces of letterhead hanging from their corners.

Standing in front of the papers, McGhee tilted his head, sipping at his mug:

Mr. McGhee,
We are pleased to accept your most recent submission for publication in the November issue.

Beside it, the second sheet was perforated, containing a check for $1,500.

Fully Meets

33
0 ◄──────────────●────────────────────► 90
4PM
San Francisco, CA 1/17/1997

McGhee sat with his hands on the keyboard of his desktop in his cubicle, but it was impossible to work: even if it wasn't three-thirty and he weren't spent already, his pending meeting with Jerry was enough to bother him. He wasn't even lucky enough to have a window next to his cubicle or even near it, let alone an actual office with windows, though he did count himself modestly lucky to be on the tenth floor, and some of the windows actually faced out and toward the Bay Bridge, or a sliver of it. He'd learned to parse his good fortune finer and finer as it ever more closely approached zero.

Standing up to look over the cubicle edge, he put his hands there, then his chin, looking at Fred.

"Yo . . . ," he said. "Smoke break?" he asked.

Fred had a shiny metal band around his head ending in foam ear-pads, listening to music, staring into his monitor. His lips moved as he read the screen, his finger tracing code there, the screen reflecting as two small blue squares in his round wire-rimmed glasses. Despite the fact McGhee knew he was in his late twenties, he looked permanently stuck in his late teens: chubby cheeks, red and freckled and acne-laden, despite the endless remedies he tried. His dark curly hair reminded McGhee of a cherub, past plump, with a passion for games and pornography, not necessarily in that order. Now and then he'd call McGhee over snickering, and he never knew what he was going to get. So when McGhee stepped around to Fred's workstation, he knew was as likely to see a cartoon or some ghastly crotch-shot of a fat woman doing something unnatural as something actually work related.

It took a minute for Fred to notice McGhee's hail, and another ten seconds to realize he was talking too loudly – recalling his earphones – and to snap them around his neck with a wriggle so he could actually hear human conversation.

"Huh?" he finally asked, staring up at McGhee.

"Smoke break?" McGhee repeated.

"How 'bout at four?" Fred asked, pointing to his screen as if McGhee could hear the code noise polluting his head.

"I got the thing with Jerry at four . . . ," McGhee said. "You know . . . the *thing* . . . ?"

It took a minute for the significance to register on Fred's face.

"*Fuck* . . . ," he said. "OK, give me a second . . . ," he continued mumbling, typing rapidly for forty-five seconds straight. McGhee was amazed how often it worked like that. He'd listen to Fred before he stood, to assess his busyness, and though there was the occasional key click, or even two or three, it was like a dam broke as soon as McGhee asked him to go. Then there was the elaborate departure sequence: Fred would pause before the last keystroke, all ten fingers up, scanning the screen, then a single, careful press of *Enter* to commit it, then another ten finger display, then he'd stand, hitch up his jeans, push in the chair, then lean in upon it to look at the screen again – twenty seconds for that – a single pat on the seat back, and a look at McGhee. "OK," he'd say, then invariably, "Shit, shit . . . ," and sit again. "One sec . . . ," and he'd type furiously ten seconds, sometimes twenty, a single key press, he'd stand again, hitch up his jeans, again, and say, "OK. Now I'm ready."

Then it was time to go, though he might say, "Wanna get Marcus? Or Kevin?" then in a whisper, "or Gwen?" (this last name usually with a snicker). "I like Gwen . . . ," he'd whisper, breathy, but McGhee would invariably shake his head.

"Maybe later . . . , we're burning daylight . . . ," McGhee would say. All together it would consume three minutes of precious break time. McGhee had learned to factor that in, it was so predictable.

An emergency door hidden at the back of the lobby led to a small parking garage attached to the building. The smokers would congregate outside the door there, huddled around a tall ashtray. McGhee liked to walk out to the edge where the sunlight came in with some breeze, if there was any. He hated to be associated with the huddled masses guiltily sucking down their cigarettes, always acting like it might be their last. As for Fred, he didn't care – he always went where McGhee wanted, acting like he was being accommodating, when the real reason was that he never had any smokes of his own. This was their understanding, and it usually went unspoken. Sometimes when Fred would annoy him, which happened often, McGhee would ask him when he'd buy some of his own. Fred would look a little hurt, McGhee would relent, shake one loose from his pack and say, "Whatever . . . ," handing it over.

McGhee stood looking out, his back to Fred a moment, taking the initial drag on his cigarette. The weather was good – upper fifties and sunny – and just outside the garage, pedestrians walked by on the sidewalk just beyond the edge of the garage. Usually he liked the parade, and it always reminded him he was a transplant: they didn't dress like East Coasters and weren't in the same hurry. Even the businessmen were more casual; the bags they'd carry had a strap over the far shoulder from where they hung, the cut of the leather edgier and less formal, even at that end of the spectrum of humanity. Mixed in were those walking even slower with no place to go, the young and displaced, strange hats, scrubby beards, army jacket or peacoat, layered in colors and textures. Even the women had the same vibe, so the differentiation of genders was smudged, almost intentionally. So usually he liked the spectacle of it, but not this day, turning back to Fred who was still messing with the lighter.

"Here . . . ," McGhee said, grabbing it out of his hand, generating a light on the first flick.

Exhaling his first draw, Fred spoke, coding his words into staccato bursts of smoke. "You seem edgy . . . ," he said, then finished his exhale. "It's just a review . . . ," he continued, shrugging and jamming his other hand in his pocket, holding his arm against his body. He always forgot to grab his jacket when they went out and always wore short-sleeved T-shirts – his uniform – so he was invariably chilled when they stood there, surrounded by cold cement in the shade.

McGhee looked at Fred, almost pitying him. He seemed so oblivious to the process, to the way things worked. In his favor, he didn't seem to care, either, rendering any possible anxiety he might feel over the subject unlikely.

"It's the most important thirty minutes of the professional year . . . ," McGhee said, drawing on his smoke again. "That's when you get the most done. That's when things happen. It's like the big clock ticks off a whole year of your life in that moment. That is, if you give a shit about such things . . . ."

"I thought that was your birthday?" Fred said, looking a little confused.

"Yeah, well, it's not . . . ," McGhee said. Staring down at his shoes, he examined their brownness against the asphalt, the swirling dark perforations decorating the toes, conservative wingtips he'd convinced himself were necessary, but his toes were complaining inside like they always did. Even on the weekends his toes dreaded Monday mornings and their return to confinement. For a moment, the shoes dissolved for him into black and brown dots against more dots of gray, senseless, without meaning or purpose, until he pulled himself back.

"You wanna walk? – you're cold anyway . . . ," McGhee said, motioning with his chin at Fred who was visibly shivering.

"No man, gotta get back and finish that procedure . . . tricky code . . . keeps blowing up on the boundary conditions . . . ."

McGhee laughed. "Sounds like my life . . . ," he said. Looking at Fred, he realized he wasn't the company that he needed anyway. Fred looked at him blankly like a dog, clueless but willing.

"Hey, I can go if you want . . . ," Fred said, bucking up.

McGhee shook his head. "I just need to walk . . . . Later," he said, crushing the cigarette under his heal. "Need to clear my head."

"I'm heading up in a sec anyhow . . . ," Fred said, shrugging again. "Don't worry so much . . . ," he called, but McGhee was already into the sunshine, heading for the coursing humanity.

⸙

Heading down the sidewalk, he looked at the faces around him. Those walking in twos were talking, laughing, their paths irregular as they'd lean in for confidences, as if their center of gravity took a wobbling path while pulling them along. Those walking alone went faster, straighter, like the distance was something to get through. But though he was alone, his path was more like the former, less directed, aimless. What he had for direction, expectations, on every front, seemed to dissipate upon inspection, fading into disquieting and inscrutable whiteness. He had his hands in his pockets as he walked but was thinking of the folded papers in his breast pocket. Two emails he had printed, from separate sources, each on his mind: one from his brother Wil, the other from Kate. And, of course, the other paper.

By the time he thought to look at his watch, he realized he'd have to walk fast to make it back in time for his review meeting. At least it was at the end of the day, so he'd be out of there before too long. The meagerness of his optimism welled briefly, but he suppressed the thought.

In the elevator on the way back up, he leaned against the wood paneling, trying to recall if he'd been there seven or eight-and-a-half years. Counting the internship it must be the latter he concluded, then shook his head. He was into xCopy Inc. a significant portion of his life already. On alternate days, that was a comfort to him – that he'd stuck it out and learned the things he had about being a manager – but this wasn't one of those days. When he thought about it, he'd been *awake* since he was about fifteen, as in not a mindless kid anymore, so of the eighteen years he'd had since then, close to half of it was indentured at this company. In this role he was learning how to be like the best managers, burning out his eccentricities like impurities right there in the crucible of corporate America. In the end, the elimination of these carbon impurities was designed to make him stronger, to even his temperament, and generate a plug-compatible manager who could fit in anywhere and work like a dutiful widget, one of a million, one of ten million copies.

When the doors of the elevator opened, he paused long enough for them to close again only realizing he'd missed his floor once the upward motion shook him conscious again. Pushing his floor button again, he decided to ride it out. That was usually fastest, though it mildly disturbed him that he knew that.

By the time the doors opened on ten again, he rushed out, nearly bowling over Olga, the Admin for the department. She giggled as she danced out of the way, clutching a three-inch stack of interoffice envelopes to her chest. "Jerry's looking for you," she said, stepping into the elevator, spinning on her toe to lean against the back and look out at him. Her smile was warm and genuine. "Good luck . . . ," she said, the doors closing as punctuation.

Jerry's door was ajar but mostly closed, so he knocked lightly twice. Some fingers wrapped around the edge to pull it open; he was on the phone, cradling the receiver against his shoulder as he talked, looking over his glasses at McGhee, waving him in and directing him to a seat across from him at his desk. He motioned to swing the door shut as he plopped into his chair with a slight huff, the leather of it seeking to release the air trapped in the foam cushions. Holding up a finger to McGhee, he indicated it would be quick, but tilted back, laughing, chin high, putting his feet up on the edge of the desk that swept around the side to give him an extra two feet of work space. To McGhee, the soles of his shoes against that edge made him look like a kid on the blocks at a swim meet.

He didn't know for sure, but he strongly suspected Jerry hadn't hit thirty yet. He looked so clean-cut: either his hair didn't grow or he got it cut weekly, neatly trimmed up the sides, swept across his forehead above a neat hairline, product holding it in place. Sometimes when he laughed, those strands in the sweep of it would jiggle but remain fixed in position. He never had to run his fingers through to keep it there, the surest sign it was unnatural, but it went with his overall image. He always wore white shirt sleeves, neatly pleated and starched, rolled up nearly to the elbow. Oddly, this casual appearance came across as premeditated, and more odd-ly still, it seemed he wanted it that way. He wore his badge on a lanyard around his neck, though most of the regular guys wore it clipped to their belts. Policy said *above the waist*, and he always thought it was best to follow it. McGhee knew because Jerry had once made a point of saying so, glancing quickly, but not so quickly he wouldn't notice, at McGhee's badge riding on his hip. Such was his general stiffness which seemed to emanate from within with some pride.

Jerry had come in about a year after McGhee and was one of the guys in his group, though he was never really one of them. He was out of one of the UC schools – Davis or Irvine, not one of the majors – and was a business guy. So while the others mostly did technical stuff, Jerry did not, looking every bit as busy as the oth-ers, though it mostly involved authoring small reports and snarky comments on other people's work. He enjoyed acting like he ran the group, which was transparent to the rest of them and a con-stant source of amusement. So when he promoted over the rest of them to run that very group, there was mild consternation among them – most notably Paul who took it as a personal affront. Paul was a good five or seven years older than McGhee (Paul never quite said, as he wasn't fond of such personal disclosures). And though

Paul had no such aspirations to run the group himself, he saw such a meritless promotion as further evidence the system was corrupt, or at least comically broken in a darkly ironic sense he once said Kafka would have appreciated. He had then proceeded to pursue a work *slow-down* policy, which, unfortunately, no one noticed. It wasn't long after that he quit outright, and not long after that McGhee and Paul went to Turkey. Paul had called it his *victory lap*, laughing when he said it.

These thoughts swirled in his head as Jerry noisily dropped the receiver back in the cradle. After one last exaggerated laugh, he swung about to come to, like a proud little tugboat, ready to pull his weight, his arms behind his head to further look like the boss he was.

"McGhee, McGhee, McGhee . . . ," he said. "How goes it, McGhee?"

McGhee wondered how much he was aware of the posturing, or even cared. Sometimes he even seemed to revel in the absurdity of it, while he simultaneously surfed it with great alacrity. It was a marvel to witness, and horrifying to McGhee, though he said nothing.

"Well?" Jerry said, tilting his head down to look at McGhee more directly.

"Was there a question?" McGhee asked.

"I asked you how it goes, my man . . . ," Jerry said, smiling again.

"I thought that was a rhetorical flourish . . . ," McGhee said, smiling uncomfortably.

Jerry laughed nervously, dropping out of his tilt to put his elbows on the desk.

"So how do *you* think you did this year?" Jerry asked suddenly, reaching into the pile of folders to pull out McGhee's, tipping the cover open so he could see the report.

McGhee adjusted his jacket which had become trapped on one side. "I think I did pretty well . . . ," he said, maintaining his pose.

"You *think* . . . ," Jerry said, leaning back again, rocking slightly in his chair.

"Yeah . . . I *think* I did pretty well . . . ," McGhee continued. He tried to prevent uneasiness from entering his voice, but he wasn't confident he was being successful, adjusting in his seat again.

"Well I *think* you did *very* well . . . ," Jerry said, putting his hands behind his head again.

McGhee relaxed slightly, tipping back himself a bit, though he was careful not to rock.

Removing the cover sheet from the report in the folder, he handed the rest of that copy to McGhee, retaining a full copy for himself, folding back to the second page.

"Let's review your MBOs, shall we?" Jerry said.

For the next twenty-five minutes, Jerry methodically reviewed each item on the *Management By Objectives* list, confirming his reading of each one, which McGhee had completed, making a little pencil check mark next to each one on his copy, mumbling *reviewed* each time he did so.

Once Jerry got down to business, his sonorous tones made it difficult for McGhee to maintain his focus. He wondered if this, too, might be some cagey affectation, but even this thought fell away, and his attention turned to the window behind Jerry's desk, to his own messy desk with unfinished work, to his apartment where Kate was busy with her life, too busy from his perspective to remember he was even in it, and his dad back in Pittsburgh in the ICU, slipping away. He imagined the machines beeping now and then to confirm he was still alive, though he had been sleeping a week already, and the end was probably near. No doubt the email from Wil was a dire update. He was brought back into the moment as Jerry leaned back and grabbed the cover sheet which had been turned over the whole time, glancing at it before handing it to McGhee.

That was the sheet where it all came together as specifics: the final rating, the yearly raise, the bonus, all chuffed out by some machine with Jerry at the handles, working it with his grin, for better or worse. And when he scanned to the corner where the rating was, he couldn't read it for a minute, wondering why he couldn't find the letters for *Far Exceeds*, which is what he expected, nor *Exceeds* either. Instead, he found the words *Fully Meets,* which he assumed was some mistake.

Pointing at the corner, he held it out to Jerry. "There's a typo here I think – it says *Fully Meets* . . . ," he said, genuinely expecting a correction.

"That's a good review . . . ," Jerry said, leaning back, putting his arms behind his head.

"Since when?" McGhee countered, leaning back in his chair, matching Jerry's pose, then correcting it to tip back down, crossing his arms.

"Everyone knows we've had rating inflation here . . . ," Jerry said. "They asked us managers to take a harder look at it this year to push on that."

"But you just said I did *very* well . . . ," McGhee said, looking at Jerry directly. He stared back at McGhee with that smile on his face indicating he was being a good manager, at least to him it seemed to mean that.

"You did do very well. You fully met your commitments, your objectives. We just reviewed them, and covered all of it. You agreed, as we went through all of them that you had done them."

"But there's more to it than that . . . ," McGhee said, returning the stare, but not smiling. As Jerry's words sunk in, their impact was landing like a scatter bomb in his head, little realizations continuing to go off each second as he thought of the impact: *What there was of his career had already stalled*, and, *Such a review would cement that path, and, How did I get here?* He caught himself falling into the spiral and pulled out again. Still, it left him seething, shifting again in his chair.

"Of course there is . . . ," Jerry said, nodding. "But it still adds up to *Fully Met*. Why don't you look at the raise and bonus numbers — they're really not bad. The money pool was smaller this year. We had less to go around. And the star performers get . . . ," Jerry continued, but stopped himself, a slight look of panic flitting across his face.

"But *I'm* a star performer . . . ," McGhee said. "I'm the best guy in the group . . . ." He knew it sounded immodest, but it wasn't the time to hold back in his estimation — it was, after all, the most important thirty minutes of the year.

Jerry looked at him, the same smile on his face, but his head tilted slightly, and he remained silent a moment, before adding, "This isn't about the others."

"You just said *star performers* . . . ," McGhee said.

"I shouldn't have said that — sorry . . . ," Jerry said, shaking his head. "Management wants to get out of that mindset entirely."

"But there are still star performers, no matter what you say, and they get a better rating."

"Well . . . ," Jerry began, tipping out of his pose to put his elbows on his desk. "There are people who do more with their potential."

"So tell me, then, what rating did you get?" McGhee asked. He let the question hang in the air until it was answered, and Jerry smiled again.

"That's not relevant to this discussion," Jerry said.

"I think it is . . . ," McGhee continued, "because your rating is contingent upon the performance of the team."

"*My team* exceeded its objectives and my review reflected that," Jerry said.

McGhee laughed. "You realize you sound like a total ass when you say that, right?" McGhee said. Jerry's smile seemed to set into his lips more firmly, but remained.

"That's not productive," Jerry said. "I think we're done here, once you sign your review," he said, folding over his own copy to expose the cover, sliding it across the desk. A little plastic tab indicating *Sign Here* was affixed to the signature line.

McGhee stared at him in silence. For the first time he felt like an old man in the presence of an upstart, but worse, he saw that Jerry had exceeded him in becoming what he himself would become eventually, a copy of a manager. Reaching into his pocket, he pulled out the three sheets, flipping past the emails from Kate and Wil to the third. Pulling out a pen, he clicked it on, pausing to look in Jerry's eyes which he deemed lifeless in that moment. Signing it, he slid it across the desk.

Reading it out loud, Jerry stopped after the single line typed in the body:

January 17, 1997
To: Jerry Schwanz
From: Francis McGhee
Jerry:
I resign, effective immediately.
Regards,

Fran McGhee

Francis McGhee

McGhee stood to go, tossed the review on the chair and closed the door behind him, pinching off Jerry's protests behind it with satisfaction.

Grabbing a box next to the copy machine, he tossed it onto his desk, then took a look around. There were Post-it notes on his monitor, a couple photocopied posters on the wall hinting at insurrection and discontent from *Calvin and Hobbes* and *Dilbert*, mounds of papers and reports he'd built over the years and never moved (but remembered where they were), a foam squishy brain he'd exercise now and then, and a litter of pens and highlighters and staplers and staple pullers scattered across and mixed into the surface like gravel in a stream. His keyboard rested atop it all, askew, fingerprinted and grimy, waiting pointlessly now. Grabbing a few handfuls of the stew, he threw it into the box, pausing at the five-year service award – the official clear-resin milestone on most every other desk – a letter opener he never remembered using, a thin report he was fond of (for his writing, not the actual content or analysis), a pair of black Converse High-Tops, and an unopened can of Coke. It was a meagre and half-hearted attempt at a career he never really wanted, and he was glad to be rid of it. Rapping on the top of the cubicle, he leaned over to look at Fred. He was staring into his screen, oblivious, and didn't look up.

Waiting at the elevator, he stared into the box at the sampling of his life, disappointed. Grabbing out the Coke and shoes, he dropped the box on the floor, sliding it against the wall under the button with his foot. When the door opened, Olga popped out, smiling at him. "How'd it go?" she asked.

"Just as I imagined . . . ," McGhee said, stepping in past her. Holding the door open with one arm, he reached down and slipped off his wingtips, gathered them in one hand and plunked them into the pile of envelopes in her already full arms.

"Don't you need them?" Olga said, surprised and laughing.

"Not any more . . . ," he said, allowing the door to slip shut, his toes finally free to feel again.

The Boney Pile

5PM
Scalp Level, PA 4/1/1978
4/1/2043

Behind the tipple, which was already sinking into decline with the rest of Mine 40, there stood the boney pile, hunched and brooding over the mine entrance, dark shoulders of waste shale and coal dust looming over the scene as the full backdrop, piled high above the buildings and the company town perched in front of it. From up on the hillside, getting off PA 56 and looking into the valley, McGhee saw the setting, the protracted mound spread like a cape in semi-circle behind the mine, as if the earth were contemplating swallowing the metal buildings and the town with it, all these years later, in exchange for all the coal that had been stolen from her. Each time they descended into the valley, he was struck by this image, or for as long as he could remember, and when he looked to his mother and father to see if they saw it, too, he was amazed that they did not seem to sense the same impending doom he did. Such seemed to be a sensation he was having more often now, of seeing what others did not, and he leaned further into the backseat, staring into the leaden clouds pushing down from above.

They had been doing the drive for as long as McGhee could remember – longer – because his father had grown up there on Third Street, just uphill from the mine, though he couldn't remember too much from the early visits. And now that Les and Wil were at school, it was just him with the parents. Since his grandparents were gone, too, (though in the permanent sense) the trips were less frequent and only to see the dwindling members of the family who were left. Most of the cousins were gone as well, though they tended to stay in the area, and Matty might still be there. He found it odd he still thought of him as Matty, even though he was older than McGhee by three or four years and had gone by Matt for some time. If he were there, which was questionable, he might have something to do, but being in the sweet spot of high school, he'd likely be out. Otherwise, he'd have to hide in the back room at Aunt Rose's watching TV while the rest reminisced in the front room.

That TV room was dark and close, and the couch felt second-hand, though it was probably just demoted to the back when the springs went. It was fated to be covered by hand-knitted afghans and quilts meant to cover the stains that had helped seal its fate as it continued its descent into utter dilapidation. Still, he couldn't complain – they had their own equivalent in their own basement, now re-upholstered in a hideous fake snow-leopard short-nap fur – and by comparison, despite its condition, his aunt's couch was comfortable and managed a certain level of homey charm. He'd be able to hide in there for some time until his aunt noticed he was missing and came to find him. She'd cajole him into the light where she could get a good look at him and remind him how much he looked like his father. By that point, he'd be sick of TV anyway and be ready for the onslaught of family attention and be in the mood to eat something.

Aunt Rose's house was on Richland Avenue, a grandiose name for a little street barely long enough to have a bend in it, almost directly across from the entrance of the mine. One might say it had a view if one was inclined to be charitable: one could stare across the street at early twentieth century industry caving in on itself, or watch the incessant coal trains at close range slowly carrying away the minerals derived beneath their feet. But those days were nearly behind it as it had finally succumbed to a shifting economy and shrinking yields, so the bright side of that collapse was that the mine was at least quieter than it used to be.

These thoughts always poured into his head as they climbed into the driveway and he saw the vaguely barn-like shape of her house, and as they crawled past the scraping brush into the parking space in the back. They'd come to rest near the separate improvised garage that never had the doors open, and went into the house, directly through the screen porch into the kitchen. That porch, too, had a bit of ramshackle feel to it, like it was added by well-meaning but struggling craftsmen making the most of limited resources and budget. But once in the kitchen, there were the inevitable kitchen smells that told him he was in an Eastern-European home, redolent of boiling ingredients uncommon to other cuisine, and despite its modest origins, it was always clean and cheerful, and Aunt Rose would always run up to Mr. McGhee, her brother, with her high-pitched wailing welcome, clapping both sides of his face to kiss him on the lips before grabbing the young McGhee for an unrestrained, all-encompassing hug. It went that way every time, and though he had always wriggled free of the endless grabbing, he liked it and the boundless welcome it meant. That is, he liked it in the half-grudging, half-sheepish way teenagers ever endure such displays of affection.

It was Sunday, so the smell from the kitchen was holubky – stuffed cabbage filled with hamburger and peppers, onions and rice – the tightly stuffed rolls simmering in tomatoes and thin broth filling the deep pan. The aroma was pungent as McGhee leaned over for a smell, then recoiled, but Aunt Rose only laughed, leaning in to hug her nephew again.

"You got a girl yet?" she asked, wrapping her arm around his waist, still holding his hand. Before he could make his exit, he found she was guiding him to the dining room table, away from his turn toward the TV. He towered over her a foot already, but she wouldn't let him escape. "Not this time, Franny . . . ," she said, her eyes smiling into his. "You gotta *talk* to me before you go hide . . . ."

Pulling out a seat at the table, she bumped him with her hip suddenly, forcing him to sit, only releasing his hand when she could see he had given up his notions of flight. "How about a sandwich before dinner?" she said, not waiting for an answer, scurrying back to the kitchen for the plate of cold cuts she had prepared.

Mrs. McGhee noticed the perplexed look on her son's face. "He doesn't have to eat *before* dinner . . . ," she said, calling after her.

Aunt Rose had disappeared around the corner, but she expected the parry. "Of course he does! He's a growing boy. I bet he eats five, six times a day . . . ," she said, reemerging with the cold cuts in one hand and a stack of buns on a plate in the other. "Just a little sandwich . . . . We won't be eating for a whole hour yet." Plopping the plate in front of McGhee, she peeled back the cellophane she'd used to keep it fresh. Balling it in her palm she rolled it with the other into a tight wad and threw it at the young man's head.

Blinking, he looked at his mother, then at his dad, who had come into the dining room, too.

"Don't look at me . . . ," Mr. McGhee said. "She's been like this for fifty years."

"Like what?" Aunt Rose said. "I just like to *feed* people . . . ," she went on. "And besides, I just want to talk to my nephew." Sliding out the chair next to him, she plopped down, nearly missing the edge but catching herself on the table and the chair back. "Whew!" she said, letting out another peel of laughter as she grabbed McGhee's shoulder, rubbing it enthusiastically. "You're such a young man now."

Looking at her brother, Aunt Rose got up again and shooed him into a seat across from his son and did likewise with McGhee's mother, before disappearing again into the kitchen. "You guys want some coffee?" she called out, returning with a pot and clattering cup on a saucer as she danced back into the room.

Mr. McGhee raised his hand to accept the saucer, only to find his sister pouring before he had it on the table. "Easy, Rose . . . ," he said, laughing.

Perhaps it had been there all along, but McGhee couldn't remember seeing his father as a sibling in a family, too. He seemed to have a comfort in his sister's presence that he hadn't noticed before. It was like he was seeing his father as one of several brothers and sisters, how it used to be when they were kids, long before thoughts of their own families ever entered their heads, and the sight of it struck McGhee as something unseen before, and he liked it. That glimpse of his father as a child in another family wasn't something he had ever thought of, not really, and the realization shifted his understanding of him, if only a little.

"Walt'll be down in a minute. He's moving a little slow today . . . ," Aunt Rose said, returning with two more cups and saucers and a glass of lemonade for McGhee, settling one cup carefully in front of her sister-in-law. "There you go, Loret . . . ," she said smiling, then got up again, still talking to her. "Don't worry – I didn't forget the *cream and sugar!*" she said, disappearing again, only to reappear seconds later. Sitting with a huff, she looked at her brother. "Now we can talk, Emil . . . ."

McGhee liked how she said his name, and could see his dad liked it, too. With Aunt Rose, everything was a little operatic as she almost seemed to sing everything, her voice rising and falling with a constant hum throughout, though it was high and not low, and never shrill. She was a large woman, packed into a short frame, always wearing an apron with a rag at her waist to dry her hands, and she was always smiling. Her teeth were gappy and not tight, further leading one to conclude she must be a comedic character in the play she was conducting, always leading the conversation into clever avenues punctuated by laughs.

"You're looking good, Rosey . . . ," Mr. McGhee said, leaning in on both elbows.

"The boys keep me busy, you know . . . ," she said, smiling again, reaching across to grab his hands. "I can't believe my big brother is here . . . ," she said, turning to McGhee. "Probably looks weird, huh, me grabbing your dad's hands, huh, but I miss him. Betcha don't do that with *your* brothers, though, huh?"

"Uh, no . . . ," McGhee said, feeling sheepish again.

Reaching over, she tussled his hair, but let her hand come to rest behind his neck, pulling him in. "Don't worry, you will. Or you better. You're gonna lose 'em some day and wish you had."

"I'm only fourteen . . . I got some time yet," McGhee said, returning her smile.

Aunt Rose broke out in laughter, tossing her head back to let it go, then looked at him again. "You got your dad's looks you know. All the girls, *all the girls*, liked him."

"You're telling tall tales now, Rosey . . . ," Mr. McGhee said, shaking his head. "It was never like that."

"How would *you* know?" she said, laughing again. "You were just a stupid *Hunky boy* back then."

"Slovak," Mr. McGhee corrected, smirking at her, "and Irish."

"She meant good looking, Dad . . . ," McGhee chimed in, but Aunt Rose put her hand on his arm.

"No, I meant like *Hungarian* or Russian – they called us that you know – mostly the Polacks anyway."

"Hey, I'm a Polack," Uncle Walt said, stepping in from the other side of the room, leaning on a cane.

"Me, too," David said, stepping in from the kitchen, with Matt in the rear.

"Me, three," Matt said.

"Four," Gene said, rolling in with his chair, nudging David aside. Grabbing David's place setting, he settled in while David took his case silently to his dad, who only smiled.

"That's what you get for marrying a Polack . . . ," Walt said to his wife, winking at McGhee, then reaching out his spare hand to shake with Mr. McGhee.

Aunt Rose sprang into action again, pushing her sons toward the table, then darted into the kitchen. Walt took the far end of the table while his sons flanked him on either side, helping him sit.

"Damned arthur-i-tis . . . ," he said, finally landing in the seat. "Woke up this morning and damn near couldn't move."

"*Walter!*" rang out from the kitchen, but had only the mildest recrimination to it.

"I can say *damn* in my own goddamned house, damn it," he said, smiling as he did so. It seemed so automatic he must have said it a million times before, but McGhee liked the subversiveness of it and smiled.

"So, lookie at this young devil over here . . . ," Uncle Walt said to his nephew. "Bet you're chasing skirts all over town with a mug like that . . . ."

"Walter . . . ," Mrs. McGhee said, shaking her head and closing her eyes. "He's only fourteen."

"Shouldn't you be twenty by now?" Uncle Walt said, winking at McGhee again.

"I guess he's slow," David said in his dead pan delivery, only the faintest smile on his lips, looking sideways at his cousin.

"David!" Aunt Rose said, returning with another plate of food, lightly slapping the back of his head.

"I was merely pointing out the obvious . . . ," David said, holding up his palms in mock exasperation.

"You only point out the obvious," Gene said to his brother, then looked to McGhee, smiling.

"So how are Les and Wil?" Aunt Rose said, changing the subject while she cleared a dirty plate.

"What about the holubky?" Matt said, leaning in.

"They're fine," Mr. McGhee said.

"They're slow, too," David said.

"The holubky or the cousins?" Matt said, smirking at his brother.

"Glad to hear it . . . ," Walt said, reaching out with both hands to slap David and Matt on the back of their heads simultaneously. "Boys . . . ," he said, but didn't bother to look at them. "We have guests," he continued, winking at McGhee. "Matt, why don't you take Franny, here, out back and show him your dirt bike. He looks like he's gonna have a stroke if he has to listen to you guys yammer any longer . . . . Me, I just turn down the hearing aids," he said, turning his head to point at his ear, letting out a laugh with a volume that bespoke the truth of it.

Matt looked at McGhee smiling the way he always did, like everything was funny if you looked hard enough. "Let's split, man . . . ," he said. "Just don't eat all the golumpki before we're back," he said, leaning over to grab his father by the shoulder for a shake.

The screen door screeched shut with a bang as Matt strode up the stony yard toward the garage. Next to it he stopped near a gray canvas tarp draped over the bike, pulling it off and rolling it up with his arms like cotton candy and threw it aside. The motion was oddly efficient and comical, and McGhee liked it. "There she is," he said proudly, but amused. "Wanna drive it?"

"Ah . . . No," McGhee said, shaking his head. "But thanks. I'd probably wreck it."

"True," Matt said, nodding, then laughed. "Then you ride bitch," he said, tossing his leg over it and patting the seat behind him. He smiled broadly at McGhee, waving him over. He'd always had that way about him: casual and friendly, irreverent but genuine. He was a lot bigger than McGhee remembered from the last visit – it must have been a couple years already – he looked like a man now, though he was only seventeen. He was taller – probably six foot – strapping and healthy, with tousled dirty blond hair and green eyes, white T-shirt, jeans, and scuffed boots. McGhee wondered if he'd be like that when he was a senior, on top of the world, confident, and with anyone else he would have declined the ride, but he found himself climbing on, only to find he didn't know what to do with his arms.

Matt looked over his shoulder with the same smirk. "Better wrap your arms around my waist or you'll fall off," he said with a short laugh at the end. McGhee put his arms around lightly, but as Matt gunned the gas, he grabbed on harder as they bounced down the rocky driveway and out onto Richland where the ride got smoother until he veered off road again to the right and into the mine lands.

The air was almost sixty, but the wind made it cooler, though McGhee didn't mind. It was nice to get out of the house and into the open. That part of the mine had been scratch land – pools and piles of stone and rock lay about, grown with scrubby weeds that had found opportunistic footing in between times when trucks or other machines moved through to rearrange the barren landscape. There were dirt trails through the obstacles, up and over small hills that made McGhee's heart stop as they'd descend again on the other side, skidding turns where Matt would let his inside foot scrape the mud and gravel to support them in case they tipped, tilting vertical again when he'd open it up on a short straight away. The trails crisscrossed and wound their way through the lot which was probably ten acres or so. Eventually, they came to the crest of a small hill, and Matt kicked out the stand and turned it off.

"I like coming out here . . . ," he said, waving his hand all around. "It's peaceful. Quiet. You can see the house from here," he said, pointing off into the distance. Sure enough, the row of houses along Richland were visible just over the edge of the weeds, mostly gray but some still red with their winter color. It didn't look so messed up from that spot: the machinations of the mine weren't visible from that little hill, nor were the unplanned scratches and piles of refuse rocks thrown without thought into that area. From that angle, it looked mostly feral and natural. McGhee could see why Matt had thought to stop and look from this place, and why it might be special for

a kid from there. From that vantage, it looked like any other
street across from a field.

Back inside after the ride, Aunt Rose was scooping holubky into a
big bowl to transport to the table. Another bowl had mashed potatoes, and another green beans, and another corn. She motioned
with her head toward the bowls. "Make yourselves useful . . . ,"
she said, laughing, but as McGhee went past she put down the bowl
and gave him another hug around the waist. "You're so much like
your dad, I love it . . . ," she said, smiling up at him, then released
him to finish loading the food.

When McGhee stepped in with the bowl of corn, David was
looking at him. "I'd say it was about ten henway, right Franny?"

"What?" McGhee said, then looking between the faces. "What's
a henway?"

"About five pounds," Uncle Walt said, and they all broke into
laughter.

Mrs. McGhee caught him around the waist and leaned in,
"Think *chicken*," she said.

"Oh . . . ," McGhee said, smiling sheepishly again.

"Like I said," David continued, "he's kinda . . . ," but was cut
short by another cuff on the back of his head from his father.

"I seem to recall you didn't get it, either . . . ," Uncle Walt said,
still chuckling.

Matt reached for one of the bowls to get started, but Aunt Rose
slapped his hand away, and looked to her nephew. "Franny's gonna
say grace . . . ."

McGhee didn't want to do it, but looked at his dad who simply nodded. "Go ahead."

Taking a sip of lemonade first to prep his throat, he lowered his head and began:

"Bless us oh Lord, and these thy gifts
which we are about to receive,
from thy bounty, through Christ our Lord."

Matt began to move again, but both Mr. and Mrs. McGhee continued the prayer, surprising him, calling out,

"Mary conceived without sin."

On cue, McGhee completed the response: *"Pray for us who have recourse to thee."*

Matt looked at his mother. "I thought it was done . . . ," he said.

"The Butler McGhees say a little extra . . . ," Aunt Rose replied.

"My mother used to say that, Matty . . . ," Mrs. McGhee said, leaning in to explain. Then noticing the slightly increasing smile on his lips, she corrected, "I mean Matt."

"He's still my Matty . . . ," Aunt Rose said reaching across the table to grab a large pinch of his cheek, which she did hard enough to leave a pink mark when she let go.

"She was actually *from* Ireland, right Loret?" Uncle Walt said. His sons were dutifully loading his plate, but his eyes were on her, smiling.

"That's right . . . about 1907 as near as we can tell."

"Maybe Grandpap was on the same boat . . . ," Mr. McGhee said to his son. "Wouldn't that be something."

"I think it was more like 1905 . . . ," Aunt Rose said. "That's what Aunt Dorothy Keblesh always said."

"That was Einstein's big year . . . ," McGhee blurted out, suddenly anxious to contribute, but just as suddenly, regretful. All talking ceased and they looked at him.

"Look who's awake . . . ," David said, dead pan as usual.

"Try to keep up, Dave . . . ," McGhee said, the faintest quiver in his voice, but everyone laughed, David included.

"You got that right, coz . . . ," Gene said, raising his glass to toast McGhee. He was the oldest of the sons, so he'd frequently ride herd on them to keep them in line, especially if Uncle Walt wasn't up to it.

"Well played, cousin . . . ," David said, actually breaking into a smile.

"So we're talking Einstein, now . . . ," Uncle Walt said, smiling broadly and leaning back to cross his arms. "So tell us *all about that* . . . ," he said, still smiling at his young nephew, amused.

McGhee shifted nervously in his seat, clearing his throat. "Well . . . ," he began, looking down at his plate, "he did a bunch of stuff that year. The theory of *Special Relativity*, and the *Photoelectric Effect* – that's what he got the Nobel for."

"The photo what?" David said, feigning incredulity. "He was taking pictures?"

Uncle Walt cuffed him again. "Let him talk . . . ," he said.

Gene shook his head. "Never mind the idiot, Fran . . . go on . . . ," he said, motioning with his chin.

"Uh, not exactly. That one was about light as both a wave and particle . . . ," McGhee said, looking between the faces.

"Jesus . . . ," Matt said, immediately moving his head to dodge the cuffing his father threw.

Mrs. McGhee leaned in: "He did a book report for school . . . ," she said by way of explanation.

"I'm not sure he really gets it . . . ," Mr. McGhee said. "I certainly don't."

A knot welled in McGhee's throat, but he pushed it down. "It wasn't a book report. It was my science fair project, and I *do* get it," he said, looking at both his mother and father, frowning. Mrs. McGhee put her arm around his shoulder instantly.

"Sorry, honey . . . ," she said to him, then to the rest of them, "He did win first prize in his grade."

"Ahhh . . . that's wonderful!" Aunt Rose said. "You McGhee boys are all so smart."

"We're not chopped liver, here . . . ," David said, his lips curling again.

"You figure that out the second or third time you took algebra?" Matt said to his brother.

"The third," David said.

"He only took it once . . . ," Aunt Rose said, laughing. "My David is such a kidder . . . ."

"Hey, it was my joke . . . ," Matt objected. "Some credit here."

Aunt Rose looked into her plate. "You sure try, Matt . . . ," she said to another course of laughing.

Grabbing the bowl of holubky, she handed it to her brother. "You better get some before the boys polish it off . . . ," she said.

Grabbing the bowl of potatoes, David grumbled, "I prefer to think of it as *Pole-ishing* it off, but whatever . . . ."

Uncle Walt toasted his son with his glass, "And never forget it!" he said.

The table set to loading their plates, tearing into freshly baked buns and using them to lap-up the juices running from the stuffed cabbage. Even McGhee took a holubky, though he remained unclear on his appetite for it: the semi-transparent cabbage rolls, stuffed as they were with meaty and chunky and squishy innards sometimes reminded him of primitive animals from a primordial sea, crawled up onto the plates, eyeless and immobile, to be rendered by forks into sprawling displays more appropriate for a bio class than dinner. Still, their savory flavor did draw him in once he'd dispensed with the disposable cabbage wrapper. The hot tomato broth, oozing from the hamburger and rice, helped infuse it with a nice, subtle flavor he liked. And where that broth met the mashed potatoes and formed a slurry, it became a nice application for a shred of bun to collect the mixture for a satisfying mouthful. By the end of it, his plate was nearly clean except for the eviscerated cabbage carcass he had shoved to the side.

As the eating subsided into more casual grazing, McGhee felt the gaze of his father looking at him, and their eyes met. He wasn't certain, but he sensed a hint of parental regret in them, though he smiled at his son, lightly.

"What say you and I walk over to the tipple . . . ," he said suddenly to McGhee, pushing back his plate. "This stuff weighs heavy if you don't take a constitutional after."

"A couple henway at least . . . ," David muttered, still shoveling with his fork, but watching for his father's hand.

McGhee nodded, pushing his plate back, too, for though the conversation was amusing, he'd just as soon not have to endure further questioning, and the prospect of another dose of fresh air was suddenly appealing. As they stepped through the screen porch, Mr. McGhee grabbed their jackets. "It's still only April," he said. "It might get chilly . . . ."

For whatever reason, there hadn't been many walks like this, so when his dad offered, he took him up on it. There was that time they walked through the woods – he was very little – that his father had helped him over the stream, lifting him by both hands, feet dangling. The blackberries had been in season with their long arms reaching into the trail for a snag of jacket, and his dad had picked a few for him. He liked their sweetness, but not the little seeds, though he mostly liked that his dad had picked them for him. And there were the times in the yard when he'd chase after him as he pushed the wheelbarrow up past the garden to the compost pile, moving dirt and material back and forth. Sometimes when it rained in the summer, the drops were warm on his skin, and his dad would just work through it, shaping and improving the yard, one load at a time.

After a few minutes they reached the Company Store, or what used to serve that function, working out of the corner of an enormous red brick double-crested building mostly purposed for something else. Just behind that a hundred feet or so, the massive building housing the tipple and cleaning plant rose, though gravity and decay seemed to be pulling it down again. The walls were corrugated steel, colored alternately by maroon paint and rust, or natural gray where patches had gone in as repairs when they were too busy to finish the painting. Long rows of pane windows hung up near the top near the eaves, three down by ten across, repeating and spanning the length of it, then another course, on the lower level, each pane glazed in place seventy-five years before. Now many hung in pieces where the local boys had practiced their rock throwing, or aimed their BB guns. Above, the corrugated metal roof hung over five feet as cheap soffit, running up to the crest where huge exhaust caps terminated vents from furnaces within. Another building built on a long incline led up into the tipple itself, looking like a conveyor from the interior of the earth for the cars to emerge from the tunnels and unload their burden before returning below for another. Behind that, another building reached back, perpendicular to the incline, huge ducts on the roof to vent still more byproducts from the extraction process.

Mr. McGhee stood staring at it in silence, and his son looked at him, then to the huge building, then back to his father again. "Come on," Mr. McGhee said finally, picking his way around the building to the east to see if they could go in.

The spelunking began with protracted and careful stepping: there was rebar sticking from the ground, fragments of corrugated sheet metal, unidentifiable but purposeful chunks of steel formed into gears and levers and odd tools strewn about, rocks, and weeds, and a dirt that consisted mostly of coal dust. Once past it, they found their way onto a cement slab inside the shop. The door remained open on either end, letting light into the area that for so long had been the protected and dark heart of the operation. Metal tracks led into the middle of the room, continuing through a huge donut of steel wrapped around the track. Off to the side, a large metal lever stood, disappearing into a gap in the floor where it seemed to operate the contraption. Mr. McGhee walked over to it, staring into the gaping hole.

"What is it?" McGhee said, stepping up to stand beside him.

Mr. McGhee looked over at him, then back into the maw of it. "Never actually saw it before, I don't think. I musta sent a hundred ton of coal through that before I was done, though. That, there, is the actual tipple," Mr. McGhee said.

Grabbing the lever and pinching another handle near the top, he was able to move it a couple inches before rust intervened, but it brought a tired smile to his face. "The operator would wait 'til the mine car was in there, then throw this lever here to make the whole thing spin, the car and everything. The coal would spill down below. That's why they called it a *tipple*. Gravity fed, right down into the train hopper cars down there," he said pointing through a seam in the floor toward tracks still visible below. "Then he'd turn it the rest of the way upright again and send it on its way until the next car came in. Back in the day, they were coming in one after the other, all day long.

"The mine cars were short, maybe three feet tall," he continued, holding his hand off the ground to illustrate. "We'd have to shovel into 'em. We'd be on our knees – the galleries were only four foot or so – so there wasn't much space to shovel in. We'd be in there drilling bores for the blasting then move back until they shot the face, and then we'd go back in to shovel it out, over and over again."

"Weren't you scared?" McGhee asked.

Mr. McGhee laughed. "I was too tired to be scared, most of the time. Besides, everyone I knew was doing it, so it seemed . . . natural."

"So how'd you get down there?" McGhee asked, looking around for an entrance.

Mr. McGhee put his arm around his shoulder and led him back to the door where they'd come in. "See that big wheel over there?" he said, pointing to a large pulley-type structure on a tower. "That's the headframe, and the wheel is the pit head – we'd load into the basket and go down. Sometimes in winter we'd never see daylight the whole day. We'd go in at five and come out at five, and it was dark on both ends of the shift."

"How far down was it?" McGhee asked, stepping back out into the yard.

"Depended where we were working," Mr. McGhee said. "Toward the end I was mostly at 1,500. But once you're down there, it doesn't matter much. It's all the same – dark and dusty and noisy and miserable. So when the war came, I went for that.

Didn't figure it could be any worse, and seemed like the thing to do anyway. I sure hope you never have to endure that, either . . . ," he said, his voice trailing off. McGhee couldn't recall him ever saying more than that about the war, though he'd asked a few times, and wondered if he'd ever know more of it, but he knew not to ask.

"Come on . . . ," Mr. McGhee said, picking back through the yard, past the cleaning plant and the outbuildings, across the tracks further back where a few of the mine cars remained, waiting, and on toward the looming boney pile. "We used to walk this way to school every day . . . ," Mr. McGhee said finally, when they'd gotten to the nearest edge of the pile. "I wanted to do it again . . . ," he said, looking over at his son. "Are you game?"

McGhee nodded, striding past him to start the climb. What had looked like a regular hill from a distance suddenly looked much more formidable, consisting of small chunks of shale with coal mixed in and bits of ash. After a few steps up, he suddenly realized how hard it was and turned to look at his father who still stood planted below him, both hands on his hips.

"Harder than it looks, huh?" he said, starting the climb himself. He splayed his feet outward automatically, his muscle memory reminding him how to do it, crunching deliberately with each step, rocking back and forth, crunch, crunch, until he was even with his son, though he wasn't as out of breath. "Let's go," he said, marching ahead, leaning in toward the hill to allow his shifted balance to assist with the climb. Mimicking his father's steps, he found it easier to make progress. But though he had age on his side, he still had trouble keeping up as his father opened up a lead of ten yards, then fifteen, continuing his methodical climb. As he trudged upwards, the rocks tumbled below, or slid as scree with the high-pitched whine of shale on shale. After another ten minutes, McGhee finally got to the summit to find his father staring off toward Windber on the other side of the hill.

"That's *St. Cyril-Methodious*," he said, pointing off toward the distance. It must have been another mile, down in Windber itself, but they'd have to climb down the other side of the pile before wending through streets to climb the hill where it rested if they were to walk there. "We'd have to walk this way every Sunday," he said, "to get to church. Then back again after." Wiping his brow, he laughed, looking over at his son. "You can't imagine that, right? It was either that, or walk the whole way around, but that was a couple extra miles at least," he said, but the younger McGhee was too out of breath to answer right away.

When he finally caught his breath, he stretched his back, pushing a hand into his side. "You mean your whole family had to do this – even Grandma?" McGhee asked, still wheezing a bit.

"Even when it rained," he said. "Or snowed. You should try this when there's ice on the rocks."

Turning around toward where they had climbed, Mr. McGhee sat down on the peak and patted the rocks next to him. "Take a load off . . . ," he said, smiling weakly at his son.

Looking back, the whole of Mine 40 and Scalp Level opened before them. They were several hundred feet higher than any of it and it looked something like a fixture on a train board: a small town nestled into the elbow of the industry that created it, supported it, defined it. The Stony Creek, which fed the mine and the town, wound its way through the whole of it, giving shape and meaning to the otherwise arbitrary layout of the entirety. From above, the heavy clouds remained motionless and gray, barely differentiated where one cloud ended and the next began, unbroken and pressing down upon the whole of it.

The young McGhee picked up a dark, chunky, flaky rock and showed it to his dad. "Coal, right?"

Mr. McGhee reached over, gently lifting it from his hand. "Yep. Bituminous coal . . . ," he said, gingerly rolling it around in his palm.

"Versus?" McGhee said, grabbing another small chunk to do the same.

"Anthracite. Anthracite is *hard* coal. This is *soft* . . . ," Mr. McGhee said, holding it up, then pressing with his thumb around the edges to crumble off a few pieces.

McGhee tried to do the same, but his piece wouldn't yield so readily. "I wouldn't make a pillow out of it . . . ," he said, still struggling to match his father. "So what's it doing on the pile?"

Mr. McGhee laughed, adjusted his heels deeper into the rocks, sending a few rolling, to improve his position. "Well, some got through I guess . . . ," he said. "What you're sitting on, this huge mountain, is the byproduct of a generation of men scrambling underground. More likely, two or three of 'em."

"So this is what's left of them, then?" McGhee said, looking at his father. "And that?" he said, pointing at the crumbling mine buildings. Mr. McGhee laughed lightly, though it wasn't so much from humor as from memory.

"I wouldn't say that . . . ," he said, motioning with his chin toward Scalp Level. "We lived on Third Street, over there. Most of the way up the hill. My dad worked a good part of his life under here, until he couldn't no more. Started finding it hard to breathe, so he had to stop. But he built a family in the process. We were poor, but happy. His labor allowed me to grow up and start my own family. They did their part. There was a lot of give and take with this here mine. We were thankful for it. I know it doesn't look that way to you, but I remember happy times here."

"Even underground?" McGhee said, tossing his coal over the edge, watching it roll down below.

"Not so much underground, but even that had its moments. I trusted those guys. Had to – my life was in their hands, and vice versa . . . ."

"Sounds like the war rather than coal mining . . . ," McGhee said, looking at his father. His eyes seemed to well, slightly, but he swallowed it, nodding, but not looking at his son.

They fell silent a few minutes, surveying the scene. An old truck made its way along Richland in the distance, around the bend and past Aunt Rose's, turning into the rest of Scalp Level, rolling up one of the streets in the small grid, stopping about half way up. Mr. McGhee watched, too. "My friend Viener Schlongka lived about there," he said, a smile coming to his lips. "Nicest kid you'd ever wanna meet. Met him in gym class – really got to know him there, anyway." He talked about Viener a few more minutes, and they laughed at the recollections. To McGhee it seemed like maybe the first adult conversation they'd ever had – more like peers than a son with a parent – and the feeling welled in himself that he was finally growing up.

After a few moments of silence, Mr. McGhee looked at his son. "I shouldn't have said that at dinner . . . ," Mr. McGhee said. "I have no idea how smart you are or what you know. Scares me sometimes . . . ," he said, picking up another stone and tossing it down the pile.

"Thanks," McGhee said, swallowing hard himself, looking off toward the still-bare trees flanking Richland. McGhee started to stir as if they were ready to go, but Mr. McGhee put his hand on his shoulder to settle him.

"Listen Franny . . . I brought you out here for a reason . . . ," he began, the pieces coming in parts with some difficulty. McGhee looked at his father, but he remained quiet for a minute.

"Your mom and I . . . we're having some issues," he resumed, but faltered again. This time the welling in his eyes required he use a hand to hold back the emotion, pushing in with his thumb and fingers before drawing his forearm across. Looking back out over the mine, his eyes looked tired and red rimmed. "I'm not as worried about Les and Wil. But you . . . you were always a little different. More tender."

McGhee picked up another piece of coal to stare into it. His eyes felt hot as they examined it, collapsing in their focus until they saw nothing but the mineral, and then only its darkness, in his hand. The words he was hearing wouldn't stick together – or couldn't – and he struggled to comprehend them. They embodied his childish fears which he had become convinced were baseless, universal, like falling nightmares or parents dying, but he was hearing them, and despite what he did to push them out, the sense of them seeped in, chilling him.

"So you're splitting then . . . ?" McGhee said, finally mustering the words.

Mr. McGhee had regained his composure and picked up another rock, tossing it down the pile. "I don't know . . . ," he said. "I'm not sure we'll make it. I just thought you should know. In case we don't."

McGhee waited a moment before speaking, but looked at his dad. "So what is it?" he said.

Mr. McGhee smiled wryly, sadly, and shrugged. "Hell if I know . . . ," he said.

"So it's Mom then?" McGhee said. His eyes were on the stones around his feet, and he picked one up with some heft, but light enough to throw. Sensing the same impulse, Mr. McGhee picked a rock and got to his feet first.

"I didn't say that . . . ," he said, launching the rock toward the nearest building, far down the hill, but it fell just short. McGhee watched the flight of the stone, then got to his feet, steadying them in the rubble on either side of the blunt peak. He'd learned from his father's throw and leaned into it, throwing in a higher arc, hard. *Bang!* it went, barely on the edge of the corrugated metal roof, rattling the metal with a satisfying thud before it rolled off the edge.

"Nice throw . . . ," his dad said. "Better-n mine. My turn."

As Mr. McGhee reached for another rock, McGhee grabbed up another, ready again. "So what is it then, I mean, if you can tell me . . . ," he said.

Launching the rock, Mr. McGhee threw harder and with a higher arc, well past his prior throw, until it banged on the side of the building just under the row of windows.

"Dang . . . ," McGhee said, shaking his head. "First glass then?"

"You're on . . . ," Mr. McGhee said, picking up a rock quickly and launching it.

"Hey, it was my turn . . . ," the younger McGhee said, launching his own. Neither even hit the building.

"Go ahead . . . ," Mr. McGhee said, tipping his chin.

McGhee selected another stone, and once in his hand it seemed to have just the right heft, but looked at his father. "You didn't answer my last question . . . ."

Tossing the stone in his hands back and forth, Mr. McGhee lowered his head in thought. "Ever wonder what it's like to get old? I mean . . . what it really *means* to get old?"

McGhee shrugged. "You just *get older* I guess."

Mr. McGhee laughed quietly, lowering his head, then looked at his son. "That's right . . . but what does that *consist* of?"

McGhee shrugged again. "Lots and lots of days, I guess . . . ," he said, smiling back.

Stepping over, Mr. McGhee put his hand on his shoulder. "That's right. Lots and lots *and lots* of days . . . ," he said. "Ever have two that were just the same?"

"Pretty close . . . ," McGhee said. "I mean almost."

"Good answer. It's that *almost* I'm getting at. Those add up. And before you know it, you're somewhere new. Even if you're in the same place. Understand?"

McGhee looked at his father. "Not exactly," he said, then turning toward the building, let the rock fly. It was a hard throw – he could feel it in his shoulder this time – lower than the last, flying on a good trajectory, toward the windows, but found an empty pane and sailed through, soundless.

"Doesn't count," Mr. McGhee said.

"But it went through the window . . . ," McGhee complained, smiling but annoyed.

"Hey, you're the one who said *first glass* . . . ," Mr. McGhee said, smiling again. McGhee was about to object, but it was good to see his father's mood lighten, so he relented. Seeing the thoughts flit across his son's face, he stepped over to him, wrapping an arm around his shoulder.

"It was a nice throw though . . . Let's keep going."

"So that's it . . . ?" McGhee said, getting back to the thread of their conversation. "Age is just the residue of a lot of days?"

Mr. McGhee looked at him and smiled. "Nicely put . . . sometimes you say things just right. I'm gonna have to write that down and tell Mom."

The thought of them speaking about him, in light of their recent discussion, crossed over his face like a shadow on a field. But as he thought of it, any such talk was good, and he brightened at the prospect, until he realized he still didn't have an answer.

"So how does that answer the question? I mean . . . about what happened?"

Mr. McGhee shook his head. "Doesn't really . . . except one day you wake up and wonder who you are, maybe wonder who the person next to you is, too. Never thought it'd happen to us, but with Les and Wil leaving, maybe it was bound to. I mean, once your kids are gone, what was it all about?"

McGhee looked at his dad. "Are you sure you should be talking to a fourteen-year-old like this?"

Mr. McGhee looked to his right, then his left, then at McGhee. "Don't see no one else to talk to . . . ," he said, smiling. "Sure feels better getting it out there, though, I tell ya. I've been dreading this for weeks . . . but now that I told you, it feels better. Like maybe it'll even work out. And I'm especially glad I told *you* . . . ," he said, pointing at his son.

"Why's that?" McGhee said, staring into his hand at another rock he was rolling around.

Mr. McGhee shrugged. "Dunno, really. Maybe's it 'cause we never got to spend much time alone together. After your brothers, I was tired. But maybe it's something else . . . ," he said, his voice trailing off.

"Like what?" McGhee said, discarding the stone as too light for the task at hand.

"Like maybe you're more like me than anyone else, that's why . . . ," Mr. McGhee said.

Stepping away again and steadying his feet among the rocks, Mr. McGhee made another throw, though as soon as he released, he grabbed his shoulder. "I think that's it for me . . . ," he said, shaking it off. It was a good throw, far and true, but landed just to the side of the windows, hitting the metal with a huge *thunk*. A loose pane adjacent to the strike, fell out, tumbling thirty feet to the ground with a crash. He raised his arms in victory, but seeing the look on his son's face, he lowered them again.

"I don't think that counts . . . ," Mr. McGhee said.

Looking over at his dad, McGhee saw what he was doing and fell silent, allowing himself to be fathered.

"Go ahead . . . give it another shot," Mr. McGhee said, urging him on.

Reaching down, McGhee found a dense, small rock, more like a river cobble than something from the mine. Adjusting his feet, he concentrated on the windows, the rest of the image blurring then disappearing for him before he let it fly. Once it was gone, he knew his shoulder was done, too. Out the rock flew, out and down, falling, aided by the height, until it landed just beside where his father's had, enough to the left, where it crashed through the next pane over, throwing shards, landing inside where it stuck some sort of metal drum, resonating.

Mr. McGhee smiled at his son, proud.

The two stood looking in silence, surveying the scene: the mine with its buildings, the town waiting at its feet for the mining that would never come back, and the boney pile.

"Sure do miss those days," Mr. McGhee said, stepping off to crunch his way back down the pile of miners' labor, taking care to mind his steps.

Sixty-five years later, when McGhee stood on the hill looking down into Scalp Level near PA 56, Mine 40 was nearly all gone. Only the building for the Company Store remained, and the thick blanket of cloud cover. What had been a mine had been reclaimed by the earth, leaving an inexplicable blank spot across from a small town crowded into the crook of a hillside's elbow, perched over nothing at all, except memories. And he knew what his father had meant by days and days, only he knew something else, too, that his father hadn't told him, though he was sure he had known it: there was no getting any of it back.

Soldier's Wounds

33
0 ◄————————————●————————————► 90
10PM
Butler, PA 1/21/1997

As he stood at the door, he looked back into the apartment –
Kate was somewhere in the other room out of sight, though
he could hear bustling. She was getting ready herself for a trip to
LA, and they were dodging each other in their separate preparations for travel, each lost in their thoughts and personal reminders,
acting oblivious of the other. He thought of calling out but the
words caught in his throat. Pulling the door shut, he jogged down
the stairs to the building entrance and out onto the steps. It was
cool and clear, though he couldn't see his breath, despite the fact
it was January. He knew, however, he'd be seeing his breath by
evening when he landed in Pittsburgh.

Though it was only 7:00 a.m., he ordered a drink from the
cart when it went by – two tiny bottles of Jack Daniels – to calm
his nerves. He hadn't done that in years he thought, but it seemed

appropriate and necessary. The call had come the previous morning at first light: when he picked up the phone and heard both Wil
and Les on the line he knew before they said anything beyond *Hello*
that his dad was gone. It was about that same hour, on the East
Coast, when he'd passed away at the VA hospital, alone, so by the
time he got the news three hours later, his father was surely cold
already and on his way. Though he couldn't sustain the thought,
an image of pearly gates flickered momentarily in his head: despite
hopes for an epilogue, there would be none. So a little whiskey was
called for, even if it was early and the sun barely up.

Everything seemed higher contrast, etching into his head
with greater significance: the lock of the landing gear pulling
into the belly of the plane, the tug of gravity pushing him in the
seat, the plane banking out over the Pacific, then curving back,
pushing hard against that momentum to swing east, the blast of
light through the shade, the sun low but bright bursting up over
the distant Sierra Nevada, the roar of the engines, the slap of
sunshades by cranky would-be sleepers, the whistling AC vent
overhead, the smell of coffee from the metal urn on the cart, the
smile on the flight attendant's face that went slack when their
eyes met, the extra bottle she gave him, unasked. He wasn't one
for melodrama, but significance oozed from everything like an
existential miasma: this would be the last time he'd see his father,
but there'd be no conversation, no further refuge to take at home,
albeit sometimes it was taken reluctantly. It had always been like
touching base in a game where it was safe, would always be safe,
though that memory felt gone now, too. And though his mom
was there, the illusion of sanctuary was punctured, and it was
only a matter of time before she'd be gone, too, and with her any
hope he could go home again, really home.

Wil was driving over that morning and Les was flying in that night, so at least he'd have them as company. For once, he felt lucky to be the youngest. The hardest parts would fall on them – they'd surely take lead – so he could go on automatic if he needed to. Then again, there was no escaping that the loss was as much his as anyone's, except perhaps his mom, so there wouldn't ever be any genuine escape, not really. He was thus reconciled to inescapable sadness, and it descended upon him like the pall it was.

The alcohol was finally entering his system, taking the edge off. He normally hated that feeling –losing control – but he liked the dulling effect it was having. The hyper-awareness was subsiding, and he put his head back on the headrest to nap. It'd be six hours yet, and the prospect of alcohol-driven sleep almost made him smile, though his lips couldn't form it, remaining just as stoic as they had been.

The wheels hitting the tarmac in Pittsburgh jarred him awake. He didn't think he had fallen asleep, not really, except the drool line from the corner of his mouth begged to differ. Wiping it with his sleeve, he stole a glance at his neighbor whom he hadn't thought to look at before: an older man with silver hair, his arms crossed, eyes clamped shut (though he didn't appear to be sleeping), wearing a headset connected to a CD player in his lap. Judging by the cashmere sweater and button-down shirt and neatly trimmed hairline, he didn't quite belong in coach, so he figured he wouldn't have cared to notice him anyway, since the man had seemed to take measures to notice nothing by intention. And by the window, the college student looking out the glass seemed oblivious to anything else. When she looked away from it, slightly, he could see her eyes were wet, so she had her own problems to keep her occupied.

He wasn't sure how he was going to make it up to Butler from the airport – he hadn't arranged for a rental car – but noticed he had a voice mail waiting when he turned on his phone. Standing in the aisle as soon as the *Fasten Seat Belts* sign binged-off, he cradled the phone against his shoulder while he pulled out his bag from above. It was Wil – he'd gotten an early start and could get him at the curb, he just needed some notice. Glancing at his watch, the timing seemed about right for a drive from Jersey, so he called him. He'd already assumed it'd be OK, and he was nearby at a *Dunkin' Donuts*.

When the doors at *Arrivals* snapped open, the cold hit him with stinging immediacy, his eyes watering instantly, his breath catching. *Must be about fifteen* he thought, but he opted to wait outside. He had a love-hate relationship with the weather there, though he always missed it. The climate was always more temperate in California, both in heat and cold, but never felt like home. Every time he felt that cold, or the peculiar heat of the summer, he knew he was back, like some magnetic thing in his bones aligned with the place, setting him a little straighter. The sky was nearly dark already with just the barest remnant of blue in the west near the horizon. He always hated flying east, losing a whole day in the process. It felt like the day had been stolen, like he was being lined up to go to bed early, just like when he was a kid and dreaded lying in bed, awake, alone and unable to sleep. Luckily these thoughts didn't last long. A quick honk on the horn and a flip of the lights indicated Wil pulling in, splashing up a gusher of cold slush, just narrowly missing McGhee who barely stepped back in time, the automatic winter defenses surfacing from the recesses of his muscle memory. Rolling down the window, Wil waved.

"Welcome to Pittsburgh," he said smiling, though it was weighed in each corner by prevailing gravity.

Tossing his bag in the back seat, McGhee jumped into the passenger side. "You want me to drive? You've been driving all day. Thanks for the lift, by the way."

Wil patted him on the shoulder. "No, I'm all right. And, of course, it's better to have company. That drive across Pennsylvania was pretty long, all alone . . . ," Wil said, but stopped talking suddenly.

McGhee turned to look at him. It was clear he was choking down emotion. "I bet . . . ," McGhee said. "I had a couple JDs and slept the whole way."

Wil laughed. "Smart," he said. "But the cops frown on that for drivers . . . . So . . . how you holding up?"

McGhee shrugged, feeling the emotion welling. "I managed to not think about it the whole day. I just can't believe he's gone. I mean, I knew it was coming, but . . . ," his voice trailing off. "Did you see Mom yet?"

Wil shook his head. "Came directly here," he said. "I thought it'd be better if we saw her together."

"When is Les getting in?"

"About thirty minutes. Did you guys coordinate?"

McGhee shook his head. "Just lucky I guess. I could use some coffee though. Is that *Dunkin'* close?"

"Close enough . . . ," Wil said, pulling away from the curb.

Just outside the grounds of the airport, Wil pulled into a grungy little strip of stores anchored by the doughnut shop. Despite the hour it was nearly full with only two open stools at the end of the counter. The rest of the space was occupied by street people escaping the cold, nursing coffee to avoid going back out into it. The counter attendant seemed powerless to do anything about it, pouring carafe after carafe of coffee going down the line, return-ing to setup a new pot after each run, the only break being the ninety seconds it took to refill the basket and watch the water run through. When he got down to Wil and McGhee, he looked worn out and paused to look at them.

"Please have a doughnut . . . ," were the first words out of his mouth. He glanced back up the line of homeless men, then back to them. "I've been working four hours and I have thirty cents of tip so far. These guys are killing me."

"I'll take two, then," McGhee said, fishing out his wallet, "and these are on me," he said, holding it up to show Wil.

"How magnanimous . . . ," Wil said, his familiar sarcasm re-turning. "Me, too, then, since he's buying," he said to the atten-dant, pointing at his brother with his thumb. "Two classics," he said.

The attendant nodded, tilting his head slightly with disapproval. "Not exactly *creative*, but it's a start."

"So what would *you* recommend then?" Wil said, crossing his arms.

"Definitely Boston Crème. Maybe Dutch Apple Crumble if you can handle it," he said immediately. "I mean, you *are* in a doughnut shop . . . ."

"It's a *Dunkin' Donuts* . . . ," Wil objected, but the attendant held pat.

"Whatever . . . ," he said, scribbling down the order, saying *two plain doughnuts* as he did so, before looking expectantly at McGhee.

McGhee looked sideways at this brother until he returned the glance, then looked at the attendant. "I'll take a glazed chocolate cake doughnut . . . ," he said, waiting for the reaction.

The attendant nodded, scribbling. "Not bad," he said, looking up. "And the other?"

"A glazed blueberry cake doughnut . . . ," McGhee said.

The attendant's shoulders caved in. "Really?" he said. "That's the best you can do?"

"And a Boston Crème . . . ," he said, to the delight of the attendant. "And coffee for both of us."

"Sure thing, slugger . . . ," the attendant said, spinning on his heel to retrieve the order.

"Three doughnuts, Fran?" Wil said, smirking at him.

"I didn't eat all day . . . ," McGhee said, leaning in on his elbows. The weariness of travel suddenly caught up to him, and he felt a wave of exhaustion descend.

When the cups arrived, Wil twisted his in the saucer, staring into it. "You know Mom wasn't there, right?" Wil said, still staring into the blackness.

McGhee looked over at Wil. He looked older all of a sudden, more than the eight years separating them would explain.

"They called her, just before… but she didn't go," Wil continued, finally raising the cup to his lips.

"What? Why not?" McGhee said, but Wil only shrugged.

Looking at his watch, Wil swiveled on his chair, "Ready to get Les?"

Nodding, McGhee downed half a cup of coffee in two gulps, and grabbed the last doughnut and a half for the road.

Back at the airport, they pulled into the curb near *United Arrivals* to wait. That was pretty much the best option out of Casper, the closest airport to Rawlins, connecting through Denver. Opening the door a crack, McGhee looked at Wil. "I'm stepping out for a smoke . . . ."

Wil's face darkened. "I thought you quit. Besides, it's probably ten degrees out…."

"Long flight . . . ," McGhee said, stepping out. "Put the window down a couple, will ya, so we can talk."

Wil pressed the button, putting the window down five inches.

Igniting the cigarette, McGhee took a deep drag and held it a moment before expelling it up and over the car. The exhalation was as much steam as smoke in the cold air. McGhee could feel the inside of his nose crinkle with each breath, which he liked a few times until he remembered the pain that went with it, opting to breathe through his mouth instead. The infusion of nicotine was welcome, as was having something to do. He found the distraction of smoking as compelling as the actual addiction, and in moments like this, relished it.

"You talk to Mom at all?" Wil asked, leaning over to the passenger seat to speak through the window.

"Just for a minute, yesterday. She didn't seem to want to talk. She said she was fine. It was a little weird, really."

"Yeah . . . ," Wil said. "I had the same talk. Both yesterday and this morning. It's kinda like nothing had happened. She sounds the same as last week . . . ."

Just then, Les came out of the sliding door onto the sidewalk, a bag on his shoulder and a duffle in his hand. Looking over, he saw them immediately and shuffled over.

"Jesus, Franny, I thought you quit . . . ," he said, plopping the bag by his feet. "Gimme one of those . . . ," he continued, reaching out to McGhee.

"Et tu, Les?" Wil shouted out the window, then thinking better of it, got out of the car.

Les left the unlit smoke in his lips, smiling, then hugged Wil, then after a moment, McGhee. "Good to see you guys . . . ," he said, but his brows were strained. It was clear the circumstances were bad and didn't need stating. Lighting up, he blew the smoke up in a quick motion, the thin cold breeze breaking up the steam, though the smoke hung as a cloud, floating away. "You guys talk to Mom yet?" Les asked, sucking another drag from the smoke. He jammed his hands into his pocket, jumping a little bit like a pogo stick. "It was in the forties back in Wyoming . . . ."

"Yeah . . . ," Wil said, motioning to McGhee. "We both did, only it was short."

Les, shook his head. "Did she sound weird to you guys, too?" Wil and McGhee nodded.

"Like nothing happened," McGhee said. His eyes met with Les and they locked momentarily. He could see they were red on the edges, more than the cold would explain. All color had left the sky with just the harsh white lights of the terminal overhang to enlighten them. "How you holding up?"

Les, laughed, looking at Wil. "I should be asking you guys that. I'm the oldest after all . . . ."

Wil nodded, pressing out a slight smile on his lips. "You guys done yet? I'm freezing . . . ," he said, nodding to the car.

"Pop the trunk, then," Les said. "We'll be in in a sec . . . ."

Wil jumped in, the dull thunk of the trunk-release echoing slightly.

Les moved over to McGhee and put his hand on his shoulder. "This must be hardest on you . . . ," he said. It had become clear over the last few years that McGhee had been the closest with their father, though they all were. McGhee appreciated the acknowledgement, smiling himself, though it was tempered.

"We all lost Dad . . . ," McGhee said, taking a last drag of his smoke before dropping the butt on the curb, crushing it under his heel.

"I know . . . ," Les said, pinching McGhee's shoulder slightly. "But I had ten more years with him, Wil almost as much. And you're younger."

Tears welled in McGhee's eyes, but he wiped them away, unwilling to break down. "Let's get to Mom . . . ," McGhee said, stooping to retrieve the butt for the trash can.

———— ⠀⠶⠶⠶ ————

McGhee fell asleep in the back seat on the way up to Butler, Les and Wil falling into discussion over something unintelligible up front, the noise of the car making it impossible to follow. The familiar crunch of gravel and swing up the hill into the driveway with the changing engine load woke McGhee. The light in the picture window was on as always, and he was home, though for the first time in his life, his father could not be.

After hugging her sons, each in turn, Mrs. McGhee corralled them around the small round kitchen table, against their protests to the contrary, for sandwiches. The truth was they were hungry, however, and it immediately seemed better for her to stay busy. She'd spent the day cooking them a meatloaf – something she'd never do just for herself – expecting the scene to play out exactly as it was. The three of them hadn't been home at the same time for a few years, each taking turns coming in to spend time with Dad, spreading out their visits to cover as much ground as they could. For her part, Mrs. McGhee was enjoying their company, recalling the visits she'd had from neighbors and phone conversations with relatives from the last twenty-four hours. Spilling the loaf out from the tin onto the cutting board, she pulled a long, thin bread knife from the drawer and began cutting slices, talking over her shoulder as she did so: neat quarter-inch slices through half the loaf. Loading them on a plate, she shuffled over to the table before returning for plates for the boys, and utensils and napkins and ketchup, and glasses. Wil stepped around her to get to the fridge, pulled out a six-pack of Diet Coke he'd stowed from his last visit, plunking it on the table just as Mrs. McGhee got the rest of it ready.

"It's so nice of you all to come – to be here . . . ," she said, getting up again to get the sandwich buns she'd forgotten from the refrigerator. The brothers exchanged glances, but said nothing, watching their mother.

"Your dad would have liked to see you boys together. You've always gotten along so well." She had to tug at the door three times to get it open – the seal was giving her trouble these days, exceeding her strength – and she poured the cold bread into a wicker basket before returning to the table again.

For each of them it was a familiar ritual and they took their first bites in silence.

"Mmmm," Les said, smiling at his mother. "You always made the best meatloaf . . . ," he said.

Wil and McGhee nodded, though McGhee had never really liked it. It was always dense and, other than some onion and green pepper, seemed like a hamburger in different format, cold and unseasoned at that. Still, he liked the community of the moment and ate it dutifully, soaking in the company. Each of the details became more significant to him – the sounds of his brothers chewing and pushing gulps down, his mother's half-sized plate with a dry cookie on it, broken, crumbs sprinkled about. Her tea cup steaming – she had tea ready at all times, or so it seemed to McGhee – her tentative sipping at the edge, the tilt of her head when she looked up at each of them, like she was recording the moment, too, her smile sad and tired. Above Les, there was a picture of the *Last Supper* with a few dried palms trapped behind the corner, bent back to contain them in loops. Behind Wil, a black metal key and rooster affixed to the wall where they had been thirty years. And above it all, a ring of fluorescent light humming in the fixture cast cold sterile white light on it all with no warmth and only cheap utility.

"So how you doing, Mom?" Wil said, setting his sandwich down to grab a can of soda.

"Oh, I'm fine, considering . . . ," she said, pinching off a piece of cookie. She nibbled the edge like a mouse, her eyes magnified by her glasses. McGhee caught the glint of light in her eyes from the replacement lenses her cataracts had required. Despite the sadness of the moment, however, they remained dry and her sadness seemed more like resignation than deep trauma. "I just wonder what will happen to me now . . . ."

Les's eyes looked at Wil, then McGhee, but he didn't move his head. "What do you mean, Mom?" he asked, taking another bite of the sandwich, but chewing quietly.

Mrs. McGhee sipped at her tea, averting her eyes, watching the cup land back in the saucer. "You know . . . ," she said, sticking her bony finger under the edge of the cookie to break off another crumb to nibble. "I've always had your father here. To take care of things, the house."

"Let's just get through the next few days . . . ," Wil said, reaching across the table to lay a hand on his mother's. She didn't release the cookie, but put her other hand atop his, patting it lightly.

"It's so good to have you boys home . . . . Now it's better," she said, forcing out another smile and scanning their faces again.

"We'll take care of everything, Mom . . . ," Wil continued. "I called Geibel this morning on the way in. We have a meeting with them tomorrow morning to set the arrangements." Pulling his hand back slowly, Wil looked at Les, then McGhee.

"Can you handle writing the obituary?" Wil said, his eyes catching with McGhee's.

A lump welled in his throat at the thought of writing it, but he pushed it down again. "As long as you guys help . . . ," he said, looking back and forth between them. They both nodded.

"Of course . . . ," Les said. "But you're the best with words. And Dad would like it that way . . . ."

"So what time tomorrow?" Les asked, though Wil had mentioned it in the car already. McGhee had heard that part – the rehearsing of the chat with Mom, to cover the details, with special attention to keep it low key and easy – but it was different to see it real-time. Mrs. McGhee looked from boy to boy as they spoke, but the words only faintly registered.

"Ten . . . ," Wil said, continuing the script. "We'll need to pick the casket, finalize the obit, set the wake – the Director suggested Thursday evening, burial Friday."

"And St. Paul's?" Les said. "We'll need to talk to them."

Wil nodded. "Called them, too. Spoke with Father Harry. They put me right through to him. I guess they got a call from the VA already. He wants to do the ceremony."

"Ahhh . . . ," Mrs. McGhee said, brightening. "Emil would like that... he always liked Father Harry. He's such a good man."

The three boys nodded but couldn't speak. McGhee took a bite of his sandwich, glad to have an excuse not to say anything. Wil drank from his soda. Les looked at his mother.

"You don't have to come in the morning if you don't want to . . . ," he said to her. His voice seemed to run out of breath near the end of it, but he held firm.

"Thanks Les," she said, reaching out to grab his hand with both of hers. "I'll see in the morning . . . ," she said. "Now, you boys keep eating. I'm going to go get my jam-jams on and get ready for bed . . . ," she said, standing, using both hands on the edge of the table to push herself erect. All three sons partially stood, though she waved them back into their seats. "Don't be silly . . . ," she said, annoyance creeping into her voice. "I've been standing up for seventy-three years and don't need help just yet." Seeing she'd been too sharp, she forced another smile at them. "Now, go on and talk. I like hearing the sound of it."

Once she was down the hall, Les moved over to the cutting board. "You guys want?" he said, turning to point at them with the long knife, then realizing it was an odd pointing instrument, waved it playfully in the air at them like a sword, thrusting lightly in Wil's direction, across the room.

"Sure," Wil said.

"Franny?" Les asked, pointing to him next, but he shook his head to decline. "Sure?" Les said, giving him another chance. "You always loved Mom's meatloaf . . . ."

"I'm good," McGhee said.

"What?" Les said, staring at him. "What's that even mean?"

"It means I don't want any," McGhee said, pushing his plate back and crossing his arms on the table.

"Since when?" Les said.

"Since I already had a sandwich," McGhee said, looking over at Wil. For his part, Wil had no intention of intervening and shrugged.

"No, I mean, since when does *I'm good* mean that? Or mean anything, exactly?"

"I don't know . . . ," McGhee said. "People say it in Cali all the time . . . ."

"Ohhh . . . ," Les said, shaking his head back and forth, wiggling the knife in the air as he said it. "In *Cali* . . . ."

"You know, the big long state on the West Coast," McGhee said, taking up the challenge.

"Hey, am I ever gonna get more meatloaf here?" Wil said, chiming in, looking over at McGhee, then back to Les. He wasn't sure, but McGhee thought he saw a quick wink when he did so.

Les kept shaking his head, but set again to slicing the loaf slowly in thin wafers, just like their mother had done.

From the distance Mrs. McGhee's voice rang out: "Franny... Can you come here?"

Thankful for the intervention, McGhee stood and walked down the hall, passed the room where he'd slept in high school, turning just before his childhood room into his parents'. She was in front of the dresser, the bottom drawer pulled out.

Seeing him enter, she motioned to the drawer. "Did I ever show you boys that?" she said.

Neatly folded inside, something filled the drawer from side to side, light yellow and natural cotton. It wasn't familiar, so he got on his knees to view it. "Is it some kind of quilt?" he asked, looking back and up at her.

Putting her hand on his shoulder, she looked in, too. "Take it out, please . . . ."

Sticking both of his arms into the drawer he was able to pull it out, still folded, placing it on the bed. It appeared to be folded to expose the underside, small flowers on an unbleached field. Tugging at one end, she unfolded the top, then unfolded again, opening it larger until it remained folded once. "Can you lift it up now, Franny? I wanna see it again."

Grabbing at the free corner, McGhee tossed it open to reveal the front, covered in women with hats, standing in a crowd, with one in front, her face crafted from many pieces, shadows on her eye line and cheek and nose, smiling slightly and proudly. Above her in

Art Deco letters was a *1920* in charcoal gray, and in similar letters below, the word *Suffrage*.

"Wow . . . ," McGhee said, still holding the corner. "I remember *this*... Where has it been?"

Mrs. McGhee lightly smacked him on the back of the head. "In that drawer, numbskull," she said, but it was affectionate.

"Hey guys . . . ," McGhee called out. "You gotta see this thing . . . ."

Les showed up first, still munching his sandwich. Pushing the bite into his cheek, he spoke through the meatloaf. "I remember that thing . . . ," he said nodding.

Wil looked around the corner. "Oh yeah . . . I forgot about that. Where has it been?"

"In there . . . ," McGhee said, pointing at the yawning drawer at the bottom of the dresser.

Wil stepped into the room, grabbing the other edge, unfurling the rest of it, stretching it across his chest and craning his neck to get a better look at it. "That's amazing workmanship . . . . I remember you in the basement working on that for months . . . ," he said. "I always liked the look on the woman's face."

McGhee leaned in to have a look at the woman, staring. "Is that Susan Anthony?" he said, looking over his shoulder at his mother.

She put her hand on his shoulder. "Sure is . . . ," she said. "Got fired over this damn thing, too...," she continued, nodding defiantly.

"What?" Les said from the doorway, dropping his arm to his side, pushing the last bite down. "How? Where?" he said, like it was a fresh affront.

"From the rectory, back in '71. The Monsignor."

"Spiegel or McNulty?" Wil asked, looking from his mother to Les and back again.

"It was McNulty, by then . . . ," Les said.

"He was still new . . . ," Mrs. McGhee said, sitting down on the corner of the bed, tracing the edge of the woman's dress with her finger. "I worked so hard on it. It was for the bake sale, to raise money."

Wil laughed, shaking his head. "Man, that was *ballsy*, Mom."

"*William!*" she said, but kept looking at her handiwork.

"Sorry, Mom. But it was," Wil said, snickering.

"Yeah . . . ," Les said, shaking his head. "And pretty awesome. What made you think of it?"

"I was a bit of a firebrand, in those days. In my way . . . ," she said. "But you boys don't remember."

"I remember you yelling at the TV during Watergate . . . ," McGhee said suddenly. "So I saw it."

Mrs. McGhee looked up and smiled. "The good old days . . . ," she said. "He wasn't a bad man – the Monsignor – but he didn't want to make waves. He said it wasn't time for that, that there was enough upheaval. I never told your dad that part. Maybe he was right . . . ."

"Which part?" Wil asked. He, too, was tracing the lines in the quilt, the beautiful hat Susan Anthony wore, with the feathers stretching proudly back, arched.

"About the debate with the Monsignor. It was hard enough to tell him I lost the job. We needed the money."

"Debate?" Les said, smiling, leaning against the doorframe. "I'd give anything to have heard that. Was it heated?"

Mrs. McGhee laughed at the thought of it, shaking her head. "Discussions like that were never heated. You forget what it was like. They were important men in an all-male system. And I was just the rectory secretary. It was enough to ask him *why*, and to ask him when *would* be the time for women to speak up."

"So did he fire you right then?" Wil asked. Les leaned in to smack him on the back of the head.

"Les, don't hit your brother . . . ," Mrs. McGhee said, accessing a familiar recording in her head that had been dormant for decades, but her focus was on Wil. "It wasn't like that . . . ," she said, pausing. "He seemed rather surprised I spoke up, and he looked uncomfortable. He'd just come back in from the Cowoski's. They'd just lost Billy in Vietnam – he'd been MIA a few months, but they'd gotten the news that morning he'd been converted to KIA – so he'd been with them. Of course, I had no way of knowing when I went in that morning it'd be one of those days. It was tough on the Monsignor. I think that was the first one he had to do – Monsignor Spiegel had two or three of those during his time.

"So when he saw the quilt, I think it pushed him over the edge. It was too much. And the parish was having some money troubles, too – the parishes were shrinking by then, but the costs to run them weren't. It all fell on him. So the last thing he needed was another front to fight upon, and he was thinking he had to let me go anyway. That just made it easier. At the end of the day he called me into his office and gave me the news.

"I told him I could work fewer hours, but he just shook his head. He said he had to learn to do for himself, at least until things got better. Maybe then I could come back, but I knew his heart wasn't in it, either. He couldn't see past the bad times. All he saw was unravelling. That's how he put it. *Unravelling*."

"So then it wasn't the quilt?" Wil asked, looking from his mother to Les and McGhee and back again.

"It was timing . . . ," Les said, shaking his head. "Maybe any other day would have been better."

"But you hid the quilt all these years . . . ," Wil said, still processing.

Mrs. McGhee shrugged, but was looking at McGhee, smiling sadly. "You remember that car wreck, Franny?" she asked. "That's when I told your father."

"So the wreck was *his* fault?" McGhee asked.

Mrs. McGhee grabbed his hand, stroking it. "Heavens no! But like Les said... timing. My timing always seemed off those days. Even with you, Franny . . . ."

Wil and Les looked at each other, but said nothing.

"Your dad and I were gonna stop at two . . . ," she said, her voice trailing off. "Surely you realized you were born almost nine months to the day after Valentine's."

"*Jesus* . . . ," Les said, shaking his head again. Mrs. McGhee shot a look of disapproval at Les, but relented.

"Timing . . . ," she said again, removing her hand from McGhee's to pet the quilt again. "Not that we were unhappy about it. We were kinda hoping you'd be a girl, though . . . ," she said, looking at McGhee, tilting her head.

"Well, you got that right," Wil said, reaching over to push McGhee on the shoulder.

"*William!*" Mrs. McGhee said, though she laughed through the admonishment, removing any hint of genuine frustration. "All right... time for bed. Help me get this back in the drawer..." she said, slowly standing.

"No way . . . ," Wil said. "It's never going back in there."

"Damn straight . . . ," Les said. His mother looked at him to provide reproach but smiled instead.

"Can I put it on my bed?" McGhee said, running his hand over it.

"I vote that *the mistake* gets to use it . . . ," Wil said, raising his hand.

Mrs. McGhee raised her hand to yell at him, but Les intervened: "Seconded . . . ," he said, stepping into the room, past Wil, to gather his mother in his arms. "You're still full of surprises, Mom," he said, pulling her close.

Rising, Wil and McGhee joined them, and they were all glad to be together again, if only for a while.

The viewing room at the funeral parlor was hot and stifling set against the bitter cold still outside. The three boys stood together by the door waiting for friends and family to arrive. Mrs. McGhee sat alone in a chair near them, a piece of tissue clutched in her hand, another tucked into her sleeve at her wrist, though her eyes remained dry, staring. Each of the brothers tried to avoid looking toward the long end of the room where their father lay in the box because it was too hard, but they knew it was time.

Les moved first, nodding at his brothers as he walked by, but halted five feet from the casket, dead in his steps. He'd been strong throughout, but his shoulders weren't holding up his suit as they used to. McGhee had never thought of Les as old before that moment, but the weight of it seemed to descend upon him right then, slightly crushing him into his shoes. A slight shaking became apparent across his shoulders as his head dipped. Wil and McGhee instinctively walked over, putting a hand on either shoulder, focused on their brother, but the weight hit them, too, as they each in turn looked toward their father. McGhee patted Les, then dropped his hand, moving closer.

His father's eyebrows had grown bushy over the years, his features thickening with age, lines deepening. But the gravity he'd seen in those features the last year, growing heavier, was gone like he'd found rest after all and the burden of slowly dying was finally lifted. His brows had the slight look of surprise like he used to have, where his humor perpetually resided; with his eyes closed it looked like he was in the midst of a good dream, reluctant to wake. He knew it was the effect of those skilled in preparing the dead for viewing, but he was thankful for it, that they'd found who he was again, somehow, and brought forth his happier self in that moment of ultimate repose.

"He looks good . . . ," Les said, coming to rest beside McGhee, Wil flanking him on the other side.

"I wonder how they did that . . . ," Wil said. He didn't need to explain, for they all saw it, their essential father, resting.

"I don't think I believed it until this moment . . . ," McGhee said. "He's gone."

"Yeah," Les said, Wil nodding, his eyes wet and flowing, though no sound emerged.

McGhee felt a tugging on the tail of his jacket and turned. His mother was looking up at him. "Me, too . . . ," she whispered, pushing a tissue over her lips.

"Oh gees . . . ," McGhee said, wrapping an arm around her. "Make room, guys . . . ," he said, ushering her in front of himself, Les and Wil on the sides. She was short, so he rested his chin on top of her head, folding his arms in front of her.

"Dad looks good, huh?" he said.

"Oh . . . Yeah . . . ," she said, but he could feel her going slack in his arms, her shoulders heaving, finally, as the tears came as quiet weeping. Les and Wil wrapped their arms around McGhee's shoulders, joining in the front, the group relying on the strength of the others to remain standing. They were now only four.

Over the next two hours, visitors streamed in filling the room, carrying with them cold in the folds of their jackets and scarves, and the light smells of old people and their cloistered homes where they usually hid from view except in times necessary to make trips such as this. It became the intersection of the various lives their father and husband had lived: at work where he had toiled thirty-five years as a craftsman in the backroom of a jewelry store adjusting baubles, tightening prongs to protect shiny stones from loss, gilding rings where wear showed lesser metals underneath; at the *KofC*, where the *Knights of Columbus* toiled at *Friday Fish Frys* to raise money for the church and its charity, old men channeling lost camaraderie from WWII army days in service and memory of what they fought for but that they were forgetting more and more as those days receded, lost; at the church, where he kept vigil on the Eucharist Thursday evenings in solitude; on the streets of Butler, where he'd forged thin but durable relationships in occasional but years-long chance encounters; at ball games, where he'd worked with other fathers to induct their sons in team sports of baseball and football, those sons now long grown and cast about as diaspora beyond those hills to places that wouldn't believe such things still happened, at least in the way they did; to park benches, where he'd had his lunch baloney sandwiches and fed pigeons with others inclined to scatter seeds like he did, amused at the pecking and dumb glances hopeful birds shed, skittish, at their feet.

They all streamed in and found the brothers, pulling them aside to tell their small tales, vignettes of kindness from him and how he'd touched them – an endless stream of them – and how they wanted to pass this knowledge along and feed it back into the family, lest it be forgotten, that he'd be forgotten, because they were the only connection now, and their own candles were flickering low, and this would be the only opportunity to share those moments, when all those timelines and connections would fold into a momentary coincidence. And once these stories were related, their brows would relax, unburdened and relieved, and after one last handshake, they'd recede back into the crowd as the next wave washed in to absorb them, to disgorge their stories, too, and repeat the washes, layer upon layer of nuance, sketching in his hidden and quiet life, that they'd always suspected but never knew in any detail. Until finally their numbers dwindled, and the brothers and their mother and funeral director were the only ones remaining to wait for the last hour of viewing, and it was time for them to do the same with each other.

The brothers pulled a few of the neat folding chairs out of their rows to form a small circle around their mother who had already taken a seat along the edge, exhausted. Her eyes were dry, though she had tissue ready, clutched in her hands while she stared into the distance, well beyond where they peered toward her feet.

"I can't believe how many people came . . . ," Wil said, looking over at Les.

Les nodded, leaning back in his chair, the wood groaning slightly. "It's pretty amazing . . . ," he said, sighing. "Reminds me of the small town I remember, way back."

"Yeah . . . ," Wil said. "I think they still live there, only I'm not sure it's really here anymore."

"It is," their mother said, her eyes remaining lost, unfocused. "For those of us who never left."

McGhee looked at Wil, then Les, wondering if there were any reproach to it, but it didn't feel like there was, so much as a tinge of unavoidable regret. Still, it seemed to have wisdom to it, wisdom that could never have been accessible to them as young men, anxious to get out and on with their own lives.

"What you boys seem to forget – or never knew – was that we chose to come here, from where we lived before, just as you chose to leave. So perhaps you have it where you live now, though you may never know until someone tells you."

The brothers glanced at each other – she wasn't prone to making such pronouncements, especially ones with self-awareness. From their perspective, this had been home and not a new start. But upon recollection, which they each were doing, their father had come from the coal fields of central Pennsylvania, and she had come from the city – Pittsburgh – so that very beginning for them, their flight from their birth circumstances, was likely lost on them unless they kept it in view with great intention and effort. When they had come and settled in Butler, this life they knew as home was no such thing to the elder McGhees, though they built it, seamless, an envelope to hold the family and their baseline for peace of mind, their nest. The brothers knew little of what came before except in the abstract, so they were all, in actuality, wanderers, and she wanted them to know it.

It was late by the time they made it back to the house – past ten – so with a few hugs, Mrs. McGhee made her way to her room, prepared for sleep and cut off her light just as her door snapped shut for the evening. Emerging from the basement steps, Les held up half a bottle of bourbon and three glasses to the approval of the brothers. Moving to the living room, they set about filling their glasses and collapsed in chairs to unwind from the official wake to have a private one of their own.

"I remember when Dad bought that bottle . . . ," Wil said, wincing at his first sip. "It's been open fifteen years, anyway . . . ," he said. "Got it for one of those family picnics."

McGhee sipped his glass but remained silent, looking around the familiar room with less familiar eyes than they had been in his youth. The peach-colored walls hadn't bothered him when he was young – it was the natural color of home – but since then he'd come to realize it was a little too peachy, though the effect remained his baseline. The Berber carpet was unusual, too, a shade between taupe and brown, beaten down and worn from forty years of wear. He remembered the couches from the earliest years – maroon and stodgy and scratchy, then streamlined and hard and olive with wood accents and tubular bolsters, then the current set, bright with floral patterns in a cheap print, devoid of texture, stretched over firm unforgiving foam cushions, hidden under white protectors their mother had fashioned from recycled cotton sheets. Then there were the built-in shelves where the fireplace should have been but their parents had disdained, since the modern romance with fireplaces still remained subordinate to their memories of dirty coal stoves well before any of the boys' experience. A wooden ship – *The Bounty* – remained in the cubby above the middle where the stereo resided instead of the fireplace, all done in pretty maple but covered in yellowed varnish applied in the mid-fifties.

"It's all coming to an end . . . ," Wil said. He had been watching McGhee survey the room and could read his thoughts, perhaps better than anyone. "This world won't last much longer...."

McGhee took a large sip from his glass but held it in his mouth, stinging. His eyes met Wil's, and he saw the same sentimentality he was feeling. Wil was starting to gray in his temples, and though he'd always looked boyish to McGhee, he could see the years mounting in his face. More freckles than there had been, circles etching their way beneath his eyes.

"Has Mom mentioned her plans?" Les said, finishing his glass and immediately pouring another couple fingers.

"Plans?" Wil said, looking over. Les motioned his glass around the room but remained silent.

"You heard her. I don't think she has *plans* . . . ," McGhee said, leaning back in his chair. The bourbon was starting to feel warm in his stomach, and the glow was welcome. "I think she'll stay here."

Wil nodded, sipping his glass. "Yeah, we have time for that. I just want to get her through this process."

"*Process?*" McGhee said, turning his attention to Wil. They didn't often find themselves at odds, but it seemed so indelicate to McGhee. "You mean *burying Dad*, that *process?*"

Wil immediately raised his hands in surrender. "Sorry. Can I get a do-over on that one?" His eyes were on McGhee, his mouth formed into a light smile, though tempered. He knew better than to raise his younger brother's hackles from years of experience. He was the baby in the family, after all, requiring occasional special handling.

"No… it's me," McGhee said, shaking his head. "This whole thing has me . . . . It seems we're losing Dad in the whole… *process*… so it struck a nerve."

"That's exactly what's happened . . . ," Les said, slightly clueless, swishing the bourbon around his glass slowly.

"I know what he means . . . ," Wil said, holding out his hand to stay Les's pragmatism. Les shrugged, taking a small sip from his glass noisily.

"We haven't said one thing about Dad. It's all been other stuff. It's like we're already forgetting . . . ," McGhee said, raising his hand to cover his eyes, pushing his glasses up to catch the tears forming but not yet falling.

"I think it's hardest on you . . . ," Wil said. "You spent the most time with him near the end . . . ."

"You came out three times this year, right?" Les said, becoming more conciliatory.

"Four . . . ," Wil said, correcting him. "Franny came out four times."

Wil and Les fell silent, watching their brother. Wil leaned across, putting a hand on his knee a moment, like their dad was fond of doing. McGhee's shoulders heaved, but he pushed the tears back again. He wanted to remember and for the moment to be about their father, not consolation for him. After another sigh he composed himself, looking at them.

"Last time I was here, I sat with Dad in the VA, by his bed . . . ," McGhee began. He took a sip from his glass, the burn feeling good as he pressed it back into his throat. "I don't know about you guys, but he never talked about the war. Not with me, anyway . . . ." Les and Wil shook their heads, but remained silent.

"One night – it was almost time to leave – Dad started crying. It wasn't just a little either. He was totally balling his eyes out. I don't think as long as I knew him I ever saw him cry before. Not like that. Maybe a little moist during a movie, but no real crying. So this was different.

"I gave him a few tissues from the box by the bed, but he just held them in his hand and let the tears roll down his face. Then he related a story from when he was on Leyte in the Philippines. It had been raining a few days straight, probably a monsoon or something. Just pissing down . . . ."

"He didn't say *pissing* did he?" Les said. McGhee shook his head.

"Probably not. Pouring more likely . . . ," he said, nodding. "It's important to get it right. So it was pouring for three days I think he said, and they were all covered in mud and shit – crap – and suddenly the clouds broke. There were rays of sun and the trees were dripping, the drops shining like silver, and the guys started laughing. Standing up, spreading their arms in the sun, jumping in puddles, like they were kids.

"He was leaning on his gun – the BAR – since he was on point out at the perimeter, talking to his buddy Joe Meckelman. Joe was saying he was gonna take Dad to New York City when then got back – something about pizza . . . ." McGhee went silent a moment. Wil leaned over again, patting him on the shoulder.

"So he was holding his hands apart to show him how big the pizzas were, and a round came in. Hit Joe in the right eye."

"Man . . . ," Les said, shaking his head. "I can't imagine that."

"So a guy comes out of the bush right near them onto the road, running toward him, maybe thirty feet away. He was pulling a pin on a grenade and screaming. Dad said he could see his eyes when he shot him… the look of surprise he had as the rounds hit him, at the look he had when he dropped the grenade, stopping, how he stood there looking at it before it went off, and the cloud of dirt and red mist that was left behind. It was the only man he was sure he killed in the war."

"Jesus . . . ," Wil said, leaning back in his chair. "He certainly never told me *that* before."

"Me, neither," Les said, shaking his head.

"You know… It explains a lot about Dad," McGhee said, twisting his glass on the table. "He had a memory like that in his head all through the years. He was so gentle. He did so much to help people, to teach us. Maybe it was because he knew how bad it could be. How he could be driven to do such a thing."

"Well . . . ," Les said, leaning in. "It was either him or Dad . . . ," he said. "It was a war."

"Yeah . . . ," McGhee said, "I know. But in that instant, it was just the two of them. It was very personal. He said he didn't regret that he did it. But he did regret that he was *made* to do it."

"I never had a conversation like that with Dad . . . ," Wil said, his brow wrinkling.

"All I remember Dad confiding to me was about his friend Viener Schlongka – said he had a dick like a pencil."

McGhee and Wil looked at each other, then Les.

"What?" Les said, looking back and forth between them.

"How's that the same thing?" Wil said, suddenly recovering, McGhee laughing outright, though his cheeks were wet.

"Yeah, Dad told me that, too . . . ," McGhee said, "back in Mine 40 one time . . . ."

"No, I mean, you know, the candor. He always kept stuff to himself," Les said, relaxing into a sad smile.

McGhee raised his glass, looking at his brothers, glad to be in their company. They raised their glasses too, waiting.

"To Dad and the Greatest Generation . . . ," McGhee said, downing the rest of it in one gulp.

McGhee was in his dark suit on the porch at the funeral home, smoking. The wind was coming out of the east, cold and hard, stinging his face in little gusts, but he liked it. The wind rarely came from that direction, but he saw it as a sign of something. With the passage of his father, he suddenly felt like the wind was hitting him more directly than it had been before, like his security, such as it was, had finally gone. Perhaps it was an homage to a great man, the weather offering a begrudging acknowledgment of the loss of another soldier.

McGhee looked out the window of the black limousine in the procession to the church. St. Paul thrust its spire into the sky, blackened with the soot of a hundred years of steel industry, recently gone dark, as the rest of the town was being slowly reclaimed by the earth, dead. The sky was leaden, pushing down upon them with grayness, its only relenting being that it couldn't snow, for it had cried out its moisture already.

Les, Wil, and McGhee, with a couple old men wearing garrison caps and jackets from their army days, collected around the casket, sliding it onto the gurney at the top of the stairs for procession to the altar. It was dim inside, as it always was, perfumed with incense floating in the air, blue, above their heads, stirring slowly. Father Harry waited on the step there, mumbling prayers, his head lowered but arms raised as the casket came to a stop before him and the boys filed away and into the pews. Muffled sobs emanated from those about them. Aunts reached out to their mother to tug at her elbow, tissues already planted under noses to contain the flow. When McGhee turned to look at her, she looked lost and small, clutching a rosary in her thin fingers, her worried eyes focused somewhere mid-distance that no one else was capable of seeing.

So when it came time, Father Harry motioned to McGhee, and he shuffled out of the pew, past his brothers up the marble steps to the lectern. Unfolding a paper from his pocket, he looked out across those gathered. He'd never had that vantage before – unlike his brothers, he'd never tended altar in his youth – and the perspective surprised him. There sat maybe a hundred, perhaps more, gathered to remember his father. It occurred to him he'd never have that number himself, nor likely would his brothers, though his mother might. Toward the back of the church were the city friends – not even Catholic some of them – intent on witnessing the passage. He saw the balloon man from the park – he'd never connected them before. Or the counter lady from the *Hotdog Shoppe*. Or the janitor from his elementary school, back when he ran down the hill. Closer in were people from the neighborhood, from the houses that had names like Miller and Rodgers and McCaw and Thompson: even though most had moved away by then, they'd come back for this. Then closest were the close friends and relatives, such as they remained. Mrs. Sanderson and Eddie and David, watched him, waiting for the words to come.

Looking at the paper in his hands, he smoothed it out, hoping he'd make it through but wasn't sure he could. His eyes were welling and there seemed no stopping it, so he waited, pressing the pages flat.

Les and Wil, seeing his distress, slipped out of the pew, collecting by his side. Wil wrapped an arm around his shoulder, Les wrapping an arm around his waist. "Go ahead . . . ," Les whispered, leaning over.

Looking out, McGhee cleared his throat, his voice wobbly at first, but gaining strength as he read:

Green Ash
Gray Ash
What once was wood
dense grained, heavy green
did lose its sap
to many winded summers
and blustery fall.
When dry, fire consumed it
through blaze, crackle and ember
until the lightest ash remained
to ride those self-same breezes
away where glances lose them
except in memory.

Wil leaned in to McGhee and whispered. "I couldn't have done that . . . ," he said, slightly pinching his shoulder and patting him.

"Dad would have liked that . . . ," Les said.

At the airport, McGhee stood at his gate as they called his flight, staring at the boarding pass. It'd take him back to San Francisco, it said so, but it wouldn't get him any closer to where he needed to be. Dropping it in a waste bin, he stepped out on the curb to stare into traffic, raising a thumb. It was cold, so cold it numbed him, but he'd had enough. Mexico should be nice that time of year.

McGhee's Road

55

0 ◄─────────────────●──────────► 90

9PM

CA-395, CA 8/9/2019

It was hot in the Central Valley, but McGhee wasn't through with the heat when Friday came and was time to go home, back into the city where there wasn't anything, or anyone, waiting for him. It'd be cold there, and he wanted warmth, baking heat, to remind him it was summer and of summers gone by. And though he loved San Francisco, one thing it didn't have was that. Then, too, he imagined his breakfast dishes on the small round table in the kitchenette where he'd left them Monday morning, before first light when he'd set out. They'd still be there, too, for there was no one to disturb them: each fleck of egg remaining where his fork last touched it, crumbs from toast, a dab of blueberry freezer jam stretched in a swath across the plate ending in a small blob he didn't quite collect, a quarter cup of apple juice in the small juice glass, a knife coated in condiments, a crumpled napkin. At the time it was just breakfast, but through the week it had set into memory, to re-emerge as a reminder of what he had, and didn't, and the prospect of driving back into the damp and walking into this still life had him sitting in the lot with the engine running but no desire to return home.

Closing his eyes, he tipped his head back against the headrest, sighing out some of his remaining stress. He could feel the hot sun through the windshield landing on his chest, but the AC chilled him anyway. Eyes closed, he felt for the window control and lowered it, a warm cushion of air entering immediately, and it felt good. It reminded him of other times and other places, of the warm sun on his face when he was able to find the moment and relax into it, and by degrees, the tight feeling subsided. It'd be good to see scenery like that again — scenery that exuded summer swelter — and he recalled his favorite highway not so far to the east. The sun wouldn't set for at least another four hours, and he'd be well into it by then if he left immediately. So he took pleasure passing the entry ramp to head west, heading east instead on US 50, out of Sacramento, onto the plains east of the city, past the spreading suburbia, the unzoned sections of Rancho Cordova, past the wide spot of Folsom, and up the first naked foothill, up and out, away from humanity to get lost in the Sierra and beyond.

It took more than an hour to wind through the foothills, past the big bend at Twin Bridges and up toward Echo Summit, before he could descend again on the far side of the Sierra, hugging the mountain. He hadn't seen Tahoe in at least ten years — he couldn't recall the last time exactly — and it looked so blue in the distance it reminded him of the first time he'd seen it and the effect it had and the smile it forced upon him, the lake still cast in sun, though mountain shadows approached the edges. He wouldn't make it there, though, turning just to the west of it, south, cutting through passes on 89 and 88 and 89 again, sliding east and south on the Alpine State Highway past Woodfords and Markleyville (he had fond memories of the hot springs there, and just being near it reaffirmed his decision to drive), until finally, cutting east again with another leg of 89, he emerged at a crossroads where it dumped into his highway, and he sat looking at the sign, black and white but cast in sun, saying CA 395.

He must have been in his twenties the first time he drove it, but he couldn't remember the circumstances that landed him there. Had he been in Carson City? Had he found it further south, exiting from Yosemite's east side? The memory was lost, except that the number 395 had remained as something worth recalling. Since then he'd travelled it several times, sometimes to get somewhere, like a trip to Texas he'd made to pick up a truck he'd bought, but other times it wasn't about getting somewhere as much a being somewhere. This was one of those times and he was glad to see it, and especially glad to have no reason to drive it other than simple desire. Smiles had never come to him naturally, but he felt one beginning to show in the corners of his lips.

There was no traffic at the intersection, two roads meeting in the middle of nowhere, no traffic behind to push him, nothing but emptiness, and he took solace in the desolation. To the east, the plain opened, mostly scrubby desert, green lines trailing in the distance where cottonwoods marked a trickle of water. The sky was blue, deep blue like he'd only seen in that part of California and the West, a few light clouds scudding above, throwing dark shadows onto the scrub miles out where the gray and dusty green and taupe of the landscape met the sky as a thin blue range marked the far end of the basin. On his right, as he moved onto the road, slowly picking up speed, the route traced the eastern edge of the Sierra, poking up into the sky, still harboring small patches of snow in the eastern recesses of the peaks that only saw tepid morning sun, reaching up to ten thousand feet or more. He liked being on the edge of a continental conflict between the desert and the range, tracing that meeting two hundred miles, where human beings knew their place and clung to their dry perches at the mercy of nature.

Rolling down the rest of the windows, McGhee turned off the AC to let the warm air tousle him from all sides. Little bits of airborne grit sometimes came in to sandblast him, but he wanted that, too, to abrade whatever ill-humor still might remain out of him, and the occasional sting on his cheeks was welcome. Laying one hand lazily over the wheel, he adjusted in his seat for the long ride, and could finally get down to thinking, which he was remembering was the true purpose of any road trip.

The gig in Sacramento was winding down – there'd only be a few more weeks of it – and he'd be glad to let it go. He'd been doing the work for more than twenty years, so the engagements weren't novel anymore. This project wasn't much different than the usual, and it made him tired: he'd been collecting data from around a hospital network, pulling it together in a database, doing analysis, sifting – simple stuff to him – but they were always surprised what he could tell them about their operations. As usual, it was new people, a new company, realities to face (which meant politics), budget issues. It was better, though, as an outsider – he could always see a way out, so he didn't feel the pressures he used to feel at xCopy Inc. – and he liked that. He liked never belonging anyway, never felt like he really did. Within a few weeks he would disappear from them forever. Still, it was getting harder to take those engagements, and though he was good at it and it paid well, he was always reminded (by himself in the quiet moments at night) that he was solving other people's problems. That left him feeling like he wasn't doing the right thing – that he had never found his own way and was still waiting for something to call him, to become his righteous focus, deserving his full attention. He could never shake the thought that he was an impostor in their world and he needed to be someplace else, and his dreams reminded him of that, when he'd wake in a panic that he was out of position, that he was a disappointment, that he had squandered his potential. As usual, though, when the reverie faded he came up dry at the end of this line of thought, and was left looking at the scenery. Glancing at his watch he saw he hadn't even been on the road three hours yet, so he had more to get through before he was done.

To the east, past Bridgeport, some farms dotted the edge of the road, ending in tubular metal fences and cattle grates. Cows stood in the distance, poking at the meager grass, or clustered in the shade of the cottonwoods, looking, ruminating. Cheap metal watering bins sat nearby, rust stains painting their sides, cattle chutes next to them built of gray, wind-dried wood standing where they had been for one hundred years. Now and then a tractor would appear, scraping at the surface, leaving a cloud of dust behind. There were farms, too, on his right, rising up into the flanks of the mountains. Squat corrugated roofed buildings came down near the road at angles, rust painting swatches of orange and black where the spare rain had found a way into the steel to begin its decay. It wasn't clear what they might grow, or could grow, given the dry conditions, other than cows. Somehow these people scratched out a living, and the thought of that simplicity helped McGhee settle again, looking back toward the road which wriggled along that edge and headed back into some slight hills. They were covered in short yellow grass and clumpy scrub, a light breeze playing through it. He could see the wind moving there, an invisible hand brushing through the heavy heads, rendering them silver as they tipped before righting again.

Off to the left in the middle of a roadcut, another road opened revealing a route leading to Bodie, but he wasn't heading there this day, though his thoughts went there as he continued driving: that road traced east another ten or twelve miles over the high plains with Russian thistle and short grass, crawling through the rolling hills, gradually climbing until the view opened again where the mine was and Bodie sat at its feet, like a dog. It was still waiting for life to come back from whatever death befalls a mining town when the ore runs out or the value of what comes from the ground can't get men to do it anymore, and they throw it away with disgust, resolving to move on, looking to the horizon for what's next. So the buildings waited for the men to return, dutiful, but they didn't. Their wood dried in the desiccating wind, the gritty gusts carving out the grain of it, but it wouldn't fall, mummified in place, wood creaking at the square nails wriggling their holes bigger but not big enough to ever escape. Even the church with its pews and dusty sunlight looked like it was abandoned on a whim one morning, hymnals in place, the upright piano with its bench still askew from the last organist with song book splayed open. It all waited for the masters to return, but they didn't, until more recent voyeurs came to pretend they were miners, too, in station wagons and kid-laden cars for daytrips as long as they could get home by evening. But on this day, McGhee was content to remember prior visits there, and to keep to his road, for driving was what he had on his mind, and his own history, not that of the long dead.

He couldn't say why he loved the road so much except that it fed his loneliness, elevating its painful sweetness like a toothache, and allowed him to think and remember. Somehow it reminded him of his mother, too, though he didn't know why. They certainly had never discussed it. Still, something about the solitariness of that stretch brought her to mind and she swam to the forefront of his musings. It had been ten years since she passed, but her memory had become complicated by the actions of Les. Usually when his mind tended to think of her, those unpleasant recollections intervened and he steered his thoughts away from them. He hadn't quite realized it until then, but it had been some years since he had thought of her – just her, outside that context of Les's maneuvers – and he found himself tumbling back in time.

One morning when he was four or five she took him into the yard to play catch, because it seemed that she felt bad for him, that he was alone since his brothers were so much older. Though he couldn't have said those words himself at the time, he sensed it, wordless and sad. She tossed him a plastic ball from a few feet, but had turned away to look at the neighbor's yard, flushed and crying. She must have been forty-five then – the thought that he was now ten years older than she had been felt odd – not so old as she seemed back then, but old enough to be struggling with being a middle-aged mother with a young son, feeling she was too old to play, and that he was so young and should have some diversion anyway. It must have been nine in the morning – the light had that harsh glare of a sun still rising into a waking day – sometime in the spring when the plants still had dew and the shadows sparkled with it in the grass. His father's impatiens were bursting under the window in pinks and oranges and whites, still waiting for the light to hit them. Behind her, the huge Baldwin apple tree hung above the screen porch, limbs heavy with small apples: perhaps it was early summer, then, if there were apples already, and he slid forward in the timeline to collecting those that fell in five-gallon buckets to throw on the compost pile at the back of the yard. Sometimes instead his brothers would help him make apple throwers with long switches of stripped limbs, arms long, apples skewered on the end, to throw them yards away in high arcs past where he was allowed to roam. Somewhere in his arm muscles he felt a faint twitch of recollection.

Then there were the holes he dug up by the sassafras tree. She had made him return the three pennies he got selling clay to his friend Sammy from across the street from one especially deep hole, saying it wasn't right. So it had been hard for her but she had been there and he suddenly remembered all of it, and he had the impulse to call her and tell her so, and had his phone in his hand before he remembered he was ten years too late to do so. He still had her number there and was poised to call it anyway and wondered what would happen if he did, but stopped, because he thought a different old woman would answer from some other kid's life who hadn't faced that loss yet, and he couldn't bear to hear it. Still, it felt good to remember, and thoughts of his mother remained for some time, lingering.

The road had turned again, climbing into more hills until he reached the crest and the view opened to the south as 395 crept through the pass and began its descent. A pullout opened to the right for a vista and he veered in to see, stepping out to stretch and breathe. There were no other cars there and it was quiet except for occasional gusts of wind. The sun was still above the mountains to the west, though its glare had relented, easing into the evening, casting its light across the valley and its magnificent view. By the edge, below the rail, spare yellow stiff grass caught the breeze, reluctantly bending when the wind got strong enough. Down below in the distance Mono Lake stretched wide across most of the scene, a sprawling blue patch embedded in a dry and inhospitable landscape, prehistoric and forbidding, yet lovely in its oddly misplaced and unlikely existence. Each time he saw it his reaction was the same: it should not be there, but was, and persisted, in spite of the harshness.

It felt good to stand in the air and survey the valley, the lake, and the mountains. Though the car was still running – he could feel it as he leaned on the hood, the engine humming softly – he wasn't ready to move on yet. He was softening in the sunshine and breeze, more stress easing from his shoulders.

The solitary nature of that scene suddenly reminded him of a conversation he'd had with his friend Kovach in high school, about seeing the Grand Canyon, and how he said he didn't care to see it. He'd said it would just remind him of all the things he couldn't do, just open a box he'd prefer to ignore. At the time, that sentiment was unimaginable to him and he set to convincing Kovach otherwise. It all seemed so obvious to McGhee. So looking out over the valley, he wondered for the first time if he was right after all, wondered if Kovach had ever seen the Canyon, like he had, if he still had the same perspective, if he was even more convinced he was right. For McGhee's part, he wasn't sure the trade he made was good after all, even though there was little personal contentment on the other side of the balance to trade for being a roamer, not really. He had largely resisted the temptation to settle down, with the exception of Tess, which he considered a bit of temporary insanity that had only lasted a few years. And when he thought of Tess, it left him empty – there was no more fondness there than he'd have for a stranger, which didn't tend to be much unless they were good for a solid conversation. With Tess, it turned out, she wasn't, but that had been the point. That had been the basis of their relationship at the time, that she didn't remind him of his deeper self at all, and he was able to skate across the pragmatics and logistics of an ordinary existence which remained for that interval unexamined. So when it came back to him, he wondered how he could have lost such utter contact with himself, but then came to the same conclusion he always did, that it seemed to be what he needed at the time. So Tess didn't add much to the balance after all, but when it came to Kate it was a different matter.

Each time his mind turned to her, he always sighed, and he noticed himself doing it again. It was all so sweet, making the unravelling that much more intractable, even if it seemed inevitable. At the time, he couldn't see his way through it, through the growing apart, through his coveting of her success, to the pain this envy caused him and that she couldn't understand his plight, or worse, that she chose not to. It was too hard, and she was willing to let it go, though eventually he was, too, even though it fell to her to leave. Sure, he'd gone to Mexico after his father's funeral, but he had called her, and she was in LA anyway when that call landed on the machine. He always wondered if he should have taken her back east with him, but he was afraid she couldn't go, or wouldn't. So by the time he got back to San Francisco it was as if they had already decided it was over, and she just said she'd be spending her time at the South Gallery, and that she was sorry. He could still hear her saying goodbye to Mr. Chung out on the sidewalk a few days later as she walked away, while he hid back in the apartment staring at the empty spaces, relieved and broken. So perhaps he had engineered their demise at some level, through neglect or insecurity, allowing it to die without a proper fight, but he didn't have it in him, so he had found himself alone, again, and was content, if resigned to this fact, until Bordeaux. They'd shared most of that day together, though not the night, but it was enough to remind him of his sense of loss, which over time, only grew. So perhaps there had been sacrifice for this solitary path, ballast for the Kovach balance.

That, it appeared, had been the predominant theme of his life – making short term decisions and surfing the consequences – not that he regretted the approach in general, except in times like these when he examined the overall contours of his life and sensed a directionless meandering that might not ultimately amount to anything. It seemed, too, that when those feelings mounted his only solace was to synthesize those thoughts and that meandering into something written, and thereby render some tangible product from what seemed was otherwise random swatches from a remainders bin.

Then again, he wouldn't be there nor in that moment if he had taken the other path, and he was resolved it was the place he needed to be, regardless of the path he had taken to get there. Such was the swinging of his ruminations between extremes like some ponderous pendulum touching each of the corners of his mind. Standing from his seated lean against the hood, McGhee walked over to the guard rail. It swung the full sweep of turnout, a couple hundred feet, on the slight uphill edge where the asphalt ended, transitioning into nothingness, the gray steel backlit against nothing but perfect blue sky. At the edge he could see the hill dropped off there where the rocky bluff continued its descent downhill, where it again intercepted the next sweep of the switchback of 395 crawling down the face of the mountain, stretching out again after the slalom to trace the edge of the basin where it washed up against the foot of the Sierra.

Sights like those reminded him of a time when the road had only been a concept, that someone somewhere, probably in DC, had been convinced by a local western advocate – a lover of this place – that it would be good to construct such a road. He knew it dated from the 1930s but not much more than that, so he imagined it had been yet another output from the CCC or other such program, dragging the dusty men of Steinbeck fiction away from their picking fields and canneries out into the wild Sierra in vast and endless convoys of trucks. They'd set to carve the route laid out by surveyors, peak to peak, with picks and shovels and steam-shovels and dozers, such as they had, to cut into the face of rocky potential a path for future generations, one mile at a time. Those men were long dead, but their contribution endured as that thin ribbon, a testament to man and what he can do when he sets his mind to it. That made it all the more improbable to him that he could be there, seeing this particular landscape, and he was in awe that circumstances had conspired to allow it.

Seeing that slalom down the rocky hillside reminded him of young Les all of a sudden, but he was able to see past the rancor, or actually forgot it for once, as he recalled that Saturday evening late in '67. The phone rang in the McGhee's kitchen, and it was the hospital with news of their eldest son. He'd been tobogganing in Alameda Park with friends, but hadn't bailed out with the others when it went off course, choosing to ride it down, his tibia discovering the limits of its flexibility in dramatic and compound fashion. His mother had taken the call – McGhee saw it – and the blood drained from her face as she handed the receiver to her husband to clutch her face in tears. He'd pulled her to his shoulder with his other arm, cradling her as he grabbed the phone, his face dark and serious as he took in the news, until his brows relaxed as he heard his son was asking for milkshakes already and would be fine. There were pins involved in the repair which would need to come out eventually, but they expected a full recovery. Mrs. McGhee wriggled free to get their coats – it was February and dark and cold – but they'd drive into town to see him, even though visiting hours had passed.

Wil had been allowed to go in for a minute, but McGhee wasn't: they were concerned it'd be too much for him, tender as he was, once Mr. McGhee had emerged from Les's hospital room and

shook his head *No* when Mrs. McGhee had asked. He was only four
or five and had never seen a waiting room. He crawled around on
the chairs while she tried to keep him occupied, until she swapped
with Mr. McGhee, and one stern look from him was enough to
keep him glued to a chair, though his feet continued swinging.
Still, his father's face was relieved after seeing Les, and he took to
tickling McGhee, and telling him to stop wriggling, by turns, to
entertain him. Wil looked blank when he came out, his face white
and slack, but Mrs. McGhee kept her arm around his shoulder. He
was old enough that he wouldn't usually let her hold him close anymore, but on that occasion he didn't resist, leaning in for the hug.

Looking back, McGhee saw another car pulling into the turnout. His privacy gone, he resolved it was time to continue down
the hill and out onto the plain.

The air was cooling into the low eighties, but the wind of driving seventy miles an hour provided a warm and blustery tussling.
Mono Lake was emerging on his left with its odd pillars of tufa
lining the shore, but he didn't stop to see. He'd climbed around
there years ago on its sharp edges and the memory of his scuffed
hands was fresh enough he didn't need another. Lee Vining was
just ahead and it seemed he'd forgotten to eat anything in the four
hours since leaving Sacramento. RVs and campers and cars were
spilling from 120 out of Yosemite and into 395, cars barely breaking for the turn as they sped south. They weren't focused on their
driving, distracted by kids inside or tired spouses, juggling phones
or maps or snacks, and they were oblivious to the fact they were
hurtling fifty miles an hour into a pre-existing stream of traffic,
albeit a light one. McGhee could feel his hands tighten around the
wheel as he watched, managing his own car. On the left, a man on
a horse near the intersection was yelling at a dog trailing behind to
keep him in line and out of the road. A kid on a bike was making a

slow, wobbly loop in front of him. It used to be he'd sail through such endless distractions unfazed, but he could feel his brain processing the parts, assessing risk, sending uncertainty to his foot on the gas, to his hands on the wheel, and he slowed. Five years ago he wouldn't have done that, not without more indication of impending risk, but he could feel his mental grip weakening slightly and he felt his age. So as he slid past the intersection and the cars merged in, and the horseman sauntered past, and the kid regained control, and the dog fell in line, he resolved it was time for dinner and perhaps some coffee to fortify his senses.

Less than half a mile back he'd passed the closest thing to a restaurant he'd seen in a while, and the town was already petering out, losing whatever sense of urban format it had, returning to the lonely stretch of pavement it was, so he swung the car around to head back. The man on the horse waved to him as he passed, as did the boy on the bike, both smiling like they knew what he was thinking: finding disappointment on the edge of town, resigned to the best he could find, which was their humble *Nicely's*. It looked like it had been built for a one-off coffee shop years before, a precursor to *Denny's*, and had changed hands over the years, each time getting a new coat of paint, as if that would make a difference. From the roof, a huge pointy pole thrust up thirty feet, with signs skewered on it like checks on a spindle – perhaps that was the point – announcing *Nicely's* and *Restaurant* and *Pancakes* and *Salads* and *Steaks* as tags on the pole, sticking out opposite sides, with the last sign, shaped like an eye and skewered dead center, stating *Lounge* at the bottom, like the ultimate enticement. Oddly, though its style was a campy relic from the fifties, the signs were immaculate, like they knew it for the lure it was, a beacon to strangers that this was as good as it gets in those parts, and they'd better just settle for it. So McGhee turned in, too, crunching to

a stop in their gravel, along with everyone else who hadn't chosen
better earlier, or who were so desperate after the desolate drive
out of Yosemite's back end that they actually thought it was what
they were looking for.

Inside, McGhee slid into one of the brown Naugahyde booths
near the window, squeaking as he slid toward the middle. Each
adjustment yielded such a squeak, to the amusement of the kids
the next booth over, so he resolved to be still, concentrating on the
laminated menu. Scanning through the dinner section, his eyes
settled on beef liver (with onions), which caused him to shudder
involuntarily. His dad had used to eat that, as did he before he
knew better, with lots of ketchup. At the time it seemed natural to
bathe it in a cup of ketchup until he realized it was necessary to use
that much to disguise the taste. He believed that might have been
the first time it occurred to him he could decline eating certain
foods on the basis of revulsion, which in retrospect was a pretty
useful life lesson. That said, he also recalled the smile his dad had
while eating it, like it gave him comfort, like it reminded him of
his earlier times, when they had liver on their *good* days during the
Depression, versus scrapple – fried blood – which they could get
for free from the butcher because he was just going to throw it
out with the offal anyway. McGhee could even remember his dad
making scrapple once, its acrid taste of copper pennies and bitter
earthiness, grim and soft and suspended in fat. Even that scrapple
his father liked, but he had to turn away from it, from its terrible
grayness congealing in the pan. So he wouldn't be having liver and
onions, but it did bring a smile to his face as he settled on chicken
fried steak, the closest he could allow himself to get to authentic
local cuisine.

Les had never liked it either, the liver, but he ate it dutifully because it was available. Wil, on the other hand, had always been picky

at the table. He'd pick at the succotash those nights – the standard accompaniment – and the buns if there were any – but it wasn't as if his diet was any better. One of his inventions, which became a staple for some time, was butter and pickle sandwiches, which really used margarine because they never had butter. Mrs. McGhee would never have it in the house because her mother had hated it, and she had vowed at an early age to honor her Irish mother's disdain for it, out of loyalty. So he'd slather Wonder Bread – untoasted or otherwise prepared – with margarine and carefully lay out dill cross sections like stars on the flag, olive green in a field of pale yellow, before slamming the halves together and stuffing it into his mouth with great enthusiasm. He'd make satisfied moaning noises while he ate them, too, exaggerated orgasmic sounds like it was the best edible concoction ever created, but no one actually believed he liked them. McGhee heard his parents discussing it, right after they looked at each other in disbelief, like they were observing some odd species just discovered from the Galapagos, finely evolved to subsist on margarine and pickles and Wonder Bread. In retrospect, it was probably one of those parental moments in which parents discover yet again they were utterly unprepared for the creative insanity of their progeny. Yet no one believed he actually liked them because the manner in which he ate them looked too studied and artificial to be genuine, like he was pretending to understand what hunger meant or the act of finding true satisfaction. From these glimpses and bits overheard from his parents, McGhee inferred his brother was strange, at least while he was young, and contrary. This latter part blossomed as he became a teen, or so his parents used to say. From McGhee's perspective, this had eased as he matured, the only vestiges of which lurked in his language, which still wriggled upon inspection, unwilling to be pinned down.

McGhee pushed his fork into his mashed potatoes, carving a path from the cinder cone containing the gravy to let it run down the side, like a flow of lava onto the unsuspecting peas living peacefully on its flanks, adjacent to the chicken-steak republic unaware of its impending doom. He imagined Les and Wil at the diner with him, though they hadn't eaten dinner all in one place for many years. They'd always been much older and beyond the stage of needing fantasy to make it through a plate of food by the time he had come along. Still, he liked to imagine they had been kids together though it had become something of a conceit in his head it ever was the case.

Just then, after that awareness, or perhaps the sudden scent of maple syrup, he felt the process begin. The clouds were gathering in his head, or maybe parting, his vision narrowing, and with a sudden impulse, he moved his plate and glass to turn over the paper placemat. He still had his blue pen in his pocket, and he clicked it open, the tip hovering over the paper. Sometimes when it happened, it felt like getting sick, in those moments when you grip the bowl and know it is coming and resignation sets in, with a secret relief it'd be over soon. It would just be a few moments of torment, when he'd wink out of existence, some more primal part of his brain pushing him aside to use the pen to disgorge its discomfort, lest it consume him. He'd watch the pen, too, to see what this troubled self had to say. These musings had been like a huge pile of yarn all afternoon, tangled and heaped and unsorted, until that moment, when he saw the end of one thread as a few words to pull upon. He began scribbling lines, folding in the distillation of thoughts into their essence that had been particulars but finally meant something else, falling like the lightest rain:

This road is hard but lovely,
so lonely, but so lovely
how can I take it
with some comfort
when I fear its tread?

This thing in me
has my throat,
butterflies Sunday,
harpies Monday,
one day a tickle,
the next, torment.
One day I think I've found my path,
the next I'm lost,
always searching, searching
each twilight, further.
When all seems lost,
my friend had said:
"Remember the sea."

I pinch eyes tight,
draw in the air
when mind falls weak
the blood takes the handle,
to search for
brackish calm,
but it eludes me,
no moist solace,
a dry flood of
recollection instead.
The tumult comes

breaking white on
my hard edges:
crying mothers,
broken brothers,
countless questions
can they see behind my stare?
Am I watching,
or watch checking,
am I really
anywhere?

What were those finger touches,
who were those old men and howling dogs,
what are these fecund blossoms,
clamoring to be remembered,
for just me to hear
in the in-between?
So do we laugh
when we dance and turn
our ring-around-the-rosey
and smile with knowing
it was us chasing us
all along?

How can I embrace it,
accept this road of mine,
so lonely but so lovely,
this lonely road of mine?

McGhee looked around the restaurant, wondering if they had watched him, wondered at the man writing feverishly on his placemat, but they had not. A family across the way was eating and conversing, the boy playing with something from the park gift shop. The waitresses were clustered by the register, chatting, laughing, one holding her hand over her mouth as she finished the story. An old local man sat at the counter, his finger through the loop on his coffee, huddled over it, alone in his thoughts. It was as he'd left it ten minutes before, and a calm settled over him. That's how it was and how it needed to be. It was time to get on with it, for it would only ever matter to him, and that was suddenly OK.

Signaling for the check and a coffee refill, he rested his elbows on the table and smiled lightly. He wanted to remember that sequence of events leading to that moment of creation so he could have it again. Though the rest remained unsorted, that part was clear, and he sought to remember it.

He was glad for the coffee – he was hoping to get further south on the highway before dark, because the light was fading. The sun had gone behind the Sierra just as he'd sat down for dinner, though it'd take another ninety minutes to get fully dark. It wasn't like he had any particular destination to reach, but he did want to drive into the darkness before stopping. Flipping a twenty on the table he headed for the door, but was caught just outside by the waitress; he'd forgotten his wallet on the seat, and she smiled when she handed it to him, but said nothing.

Heading back out onto 395, the air was cooler, but still warm, retaining vestiges of the hot afternoon. It was McGhee's favorite time to drive, when the landscape settled into evening, animals nestled for the night, when the sky got white by the horizon, a little pink toward the west if he could see it, graduating into blueness the further up he'd look. He thought he might make it to Big Pine for the night – he'd found Baldwin apples there once, and it reminded him of the trees in his yard, the remnants of the apple orchard that had been sold to build houses for the GI Bill. They'd had an odd sweetness modern apples didn't have, wilder, closer to what nature might devise than men.

His phone was on the passenger seat and a thought called to him. It'd be good to talk to Les – it had been long enough – he still had Les's number, way out there in Wyoming where it was surely dark already. It'd be good to hear his voice again. He missed the gravelly sound it had and the laughter in it, and perhaps, most of all, the comfort of talking to his oldest brother, but after a few seconds saw he had no signal, and resigned himself to being all alone, again, and just drove, further south where it seemed he needed to be.

The Math Idiot

36

0 ←————————————————●————————————————→ 90

2PM
San Antonio, TX 8/31/2000

H e hoped if he lay still enough the oppressive heat would leave him alone, but it wouldn't, and if he would admit it, he wanted it that way. The air itself was in the mid-nineties, but was also laden with eighty percent humidity. Not quite as bad as the air had felt in New Orleans, at least in his recollection, but bad enough to be uncomfortable. Still, he wanted air that was different than San Francisco – heavier and thicker enough to remind him he was some place different with every breath, not that he didn't like that city any more, but he'd had enough of it, for the moment. He'd been in San Antonio a month already – five weeks really – and it was still new enough, and different enough, to be a welcome distraction. But if the heat weren't enough to disrupt his nap, the moving dapples of sunshine crossing his face were, and despite the fact the shady grass under the pecan tree had looked inviting, these things combined to keep him just out of sleep, nipping at it, but not falling into it deeply.

McGhee's backpack didn't make a good pillow, filled with heavy books as it was, but it suited the moment. He still had the database management book spread open on his chest where it had defeated his ability to remain awake, though he liked the pressure of it there, reminding him in his sleep that he was doing something, finally, to alter his path, which until then had been meandering for what seemed like forever. It was good for him, he thought, and he liked to remind himself of that, and hoped such reminders would help grow his resolve from pragmatic decision to passion, or something closer to it than he had. And though he was hovering in that woozy state just before sleep, his ears continued listening, amused by what they heard: he had found Woodlawn Park on one of his incessant evening drives, and had found himself returning to it as one of the first destinations he had accumulated in the area. Off in the distance, a pickup basketball game was progressing, good natured jibes among the players, black and white and Mexican, as they jostled under the hoop, shoes squeaking until the jingle of chains indicated a basket and cheers rang out among them. Along the edges there, down to the water and hidden in the trees, crackles offered popping commentary as they gathered in the afternoon. A cart nearby tinkled a little bell as a man peddled, calling out in thick Mexican-English, "Shave ice, shave ice," as kids chased after it.

After another thirty minutes, McGhee gave up, leaning up on one elbow, but he was glad for the break, even if it wasn't the restful nap he had been seeking. Wagner had office hours coming up, and even though he didn't have any specific coding questions to ask, he liked going in anyway. Though he hadn't known him long, it seemed they had already discarded the traditional faculty-student relationship in favor of something else bordering on friendship.

When he thought of it like that, it made him pensive, for it wasn't exactly that either – friendship – because McGhee had found he wasn't so sure how to have that, either. When he thought back on it, it stemmed from their very first encounter in class when Wagner had pulled him out of class into the hall, towering over him with all his lankiness, his left arm threaded behind himself to hold his right elbow, looking down on him like a vulture eyeing roadkill.

"What?" McGhee had asked.

"So are you some kinda plant in my class or what?" he had asked, staring down at him, blinkless. It was a strange introduction, but portended everything after in that one sentiment: directness, paranoia, insecurity, curiosity and utter naiveté. He had only asked what he had thought was a simple question on recursion, and that one question pushed Wagner over the edge, past all the potential foreplay of friendship with its gradual discovery, to the core question of it, at least in that moment for Wagner, who then relented when he saw the confusion in McGhee's eyes in that moment. "Oh . . . ," he had continued, sniffing and rubbing his nose in what was to become his signature phlegmatic gesture, "You're just old."

McGhee did stick out in the class – thirty-six among twenty-year-olds – and by virtue of that acted differently. He was actually present, for instance, listening to Wagner's running commentary and jokes, even laughing when others didn't (because he was paying attention and was old enough to get the references), but these things constellated for Wagner momentarily as suspicion, until they faded, though the cast of their relationship was set in that instant as something uncommon.

For McGhee's part, the sudden overture of challenging familiarity caught him off guard, but it tossed their interaction into a different trajectory than he expected, and he liked it. It had been years since he had felt that kind of immediate intellectual engagement

– he could feel the thirsty roots of his brain jarred by the encounter, and their desire for more.

Under the tree, McGhee laughed to think of that encounter, stuffing the book back into the bag which had trouble accommodating its heft, bulging to capacity. It was funny that Wagner had called him old because he was having exactly the same image form in his mind of his professor – that he was old – though the concept was inchoate and inconsistent with the quick probing of Wagner's mind. He was at least sixty-five, or looked it, short gray hair shaved on the sides, tousled on top like he'd slept it that shape, bags under the eyes, red, and frosted beard, reddish and gray and black and white, short, crawling down his neck over his Adam's apple to hide beneath a white T-shirt which in turn disappeared into his Penney's short-sleeved shirt, pinned in place by his belt buckle at his waist, which seemed to hold the package together, like the string bowing a kite to keep it taut and kite-shaped. He was that insubstantial in his clothes that they hung from him, neat and tidy, but impossibly loose as his frame approached zero. In short, he was the epitome of a computer science professor if he were to imagine one, and he had thrust himself into McGhee's psyche, like it or not, demanding attention, and he was glad for it.

When he stepped into Wagner's office, the professor was staring into his monitor and started talking immediately mid-sentence, as if he'd been expecting McGhee and he was late. It was some cryptography thing the government was working on that bothered him, and he leaned back to expound on it as he did. When he spoke, he always stated his thoughts as if they were obvious to the listener, and he'd only now understood them himself – they had that self-deprecating flavor to them – regardless of how esoteric the subject, or the impossibility the listener had conceived them first, or even understood them. McGhee did basically understand them, though, but more importantly, was willing to go along with the conceit as necessary for the health of their budding friendship. In fact, the utter novelty of those topics (as compared to the usual things he heard) was so welcome, it was no trouble at all to go along, and in fact, he wanted exactly that.

During their initial meetings, McGhee had taken to calling him professor, but eventually McGhee noticed his friend winced a bit every time he said it, so he paused once as the spasm crossed the professor's face. Cocking his head, he said, "Neal. Just call me Neal. The professor shit weirds me out. In here. Just in here. While you're in my class anyway, but in here . . . ," he continued, gesticulating at his desk, then then walls, floor and ceiling, then a quick swing around his head, "In *here*, call me Neal . . . ." So after that McGhee called him Neal – in the office that is – though the professor persisted in calling him McGhee from the beginning and seemed to take pleasure in it, like they were players in some fiction in his head, colleagues at a prep school playing at being adults. With Wagner, it was always a bit like being in an absurdist play.

McGhee suddenly realized Neal was staring at him and had resorted to rubbing his nose and hacking at his throat, cycling from one to the other, while continuing his gaze.

"What?" McGhee said, seeing he had missed something.

"I was just asking you about class, and the assignment. You don't need help on that or anything, right? I mean *you* don't need *my* help, right?"

"Not really, no . . . ," McGhee said. "I just wanted to drop by."

"Good . . . ," Neal said. "I mean, you can ask, and I'd help, but I'd really rather not. I mean, I would, but it seems like we're beyond that. I wanted to ask you about that thing with Sonja."

"Who's Sonja?" McGhee asked, confused.

"The folder thing . . . ," Neal asked, his face slack. "The *submissions* thing. *Stealing* the folder."

"I told you that?" McGhee asked, adjusting uncomfortably in his seat. Neal exploded into gestures, stretching out his fingers to act it out.

"Seriously, you don't remember telling me *that*? You don't remember *foolishly confessing* that larceny to me? From your college days? At *Yale*?"

"If I remembered everything I said, I wouldn't have room to store anything else," McGhee countered.

"Your brain works like that?" Neal said, cocking his head again.

"Apparently, or I'm lazy . . . ," McGhee countered, shrugging.

"Or you don't care. I'm like that with things I don't care about. Checkbooks. Bills. Lesson plans. Student names."

McGhee nodded. "Yeah, that's more like it. I don't always have the recorder *On*. So why did I tell you *that*?"

Neal leaned back in his seat. "You're amazing. And a little appalling. But fascinating."

McGhee shrugged again, smiling. As usual, the exchange was amusing, so he settled into his chair, crossing his legs.

After a few more seconds, Neal continued. "So, I was telling you about encountering a man who I was absolutely sure was my superior. He was literally better at *everything* than I was. I told you my story, then you told me yours, which was, like, a hundred times better, and you don't even remember *that*?"

"I remember the story, and now that you remind me, it's coming back," McGhee said. "I wasn't trying to one-up you or anything."

"Fuck that! It was just better . . . ," Neal said, rubbing his nose again, but keeping his eyes locked on McGhee. "At least yours had some dialogue. It was *real*. You actually confronted your superior and confessed it. My god, it was awful and great."

"I object to your usage of *superior* . . . ," McGhee said casually, re-crossing his legs the other way.

"Moral superior . . . ," Neal clarified. "You wronged her, both professionally and personally, so it's not a stretch."

"Now I feel bad . . . ," McGhee said coyly, smiling lightly.

"Ahhh . . . ," Neal said, grabbing his own head, then looking back intensely. "You're messing with me, right?"

"Right," McGhee said, smiling more broadly.

"Jesus, McGhee . . . ," Neal said leaning back in his chair. "You're so perverse." Leaning on his desk with both elbows, he stared at McGhee.

"So, what about it?" McGhee asked, finally resuming the thread.

Neal leaned back again, wrapping a bony arm across his stomach while grabbing his chin with the other hand to stroke his beard. "OK . . . ," he said finally. "So did you ever talk to her again?"

"No," McGhee said shaking his head. "I saw her around, but we never spoke again."

"Did you ever make eye contact at least?" Neal asked, unwilling to let it go.

"Once . . . ," McGhee said, lowering his head at the recollection. "At Yale Station, by the mail boxes. I nearly ran into her. She had her arms full of posters and a roll of masking tape."

"And you didn't speak?" Neal asked.

McGhee shook his head, still lowered. "When I looked at her she was smiling – she had a great, wide smile. Fresh and wonderful, like Mary Tyler Moore at the beginning of her show on TV. Only when she saw me, it dimmed. It didn't go away, and she tucked a strand of her hair behind her ear – it was such a nice color of dirty blond, with a little silver cast to it – and her eyes. That was the bad part. They got sad all of a sudden when she recognized me. If I'd been a stranger, it would have been the full smile. But since I wasn't, and because of what I had told her, I wouldn't get even that. I was less than a stranger to her."

"Jesus . . . ," Neal said, leaning back to put his hands on his head. "There's a whole novel in that moment. You should write *that* . . . ."

"I'd rather not . . . ," McGhee said, raising his eyes to meet Neal's.

"Why the hell *not?*" Neal said. "I wish I had something like that . . . ."

McGhee shook his head. "No you don't. There's too much shame in it, and I don't want to wallow in it."

"You should have thought of that before taking the folder . . . ," Neal said.

"Yeah . . . ," McGhee said, his voice low.

Neal suddenly seemed to realize the conversation had taken a serious turn, and adjusted in his seat, grabbing his chin again.

"So . . . , why did you take it, anyway?"

McGhee uncrossed his legs, sitting up in the chair to stretch. He caught his hands behind his head, clasping them behind his neck, pulling his elbows forward slowly.

"I guess that's what I don't want to remember . . . ," he began, pausing a moment to look around the office. It was on a corner with windows looking south and east, the outside blazing in sunshine. Inside, it was a mess, papers stacked on every surface, books spread open, with books spread open upon them. It reminded McGhee of the rooms he had once he'd lived in, disheveled but showing an active, wild mind. It made him comfortable, and through its familiarity, safe.

"At the moment – when I grabbed the folder – it felt delicious and righteous. It felt so good; that's how I knew it was wrong. Anything that seems so righteous has to be wrong. And it was."

"Did you look through it?" Neal asked, fingers still on his chin. "Look through the folder, I mean?"

"I think I read a few things."

"And they sucked?" Neal asked. "I mean, they were pretentious crap, right?"

"Yeah, but it didn't make me feel any better. I mean, who knows – maybe some of it was decent. It would have been better to find something good, though, to make it a crime against that *thing*, but I didn't. It was all ordinary."

"Like the usual stuff. The stuff they printed. So you should have felt vindicated," Neal said, "or maybe not."

"That's the thing. It made the crime that much more abstract. It was the act of doing it, rather than the items taken. It was that *I did it*. That I succumbed to the impulse."

"Yeah, right. But that still doesn't explain the *why* of it, does it?" Neal continued. He rubbed his nose and cleared his throat twice, but didn't expand the thought.

"I guess not . . . ," McGhee said releasing his hands from behind his head, grabbing the arms of his chair. "That's the hard part. There are a lot of pieces to it."

"Such as?" Neal said, his eyes anchored on McGhee's. There was no judgement in them, but genuine curiosity, as if he were gently watching the unpacking of a human being and didn't want to scare the subject or disturb his progress.

"Well, I was young then. And I was discovering . . . all sorts of things about myself. The whole place and everything about it – Yale – was mind-bending. I was from a little corn and steel town.

It was the big leagues. There were many dimensions of shear force shredding my identity."

"Nice image . . . ," Neal said, gesticulating. "Like being rendered by some huge tallow machine . . . . Maybe it was just being tossed in with rich preppie kids . . . ," Neal guessed, relaxing his pose to fold his arms in his lap.

"Yeah, you'd expect that, but it wasn't like that, or I couldn't see it. Most of that seemed kind of invisible. Richness turned out to be experiences and assumptions and known things I didn't know, so I couldn't really tell if it was that, but I could sense things there. Or other realities: everyone was so damned smart, even the assholes."

"That would be annoying," Neal said, snorting, rubbing his nose again before settling back into hands in lap.

"So I was kind of blundering into all this thinking I was pretty smart, and I was, but I wasn't prepared to be average."

"But you *weren't* average," Neal corrected. "You were in a different population."

"Spoken like a statistician," McGhee laughed. "But relatively, I was, and it scared me. So it was really the *fear* that got me."

"Fear?" Neal asked. "I'd describe you many ways, but not that one."

"That's pretty funny. That seems to be my defining feature," McGhee said, laughing.

"Me . . . I'm afraid of everything, even though I know it's all meaningless, but with *you*, with *you,* it doesn't look that way from the outside," Neal said, scratching at his neck a moment, doglike, before resuming his pose.

"You probably don't hear this music, either . . . ," McGhee said, tapping his head.

"Point taken," Neal said, nodding. "My thoughts are loud, too."

"Exactly. So it was the fear that was eating me."

"But how does that translate into stealing a folder?"

McGhee shifted in his chair again, then rose suddenly. "Mind if I pace a little?" he asked.

"Just don't break anything," Neal said, waving his hand.

McGhee paused at the bookshelf immediately behind him. Aside from being crammed with books on CS, and crypto, and math, other objects fronted the publications along the edge: a green plastic army man, a ball bearing, several magnets, a plastic block. Picking up the Lucite block he stared into it where a crystal wedge of amethyst remained suspended.

"This is neat," he said, turning back to show Neal.

"Yeah, it's purple. But we were talking about fear. I don't quite get the connection. Or were you afraid to submit to the publication, for fear of rejection, when you felt it was shit? The paper I mean. Or did you think your stuff was shit, too?"

"Yeah, that's pretty good. That's about right . . . ," McGhee said nodding, tossing the Lucite block in the air and catching it repeatedly.

"So the publication . . . what was it called by the way?" Neal asked, stopping.

"Zirkus, I think," McGhee said. "Yeah, Zirkus."

"Perfect. I mean, really, could it be more perfect? − if you were writing a book you'd pick a name like that. You were afraid of the *circus* of it. Afraid of being banned from it, and hating it if it accepted you. It really is perfect."

"I'm glad you find this so amusing . . . ," McGhee said, his smile returning, though tinged with doubts.

"No, I mean, you'd say that if it wasn't your story. Come on. Right?"

McGhee nodded. "Yeah, I guess I might."

"So this thing takes on mythical significance to you. It's the arbiter of your talent, and you hate it while you crave its approval."

"I didn't exactly say that . . . , but that's a pretty good summary."

"So you strike out at it in the only way you can . . . stealing its voice, if only for a moment."

"Who's writing the fiction now?" McGhee protested, but amused.

"No, no – this is great. You've really got to write that. It's so . . . ," Neal said, his voice trailing off, his eyes going out of focus as his head tilted back to look at the ceiling. "Maybe it should be a screen play – or just a play. It's like Ibsen. Or maybe more like Henry Miller. Or maybe absurdist, like Beckett's Godot."

"I'm more of a Kafka man, myself, but you read plays?" McGhee asked, hoping to nudge the subject away from the running psychoanalysis.

"What, you think I'm just a math idiot?" Neal asked, though his voice lacked temper.

"I doubt that sentence has ever been uttered before," McGhee said, pointing at Neal with the Lucite block.

"I say that every day. Just to other people. It didn't seem necessary with you . . . ," Neal said.

"No, I don't think you're a *math idiot*, though I love the image. We just never talked about lit before," McGhee said.

"Sure we did – you just don't remember. Your head is a sieve, remember? – scratch that. Of course you don't." Neal, rubbed his nose and cleared his throat, rubbed his nose again, and cleared his throat again. "Well, yeah, of course. I did have to take the occasional English class. Though I liked the Germans more. They're so humorless I find them amusing."

"I only read some Goethe, and a few Hesse. And Nietzche – talk about humorless."

Neal laughed. "Right? But, really, you've really got something good there to dig into and mine. You could go deep with that. All I got is this stupid science fiction stuff – at least you might get something published."

McGhee plopped back into the chair, sighing. "I just don't feel it . . . ," McGhee said.

"Write it anyway. Gardner always says you just have to push through it – do it – especially when you don't feel it. Then eventually you will. Writers are those people who do that, who push every day."

"I don't work that way," McGhee said, shaking his head. "Besides, I'm doing comp-sci now. I need to focus on that. Now that I think of it, it's funny my CS professor is lecturing me on being a writer."

"Really?" Neal said. "Why not do both?" he continued, ignoring the jab.

"My head . . . ," McGhee said, shaking it slightly, "it needs to be very still to write. There can't be distractions or worries or anything. The thoughts are loud, but the writing voice is very soft. It's like I have this pond in there, and the waves have to subside until it gets very smooth and I can sense the tiny ripples from the little voices. Then I can focus. Then I can write."

"Uh huh . . . ," Neal, said. "Maybe that's still the fear talking."

"It certainly has gotten more insidious over time. It gets harder and harder, or conversely, it gets easier and easier to make excuses not to. Only I feel shitty about it."

"That's not really *converse*. More like *inverse*. Anyway, yeah, Gardner says that, too. He says it's all about demons – personal demons – who don't want you to tell the truth. To push yourself and get it out. Who lull you into being silent. Anti-muses who drain you and urge you to be ordinary. To let go of the impulse."

"Who is this Gardner anyway?" McGhee said, sitting up again. "You're always quoting him."

"A writer – he used to do workshops and stuff. I think he's dead now."

"Figures – I hate writers," McGhee said, smiling again.

"There's some irony in that."

"Not so much *irony*. More like *misanthropy* with a touch of *autophobia*," McGhee said, smiling again.

"*Are you sure?* Wait, what? – you goddamned English major . . . ," Neal said, equally annoyed and amused, briefly reaching for a dictionary before waving it off to cross his arms again.

McGhee shook his head. "I think that covers it."

"You are complicated . . . ," Neal said, smiling as he sat back.

"One of the last stories I wrote, at least that I finished, was about the greatest writer in the world," McGhee said. "A young writer travels to South America to see him and get some advice."

"Where in South America?" Neal asked.

"I don't know. It doesn't matter . . . some vague South American country. So he goes to see him and they have this dinner, and the young writer is anxious to talk about writing, but the old writer keeps putting him off with courses of dinner and wine and desserts and port and so on. Out in the square below the terrace, there's a festival going on and they locals are dancing, and it gets wilder as the night goes on. They lead a cow into the square, dancing all around it. They put ribbons on it and bells on the horns."

"A bull then . . . ," Neal interjected, raising a bony finger.

"Some cows have horns . . . I checked . . . ," McGhee countered.

Neal shrugged, lowering his finger. "And?"

"Eventually, several of the men circle the cow, you know, swinging their machetes in the air as they dance around it. Just as they are about to set upon the cow, the old writer leans into the table and looks the young writer in the eyes. He says, 'Do you want to know why I'm the best writer in the world?' to the young man. By this time, the kid is drunk with the drink and wild ceremony and the commotion, but manages to nod: he wants to know. The old writer says, 'Because I write *nothing*', and then *BAM!*" McGhee said, slapping his hand on the desk, "The cow cries out as they sacrifice it in the square."

Neal sat back in his chair and shook his head, like he'd had a shot of liquor, then refocused on McGhee. "Wow. I mean . . . *wow!* So that's your explanation then? For not writing?"

"Better to write nothing than to write clutter. If it comes, it comes, but I won't produce more crap for the world to read just because I want to write. Too many do that already."

"Jesus, you're a complicated kid . . . ," Neal said, crossing his arms again. Reaching up he rubbed his nose and cleared his throat before rubbing his nose again, then re-crossed his arms.

"I'm thirty-six . . . ," McGhee responded. "And you called me old."

"Everyone's a kid when you're sixty-five . . . ," he said. "Even the old ones. And you stick out in class — an otherwise undifferentiated heap."

"Flattering . . . ," McGhee said. "So I should probably get out of your office. You're probably busy."

"Not really. I have some crap to grade . . . ," Neal said motioning to a pile, disgust evident on his brow. He rubbed his nose and cleared his throat, looking back at McGhee. "You wanna grade it?" he asked hopefully.

"Uhhh. No."

"Shit . . . ," Neal said, scanning the pile again, then looking back at McGhee. "Well, then go write something. *The Force* is strong with you . . . ."

"Really, *Star Wars* Neal?" McGhee said, rising to go.

"Seemed like a good thing to say . . . . When in doubt, go with science fiction. There are no consequences," Neal said, staring at him blankly.

Back at Woodlawn Park, McGhee found his tree again and leaned against it, unzipping his bag to grab a book, but thought better of it, closing it again. There was a light breeze to take the edge off the heat jingling a wooden wind chime in the distance with a repetitive light thunking of different tones. Readjusting the bag, he settled back in for another nap, dapples of light playing on his face, though it wasn't as strong as before, just barely making his eyelids pink now and then, but not disturbing him. The chat with Wagner had settled him, making it easier to sleep. He immediately drifted this time and was nearly out when he heard slight footsteps approaching.

"Mind if I share your shade?" a woman's voice said.

He didn't open his eyes, but tilted his head in its direction. Her voice had a song in it, merry but serious, and he liked the sound. "Please do . . . ," he said, tipping his hat down over his eyes.

"Thanks . . . ," she said again, leaning against the other side of the tree. "My name's Tess . . . ," she said, and something about the sound of it made him smile as he drifted off, dreaming.

A Dublin Homily

```
44
0 ◄─────────────●─────────────► 90
            2AM
     Dublin, Ireland 4/19/2008
```

McGhee stood surveying the street, lost and without a plan. *April is better in warm cities* he thought, looking down the avenue, hoping to discern a course for his walk, to learn the city, or at least feel it, the beat of it. He felt in danger of glancing-off its veneer, having been there without actually penetrating any but the most superficial level. Such was his fear in Dublin so he sought a bench just inside the park behind Fusilier's Arch to think. As he sat, he pulled out the city map folded in his pocket for another look, spreading it in his lap as he plopped onto the bench, already spent, though he'd only been walking an hour. Hunching up his jacket he pulled it closer about his neck to ward off the chilling breeze.

Staring over the map, reading street names and park names and even bridges over the river Liffey, he looked for inspiration, but it wasn't coming. He thought to himself he should have done some research before the trip, but he had thought it would be easier, that the city would open itself to him, perhaps because he shared its heritage and he'd understand it, making such reconnaissance unnecessary. Some cities do that, just open themselves for exploration, inviting the wanderer to partake of their delights. Rome had done that. Paris. Even Istanbul. Certainly London. But he took the blame into himself for it, annoyed he hadn't done a better job, hadn't thought ahead. *Then again, perhaps this is one of those cities better done with a companion* he thought, but it didn't make him feel any better, for he was alone. His preferred means of travel was solo anyway because he felt it harder to bring his context with him that way, which from his perspective was exactly what not to do when traveling. But this time he could use the company, and it occurred to him he should have thought of it when it could have made a difference. Then again, how could he have known – the necessity for the trip had arisen suddenly – and besides, he had no one to ask – Paul certainly wouldn't come – and it'd be better in the company of a woman anyway, though he didn't have one of those to ask, either. Such was his deliberation, settling nowhere except upon continued discontent.

Lost in these thoughts, McGhee didn't notice a man had alighted at the far end of the bench, hunched slightly. He was sitting sideways over the far end of the seat, not in the normal direction, with his back to McGhee, as if he didn't want to intrude, or perhaps, wanted privacy himself. Something about the man caught McGhee's attention, for he looked up from his map to glance down bench at him, as the map hadn't provided sufficient guidance to hold his attention any longer.

The man wore a tan trench coat, with epaulets buttoned at the shoulders and a belt at the waist, hanging loosely in the loops there to gather it, the ends undone. He wore a woven newsboy cap, a light brown wool herringbone, but there wasn't much to see from behind, as he seemed working on something in his lap, but out of view, the only evidence being the sound of paper crinkling. Suddenly the man stopped and raised his head, continuing to look straight ahead.

"You're an American, aren't ya?" he said, not turning at first, but eventually swinging his head around. McGhee wasn't sure the man was addressing him but eventually looked over, by which time the man had twisted around to look at him, though his legs remained off the side. In that twisted pose, he looked uncomfortable, using his arm to maintain the angle and get a look at McGee. His mouth remained open from the strain of it, his lips red and days of black growth on his cheeks showed the contours of his face. Based upon his dress and level of hygiene, he didn't appear to be a vagrant, even though it did occur to McGhee he wasn't sure what the Irish variety would look like. He had the nose of a boxer, formerly straight but adjusted, dark bushy eyebrows and dark eyes, brown but tending toward black, and a squint. Turning back over the side, he continued messing with the thing in his lap, then threw his legs back over the front of the bench, finally, and looked over to McGhee and smiled.

"Gotta get the bag right, or the cops will hassle ya . . . ," he said holding up the bagged bottle in his grasp. The top was folded down three turns, neatly set to expose the neck of a bottle half an inch, with the paper edge twisted to keep it in place. Breaking the metal seal he merrily spun the cap off, still looking at McGhee. "Here's lookin' at ya . . . ," he said, tilting the bottle back for a quick swig. He closed his eyes and winced as he pushed down two gulps, loud, and let out a sigh.

"How'd you know I was American?" McGhee asked, looking over at him.

He smiled again at McGhee and took another swig. "Fuggin' obvious, mate . . . ," he said, replacing the cap on the bottle, then thinking better of it removed it again, extending it over to McGhee to share.

McGhee looked at the bagged bottle, then at the man, unsure.

Pulling his arm back, the man wiped the neck on the sleeve of his jacket, smiling and shaking his head. "You Americans . . . ," he said to no one, then extended the bottle again. "It's alright, I ain' sick . . . ."

McGhee crushed the map, tossing it onto the bench, grabbing the bottle from the man to peer in, but couldn't see. Sliding the paper down he saw it was a pint of Jameson whiskey, and he smiled back at the man, tilting the bottle up for a swig. It was sweet but stung with the first gulp of it, then he had another, smaller sip, mindful of the hospitality and handed it back.

The infusion of the liquor was warm and welcome washing down McGhee's throat, then beyond, leaching into his stomach, then slowly into the rest of his body. Almost immediately the cool in the air was gone and he could feel the flush in his cheeks, and the warmth was good. If nothing else, the weather explained some of the drinking these people were known for.

"Name's Mulligan . . . ," the man said, stretching out his hand. His grasp was firm and steady, one shake, then he let it go.

"McGhee."

"Ahhh. So you're Irish then, by blood?" Mulligan said, his eyes wide with the question.

"Half," McGhee said, leaning back on the bench, tossing his left arm over the back.

"The good 'alf, I s'pect . . . ," Mulligan said, replacing the cap on the bottle.

"And Slovak . . . ," McGhee said, "not sure which is the good half yet."

Mulligan laughed. "Those Slavs aren't bad. Worked with a couple in the service . . . ," Mulligan said, his voice trailing off. Looking out past the gate Mulligan leaned forward a moment, then plopped back again. "So ya travellin' then?"

"Something like that . . . ," McGhee said, motioning for the bottle again. Mulligan just looked at him but didn't hand over the bottle. "It's a small one, mate . . . ," he said, then smiled, handing it over.

McGhee took a longer drink, deeper, and held onto the bottle. "I'll get the next one . . . ," he said.

"So you alone or with fam'ly?" Mulligan said, leaning back himself.

"Alone . . . ," McGhee said, but didn't look over. Standing suddenly, Mulligan walked over to the bushes a few feet from the bench, looking back and forth, before facing into the brush to unzip his pants.

"So what is this place?" McGhee called over to him.

Mulligan looked annoyed to be disturbed while pissing, but answered after getting his stream going. "*St. Steven's Green* . . . ," he said finally, turning to look back into the bush he was watering. "It's famous fer something, but I'll be damned if I can remember what . . . ." Once finished he returned to the bench but remained standing, just off to the side where McGhee was sitting.

"So what's your plan then, McGhee?" he asked. His hands were grabbing his waist and he stood staring down at him. He wasn't a tall man but was stalky, a bit barrel-chested and sol-id. He was wearing a tweed suit under his jacket – something McGhee hadn't noticed before – including a vest with a gold watch chain dangling. His shoes were modest but polished, and all together he looked more refined than McGhee had expected from their introduction.

McGhee looked up at Mulligan, throwing his other arm over the back of the bench to stretch out. "So what are you doing out here drinking at five on a Saturday evening?" McGhee asked. Remembering he had Mulligan's bottle, he unscrewed the cap and took another swig before handing it back to him.

"Got sacked yesterday . . . ," Mulligan said, tipping the bottle back. Wiping his lips on his sleeve, he smiled down at McGhee. "Nineteen years and some. Counting numbers and such, and then bam. So I figured this here would be the perfect time to get a little legless . . . ."

"Legless?" McGhee said.

"As in *fluthered* my friend. *Trousered*, *polluted*, *pissed* and otherwise *shitfaced*."

"Nineteen years?" McGhee said.

"And some . . . ," Mulligan said, "and so I says, 'That's it then?', and Seamus says, 'Yeah, that's it then,' so I says, 'I've been meaning to tell you, Seamus, at least ten years now, maybe fifteen, that you are a total *prick*,' and he says, 'I thought we was friends,' and I says, 'So did I,' and walked out."

"So why didn't you get pissed yesterday?" McGhee asked. "It seems kinda late now."

"It's never too late, my friend. And who says I didn't anyways?"

McGhee looked at him and Mulligan smiled. "You know our food sucks, right?" Mulligan said.

McGhee shrugged, "It's not world famous."

"I just didn't want you to get the wrong idea, but we're gonna get some dinner," Mulligan said, and started walking. He was a bit unsteady, but stopped to right himself, brushed his hands down his vest and tugged the edge, then adjusted his coat on his shoulders. "Come on . . . ," he said, resuming his walk toward the gate, steadier but not steady. "Besides, you're buying . . . ," he called over his shoulder, but didn't wait to see if McGhee was following.

"But I didn't drink that much, did I?" McGhee called after him, grabbing his map and hurrying to catch up.

Though he was a full six inches shorter than McGhee, Mulligan walked at a brisk pace, once he got his feet moving, and McGhee had to struggle to keep up. Walking down past the park, the buildings facing the green were all varieties: some classical architecture, others modern, one decent, then one drab, varying one to the next, no seeming pattern to it. After a quarter block jog east, they cut into Baggot Street, continuing the march. It was tree-lined, offering shade though the low-ceilinged sky didn't demand it, but the breeze in the trees made a pleasant sound that reminded McGhee of fall. The neighborhood felt more residential, as if they were moving away from businesses, until just when McGhee was going to comment, the street gave way to commerce again and Mulligan spun on his heel (nearly falling), and pointed to a small establishment tucked in among the buildings.

"I give you *Doheny and Nesbitt* . . . ," Mulligan said proudly, presenting it with a sweep of his arm.

"Is it famous or something?" McGhee asked.

"It most certainly is not," Mulligan replied, shifting on his feet.

"Is the food good, then?" McGhee asked, looking from the place to Mulligan and back again.

"It most certainly is not," Mulligan replied, still proud, "but it *is* where I drink, and they extend me credit."

Opening the door, Mulligan ushered him inside, instantly waving to the bartender who looked up to see him enter. "So how is it then, John?" Mulligan called out.

The bartender looked at Mulligan and shrugged, continuing to towel his glasses.

Mulligan made his way to a table in the rear, across from the bar. It had a bench near the back of it, built into the wall like cabinetry, and several stools in front. McGhee would have preferred a smaller table, but Mulligan was on a mission, tossed his cap on it, and kept walking toward the far back of the bar. "Ahh... here's me pew, then. Order me a pint, mate . . . I'm hittin' the lav'," he called back, to either the bartender or McGhee.

John looked over at McGhee and shook his head. "Got it," he said, and slowly strolled back to the tap to pour it.

"Given me a Harp, then . . . ," McGhee said, walking himself over to the bar to retrieve their glasses. The inside was brightly lit, with pictures and paraphernalia all over the walls, covering every bit of surface, and the ceiling, too, where space permitted, though the center vaulted up, coffered on the edges, with windows facing out. McGhee was still staring up when Mulligan returned and slapped the table.

"Better get drinking, McGhee," he said, lifting his pint to his lips, tipping it lightly so as to catch every drop, gulping and tipping, gulping and tipping until the last little bit of foam drained into his mouth. "Ahhh . . . ," he said, satisfied. "John?" he called out, but the bartender was landing another pint in front of him already, wiping the wet circle where the last glass had stood.

Shaking his head again, John looked at McGhee. "How long you know this bore, anyway?" he asked, slinging the rag over his shoulder.

"About thirty minutes . . . ," McGhee responded, looking between them.

"That should about do it, then . . . ," he said, patting McGhee on the shoulder, then turning to Mulligan, "Better pace yourself, mate . . . ."

Returning to the table, the bartender dropped off a few menus. "You boys should get something in your stomachs to hold the beer down . . . ," he said, stepping back to the bar to lean on his arms and watch them. Another young man appeared from the back with a rack of glasses and began putting them away, but John kept watching like a sentry. After a few minutes he cleared his throat.

"You gonna order, then?" he called out. Neither McGhee nor Mulligan had opened the menu, but took the hint.

"Sure thing, boss . . . ," McGhee called back. "Give us a minute."

Mulligan snickered into his beer, talking into his glass. "He thinks he's our mum . . . ," he said, sputtering into his drink, then waved John back over.

"Give us some bangers and mash . . . ," he said, "and McGhee'll have . . . ," he continued, leaving a gap for McGhee to complete the sentence, and holding out his hand to prompt him.

Looking up, McGhee saw John waiting on him, and he smiled. "I'll take the Shepherd's Pie – is it good here?"

"Pure shite, mate . . . ," John said, "but it sets up a nice dike in your gut against the beer that's comin', so it'll do . . . ."

So it was they got their orders in just in time, though there was no one else in the bar. McGhee couldn't see a reason for the hurry, but he knew enough to shut up. As for Mulligan, he pushed his glass aside, half finished, to give McGhee another look.

"So I just wanna tell ya, a bunch uv me buddies are gonna be here any minute . . . an' whether ya wanted ta see the vile underbelly uv Dublin or not, you're gonna see it shortly."

"Perfect," McGhee said nodding. "I guess I came to the right place, then."

"I like you, McGhee," Mulligan said, raising his glass to toast him, but set it down again, without drinking. "You Cath'lic by the way?"

"Not exactly . . . ," McGhee said, "Why?"

"You're goddamned right I'm Cath'lic," Mulligan answered though no question had been asked, smiling again. "Fat lot-a-good it did me, though."

"You're not dead yet, Mulligan," McGhee said, leaning back on his stool for a stretch.

"What?" Mulligan said, scratching his head. Standing half way from the booth, he had a good scratch of his buttocks, then sat again. "Maybe ya oughta get over here on the bench coz those arseholes are gonna get here and take all the good seats, and we're gonna be 'ere a while."

"All right . . . ," McGhee said, sliding his glass to the other side of the table, shifting to the bench side. Almost on cue, the door swung open with a bit too much energy, banging into the wall behind it, two men stepping in, unsurely.

"Doc, what'd I tell ya about that door, again?" John the bartender called out to the man in front. Righting himself, the man stood taller, gathering his faculties, smoothing his vest, though even erect he barely made it five feet tall. Behind him, another man trailed, tall and thin, barely occupying his suit, his wrists three inches out of his sleeves and a huge Adam's apple bobbing at his throat, under a slack smile.

"Good evening, John," he said slowly from above Doc's head. Doc Phelps tilted his head back to see him, nearly losing his balance.

"You're such a dolt, Degney . . . ," Doc said, lowering his head to focus on level, allowing his eyes to collect on the bartender again. "We're dry here, John, practic'ly dead wid it, an' if ya don't get us some hydration quick our souls'll be on your 'ands."

"What souls?" John grumbled, tipping back the tap to fill a couple glasses.

The door had barely closed behind Degney when it opened again, cautiously, a priest sticking his head in, looking.

"You're letting fresh air in, Fadder . . . ," Mulligan called to him.

Shuffling over the priest removed his black felt hat while shaking his head and clucking. He unwound a scarf from his neck, revealing his scapular cloak and white collar, adjusting his white bushy hair where his hat had misshapen it. Smiling good-naturedly, he signaled to the bartender for a glass of his own.

The priest sat on the stool across from McGhee, tossing his hat and scarf onto the bench. As he leaned across, McGhee caught the hops in his breath that let him know Doheny hadn't been his first stop.

"So you American, then?" the priest said extending his hand. "Father Linus."

"Or ya can call em Jiggs," Mulligan said, leaning in helpfully. "He'll eat anything long as it's boiled."

McGhee halted momentarily as he reached across, then took it for a quick shake.

"Haven't et anything yet that ain't better boiled, Sean," he said, continuing to look at McGhee. He seemed to be studying him like a project, but he only smiled, kindly and open.

"Fran McGhee . . . out of San Francisco, Father," McGhee said when there was finally a gap, their eyes remaining locked.

Fr. Linus slapped the table lightly. "I knew it . . . ," he said, proud of himself. "You have that American way about you."

"What exactly *is* that?" McGhee asked, his lips curling at the edges. He preferred to remain anonymous as a traveler, observing, but it seemed his cover wasn't working.

"Americans always look like they got a stick up der bum . . . ," Degney said.

Leaning diagonally across the table, Doc leaned in: "Ya don't look like a flaming arsehole to me, so I don' see it," he said, then smiled slyly. "Doc Phelps," he added after a beat, extending his hand, "an' this numbskull is Degney," he said throwing his left thumb over his shoulder to an empty spot, then noticing the gap, threw it over the other shoulder at the brooding man. Degney nodded but his smile remained slack and he said nothing, though he didn't seem hostile.

"You boys gonna eat?" John called from behind the bar. He was still watching, both arms straight against the edge, like a bulldog on duty. Doc nodded for the group and waved him over. Strolling slowly, John pulled his order pad from his apron but didn't offer menus.

"I'll take me regular . . . ," Doc Phelps said, looking up into John's face, though he didn't return the glance and just wrote on his pad, "an' another pint when ya get a chance." Holding up his glass with a little wiggle, he showed it was empty already.

"Me, too . . . me regular," Degney said, and then almost as an afterthought, "an' another pint while you're at it."

When John got to the priest, Fr. Linus waited patiently for his look, which annoyed the bartender because he had to remove his eyes from his pad, but he was used to it. "Fadder?"

"I'd like the boiled cabbage and corned beef, please. An' some more a da holy water when you can . . . ," he said, folding his hands on the table in front of himself.

"Jiggs . . . ," Mulligan said.

"Jiggs . . . ," Doc said, then Degney.

"What's this Jiggs business?" McGhee asked, turning to Fr. Linus.

"Oh, it's nothing Francis. Just an old comic in da paper back in Nova Scotia. Made da mistake a tellin' these fellas once and now they won' forgit it."

After some time and conversation, the food arrived and they set to eating, the banter subsiding into the small clinks of knives on forks tearing meat, or forks on teeth busily shoveling the morsels gut-ward. When he thought to twist his wrist to note the time, McGhee was surprised to see it was nearly eight already.

About the time they were pushing back their plates – though Fr. Linus was slower than the rest – another face appeared at the table, her fists resting on her hips, scanning the group.

"You boys still fishing off stinker's bridge, or can I join ya?" she said, smiling, then reached over to punch Degney on the shoulder.

"Oh Jesus . . . ," Fr. Linus said, blessing himself. "That's some mouth you got, Arlene."

"Like it, Fadder?" she said, pursing her lips and batting her eyelashes.

"I like it . . . ," Mulligan said, leaning over to purse his lips at her, but she put her palm over his face to push him back into the bench.

"Down, boy . . . ," she said. "I ain' dat desperate yet," she said, "an' 'sides, I got a deal with Degney here to shoot me first afore I git der anyways."

Degney nodded. "She ac-shully does."

"So who's dis American, then?" Arlene said to the group, motioning to McGhee with her chin.

"Dat's just McGhee . . . ," Degney said. "Mulligan found em in a park, an' ya know how he likes his strays."

McGhee was lost pondering his gut, where the Shepherd's Pie was doing its best to quell the mounting lager, but losing. Noticing he had become the topic of conversation, he swung his head to look at her and was surprised to see her staring back at him. She had short black hair, cropped close on the sides, bangs in front, but attractive, with sharp features and fine eyebrows, slightly fierce but clean. Her sleeveless black blouse was snug and revealed her shoulders and arms, strong and taut, like the rest of her seemed to be, the net impression slightly defensive, and he liked it.

"So ya dumb, then? Arlene asked him, her lips curling on the edge into the slightest of smiles.

"Not usually . . . ," McGhee said, "except when faced with profound beauty . . . ," he continued, and after a pause, "or a total wanker, as you call it." His smile broadened at her, and their eyes remained locked.

"Definitely a wanker, then," Doc Phelps said. Doc Phelps wrapped his arm around her shoulder and pulled her in for a hug. "She's the worst boy in the club, McGhee, but the only one who smells 'alf-way decent."

Arlene still had her eyes on McGhee, but they had more of a smile to them than before, though in their blueness remained piercing. "So what brings ya to our little hole, den, McGhee?"

"Poor judgement," he said instantly, "and a desire to see where Guiness comes from."

Mulligan leaned over, cupping his hand, but spoke loud enough for the rest to hear, "But you're drinkin' Harp, mate."

John the bartender perked up, drawing a fresh draft and walking over. "Easily remedied," he said, sliding a dark pint under McGhee's nose, its head still building, "So young I cut the umbilical myself a second ago."

"No, really . . . ," Arlene persisted. "Why you in Dublin?"

"Wanted to see it for myself, and got some questions to answer . . . ," McGhee said, lifting the Guiness for a sip. The foam was thick and earthy, the beer below hoppy and strong.

"Such as?" Degney asked, finally weighing in. His front teeth seemed a bit large for his mouth, keeping his lips slightly parted even when his mouth was closed.

"All right, then . . . ," McGhee said, leaning back in the booth. "Such as . . . why does every corner seem to have two churches and two bars on it?"

"Three bars would be kinda excessive, doncha think?" Doc Phelps said, the others breaking into laughter.

"An' three churches would be kinda sad . . . ," Degney added, sending them into another roll of laughter, though Fr. Linus only smiled. "Sorry Fadder," Degney added, raising his glass to him.

Mulligan reached over to put a hand on Fr. Linus's elbow. "Ee's up a diff-rent tree, anyhow . . . ," he confided, which brought more than a smile to the priest's face, finally getting him to join in the laughing outright. Encouraged, Mulligan continued. "Not that there's anything wrong wid it . . . ," Mulligan said, tilting his head and sticking his tongue out the corner to indicate otherwise.

"Here we go ag'in," Doc Phelps said, "an' I like my tree just fine, thank yerself. We don' need no red vicar telling us what *He* has to say," he said, throwing his thumb up toward the ceiling, "an' the only Pope *I* listen ta wrote decent verse. Asides, when was da last time da inside a church ever saw da likes a you, anyways?"

"This is my church . . . ," Mulligan said, extending his arms to encompass the whole of the bar. "Our Lady of the Sudsy Brew."

"Our Lady of the Stiff One . . . ," Degney threw in, smirking.

"I like the sound o' that . . . ," Arlene continued, nodding.

"Boys . . . ," Fr. Linus said, and after a pause, "and Mulligan . . . ," he continued, crossing himself and mumbling in Latin.

Turning her attention back to McGhee, Arlene's gaze settled upon him again. "So really, McGhee, what brings ya to our fair city?"

"You're like a dog with a bone . . . ," McGhee said, holding pat. He was enjoying her persistence and smiled again, though she resisted it, but with evident struggle.

"You have *no* idea . . . ," Degney added, the crew laughing again.

"You're not getting off that easy," Arlene said, leaning in on an elbow on the table.

"All right . . . ," McGhee responded, returning her gaze. "My uncle Joe died, and I came in for his funeral. Last of my dad's brothers. Figured I'd stick around Dublin a few days to get the feel of it."

"Where your family from, then?" Fr. Linus said, looking over.

"Galway, or somewhere near it," McGhee said.

"Gees – all turf-cutters and pot-lickers over der," Degney said. "Ain' got two sticks to rub together, they don' . . . ."

"My grandad left there around 1906 and went to western Pennsylvania to be a miner," McGhee continued. "I don't remember much about him except that he grunted a lot, and was in his cups Fridays. Seemed like a tough life."

"A Cat-lick coal-cracker, den," Degney continued.

"Charlie . . . ," Fr Linus said, shaking his head lightly and tapping the table in front of him.

Mulligan leaned over to McGhee. "Degney's from Belfast, so he's still a little *troubled* . . . ."

"Well, at least I ain' a *Fumbling Dublin*, then . . . ," Degney retorted, his smile waning.

"Like you been employed nineteen years in your whole bleedin' life, Degney," Mulligan said, getting defensive, a little lather gathering at his mouth's edge.

"Boys, boys . . . ," Arlene intervened, raising her hands. "I believe Mr. McGhee is presently on the witness stand."

Swinging around to face his interrogator, McGhee crossed his hands in front of himself. "Mum," he said, adopting a serious air.

"So what's your verdict, then, McGhee?" Arlene continued, comfortable with the cross examination role. Her smile was slight, but her look intense.

Leaning back, McGhee stretched his arm along the bench. "I'd like to speak to the zoning board, for one thing."

"What's a zoning board?" Degney asked, looking back and forth between Mulligan, Doc Phelps and Fr. Linus.

"I think we just been insulted as ugly . . . ," Doc Phelps said, then corrected. "You guys, I should say, since teck-nik-ly I'm still a Brit."

"You're about as British as my bung-hole . . . ," Degney said, shaking his head.

"You got a British bung-hole, Degney? – might explain some things," Mulligan said.

"Oh, sot off . . . ," Degney said, looking back to McGhee.

"It's *sod* off, mate . . . ," Doc Phelps said, leaning in helpfully.

"Oh, go fug yerself, Doc. I wanna know what McGhee means by dat remark . . . ."

McGhee shifted in his seat slightly, but didn't change the light smile on his face. "To answer your question, Mr. Degney . . . I mean the city seems to have an odd *aesthetic* to it . . . ."

"Like I said, he's sayin' Dublin is a bit uva cow . . . ," Doc said. "Ain' whatcher sayin'?"

McGhee laughed. "But she has a nice personality . . . ," he said. The boys were silent, but Arlene leaned in for a look.

"Rather ballsy . . . ," she said, frowning, but couldn't hold it, stretching out her hand for a shake. "I like *this* McGhee . . . ," she said nodding. "Not bad for an American. What else ya got?"

McGhee held onto her hand after shaking, turning it over to see the back of it. Her age showed there a bit, though not in her face or neck, and he stroked the back of it with his thumb before letting it go, but she didn't recoil.

"Looks like Arlene's got 'erself a new fella, if I'm readin' right . . . ," Doc Phelps said laughing, only to receive a punch in the shoulder from her.

Ignoring the comment, McGhee continued, motioning for the bartender to bring another round for the table. "All right then . . . ," he said, scratching his chin. He'd forgotten he had a few days' growth there, and the stubble was strong and dark, pushing back like short wires. "Seems like the only thing made in Ireland is Guiness . . . ," McGhee said finally after some thought. "Judging from the signs everywhere . . . ."

"What's wrong wid dat?" Doc Phelps asked.

"An' Harp," Mulligan said, raising his glass. "Don' fergit Harp."

"An' Jame-son," Arlene added, looking back and forth between Mulligan and Doc Phelps.

"An' a nasty-strong brand-a Catholicism . . . ," Degney threw in, stiffening again for the retort. Fr. Linus immediately tapped on the table in front of him, shaking his head.

McGhee nodded. "So that's it? -- religion and alcohol?"

"Can't have one widout drinkin' da udder . . . ," Arlene said.

Fr. Linus laughed. "Now dat's clever, Arlene. Whoever sez you're slow never heard ya say dat."

"Who sez I'm slow?" Arlene said, leaning in to see Fr. Linus better, but Degney answered.

"Paddy Finnegan, fer one . . . ," Degney said, raising a finger.

"Fuggin' hell – he's slow in the head and quick in the pants, that sot," Arlene retorted. "More likely ta shoot off a toe than make a girl 'appy wid dat gun-a-is."

"'Eard it's a Derringer anyhow . . . ," Degney said. Arlene clinked her glass on his, then noticing it was nearly empty, he gulped the last down and held it up for John the bartender to see.

"Did somebody say Finnegan?" a large man said, putting his head between Degney and Phelps and throwing his arms over their shoulders. He was red-faced, with even redder cheeks and howling orange hair and freckles, strapping and tall, dwarfing the men on their stools, beads of sweat on his brow, and his blond eyelashes batting, like they'd clear the fog he already inhabited if they blinked hard enough.

"Yer ears musta been tingling, Paddy . . . ," Fr. Linus said, raising his hand to wave at him.

"More likely his crotch . . . ," Mulligan said, tipping his glass toward Arlene and winking.

"Mulligan . . . 'eard dat company a yers finally came to its senses," Finnegan said, weighing heavily on the shoulders of the boys, his eyes focused through the haze on him.

"Cripes, yer manky . . . ," Doc Phelps said, freeing his head from the crook of Finnegan's elbow. "Time for your monthly . . . ," he continued, pinching his nose shut. Unbalanced, Finnegan stood, putting his weight with one thick hand on Degney's shoulder, but Degney tipped it off.

"Carry your own weight, Finnegan," Degney said, "fer once."

"Can't we get that tap-jockey over 'ere, I'm parched . . . ," Finnegan said, ignoring the insults.

"I'd like to hear ya say that to John . . . ," Doc Phelps threw in over his shoulder, then turned to smile wryly at Mulligan. "Betcha'd eed go arse over 'eels out . . . ."

Holding his beefy arm up, Finnegan signaled for a beer. Turning back to the table, he spied McGhee on the bench and his face went slack. "So who's the 'Mer-can?" he got out, a bit of slobber on his lip.

"Name's McGhee," McGhee said, extending his hand, but Finnegan was slow to take it.

"An FBI then?" Finnegan continued.

"Only aff," Mulligan said, then leaning to McGhee, explained it meant foreign born Irish.

"What's the other aff, den?" Finnegan continued.

"Slovak . . . ," McGhee said cooly, retracting his hand.

"Fugg me arse, I dunno if der's even a word fer dat. You ain' no McNugget, or McChigger. Ya ain' no McSpic neither, an' not a McKraut . . . ," he said, rubbing his chin in mock thoughtfulness.

"That's quite enough, Paddy," Fr. Linus said, tapping on the table, but Finnegan was on a roll.

"I guess we'll need a new one then . . . How's abou' McSlav. Dat oughta work."

McGhee eyed him cooly, leaning back again, looking over at Mulligan, then back at Finnegan. "So ya still a chronic masturbator then?" McGhee said.

Finnegan stood erect, blinking. "Wha'?" then reconsidered. "No."

McGhee smiled wryly. "Glad to hear ya quit, then," McGhee said, raising his glass to toast him.

Finnegan stood blinking, brooding and processing, gradually breaking into an uneasy smile.

"Good un, McGhee . . . Ya got a pretty little mouth on ya . . . Jus' lemme know when yer ready ta get ta work proper . . . ," Finnegan said.

The table settled into an uneasy silence, McGhee and Finnegan looking at one another, but Fr. Linus leaned in. "Which reminds me . . . 'Erd a good one today. Wanna hear it, boys?" he said, scanning their faces.

"I can't imagine a Fadder tellin' a good un, so let's 'ave it, Jiggs . . . ," Doc Phelps said.

"Seconded!" Arlene said, raising her glass.

Gratified, Fr. Linus lowered his head and cleared his throat, then looked up again. "OK den, it goes like this . . . ."

"Too much preamble – ever tell a joke afore, Fadder?" Degney said, but Doc Phelps gave him an elbow to the ribs to shut him up.

"What do a flyswatter and a pretty girl got in common?" Fr. Linus said. The group set to thinking, quiet.

"Der both thin?" Degney said. Mulligan lowered his head, shaking it.

"I bet it involves swallowin' . . . ," Finnegan said, shifting the weight on his feet and crossing his arms.

"'Ow would a . . . ?" Degney said, his face screwed up in confusion, his voice trailing off.

"Not if you shot gin and tonic, mate," Arlene said. Doc Phelps looked at her and snickered. The rest leaned in, expectantly.

Fr. Linus leaned back. "They both lead to a fly's undoing . . . ," he said, happily clapping his hands together.

The table groaned in unison. "Lame," Degney pronounced. "'Erd dat one in grade school."

"Where'd you hear that anyways?" Doc Phelps said, leaning in on one elbow.

"The confessional . . . ," Fr. Linus said before tipping his glass for a sip, then as an afterthought, "a politician I think . . . ."

"Yous tell jokes in confession?" Degney said, looking confused again.

From behind, Finnegan suddenly broke into laughter. "Right!" he said, shaking merrily, "Fly's undoin' – I get it."

"Yer as thick as da book they named after ya . . . ," Doc Phelps said, looking back at Finnegan. Arlene removed his cap and kissed him on the bald crown of his head and replaced it. Looking up at her, he smiled. "Thanks, love, but I'm just statin' the obvious."

As the banter continued, McGhee looked around the table, taking stock of his company, wondering if this happened every night, if they were all fixtures, and how they got there. It seemed a strange and uneasy mix, like what you'd find in the trap of a drain – odds and ends that fell out of the normal flow and current to collect there, unsorted.

As Fr. Linus noticed his silence and scan of the group, his gaze fixed again on McGhee. Leaning over, he whispered: "So whatcha think of my flock?"

"Not sure what to make of it, Father," McGhee said, "but you got your work cut out for ya."

Fr. Linus smiled, lowering his head, picking at a rough spot on the table with his fingernail absently. "So what's your story, then?" he asked, looking back at McGhee.

"Not sure how to answer that, Father . . . ," McGhee responded.

"Got a girl back home? Fam'ly?"

"Not really, no," McGhee responded, shaking his head. "Used to have a wife, but it didn't work out."

Fr. Linus nodded. "Thought that might be the case . . . ," he said, pursing his lips and looking at him sideways. "Ya got dat look to ya yet – like you was hurt and still not quite right."

"That obvious?" McGhee said, tilting his glass on its edge to stare into it. Fr. Linus shrugged, but looking back at McGhee nodded slightly.

"In my line-a work I see that a lot. More than I'd like. Nothin'll wreck a life so thoroughly as a bad marriage."

McGhee nodded, but tilted his head. "It wasn't that bad. It just wasn't right. For either of us. We just needed out."

"I see . . . ," Fr. Linus said. "So you got faith on your side, then?" he asked hopefully, his bushy eyebrows raised.

It was McGhee's turn to shrug. "Not really, Father, no . . . ," he said.

"But ya grew up Cath'lic, I tink . . . ," Fr. Linus said, his eyes meeting McGhee's.

"I must be an open book . . . ," McGhee said, laughing lightly, Fr. Linus joining him.

"Pretty much. But I've got pretty good readin' people over da years. Been a priest almost fifty years now, so I've seen most of it. You got a familiar aspect . . . ," Fr. Linus said, looking back down at his fingers, still scraping at the surface.

McGhee hunched up his shoulders to lean in on his elbows, staring at the priest. "A familiar aspect?"

Fr. Linus nodded lightly again, his eyes returning to McGhee's. "A familiar aspect," he repeated. "Seen it a lot. I call it *the smart man's disease.*"

"You need a better name for it. Maybe *intelliosis*. Or if it's more serious, a cancer, maybe, then *intellioma*," McGhee said, playfully, but Fr. Linus wasn't playing back.

"Oh, it's serious . . . ," Fr. Linus said, tilting his head to the side, nodding. "*Acute intellioma*, then."

"Tell me doc, how long do I got?" McGhee continued, smiling back into the analysis.

"Oh, I'm afraid it's permanent, without some kind of intervention," Fr. Linus said, raising a finger to wag at him. "You think I jest, but it's serious business. Tell me – doncha believe in God at all?"

McGhee looked back into the Father's eyes, pondering his answer. Sometimes such attacks bothered him and he weighed into the fray, but he saw goodness there, and kindness, and didn't care to offend, so he deferred his stronger defenses in favor of civil conversation.

"Not really, no . . . ," McGhee responded finally, shaking his head lightly.

"So dat's part of it den . . . ," Fr. Linus said, "but not da *big* part."

"What *is* the big part, then, Father?" McGhee continued, sensing a more interesting analysis than he expected.

"Well . . . ," Fr. Linus said, sighing, "I'm willin' ta bet ya don' believe in yerself, neither. Am I right on dat, son?" His eyes were watery and blue and McGhee stared into them, into their depths, wondering what they had seen. His face was weathered and wrinkled, his eye brows bushy and untamed, but the effect suggested he had spent more time smiling than otherwise and was pleasing.

"I'm not sure what that means," McGhee objected, but smiled at the priest. John the bartender arrived with refills for them, and he took a sip from the new glass. He was glad to have something to do as his old glass had run out of diversions.

"Easier said dan explained . . . ," Fr. Linus said, nodding his head, "but it goes back ta why it's called the smart man's disease. Are ya listenin'?"

"Definitely," McGhee said, sipping from his glass again. "This is getting good."

"I'm glad yer entertained, boyo," Fr. Linus said, raising his glass to toast him. "Da nice thing about stupid men – take Finnegan here . . . 'e's permanently inoculated – is dat dey know when to stop asking questions and take things on faith, because they have ta. Fer dem, it's *Why are rocks hard?*, or *Why is the sun warm?* – simple stuff. Dey learn early on dat der never gonna know da answers to most-a der questions, and dey get comfy with dat. Der content. Even fer udder people, non-stupid people, eventually dey find der limits and can be content wid dat. Den der are guys like you. Sound familiar so far?"

"Not bad . . . ," McGhee said, frowning but still amused and nodding.

"Right. So guys like you go beyond dat. Da simple stuff isn't good enough. You go to da hard stuff. And even most-a dat you get. So you keep goin'. Pretty soon, it's the *goin'* dat keeps you goin', more dan da answers, follow me?"

"Yeah, I think so . . . ," McGhee said, nodding.

"Eventually, ya get to da God question, an' based on everything yav seen, even dat's not so hard for ya, am I right?"

"I wouldn't say that, *exactly*, but keep going . . . I don't recall ever being dissected over beer before. It's an odd sensation . . . ," McGhee said, nodding.

"Right. So, after dat, everythin' opens up. Der are no bounds. Some men just keep chasin' da horizon and it never ends. Der what you might call da sociopaths uv da world. But fer udders – men such as yerself, smart men *blessed with a conscience* – dat scrutiny turns inward. *Dat's da* big part."

"Uh oh . . . ," McGhee said, smiling more broadly. "I think I'm in a trap. Or pinned out, like a patient etherized upon the table . . . ."

"Now *der's* a poet . . . ," Doc Phelps said, nodding, then apologized for the intrusion with a finger over his pursed lips.

"Only a trap of yer own devisin', son, only of yer own devisin' . . . ," Fr. Linus said, nodding, "fer dat's when da real fun begins. Dat's when ya peel yerself, layer after layer, lookin' for the hard kernel in the middle where ya can stop. Only ya don't know how to stop, and before ya know it, there's nothing left to peel. There's no heart in da middle and yer left undone."

McGhee nodded slowly, thinking. "That's a nice analogy, Father. I'd say there's some truth to that, only I think it's more complicated."

Fr. Linus frowned, looking sad. "Indeed it is, boyo, butcha gotta go all da way back ta da beginning ta see it, an' it's hard to fix once ya broke it."

"What's that, Father?" McGhee asked, twisting his beer on the table in its wet spot.

Fr. Linus leaned back a bit, rubbing a hand on his neck. "It's faith, son," he said, his eyebrows going up.

"Faith?" McGhee asked, lifting his glass for a sip.

"Faith," Fr. Linus repeated, nodding. "I'm sure you let dat go near da beginning. Even before God got da boot, am I right?"

"I guess so . . . ," McGhee said, nodding. "It mostly seemed necessary to answer the God question," McGhee admitted, slightly unsettled. He'd become aware that the others at the table had ceased talking and were listening in, and the sudden spotlight made him uncomfortable.

"*Dat's* where yer wrong, boyo!" Fr. Linus said, triumphantly, smiling and raising his own beer for a sip.

"What's all this faith business, then?" Finnegan said, leaning in.

"Hey, I think there are cartoons on the tele back der for ya . . . ,"
Doc Phelps said, snapping his fingers in front of Mulligan and pointing toward the back.

"Last call, gents . . . ," John the bartender called solemnly,
wiping the bar where no one had been sitting.

The table grew quiet again, and Fr. Linus leaned in on both elbows. "Faith *ain't about believin' in God*," he said, almost whispering,
"It's just about believin' in *somethin'*."

"Jumpin' Jesus," Mulligan said. "Dat makes me 'ead 'urt."

"Only fer a dolt such as yerself," Degney said to Mulligan, shaking his head. "Go on, Fadder . . . ."

"Tanks, Charlie . . . ," Fr. Linus said, tapping the table in front
of him. "Dat's pretty much it, Francis," he said turning back to
McGhee. "When you killed yer faith, you killed yer faith in yerself,
too, an' dats what ya need ta git back."

McGhee sat quietly looking at the priest, then at the others
who were all staring at him.

Doc Phelps leaned in toward McGhee. "He's pretty fuggin' an-
noyin', idn't-e?" he said, tossing a thumb toward Fr. Linus.

"I think I like you, Doc," McGhee said, smiling at him, the others laughing along with them. Once it subsided, McGhee looked
back to Fr. Linus.

"So Father . . . about that onion . . . ," McGhee said, leaning
back again. Fr. Linus nodded.

"Perhaps we should make dat an apple . . . ," Fr. Linus said,
raising his finger.

"You're the one talking in layers, Father. Not fair to change the
parameters now . . . ," McGhee said.

"Yeah, param-ters . . . ," Degney said nodding, but Doc elbowed him again.

"Granted . . . ," Fr. Linus said, bowing his head. He'd gotten the apple into evidence, even with instructions to the contrary.

"How do you ever understand the onion without taking it apart to inspect it and look for its heart?" McGhee said.

"I don't need to take apart the onion to understand it . . . ," Fr. Linus said, shaking his head. "It's more than the sum of its parts."

"So onions got souls den, Fadder?" Arlene said, winking at McGhee, but the priest ignored her.

"I got dat ghost on me breath now, Arlene," Mulligan said, blowing toward her.

McGhee nodded. "I agree the onion is more than the sum of its parts, but aren't you compelled to learn that for yourself?"

"There are mysteries I know enough to leave alone . . . ," Fr. Linus said.

"Fair enough . . . ," McGhee said nodding. "Only *how* do you know that?"

"Faith has no epistemology, son . . . ," Fr. Linus said, his smile fading. "Dat's da point-a it."

"Wha' da fuggin' 'ell?" Finnegan said, leaning in again. "I don' think I understood a single letter-a dat whole sentence."

"See . . . ," McGhee said, "that I can't abide. Seems like an abdication to me. Like it's your duty to seek understanding, otherwise you're wasting god's gift to you, aren't you?"

Fr. Linus shook his head strongly, growing more serious. "Not atall son, not atall. Dat's what da garden story is about – knowin' yer bounds an oversteppin' em."

"By what authority, Father, are those bounds set?" McGhee said.

"By *God*, son. By *God Himself*," Fr. Linus offered, his nail resuming its prying at the table surface.

"OK," McGhee said, nodding. "Suppose I grant you that . . . Where does *his* authority *come* from?"

"Ours is not ta know da mind-a God . . . ," Fr. Linus said, shaking his head.

"That's not a fair argument," McGhee said, "and who says so?"

"The Bible says so," Fr. Linus said, "an' it's da Word-a God."

"So God grants his own authority, then?" McGhee said, looking at each in turn, but the faces were blank.

"Ya guys lost me at episte-whatever dat was . . . ," Degney said. He tilted his head tentatively, his eyes on McGhee. "*But* . . . ya do sound a bit ungracious, wid dat . . . ."

Fr. Linus leaned in again, his face resuming its kindly look. "It all goes back to da smart man's disease . . . ," he said, "and our original sin."

"So that's what the sin was? – curiosity?" McGhee asked, raising his glass to drink. "Seems like a bad deal to me, to be given a brain and then told not to use it too much. What kind of a god does that?"

"So you're angry wid em den?" Fr. Linus said, raising his eyebrows. "He's gotta be der ta be mad at, right?"

McGhee laughed. "Nice try, Father," he said, draining his glass and setting it on the table.

"It's a start . . . ," Fr. Linus said, reaching out to grab McGhee's arm for a fond shake as they rose to leave.

"No need a church tamorra," Mulligan said, rising, too, "fer it seems we jus 'ad it . . . ."

Out in the street, the air was cool, and when he checked his watch, it was already one thirty in the morning. They shook hands as they buttoned their coats, wandering off into their various directions, some more directly than others. A street cleaner was moving down the edge of the curb, its brushes clearing away the detritus from the margin of the avenue. Near the end of the street, the cleaner stopped where a man sat on the curb, elbows on knees, head drooping. Stepping out of his cab, the driver helped him to some steps nearby before finishing the sweep, disappearing around the corner, the hum of his brushes drifting off to silence.

As McGhee walked, he realized he wasn't sure which direction his hotel was, but was content to wander, his thoughts simmering, hands in pockets. He didn't get very far before he heard light and quick footsteps behind him catching up. Stopping, he found himself in the cone of light thrown by a street lamp, partially shaded by a sycamore. The approaching steps slowed and the dark figure spoke just while stepping into the light.

"Isn't your hotel the other direction?" Arlene said, strolling over to him, looking up at McGhee and smiling.

"And how would you know that, exactly?" McGhee asked playfully.

Shrugging, she smiled but didn't answer, instead looping her arm through his elbow. "I make lousy tea . . . ," she said finally, "but it's hot. Care to have some?" She tugged lightly at his arm, breaking out his feet frozen to the flagstone.

It wasn't more than a block or two to her place, around the corner and in an alley, pleasant and quiet and inviting, a little apartment above a bakery. Tossing her keys in a bowl by the door, she bustled into the darkness, bumping into a table, the noise receding as she disappeared within, finally turning on a light in the kitchen. She wasn't visible, but he could hear her running water and she called out for him to come on in.

It wasn't a large place but was cozy and neat; a framed portrait of a family sat on the wall over the small mantle above an equally small fireplace. Bookshelves lined that wall, stuffed with books, though they weren't so tidy as the rest of the place, jammed in at angles, stacked as if recently moved, others standing in proper order, still other magazines and articles stacked along the edge. In front of them, an ancient loveseat sat facing into the fireplace, tables on either end with mismatched lamps to illuminate their part. In all, it seemed familiar, rather like his own place, and he liked the feel of it.

In the kitchen, Arlene had an old fashioned teakettle directly on the stove, the high flames licking up the side.

"You might wanna turn down the burner a bit . . . ," McGhee said, stepping in, leaning against the counter.

"I'm not very domestic . . . ," she said, reaching awkwardly to lower the fire. She fiddled with the knob to get the flame right, pounding it with the heel of her palm.

Reaching around her, McGhee gave the knob a twist, adjusting the flame, leaving his arm there. Leaning back, Arlene fell into his chest lightly, and she wrapped her hand around his.

"I don't wancha ta think I ask just anyone back . . . ," she said, without looking at him. Wordless, she reached for his other hand and gathered it with its mate in front of her. Resting her head on him, he could smell her hair – light and clean – and feel her nervousness through their slight embrace.

"And I don't want you to think I accept all invitations, either . . . ," he said lightly into her ear, her body relaxing against his as he said it.

Turning off the burner, she turned to face him, her face close to his. Her skin fair and her eyes deep blue, she looked at him from below her dark bangs. "Perhaps the tea can wait . . . ," she said, standing on her toes, her lips parted slightly as invitation to kiss her. Her breath came in small puffs as her lips probed his, insistent yet delicate, unrestrained yet playful, her smile evident through her kisses. Her body was warm against McGhee, her breasts pushed against him as she fell into him.

Her bed seemed to be endless layers of sheets and quilts and thin blankets and duvet, the bed cool to their skin as they climbed in, their embrace reaching some mutual urgency and satisfaction, each finding something they needed in that moment. And with release came lassitude and they fell into light napping, the moment extending into an hour and a bit more, Arlene resting in the crook of his arm, playing lightly with his chest hair.

For his part, McGhee was lost in thought, one arm tossed behind his head. Arlene looked up at him, then went back to rubbing his chest lightly. "Don't let what da Fadder said get ya down . . . ," she said. "I don't think he knows ya at all . . . ," she continued, resting her head on him again.

"Maybe he's right . . . about some of it," McGhee said. "It was certainly very personal."

Adjusting herself, Arlene got up on one elbow to look at him. "You wanna know why I chased ya down?" she said, her eyes tracing the path of her fingers on his chest. McGhee didn't answer, but watched her. He liked the sensation of her attention and her pursuit, and it warmed him.

"I liked the sense of hopefulness in yer eyes . . . ," she said. "Ya may not be a man of faith, but ya 'ave dat . . . ."

McGhee chuckled. "That's a pretty fine distinction," he said, adjusting lightly to look at her more directly.

"And I don't think ya lost your faith in yerself, neither . . . ," she said, "but I know what he's talking about. Ya *do* 'ave a look to ya – a little lost, a little forlorn. Like you're searching for somethin' ya lost, or maybe somethin' ya always wanted. But dat's not the same as what 'e said."

"Yeah, that sounds about right . . . ," McGhee said, "only I don't know what it is, either. I just don't feel like I'm doing the right thing most of the time."

Arlene continued the slow rub of his chest, thinking. "So how long ya feel like dat?" she asked.

McGhee sighed, pondering the question. "At least since college. Probably even freshman year – Yale really messed me up while it was fixing me. I had a lot to unlearn, and much of it was about me. I'm not sure it was a good trade."

"You went to *Yale?*" Arlene said, pounding him lightly on the chest, surprising McGhee.

"What?" he said, looking at her.

"Dat's not some backwater school yer talking about. It's no wonder it messed with you. I'd guess it messes with everybody."

"Not everybody . . . ," McGhee said, shaking his head.

"But doncha see?" Arlene said, grabbing him by the chin. "If ya can make it der, even survive, then ya can make it pretty much anywhere. Ya just have ta figure out how to make it yer own. Long as ya measure yourself by someone else's yardstick, ya won't be happy."

McGhee smiled. "Easier said than done . . . ," he said, looking back at her.

"Maybe not . . . ," Arlene said, returning to her finger tracing on his chest. "Ya just need to forgive yerself fer . . . ," she said, her voice trailing off.

"Forgive myself for what?" McGhee said, reaching over to turn her chin toward him, lightly caressing her cheek.

"Fer letting yerself down . . . that's what I was gonna say, but maybe that's goin' a bit too far. But you were young, and it's all so confusing then. It's alright ta be mad at yerself a while, but I tink you could cut yerself some slack."

McGhee sighed, thinking. "Actually, that sounds about right, too," he said.

"But here's da good thing . . . ," Arlene said, her eyes locked on his again. "It's never too late. And ya got that hope thing I saw, too, so I know it's in there," she said, tapping his chest lightly. "Ya got a good heart, McGhee. Anybody could see it . . . . Just use it once fer yerself."

Out on the steps, she grabbed the collars of his jacket and got on her toes again. Retrieving a small paper from her sweater she folded it and stuffed it into his jacket.

"What's that?" McGhee said, smiling down into her eyes.

Arlene smacked him lightly on the shoulder. "It's fer when ya wake up. Ya need to see the city proper before ya go, and 'ave a 'alf-way decent guide ta do it . . . ," she said, smoothing the pocket closed with a tap.

McGhee caught her hand, pressing it to his chest, smiling. "It's a date, then," he said.

Arlene's brow crinkled as she grew serious again, staring into his eyes, from one to the other. "I know you'll find it if you keep lookin', McGhee . . . ," she said, kissing him before letting him go. The smile he had seen on her lips earlier returned, only this time he knew he'd remember it fondly for a long time.

The sky had moved from black into a deep blue suggesting the night had turned toward morning. Though the streetlamps were on yet to light his route home, it'd be some time before he got there.

The Baptism of Frosty McGhee

9AM
Andrew Gulch, Ruby, AK 10/1/1986

It was late – almost 3:00 p.m. when McGhee left the cabin – heading in to Ruby to get the case of beer for the guys at the mine, and he felt guilty, wondering if they might even wonder if he'd return at all. They didn't know him, either, except that he'd represented himself as a friend of Big Mike's step-son Matt, and that somehow Big Mike had heard some kid might be coming out for a look.

The day before, he'd gotten out there late to Andrew Gulch, which seemed to be a recurring pattern for him, to have a look around, only the sun was set already when he got there, and at that latitude in September, the sun was timid about rising at all, or so it seemed to McGhee. So he didn't get to look around, except for a bit by the shack, which wasn't very satisfying for a gold mine visit, and he resolved to come back. In fact, it seemed like the guys were discouraging him from looking around at all, which itself was difficult to swallow after seven miles over a rutted mud road at five miles an hour in a crappy pickup, ten in the good spots, but it did seem to be for the best that he just go home to the cabin. And it seemed almost coincidental that they said he could come back, of course, tomorrow, which the more they suggested it – early start and all – would afford a better chance to knock around and get the lay of the place. And further, if he was going to be coming back, would he mind bringing them a case of beer because they'd just run out of Oly anyway – *Olympia Beer* that is – and it just wasn't the same running heavy equipment if you didn't have a buzz on. They snickered at the last part, only he didn't realize they were kidding, or mostly, because such folly would likely be more fatal than amusing, and none of them wanted to die in the cold mud, no matter how much money might be involved, even though it wasn't so much, they said. So he agreed.

Only, he didn't get to Ruby early, and in fact was getting out late again for some reason, not that he had any excuse for that. Add to that the fact Ruby was several miles in the opposite direction, over better but still crappy road, and he didn't see how he was going to make it out, but he was still going to try. The guys had looked so happy: as soon as he had said he'd be willing to do it, the men spontaneously turned out their pockets, throwing mostly ones into a pile, that after some effort and extra cajoling of Joe, who it seemed had a rep for holding back but eventually threw in a five, reluctantly, amounted to exactly twenty-two dollars, which apparently was the going rate for a case of the stuff. So he dutifully counted it, given the gravity and investment of the situation, folded it neatly (after removing the wrinkles) and stuffed it into his pocket with a solemn nod. Feeling his pocket for the wad of bills he paused at the door before pulling the knob shut, lost in thought. It was late and he'd better just get going. He didn't know why, but his head felt cloudy inside, so through sheer force of will, he pushed through it and left, feeling instantly better behind the wheel, driving forward.

He was relieved when he saw Ruby spread in the valley below him as he slid down the mud hill into it, though it was later than he'd like. Sprawled on the banks of the Yukon, it seemed carved out of the mud itself, a ramshackle collection of corrugated metal buildings and cheap wood-frame houses, set back and down from the elevated mud roads separating it out like an ice tray. Only the very center of the main drag looked slightly more normal, with the buildings at street level, such as they were. Most of those were houses, and it didn't have the flavor of a bustling center of commerce, quite the contrary. About the only building there that seemed to be something official contained the general store in one part and the post office in the other. The only other official building – official, meaning it looked like it was built according to some plan and with state money – was the laundry, which represented the absolute pinnacle of civilization in the otherwise struggling lichen of humanity clutching at the rocks there. In short, it was a tough town the winters did their best to erase, but which through some miracle and a lot of stubborn tenacity, survived in spite of them.

Pulling up in front of the general store, McGhee wasn't sure where to park, so he parked in front of the door. An Athabaskan leaning against the building at the top of the stoop, which was only two steps, shook his head. "Can't park there," he said. McGhee looked at him, then the street, which was otherwise empty, but acquiesced, getting back in, and moved the truck thirty feet, before walking back.

"Can't park there, neither . . . ," the man said, pushing his wire rims up, which were held together in the middle with a thick wad of surgical tape. His insulated flannel shirt was blown out at the shoulder seam, but he looked solid nonetheless, jeans and boots scuffed and broken like it might be his only uniform.

"Oh, come on . . . ," McGhee said, putting one foot on the cement step, but the man remained stoic, arms crossed, until when it seemed he was actually serious, he opened the storm door, yelling in with some local language, laughing, then, looking back at McGhee, motioned in with his head. "You coming in then?"

Just then a man came walking out, dirty blue coveralls with an engineer's cap, but otherwise naked underneath, or so it appeared. Stepping down, he threw open his arms and hugged McGhee.

"Hey kid . . . ," he said, holding him at arm's length. It was Junior from the mine, the cook – he'd only met him yesterday, but greeted him like a long lost uncle. He was probably in his forties, but looked much older: stubble on his chin, wrinkles, like he'd stared into a hard blowing storm for years straight, bags under the bags under his eyes, which were red where the white should be but bright blue otherwise. Based on how his mouth over-closed and the softness of his voice, loud as it was, it seemed he wasn't wearing his teeth, either, none of which dimmed his aspect. For his part, McGhee was glad to see him, as it suddenly seemed he might still make it out to the gulch after all.

"Junior! Whatcha doing in town?" McGhee asked, matching his enthusiasm, which seemed to be the thing to do.

"S'plies," Junior said, nodding, then shaking his head, then nodding. "Eggs-n-whatnot . . . an' you?"

Junior hadn't been part of the band that had approached McGhee, so he pulled the wad out of his pocket and showed him.

"The guys gave me money for a case of *Oly*," he said, wiggling it between his fingers. "You heading back to the mine tonight?"

"Wuz just . . . ," Junior nodded, smiling. "Better git movin' if you're goin' out yerself" he said, tilting his head, raising his eyebrows for emphasis.

McGhee nodded, lowering his head. "It's pretty late though. I was kinda thinking I might go tomorrow."

Junior nodded, "Yeah, well . . . ," but didn't say anything else. McGhee looked into his watery eyes, a thought forming.

"I don't suppose . . . ," he began, but Junior was ahead of him, grabbing the wad of bills, turning to go back up the steps.

"I'll take it. You come out tamarra . . . ," Junior said, smiling and waving back at McGhee before disappearing into the store under the Indian's arm.

McGhee laughed, smiling at his good fortune. The Athabaskan was still holding the door open, and shrugged. "You coming in then?" he asked again, looking disappointed McGhee wasn't.

Unlike the previous few days, McGhee made an early start of it and was out just after eight and to the mine just before nine. The earliness of the hour had the mud firm tending toward crunchy, versus the moist mess he had contended with his previous trip. Pleased with his progress, he made his way to the shack, but two of the guys made it to him first, two others close on their heels: Little Mike (no relation to Big Mike as it turned out) and Jimmy — two of the younger crew members, both in their early twenties, black hair and sparse Indian mustaches — who seemed especially anxious, stepping over puddles, watching their boots as they danced toward the truck, until Jimmy, then Little Mike went six inches deep in the very last puddle.

"Shit," Jimmy said.

"Fuck, that's cold," Little Mike said, but they looked up, bright and hopeful at McGhee.

"Where's the Oly?" they asked in unison. Joe and Dave came to a stop beside them, Joe holding his cap in his hands, like Oliver Twist, his eyes expectant.

"Guys, it's like 9:00 a.m. . . . ," McGhee said, smiling across the four of them, from one end to the other. "Besides, didn't Junior bring it back? Ran into him town yesterday and gave him the beer money."

"Fuuuccck . . . ," Jimmy and Little Mike said in unison. Dave and Joe thunked their heads.

"Jesus, kid," Joe said, looking sadly at McGhee.

"No wonder he's MIA," Dave said, shaking his head. Finally making it out, Big Mike caught up to the rest of them. Wheeling around, Dave stepped over to him, tall and lanky, his hunched shoulders registering disappointment. His stringy blond hair hung down from his dirty cap and might have been a pony tail if he'd cared enough to bundle it, but didn't. Big Mike was his younger brother, but ran the operation, so it fell to Dave to share the news. "The kid gave the beer money to Junior," Dave said, once he came to rest in front of him.

"Jesus, kid . . . ," Big Mike said, shaking his head. "You know he was *on the wagon*, right?" He put both hands on his hips for emphasis.

Dave leaned toward McGhee. "He was out here to dry out . . . ," he explained. "First trip inta town in six weeks was yesterdee."

McGhee's former glow faded to black immediately. "Well, fuck me then . . . ," he said, scratching his head. "Sorry guys."

"You got that right," Jimmy said, nodding.

Big Mike stepped forward, looking at McGhee. "Worst part, son, is Junior was our cook. . . ."

The other guys nodded, then shook their heads. "Maybe not the worst part, but bad . . . ," Joe said.

Big Mike held his gaze on McGhee, steady. "So now we don't have a cook."

"Gees . . . ," McGhee said. "That kinda sucks."

"Only, we kinda have a rule around here . . . ," Big Mike continued. "You mess with the cook, you own the kitchen . . . ."

McGhee stared back blankly. "Uh huh . . . ," he said, not getting it.

Dave leaned in again to clue him in. "So, now you're the cook," he said, his smile as much a grimace as anything.

McGhee let out a snort and the others laughed, too, McGhee laughing hardest of all. "That's fine guys . . . ," he said finally, "but I don't know how to cook."

"Doesn't matter . . . ," Big Mike said, his gaze still fixed on McGhee, smiling but serious.

"No . . . ," McGhee said, holding up his hand in protest. "I *really* don't know how to cook."

Dave leaned in again, but paused. "It *really* doesn't matter," he said.

Stepping over, Big Mike put his hand lightly on McGhee's back. "Better come in and get situated then . . . ," he said, the matter settled.

As McGhee was discovering, his timing was fortuitous – the night shift hadn't eaten, and the day shift was getting ready to head out. Walking in, he took stock of his new home: a twelve by twelve shack of plywood, of various vintage, quality, color and use, one window – a two-foot square near the tin roof, cut hastily with a saws-all by the look of it, with Visqueen for glass, stapled, edges trimmed with a box cutter, approximately. Inside, it was dark, except for the light coming in from the window in a narrow, dusty band, illuminating his place of indenturement: the only operational appliance of any kind in the shack, not counting a derelict small freezer box which appeared to be a freezer in name only, an ancient battered and nicked gas stove, jury-rigged with bendy-pipe to a propane tank on the floor. Along the walls, bunks stacked by two, accommodating four sleepers at a time, and in the middle, a weathered wood picnic table which provided the mess hall, meeting area, and recreation space. Suspended from the rafters, a kerosene lamp hung from a thin rope, swinging slightly, but dark. Sleeping bags were smashed into the corners of each of the bunks with pillows stained by muddy and sweaty heads twisted by hard-fought bouts of sleep between harder-fought shifts of work.

McGhee stepped over to the stove but had no idea where to start. To the left was a makeshift open cabinet of three shelves fashioned from two by fours and plywood, stacked with all manner of pans, only varying in diameter, and two pots, no doors or walls necessary. To the right, the freezer awaited, and another small open cabinet with three shelves which Big Mike called the pantry, though that seemed a charitable name to call it. Joe grabbed a sack of pancake mix from there – it said so on the side in black marker, with a *3:2* underneath – and handed it to McGhee. "Best get started, kid. We're hungry . . . ," he said, a wry smile on his lips. All of the guys lined up and sat at the picnic table as if breakfast was imminent, as did Big Mike himself after putting three skillets on the stove and handing McGhee a bowl.

McGhee opened the freezer. "I wasn't kidding, you know . . . ," he said, pulling out a package of bacon and a stick of butter.

"It doesn't matter," arose as a chorus from the table, the guys chatting among themselves as they waited.

Jimmy, impatient with the progress, got up from the table, twisted the valve on the propane tank, then lit a burner under the medium pan. "Bacon," he said by way of instruction to McGhee before sitting again.

Dutifully, McGhee threw the entire lump of bacon in. Leaning out from the lineup, Dave motioned with his chin. "Ya prolly wanna separate those . . . ," he said, motioning to the lump in the pan that was already starting to sizzle, but McGhee was busy already with the pancake mix. There was a coffee cup in the sack, so he scooped out three or four loads and poured in a bit of water from a pitcher sitting atop the pantry, mindful of the 3:2 on the front. A wood spoon there, crusted with previous pancake mix appeared to be the implement for the job, but he stared at it, unsure it was safe.

"Just use it, kid," Dave said, still watching. Turning to him, McGhee looked to see if he was serious, but there was no hint of sarcasm.

Firing up another burner under the other two big pans, he scooped a giant chunk of butter in each to melt while he mixed. A minute later he was pouring blobs of batter into the pans to make as many pancakes at a time as possible. "Spatula?" he called over his shoulder at them.

"Wall above cabinet," two voices called back, Jimmy and Little Mike dealing out a hand of cards to most of the guys there. Joe had his head in his hands and wasn't playing, and neither was Big Mike, who was talking at him.

The lump of bacon wasn't cooking evenly, so McGhee turned up the heat. Neither were the pancakes, so he turned those burners up, too. "Maybe pull the bacon apart . . . ?" Dave called out again, McGhee hearing him this time. There was a used fork sitting near the pitcher, so he grabbed it, unceremoniously wiping it on his shirt, then deciding it probably didn't matter, either, used it to pull the meat strips apart. The middle looked a little frozen, which made him wonder about the freezer again, but he didn't have time to ponder the details.

Smoke was beginning to rise from the pans, all three of them, mostly blue in the stream of sunlight, and collecting in the rafters, but he was too busy to manage that: time to flip the pancakes already – bubbles in the pan meant something, he recalled, only discovering then that the pan-side of the cakes were well beyond the golden brown he remembered from his mother's stove, tending toward black. Still, it was progress, and by the time he had the eighth turned, it was time to wrangle the bacon, which had gone beyond mere smoking to minor grease fire with flames licking around the pan to set off minor explosions of crackling fat. The bacon, too, was black on the edges, though barely warmed in the middle past defrosted, but it seemed that would have to be good enough, figuring it might average out. So by the time he had that on a plate – which he had to search for and found on top of the cabinet – the pancakes had achieved a nice black crust on their nether sides, too. So in a flurry of elbows, McGhee slid the two plates of steaming – but mostly just smoking – piled food onto the table in front of the guys. Though they kept talking and playing cards and Big Mike still talked at the top of Joe's head, there were looks among them, Jimmy coughing and Little Mike seconding it. One of them had mercifully grabbed the plates and utensils and some butter and syrup from places McGhee didn't see or know of yet, so at least they had the tools required. Jimmy took to sawing through a pancake with his knife, and though initially rebuffed by the tough crust, kept at it and stuffed it into butter, then syrup, then after inspecting it and smelling it, more syrup before finally eating the first bite, chewing with determination and swallowing with a grimace and something of a low groan. Observing the process, the others set to their own plates, heads down. Dave crunched on a piece of bacon which shattered into a hundred black shards, but said nothing.

"You figure Junior's coming back?" Little Mike said to no one in particular, and the table set to roaring in laughter, even Big Mike.

"You know the rule, Mikey . . . ," Big Mike said finally. "The kid'll get it . . . ," he said charitably, smiling at McGhee as he chewed some of his own pancake, then added, "I hope."

The table set to laughing again, but no one complained. McGhee sat at the end near the stove, taking the last of the cakes and the last piece of meat. It was awful, but McGhee kept chewing, then broke into a smile. "Told you I couldn't cook . . . ," he said finally.

"It doesn't matter . . . ," arose as a chorus from the men, but he could tell their hearts weren't in it, even as they laughed again. Dave leaned over toward McGhee. "Maybe turn down the heat a little bit next time?" he offered, holding up his fingers an inch apart.

It wasn't but a couple more meals before the smoke grew less, then not at all, and the food crossed the threshold from bad, to acceptable, to decent, four times a day, sometimes allowing McGhee to take catnaps in between. It was close to the end of the season anyway, so it was the final push before the ice would call an end to it, but McGhee was glad for the work. He'd driven up the Alcan in early June, just after getting out of school — for the last time — and met up with his friend Matt on the spit in Homer by some wild stroke of luck. It was a long way to drive without any kind of plan, twice as far really: he was in the parking lot of a Seattle *McDonald's* when he discovered he was only half way there. And his summer job in Anchorage didn't generate much cash, so a little surprise income at the mine would be welcome, though he didn't actually know what his wage would be. Really, it was mostly having something to do, in the company of other people – that was the valuable thing – for he was discovering too much solitude, alone in Matt's cabin, might not be a good thing. Matt had disappeared onto a Yukon river barge shortly after McGhee arrived, and after Karl dropped off the quarter moose as payment for the raft help, it had been quiet, very quiet, except for the wolves at night, which he liked but wasn't exactly what he'd call good company. Sometimes he'd take to watching the northern lights out in the cold air, green curtains shimmering, fringed with magenta and yellow, with only those howls in the distance, and he felt alone. For as much as he loved solitude, he realized he'd never truly had it before, and he suddenly had too much a good thing.

So between shifts of food prep and clean up, McGhee found himself hanging with the off-shift crew while the others pushed heavy equipment just down the hill. They were running rotating eight hour shifts around the clock and had been on it since late August – before that, they did two tens with a gap in the middle during the night, but they couldn't afford that anymore. So every eight hours around the clock, he had to get a meal together at least, with lunch in between, but he was getting the hang of it: moose steaks, salmon, eggs, pancakes, bacon, sausage, the guys rolling through days and evenings and nights, one on, one off, McGhee a fixture in all the sit-downs, fixing meals and sitting at the table as they ate.

A couple days into McGhee's routine, Dave came in and called an *all hands* down the hill – they needed some help and could use all the bodies they could get. It was good for McGhee as he had been spending most of his time in the shack. It wasn't very far over the hill – a couple hundred yards at most – to where the action was. It was pretty simple, really: they had a sluice box where they'd load the pay dirt, which connected on the downhill side to a trickle trough which included riffles, or metal fins, running about forty feet before dumping out as tailings. Up on the edge of the sluice box, they'd mounted a monitor water nozzle connected to a high-pressure pump which sucked water out of an intake pond fed by springs. One of the guys would feed pay into the box with a front loader, while another would operate the monitor, seriously agitating the pay with the jet of water, creating a slurry of mud and rock that only had one place to go – downhill through the trickle trough and over the riffles. Under the riffles, they'd set miner's moss mats to collect the heaviest materials which settled there, hopefully including gold.

Big Mike had been operating the D-7G dozer but got stuck in some mud as he was clearing overburden to expose more pay. Little Mike and Jimmy were using the front loader to push it out, when Dave noticed the riffles had become packed, so while the rest of the operation was freeing the dozer, he wanted to clear the riffles. McGhee wasn't sure what he could do, so he stood watching until Dave saw him, handed him a screw driver, and invited him to work the trough, too.

The fine sand and mud had packed hard into the riffles, but the guys were used to it. Jamming their own levers or knives or crow bars into the material, they worked across each row, prying it up, careful to make sure they didn't lose it in the process or bend the fins. Since it had become packed, they couldn't be sure it didn't have gold in it, so they'd be running more water through it, or so Joe explained to McGhee, working next to him. Simple as it seemed, there was technique to it, and Joe clued him in. The screwdriver wasn't great for the task – the others had the better tools – but he kept at it, rewarded eventually with a shiny little nugget the size of a molar filling, which he proudly held up in front of Dave between two fingers, and who, upon inspecting it, dropped it into his breast pocket. "Thanks, kid," he said, ignoring McGhee's disappointment.

Trudging back up the hill, McGhee walked with Joe. There was something about him McGhee enjoyed, and he'd taken a shine to McGhee, too. He looked to be in his fifties, stalky, and walked with a lumbering gate. He wore blue-jean coveralls that seemed to be weeks, if not months, past their last laundering, grime pushed into the fabric with brute force, then pushed in again. All the edges had an extra layer of grease to hold the dirt in, while the sweat tried to push it out. They had achieved a balance there, changing the nature of the material itself, making it a matrix for soiling agents, bending more than wrinkling with his movements and tired strides. Underneath, his white Henley was white no longer, now brown and yellow, the waffling catching all manner of debris and stain. His hair was dark and matted to his head: when he removed his cap, his hair didn't stir, cemented in place by smears of sweat and mud. Still, his eyes smiled when he talked, even when he was swearing, which he elevated to a form of art, his thick cheeks folding in crenulations of skin that showed some age.

"Fuck . . . I saw that, kid . . . ," he said, once they were beyond earshot of Dave. He was shaking his head when he said it, looking sideways at McGhee.

"You mean the nugget?" McGhee asked, his tone still low.

"Yeah, I mean the fuckin' nugget . . . ," Joe said. "Shoulda let ya keep it, the cocksucker . . . ," he said, continuing to ruminate. "It's their mine, though . . . ," he said finally, shrugging, then laughing.

McGhee nodded. "Yeah, I guess . . . ," he said, though it was unclear which part he was agreeing to. Joe patted him on the back, then reached around his shoulder to pull him in, laughing under his breath like they shared a joke, and though he wasn't sure what that was exactly, McGhee liked it.

Back in the shack, McGhee set to making some lunch. He'd mastered the basics, or at least learned not to burn them, so he turned to a challenge. There was a large, opened can of tomatoes, half-full, and something that appeared to be moose burger meat, and beans, and some onion, and some dried pepper flakes. Joe observed from the table as McGhee assembled the ingredients.

"Finally, somethin' fuckin' diff'rent . . . ," Joe said, leaning on his elbows. McGhee swung around to assess the comment, but Joe was smiling, in his way. Ornery seemed to be his default setting, though McGhee sensed everyone discounted that within ten minutes of meeting him anyway. Despite his prickly comments, there was something about Joe that made it hard to take him seriously, or more precisely, to read his criticism as anything but humor. He'd seen it happen with some of the guys: Joe got bent out of shape and was railing at Jimmy, who'd taken his hat and was wearing it at an angle to mimic the way Joe himself wore it, and even though Joe let loose a torrent of swearing and chased him around the table, which was pointless, because he was an old lumbering bear chasing a young lynx with no hope of catching it. The more it went on, the more everyone laughed, especially Jimmy who nearly let himself be caught by laughing too hard to run, and when Joe nearly had him, he relented anyway, knowing what everyone else knew already and permanently: that if he was a bear, he was nothing more violent than a teddy.

McGhee had the moose sizzling in an ancient black iron pan, the other parts going into the large pot, while the others streamed in. Jimmy crashed on his bunk, while Dave and Big Mike settled at the table, talking about the Cat and the riffles and taking the black sand in for processing later that week. Reaching over, Joe grabbed a belt loop on McGhee's pants for quick tug. When he looked down, Joe signaled quietly for him to watch. He waited a moment for the conversation to lull before interjecting.

"So . . . Dave . . . ," he started, waiting for him to look over. Dave required notice like that to get his attention, usually lost in his thoughts. So when he finally swung his blank glance over, Joe continued. "You show Big Mike the kid's nugget yet?" he asked casually.

"Nugget?" Big Mike said, perking up. "What nugget?" Dave's eyes met Joe's and he mouthed the word *fucker*, but no sound came out as he fished into his breast pocket, beneath the pearl snap. Holding it up, the guys let loose an involuntary *ahhh*, Little Mike looking over to the stove: "Nice one, Cookie."

"Let's see that . . . ," Big Mike said, reaching across the table. The nugget stuck in Dave's fingers a moment, then he dropped it into his brother's palm. Grabbing it with his other thumb and pointer, he held it up to the kerosene lamp, rolling it between his fingers. "That's a couple pennyweight, anyway," he said, dropping it into his own breast pocket, before folding down and smoothing the flap over it. Looking over his shoulder at McGhee, he nodded. "You're a real miner now, McGhee. A good thirty-five dollar picker, that one . . . ."

McGhee looked at Big Mike, then Dave seeing the same disappointment register on Dave's face he felt half an hour before. When he finally looked at Joe, he was smiling ear to ear, and nodding. "Fuckin' A," Joe said, tipping his cap to McGhee. Turning back to his stove, McGhee took to stirring the chili, smiling to himself.

The day shift headed back out after the chili, most having a second bowl, Jimmy collapsing back into the cot again while Little Mike dealt out solitaire at the other end of the table. Grabbing some coffee, McGhee sat at the table across from Joe to nurse it. Joe leaned in. "That was pretty fun . . . ," he said, laughing out loud. Little Mike looked up, but seemed oblivious. McGhee took a swig from his cup, toasting Joe in the process.

"Yeah, that was sweet . . . ," he acknowledged. "But how did you know Dave was gonna keep it?"

Joe's jaw dropped open. "Coz I'm not a fuckin' *idiot!*," he said, then realizing McGhee didn't follow, added, "Don't worry kid. You'll grow out of it . . . which is more than I can say for *shithead* down there," he said, tilting his head toward the other end of the table.

"Hey," Little Mike said, keeping his eyes on the cards. "Looks like you're covered in shit, just like me . . . . Only you're, like, forty or something . . . ."

Frowning, Joe opened his hands, looking back at McGhee. "It speaks . . . ," he said.

"But it was pretty sweet . . . ," Little Mike said, looking up at them, his next card suspended mid-air.

"Vindication!" Joe said, raising his hands, but turned back to Little Mike. "And what's this *something like forty* shit, then? I'm fifty-seven come November . . . ."

Little Mike looked back to his game, playing his card, with a smirk. "Yeah, old, like I said . . . ," he muttered. "You're practically dead . . . . Surprised you haven't collapsed yet."

Joe stood, half lunging toward Little Mike, but there were smiles all around.

"What day in November?" McGhee asked, catching Joe's eye again. "Mine's the twelfth."

"What year?" Joe came back, his eyebrows up.

" '63," McGhee answered.

"*Shit*. I'm older then. '29."

McGhee thought to answer, then realized he was being stupid, smiling sheepishly.

Using his fingers, Joe counted like he was slow, screwing up his face sideways to look at McGhee. "So, you're, like *twenty-three?*"

McGhee nodded. "Just about."

"So where you from?" Joe asked, continuing the examination. Stepping over to the stove, he grabbed the camp pot and poured himself some coffee.

Both the pot and cup were blue, speckled-white enameled metal pieces, and ancient. It reminded McGhee of pictures he'd seen of life in the bush, and the camp pot Julie had used, but he just smiled at the thought. "Pennsylvania," he finally answered.

"Never been," Joe said, shaking his head.

Little Mike let out a little *pfft* with his lips, shaking his head.

"Oh, like you been, *world traveler?*" he said toward Little Mike, but he didn't take the bait. "So what's it like?" Joe said, turning back to McGhee.

"Cold," McGhee said, sipping his coffee, Joe immediately laughing.

"No, kid," he shouted, "*this* place is cold!" he said, tapping the table with both pointer fingers.

McGhee smirked. "Now you're the one slow on the uptake, dude . . . ."

Joe leaned back, laughing, then looked back at McGhee, smiling. "Time to sluice our heads, kid," he said, standing up. "You're about to get an *entirely new* definition of cold." Little Mike tossed his cards onto the table and stood. "You, too?" Joe asked, extending the invitation.

"Fuck no . . . ," Little Mike said, "I just wanna see Cookie do it." He was rubbing his hands expectantly.

Joe extended his arm outward toward the door, inviting McGhee to step out. Next to the steps stood the water collection barrel, a 55-gallon drum. Hurrying around McGhee with tiny running steps, Joe leaned against the barrel, smiling widely, pulling on a leather glove. Little Mike leaned against the door jam, watching. Joe motioned to the barrel with his chin. "You wanna go first then?"

McGhee looked at the barrel, then smiled. "Ahh, man. Can't . . . ," he said, motioning to it with his hand. Across the whole surface a layer of ice had frozen it closed.

"Oh, sorry . . . ," Joe said, suddenly punching the surface with all his might, crashing the ice into half-inch-thick pieces with his gloved hand, chunks floating at angles, stacked and random, but exposing the water underneath. He smiled at McGhee, then with both hands on the side, dove in down to his shoulders, twisting under the surface a few seconds before pulling his head out, face red, shaking off the water like a dog. "Whew!" he shouted. "Now *that's* refreshing!"

McGhee watched with dismay, knowing he had to do it, which made Joe all the merrier.

"Your turn, Cookie . . . ," Little Mike said, his arms folded and watching intently.

McGhee smiled back at Joe. "All right, then . . . ," he said, getting up on the step to go in even further, plunging in even past his shoulders.

Time stopped. To his surprise, cold was not the first sensation he felt, but instead, it was burning, like a million hot needles had converged on his head and face, pushing in instantly, painfully, so deep it seemed to stop his heart, so sudden all thought vanished, and for one gleaming instant, all he was was a single sensor of pain, paralyzed, trapped, utterly under the control of his senses, incapable of even a reflexive urge to pull back out. There he hung for what seemed hours, eyes closed, his impulse to breathe frozen shut, his head delivering what warmth it had to the water – which drank it thirstily – until finally, he felt as cold as it was, and the absence of heat washed over him like a wave, draining him of all his remaining strength, leaving him to flicker on the edge of total darkness.

He barely felt Joe and Little Mike's hands on his back, pulling him out, and when he opened his eyes again, he found himself sitting on the steps, Joe and Little Mike stooping below, staring up at him, both their faces slack.

"Jesus, kid . . . ," Joe said, then seeing McGhee blink, laughed and laughed and laughed. McGhee smiled weakly. Little Mike retrieved a dirty towel from the shack and dropped it on his head, which he accepted languidly, then gradually, squeegeed the water from his hair.

"So . . . ," Joe said. "Pennsylvania's cold then?" he asked, which pushed Little Mike over the edge, and even he laughed.

Later that night, while McGhee cooked, the story of his baptism got told and retold, first by Joe, then Little Mike, then Joe again, as the others laughed, requesting parts be retold, even as short as the story was. Somewhere during the retelling, Joe took to calling him Frosty, which drove the laughter higher, Joe's tenor voice the highest and merriest of all. Big Mike stepped away to his private stash, returning with a couple shot glasses and a half-bottle of rum. "*Frosty*, get over here . . . ," Big Mike called over his shoulder. Big Mike slid a shot across the table from him, looking at Dave, who then shooed the other guys down to make a place for McGhee there. Little Mike grabbed some plastic cups, and Big Mike slid down small samples to the rest of them.

Big Mike raised his glass to McGhee: "To Frosty McGhee . . . ," he said, then paused, looking down the table, "the only one *stupid* enough to take Joe's challenge . . . ." The men cheered and laughed and even Dave patted him on the back.

McGhee drained his glass, the warmth sliding down to his gut, fanning out, displacing the cold that had settled there. The guys laughed, and McGhee did, too, finally a member of the company, telling stories like the rest of them, and it was good.

Kite Weather

66

0 ◄──────────────────────────────► 90

8AM
San Francisco, CA 7/12/2030
Missoula, MT

A wakening, it was less breaching the surface like a whale than a gradual emergence from the depths, like a turtle that one moment isn't there but the next is, that McGhee emerged from his nap, light and floating, bobbing at the edge of wakefulness, something inside finally rested and restored like it hadn't been for as long as he could remember. It was in this state that he awoke, smiling. It was six in evening and his nap had begun rather fitful and restless, but something in the course of it broke that fever, though it wasn't of body so much as mind, and he rose as if from the dead, awake.

The curtain still had light in it, and he swept it aside to look out at the street and down the hill toward the water. He could just see the edge of it, and out into the bay where he could see a small red light in the distant haze blinking sleepily. Tossing off the sheet around him, he threw his feet over the edge, anxious to get out and roam his city.

The air hit his face with a freshness he couldn't recall remembering, and it felt good. Even in July the San Francisco air never had much heat to it, but it filled him like a sail, and he was content to walk with it, buoyed by its goodness. He had his canvas satchel with his pad inside – he felt for it in those first steps to assure it was there – and he thought he might pull in for some coffee eventually when his feet tired, to do some writing. Perhaps his wellbeing came in part from the story he'd written the night before, and he thought of it as he walked, remembering the course of it. Usually he found the exercise difficult, each step unsure and halting, but this story hadn't been like that at all. It started with the image of a woman in a coffee shop and told itself from there, and he was anxious for each paragraph as it unfolded, telling him the story, too. So by the time he got to the end of it, he felt its sweet sorrow strongly, wiping tears from his eyes surreptitiously (for he was in public, writing at a neighborhood coffee shop as was his way), and when it was done he stared into it as the haze of it lifted from his mind, and he suspected he may have finally done it, got it on the page as it was meant to be. Yes, perhaps that was the beginning of his mood after all, and he laughed to himself to think of it. Stopping to lean against a parking meter, he pulled out the pad to make sure it was indeed there, and it was, and he spent the next twenty minutes reading the last ten pages of it, to see if it was as good as he thought, and when he finished and his eyes were wet again, he was pretty sure it was, and his breath came up short with something close to happiness and relief.

The next hour he walked, thinking of it, wondering how it happened as he wandered down streets, then back up again the next block over, then down again, thinking. It was a pleasant rumination, recalling how the bits had come together, stringing themselves like pearls in nice sequence on their own without the slightest intervention from him. That sensation of watching over it, floating, as it came out, easy and effortless, filled him again and again with a sense of light giddiness, like he was a little high, except the good part of it was the highness came from within, and he sighed again, satisfied.

It was seven or seven thirty, and he found himself far away from his place in a neighborhood two hills over or maybe three. He hadn't walked there before, but his feet had found it, or perhaps it was the wind that blew him this way, but he was content to have followed it. From his gut he got signals it was time to eat and his thoughts turned to food. It was a Friday evening, so he thought he should find something different, something special to go with his mood, but the territory wasn't familiar, so the usual stops were out, but that was for the best. As he became more aware of his hunger, he also became clearer that he hungered for something he couldn't identify, but that he must have it - otherwise the opportunity would be wasted on the ordinary. So this hunger became something like a mission, and he was content to walk as long as necessary until the right thing presented itself to fill that hole within.

It was a mixed residential and commercial neighborhood as that part of the city was, so as he clicked through the options in his head – Chinese, Indian, Italian, Greek – he continued walking, coming to a new street he wasn't sure he'd ever explored before. The edifice of a grocery wrapped around the corner, and as he turned it, he found himself on a tree lined block, pleasant with leaf rustle, as there was a breeze coming down the avenue to stop him in his tracks, just in case the shop, with its sign swinging lightly in the wind didn't do it on its own.

It was an eclectic sign, forged of tin and wood and paint, a strip of small black and white photographs crossing at an angle, a dog moving in a sequence toward someone, with a larger image of a woman smiling, windswept, across most of the sign. The shop name, *Proof Negative*, appeared in two parts – "Proof" in black block letters, stencil style, and "Negative," cut through the sign, absent. It was clever and well-designed, but that wasn't what caught his attention: the picture of the woman – that was *his* – he had taken it on a beach in France – Pylat Dune – more than twenty-five years before.

As he stood staring up at the sign, the door to the shop opened with bustling and commotion, the woman exiting carrying various bolts of fabric in a short basket, their centers of gravity spinning them toward tumbling out. Even if she had been paying attention, which she was not as she talked to someone back in the shop, the net effect was that their tumble caught her attention enough to divert what little she had left away from her continued launch into the street. The collision was complete and absolute, dead on with neither aware of their intersecting paths until they had fully intersected, bolts of cloth spilling out, unfurling down the sidewalk several yards worth. For her part, she had fully stepped from the step, committed to her expected landing, hitting McGhee with her full weight, throwing him almost flat out on his back, his fall only broken by his cloth satchel and an unfortunate wrist caught in the strap and pinned underneath him, secured by his weight, and that of the doubly surprised woman on his chest, exasperated then re-exasperated as she smiled at him.

"I'm gonna guess it was my fault . . . ," Kate said looking him in the eyes, first one eye, then the other.

"I played my part . . . ," McGhee responded, wincing as she adjusted her weight upon him to put her elbows on his chest. Behind

her, the shop emptied of its contents: one customer and two attendants in their aprons, rushing out to lend aid, but befuddled by the
sight of their leader, pinning a man to the sidewalk, evidently with
some comfort, sprawled atop him.

"Kate, you really nailed that guy . . . ," the young woman attendant said, reaching her first, offering a hand under her shoulder
to help raise her, though she seemed oddly content where she was.
Only when McGhee let out a little yelp did she run pale, throwing
her hands to her face, lending more weight to the situation and a
more insistent yelp from the pinned McGhee.

Regaining her senses, Kate slid off, leaning over McGhee,
staring into his eyes. "Sorry . . . ," she said, reaching under his
shoulder to lift him, but the effort brought forth an audible gasp
from McGhee as he passed out momentarily. The male attendant
from the store leaned in helping Kate clear McGhee without further damage, then looked to McGhee. He could tell through the
jacket something was wrong and looked up at the circle of women
around him.

"I think it's probably just dislocated . . . ," he said, forcing a
smile at Kate.

Kate looked at the customer who was watching, horrified.
"Oh, it's alright. I think. George is studying for his EMT exam,
right George?" she said, looking back to him, but he looked a little
pale, too.

McGhee was stirring and struggled up onto his right elbow,
his left arm hanging useless. George put his arm behind his back,
careful to avoid the bad shoulder, to help him sit up. He had landed near an open square on the edge of the sidewalk where an or-
namental tree grew up, thin but strong, and George helped him
slide over to it so he could lean against the trunk. Kate sent the
young woman inside to call for help. Kate was kneeling in front of

McGhee, alternating between contrition and awkward smiles, the others spread around the pair, watching. George handed his apron to the young woman who went back in to close the store and take care of the customer, remaining by his side until help arrived.

"So . . . ," Kate said, resting back on her haunches, kneeling. "What brings you by, Fran?"

George looked at her, surprised. "So, you know the victim, then?" he asked.

Kate laughed. "Oh, I know the *victim* all right . . . ," she said smiling at George and putting a hand on his shoulder. "This is *McGhee*," she said, tilting her head, nodding.

It took a few seconds to register, but as he looked at McGhee his expression changed and his eyes got big. "*The* McGhee?" he whispered, looking back at Kate. She nodded, tears forming in her eyes.

"You guys know I can hear you, right?" McGhee said, forcing a smile. As long as he didn't move it, his shoulder didn't hurt too badly.

"Oh, gees, sorry Mr. McGhee . . . ," George said. "Can I get you anything while we wait?"

McGhee winced, adjusting his position, but found one of more comfort and looked at George. "Just let me chat with Kate, OK?" George shuffled back and moved over to the steps to sit.

McGhee found that if he cradled his left elbow in his right hand, it relieved some of the pressure on the shoulder, improving the pain markedly. He looked into Kate's eyes, the sadness there with the tears, but saw something else, too, he couldn't quite put his finger upon, but he liked it. It had been a very long time since he had seen her. There were slight wrinkles at the edges of her eyes, but her eyes had the same gray color with green edges and life to them he remembered. Her smile – he recalled in that moment it was the benchmark smile of his life – her smile was the same, if a little wiser than it had been.

"You won't believe me," he said, still staring into her eyes, "but I just stumbled on your sign, right before . . . ,"

"Right before I stumbled into you . . . ," Kate said.

So they talked the whole time until the ambulance arrived, and she insisted she ride with him to St. Francis Memorial and wouldn't take *no* for an answer.

Kate covered her eyes when the doctor relocated McGhee's shoulder while he passed out again – the doctor thought it would be a good idea for Kate to distract him, and she certainly did. The nurse caught him before he could slump over and had a smelling salt ready to pull him right back to consciousness, which it did, his first word being, "Ow . . . ," upon being revived. Kate stared at him, still looking guilty, while the nurse and doctor wrapped his arm to his body to immobilize it with a very long ace bandage anchored with little toothed grommets to hold the wrap in place. His good arm went through his sleeve, but the other hung empty, his wing trussed up under the shirt to heal.

He smiled at her ironically, rubbing in her guilt. "You know, I won't be able to feed myself now – I hope you're happy . . . ."

"Have plans, did you?" Kate answered, playfully skootching forward in her chair, balancing on her arms to her sides.

"Big plans . . . ," he said, nodding.

"But I thought you were right-handed?" she pointed out, motioning with her chin to his bad shoulder on the left.

"That's my buttering hand you took out . . . ," he said, "and you know how I like my bread."

The doctor and nurse helped him stand from the exam table, but he was unsteady. "Whatever that shot was, it's working . . . now . . . ," McGhee said.

"You wanna wheel him out?" the nurse said to Kate, pulling a chair over to position for him. The doctor handed him a scrip, then helped him sit. "That'll be sore for a few days. And you'll need to take it easy with that arm the next month or so. You can take the wrap off Sunday."

Grabbing the doctor's sleeve, Kate leaned in. "I'll make sure he keeps in on 'til then . . . ," she said smiling.

Rolling back out through admitting McGhee leaned his head back, looking up at her. Her white blouse opened at the neck with a large collar, and she looked good to him in that moment, comfortable in her skin, and despite the circumstances, happy and in control. He was content to remain in her care, even reveling in it, though he thought it might have been the Demerol smoothing out the edges.

Parking him by the door, she went back to the admitting desk to ask the attendant to call for a taxi. McGhee wasn't watching, but he heard another man's voice there, deep and warm, and he offered to give a ride as he was heading that way, if they didn't mind sitting in the back of his patrol car. Walking over, she leaned over to tell McGhee the plan.

He looked up at her, then at the officer. He was older than the last time he'd seen him – his short hair was frosted where it had been brown before, and he had a bit more weight in his face, but had the same expression, and he was smiling at him.

"This is getting to be a habit with you McGhee, isn't it?" the officer said.

McGhee smiled back. Kate looked back and forth between the two men, confused. "This here is my oldest and most imaginary friend . . . ," McGhee said, "Officer Bill Kennedy." Still confused, she looked to the officer to explain.

"It's alright, ma'am . . . ," Officer Kennedy said. "He's not a perp, far as I know, anyway . . . ," he said chuckling. "McGhee here and I met about twenty years back, right here in fact. Turned out when he was a kid he had an imaginary friend with my name. Never forgot that."

For the second morning in a row, McGhee surfaced from sleep with a light floating, and though he didn't recognize his surroundings, he wasn't alarmed, for he recognized the perfume. It was light and floral, mixing with the glimmers of dawn to make him dream of waking on a farm, briefly fading in and out, such as he'd done once, he thought, when he was very young – it had that inchoate feel to it, barely observed but enjoyed. The bed he was on faced into a corner filled with windows around the edge, opened, the light sheers riding the breeze, tentatively illuminated by the rising sun.

Almost in silhouette, Kate sat beside him, her hand on his bare thigh stroking it lightly. She wore the same blouse as the evening before, though unbuttoned to the bottom, her sheer dark bra peeking out. Her knees were curled in with her feet tucked in behind her and under her slip, just the way she used to do back when they were young, McGhee thought. She'd lost none of her loveliness over the years, her natural way, though she was obviously older. Her hair, which had always been difficult to capture in words looked almost the same, though there was gray swirled through most of it. Like the rest of her it bespoke a graceful aging he liked, neither denying her age nor succumbing to it, a perfect reconciliation of acknowledgement and defiance.

McGhee cleared his throat to speak, but Kate leaned into him, kissing his lips silent. Her breath was warm on his, her lips soft and absent pressure in their light probing. Pulling back, she looked into his eyes, her body warmly pressed against his, a strand of hair escaping its place behind her ear to dangle in his eyes. Wriggling a bit, McGhee adjusted, looking back into her eyes, but she shook her head lightly. "Let me . . . ," she whispered, at once commanding and pleading.

His shirt had been removed since his last recollection and she kissed his chest with light caresses, sliding down further, her lips catching on his skin as she threw occasional playful glances toward him, slightly laughing as she titillated him, showing her pleasure, too, moving lower, slowly, making her ultimate destination deliciously inevitable. Pausing to look him in the eyes, she freed him slowly, taking her time. There was no hurry to it, and only the greatest care and longing. For McGhee, it wasn't even something he knew he needed, or had put into thought for as long as he could remember, but in her caress found it was that thing he longed for and had nearly forgotten, not the touch but the person touching, offering careful caresses, loving mindfulness and an extended expression of devotion.

Bound as he was and on his back, McGhee knew he must surrender for the moment was as perfect as the moment could be: the sheers were floating above him on the breeze, light sun gilding their edges where they floated; the barest city noises reaching in as a beautiful city awoke in a beautiful day, bay horns warning fog but far away and safe, and in the company of one he'd lost but found unexpectedly, their distance finally wiped away and forgotten in the greater sweep of time, so that one thing remained, their closeness and fondness, forgiveness and charity, mutual longing and regret, all sublime in that instant, disappearing like a mist rises all at once, gone, leaving them floating perfectly in the moment, no time before and none after to worry for, perfect and bursting, complete.

Just down the block and a few steps over they found a café and bustled in for breakfast, McGhee remembering he had missed his dinner, and with his appetites restored had a great desire for further sustenance. It was early enough to get a table by the window which slid open to offer breeze and a view of the passersby. Reaching across the table, Kate offered her hand and McGhee took it, no thinking required. It was warm and moist, and he leaned across to kiss her, catching the saltiness of her lips before she pulled back, demure and blushing.

"I need coffee . . . ," she said, looking down at her cup and saucer to stir the black fluid, steaming.

"No you don't . . . ," he said, rubbing her palm lightly with his thumb. Her fingers curled around his and she returned his gaze, smiling.

"What'r you gonna have?" she asked, retracting her hand to open the menu.

"Everything . . . ," he said, opening the menu himself, then closing it again, leaning back to relax. He suddenly became aware of his shoulder again, wincing slightly as he adjusted. Reaching into his right pocket, he found a pill case there and pulled it out, looking at her. "You think of everything . . . ," he said, struggling to open it with one hand.

Reaching over, Kate opened the bottle and took out a capsule. "You were pretty out of it last night . . . ," she said, moving his glass of water over where he could grab it with his right hand.

"Did we really ride in a cop car last night?" he asked before swallowing the medicine with a gulp of water.

"With your imaginary friend?" Kate asked, laughing. "Yes, we did. Very nice man, that Bill Kennedy. He told me the whole story, too."

"What a weird night that was . . . ," McGhee said, shaking his head. "It's like the whole thing was a dream . . . ."

Leaning over, Kate looked into his eyes. "A good one, I hope," she said, grabbing his hand again.

McGhee smiled. "Perfect . . . ," he said. Squeezing his hand, she let it go again.

"So tell me . . . ," she said, taking a bite of the buttered toast that had arrived. "Where have you been all this time?" she asked, through her chewing.

McGhee shrugged. "Waiting . . . ," he said, his eyes on her to see her response. Smiling, she covered her mouth.

"Not for me, I hope . . . ," she said, then laughing, "pining . . . ."

McGhee laughed. "Not exactly . . . ," he said, toasting her with his coffee.

"Perhaps a little?" she said, holding up two fingers to peer through the gap, smiling.

"You're more playful than I remember . . . ," McGhee said. "It's nice to see."

Shaking her head, Kate wiped her mouth with her napkin. "I got tired of having a stick up my ass . . . sweetheart," she said, slightly exasperated. "I woke up one day and realized I was missing the point."

"Sweetheart?" McGhee asked, his smile curled in the corner of his lip.

"Too corny?" she asked, leaning in, her elbows on the table, her blouse billowing open two buttons down.

"As long as I'm the only one . . . ," he said, motioning with his chin toward the opening. Looking down, she noticed the reveal, but just looked back at him.

"Oh, you're definitely a finalist . . . ," she said, smiling coyly back at him, content.

"Like a sweepstakes then?" McGhee said, grabbing his own toast for a bite, but she only smiled, sipping at her cup.

"So what's this 'the McGhee' I heard that guy mention last night . . . ?" McGhee said, scratching his head.

"George? He's such a blabbermouth . . . ," she said, shaking her head and putting her hand to her forehead, finally looking back at him. "Well . . . ," she said, haltingly, "there's something of a . . . shrine . . . back in the shop."

"A *shrine*?" McGhee said. "I have a *shrine*?"

"No, I have it, a little thing . . . you know, some pictures and whatnot. A little thing," Kate said, blushing. "It's not like a *big* thing. It's a little thing."

"A *shrine*?" McGhee persisted, but his delight was evident, despite his attempt to conceal it. Kate took to handling the salt shaker, spinning it slowly on the table.

"The only pictures . . . ," she began, "of me, that I permit in the store, at all, are ones you took . . . ."

"I noticed the one on the sign. I think that caused our crash . . . ," McGhee said. "I was shocked to see it, waving there at me."

"Yeah . . . ," she said, still spinning the shaker. "That's one of them. There are others. Remember, you grabbed my camera? No one ever got me . . . not like you did. And those pictures . . . ," she said cocking her head, "that's the *me* I like to remember."

"We wasted a lot of time . . . ," McGhee said, his smile pressed and thin. "Why did we do that?"

Kate shrugged. "Life got in the way, I guess . . . Or me," she said, sadness in the corners of her eyes. "I'm sorry."

Though it was difficult, McGhee leaned over the table, reaching behind her head to pull her in gently for a kiss, tender and slow, releasing only when it was finished. Settling back into his seat, he looked at her.

"One should never apologize for one's youth . . . ," he said, "and that's what it was. Mine, too. I really think it was me, anyway."

Kate wiped her eyes, which had become moist, and recomposed herself. "So what should we do today?" she asked, smiling, open and raw, then barely and almost in a whisper, "and tomorrow?"

McGhee smiled. "Let me show you . . . ," he said, extending his hand across to her.

It was light but not yet sunrise as they crossed into Montana from Idaho, following I-90's winding way toward Missoula. It was cool, but Kate had the window down anyway, though she pulled her collar closed on her jacket and held it there with her hand. Coming around a bend, the shorter foothills gave way to a broad vista to the east where they could see the horizon, and McGhee pulled into a pullout, drifting to a stop. "Let's look at the map," he said stepping out.

Spreading the map on the hood, he traced their path, thinking. "We should make it to Missoula in another hour or so . . . ," he said absently, but Kate wasn't paying attention.

Tugging on his sleeve, she turned him around to face east and the mountains where the gold of the sunrise was just cresting the ridge. "Stop talking and just look . . . ," she said, wrapping her arm around his shoulder.

The sky was big and clear and cloudless, deep blue down to the ridge where the sun was pushing it back. Tall, dark pines thrust their way up into the sky, junipers and spruce scenting the air, a stream down below plowed white over boulders, rushing and frothing, carving into the pristine landscape. And as the highway noise subsided, and only breeze in the pines was audible, they looked into the sunrise, wordless and floating in a present without worry.

Signal and Noise

It was hot for May in Butler – almost ninety – and the air conditioner in the Volaré was having trouble keeping up with the heat. Luckily, McGhee was able to park on the shady side of Main Street as he waited for his father to come out of the store where he worked and avoid the beating sunshine. The real problem was the moisture in the air anyway which was oppressive and thick. But his thoughts were elsewhere as he worked on his graduation speech – he'd be on stage with the other students in a week, but would go last – and he wanted his speech to have some significance to it, an anchor that would make it memorable. That said, the thought of actually delivering it to a crowd of parents in the stands at the football stadium made his stomach wrench uncomfortably.

Retrieving his father from town had been a chore for as long as he could remember – his mother had done it before any of them could drive, then his brothers, Les then Wil – picking up Mr. McGhee from downtown after work. They only had one car, so if there were errands to run during the day, he'd be dropped off and picked up so Mrs. McGhee could run them. Still, McGhee didn't mind, for since he could drive, he'd find any excuse to get out and do it. In fact, once he'd had a taste of it, he didn't know how he could tolerate being stuck at home before, remembering his childish self and shaking his head. Such were his thoughts and growing restlessness.

Mr. McGhee slipped into the passenger side and looked at his son. "Let's go . . . ," he said, clicking in his seat belt, then tossing his arm over the bench of the front seat, looking at his son again. "Still working on the speech?"

McGhee nodded his head, sliding into traffic, but didn't answer otherwise.

"Still stuck then?" Mr. McGhee said, reaching to adjust the vent to blast at him more directly. "Sure is a hot one. Seems like it was just winter . . . ," he said, leaning into the vent for relief.

Tilting his head, McGhee held onto the wheel with both hands. "I'm thinking of using a quotation in it – maybe something from Hemingway or maybe even Faulkner – and you think it's OK I talk about science in the speech? I mean, how they teach it?" he asked, looking over at his father.

Mr. McGhee laughed lightly, mopping some sweat from his brow using a handkerchief from his breast pocket that he always carried, folding it and replacing it in his pocket again. "I can *guarantee* you'll be the only one to do it . . . ," Mr. McGhee said, but he could instantly see his tone was lost on his son. "If you think it needs to be said . . . ," he continued, "then say it. Just make it constructive."

McGhee's grip on the wheel tightened at the thought of delivering the speech, and he shook his head. "I don't like to think about that part. About standing up there . . . talking. . . out loud."

Mr. McGhee put his hand on his son's shoulder. "You'll do fine."

McGhee shook his head again. "I'm not sure *fine* is good enough . . . ," he said. "Mr. Woods will like it, but it's likely to piss Porky off...."

"Jesus . . . who ever gave him that nickname?" Mr. McGhee said, shaking his head. "I bet it was Wil."

"Fits though . . . ," McGhee said, looking over to his father, then back to the road. "Red curly hair. And something about his face. Kinda flat . . . puffy and pink, and that nose. You've seen him, right?"

"All right, all right . . . ," Mr. McGhee said, raising his hand. "Just make sure you're not *trying* to make him mad . . . ," Mr. McGhee said, then after a pause, "You're not, are you?"

McGhee shook his head, but his words weren't entirely convincing. "I don't *think* so . . . ," he said, looking over at his dad.

"How about you show me the speech when we get home then. You got it written down, right?"

"Mostly . . . ," McGhee said. "Yeah . . . that might be good."

"I'll be your sounding board – just in case. That way, by the time you give it, it won't be a big deal."

McGhee looked back and forth between the road and his father hoping he was right, but fearing that moment nonetheless.

It was cold even by December standards when McGhee and Troy got to Russ's house, running a few degrees below zero. Walking up to the door the snow squeaked beneath their tennis shoes like Styrofoam, and the insides of their noses froze with each inhalation, thawing again as they exhaled in plumes of steamy exhaust, instantly absorbed by the heatless air.

Mrs. Russo met them at the door and invited them in, but Russ bustled out, pushing both of his friends with him.

"Mom. Mom . . . it's OK. They've eaten. We gotta go . . . ," he said, leaning over to kiss her on top of the head.

Letting the door swing shut she put her palms on the window, looking out. "But it's so cold . . . ," she called after them, looking forlorn behind the storm door which was already fogging from the moist air inside.

Russ climbed in the back seat, immediately leaning over to release gas, contorting his face in the process, though it was soundless.

"Couldn't you do that outside?" Troy said, leaning over the bench of the Volaré, then recoiled, covering his nose. "Oh gees . . . ," Troy said through his shirt, "what the *fuck* did you eat?"

"Christmas turkey . . . ," Russ said, proud of himself.

"Again?" McGhee said, looking into the mirror to see him. "That's three days running . . . ."

"It was a big turkey . . . twenty-five pounder," Russ said, smiling. "Hey, you figure they eat turkey in Turkey?" he said.

"Only you would think of something so stupid . . . ," Troy said, laughing. "That's rank, man. Totally rank."

"So where to, gents?" McGhee asked, turning out of the housing development onto the main road.

"Just drive, man . . . ," Troy said, leaning back. "We can get some chew later at *7-Eleven*."

"Yeah, and I wanna burrito . . . ," Russ said, leaning up against the bench.

"No . . . ," McGhee and Troy said in unison.

"Why not?" Russ whined, "And by the way, you won't be needing any fuel. I'm gassing up the car now," he said, leaning over to release more foulness from his angry bowels.

McGhee was pulling onto New Castle hill and gunned the engine for the climb.

"Arctic blast, then . . . ," he said, looking over at Troy. Both cranked down their windows as fast as they could, purging the car of the fumes, sending a torrent of icy wind through the car, flooding the back seat with a heat-sucking wave that left Russ gasping. Rolling them back up, McGhee and Troy were laughing while Russ rubbed his cheeks to regain some heat.

"There will be no more farting in my dad's car . . . ," McGhee pronounced.

The class was settling at the lab tables when Mr. Swinson came in, carrying an armload of books and materials, pausing to survey the student humanity before plopping his load on the long demo bench that was his lecture area at the front of the room. He scratched his curly hair, rubbed his nose and adjusted his glasses before planting his fists on his sides at his waist. He wore a white JC Penny's short-sleeved shirt with a light plaid print that made him look vaguely topological, three pens clipped in his pocket. His brown polyester pants didn't quite make it down to his dark socks and Buster Brown shoes, but he adjusted the belt at his side to hitch them up anyway. Standing especially erect, he waited for the students to get quiet, his rigid pose calling to mind a stalky fireplug, with just a hint of belligerence to his expression to encourage their immediate compliance. Scanning those assembled, he stopped at McGhee and shook his head.

"Nice to see you dressed for the occasion, Mr. McGhee," he said, staring at him.

"*What?*" McGhee said, defensively, then moderated his tone. "How so?" he asked, more conciliatory, but the original tone lingered, and the rest of the students grew quiet immediately.

"*That* . . . ," Mr. Swinson said, motioning at McGhee, then realizing he wasn't being clear, added, "That *shirt* . . . ."

"What's wrong with my shirt?" McGhee said looking down at it. It was an ancient flannel, threadbare and ripped in a few places, his favorite, and he saw no problem with it. He had to be careful putting it on to prevent ripping it further. It had been one of Wil's shirts from college ten years before, so he liked wearing it as it reminded him of his brother.

"It's barely hanging on you, that's what . . . ," Mr. Swinson said, shaking his head. Sliding the stack of material five feet across his desk to the middle, he came to a rest, leaning on his arms, puffing up his cheeks, pausing.

"This is *not* my favorite unit to teach . . . because, frankly, you don't have the *math* for it, and I don't have the time to teach it to you, but this is *AP Physics*, and we're gonna try to discuss signal processing without any calculus."

"That sounds like a bad idea . . . ," McGhee said, and the class grew even quieter.

"*McGhee* . . . ," Mr. Swinson said, lowering his head, "can we *just* get *through* it?"

"I was *agreeing* with you . . . ," McGhee said, leaning forward on his elbows.

"*McGhee* . . . ," Mr. Swinson said, and looked at him. "Not again . . . ."

McGhee drove as Troy fiddled with the radio, leaning back when he'd tuned in a Rush song – *Tom Sawyer* – then leaned back in to crank the volume, singing the lyrics and drumming on the dashboard. Russ shared his enthusiasm, drumming on the back on the bench. Troy switched to air guitar and bass and keyboards as needed, though Russ continued drumming at the air, content to take the Neil Peart part. The music wasn't to McGhee's taste, but he enjoyed their passion for it even as he strove to contain it, which appeared to be his role for the moment.

Reaching for the radio knob, McGhee paused. "Perhaps I can find something *decent?*" he said, but Troy batted his hand away, in time to the music.

"Bite your tongue . . . ," Troy sang, shaking his head.

"Yeah . . . ," said Russ, still drumming.

West of town they passed through a small village named Meridian and McGhee cut off the main highway onto a road wending into the trees. There was a way to cut through to Route 8 and south toward Pittsburgh, but he could never remember which road did it. Troy was nodding, for he knew the impulse – they'd done it before – and they both enjoyed the discovery of it. Neither would take the time to find a map and see which road it was; they agreed that wasn't the point of cruising, which they'd discussed at great length. It was a worthy goal to discover that passage, even though they'd found it before, by chance, and it was the impulse to explore they were after. Sometimes it even seemed they forgot willfully so they'd have the pleasure of discovery all over again, but Russ wasn't quite following the flow of the moment.

"Oh . . . if you want to get to Route-8 . . . ," Russ began, leaning into the bench, "you need to . . . ," but Troy cut him off.

"Na na na na . . . ," Troy said, looking over at him. "We're not here to follow directions. We get enough-a that . . . ."

"*Two roads diverged in a yellow wood, And sorry I could not travel both, And be one traveler, long I stood . . .*," McGhee said, looking at Troy, then at Russ in the mirror, but neither reacted. "Cavemen, the lot-a-ya . . . ." he continued, his voice trailing off.

"But I know the way . . . ," Russ said, objecting. "My dad-n-I went down November when Buck opened . . . ."

"Tut tut . . . ," Troy said, raising a finger in his face. "And besides, that's such a *caveman* thing to do . . . ," Troy said, nodding to McGhee. "The only civilized hunting is done with a pole and bait . . . ."

McGhee looked into the mirror. "Unless you're gonna tackle it and use a club, where's the *fairness* in it?"

"Naa . . . ," Russ said, shaking his head. "You guys don't get it. The challenge of stalking your quarry. Walking through the woods at first light with your dad, fanning out to track them, sneaking up until you can get yer shot. It's pretty awesome . . . ."

"Right . . . with a scope at five hundred yards," Troy said.

"That'd be a hell of a shot . . . ," Russ said, laughing. "Two hundred maybe."

"Which circle of hell is this?" McGhee said, but they were used to ignoring such outbursts.

"Don't be *dense* . . . ," Troy said, smacking Russ with his cap, then putting it back on his head. "Hey, that looks familiar . . . ," he said suddenly pointing at a branch in the road.

"That's not fair . . . ," Russ whined again from the back. "Why does he get to tell . . . ?"

"Coz I don't actually remember . . . I'm using the *Force*," Troy said but didn't turn to look at him.

"Right. The *Force* . . . ," Russ said. "More likely the *bull-a-shit...*," he went on, laughing, looking back and forth between them.

"The *Force* is *weak* with this one . . . ," McGhee said to Troy, motioning with his head toward Russ.

"That's right, the *Force* . . . ," Troy said, nodding.

"Whatever . . . ," Russ said, leaning back and putting his hands behind his head. "You missed the turn five minutes ago anyway . . . ," he said, smiling broadly.

"Fuck . . . I'm callin' it . . . ," Troy said, looking over to McGhee. "Let's go to *7-Eleven*."

McGhee nodded, shrugging. "I hate to admit it, but Russ was right . . . he's like a farting harpy back there . . . ," he said, smiling as he glanced over the bench to the backseat.

"What was that?" Russ said, leaning up to the bench again. "I didn't quite hear that?"

"He called you an asshole . . . ," Troy said, laughing, but it didn't bother Russ.

"I don't know what you guys see in driving around lost all the time . . . ," Russ pronounced, putting his hands behind his head again. "Give me a map any day . . . ."

"Being lost *is the point*, doofus . . . ," Troy said, laughing. "That's what makes it fun. Being lost together with your buddies."

"Hey, didn't you say Kovach would be around tonight?" Russ interjected, ignoring the sentiment.

Mr. Swinson pushed up his glasses again, staring at McGhee. "All right," he said. "Let's have it."

McGhee leaned back in his chair. "Like I said, I was just agreeing with you. We should do the math. Otherwise, we'll miss the point, right?"

Mr. Swinson lowered his head again, then raised it. "It's OK for *me* to say that . . . ," Mr. Swinson said. *"I'm* the *teacher.* Ostensibly, *you're* the *student,"* he said smiling sweetly.

McGhee shook his head. "What's wrong with *agreeing* with you?"

Standing upright, Mr. Swinson crossed his arms, staring at the young man.

"Because I actually *know,* that's why," Mr. Swinson said, holding his pose a moment as if the discussion were over, then after a pause reached for the book to open it to the right place, mumbling as he flipped pages.

"Actually . . . ," McGhee said, pausing, "I *kinda* know, too . . . ," he said, opening the text to a bookmark he had at the chapter.

"And how is that, *exactly* . . . ," Mr. Swinson said, pointing at him with a thumb before crossing his arms and leaning back against the green blackboard, yellow chalk dust in the tray rising in a light puff. His pose was calculated to appear casual and confident, but looked stiff.

McGhee raised his palms in surrender. "Sorry, Mr. Swinson. As for the material, I read the chapter last night. It has calculus references all over the place – way past what we're doing in Camissa's class," he said waving down the hall.

"You actually *read* it?" Mr. Swinson said, squinting at him. *"Francis McGhee* actually *read* something?"

McGhee shrugged. "Well, yeah. It looked neat. And I liked the philosophical implications. Very cool."

"It looked *neat* . . . ," Mr. Swinson said, "and *cool.* And you liked the *philosophy* of it . . . ." Turning back to the text, he paged further through the book, but abandoned it again. "How could you tell that, *exactly,* without the math?"

"They explained most of it in the text, and I looked over the equations. Those were pretty tough, but I think I got most of it . . . ," McGhee answered, careful to keep his tone in check. He had become skilled in reading the body language of his teacher over the semester, not that it required great observational ability, but he didn't want to push him over the edge. It had become something of a contest that emerged now and then, a game which Mr. Swinson was all too willing to play.

Mr. Swinson smiled thinly. "So, maybe *you* wanna teach the class, then?" he asked, tilting his head.

"You really want me to try?" McGhee asked, pushing his chair back. "I'm not sure I got it *that* well, but . . . ."

"Sit," Mr. Swinson commanded, pointing with his thumb again.

It was a warm Saturday night in May, but McGhee couldn't sleep. Despite the oscillating fan, the heat was building, giving the sheets a film of sweat as he moved to get cool, but couldn't. Out the window, behind the motionless sheer, he could hear the trucks groan out on 422 climbing the hill, heading west, beyond Ohio, perhaps, where his thoughts would usually wander. It wouldn't be long, he thought, before he could find out where they were going, see it for himself. But despite that distraction, his mind drifted elsewhere, and he threw his feet over the edge and onto the cool wood of the floor. Feeling for his shorts in the dark, he pulled them on and stood to stretch.

In the kitchen he filled a bowl with cereal, the little boluses of corn ringing as they fell. Crunching on the hard cereal he looked at the clock – 2:00 a.m. – it was about time, so he gulped the milk from the bowl and rinsed it quietly in the sink before stacking it on the dish towel. Usually he'd be doing this for a meteor shower or an eclipse, but this was something even rarer he wanted to see.

Outside, the air had a heavy moisture in it but it was cooler in the open, stirring very slightly, crickets scratching their itches slowly as they slept unseen in the dewy bushes. Grabbing his bike – he didn't want to alarm his parents by taking the car at that hour – he checked the tires and brakes and it was ready. It had been a while since he had ridden it, and the act of throwing his leg over the bar reminded him it had been his transportation until just a year before. Rolling down the driveway, the breeze was cooler and welcome, the muscles of his legs becoming accustomed to propelling him forward as they had used to do. Now that he was old enough to drive, he felt a little self-conscious on the bike, like it was a vestige of his self that he was leaving behind. It was fitting, though, for his mission.

At the corner where Westwood Manor dumped into Duffy Road, it was quiet. Under the street light he looked over his shoulder at the Sanderson's house, but all was quiet there, too. Mr. Sanderson wasn't up yet, if he was working, so there was no one to see him as he veered onto Duffy, out of the cone of light and into the darkness of Duffy hill, gaining speed as he plunged faster.

The air hovered at the edge of fogginess, picking up some of the half-moon-light, allowing him to see just well enough to avoid obstacles – his bike had no light – so as he glided out of the well into the upswing he sighed. Maybe it wasn't a good idea to bike at that hour, but the most perilous part was past, and his legs were warming to their task as he pumped up the next hill.

Some words of Frost rang in his head as he plunged through the darkness:

I shall be telling this with a sigh
Somewhere ages and ages hence

He liked the sense of it, the loneliness of his adventure, and felt it was good.

Stopping at the top, McGhee turned around to look – still no cars. Off to the west, over the little valley, he could see his neighborhood, sleepily nestled against the slight incline on the other side. It wouldn't *be his green valley* much longer, he thought, and the notion filled him with a sweet but sad sentiment as he could feel the passage of time in that instant. Leaning forward, he pushed on, over the hill, cutting through the neighborhood to avoid the big traffic light near Montgomery Ward.

It was late May as McGhee waited behind the little hill near the field, waiting for the instant of his entrance, his shirt covered in yellow feathers. The feeling of the moment swelled in his chest as he felt the hero – Achilles destined to slay his foe – and he loved it. It was all part of his plan to psych-out his friend Hector, the unofficial captain of the other intramural soccer team.

Their teams had been on a collision course all season, and the last meeting had been a disaster for McGhee and his cohort – a 7-1 blowout. He and his buddies from the official soccer team had split up for intramurals. The idea was to spread the real players among the other kids to make the games fairer, and it had mostly worked, except Hector's team, the *Trojans*, somehow managed to have three or four, enough to tilt the scales heavily in their favor. In contrast, McGhee's team, *The Simians*, only had one, and further, most of the team were just buddies from Highfield, names ending in *sky* or *ich* or *nik*, who were in it for the fun of it, for whom it was just another round ball, an alternative to hanging out at the Hall playing hacky sack on the dusty edge of the baseball field. So going into the championship, which by some miracle they'd managed to reach, they needed an edge.

Hector had been gloating at the table in the morning for the last week. How bad they were going to beat them. How *The Simians* didn't stand a chance. How it was going to be almost "anti-climactic" – Hector's word – so maybe they should hold back to make it close.

Hector was nodding, looking at McGhee knowingly. "You're the only shot they got, McGhee," he said, tracing with his finger on the table. "And I'm just afraid you're not enough."

The suit he wore for *Awards Night* was tight in the shoulders – it was cheap and he knew it, but that was OK as it was what they could afford. Spread as far as he could see, back into the depths of the dim room, ninety round tables seating ten each dotted his view, thick white table cloths draped over the edges, blue and gold napkins folded at each place setting, exuding a little too much school spirit for his taste. Above the podium in front, a blue banner announced *Golden Tornadoes, Class of '82* in yellow block letters, not quite the same shade of gold as the napkins, the sight of the mascot causing McGhee to wonder how he'd explain it to future colleagues.

In an effort to be efficient, seating was alphabetic, so he didn't know anyone at his table, but luckily one row back and one over had Troy. With a little switching, to the annoyance of the kid sitting there, McGhee was able to adjust his seat to be closer to the other table. Troy did the same, so they were able to chat, if only occasionally, because it was still ten feet between them. And when McGhee did turn to sit properly at the table, he found his tablemates looking at him, mumbling congratulations. One kid sitting next to him – Mike – he recognized from gym class freshman year, but they'd never had any other classes together. He wore a flannel shirt under a tan corduroy jacket and jeans – the only one not in a suit, and fidgeted self-consciously. He stuck out his hand to McGhee, to reintroduce himself.

"I don't know if you remember me – we had gym together . . . ," he said, shaking McGhee's hand. "Congratulations . . . I had no idea I was playing dodge ball with a celebrity . . . ," he said smiling slightly. McGhee could sense he was uncomfortable in the presence of so many people, and it invoked his protective instinct.

"Sure, Mike. I remember. And I'm hardly a celebrity . . . ," McGhee said.

Mike held onto his hand and leaned over. "I was the one who pulled Bruce off of you in the locker-room," he said, leaning back. "He was such an a-hole . . . ."

It had been the sole fight of his high school career, when he walked around the corner and got sucker-punched by Bruce Rohonic over a grievance on the basketball court. "Well then, I guess thanks is long overdue . . . ," McGhee said, shaking his hand again.

Just then, someone tapped him on the shoulder. His history teacher, Mr. Schmidt, was leaning down to say something. "I'm glad it's you . . . ," he whispered rather cryptically, patting McGhee on the shoulder.

McGhee hurried through two plates of food, slightly offset since his speech lay there awaiting his attention. It was dog eared and bent with effort, written longhand on notebook paper, with plenty of corrections, arrows and cross-outs. Looking over at his dad, McGhee frowned. "I'm not sure how you're gonna read this . . . ," he said, shaking his head, holding it up for inspection.

Mr. McGhee laughed. "Don't worry . . . *I'm not* . . . . *You* are," he said, wiping his mouth, pushing his plate back half finished. It was Mrs. McGhee's meatloaf, but there was only so much ketchup could do to rescue it, though he never complained.

"Gees . . . ," McGhee said, laying it flat, lowering his head to rub his neck.

"Fine . . . ," Mr. McGhee said, relenting, extending his hand over. McGhee handed it to him and started to explain how to read it, but Mr. McGhee raised his hand to stop him. "I'll figure it out . . . ."

McGhee couldn't wait for him to finish and interjected. "Mr. Woods said good speeches are personal but put things in historical perspective. I was thinking maybe Conrad, or Kafka. Maybe Melville. Something about the whale . . . ."

Mr. McGhee looked up, foggy. "What? I thought you said Hemingway, or . . . that other guy?"

McGhee shook his head. "That was last week. Besides, I want more punch than that . . . ."

"More punch than *Hemingway?*" Mrs. McGhee chimed in, skeptical. She was clearing the dishes but monitoring the process. Striking a pose, her voice rang out: "For whom the bell tolls, it tolls for thee . . . ," she said, ending with a flourish of her fist.

"Jesus, Mom, that's John Donne. Hemingway just stole the title . . . ," McGhee corrected her. She leaned in: "Language . . . ," she said, pointing at him with a bony finger, but smiled. "I *knew* that . . . ."

Mr. McGhee kept scanning, his finger jumping occasionally to follow arrows, his head tilting to assemble the sentences, nodding slightly, until his finger stopped at the end of a paragraph. "*Man* . . . ," he said. "That's some *strong language* you got there. You sure you want to say that?"

McGhee leaned over to see where he was, then plopped back into his seat. "What?" he said.

"Maybe you don't want to burn *all* your bridges . . . in one speech, I mean," Mr. McGhee said, chuckling. "You sound a little . . . *bitter.*"

Mrs. McGhee leaned in to see, brushing Mr. McGhee's hand aside three times, until he noticed her expression, and leaned back. Scanning the paragraph, she mumbled as she read, following the arrows, but more easily followed the flow than her husband. Looking at her son, she frowned. "Oh honey . . . ," she said, looking at him. "You'd better sleep on that one . . . ," she said, retreating to the sink.

"Jesus . . . ," McGhee said, throwing his hands behind his head, pulling his elbows forward. "Maybe I should just shit-can the whole *thing.*"

Mr. McGhee looked at his wife, and they looked at McGhee, stifling their smiles. "Language . . . ," they said in unison.

Mr. Swinson walked slowly around the corner of his desk, strolling back to the middle, leaning against it to cross his arms again. The students knew the gesture – they'd seen it before – and closed their notebooks. It had been a confrontation months in the making and they settled in to watch.

"You know . . . I've been teaching physics a long time. A *long* time," he began, "and I've seen some really *good* students. Back in Wil's time," he continued, nodding toward McGhee. "That was

McGhee's brother," he said to the rest of the class. "There was a guy named Gunter – exchange student from Germany. And a kid from Japan, Tamatsu, and a girl named Patty. *Man*, they were *sharp*. Really *sharp*. Wil, too," he said, nodding some more. "They were the best physics students I ever had. And I guess I'd have to put you in that group, too, McGhee," he said, looking over at him. "But I worry about *you* . . . ," he said. "*You're* the one I *worry* about. It's funny this should come up when we're talking about signal processing. I mean, really, there couldn't be a more perfect time for it. In the end, it's all about *signals*, isn't it?"

McGhee shifted uncomfortably in his seat, crossing his legs. "I guess so . . . ?" McGhee said, unsure where it was going.

Mr. Swinson laughed, looking at him and pushed his glasses up his nose. "I don't know if you're playing *dumb*, or you don't know," he said, "but I'll play along." He began pacing back and forth in front of his desk, constructing his argument. "Well, from where I stand, here's what I see . . . . You're about eighteen now, I'd guess. You sure act like it. And you're in your senior year. It's all come pretty easy for you I think . . . ."

"I work pretty hard . . . ," McGhee said, shifting again.

"Yeah, sure, yeah – I'm sure you do. I'm sure you do. But when it comes down to it, it's all been pretty easy to understand for you, right? I mean, all that extra effort, it's been to work the system. Make sure you count your points and hit ninety percent, right?"

"That's part of it . . . ," McGhee admitted, wary.

"Right. Keeping teachers happy. Laughing at their jokes. Pretending you care about their *little hobbies*," he said, raising his fingers to wiggle them. "It's all part of it. But at the core of it, the subjects weren't so hard for you, *right*?"

"There were some challenges," McGhee answered, "but yeah, it was mostly just a matter of reading the material and keeping up."

"*Right*," Mr. Swinson said, nodding. "No *real* struggle. No *real* challenges, right? And you've spent your entire life in Butler, right?"

McGhee shrugged but didn't answer.

"*Right*. So you're this fish swimming in this pond, with your fellow classmates. And you're the big fish. There aren't any bigger fish, right? I mean, you *are* the valedictorian in your class, right?"

McGhee shrugged again.

"*Right*. So as far as you know, you're the *biggest fish in the world*. Isn't that right?"

"I wouldn't say that . . . ," McGhee answered, crossing his arms.

"Right. You wouldn't *say* it. You're too smart to say that *out loud*, but you can't help but think it. I can see it. It's on your face. All the time. Every minute I look at you. And as far as you know, that might be the case. And you're proud of that. Very proud. Only I wonder what happens when you find out otherwise . . . . All the *signals* you're getting," he said, pausing to accentuate the word, "suggest that might be the case. Am I *right*? Captain of your soccer team. Awards. Even some of the other students look at you like you're some kinda *hero* . . . ."

"I don't . . . ," Hector said from the back row, to a course of laughter from the other students.

"Stifle!" Mr. Swinson threw to the back of the room, then continued his gaze at McGhee. The other students laughed, Hector squirming in his place, McGhee pinned for dissection.

The car was packed, waiting in the garage for the McGhee's departure the next morning. New Haven would be a ten-hour drive, but he tried not to think about it. An informal going away party was brewing at the house – Russ and Troy were already there looking hungry, and Mrs. McGhee was moving with speed in the kitchen to rustle some sandwiches to buy her time. McGhee heard the can opener whirring in the distance, so he guessed it'd be *Manwiches* again, her go-to dish in a pinch. It was already almost eight o'clock as the day had been absorbed with last-minute packing and trips to the store for various bits, *just in case.*

Russ was offering commentary as usual, and Troy countered, but McGhee was having trouble focusing on the flow. When the phone rang it presented something immediate to do and he made it there before his father, who was lost watching his wife prepare food, helpless.

"Hello, this is the McGhee's."

"Hey . . . ," was the response. It was a small sample of voice to go on.

"Hey . . . ," McGhee responded, but there wasn't any further response for a moment.

"I want to see you . . . ," the voice said, and after a moment McGhee knew it was Wanda. She sounded a little drunk and agitated. "Can I come over?"

McGhee thought a moment. It wasn't the right time for one of those conversations. "Actually, it's not such a great time. I'm leaving tomorrow and there are some people over . . . ," he said coolly. Reconsidering his tone, he added, "Sorry . . . ."

"I *really* need to see you . . . it won't take long," Wanda said, persisting.

"Gees . . . I *really* can't spend much time. I'm kinda hosting the party . . . ."

"*Party?*" Wanda said, her agitation mixing with hurt. "I'll be there in five minutes."

"Wait . . . ," McGhee said, "Where are you calling from?"

"*Wards*," Wanda said, then disconnected.

McGhee hung up the phone but left his hand on the receiver.

"Who was that?" Mr. McGhee asked, moving over. He was rubbing his hands in a dishtowel, even though he hadn't been doing anything.

McGhee looked at him, frowning slightly. "Wanda . . . ," he said. "She sounded a little . . . ."

"Inebriated?" Mr. McGhee said, smiling slightly.

"Maybe . . . ," McGhee said. "How did you know?"

"I could hear her shouting from over there . . . ," he said, motioning with his head.

"She's coming over . . . ," McGhee said. "She was very persistent."

Mr. McGhee laughed, patting his son on the shoulder. "Good luck with that . . . ," he said, turning back to look at his wife, who was asking him to get buns out of the refrigerator.

Back with Troy and Russ he remained lost in thought. Russ was expounding on what's wrong with America, but Troy wasn't listening any longer.

"Was that *Wanda?*" he whispered, leaning over. McGhee nodded.

"*What?* – nice timing . . . ," he said, laughing. "What'd *she* want?" He'd heard the whole story, at least the last few chapters, culminating with the breakup just before prom, which had seemed like the end of it.

"She's coming over . . . ," McGhee said, head lowered.

"*Jesus* . . . ," Troy said.

Mike smacked McGhee on the shoulder. "Hey, she's talking to you . . . ," he said, motioning to the stage. McGhee looked at the podium to see his friend Kathe, laughing, pulling something out of a cooler, dripping.

"This . . . ," she said, careful to keep the mess over the cooler, "was supposed to be frozen." She held it up for everyone to see, but no one got the joke. She read the packaging: "THIS," she said, "is an *Eskimo Pie*." She showed it to the right of the room, then the center, then the left, where McGhee sat. "You'll notice it has *vanilla* ice cream – that's what I'm dripping all over myself . . . ." A hoot emerged from a deep male voice in the audience. Everyone laughed at that, even Kathe.

"Down boy . . . ," she said, smiling broadly, laughing so hard it was difficult to continue. "This is for Fran McGhee . . . ," she finally continued, walking over to his table with the cooler and mess dripping down her arm. She had to shout, since she was away from the mic, but she was comfortable doing it. She was that kind of girl.

"I just use it as proof that Mr. McGhee here can be *wrong* on occasion. We had no less than *three* arguments over whether they had *vanilla* or *mint* ice cream inside. I offer this as *Exhibit A*," she said, extending her arm to McGhee.

McGhee looked up at her smiling face, the melted ice cream running down her arm. She was blushing with her performance, her hand wiggling in front of him to take it. Standing, he accepted the package by the cleanest corner gingerly, but it was squishy.

Unwrapping a corner, he took a bite, waving to the crowd. "Anything for free ice cream . . . ," he shouted to general applause. Grabbing his gold napkin from the table, he handed it to Kathe to clean up, leaning in. "You're *sooo* annoying . . . ," he said, smiling at her, and she laughed and laughed.

As she leaned in for a hug, she reached into her rear pants pocket, pulling out a small envelope, straightening the corner. "Here . . . ," she said, sliding it into his palm, out of view of the crowd. Her laughing had subsided into a warm smile.

"What's this?" McGhee said, quickly peering into the envelope to note the edge of a photo inside.

"Something to remember me by . . . ," she said, patting him lightly on the back.

Mr. Swinson stared hard at McGhee, but McGhee didn't relent.

"I'm not following . . . ," McGhee responded.

The class bell rang, surprising, Mr. Swinson. Closing the book, he scanned the class. "All right everyone – just read the chapter, and we'll start next time . . . ."

The students filed out of the room, but McGhee stopped at the desk in front of Mr. Swinson. "Why did that make you so mad?" McGhee persisted.

Mr. Swinson forced out a smile. "Perhaps I should have done that in private. I'll give you that. But you sure know how to push my buttons. *Philosophy.* That was *precious.*"

"That was the best part . . . I really liked the definition of signal – it all seemed so . . . subjective. Maybe sometimes people get confused which is which. And how you pick out the signal from all of it – I loved that. Sometimes I miss the signal – I have a lot of trouble with sarcasm . . . ," McGhee continued, crossing his arms in front of himself to lean against the desk there.

"You know damn well you were talking about the conversation we had a couple weeks back – me adding in calculus to the class, and how I couldn't do it."

"Really?" McGhee said, pausing to think of it. "I guess that was *maybe* in there, but I really did like it, like the material. So mostly I was *agreeing* with you. But maybe that was in there. Yeah, I guess it was to some extent."

"Listen, McGhee . . . ," Mr. Swinson said, leaning in. "They don't pay me enough to do that, and besides it's not my job. It's not my fault the curriculum is screwed up. And I don't appreciate you trotting it out like that either – in front of *your* friends. Not everything is so goddamn simple as it looks when you're eighteen. You're mistaken if you think I can just wave my wand and do what I want. Adulthood doesn't work like that. You just haven't learned that yet . . . ."

"*You're* the one who said it didn't make sense to teach it like that," McGhee said, shifting his weight. "I thought we were on the same side?"

"We are . . . ," Mr. Swinson said. "We are."

"Then what are you *talking* about?" McGhee said, scratching his head, staring back at Mr. Swinson. The next class of students was filing in, filling the desks, murmuring at the door to catch the conflict in progress at the front of the room. They'd seen it before, and didn't bother opening their notebooks.

"Let's walk over the *VA* . . . ," Troy said, pushing out the door of the *7-Eleven*, but Russ was quick to object, juggling a hot microwave burrito from one hand to the other. McGhee handed him a napkin from the counter so he could wrap it.

"It's like fuckin' two degrees or somethin' . . . ," Russ said, already tearing at the tough plastic wrapper.

"But I wanna chew . . . ," Troy said, holding up a bag of chewing tobacco. It had become their tradition to walk the grounds of the VA hospital, talking, even in the winter. The chain on the gate at the back entrance was loose, so they could squeeze through.

"All right," Russ said, "but let's drive over there."

"It's only like five hundred yards . . . ," Troy said, laughing.

"Like I said, five hundred yards isn't so close, is it?" Russ said, pointing in Troy's face, laughing, looking at McGhee for confirmation. "Besides, we can cruise by Kovach's and see if he's out."

Kovach was on the far end of McGhee's friends, mostly connected to Russ, who, in turn, McGhee had met through Troy. They'd had a few classes together, but McGhee didn't know Kovach that well. He was a bit of an unknown quantity – quiet – but the things he did say weren't stupid, so he was disposed to like him.

Across from the VA gate, McGhee turned into the neighborhood – similar to his parents', houses of about the same vintage, built on the GI Bill. Mostly red-brick ranches on half-acres, the yards had mature trees and bushes, street lights every couple blocks to barely lighten the sleepy streets stretching back into the woods and over the hill. Troy directed him to stop in front of one of the houses, large junipers crowding the front porch, the picture window flickering with the variable light of a television.

Russ grumbled, climbing out into the cold, crunching over the snow of the yard, realizing half way he could have walked up the clean driveway instead. McGhee watched the process, Troy laughing the whole time, narrating the misfortunes of his friend as usual. And just as he reached the porch, shaking the snow from his tennis shoes, the door opened, and Kovach came bounding out on his own. Russ turned to look at the car and could see McGhee and Troy laughing, though the closed car windows mercifully cut off any noise from it.

Kovach scampered down the sidewalk and driveway, avoiding the snow entirely, while Russ retraced his tracks across the snowy lawn, swearing the whole way, Kovach jumping in the back seat before him.

"Boys . . . ," Kovach said smiling in a gappy grin, which turned sour. "What the *hell* is that smell?" Just then, Russ arrived sticking his red face in the back, puffing, mumbling *fuck, fuck, fuck* between his gasps.

"You're looking at it . . . ," Troy said, throwing his head toward Russ. "Russ has gas . . . ."

"You'll get used to it . . . ," McGhee said.

"I don't *want* to get used to it . . . ," Kovach said. "Let's just walk from here – I can't stay out too late anyways. Got shit in the morning."

"Are you *goddamn kidding* me?" Russ said, stopping before he got the whole way in. "My lungs feel like plastic already . . . ."

The neighborhood at the top of the hill was dark and quiet, but his legs enjoyed the break from the climb up Duffy. His path was tracing his old grade school bus route backwards so it felt vaguely wrong to do it, but he liked the sensation. And when he was on his bike, rather than driving as was his default these days, he felt so much further from home, which added to the sense of displacement. The solitary effort in the darkness also gave him time to mull over his speech which was becoming a boulder for him he'd been rolling uphill each morning, only to become dissatisfied at night. Perhaps this rumination would set that straight.

The street lamps in that neighborhood were much further apart than where he lived, making it that much darker. Taking the turn, he glided down the street, coasting. The houses were different than the ones in his neighborhood, too – closer together and framed versus brick — and he suddenly realized it made them more affordable. That was the word polite people would use. The thought had never occurred to him before, that these were people of even more limited means than his family, not that his family was rich. To the contrary, they were hanging on to a lower rung of the middle class themselves, but he didn't have many occasions to look lower on the ladder, for the implicit instruction was always to look up. But back when he was on the bus, they were just the other Catholic kids, and come to think of it, it was where the only black kids he knew lived, and despite his reluctance to think it, perhaps that meant something.

Half way down he passed Norma's house, and he thought about her necking in the back seat with Stuttman in eighth grade. By then he was one of the older kids on the bus, but it still seemed a little scandalous. They'd duck their heads below the green Naugahyde benches of the seats to evade detection by the driver, but he didn't seem to care anyway, driving being at the very edge of his faculties. And when they'd finally sit up again, they had that glassy look in their eyes, emerging marks on her neck, slobber making both of their oblivious faces glossy. McGhee would take furtive glances back, curious and appalled, covetous but guilty, the prospect of that for himself at once appealing and repulsive.

Further down, he passed Strudel's house — his friend in fourth grade. It was the darkest depth of the neighborhood before the road swung back to the light again. Their house was strange and different, hidden back in the trees on the corner, where the street took a weird angle, like a broken leg. That intersection — the confluence of four streets, but not at right angles, seemed haphazard and arbitrary — was the heart of that place, but he never got to play there, not really. Somehow most of the playing had been at his house, for that brief period when their paths aligned. He wondered

what had happened to him – in high school, he had mostly disappeared, even though he had never actually gone anywhere, except
being swallowed in the immensity of the ordinary.

Around the far bend and up at the stop, he took a left near the
Grutenberel's. He was the kid who was into taxidermy by age
twelve. That neighborhood had something happen to the trees, so
there weren't any, and all the bushes were short and spaced, still
growing into their planters and aspiring to hedge in their old age.

Finally emerging by the bar at the corner, McGhee came to a
stop, winded, but nearly free of the underworld. New Castle was
dead, but the traffic lights still cycled, eerily permitting ghost cars
to transit before stopping them for others to cross empty intersec-
tions. Fog nearly hung in the distance, not quite visible but distort-
ing, ringing lights in extra glow, sleepily. It wouldn't be much
further, he thought, stepping into his pedals for the last push.

On the porch to catch her, McGhee was relieved to see Wanda
wasn't driving – it was her friend Missy – pulling up the driveway with a groan in a rusty copper Gremlin. When Missy turned
the key, the car kept idling twenty seconds, reluctant to stop, but
ended with a final sputtering cough.

Getting out of the car, Wanda got hung up in the seatbelt,
nearly falling into the yard. McGhee looked back through the
storm door on the house to see where his parents were, but they
were busy loading items onto the dining room table and hadn't
seen anything. Jogging down the steps from the stoop, he sat on
the bottom step, elbows on his knees, looking. Wanda was looking
back at him, but waited for Missy to join her at the front of the car
before approaching. She seemed unsteady, but due less to alcohol

than something else. Missy wanted to hang back, lean against the car, but Wanda wouldn't have it, grabbing her hand, pulling her upright and forcing her to trudge up the driveway.

Standing in front of McGhee, Wanda looked a little red in the face, her smile a bit forced, though her nervousness was evident in her pose which shifted foot to foot. Missy stepped forward, sticking out her hand.

"Hey . . . ," she said a little self-consciously. "Sorry to barge into your party."

Rising from his position, McGhee took her hand and smiled. "No worries, Missy – I think you were a year ahead of me at St. Paul's. How have you been?"

She smiled sheepishly. "That was a long time ago . . . ," Missy said.

Turning to Wanda, McGhee looked in her eyes. He'd always marveled at them – bright green, with rings of blue. They seemed sad and a little scared in that moment, so he stepped forward to hug her.

"I didn't think you wanted to see me again," Wanda said into his chest, muffled. When she pulled back, his gray T-shirt had wet marks where her eyes and nose had touched it, and she leaned back in to brush it away but it only smeared. "Sorry . . . ," she said, her eyes welling up. Though she'd been drinking, it seemed it was just to take the edge off.

McGhee sighed, looking at Missy. "There's some food inside. Why don't you get yourself a plate."

Missy looked at Wanda, then back at McGhee and shrugged, walking up the steps and inside.

Wanda was staring up at McGhee, looking sheepish. "I just had to talk to you . . . ," she began. "I didn't like how we left things . . . you know . . . back there." She motioned over her shoulder like it was a literal place, then looked at him again. "Can we take a little drive? You know, like we used to do?"

"What about Missy?" McGhee said, motioning up the stairs. "And my friends? Seems like bad form . . . leaving your own party."

"Missy knows . . . ," Wanda said, reaching out to grab McGhee's forearm. "Just a short one . . . *please?*" She stroked his forearm affectionately. McGhee looked up the steps, then back at her, then up the steps again. "And we'd have to move the Gremlin to get the Volaré out."

"We can take Missy's car . . . ," Wanda said, jangling the keys in her hand.

"It really has to be short . . . ," McGhee said, running back inside to tell his parents.

Busboys and girls were clearing the plates as quickly as they could to keep the event on schedule, quietly stowing them into black plastic bins, careful to minimize the noise. The various administrators were droning on with speeches to commemorate the class. McGhee wondered how they did it year after year, finding new cute things to say each time. Maybe they didn't, he concluded, and just use the same speeches over and over again. Who would know? – maybe it's just a joke among them that it's all the same, only each class doesn't know. He found the thought amusing and laughed lightly to himself.

Mike leaned over. "Are you kidding? That was, like, the lamest joke ever . . . ," he said looking at McGhee, then realized it must have been something else.

The room erupted into applause all of a sudden, everyone at his table clapping, so McGhee clapped, too. Mike leaned over again, "They called your name, *dipshit* . . . ," he said good-naturedly.

McGhee blushed, leaning back to him. "Why?" he asked.

"Most studious or something . . . ," Mike said. "I think you're supposed to go up there."

McGhee looked to the stage and all the eyes were on him, everyone clapping. It looked like they intended to clap until he grabbed the award, the principal at the podium motioning for him to rise. As he did, the clapping redoubled in intensity, the principal leaning over to hand him a large manila envelope and to shake his hand. "Better get used to it, son . . . ," he said, letting his hand go.

Back at his seat, he peered into the envelope. Inside it had a thick piece of cardstock, printed with the high school name, arching across the page in fancy letters, with his name in the middle, and just below, *Most Studious 1982*, in bold Helvetica. The others at the table asked to see it, so he slid it out, performing a seated curtsey as he did so, to their laughter.

At the podium, the principal tried to pick up the pace, handing out a few awards in quick succession, then looked back to McGhee's table. "All right, superstar, you'd better get back up here . . . ," he said, but McGhee kept sitting. "*McGhee?*" the principal said, then leaning into the mic, "Probably the smartest guy in the room and he doesn't recognize a compliment when he hears one . . . ," he said, the room bursting into laughter and applause.

As he rose, McGhee felt a little light headed. He tried not to look at the students around him, looking at him with that look, those looks, and focused his attention on the podium. The principal kept talking:

"Blah blah blah – looks like he won everything . . . ," he mumbled into the mic to more laughs. "Most Likely This, Most Likely That . . . oh, and by the way . . . ," he continued, pausing for effect, "he's your *Valedictorian*."

When he got to the podium, the principal handed him a whole collection of similar manila envelopes and leaned over to whisper again. McGhee couldn't understand what he said but smiled in response, the principal patting him on the shoulder. Just as he did so, McGhee noticed a figure who had been hidden from his view by the podium. Tucked in the corner was Mr. Swinson, and though he was clapping with the rest of them, his eyes held a sadness which seemed to foreshadow something beyond the edge of McGhee's view that he was afraid to think of.

It was in one of those gloating moments in the cafeteria, with Hector quietly reveling in his pre-ordained victory, that McGhee first realized he needed to expand the battlefield to level it, if possible, through cleverness and guile. So as Hector rattled on, trying his best to hide his unhidable pleasure in the inevitability of his impending victory, it became apparent to McGhee he'd need to neutralize the core of Hector's delight, which he knew was his personal victory over McGhee himself. It would require a bit of mental jiu-jitsu – reversing his opponent's momentum to his own advantage – and McGhee very nearly smiled as he had thought of it, two mornings before the contest.

"I have some bad news . . . ," he had said to Hector, hanging his head, in part to hide his eyes from inspection until the trap was set. After a pause, he continued. "I'm not going to be able to make the game."

Hector was dumfounded, then suspicious, then disappointed in a swirl of annoyance. "*What?*" he had said. "*No . . .* ," he continued, shaking his head. "It's some kind of trick. You *havta* be there . . . ."

The quick evolution of his thoughts was evident, but he needed to set the hook better and deeper, to make the fiction work and to ratchet up the rancor of it.

"Sorry . . . ," McGhee said, shaking his head. "There's a thing. In Pittsburgh . . . ," he continued, lowering his head again. "A *Yale* thing . . . ." It was everything he could do to contain his delight in the fiction, for Hector's other favorite topic of conversation, when he wasn't talking soccer, was the impending yuppification of McGhee once he fell into the arms of the Ivy League monster. He knew at the core of it, his acceptance at Yale rankled Hector, and this diversion would sow seeds of consuming disappointment, hollowing out his anticipation of sweet victory and replacing it with a cavity of decay and emptiness, all powered by the low hum of a small but warm core of envy.

After some seconds of letting the lie hang in the air, McGhee was able to look at Hector directly as he pressed his smile into a slight frown of manufactured disappointment. "Found out yesterday afternoon," McGhee continued. "Got a thing in the mail – mandatory meeting for incoming students." Then after a pause, added, "Sorry."

Hector's eyes finally met McGhee's as he swallowed the bait. "*Fuck . . .* ," he said, banging his fist on the table, sliding back his chair, squealing on the linoleum, and throwing his arms behind his head before coming to a rest with his elbows on his knees, looking at McGhee, his heart almost audibly cracking at the news.

By second period, McGhee was getting queries from opponents and team members alike – the news developing into a voracious cancer sweeping more effectively than he could have hoped, replacing tumescent confidence in its wake with limp pointlessness. For those on his team, he offered hope without explanation, to keep his counsel close but maintain morale, but for the others, he offered additional details as needed to bolster the fiction, which grew and metastasized as it ate his opponent's zeal with a surprisingly efficient disappointment. So by the morning of the contest, Hector's dejection was complete, his previous smiles of delight replaced with an indelible frown.

As he had thought of it the previous evening, McGhee considered the absurdity of it, reveling in the subterfuge, then hit upon the ultimate insult to heap upon injury – to dress for the occasion in some manner, to manifest the lie as mockery with a durable and constant reminder. His mother was dusting in his room with a yellow feather duster as he pondered how to do just that, when the thought occurred to him: to dress as a chicken – illustrating with silliness the absurdity of the battle, throwing the game sideways into some other contest entirely. And though his team wasn't so skilled in actual soccer, they enjoyed buffoonery and were able to keep a secret, and he discretely let it be known he would indeed be there, to lead them as the grand chicken superhero, and they all laughed and laughed at the thought of it: Pawluk laughed out loud in calculus to Mr. Camissa's repeated polite calls for order, and Chepelsky kept repeating, "Oh my god, oh my god, that's fucking *brilliant* . . . ," in the hallway after fourth period.

So as McGhee heard the repeated whistles to call the game to order from behind the hill, he checked the yellow feathers glued to his shirt and affixed his beak over his face to run over the crest to join his comrades in battle and lead them.

This was the setting as he raced down the hill toward the field, screaming, his teammates raising a call of welcome to him, his opponents turning to see what they secretly feared would happen. He couldn't have anticipated the effect his deception would cause, for as it turned out, several members of the *Trojans* had decided the effort was no longer worth attending, their numbers less than the full eleven. Hector, out on the field, languidly marshalling his troops turned to see the spectacle emerging, hearing the hoopla, the disbelief registering simultaneously on his face and in his collapsing shoulders.

For his part, McGhee raced onto the field running in wide circles, feathers flying from his hasty costume, leaving yellow fluff in his wake, Hector taking his protest to the ref, the high school coach known to both Hector and McGhee, who laughing, replied he was unaware of any rules prohibiting such silliness. His ruling, absolute and laughing, turned the blade in Hector's heart with finality and mortality, when he turned to his friend, broken.

"I knew it was too good to be true . . . ," he said to McGhee. "I just can't believe you *lied* to me," he said, hands on hips, looking at him. "*Jesus* . . . . You're *diabolical*."

And so it was they played, *The Simians* rising to the occasion, playing well above their level, and *The Trojans*, demoralized, playing below theirs, with *The Simians* scoring three times quickly, delighting in the absurd route. Unorthodox boots trapped balls, feeding their center chicken hero, who charged the net, firing the ball past the befuddled goalie, who didn't know whether to laugh or cry, in the wake of protracted cries of *Goaaaaal* from *The Simians* rolling in delight at the emerging victory McGhee had forged from the threads of absolute chaos.

It was only in the afterglow, as teams gathered their things to retreat home, that he noticed Hector standing – the look of betrayal played across his face – that McGhee felt the first twinges of regret, and he couldn't remember ever hearing whether Odysseus suffered this effect of his guile, or how he might suffer himself.

It was an odd sensation, peddling through the light stuck on green, into the high school campus. Light fog hung on the fields where they played intramural softball and soccer, the heavy spring air too thick to remain invisible at that temperature. And though it remained still, the parking lot was full at 2:30 a.m. Swinging into the large oval, surrounded on three sides by buildings where the busses let out their masses, it was dead, except for the glow emerging from the cafeteria, where the dull thud of music leaked from the prom.

Coming to a stop, McGhee leaned on one foot astride his bike, observing. The windows had steam in the corners. Inside, the girls were dressed in after-dinner mint colors, wrist-corsaged, while the boys danced stiffly in tuxedos black and white and tan and blue, frilly-chested shirts below jacket-matching clip-on bowties. *Spandau Ballet* was belting out *True* as they danced slowly and sleepily, leaning into each other to stay erect. Others lined tables at the edges, circles of boys and girls leaning back in their chairs, exhausted by the production but swept into the milestone of passage. He could have been in there, too, but was rather glad it worked out the way it had, thinking:

> *Two roads diverged in a wood, and I——*
> *I took the one less traveled by*

Hector was one of those on the edge near the window, his jacket folded over the chair next to him, his arm over the back. Looking out, he noticed McGhee looking in and smiled lightly, waving slowly. Raising his hand, McGhee waved back, returning the slight smile.

In that moment, McGhee had found comfort just outside the flow of things, and as he stepped on his pedal to leave the prom, he was glad he had seen it, if only through the window.

McGhee pulled the Gremlin onto 422 – it seemed better he should drive, even though she wasn't as drunk as he thought – but he wasn't sure it was capable of highway speeds, due to the shaking around forty miles an hour, though it evened out at fifty. Wanda was curled up in the corner of her seat, knees to her chest, staring at him out of the darkness. He could feel her looking, though he had to stare at the road, and was glad for it as it gave him an excuse to be distracted. Eventually he had to relent, however, and he looked over and could see her eyes big and moist, staring back.

She'd graduated the year before, but their history went back to his days as a freshman in biology. Since then, they'd gone out periodically, though it was always troubled. So it was with some surprise she had called him earlier in the spring to go out, and to his relief that it was pleasant, if not particularly passionate. There had been some discussion of going to prom and consummating their relationship, finally, but it had never gone much further than some necking, and in retrospect, he was rather glad it hadn't. And again, as was their way, there was an argument back in May – he lost his tuxedo deposit – and it seemed like it had been their last chapter. That is, until twenty minutes before when she stumbled onto his lawn.

"So . . . ," Wanda began, her voice cracking, "you're leaving tomorrow?"

McGhee nodded, looking back to the road. "Yeah . . . ," he said. "First light," but she seemed to be intent on something else.

"So . . . ," she continued, "I was thinking . . . ," she said, then pointed to the rapidly approaching exit. "Take this, take this . . . ," she shouted, then recoiled, surprised at her volume. "Take this exit . . . ," she said more rationally, her hands to her face. It was a familiar pathway for them, when they decided to park and *talk* – their euphemism for protracted wordlessness.

The sudden diversion made McGhee uncomfortable, but he exited the highway, veering off the road into the cemetery where they'd go. Though the gate was closed, it was usually unlocked, so any late visitors could escape if they were caught inside. Pulling up to the gate, he turned off the lights but stayed inside the car.

"I don't think it's a good idea . . . ," McGhee said, looking over at her.

"So . . . I was *thinking*," Wanda continued, ignoring him again. "I think I'm ready." Leaning forward on her knees on the bench, she leaned in to kiss McGhee on the ear, licking it lightly as she pulled back, her fingers threaded through his hair. Her breath was warm and moist and lightly sweet with some liquor, her words inaudible though her meaning was clear. She stared at him from a foot away, raising herself to push against him, expecting kisses on her neck, but they didn't come. After some moments of disappointment, she leaned back on her haunches to look at him.

"What's wrong?" she said, pouting slightly.

McGhee had his wrist dangling over the wheel as he stared out the windshield, sighing.

"I think we missed our window, Wanda. Our time. It's too late now. I'm leaving tomorrow. And it seems best not to start something now."

"*Start* something? We've been doing *something* for four years now . . . ," she said, crossing her arms, then wiping moisture from her eyes before re-crossing her arms again. "And I don't want to *lose* you."

"Jesus . . . ," McGhee said, shaking his head, laughing slightly. "I can't believe it."

"You think it's *funny?*" Wanda said. "I'm offering *myself* to you, and you think it's *funny?*"

McGhee held up his hand, then patted her on the thigh lightly.

"No, Wanda. It's really sweet . . . ," he said, finding her hand in the darkness to hold it.

"What then?" she asked, her voice hitching at the end.

"It's *our* timing . . . ," McGhee said, shaking his head. "We've never been in sync, have we?"

Lowering her head, Wanda wept quietly. "I guess not . . . ," she admitted, digging in her pocket for a tissue. "Missy told me it was a bad idea, but I said I had to try. I wanted to *lose it* with you. But now I just feel *stupid* . . . ." Her tears returned and she wiped them, blowing her nose into the tissue for emphasis. "She said I should just leave you go."

McGhee rolled down the window to let in some of the evening air. It had a bit of crispness in it, containing portents of September he couldn't miss, and it pulled his focus inexorably forward.

"We never got it right, did we?" she said, composing herself. "I was kinda surprised you wanted to go out in the first place. We're *sooo* different . . . ."

"I always liked that," McGhee said, reaching over to brush the hair from her eyes. "And I was surprised a cheer leader would go out with *me* . . . ."

"*Right* . . . ," Wanda said, snickering. "There were lots of girls who were after you."

"I guess I was pretty oblivious to that, if it's true . . . ," McGhee said, smiling.

"*Oblivious*? – yeah . . . ," she agreed, nodding. "You were always in your own little world. But you got what you wanted."

"How so?" McGhee asked, leaning his head back against the headrest.

"All this . . . ," Wanda said, spinning her hand in the air. "Getting to the top. *Yale*. All of it."

McGhee closed his eyes, thinking. It must have looked that way on the outside, to those around him, only it was so muddled in his head, his feelings drawn and knotted. The thought of it made him sigh.

"What is it?" Wanda asked, sniffling slightly.

McGhee rubbed his eyes, speaking from behind his hands. "I'm just so afraid, Wanda," McGhee said, his voice catching, too. "Maybe I don't want it after all . . . ," he said, his voice breaking off. The sudden emotion surprised him, and he wiped his eyes into his shoulder.

"What are you afraid of?" Wanda said, leaning in slightly, placing her other hand on top of his.

Recollecting himself, McGhee looked out the window, then back to her. "What if it was all an illusion . . . ," he said, his voice trailing off. "What if I got a prize I don't really want? What if I went down the wrong path? What if I screw it up? What if I'm an *imposter*?"

Raising his hand to her lips, she kissed it lightly. "If you're an imposter . . . then God help the rest of us . . . ," she said, gently laying her cheek on his hand.

Mr. Swinson looked to the gathered class and told them to read the next section and turned back to McGhee. He pushed up his glasses again, squinting at him, his cheeks reddening.

"What are you so mad about then? I was probably the only one who actually *read* it. I just don't get it. I don't know why I rub you the wrong way," McGhee said.

Mr. Swinson leaned in to whisper. "Bullshit . . . ," he said, leaning back again. "You like to play this little game where you don't know what the other side of your head is up to, but I think you do, and I'm sick of it." McGhee stared back but didn't respond.

"You rub me the wrong way . . . ," he continued, "because you play at humility, when just underneath there's something else. Another process running – needling, competing, critical – some urge to show us you're so *superior*. And it's just a huge waste of time and effort. And that effort should be going somewhere it would do some good, and it's galling to see. *Galling.*

"I don't think I do that . . . ," McGhee objected weakly, but Mr. Swinson ignored him.

"You, my friend, have a lot of *potential*. But that's what it is . . . *raw* potential. Only you're not willing to work at it. Develop it. And this school . . . ," he said, whirling his finger in the air, "hasn't forced you to. Only, *sometimes*, it's not up to the school to do that. It's up to you. Only it seems like you're not willing to do that. Maybe 'cause you're scared to try, in case you fail. That's what I see – fear – and it's going to eat you. When I look into your eyes, I can see – way down inside – a little crack and a little trickle of doubt. I can see it. I can *see* it. And I worry what happens when that crack opens up. I wonder what will happen then. If you'll fall apart. You want it to be easy, like some kinda gift, only it doesn't work that way. You want to be some kinda *genius*, only you're not."

McGhee stared back, but didn't say anything.

"Listen, son," Mr. Swinson said, softening slightly, "Stop talking long enough to listen. You don't know everything. A little humility would do you good, and a little hard work would do you better. At least you'd know you *tried*, and some day that will matter to you, and if you don't it will haunt you. *Haunt* you. You're about to go through a *tectonic* period and it's going to be painful. The image of yourself, that you have now, probably won't survive. You have to prepare yourself for that, for disappointment. Otherwise . . . ," he said, his voice trailing off, "it'll be devastating. *Devastating*."

"But how do you *know* that?" McGhee objected, his voice quiet. Mr. Swinson looked at him, a small, sympathetic smile curling the edge of his lips.

"I just do . . . ," Mr. Swinson said, grabbing a pad and scribbling a hall pass for McGhee.

The boys shuffled up the street in the cold, blowing on their hands. Troy loaded his cheek with chew, offering it to the others, but only Russ took some, jamming in a huge wad, smiling. "Might as well . . . ," he said, chuckling as he packed it in.

The street light by the gate shed a chill, blue light, clear and bright in the thin air, humming. Kovach held up his wrist to show Russ it was midnight.

"This cold makes me wish I was in Hawaii or something . . . ," Russ said, puckering his lips to form a stream of brown spit. "Somewhere warm."

Troy nodded. "Fiji . . . ," he said, smiling. "I like those little huts on the water."

McGhee shuddered, stuffing his hands in his pockets. "Grand Canyon for me. Right there on the rim, looking out. Mid-summer warmth."

Russ nudged Kovach with his elbow. "How about you?"

Kovach shrugged, smiling. "Here's good."

"*What?*" Russ said, laughing. "It's frickin' *cold.*"

"Really, Russ?" Kovach said, looking at him. "Are you *sure?*" Russ looked confused by the response and stared back, slack jawed.

"Yeah, it's cold . . . ," Russ answered, unsure. Troy laughed, bending down to slap his knee.

"Russ, you're such a doofus . . . ," Troy said merrily, smiling best he could, the chew deforming his cheek, brown saliva escaping the corner.

McGhee leaned into the circle, looking at Kovach. "What gives? I don't get that *at all* . . . ."

Kovach smiled back, shrugging again. "I like it here . . . ," he said.

"Sure . . . ," McGhee said, shrugging. "It's OK I guess . . . ," he continued, smiling at Russ and Troy before looking back at Kovach. "But don't you want to see Fiji. Or Hawaii. Or, god forbid, the Grand Canyon?"

"It's not really about that . . . ," Kovach said, shaking his head. "There's nothing wrong with those places. There's just nothing wrong with here, *either.*"

"The Taj Mahal? Istanbul?" McGhee continued, but Kovach just kept shaking his head.

"They're fine, too, I guess, only it's the same thing. It doesn't really matter to me."

"Really?" Troy said, dancing from one foot to the other. "No desire to get out – explore. Discover shit. See the sights. See the cool things of the world?"

Kovach shook his head. "Not like for you and McGhee, apparently . . . ." Kovach lowered his head and started pacing in a little circle, tamping down the snow with his toes, thinking out loud. "I dunno . . . ," he began, continuing his rumination. "When I hear you guys talk, it sounds like you're running. Like this is somewhere to escape. Only . . . most of that has to do with stuff you got going on inside. Like you're running *from* something, rather than *toward* something, and it's stuck to you, whatever it is. I don't have that. It's like you're a little possessed."

Troy laughed, shaking his head.

McGhee laughed. "That's not a bad way to describe it I guess," McGhee said, tottering foot to foot.

"Yeah . . . so maybe I'll see it one day. It just doesn't matter that much to me. And besides, what if I see those things and they make me unhappy with what I got? That's what I'm really afraid of. Do you really think having that drive makes you better off? Makes you happier?"

"It never seemed like a choice to me," McGhee said, shrugging. "I've always had it. Listening to the traffic sounds on 422 at night, I always wanted to know where they were going, and I wanted to go, too. It made me restless . . . ."

"But would you trade places with me if you could?" Kovach said, "I mean, if you could be satisfied with what you have and where you are, would you do it?"

McGhee began pacing, too, thinking. "I have no idea . . . ," he said. "I've always had it, for as long as I can remember. It's a big part of who I am. And my brothers had it, and they left, so it seemed to be the way of the world, of my world, anyway."

"Yeah, but that doesn't answer the question, does it? All that exploring seems like procrastination to me. Like an excuse for not getting down to business and living . . . ," Kovach said, smiling again.

"Not *living?*" Troy said, leaning in. "That *is* living, isn't it?"

"Not unless you stay there, somewhere. Get a job. Start a family. I got college to do, then probably grad school. I don't know about you guys, but I got a lotta work to do."

"Jesus . . . ," Troy said, shaking his head. "What's the big hurry to get *settled?*"

McGhee nodded. "Yeah, what's the hurry?"

Kovach shrugged. "I think that's what will make me *happy,* that's what."

"It's mind boggling, that's what *that* is . . . ," Troy said laughing before leaning over to spit a thick brown stream. Wiping his lips on his sleeve, he shook his head, laughing. "You're only eighteen."

Russ shrugged, looking back and forth between them. "I think Kovach has a good point."

"Perhaps . . . ," McGhee said, trying to get his head around it. "It just seems so . . . disappointing. And you're never gonna go anywhere? Never go on vacation or anything?" McGhee continued.

Kovach shrugged again. "Not the way I see it. I'd rather get things set first. Then maybe later I can go, once I know I have something to come back to. If I go now and see all this stuff, it'll make me unhappy with what I got, so I'd just rather not even think about it."

"What?" McGhee said.

Troy leaned in: "That *there* is some *fucked up* logic."

Kovach shook his head. "Naa. It's not. Oh, and I'll still go on vacation," he said, smiling again.

"Where?" McGhee said.

"Myrtle Beach," Kovach said. "My parents got a timeshare, so I can go there in the meantime."

Troy was beside himself laughing at the thought of it until some spit went back down his throat and he gagged, leaning over to throw up in the snow. Russ stepped over, putting a hand on his shoulder to look after him until he was well enough to walk back.

———— ⚬❧⚬ ————

McGhee looked up into the stands, the tassel on his mortar board blowing slightly in the breeze. Spread before him, two thousand parents and children and faculty and friends waited for him to speak, languidly captive until the ceremony's end. It was a humid June evening, gray clouds looming and heavy, but the warm and balmy breeze seemed to hold them up in place, floating. McGhee looked down at his unfolded paper speech, flapping lightly at the corner, unspoken.

His thoughts were welling fast and tangled, and he gripped the edge of the podium to steady himself against the torrent: flashes of ninth grade, bleeding in the principal's office; the smell of Wanda's perfume and her kindness; the countless hours driving in commiseration with friends he was leaving behind; the exuberance of victories commingled with the regret of his guile; the swelling emergence of potential polluted by the festering decay of doubt; the impending loss of home through his drive to abandon it; empty awards and meaningful silliness — all wound and taut in a ball of ambivalence, jammed sideways in his head, stuffed yet hollow, stuck. All these things pushed at his back, his feet on the crumbling edge of a precipice, in that moment at the end of his time.

Looking up, he spoke, finally clear on the only thing he could think to say:

"*This is the way the world ends: Not with bang, but a whimper,*" he said, staring at them, then went back to his seat.

And with that, high school was over.

The Dust Magi

0 ◄──────────────────────────────────── ● ──► 90

86

4AM

Grand Canyon, AZ 3/20/2050

I t was endless trees — that's what he always remembered — and this time was no different. McGhee couldn't remember how long it had been since his last visit — their last visit — it could have been fifteen years or more, but he pushed the thought out of his head. He'd gotten the last flight into Flagstaff, which was of course delayed getting into Phoenix and he nearly missed the connector, only getting on the flight by preying on a college kid's sympathies, and throwing him a hundred bucks to take his seat. It wasn't even a jet, and he wasn't aware there were even turboprops running anymore, but apparently there were, at least on this leg, out into the middle of the dark just south of the dim edge of Flagstaff, but that was how he liked it.

He crashed in a motel a few hours, getting out just before 2:30 a.m. It was a cold and crisp twenty degrees. Stepping around the building at the motel to get a better look at the sky shielded from the mercury lamps, he saw the Milky Way stretching over him – broad and complex – and once his eyes adjusted to the dark, he found an old camp chair discarded there, one of the legs loose from its foot, but it'd suit his purpose well enough. He had no intention of sitting on the stone directly, and it seemed to meet his needs: a little banged-up, much like he felt, especially at that temperature and what it did to his joints, but he liked that, too. He liked the luck of it, of making due with what he found. That had been his way, more or less for as long as he cared to remember, and everything else could just go fuck itself.

Five miles out of Flag it got dark and might as well have been out in the middle of anywhere, and all he could see was trees, trees, an occasional hill and more trees, but he liked that. He liked the sensation of driving out to the edge of the world, which was exactly what he was after – the edge – and the more trees the better. The further it was, the better. Endless pines, leaning out to the road, the pavement old and sunbaked, the lines barely visible except for the occasional reflector, and the cattle grate to wake him up at eighty-five miles an hour. Half way to Tusayan he nearly hit a cow jogging down the center line: by the time he saw it, trotting in the same direction he was going, its ass was passing his side-view mirror and he didn't even tap the brake. That would have been some way to go – hamburger everywhere. Some of it the cow, and some of it him. So he just pushed the accelerator down and got her up to ninety, and the trees looked just the same, only a little faster as they whipped through his lights and into his tail lamps' red glow.

Reaching into his bag, he pulled out a music player and started up his collection, blasting *Baba O'Reilly* through the speakers. He had the heat on so he could roll with the windows down, and he liked the swirl of heat and cold mixed with the speakers throbbing

The Who, and it was good. He would have gone the whole way to the gate, too, if he didn't realize he needed to piss – he had the kidneys of an old man – and needed some supplies anyway. Luckily in Tusayan there was one convenience store still open, so he was able to buy a blanket and a thermos of coffee. The attendant looked out at the old man in the car as the music started blasting again when he turned the key, but he only looked back at the attendant while he pulled out and didn't turn it down, throwing some gravel as he got back on the road for the last couple miles to the park.

The guard station wasn't manned so he winged on through, slowing to fifty – his compromise at seeing signs for twenty-five miles an hour. He figured rangers weren't paid enough to stake it out at night to catch him, and he didn't care anyway. There wasn't anything to hit – it was too late for pedestrians and too early for elk. It did remind him, though, of the time he nearly hit one of the latter coming out of Yellowstone – must have been fifty years before, he thought, disdaining the exact math for approximation. He was in Wil's *Datsun 210* at time, braking hard right to miss him, the strong muscles of his hindquarters evident just over the hood of his car as the elk broke into full gallop, looking over its shoulder at him as it ran. He must have been galloping forty-five miles an hour by the time he cut left again and out of the path of the Datsun. It was scary but thrilling and reminded him that the best times of his life had come thirty seconds at a time, and when compressed together might have filled a moderately busy two weeks. That was how he had come to see it. So perhaps it would be one of those thirty seconds in which he met his end, but that was OK with him. And besides, there might not be much more time to fit that catastrophe into. He wasn't sure yet.

Half way into the park came the turn – he didn't want to go to the usual South Rim location everyone else went to. He wasn't looking for company. Turning east, the sign appeared – *Desert View 25 miles* – that was his destination. He'd found it was a better place to be alone with one's thoughts. A little wilder. A little lonelier. And there wouldn't be the flood of people to deal with. The couples taking pictures. The Germans who were still exploring America. The Japanese who were still recording it. No, there'd be some good old fashioned peace and quiet and solitude, which is what he had in mind. As for the usual mayhem of the South Rim – that wasn't what he was after at all.

It was almost 4:00 a.m. when he got there, swinging into the entrance. There were a few RVs parked at one end of the lot – their presence bugged McGhee, but there was nothing to do – and blew past them, way up to the closest slots, shutting down the car. Opening his suitcase in the backseat, he shuttled some items to his backpack to carry over to the wall: some gloves, a hat, a flask of good Haitian rum, a thin book of twentieth century poetry, a little flashlight, a small Tupperware container. Stuffing in the thermos of coffee, he zipped it shut, collecting the camp chair and blanket under his other arm before shutting the car door, but he didn't bother to lock it. It might be easier that way, he thought.

Walking along the canyon-edge trail just off the parking lot, he let his hand slide along the pipe capping the cyclone fence protecting the walkway. The metal was cold on his hand. Looking over the edge, he could see nothing except darkness, though the vastness of emptiness was there, stirring and unseen. Further down, as he remembered, there would be chances to divert into the stone outcroppings at the lookouts. There was one, near the end, a special one he had in mind that stuck way out, where he could sit and watch and listen and think.

McGhee was glad to see his destination was empty and walked down the steps and out to the edge where the rock protruded from the canyon wall, stretching out into the nothingness. Dropping the chair and blanket, he set the pack down more carefully, mindful of the bottle inside, stretching. He couldn't stand quite as straight as he used to, certainly not as tall. The drive was always just a little longer than he thought, and the stiffness had settled into his thigh where his sciatica was waiting for it, ready to send twinges down his leg. The stretch helped it, as did some Tylenol he washed down with some coffee from the thermos, still hot. They'd only had some of the powdered creamer at the store, which wasn't as good as half and half, but it was satisfactory. The infusion of warmth was welcome as it was still below thirty degrees when he got there. There was no differentiation yet on the horizon – there was no horizon actually – and he settled into his chair, wrapping the blanket over his shoulders.

The last ten days had been a blur, starting that Thursday when he awoke, but she had not. Kate slipped away during the night, right next to him, and when he couldn't wake her and reached to shake her, he knew. It just looked like she was sleeping, but she wasn't, and he crawled back into bed to sleep it away, but fifteen minutes later, he got up, leaned in to kiss her cold lips, and knew it was true.

Her friends showed up as if by magic and handled most of the arrangements while he sat in his chair, watching the preparations. Now and then they'd stop and lean in to check on him, but he wasn't in the mood to be consoled, and they soon gave that up. Even at the viewing most seemed to know to leave him alone, though some well-wishers leaned in with those looks, teary-eyed, tissues tucked in at the sleeve to hold his cheek. Later that day he came back for the ashes in a little urn, and he had to sign for them, like a FedEx package. It was about then he hatched this plan, only it required another five days to tidy things up.

It wasn't long before the gloaming started, first with a breeze coming up the cliff. Though he couldn't see them yet, he could hear the swifts riding those currents with their little squeals of delight, darting closer then farther away, but always unseen. The immensity before him began to reveal itself with the subtlest variation imaginable, moving from absolute blackness to the slightest differences. In the far distance, the edge became deep blue just above the blackness, barely discernible.

Opening the rum, he poured an inch into the cap of the thermos to drink, draining it in three gulps before replenishing it to sit with it a while, ruminating. Though he wasn't tired, he was weary and it made him sigh. Closing his eyes, he leaned his head back to remember all the wandering, all the people he had known. Most of them were dead by now he thought, recalling their faces: Joe at the mine, Karl on the raft, Bud at Rushmore, Arlene in Dublin – and that look of hers; Bernadette in New Orleans, though she went by Molly; Honey; Yannick in Bordeaux – *whatever happened to him?*; Neal, whom he had lost long ago; Kovach – had he ever made it?; Chepelsky and those cold streets; Jaime and his warm heart. And then there was his family, which inspired yet another gulp of rum.

He'd lost Dad first, then Mom. Back on the boney pile, he'd had that moment with him, looking over the valley which was already sliding into history. That was hard losing him, but perhaps even harder losing her, though Les fucked it all up. He still felt the rancor of it, that he wanted to hug his brother but was too mad to do it, then lost the chance. The senselessness rankled him, and he had a drink to erase it, though it had never worked before, and wouldn't this time. And Wil – just last year he'd seen him, a month before he passed. So it had just been him and Kate, and he planned to go before her, or expected it, though it didn't work out that way.

Pulling out the Tupperware, he sat it on his stomach, slouching in the chair. Shaking it slightly, he could hear the light rustle of it, and it reminded him of their poem, and the sad prophecy of it:

In the gloaming, oh, my darling,
When the lights are dim and low,
And the quiet shadows falling,
Softly come, and softly go;
When the winds are sobbing faintly,
With a gentle, unknown woe;
Will you think of me and love me?
As you did once long ago?
In the gloaming, oh, my darling,
Think not bitterly of me.
Tho' I passed away in silence,
Left you lonely, set you free;
For my heart was crushed with longing,
What has been could never be;
It was best to leave you thus, dear,
Best for you and best for me.
It was best to leave you thus,
Best for you and best for me.

They'd always liked this time of day best, so when they'd found the poem *In The Gloaming* by Meta Orred, they'd both said it should be their secret to share. He'd always thought it was from him to her, but in her last prank on him, she'd turned it around, without even a good-bye. She'd only said she loved him before they went to sleep, and that night he'd forgotten to admire her as she drifted off, as he usually did secretly, though she really knew.

They'd never discussed what to do with the ashes – they'd had so much living yet to do, it never seemed the time. So when the moment came, he was at a loss: putting them in the ground certainly didn't make any sense. He knew she didn't belong there, but it was only when he found a photo in her box from the shop, of her standing on one foot leaning out over the edge of the Canyon, that he knew. He was on a plane that night – barely ten hours before that moment – and the rest was frenzied driving to get there. At least this time he remembered to pack more than a toothbrush.

The sky was definitely lightening, though it was still subtle. Above the horizon, the blueness had shifted from a deep indigo to a deep royal blue. Below the edge it was still blackness, though if he turned his head, or re-looked at it fresh, he would swear he could see the beginnings of structure to the blackness of that sea. Venus had risen, but it was too early for Mercury. The moon beat them all, ten degrees above the horizon – it was still astronomical twilight, but if he stared into his lap, he could just barely see his hand holding the cup.

Looking at his watch, he saw it was 4:50 a.m. It was old, and had a leather band. Kate and he had seen it in a shop several years back, and he remarked it had looked like his dad's, which he'd said he had lost, more or less. She knew enough not to ask, but later that year, on his birthday, it had shown up in a box. He'd never worn a watch through his life – the passage of time always bothered him, like he was wasting it – but he wore this one. He'd usually forget to wind it, so it wasn't much good for time, but he liked the heft of it on his wrist, the feel of the leather, and the look of those hands trying to keep up.

Sipping his rum, he sighed. Reaching down, he switched his music player on again and scanned for a song from Neil Young he liked. Fixing his earphones in, he heard the initial melody of

Expecting to Fly, and it filled him with emotion to hear it, and he cried. It might have been the first time he really cried since she had passed, and he clasped the plastic container in his old hands, sobbing. It was about time.

Gulping the last of the rum in the cup and tossing the blanket aside, McGhee stood, stiff from the cool air and sitting. At the fence the pipe along the top dipped slightly and seemed like a good place to climb over. The outcropping continued another ten feet out before dropping off to nothingness. Clambering over was surprisingly easy, even holding Kate in one hand. It was breathlessly still as he made it to the edge to look over. Down, down, down the ledges cascaded into the valley, disappearing into the darkness still nestled in the recesses. The sky was brighter now and he could see it all, spread before him. The swifts were whistling in front of him, diving out from the ledge in barrel rolls of glee, and he wondered what it would be like to fall, if it would hurt, if he'd be thinking the whole way, if he'd see the ground rushing up at him, if it'd be cold to fall fast through that rarefied air.

Opening the container, he stared in. It'd be the last time he ever saw any part of her, but his eyes were dry. It was over already – the rest was a formality – and he tipped the container, spilling her into the vastness where she had played at losing her balance. For a moment she seemed to hang as a cloud there, drifting off to the east, until the slightest breeze there swirled through and she disappeared, like she had never been, gone. It didn't seem fair she'd gone before him, but it had never been about fair, had it? With the good times and the bad, it simply was, that was the message of it, and he stared into the abyss, thinking it was his time, too.

Peering down, he could feel the breeze on his face. It'd only take a second of resolve. One step out and it'd be irrevocable. The far horizon on the north rim had just the barest hint of light to it, and the gloaming was ending. It was the time for action, to stay in the moment with her, forever.

As McGhee had these thoughts, a slight noise off to his right caught his attention. On the next outcropping over a young man was clambering over the fence, and once the ringing of the fence died, he could hear other sounds from him, just barely audible: whimpering. Stumbling out to the edge, he had his fists in his eyes, and his steps were not careful nor planned. McGhee suddenly hoped he would stop, but he seemed determined and not tentative.

"Wait!" McGhee called out to him, almost startling the young man over the edge. Surprised, he looked over at McGhee but didn't say anything. "Wait . . . !" McGhee called again, moving back to his fence, then climbing over, tossing the container into his chair before climbing the steps from his outcropping to the trail, then hurrying down the path. "Wait . . . ," he called again, though less shouting than speaking loudly. The young man looked at him in disbelief, wiping his eyes, but halted.

McGhee was slow climbing down the steps – the stiffness in his joints had matured into an ache – but he kept his gaze on the man, ambling up to the fence close to him. "What are you *doing?*" McGhee asked softly.

"What's it look like?" the young man said.

McGhee looked at him. "It looks like you're about to do something you'd be sorry for . . . ," McGhee said.

"Technically, I wouldn't," the young man objected.

"Ten feet above the ground, you would be . . . ," McGhee countered. "Trust me – I was just thinking about that."

The young man caught his breath, wiping his eyes again. "You were gonna jump, too?" he said.

McGhee nodded. "I was thinking about it, yeah."

"So why didn't you?" the young man said, putting a hand on his waist.

"Some jackass stole my moment . . . ," McGhee said, staring back at him.

Despite his wrought state, the young man laughed. "You mean me . . . ," he said.

"If the shoe fits . . . ," McGhee said, smiling back slightly.

The young man stared back, his smile fading, but his despair temporarily halted. Motioning to his pack behind the fence, he signaled McGhee with his chin. "Can you hand me the water bottle in my pack?" he asked. McGhee looked by his feet where the young man had hastily dropped his backpack by the fence.

"You want to drink?" McGhee said, looking back to the young man.

"I don't want to die thirsty . . . ," the young man responded, shrugging.

McGhee laughed. "We all die thirsty, my friend . . . ." The young man laughed again, despite his attempt to contain it. Reaching down, McGhee freed the bottle from the webbing on the side, then reached far over the fence, extending the bottle. "Better grab it before I have a heart attack . . . ," McGhee said.

Accepting the bottle, the young man opened it, but stared at McGhee. "Now *that'd* be ironic," he said.

"I'm not sure it would be . . . ," McGhee said, scratching his head. "I'd have to ask my editor. I could never keep that straight." The young man laughed again.

"Trust me . . . ," the young man said, taking a long drink from the bottle. "That's irony."

McGhee leaned with both elbows on the fence, then motioned with a sweeping gesture across the canyon. "This was our favorite place."

"You and who?" the young man said, shifting his weight on his feet.

"My wife Kate and I . . . ," McGhee said, frowning slightly. "Those were her ashes I was scattering . . . ," he said, motioning to the neighboring outcrop. The young man looked over, seeing the chair and pack sitting there, unmanned.

"Sorry I missed it . . . ," the young man said, "but I was a little busy."

"Busy jumping?" McGhee said, smiling again.

"Until some old jackass interrupted me, yeah . . . ," the young man said, smiling slightly.

"Well then, maybe I should join you . . . ," McGhee said, clambering over the fence. Alarmed, the young man rushed to him to catch him as he tumbled over.

"Jesus . . . ," the young man said. "You'll fall."

Looking at him in his arms, McGhee smiled. "That's kinda the point, right?" he said. They both collapsed along the fence, leaning back against it to look out. Sensing a bulge in his back pocket, McGhee fished out the glass flask of rum he had stowed there. Spinning off the plastic cap, he offered the bottle to the young man, but he shook his head. "Why the hell not?" McGhee said.

Reconsidering, the young man took the bottle and swallowed a gulp, wincing. McGhee reached for it back, but the young man held on to it, taking another swig. "I guess you were right . . . ," he said finally handing it over.

McGhee took a swig, twisting the cap back on. The sky was getting light, though the sun hadn't appeared yet. Looking over at the young man, he extended his bony hand to him. "Fran McGhee," he said.

"Lenny," the young man said. "Mind if I . . . ," he continued, motioning to the bottle again.

"Just Lenny?" McGhee said, handing the bottle over.

"Yeah, just Lenny," Lenny said, taking another gulp. He continued holding the bottle but draped his wrist over his knee. Now that they were sitting, McGhee could take a moment to study him. He appeared to be in his early twenties. He hadn't shaved in a while, not that it mattered much – the hairs on his chin were long but sparse and fine. His face had seen some sun, with his cheeks showing red along their shoulders. His hair was a shade of brown peculiar to the young, with the slightest look of gray in it though it wasn't gray at all, but was its actual color, unwashed and semimatted to his head beneath a green floppy hiking hat with a wide brim to keep the sun from his neck. Overall he seemed trim and compact, his solidness appearing through his shell jacket and shell pants. Somehow it made McGhee wonder how he'd gotten there, for he couldn't imagine he drove in (and he hadn't heard a car), and the hour was too early for hitching. By his general mien and appearance, McGhee guessed he was of college age, though it had become increasingly hard for him to tell, since everyone under fifty looked like a kid to him these days.

"So . . . if you don't mind my asking, why were you about to . . . you know . . . take the big step?" McGhee asked, simultaneously motioning for the bottle.

Lenny took a small sip, mindful of the dwindling supply, then shrugged. "Partly a woman, I guess . . . ," he said, looking over, squinting an eye shut. "And other things."

"Such as?" McGhee continued. The young man eyed him, and he could imagine what he was seeing: an old man, short white beard, wrinkles, a bit hunched – and the thought made him smile.

"What are you smiling at?" Lenny asked, smiling, too.

"I always used to like talking to old guys. I bet I look old to you, right?"

Lenny smiled more broadly but didn't answer.

McGhee nodded. "Yeah, it's alright. I'm old. I stopped denying that last year." Lenny laughed, lowering his head, then looked
back. "I remember once hitching to Mt. Rushmore. An old guy
picked me up – a lot younger than I am now, mind you – and I
spent the evening with him and his buddies. That *there* is a nice
memory . . . ," he said, taking a quick swig from the bottle. "I
always felt calm around old people. Like they knew something I
didn't, and my . . . worries . . . were so *little* compared to what
they saw, to what they'd actually done. I liked that. That was
one of the smarter things I did – talk to old people – it'll help
you get perspective. And all the shit you got going on in your
head . . . ," he said, reaching over to tap Lenny on the hat lightly
with the bottle, "just evaporates. I loved that."

Lenny nodded. "That does sound nice. I wish that would work
for me . . . ."

McGhee laughed. "Oh, so you're special now?" McGhee asked,
chuckling lightly. "I guess I thought that, too, until it happened
to me. Then I got it. It'll happen for you, too, if you let it. If you
don't go and do something stupid . . . ," he said, motioning to the
vastness in front of them. Lenny smiled thinly, lowering his head.

"I had this girl back at Wesleyan . . . ," Lenny began, "only I lost
her. And then everything fell apart. I ended up withdrawing this
semester. I've been wandering ever since."

McGhee nodded. "I've been wandering my whole life," he said,
"or most of it. You're too young to settle down anyway. There's *no
way* you know what you want yet."

"I want Beth . . . ," Lenny said, his eyes welling up again. "I
just can't see past that."

"I know what that's like . . . ," McGhee said. "I met a woman
named Kate when I was twenty-five, back in San Francisco in a

coffee shop. She was scribbling on a notepad, ignoring her customers. I fell in love right then." McGhee stopped talking and just stared out into the vastness, thinking.

"And . . . ?" Lenny said eventually when it was clear McGhee wouldn't continue otherwise.

"Oh, I guess I was actually talking . . . ," McGhee said, snickering. "At times I forget."

"Well, you are old . . . *now*," Lenny said, smiling back.

"Yeah . . . so we had this great love affair that went on five, almost six years, until I fucked it up. And her, too, a little, but it was mostly me. And I lost her."

"Sucks . . . ," Lenny said, reaching down to pick up some gravel, tossing out a few stones over the edge.

"You think it ends there?" McGhee said, looking over at Lenny. "See . . . that's why you *need* to talk to old people. You have no concept of *time*."

Lenny looked over a moment, then went back to tossing his stones over the edge. "How so?"

McGhee nodded and cleared his throat, rubbing his nose before sucking the phlegm back in, hockering out into space. "Sorry . . . ," he said when he noticed the spray drifting back over his young friend. "Rum loosens me up and I gotta spit now and then."

"No problem . . . ," Lenny said, squinting back at him. "Never actually had it before. Not bad."

"You LDS or something?" McGhee said, taking another swig before handing the bottle over.

"What makes you say that?" Lenny said.

"Met a guy once who was LDS. Had me write his eulogy – some kinda cancer. Funny thing was, he was a stranger. Met him on the way to my brother's funeral just outside Salt Lake. Went by Earl. Only Earl I ever met."

"So what happened with Kate, then?" Lenny asked, holding the bottle, but not drinking.

"Right. Lose my train of thought, too," McGhee said. "So . . . Kate. She really got under my skin. But in a good way. Got married to some other gal, but it didn't work out. Always remembered Kate though. Then, just when I thought maybe I was past it, ran into her – in *France*."

"*France*?" Lenny said. "Wait a minute . . . How did that work?"

"Dunno . . . just did. See, *time* works like that. Vast swirls you can't see, but they're out there. Just . . . swirling . . . ," McGhee said, sweeping his hand in the air. "It was just dumb luck. I was on this beach with a buddy, looking out at the Atlantic from the top of a hill, and there she was."

"What are the odds of that?" Lenny said. "I mean, in *France* . . . ."

"Exactly," McGhee said nodding. "What are the odds . . . ?"

"You religious then?" Lenny asked, grabbing up another handful of dust and pebbles.

McGhee shook his head. "Naa. Not even a little."

"So how do you explain it then?" Lenny said, resuming his slow toss, bouncing the small stones near the edge before they hopped over into nothingness.

"Explain it?" McGhee said, looking over. "I don't . . . . It just is."

"Not very satisfying . . . ," Lenny said, looking over. "So what happened next?"

McGhee shrugged. "Nothing," he said. "We spent the evening together . . . *talking* . . . ," he said, leaning over to nudge Lenny with his elbow.

"Right . . . *talking* . . . ," Lenny said, smiling more broadly.

"No, really, just talking . . . ," McGhee said. "The next morning I flew home."

"But you kept in touch, right?" Lenny said. "I mean, after a meeting like that . . . ."

"Nope . . . ," McGhee said. "I was about forty then."

"Jesus . . . ," Lenny said. "So that was it then?" He sat shaking his head in disbelief and McGhee stared into the distance. "That was it then?" he repeated.

McGhee picked up a handful of dust and stones and began tossing them like Lenny.

"Twenty-seven years later . . . ," McGhee began, leaning over to nudge Lenny, "twenty-seven – you're seeing the theme here, right?" McGhee said, pausing.

"Right. Time . . . ," Lenny said nodding.

"Right. Twenty-seven years later, I'm walking in San Francisco. I'd just written this story, so my head was in the clouds – it was that good. And I turn this corner and see this sign with her face on it – it was a photo I'd taken back on the beach in France . . . ."

"No way . . . ," Lenny said, his eyes getting big. "It was *Kate?*"

"It was Kate . . . ," McGhee said nodding, pausing to take a drink, then laughed. "And outta this store this woman charges down the steps and knocks me over. Had to go to the hospital."

"I suppose it was Kate . . . ," Lenny said, becoming skeptical. "How's that even possible?"

McGhee shrugged. "Dunno. But it happened just like that. And the story I had just written? – that was about Kate, too."

"And I suppose you just talked and let her go again . . . ," Lenny said, snickering.

"You think I'm an *idiot?*" McGhee said, nearly shouting. "Of course I didn't – I *married* her."

"Right there?" Lenny said.

"No, not right there . . . .," McGhee said. "I think this rum is messing you up . . . ," he said, holding up the bottle to wiggle it, a finger's worth swishing in the bottom.

Lenny grabbed his head. "I just can't believe that . . . ," he said.

"And you know why you can't believe that?" McGhee said.

"Because I'm young and stupid?" Lenny said.

"Because you're young and stupid . . . ," McGhee agreed, nodding emphatically. "You have no concept of *time*."

Lenny sighed. "Still seems highly improbable. *Highly* . . . ," he said.

"But that's the beauty of it . . . ," McGhee said. "You have no idea what all those years have waiting for you. Weird shit can happen. You never know what role destiny might play."

"And those ashes . . . ," Lenny said, looking over. "That was Kate?"

McGhee shook his head. "Not really. That's just what's left when you take out the good parts."

"But I thought you didn't believe in things like that . . . like destiny," Lenny said.

"Yeah . . . I don't really. Only I don't have a better word for it. It doesn't have meaning, but I like to pretend it does. Sometimes . . . ," McGhee said, lowering his head.

Lenny grew quiet, drawing in the dust with his finger. "So were you really gonna jump, then?" he asked, but didn't look over.

McGhee sighed. "I dunno. I thought I might . . . ."

"But why? I mean, after that speech you gave me, why would you?" Lenny said, looking up at McGhee again. His eyes had a sadness for him that he hadn't seen in a long time.

"Just about everyone I ever knew is dead," McGhee said, "and I'm getting tired. I'm not sure I see the point anymore. And I lost the one person I actually loved, and it makes me kind of mad."

McGhee's eyes moistened slightly, so he looked further north and east to hide them.

"Mad at who?" Lenny said, his voice quiet.

"*Whom* . . . ," McGhee corrected, looking back at Lenny. "And there is no *whom* to be mad at – maybe that's what makes me maddest of all.

"So you kinda wish you believed in God so you'd have someone to be mad at?"

"Perverse, isn't it?" McGhee said, grabbing another handful of dust. Tilting his palm he let it sift out, lightly falling with a patter. "I always wondered what that line meant . . . ," he said, looking over at Lenny.

"What line?" Lenny said.

"From *The Wasteland* . . . '*I will show you fear in a handful of dust.*' Now I think I know. But it's not something I will tell you," McGhee said.

"Why not?" Lenny said.

Standing up, McGhee brushed the dust from the seat of his pants and stretched. Looking at his watch, it had stopped at 4:58, but he had no desire to wind it. "An old friend from Rushmore bought me dinner once and made me promise to pass that on. Been sixty-four years and I haven't done it yet. How about breakfast?"

Lenny looked up at him, squinting. The sun had just broken the horizon, sending brilliant rays across the canyon, lighting the vastness with a stark and sudden beauty. The air was warming, the breeze quickening: swifts and swallows swam up the winds of the walls, fanning out with fervid squeals, diving down to do it again, and it certainly looked like it would be another splendid day after all.

Epilogue

A Life Imagined

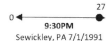

I must confess it was all a lie, or most of it. The good parts at least. And the others, such as they were, weren't quite enough. Ever since the beginning – before the beginning really – when that doctor came in my room and told me the news, I've been in shock. I actually laughed when he said it. Eventually this thing in my head – a glioblastoma or some such cranial bomb – will make my head implode. Or better yet, with much less fanfare, a fuse will snap inside my brain and I'll go dark. So, ever since that moment I mostly tuned them out and got to thinking: why should I let a simple thing like dying get in the way of my plans? And further, if I couldn't have the real thing, a real life, why shouldn't I just make one up? Have those memories I didn't get to make. Manufacture a life full of all the things a life should have: loves and loss and existential angst. After all, no one had said life is fair – I can certainly attest to that. You see, I had always played by the rules, and what did it get me? One giant shrug of indifference. So I went ahead and lived a life imagined, and that is what you have just read. I hope you enjoyed it, but the fiction is over now.

You'll notice I'm not asking for permission and not for forgiveness either. I've already done it, and you, my friend, have already read it. I don't see it so much as a mean-spirited trick as a modest sin of omission, and it is a bit of a relief to have it out. I'm sorry for that, really I am, but it seemed necessary. If I'd mentioned that up front, that this is a fiction spun by a doomed man, you would have knowingly nodded your head sympathetically, I'm sure, just as I would have, before closing the story fifteen pages in, saying, "I know this story, so why bother?" You would have moved on, because, honestly, why invest the time in another lost cause? And just so we are clear, that doesn't make me bitter – on the contrary, I'm pretty grateful, actually, that you read it. Sure, I can imagine your appalled stare into the page, the disbelief – yes, it stings, doesn't it? But perhaps now you can imagine *my* disappointment, really just getting started and ready to launch into a boundless life of adventure, only to be told to hold on a second: your future has been cancelled. Such is how fate rudely intrudes upon one's plans. But before you cast this aside in disgust, please bear with me a bit longer. Now that you're becoming accustomed to *your* new reality, you may be interested in how this all came to be and see it from my side.

If I were you, I'd still be reluctant to accept it. No doubt you're thinking, "How could he have written that? – surely there were things he couldn't have known . . . ," or, "How could a young man – barely more than a boy, really – project that far ahead into the life of his older self? When I was twenty-seven I could barely conceive of twenty-eight, let alone forty-five or sixty-five. Surely that is not possible, is it?" These are worthy questions – I would certainly have them. And it would be hard – it was hard – until I began the task in earnest. Fortunately, I had a couple strong advantages: the prospect of my demise focused my attention, and I had good support. I didn't have to do it alone – no, I'm smart enough to know my limitations – but I did have some useful resources at my disposal: you see, a hospice is good for one thing if nothing else: it contains a group of people relegated to the same circle of hell, each one similarly annoyed with his prognosis. So it was easy to find accomplices, and stories, and memories, even if they were not my own. What became *incredibly obvious* to me, after hours and hours of discussion, was how *similar* it all was, and how simple. Not simple in the content, nor in the process, but in the universality of it. We just tend to ignore our mortality because we can. For me, that suddenly wasn't possible. So I set to wondering how to invent the life I wouldn't have.

I'd have to confess my mind wandered during some of those first stories – tedium isn't as uncommon as it should be – but eventually I found I was imagining myself in their place, doing those things they related. Connecting those dots became something of a personal challenge. It turned out to be easier than I would have imagined, and the idea took shape. What had seemed like tedious detail suddenly became precious. Perhaps I could add my own flavor to their recollections, just enough *me* to make them credibly mine. In fact, once we got into the thing and they knew my plan, it became something of a diversion amongst my wardmates to hear me read my "appropriated" memories that had come from them, and for them to call out, such as they could – oxygen masks and infirmity made that difficult for some – when they heard their tales told as mine. I'd write the stories at night and read them in the mornings. Very soon, it was no longer my little fiction at all, but was *our* project, and they showed no limits to their ingenuity, helping me weave a believable tale, that by the end of it, told our collective story.

Doc Phelps (leukemia) was particularly helpful. No, that's an understatement. We forged more of a partnership – it was more of a collaboration. He'd been a college lit professor at *Carnegie Mellon* and invested less in providing memories than in structure and flow and irony – all the things that make a story credible and compelling. I had a natural inclination to that myself, as an English major (to my brother Les's enduring disappointment), but it was good to have a partner for collusion. He had a limitless well of works to pull inspiration from right there in his little bookshelf back in his room, browsing from here and there, picking a bit of Kafka or Melville or Hemingway or Dante or Dostoevsky or Cervantes, and most especially Joyce, and even some Eliot. I'd have to admit that it was mostly his idea to make the whole thing a modern *Ulysses*, only spread over a lifetime, with a little of the flavor of the Quixote, too (he always called it *the* Quixote, with some reverence). Oddly, he'd been a bit of a recluse most of the time since I had arrived, but I took care of that. Once I introduced him to Father Linus (pancreatic) – you see, I became something of a relationship broker through all of this – they got on famously, collaborating, though more than once he and Phelps nearly came to blows over Catholic theology. Doc Phelps had long since fallen away from any faith, and Fr. Linus would delight in goading him. It was marvelous to see them go at it and it became quite an entertainment for all of the guys. Phelps could get a little rabid: I'd step in once he started throwing spittle (we collectively agreed that would be the sign to intervene). It was all great fun, though as our ranks thinned, a certain grim reality tempered the general joviality of those remaining. Neither Doc Phelps nor Fr. Linus wanted me to put them into the novel, but were delighted to take sides in the debate in the Father Chepelsky *Confessions* chapter. No, that's not quite right either – they seemed compelled to take sides, almost honored and duty-bound. You should have seen them squaring off. Alas, they missed their tale in Dublin, because I wrote them in anyway. They were too important for me to leave behind, and I couldn't let them be forgotten.

From early on, the one thing I heard almost everywhere was regret. If they'd just had more time, they might have fit their dreams in. Bud, for example, had been a corn farmer up near Erie, but he'd always wanted to try potatoes. Jaimie, who cleaned the floors – he was one of the only outsiders – wanted to live in Nevada (god-knows-why), so he got his wish. Hobbs was always worrying over his obituary, so he made it in, too, but couldn't understand why I made him a Mormon, but everyone else got it: he had a thing for white short-sleeved shirts and was so nice and upbeat that we generally agreed he was fairly infuriating. Everyone liked Hobbs and told him it was a promotion, so when he passed (he was the first of us), the whole enterprise took on a more solemn direction – more important – for if it had been unspoken before, it was no longer: the most common fear among us was to be forgotten.

The Diagnosis

In case you are wondering, I did make it to California: I was there exactly fourteen days when I woke up at 3:00 a.m. on a Tuesday with a terrific headache, and when I say terrific, I mean *awful*. I was still in a hotel – my apartment wasn't ready yet – and the concierge got me a cab to take me over to the hospital – St. Francis

Memorial – so that part was true, sort of. By around 4:00 a.m. they had done the CT, and by 5:30 they had parked me in a room near the Senior Attending's office *to be more comfortable*, but he wasn't saying anything, though he looked in a few times. It gave me some time to think, but none of it looked good – I was looking for signs in the nurses who kept bringing me ice water, but they were careful. The priest who said he happened to be walking by was nice, too, but I was on to them. Nobody was saying I'd be going home soon. Mostly, I just felt like a patient all of a sudden, when I'd thought perhaps I'd simply be getting a shot when I came in, and sent along with advice to eat better or to lay off the occasional cigarette. The whole thing felt a little surreal, and I nearly convinced myself it might end soon with some innocuous explanation and my freedom. Eventually, the Attending said they had a call in to a neurologist. He walked in a minute later. He'd swung by imaging on the way up, and when he came in, he shook my hand, but didn't make eye contact – that's how I knew it was really bad. Sure enough, after some hemming and hawing, he said he'd get a consult from a neurosurgeon later in the morning. It wasn't time to panic yet. Sure.

The neurosurgeon was a nice guy – maybe fifty, gray in the temples, Indian. I had a hell of a time making out *glioblastoma* with his accent – he apologized for that – and in very polite and patient terms explained exactly, and in painful detail, how thoroughly screwed I was. I explained my situation – new in town, etc. – and after thirty minutes he suggested I just go home. Presbyterian Hospital in Pittsburgh was very good with these things, but he didn't want to sugar coat it. He tried to finesse it a bit: every case was different, but I pushed him for the numbers. Eventually he said it'd be hard row to hoe, and I'd likely be gone in six to nine months. He was very sorry to tell me, but not nearly as sorry as I was to hear it.

So I flew home and Dad got me at the airport, and after some radiation and a few rounds of chemo, they said I was done. Sorry about that. From my perspective, it wasn't even close – the conclusion was foregone – so I wasn't sweating the details. We soon went shopping for a hospice, because it wouldn't be long. It was like hunting for an apartment and signing a lease, except for the parts about resuscitation and funeral arrangements – that was different.

The Hospice

We ended up choosing *The Sacred Heart Hospice* in Sewickley for a couple reasons: it was Catholic, it was close to Butler where I grew up, and it was cheap. I certainly didn't care – it wouldn't affect my outcome one way or the other – and I found it darkly amusing Mom and Dad still wanted to save my soul. It was touching, really, so I figured why the hell not? If it made them happy, who was I to rob them of that? Hope is about all any of us ever have, right? And meanwhile, the stew was already boiling in my head. And yes, that pun was intentional. Sometimes I like to remind people of my pitiful condition, just to see their reaction. It's like sucking on an aching tooth: deliciously painful but irresistible.

An old nun signed me in when I arrived – Sr. Purgatoria. Actually, that wasn't her name at all, but we called her that when she wasn't within earshot. She was damned near deaf anyway, so we got away with it, most of the time. She managed the pill inventory, so no one wanted to piss her off. Pills were very popular on the floor. We'd compare notes, and sometimes even trade. Poker night had some awesome jackpots.

Our favorite movie became *Bridge over the River Kwai*. One of the older guys – a WWII vet named Harry – got us to watch it one night, and we saw the similarities to our situation immediately. After that, we watched it a couple times a week. It was a lot more fun (than our true lot) to pretend we were POWs charged with making the guards miserable, so we embraced the fiction whole-heartedly. And once I told the guys about my plan, it just seemed like another way to mess with the *lifers*. That's what we called any-one who wasn't terminal.

So one morning I'm sitting out in the sun porch with a pad at the big table. It was kind of early, so most everyone else was still sleeping. Doc Phelps came wheeling in and saw me working, and asked if it's "the thing." From that moment onward, that was the name of the project. It became something of a ritual that he and I would meet early to discuss it. Where it was in the story line. And I'd give him a preview of the material I'd written the night before. I'd have to say I learned more in that hour each morning than I learned in all of college at Yale: he was a firehose of thoughts and feelings and knowledge, and he wanted to share all of it, though it didn't come out in much order. Luckily, it all made sense to me.

When I had started a few weeks before that visit, the idea was pretty nebulous. The concept was to manufacture a life for the one I wasn't going to have. It would be a way to visualize what it would be like for me to get older, to mature into old age. That was the thing: I really wanted to know what it was like – not only to *be* older, but to *get* older. Especially once I got to know the guys, my sense of that need only grew. It wasn't quite enough to just imagine a lot of days. I wondered if the days were the same. I wondered if time slowed down or sped up. I wondered how people stayed in one spot their whole life and what that was like, and what it was like to move around. I wondered what was gained and what was lost. Still, it was all very abstract to me. I was staring into my pad, at the thoughts sprawling, pulling at my hair, when Doc Phelps caught me. Reaching out, he pulled the pad over to take a look, brushing my hand away. Turning the first few pages, he traced down with his finger: it was bony, and his cuticles were a little blue. Once he was done with it, he looked at me smiling and said, "Holy shit . . . ." That was the real start.

It didn't take long for the other guys to catch on. Degney cornered me in the lunchroom a couple days later, literally with his walker, and asked me what it was about. Really *about*. He almost sounded angry, his voice was so loud. Then he revealed that his hearing aids were on the nightstand – that was something I should get in there: the physical decline. He mentioned something about not being regular since Nixon, but I found that particular image unproductive. But it was much more than that, he continued. It was like the calendar was a huge piece of sandpaper, shaving off your edges one day at a time. And at the same time, it was also the opposite of that, adding a paper-thin layer to the onion. He said he didn't care if that was a mixed metaphor, either – that was part of the mystery. And when he was done, he grabbed my robe by the sleeve and dragged me over to the sitting room, one little skooch of his walker at a time. Six or eight of the guys were there, with Sr. Purgatoria handing out pills. He asked her to get his aids for him – three times, feigning forgetfulness each time she said she had to do the pills first – until she relented and went for them, down the long hallway to the end. As soon as she left, he told the guys we'd be having a reading from "the thing." Mr. Bovus looked a little confused (he generally did), but Jerry leaned in to shout it in his ear. That was the first reading, *Drift*, and from then on, right after 10:00 a.m. pills we'd do it, as soon as the staff cleared out. The next day was *Never Far Enough*, and they were on board after that. After much debate and some huffs they agreed the army hero should be changed to "Danko," for reasons I didn't quite follow, but they looked satisfied. I knew I had them then.

The next day they were a little mad when I told them I was out of ideas and didn't have a story. *What the hell else ya got to do?* Willy complained, and the others nodded, but Degney intervened: *Why doncha tell about the time I went to Turkey — that was pretty good.* Everyone else was quiet a minute, then the torrent started: *How abouts a trip to the Grand Canyon? You need to get laid in this thing! You gonna talk about Pittsburgh? I got the clap once in New Orleans . . . .* Everyone looked at Willy when he said that. Fr. Linus blessed himself but laughed anyway, shaking his head. Lucky for me, Doc Phelps had a writing pad, too, and he'd learned shorthand once back in the day at *Herbick & Held* downtown. Later that day he handed me some notes (that he'd written out for me), and we went to the sun porch to confer.

Doc Phelps liked that the whole enterprise started as an act of defiance: that, in lieu of a real life, I'd make one up, or better yet, imagine my life out to the smallest details, out to its farthest reaches. That it was a noble impulse: in the face of mortality to push back and deny it the years it was robbing from me. I must confess I didn't appreciate the full significance of his words at the time. It started as a blatant fiction, especially because I was borrowing the memories of others, but it became a lot more than that. The further it went, the more those memories became mine. The more I felt I had some idea what it would mean to be thirty-five or fifty or eighty, the more it felt real.

Initially I wasn't sure how long it would go, either, but that only lasted a couple chapters. A couple days later Doc Phelps wheeled in with a book in his lap, then plopped it on the table in front of me. You need to do an American version of that! he said.

Why *Ulysses*? I had asked, a bit crestfallen recalling its heft and the trouble I'd had navigating it. I had found it nearly impenetrable. Placing his hand on it reverently, he answered at great length, that I was on an odyssey, that my fictional self needed a voyage of self-discovery, that I was seeking to explore and map a vast life unlived and conquer death, and that I needed to become an artist in the process. In short, it would require that level of commitment to do it justice. Besides, he argued, it was about time someone wrote *Ulysses* in English. We both laughed pretty hard at that.

It would solve a few problems: it would give me a structure, it would help assemble the chapters toward a larger purpose, it would provide something of a philosophical framework, and if completed, it would certainly be significant. Those were Doc's words, because I remained skeptical most of the five minutes during his mono-logue, but by the end of it, I was mad I hadn't thought of it myself. Twenty-four chapters it would be then, spread over a life, not just a day. That said, they'd be in some other order than chronological, because the point wasn't to lay out the progression so much as the struggle itself, to capture the reader within the same existential plight as my protagonist. The same plight as mine. As I said, I wished I'd thought of it. So that's what I did. Doc Phelps sure was a clever bastard.

There was a girl who came in – a young woman really – to water the plants. She had one of those plastic watering cans with a long neck to get down into the calla lilies and the big terrarium they had on the table, with the prayer plants and dieffenbachia gushing out the hole on top. One day I was out on the sun porch working – the afternoons were some of my most productive times – and she asked me what I was doing and if I lived there. It was pretty obvi-ous I did – I had on slippers and pajamas and my maroon bath robe covered in cowboys – but I appreciated the gesture. For a second,

I almost felt normal. So I invited her to take a look. That was the beginning of my infatuation with Kate.

So Thursday was watering day, and by the next week, I'd already written her in. I was a little nervous showing her. In fact, I didn't right away, but Degney was winking at her so hard she got curious and he spilled the beans. She was nice about it. Then by the next Thursday, she wanted to see her chapter. I covered my face while she read the dicey part, but she pulled my hands away and said it was *sweet*. After that, she was another collaborator. A couple weeks later she mentioned her *ultimate, ultimate* place to see was a certain beach in France. You can see where this is going.

Unknown to me, at least for a while, some of the other guys got together in twos and threes to have their own discussions about it. I think it was more that *The Rockford Files* were on TV, or *M*A*S*H*, or *Carol Burnett* – some guys liked one and not the other – that got the groups going. During the commercials they'd discuss the plot, the over-arching themes (Fr. Linus watched everything, so he provided continuity among them), the timeline. Frankie and Jonnie (lung and lung) did tag-team on the timeline and actually drew the whole thing out. Karl (colorectal) made the list of characters so we could keep them straight. There were writing pads all over the place that they'd hide by sitting on them at the first sign of staffers. No one wanted to look at Karl's pad, for obvious reasons, so he kept it to himself.

So that's how it went. Time was short, of course, and we lost most of the guys along the way. The guys started noting when we lost someone by the chapter in progress when they went. Hobbs was CH10. Karl was CH12, but he got to see it. Frankie and Jonnie were both CH13 – that was an especially tough period. Then we had a break, until we lost Fr. Linus (CH18), which seemed to break Doc Phelps, since he lost his arguing partner (CH19). Of course there were a few new people, too, along the way. A seventeen-year-old kid named Lenny (leukemia) came in. He was really sad and even a little suicidal, but we took care of that. He wore one of those transparent green visors when we got down to business, like poker players used to wear. He took ownership of the timeline *and* the character list, so he turned out OK and even made it to the end.

The surprise of it was that it worked. Not only for me, but for all of us, even those who couldn't see it through to the end. It gave us all more time – we shared each other's memories, and they became our own. Those conversations were raucous and bawdy and we laughed a lot, hushing only when the lifers shuffled through. The years we won weren't just for me, they were for each of us, and I could see in their eyes as the story expanded and began to take its full shape how it affected them, how it affected me. It was like we were all surprised that we could have this big life right there in the tiny ward, together, in spite of our sickness. In fact, in those moments when we read together, we were not sick, and we were not mortal. In fact, we weren't dying at all – we were all young or old, at home or abroad, in love or heartbroken – we were at large, free of our bonds, boundless.

Loose Ends

I should mention this whole ordeal has been very hard on my family. Mom and Dad drive down from Butler, usually a couple times a week. Wil and Les fly in when they can, or drive. Wil lives in New Jersey, so he makes it over more often. Les lives in Denver, so at least he can get direct flights. But I hate the way they look at me. I usually forgot I'm dying until I see it in their eyes – especially Les. He doesn't cry much, but it looks like it'd do him some good if he did. Once he brought me a jar of Mirabelles preserves he got from a diner down the street from this place he liked called *The Pie Tin*. He said *It'll cure what ails ya* – then realized what he said and had to leave the room. I knew he didn't mean anything by it, but he felt bad.

I wonder what he'll think if he ever reads this thing. We were sitting in the yard at home one sunset early last summer, before the news. Mom had brought us some tea in cold sweaty tumblers rattling on a metal tray. He warned me against settling too early, urged me to get some living in before it was too late. He said I should study more – something like computer science – because he thought I might be haunted otherwise. He told me about some of his regrets and what he wished he'd known at my age. He told me he wasn't sure where his life was going, either, only he knew he wanted it to be big, or maybe really small but rewarding – he didn't know yet. He said he and I should take that trip he had planned to Alaska – he was always sorry he hadn't done it. He said there's nothing worse than living with regret. I'd have to say he was mostly right about that. He couldn't have been more right, really, except for one thing: it's worse to have that hope cut off. See, I was looking at it like he was until just a month later, when the whole thing flipped on its head. I thought all that uncertainty was bad until I didn't even have that. I'm just glad I landed where I did. Finding my life, really discovering it, with that crew of guys at the hospice saved me. In the midst of dying, I finally learned how to live.

I really wish I could thank Doc Phelps, too, for it wouldn't have worked without him. One time he looked at me all of a sudden and confided his biggest regret was that he hadn't written more poetry, and that he'd only ever written one line he really liked: *the blood takes the handle*. When I asked him what it meant, he mostly just smiled, then said: "That's why I wish I'd written more poetry, because that's how you find out." I wasn't sure what he meant at the time, but I think I get it now. And as for the rest of his help, I'd read those novels, too, of course, but I was too young to understand them when I did. It turned out they were doing the same thing as me, in their own ways. All those works we read and discussed – they were struggling with the same idea. They were just as mortal as me, perhaps even just as lost. But reading them with my new perspective, they became a series of lenses, became a microscope to peer into the small, and a telescope to peer out into the large. My god, it looks so obvious now, but it wouldn't have happened if he hadn't cleared my eyes, washed away my shortsightedness so I could finally see, see it all in focus and all at once. It required a stillness he had, and he gave that to me. How I wish I could show you – how I hope I have.

So I guess that's about it – I don't have long left myself, so I'm glad it's done. The last little bit was getting hard for me. Kate's been a big help: she and a few of her friends are typing it all now into the PC back in the office of the hospice. They have *WordStar*, so it should look pretty good when it's all done. I'm hoping to see it all printed before I go. There's something about having the whole stack of it, my whole life neatly printed, that I look forward to holding in my hands. I never expected the whole thing to go the way it went. I never expected to feel so good about it. Like I'd actually lived it. I never expected to make so many friends, or for them to like it, too. It became something of a mission for us, and they took it seriously. And I'd have to say maybe they even loved me for it. See, we were all consigned here by bad luck, and it seemed like a one-way ticket, with no escape but one. But we turned that around, didn't we? – That's what Doc Phelps said to me just before he died, and he was smiling when he passed. And as for me, I got to have that life I thought I'd lost. I got to be that writer I thought I'd never be. I wouldn't say I won, exactly, but it seems like playing to a tie is pretty good when you get those cards. Sure, it started as an act of defiance in the beginning, but it became so much more than that. I was able to bend my circumstances to my will, just a little bit. And in the end, there was a little redemption – my parents would like that.

I guess it's fitting I should end this thing while sitting outside in the garden, alone. The nurse dropped off a slice of Lenny's birthday cake; I'm not sure I'm up to it, but the icing looks good. My CD player is on repeat for *A Whiter Shade of Pale*, which seems to be all I listen to these days. I have this little picture Kathe gave me way back which is rather faded now – the two of us in tenth grade chem lab with rubber aprons and goggles – with her kissing me on the cheek. I always liked that picture: there was a whole life in it. Sometimes I used to pretend I went inside and lived it. The funny thing is, I guess I finally did.

The sun set some time ago – it's still warm, but my gloaming is fading now. Sure, it's twilight, but there's so much to see if you open your eyes. Even in the dwindling light there are mysteries to discover. It's taken a long time to struggle back into the moment, but I've finally made it. It's like floating in warm water, effortless, spinning slowly, slowly as it fades to black. I'd have to say it's actually just about perfect.

Chapter Illustrations

Additional illustrations appear on the *McGhee in the Gloaming* Facebook page at: https://www.facebook.com/McGheeITG/.

CH 1 On the Margin Lake Laberge, Yukon Territory

CH 12 Drift Raft, Yukon River AK

CH 18 McGhee's Road CA 395, Mono Lake Overlook, CA

CH 21 The Baptism of Frosty McGhee Cook Shack, Ruby AK

CH 24 The Dust Magi Desert View, Grand Canyon, AZ

Time of Day Chapter Map

Time	Midnight	1a	2a	3a	4a	5a	6a	7a	8a	9a	10a	11a
Date	12/27/1981	3/15/2011	4/19/2008	9/26/1986	3/20/2050	12/18/2023	9/21/1994	12/23/1984	7/12/2030	10/1/1986	11/15/2028	5/20/2004
Age	18.1	47.3	44.4	22.9	86.4	60.1	30.9	21.1	66.7	22.9	65.0	40.5
Year	1982	2011	2008	1986	2050	2023	1994	1984	2030	1986	2028	2004
Name	Ch 23 Signal And Noise	Ch 7 Stones	Ch 20 A Dublin Homily	Ch 12 Drift	Ch 24 The Dust Magi	Ch 9 Confessions In the Gloaming	Ch 8 The Cherry Man	Ch 3 Most of the Way	Ch 22 Kite Weather	Ch 21 The Baptism of Frosty McGhee	Ch 10 Losing Les	Ch 13 Remember the Sea
Month / Sac.	December	March	April	September	March	February Reconciliation	September	December	July Matrimony	October Baptism	November	May

Time	Noon	1p	2p	3p	4p	5p	6p	7p	8p	9p	10p	11p
Date	12/31/1988	6/15/1979	8/31/2000	11/13/1971	1/17/1997	4/1/1978	7/15/2038	6/18/1998	5/20/1988	8/9/2019	1/21/1997	10/10/1986
Age	25.1	15.6	36.8	8.0	33.2	14.4	74.7	34.5	24.5	55.7	33.2	22.9
Year	1988	1978 1983	2000	1970	1997	1978 2043	2038	1998	1985	2019	1997	1986 2026
Name	Ch 6 Kite	Ch 11 The Calendar Lagniappe	Ch 19 The Math Idiot	Ch 2 Never Far Enough	Ch 15 Fully Meets	Ch 16 The Boney Pile	Ch 14 Holy Orders of the Olives	Ch 4 One Certain Sunset	Ch 5 Old Men	Ch 18 McGhee's Road	Ch 17 Soldiers' Wounds	Ch 1 On The Margin
Month / Sac.	February Confirmation	June	August	November	January	April	July Holy Orders	June	May Communion	August	January	October

Chapter Chronology Map

#	Year	Chapter
62	2025	
63	2026	1. OTM
64	2027	
65	2028	10. LL
66	2029	
67	2030	22. KW
68	2031	
69	2032	
70	2033	
71	2034	
72	2035	
73	2036	
74	2037	14. HOotO
75	2038	
76	2039	
77	2040	
78	2041	
79	2042	16. TBP
80	2043	
81	2044	
82	2045	
83	2046	
84	2047	
85	2048	
86	2049	
87	2050	24. TDM
88	2051	
89	2052	
90	2053	
91	2054	
92	2055	

#	Year	Chapter
31	1994	8. TCM
32	1995	
33	1996	
34	1997	15. FM 17. SW
35	1998	
36	1999	4. OCS
37	2000	19. TMJ
38	2001	
39	2002	
40	2003	
41	2004	13. RTS
42	2005	
43	2006	
44	2007	
45	2008	20. ADH
46	2009	
47	2010	
48	2011	7. Stones
49	2012	
50	2013	
51	2014	
52	2015	
53	2016	
54	2017	
55	2018	
56	2019	18. MR
57	2020	
58	2021	
59	2022	
60	2023	9. CitG
61	2024	

#	Year	Chapter
0	1963	
1	1964	
2	1965	
3	1966	
4	1967	
5	1968	
6	1969	
7	1970	
8	1971	2. NFE
9	1972	
10	1973	
11	1974	
12	1975	
13	1976	
14	1977	16. TBP 1
15	1978	11. TCL
16	1979	
17	1980	
18	1981	
19	1982	23. SaN
20	1983	11. TCL
21	1984	3. MotW
22	1985	
23	1986	1. OTM 12. Drift 21. TBoFM
24	1987	5. OM
25	1988	6. Kite
26	1989	
27	1990	
28	1991	Epilogue
29	1992	
30	1993	

Cast of Characters

Ch 1. On the Margin

Rental kid	Karl
Kaskae (dog)	Matt

Ch 2. Never Far Enough

Mrs. Sanderson	Hit & Run Priest
David Sanderson	Mr. McGhee
Monsignor McNulty	Mrs. McGhee
Danko	

Ch 3. Most of the Way

Frankie	Buzzy
Jonnie	Bunny
Pat McGregor	Sergey + kids
Rabbi	Madge
Sonja	

Ch 4. One Certain Sunset

Nick	Kate
Nells	

Ch 5. Old Men

Bud Taylor	Beef
Harry Garber	Mike (counterman)
Jerry	

Ch 6. Kite

Kate	Redhead kid in shop
Mr. Chung	

Ch 7. Stones

Officer Bill Kennedy	Resident Trepanier
Attending	Nurse

Ch 8. The Cherry Man

Cherry Man	Paul
Shopkeeper (baker)	

Ch 9. Confessions in the Gloaming

Fr. Chepelsky	Ray (Rudy's)
Britney	Adams
Britney's boyfriend	Hector
Patrick O'Connor	

Ch 10. Losing Les

Jaime	Luis
Chispita (Cece)	Manny
Ximena	Earl Hobbs
Mike McGhee	Clara Ann McGhee
Wil McGhee	Les McGhee
Nam Vet	Deb

Ch 11. The Calendar Lagniappe

Willy Robinson	Honey
Freddy (tap)	Ben
Molly (Bernadette)	Jen
Waitress	

Ch 12. Drift

Karl	
Julie	

Ch 13. Remember the Sea

Yannick	Tess
Lucie	Kate

Ch 14. Holy Orders of the Olives

Baba Ganoush	Lucie
Yannick	Kate

Ch 15. Fully Meets

Jerry Schwanz	
Fred	

Ch 16. The Boney Pile

Aunt Rose	David
Uncle Walt	Matt/Matty
Mr. McGhee	Gene
Mrs. McGhee	

Ch 17. *Soldier's Wounds*

Joe Meckleman	Dunkin Donuts waiter
Viener Schlongka	Monsignor McNulty
Monsignor Spiegel	

Ch 18. *McGhee's Road*

Fran McGhee

Ch 19. *The Math Idiot*

Neal Wagner	Sonja
Tess	

Ch 20. *A Dublin Homily*

Mulligan	Arlene
Finnegan	Degney "Charlie"
Doc Phelps	Fr. Linus (Jiggs)
John (bartender)	

CH 21. *The Baptism of Frosty McGhee*

Junior	Jimmy
Matt	Dave
Big Mike	Joe
Little Mike	Athabaskan Indian

Ch 22. *Kite Weather*

Kate	Officer Bill Kennedy
George	

Ch 23. *Signal and Noise*

Mr. Swinson	Troy
Bruce Rohonic	Russ
Mike	Mr. Schmidt
Kathe	Mr. Woods
Hector	Reznick
Mr. Camissa	Gunter
Tomatsu	

Ch 24. *The Dust Magi*

Lenny

Epilogue

Sr. Purgatoria	Dr. Phelps
Lenny	Fr. Linus
Bud	Kate
Mr. Bovus	Degney
Willy	Harry
Jaime	

Acknowledgements

Writing this novel was a difficult and protracted process made possible by friends and family willing to help me do it: my brother Jim provided excellent feedback and suggestions along the way that were always thoughtful, and my brother Tom provided input on a few key chapters to make them better; my partner, Tracy Geiger, provided many insights and suggestions and cheerfully endured countless discussions that helped me understand McGhee and his struggles more personally; my son, Nathan Hazy, provided input to improve the narrative flow and philosophical depth; Dr. Neal Wagner who helped by being a friend for thirty years and an endless source of amusement and commiseration; and Doug Woods who helped as a formative English teacher in 10th grade and provided guidance I've never forgotten.

A number of readers along the way helped, too, and I can't forget their contribution and guidance: Barbara Lucey, Andrea Spear, Rob Tate, Don Faulkner, Maria Montoya, Phil Clark and Zoey Lawliss. The novel was written in a serialized manner, one story at a time, and I appreciate their patience.

Finally, I need to acknowledge the contribution of my editor and friend (I'm not sure which should come first), Linda Lucey Lawliss, who spent countless hours in discussion, character and plot analysis, reading and editing the text, re-reading and re-editing, thereby helping to wring as many mistakes and as much awkwardness from the language as possible, while making it a more coherent story. I can't express my gratitude enough for the collaboration and partnership. Most especially I thank you.

Author Biography

Photo Credit: Nathan Hazy

B ob Hazy is a writer inspired by the works of Melville, Steinbeck, Hemingway, and Dostoevsky. He studied literature at Yale University earning a B.A. and also holds a M.S. in Computer Science from Stevens. Although Bob built a career in information technology leadership and is currently an independent consultant, his real love is writing. He lives in the foothills of the Sierra in Northern California with his son, Nathan, and their dog, Gus.

Made in the USA
Charleston, SC
25 August 2016